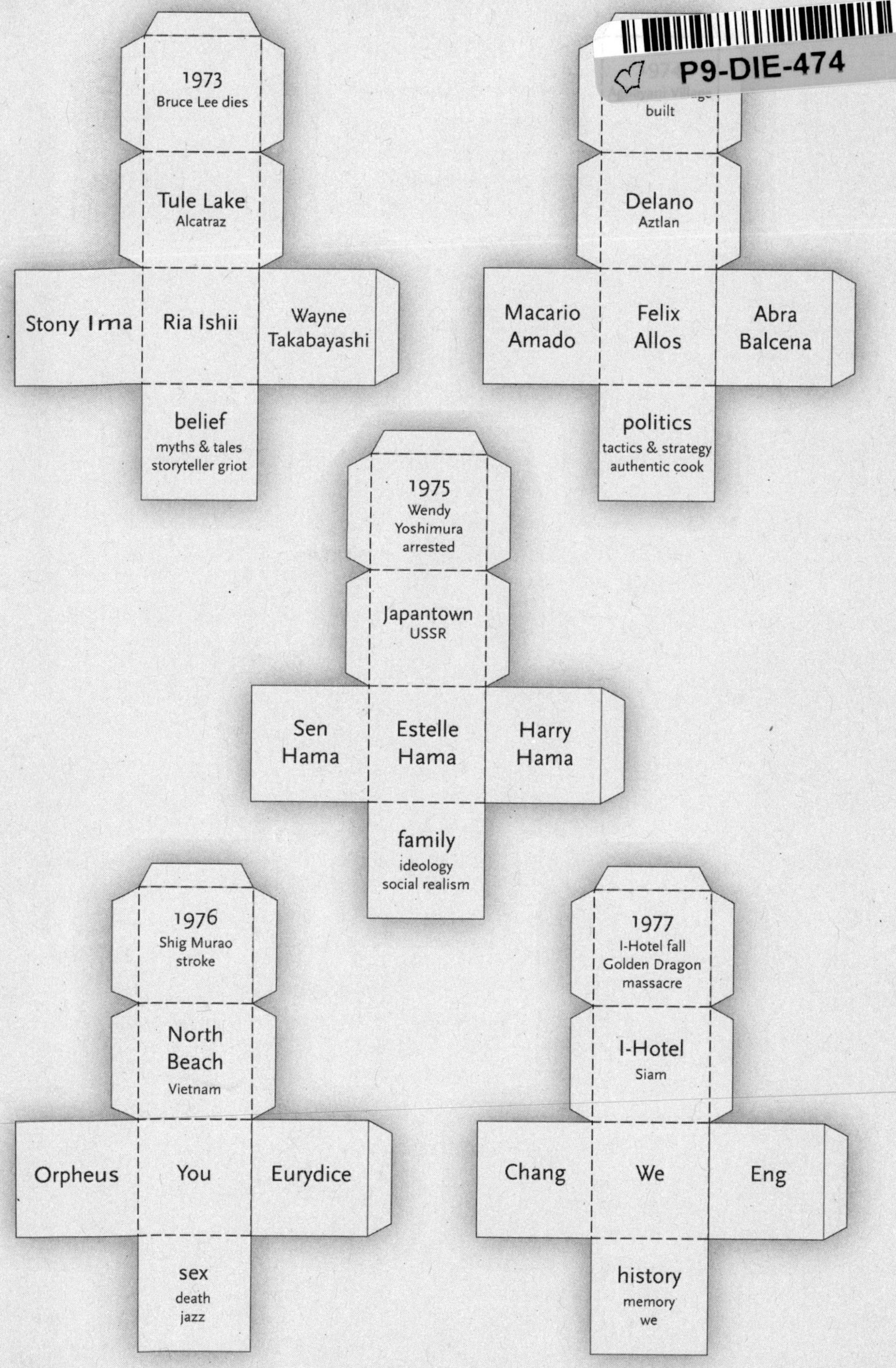

1973
Bruce Lee dies
Tule Lake
Alcatraz
Stony Ima
Ria Ishii
Wayne Takabayashi
belief
myths & tales
storyteller griot
built
Delano
Aztlan
Macario Amado
Felix Allos
Abra Balcena
politics
tactics & strategy
authentic cook
1975
Wendy Yoshimura arrested
Japantown
USSR
Sen Hama
Estelle Hama
Harry Hama
family
ideology
social realism
1976
Shig Murao stroke
North Beach
Vietnam
Orpheus
You
Eurydice
sex
death
jazz
1977
I-Hotel fall
Golden Dragon massacre
I-Hotel
Siam
Chang
We
Eng
history
memory
we

I HOTEL

ALSO BY KAREN TEI YAMASHITA

Through the Arc of the Rain Forest
Brazil-Maru
Tropic of Orange
Circle K Cycles

KAREN TEI YAMASHITA

I HOTEL

COFFEE HOUSE PRESS :: MINNEAPOLIS

COVER DESIGN by Linda Koutsky
BOOK DESIGN by Allan Kornblum

COFFEE HOUSE PRESS books are available to the trade through our primary distributor, Consortium Book Sales & Distribution, www.cbsd.com or (800) 283-3572. For personal orders, catalogs, or other information, write to: info@coffeehousepress.org.

Coffee House Press is a nonprofit literary publishing house. Support from private foundations, corporate giving programs, government programs, and generous individuals helps make the publication of our books possible. We gratefully acknowledge their support in detail in the back of this book.

To you and our many readers around the world,
we send our thanks for your continuing support.

LIBRARY OF CONGRESS CIP INFORMATION
Yamashita, Karen Tei, 1951–
I Hotel / by Karen Tei Yamashita. — 1st ed.
p. cm.
ISBN 978-1-56689-239-1 (alk. paper)
1. Civil rights movements—United States—Fiction.
2. Asian Americans—Fiction.
3. Nineteen seventies—Fiction.
4. Nineteen sixties—Fiction.
5. Chinatown (San Francisco, Calif.)—Fiction.
I. Title.
II. Series.
PS3575.A44I19 2010
813'.54—DC22
2010000382

PRINTED IN CANADA
3 5 7 9 8 6 4 2

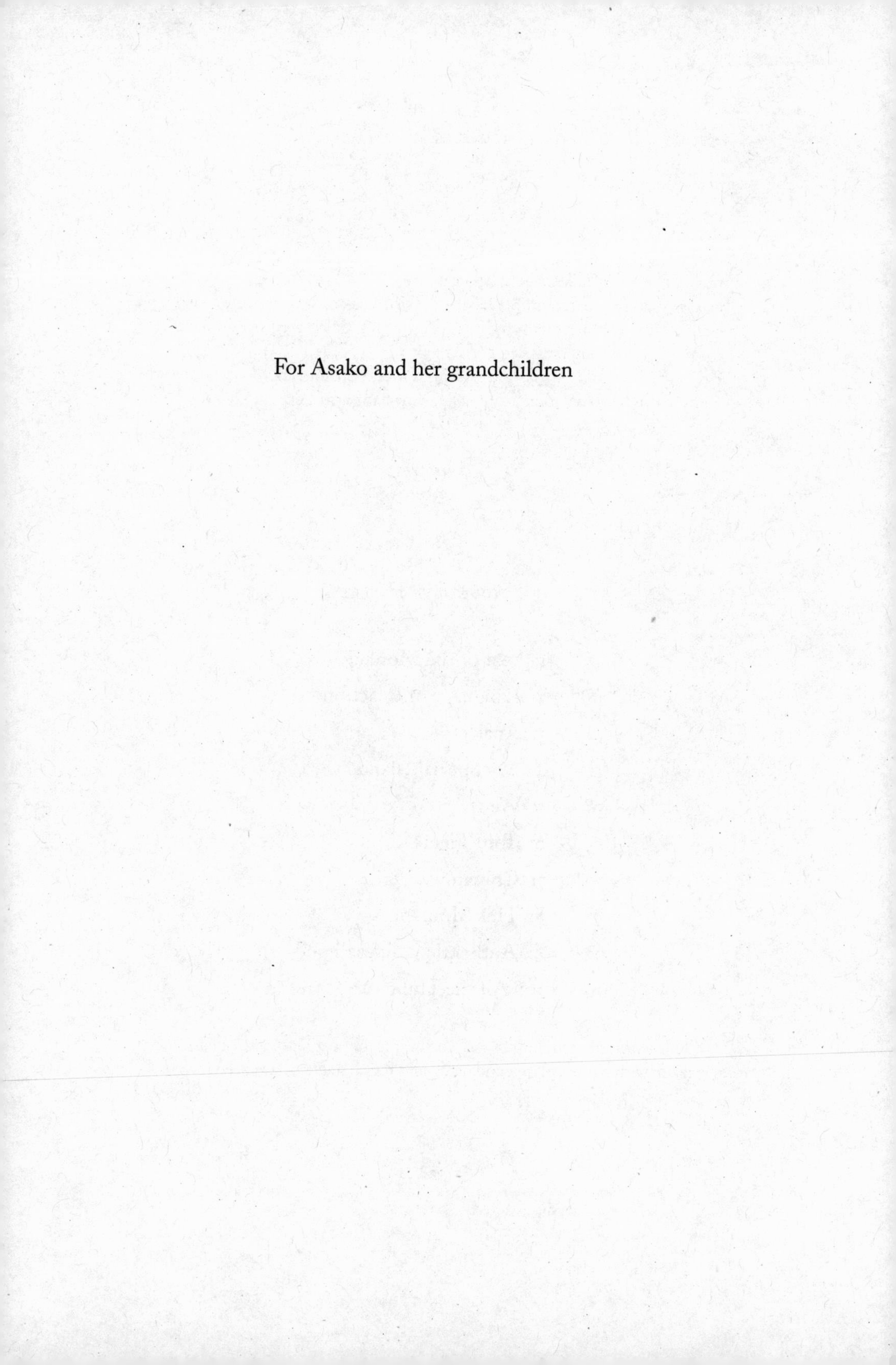

For Asako and her grandchildren

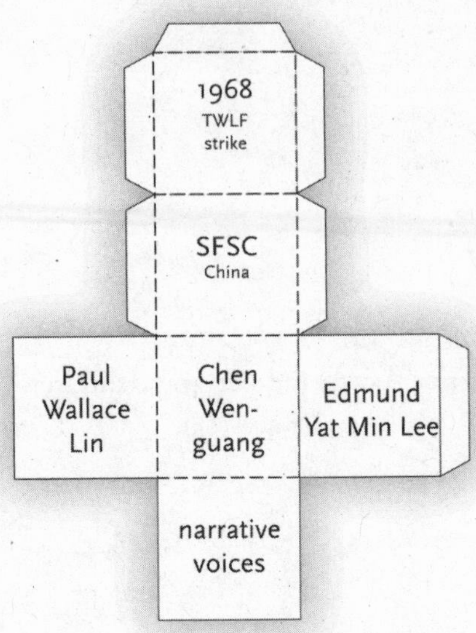

1968: Eye Hotel

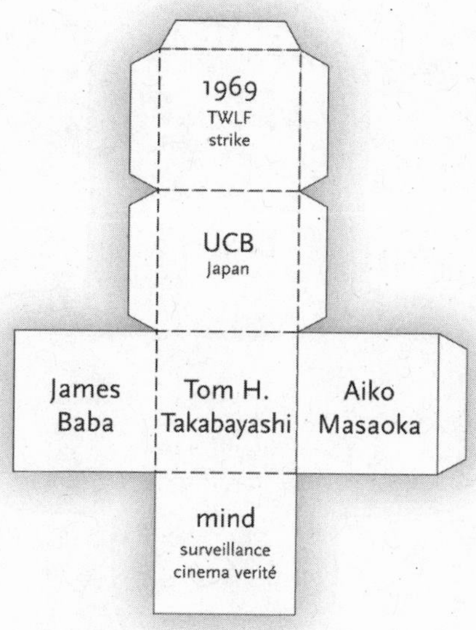

1969: I Spy Hotel

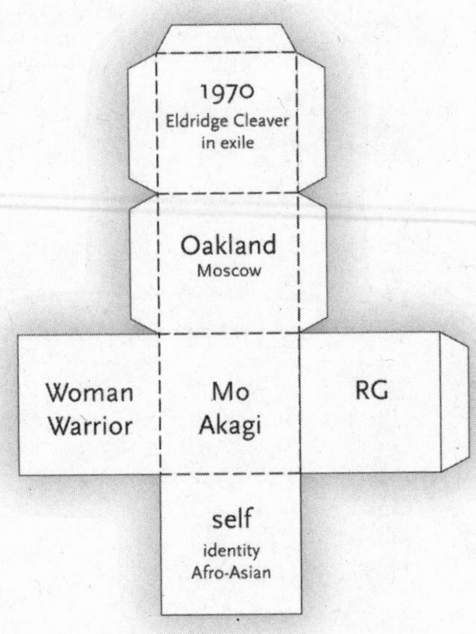
1970
Eldridge Cleaver
in exile
Oakland
Moscow
Woman
Warrior
Mo
Akagi
RG
self
identity
Afro-Asian

1970: "I" Hotel

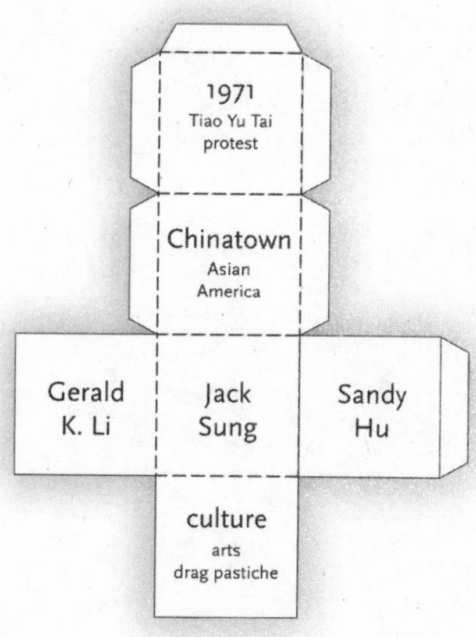

1971: Aiiieeeee! Hotel

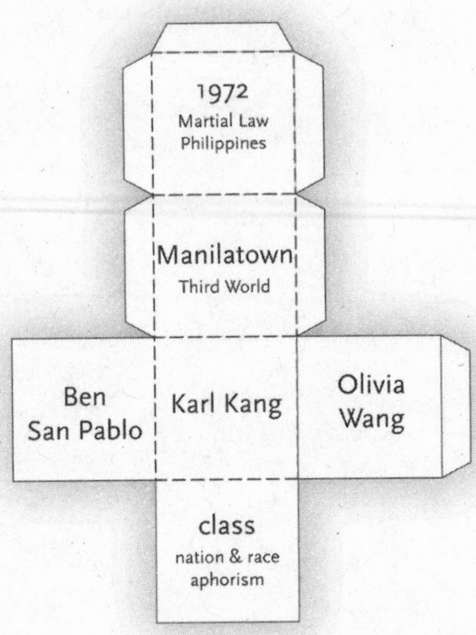

1972: Inter-national Hotel

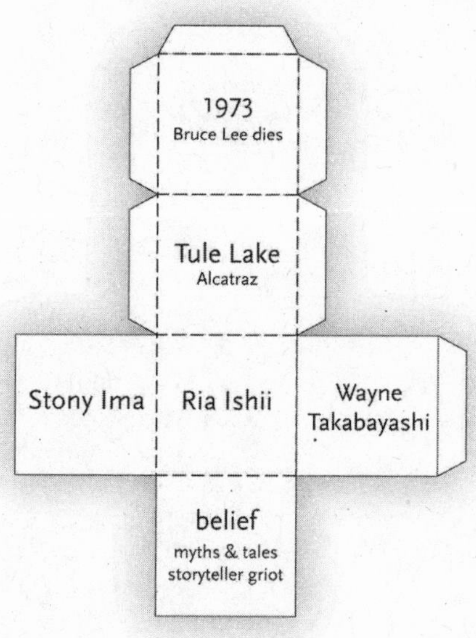

1973: INT'L HOTEL

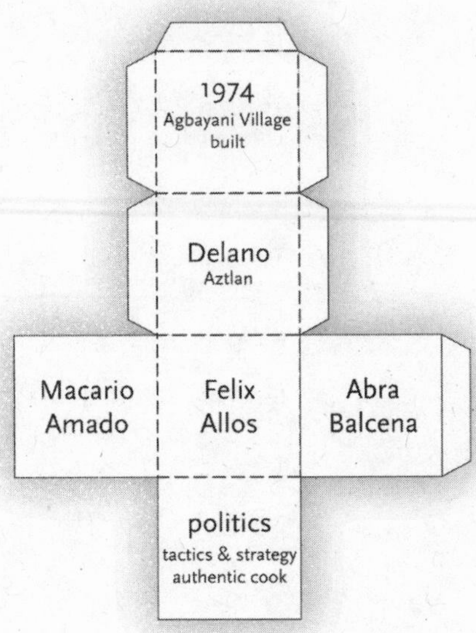

1974: I-Migrant Hotel

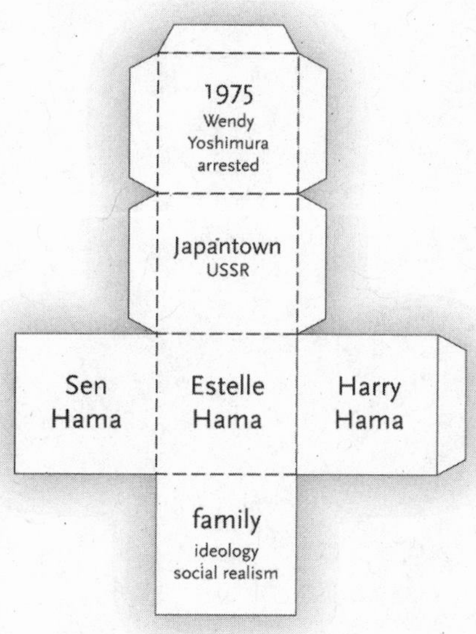

1975: Internationale Hotel

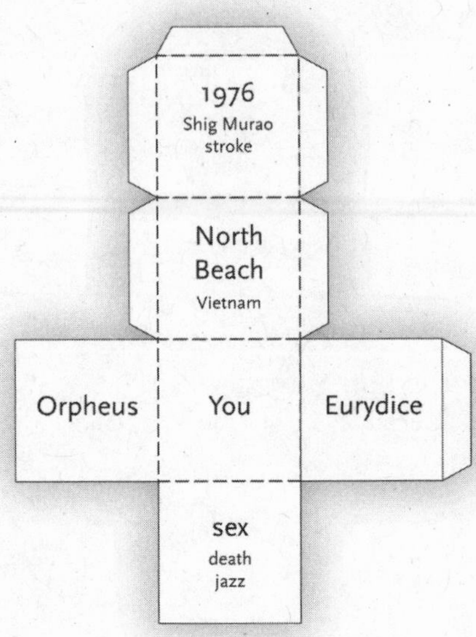

1976: Ai Hotel

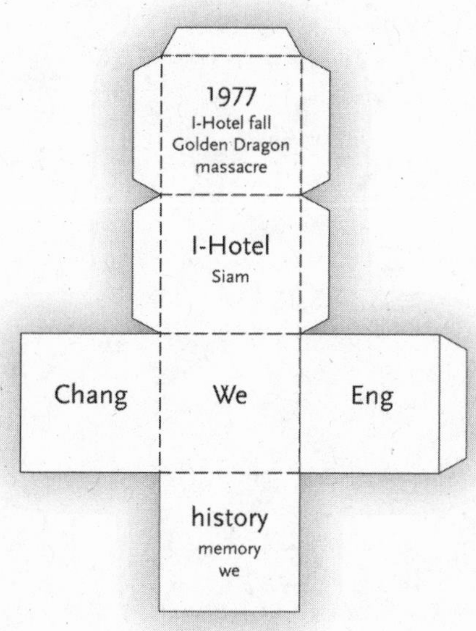
1977
I-Hotel fall
Golden Dragon
massacre
I-Hotel
Siam
Chang
We
Eng
history
memory
we

1977: I-Hotel

1968: Eye Hotel

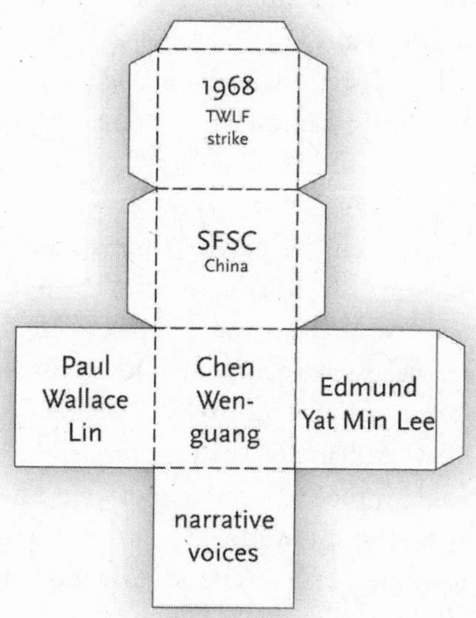

1: Year of the Monkey

So I'm Walter Cronkite, dig? And it's February 27, 1968, and I'm saying, *the* U.S. *is mired in a stalemate in Vietnam,* and *you are there.*

But whoa, let's back up twenty-nine days to the Lunar New Year. Now we know the Vietnamese call it Tet, but the Chinese own it: *New Year,* they call it. This year it's significant for Paul because on this night his dad grabs his heart like it's been antipersonnel-mined with a BLU-43, what you call *dragontooth,* like it was waiting there in one of those jungle paths, waiting for someone to put his toe on the de-toe-nator, and *boom!* There's firecrackers busting all up and down Grant Avenue, so Paul can't hear his dad cry out, but he's walking behind through a narrow in the crowded festivities and the spitting lights glittering overhead only to stumble across his dad, crumpling into a laundry heap on the sidewalk.

"Ba! What is it?"

Ba has a vision as he passes: his big mistake and no atonement. "When your mother died," he's gasping, "for your sake, I should have married again."

"What are you talking about? Help! We need help. An ambulance!"

"Just the two of us from that time on"—gasp—"Good son. Only child."

"Move away! Give him air!"

"Now, my son . . . I'm sorry . . . in the world all alone . . ."

Maybe he says this, maybe not. Paul can't hear him with all the explosions and the drumming. This Lunar New Year of the Monkey. There's a float with everyone dressed like monkeys. They're scurrying around with their wire tails bouncing. Every day for a hundred days, Paul tries to hear his father's last words. Maybe he said ". . . in the world be strong . . ." Every Chinese New Year for the rest of his life, he tries to hear his father's last words. And every year, he will hear something different.

Who's Paul? Just one of those sensitive Chinatown kids in high school, senior at Lowell, now orphaned. Isn't his story the story of every kid in the Year of the Monkey, 1968? Every one of us orphaned this year; just that Paul knows it first, a midnight orphan on the gung hay fat choy. Who are we to know that our black daddy Martin with a dream and our little white father Bobby will take bullets to their brains? By the end of the year, we are monkey orphans let loose, raising havoc; no daddies to pull the stops, temper the member; got those wired tails swinging from every rafter, we are free at last, brother, free at last.

On the Tet, boys back in Vietnam about to be orphaned too. Got their helmets fitting snug at the chin, faces smudged like football defenders, hugging those rifles for a sneak attack, all in camouflage like the VC can't see them. Must be why more Vietnamese get killed than American boys: 58,000 to 3,895. Numbers for Vietnam are rounded off to the nearest thousand. Numbers for The Boys are exact. You do the math—it's fifteen to one. We must have won. Saigon, Khe Sanh, and Hue—we get them all back. We get back the little places too, like Ben Tre and My Lai. At Ben Tre, an officer without a name says, "It became necessary to destroy it, in order to save it." At My Lai, Charlie Company gets its orders: *This is what you've been waiting for—search and destroy—and you've got it.* LBJ, the CIA, Westmoreland, McNamara, the Wise Men, they all say, let us wash our hands, go quietly into that good night. Bye-bye. See you on the judgment day.

Judgment day is here already for Paul's daddy. Wait a week to let the festivities die down, keep daddy on ice at the Cathay Wah Sang on Powell Street, over there near Jackson where the cable car makes its turn.

How many ghosts hop the cable car to make the U-turn out of Chinatown? Paul makes two calls, one to Auntie and one to the Benevolent Association, and suddenly everyone goes into action like a finely tuned machine that cranks out tradition.

"My brother, what was he thinking?" Auntie wails. "He never went to the doctor. Me, I take my pills every day. Our father died the same way."

Paul don't know what to say. Maybe it's his fault. Wasn't paying attention to the old man. But how old was he? Turning sixty-five. He was supposed to live to ninety, see Paul graduate college, get married, see his grandchildren. He was betting big-time on his only son.

Auntie's on the kitchen phone with the Cathay morticians. "My brother only has one son, and he doesn't know anything about funerals. But why should he? He's only sixteen."

"I'm eighteen, Auntie."

"Ay, how time flies. But what does it matter? He still doesn't know anything. We're going to have to take care of all the details."

"Auntie, what details?"

She waves her hand at him and continues on the phone. "You know my family, well, everyone knew our father. A modest funeral, you understand? My brother was, well, why not say it, eccentric, but we are a traditional family. Yes, Ning Yung, that's right. Someone from the Association will be in touch. I'll be there tomorrow in the morning. Yes, my nephew will come. After all, the son should be the one to choose."

"Auntie, choose what? And what about Ning Yung?"

"Chinese cemetery in Colma. Don't worry. They'll take care of everything. They're professionals. Tomorrow there'll be an obituary in the *Chinese Times.* Be sure you go and get a copy. Now, come here."

Auntie jumps up, and Paul follows her down the corridor to the study. They walk through and over the books piled with scattered newspapers on the floor. From the desk, she picks up Dad's reading glasses. She pulls one of his calligraphy brushes from a bamboo holder. "Here," she says, handing the glasses and the brush to Paul. She scans the tall shelves of books that line every wall of the study. There are books in Chinese, English, and French. There's classical Chinese literature, painting, ancient and contemporary Chinese, Western and American history, philosophy, politics, and religion. The man could read! Books are open to selected pages, annotated in the margins, wedged in every cranny of available space in the room. And behind everything else, stacked in the corners are painted canvasses. Auntie throws her hands up—"Hasn't been dusted in years. Scandalous!"—and marches out in disgust. Paul follows obediently like a dumb puppy dog. Everything is the same as it's always been. He can't remember his mother's feminine touch, her tidy ways. It's all forgotten. He looks back at the torn leather on his dad's old reading chair, and the way the wood floor is worn from the chair to the desk. He sees his dad pacing back and forth from the chair to the desk. No dust there. Not one speck.

But keep following Auntie. She's on a mission down the corridor to his dad's bedroom. She freezes at the door. Their house is a bachelor pad, so it's a shock. Clothes everywhere. More books. More canvasses. Bed unmade. You can see the shape of his body in the wrinkled sheets. That's where Auntie finally loses it. "My brother, you are gone," she weeps, grabbing the dark wood of the doorframe and slipping down into abundant sorrow. Paul bows his head, stares down at his tears spattering his dad's reading glasses and calligraphy brush. Old ink gets bloody in his young hands.

Later, Auntie sits down in the kitchen. Writes a list:

one full set of clothing including best suit
don't forget socks and shoes
reading glasses
brush
newspapers
mah-jongg set
bottle of French cognac

What else?

his favorite things
like favorite pen or favorite book
Pentax box camera

"O.K.," says Auntie. "You have to find these things. If the clothes are dirty, you bring them to me tomorrow morning and I'll wash them. Remember. His best suit. The one he wears to," she pauses foolishly, "funerals. Bring everything tomorrow. Maybe we need to get it dry cleaned, too."

"Why the favorite things?"

"We put these things with him in his coffin, to make his journey."

"Auntie, maybe he wouldn't want us to do this." Paul can't help it, but he yawns. He's been up all night in the study trying to read his dad's old letters. "Maybe he didn't believe in the journey."

"What are you talking about?"

"Camus?" he suggests. "Existentialism."

Auntie huffs, "What did he pump into your young mind? All that's irrelevant when you die in Chinatown."

Yes, ma'am, all that's irrelevant when you die in Viet'nam. To celebrate the Tet, nineteen VC commandos charge through the walls of the U.S. embassy compound in Saigon with antitank rockets. Marines hold them off until they get a helicopter of the Airborne in to finish up this mess. When it's over, you got nineteen dead VC, two dead Vietnamese civilians, and five dead American boys. And we're watching the action all on TV, dig? But that's just the embassy. The North Vietnamese have infiltrated the entire city, coming in on holiday with their ammo hid under flowers, rice, and vegetables. It's a peasant surprise. Presidential Palace, South Vietnamese Army headquarters, Westmoreland's headquarters, radio station, and the air bases all attacked. Aircraft crippled, neighborhoods reduced to rubble, two million new refugees. Ol' Walter pulls you back to the map, and you see the DMZ, line that marks North from South, and you say hey, that's a long ways away from Saigon. What's the war doing down there in the deep South? Hey, Westmoreland, are we winning this war or not? And if we are, why are twenty-six hearts and minds bleeding there on the floor of our U.S. courtyard, what you call U.S. soil?

By the time Paul's father's wake comes along, Saigon the city is under control. The war's pushed to the outside villages, which is easy because all they got to do now is destroy them. Like the lady at the front of the Cathay mortuary who is burning paper—joss paper, otherworld paper money, paper clothing, paper replicas of cars, televisions, houses, servants, everything going up in symbolic smoke to send along with Dad in the next world. Paul can see the flames go up and smolder, reflecting off the shiny brass along the casket. The pungent smell of incense and burning paper swirls through the room. Paul's dad is dressed in his best suit, sleeping on a satin bed in a beautiful box with all his favorite things.

Auntie and her husband and their five children and their children are all there. There are other cousins too, but Auntie says they are paper cousins, so do they count? If they're not careful, lady in the front might grab them, send them up in symbolic smoke.

The Association president is there. So are Paul's dad's office manager, the typesetter, and Mr. Fung, who practically does all the writing and photos for the newspaper. It's just a small operation. His dad's been publishing this local paper since his mother died maybe twelve years ago. Auntie says her brother went to hide inside that paper, use it to publish what was in his mind. She doesn't say that no one reads it; at least she never did. She reads Mr. Fung's articles about events in Chinatown, but she never understood her brother's writing—all those complicated philosophical ideas of his. Well, his friends always said he was brilliant, and they got their brilliant writing in print too. Paper comes out once a week on Friday, so today's paper's a big photo with a full-page obituary. Readers maybe don't know the whole paper is Paul's dad, and maybe this is the last issue. Auntie folds a fresh copy and tucks it in with her brother. She inspects everything: can of tea, passport, reading glasses, calligraphy brush, bottle of French cognac.

"Oh," she notices and says to Paul, "you found his old Pentax box camera." She approves. "He loved that camera and took so many pictures with it." Then she notices a book resting in the satin. "What's this?" she asks.

"Favorite book, you said," Paul mutters quietly.

"Capital?" she whispers. Even Auntie knows Karl Marx.

"Ah yeah, it was the book he was reading these days."

"Favorite?"

"He always said the book he was reading was his favorite."

Auntie's exasperated, but she smiles and looks around. She slips the book out and hugs the cover to her bosom. "Do you want to get us in trouble?" she squeaks, bowing three times.

"But—"

"Bow three times," she interjects. "Customary to do so," she instructs, and moves away with Marx under cover. Outside, she shoves the un-American book at Paul and hisses, "Get rid of this."

Meanwhile, under cover of air and artillery blasting away at the fat walls of the Citadel, Marines in assault craft ply the Perfume River to its banks to take back the sacred city of Hue. Who will bow three times to bless the blood lapping at the shore?

Next day at the funeral, Paul wears a black suit, a black waistband, and a black band on his left arm. The waistband means he's the oldest son. He knows people see it and think that that's not *all* it means. He's too young to be wearing this waistband, too young to take his father's place. Now the Chinatown community files in, solemnly bowing three times, one by one, and filling the pews at the Cathay. They've sent wreaths of flowers with ribbons naming the family, institution, or shop Paul's father did business with.

And now Paul's got to be the oldest only son, approach the casket to perform the blanket ceremony. If only there were other sons: a third son to place the white blanket of heaven, a second son to place the red blanket of life, a first son to place the gold blanket of spirituality splashed with red characters. If only there were ten sons to place ten blankets, to send his father warmly into his spirit life. But Paul's the only son, so he surreptitiously hides Karl Marx under the folded blankets, shrouds his father's traveling body with each eternal blanket, tucking the pei in to hide Dad's unfinished reading. Paul thinks, even if it's not his daddy's journey, it's their journey: Auntie's journey, Mr. Fung's, the Benevolent Association, his father's writing buddies. It's their journey, dig? It might be Karl's too. Back of the hall, paper-burning lady's going at it with the matches. Could have given her his dad's entire library plus his paintings, burn it all up to heaven.

Endless eulogies, three bows per person, and condolences take forever, but finally the pallbearers get the casket out into the long hearse. They make Paul sit in the Cadillac convertible with a giant wreathed photo of his dad. The Cathay brass band of twelve old white guys in maroon outfits starts in with their signature tune, "Nearer My God to Thee," and marches in front of the convertible Cad. Paul looks back at the hearse following. All the other cars follow the hearse. He's on parade through Chinatown. Everyone on the street is staring at him and the giant photo. Does he look like a younger version of his dad? Chinese look to see if they recognize the guy in the photo. Kids run alongside the band and then the Cad, like it's a continuation of New Year's, and tourists snap their Brownies. He can hear the tourists saying, "The band is playing 'Onward Christian Soldiers.' Can you beat that in Chinatown? These folks are Christian too. Honey, is that yellow confetti they're throwing out of the cars? How festive!" Paul grips his dad's photo and hides behind it, every nerve in his body electrocuted by an overloaded circuitry of grief and humiliation.

Suddenly, he senses a presence at his side. Someone has jumped into the Cad. "They are going to stop at the Benevolent Association first, next the newspaper office, then at your apartment."

Paul looks at the man whose agile body leaped into the moving car.

"I know this is highly irregular, but I thought you could use some company."

Paul nods behind the photo, sucks in his breath. Got to get his composure back.

"I'm Chen Wen-guang," says the agile man. "Friend of your father." He nods at the photo. "He would hate all this"—he looks around at the spectacle, "but—"

Paul finishes the thought: "It's irrelevant when you die in Chinatown." He notices Chen's white gloves. So he's one of the pallbearers.

Chen smiles. "He always said you were a smart kid."

The procession comes to a halt. Rest stop: Benevolent Association. His dad's ghost is halfway to heaven. Time to pay his last respects, eat some boiled chicken, a bit of steamed bun, maybe take a banana for the trip.

"We'll talk again later, I promise." Chen jumps out into the street, again like an acrobat. "What did you put in that casket with your dad? It's really heavy."

Two more stops: the newspaper office on Clay Street and their apartment around the corner on Commercial. Auntie's planted someone there to open the doors, make sure Paul's dad gets a good last visit, then shoo his ghost out. The doors on the back of the hearse get flung open. The mortuary director pulls out a wreath of flowers and stands at attention. The brass band plays another Salvation Army tune.

Finally they get to the edge of Chinatown. They might be a band of old white guys, but the edge of Chinatown is their limit. It's also the limit for the Cad. Paul gets out and sits shotgun in the hearse with a burning cigar of incense. A motorcycle escort takes over. It's not that Paul has never left Chinatown, but it's always foreign out there. Chinatown's his citadel. But when you die, your bones got to travel thirteen miles south outside the city to the Chinese Cemetery in Colma.

As Paul speeds away from Chinatown with his dad's spirit and favorite things, the boys in Vietnam are battling each other through the streets of Hue, house by house, block by block, hand to hand. Boys got to charge into buildings tossing grenades and wipe out the enemy room by room, meter by meter. Citadel's a concrete stonewall maze, sort of Old World castle city that American boys never seen back home. Center is the Imperial Palace of Peace, surrounded by a city maze of side-by-side stone houses of the clergy, commoners, and bureaucrats. Boys got to put up the flag at the Palace to show they won the battle, but first they got to get the tanks in there with special concrete-piercing shells to blow out the thick walls, got to destroy ten thousand houses and forty percent of the city. Vietnam boys got their own map of trenches and tunnels and sniper positions; time being, it's their citadel.

Paul stares into the pit at the coffin, throws in his black armband and his black waistband. It peels away from his waist like a thick skin, exposing his guts for one horrific moment; then suddenly, the tension in his abdomen recedes. No one notices, it seems. Bow ties and white gloves flutter down to the casket. Once again, almost mysteriously, the agile friend of his father, Chen, is at his side; he, like the other pallbearers, tosses his bow tie and gloves, and now his ungloved hand rises to Paul's shoulder. Paul wants to cry out, but he cannot. Everything gets pushed down deep. He's still trying to hear, through the fireworks, his dad's last words. There's nothing but the soft din of juniper and flowers pelting dark wood.

Far as any outsider can tell, on the one side it's American boys and Vietnam boys dying. On the other side, it's just Vietnam boys dying. ARVN/U.S. versus NVA/VC. Fighting's fierce, but the ARVN/U.S. have the advantage of their technology, the superiority of aircraft and artillery. To save lives and win the city, we shell and bomb the sacred history of Hue back to the Stone Age. Six thousand residents die in the rubble and one hundred and twenty thousand wander homeless. In retaliation, sacred history is replaced by sacrilegious history: they massacre the enemies of the state, the government officials, the sympathizers, and the Catholics; pop them off in mass graves, three thousand human lives, Vietnamese rounded off to the thousand. Meanwhile, inside the city Citadel, maggots ooze through the strewn corpses, anonymous piles of sons and daughters, mothers and fathers, spouses and lovers, rats and rabid dogs feasting on their bloated corpses, a fog of stench escaping the crumbling maze, groveling in pity at the perfumed moat.

A week later, Auntie calls and says, "We go to Colma for Ching Ming. This year it's April fifth. It's a Friday, so you come to my house after school. Don't worry. I'll get everything ready, but you pay attention. One of these days it's going to be your responsibility. You got to do this for your mother and father. For your grandfather. I say to my kids, don't let us down, especially when we're dead."

Night before Ching Ming, MLK Jr. is standing on the balcony of the Lorraine Motel in Memphis, Tennessee, gets shot through the neck. Next day, the flags are all at half mast. School's abuzz. They're rioting in DC, in Chicago. What's gonna happen here in SF? The Panthers over in Oakland calling for keeping the peace. It's not the time to go to the streets. What you want? A bloodbath? They're pretending they've got everything under control. Don't know that Eldridge Cleaver's yet to see his soul on ice and Bobby Hutton's young years got to be cut short.

Once again Paul's in a car driving to the Chinese cemetery, squeezed between Auntie and her kids and grandkids. Car smells like roast pig and jai choy. Cousin playing Sly and the Family Stone on the local channel. No assassination's going to interfere with Chinese tradition. "Better to go to Ching Ming, get outside the city," Auntie justifies. "Ancestors know better. Get outside the city."

"But what about on the way back?"

"We take safe streets. Inside Chinatown, no trouble. Here," she says, passing a box of pork bao. "I got extra for you. You must be hungry from school. Are you eating? You didn't come last week for dinner. What happened?" She nudges him. "Got a girlfriend?"

Paul's mouth is filled with bread. "Huh?"

"It's O.K. Forty-nine days are past. You can go back to your party life."

"Thanks, Auntie."

At the cemetery, other Chinese already there for the Clear Brightness Festival. Auntie becomes central command, moves her troops into action. Every kid's got a job. Sweep, rake, pick out the dead leaves, dump the old flowers, make a nice arrangement of new flowers. Stick the red candles in the soft dirt, get them lighted. Make a spread and it's a feast. Center attraction is the suckling pig's head looking all tanned and glazed. Contrasting is a whole white boiled chicken. Then the sautéed jai choy and dim sum. Auntie throws in a boiled egg, an orange, a banana, and an apple. Ancestors get three bowls of rice, three cups of wine, three cups of tea, and three pairs of chopsticks.

Paul has to light the incense bundle. "Don't blow on the fire," Auntie warns. "Bad luck." She fans the fire with a newspaper.

One of the kids is holding on to a bag of kitty litter. Auntie rips open the bag. "This is my invention," she says proudly. "Works good, you know." She pours the kitty litter into a can and demonstrates how the litter is going to hold up the incense sticks. What's tradition if you don't improve on it? It's also a good bed for burning the joss papers and the otherworld money. Next time the house's on fire, run to the kitty litter.

Now it's the ceremony: three incense sticks per person, three bows per person.

Paul does his thing obediently, but turning from the altar, he sees Chen coming forward with three sticks of incense.

Chen greets Auntie and smiles at Paul. She says, "Maybe you are interested in my brother's books. Talk to my nephew and make a visit to the house."

Chen rakes his fingers through his hair and says to Paul, "Have you walked to the other side of the cemetery?" He motions to Auntie. "Don't worry. I'll drive Paul home."

Auntie's wraps up the food offerings. "Look, you take this home for your dinner." She hands Paul a hefty shopping bag.

Paul follows Chen, crisscrossing the tombstones carved with Chinese characters. He points at the names and notes the oldest families, the earliest dates. "No paper names used here. When you die, you use your real name. Too late for immigration to deport you."

Paul nods, but he knows his name's not paper. It's the real thing. His father's story is different.

"I introduced your mother to your father," Chen says casually. "She was very beautiful, much younger, my age. Twenty years difference, but it didn't matter. At first they met with their brains. She fell in love with his mind. Well, there was more of course, since you didn't pop out of their brains. You were born right away."

"How did you know my father?"

"He was a friend of my family in Paris, but I wasn't even born. He came to Paris to paint around 1920. He hung around Chou En-lai and the others at the Pascal Restaurant, on the Rue de l'Ecole de Medicine." Chen speaks the last words in French. "He helped Chou stage a protest of the Chinese Legation, traveled around Europe with Chou to get recruits for the Chinese Communist Youth Corps."

Paul is hearing this for the first time. "Chou?" he asks.

"Yes, China's premier. The same."

"He never said."

"They parted ways. Chou returned to China to fight with Sun Yat Sen. Your father came home. What he really wanted was to return to his painting, and his family was here. His father died suddenly. Your auntie was a young girl, and he was the only son. He was a Marxist, but also filial."

Paul is quiet. He isn't a Marxist, but he already knows it's going to be impossible to be filial.

"I looked him up when I came to study. He remembered my family from those days in Paris. When I met him, he was living and painting in the Monkey Block."

"Monkey Block?"

"That's what they called the block on Montgomery at Washington. The street was a hangout for artists and writers. The building was full of artist studios. Used to be the Black Cat Café in the basement."

Paul follows Chen. Chen's a stroller, reading the stones and throwing out anecdotes. Paul's trying to grab his past as Chen tosses it over his shoulders. "Let's take that pig's head and head on home," Chen says. "I'm famished."

Paul thinks *famished* is an interesting word.

Back at the house, Chen clears off the kitchen table, washes the dishes, rummages around the drawers and finds a tablecloth that hasn't been used since Paul's mother was alive. He spreads that out, boils water for tea, sets the table. Paul's not famished, he's starving, but Chen's got to have a pot of rice too. Far as Paul knows, it's high dining. Chen fills glasses with foaming beer and toasts. "Now," he says, settling in with the food and steaming rice, "eat slowly. Think about your father. And Martin Luther King." He shakes his head. "I teach at San Francisco State. I cancelled my classes today. A great loss."

Paul sips at the foam across his glass of beer. Acid bubbles singe his senses. Suddenly it occurs to him. He could get stupidly wasted, like every other high school kid with that opportunity. Chen seems oblivious, cutting into the pig's head, relishing every bite. It's an empty freedom.

Next day, he doesn't know why, but he starts to clean his dad's house like he's looking for something. Those paintings in the corners. Dust, sweep, polish, wipe, classify. It's like he's one of Auntie's kids, commandeered to tidy up the gravesite. All summer he's into it. Auntie comes round to see what he's up to. She's pleased, but he doesn't stop. The dark grain of the wood floors and paneling is shining back at her. Smells like Pledge. "Is this healthy?" she asks timidly. She's looking at her brother's old paintings. Kid's got them hanging on the walls. "Are you having a psychological crisis? You should enjoy the summer with your friends. It's not normal to be alone inside this old house."

"I'm fine, Auntie." He's distracted. On the television, Walter's talking about Chicago. Police clubbing and gassing protestors at the Democratic Convention.

End of summer he knows the house, every shelf, every drawer, every corner, everything. House is immaculate. Day after Labor Day he steps out, locks the door. Heads off to SFSC. Got to see Chen to find the real keys to get back in.

Chen's got a class in contemporary Chinese literature. He lectures without notes. It's all in his head. This cat's amazing. Quotes passages. Talks dates, anecdotes. Like he knows the authors. Maybe he does. Paul goes home and finds the books. It's all there in his library, in Chinese and in translation. His dad's scribbling's in the margins, but it's mostly in Chinese. Paul's got to use a dictionary to decipher it, or ask Chen. Chen says, "You know Yat Min Lee? Calls himself Edmund. He sits in the back. I'll introduce you. He can read it all for you. And in return, you can lend him the books. He doesn't have the money to buy them."

Turns out Edmund is the smartest kid in class. Reads everything in the original Chinese, criticizes the translations. Paul tries to be friendly, but Edmund's too busy. He comes around when he can, hangs out in Paul's library, but he's got a job busing tables at Fisherman's Wharf. That's his routine. Got to make money to keep from taking it from his family's table. Family's loud and noisy, crowded into two rooms above a laundry. His business is everybody's. As for Paul, his dad always had rent money coming in from his properties. Now Paul's got to do the accounting every month. Two boys wishing they had the other's problems.

Today Chen's on to Lu Hsun. "Mao Tse-Tung has said that Lu Hsun is his favorite writer." Everyone perks up at this. Mao, he's the man. Lu Hsun's got to be our favorite too. Chen goes on to give the details. Lu Hsun was studying medicine in Japan when he saw these imperialist war slides of Japanese soldiers chopping off the head of a Chinese spy. What disgusted him were the bored Chinese in the pictures who were forced to see the spectacle. That's it. Lu Hsun gives up medicine. What's the point? He could study all he wanted to make his people healthy in body, but they were sick in their minds, dig. Now this might seem like a jump, but Lu Hsun thinks the answer is literature. So he starts a new life writing.

Chen pulls it out of his head: Lu Hsun's preface to his collection of short stories. He's got a photographic memory, but if you want to check, you can follow along in the book: "When I was young, I, too, had many dreams. Most of them came to be forgotten, but I see nothing in this to regret. For although recalling the past may make you happy, it may sometimes also make you lonely, and there is no point in clinging in spirit to lonely bygone days. However, my trouble is that I cannot forget completely, and these stories have resulted from what I have been unable to erase from my memory." Chen's voice trails off like he's forgotten what he's on to, but Paul knows he's talking to him. Why is the call to write so strong? Only a writer knows. You can give any excuse you want.

Paul says to Edmund, "Chinese students meeting today. You going?"

"I have to work," Edmund says. "Let me know what happens."

Later, Paul reports. It's one of the ICSA Chinese who speaks. That's Intercollegiate Chinese Students Association. Fills in for a Chinese BSU. Chinese cat wears these shades that he never takes off. Works on being intimidating. He says, "What we are trying to do is to expose the contradictions of this society to our communities, separate fact from fiction. Fiction is that the Chinese have never suffered as much as the black or brown communities. Fact is the Chinese community has the same basic problems. Difference is that we got the neon lights and tourist restaurants. Fact is the restaurants are staffed by illiterate Chinese who work fourteen hours a day, six days a week. Fiction is Chinese businessman is doing good business. Fact is this is exploitation of Chinese immigrants who can only find work in sweatshops, laundries, and restaurants in Chinatown."

Edmund says, "I'm not illiterate. What's he talking about?"

Paul says, "It's not about you. It's about the others."

Edmund says, "I am the others."

Paul says, "There's another meeting. This one is Third World. You get in if you're Chinese."

"I have to go home and work," Edmund says. He always has to go home and work. Paul doesn't have to go anywhere. And no one's waiting at home for him.

Stokely Carmichael's the main attraction. You get in to hear him if you got some color in your skin. BSU stands at the door and checks you out. Right on, brother. Paul likes this feeling of attitude rippling under his skin. Some white brother who's sympathetic wants to get in. Says he knows Stokely personally. BSU takes him aside. "Nothing personal, brother, but this is about self-determination, you dig?" Paul files the information: self-determination.

Stokely tells it like it is. In a nutshell: you got to get control over the power structure. It's not about you getting some Swahili classes. It's about getting the methodology and the ideology. We got to heighten the contradictions to politically awaken our people. Easy to die for your people, but more difficult to live to work and kill for your people.

Then some other BSU cats get up and talk about the *War of the Flea*. Get down to the strategy, dig? How we are going to wear down the man. Paul nods; this is a Chinese thing. Guerilla practice of Uncles Ho and Mao. Lao Tzu. *Art of War*. Asians the brains behind the operation.

Next day in Chen's class, it's Mao Tse-Tung's poetry. At least that's the syllabus. But Mao's practice comes to class instead. BSU and TWLF students walk in with their leather jackets, Afros, dark glasses, berets, what have you, but mostly attitude, and announce: *This class is over. We are on strike until the pig administration meets our non-negotiable demands.* Someone lights a match in the trash can, and everyone files out. War of the flea.

Month later, it's more than fleas out there warring. Buses lining up at Holloway and Nineteenth, black folks stepping out like it's a church function. All the big honchos of the community arrive: Reverends Cecil Williams and Lloyd Wake of Glide Memorial, California Assembly Rep. Willie Brown, Economic Opportunity Director and Delegate to the Democratic Convention Ron Dellums, and physician-publisher of the *Sun-Reporter* Dr. Carlton Goodlett. Besides which, some of these men are alumni of SF State. It's a we-shall-overcome protest gathering. Even so, the students are in charge: *On strike! Shut it down! We want the puppet!* They pelt the windows of the administration building with rocks. Throw garbage cans at the doors. Turn over the cafeteria tables. Throw typewriters out the windows. Run into the library and push the books off the shelves. Stuff them down the toilets. War of the flea.

Inside, the bureaucrats hide the new and acting president, S. I. Hayakawa, in the bathroom. He must be the puppet! Outside the police line up with their riot gear, batons in their fists. You can hear S. I. speaking from his post over the Big Brother speaker system. *This is your acting president. I order you to leave the campus at once. There are no innocent bystanders. I thought if we allowed you to talk you would calm down, but now this problem is escalating. I don't want anyone to get hurt.* His voice gets shrill.

Down in the field, publisher and physician Dr. Carlton Goodlett's being carried on the shoulders of his cohort. Looks like two hundred colored people with Goodlett riding on top in a sea of white students, some say six thousand. He's got his own bullhorn system, and he's yelling, "We're not subscribing to violence at this time! If the police feel that their duty is to provoke violence, all hell is going to break loose." Who's he talking to? S. I. in the bathroom? Six thousand white students? Tactical squad lined up on the green? They aren't listening. Police got their orders. They arrest the good doctor and club the non-innocent bystanders. Throw everyone into paddy wagons. Situation explodes. Garbage cans get firebombed. *Blow the motherfucker up!* Folks go on a rampage, smash the windows of all the parked cars along Nineteenth. Someone climbs up to the wires of the MUNI car and yanks them off. M looks like a giant metal insect with a wagging antenna stalled in traffic. Another group pushes a UPI station wagon into the intersection, releases the brakes, and lets it roll. Folks hysterical and running in every direction.

Paul's got his pockets filled with rocks, just in case. He's in a stand-off with others, between defending himself from and sticking with the crowd. He sees a girl being dragged by her jacket collar into a paddy wagon, and he fingers a jagged stone in the deep of his pocket. He thinks he's going to save her, but strong arms surround him from behind. He tenses, ready for his own struggle, then he recognizes the voice. "No! Don't do it!" Chen has got him in one of those kung fu grips. "Run this way," he commands. They slip away through Quonset huts faking as offices and classrooms. Paul looks back in shock at a charging cavalry of mounted police. Suddenly he sees himself multiplied, monkey orphans let loose, raising havoc. One by one, an invisible daddy cracks his multiplying monkey skulls. Who is free to be free at last?

2: Language in Reaction

There exists an unscientific attitude toward language that results in doctrinal disagreements. We must understand that problems are formulated in words, and that a change in the attitude toward language can help us become understanding listeners. Alfred Korzybski said, "A person tends to see the world as conforming to the words he has been taught to use about it." There is a system of semantic principles to guide us in the everyday thinking, talking, listening, reading, and writing that leads us to our actions. Let's examine the following story:

Once upon a time, there were two public institutions of higher learning, separated by a great bay but connected by a great bridge. The differences and the commonalities between the two sites of education were also greatly exaggerated.

Institution A considered itself a center of research and a factory for knowledge. Its president had said as much, that what the automobile had done for the first half of the twentieth century, the university could do for the latter half. The factory model of the university didn't go over too well with the students, who protested that they were free individuals who would not be cranked out like cloned widgets on a production line. One of the institution's most famous students had spoken passionately about how it was time to put one's body on the gears and wheels to stop the machine. Students didn't want to be the end product machined from a blueprint they did not believe. The factory model was probably the wrong model to choose, especially since most of the students were the children of middle-class professionals or had those sorts of hopes for their educations.

While Institution A was located in a nice white neighborhood, the surrounding neighborhoods were communities of colored people, mostly black and yellow. Families from these neighborhoods sent a few students to the university, but other colored students came from across the state. Colored students didn't want to be factory products either, but they didn't mince words about the blueprint or being free individuals; they simply wanted to control the production itself. They wanted their own classes, their own professors, their own rules, and more of themselves at the university. They argued that their history of slavery, genocide, and racial prejudice gave moral imperative to their demands, and that a public institution of learning should provide an equal opportunity for education for all citizens, regardless of race, class, or creed. And they were going to get it by any means necessary.

One day, a famous black author and leader of a black organization came to teach at the university. He aroused a crowd of students into shouting Fuck the Governor! Fuck the Governor! *To anyone who wanted to throw bricks into the gears, this was a splendid brick. Institution A decided that this man would not continue to teach at the university. His rally was not the entire reason for his dismissal, but it was a convenient rallying point. The colored students organized a protest against Institution A to push for control of their education. They organized a strike to stop the work of the university since, after all, it was a factory, and they were the worker-products. The colored students were a very small minority on campus, but the white students, the faculty, and even the staff also joined the strike. After fifty-three days of striking and four hundred arrests, including violent encounters with local police, sheriffs, and the National Guard, involving rocks, fruits, mace, tear gas, and billy clubs, Institution A agreed to establish a department of ethnic studies.*

Establishment of the department came with some fanfare and a budget just substantial enough to create a sensation of power and competition, creating political fissures between black, brown, yellow, and red students and faculty, throwing into contest what had once been idealized as a rainbow of colored solidarity. The radical white students who had wanted to throw their bodies against the gears and the black leader who could rally thousands of students to yell Fuck the Governor! *had fallen away, leaving the work of education to the bureaucrats and the folks who needed the jobs. Despite these difficulties, Institution A survived this period of turmoil.*

On the other side of the bay, Institution B considered itself a teaching college, a middling institution in a tiered system that kept the research factory on top and the two-year technical college on the bottom. Institution B was the meat in the sandwich positioned to provide the middle management, midlevel professionals, the credentialed workers of the great society. This was part of the Master

Plan. The idea that there was a master plan planned by masters outside the college didn't go over too well with the students, who protested that the plan was really much broader and began in grammar school when children were placed on tracks that headed to one of the three tiered educational institutions, to a possible fourth (prison) or fifth institution (military), or to none at all. If Institution A invoked the automobile, Institution B invoked the train. The Master Plan was a great train system chugging students along predetermined tracks. The train model was probably the wrong model to choose, especially since many of the students were the children of laborers who laid tracks, built cars, loaded cargo, harvested or cooked food, cleaned compartments, and mined the fuel.

While Institution B was located in a nice white neighborhood, the surrounding neighborhoods were communities of working-class white and colored people—black, yellow, and brown. Working young adults from these neighborhoods attended the college, and more came from across the state. Colored students didn't want to be part of any master plan either, especially if being colored might put you on a particular train from the very beginning. And they weren't interested in sharing; sharing had only gotten them nine hundred black students in eighteen thousand. They wanted to make their own plans. They wanted their own rules, their own classes, their own professors, and more of themselves at the college. They argued that their history of slavery, genocide, and racial prejudice gave moral imperative to their demands, and that a public institution of learning should provide an equal opportunity for education for all citizens, regardless of race, class, or creed. And they were going to get it by any means necessary.

One day, a black instructor at Institution B, who was also a leader of a black organization, gave a speech. He said that Institution B was a nigger-producing factory and called upon students to Pick up the Gun! *to defend themselves against a cracker administration. While this may have been a passionate cry to revolution, Institution B decided that he should be fired from teaching at the college. His speech was not the entire reason for his dismissal, but it was a rallying point, and eventually the colored students organized a protest against Institution B to push for control of their education. They organized a strike to stop the work of the college since, after all, it was a train station, and they were the worker-passengers. The colored students were a very small minority on campus, but the white students and the faculty also joined the strike. After 137 days on strike and nine hundred arrests, including violent encounters with local and mounted police and tactical squads involving rocks, bombs, arson, and billy clubs, Institution B agreed to establish a department of ethnic studies.*

Establishment of the department came with some fanfare and a budget just substantial enough to create a sensation of power and competition, creating political fissures between black, brown, and yellow, throwing into contest what had once been idealized as a rainbow of colored solidarity. The radical white students who had opposed the Master Plan and the black teacher who rallied students to Pick up the Gun! *had fallen away, leaving the work of education to the bureaucrats and the folks who needed the jobs. Despite these difficulties, Institution B survived this period of turmoil.*

These are textbook cases with semantic morals. In both cases, students got what they wanted: a department of ethnic studies. But it wasn't about what they wanted—it was about how they went about getting it. In this sense, it was all about words.

Reread the stories about Institutions A and B. Instead of worrying about whether colored students had equal access to higher education, ask yourself the following questions:

1. What is the significance of comparing Institution A to a factory or Institution B to a train station, and how do these comparisons influence the actions of the students?
2. What do you think about the provocative comments made by the black leaders to students at both institutions?
3. Is it possible or reasonable for students to go on strike?
4. Why does the narrator use the word *black* instead of *Negro*?
5. Considering the disagreements between the students and the institutions, was the violence incurred necessary?
6. Was the conflict between the students and institutions a war of words?

Jazz was our acting president's great passion. In his twenty-part jazz seminar, he spoke about the sources and characteristics of jazz, from the blues, through bebop, boogie-woogie, and gospel, to the California-New Orleans revival. Everyone had forgotten that he played the harmonica.

They only remember that he hoisted himself onto the back of a truck parked at the gateway of our once peaceful college and tore out the wires to a sound system. The truck was being used as a stage for ranting and epithets. Free speech, his tam-o'-shanter! He surprised them by climbing onto that truck, yelling, "Don't touch me! I'm the president of the college!" He jumped up and down and mimicked their ridiculous chants: *On strike! Shut it down! On strike! Shut it down!* He had a plan to beautify the campus, plant flowerbeds and pipe in swinging music on the intercom. He might have piped in his entire twenty-part jazz seminar, complete with musical examples. Instead we got this mindless ranting.

One of his colleagues yelled out his name, attaching it to General Tojo. He peered through those thick black horn-rims into the crowd. A sansei student had a sign with his caricature that said, "Tojo is alive and well and living under Mt. Tam O'Shanter." He had spent his life's work in general semantics, articulating a theory of language to fight precisely this sort of fascism. He fired that colleague Chen on the spot. Later he had to capitulate. He told Chen he had meant to say "Shame on you!" but after all, didn't he understand his fury?

Someone had ripped his tam-o'-shanter from his head. He saw it spinning in the air, tossed from hand to hand. This was typical of the disrespect he had to contend with. As he said, the leadership of the SDS and the BSU had shown themselves to be a gang of goons, gangsters, conmen, neo-Nazis, and common thieves. And he was Tojo?

This was precisely the sort of semantic error he tried to point out in his comments to the faculty senate when he said, "I wish to comment on the intellectually slovenly habit, now popular among whites as well as blacks, of denouncing as racist those who oppose or are critical of any Negro tactic or demand. If we are to call our college racist, then what term do we have left for the government of Rhodesia?" He must have heard someone yell out, "Racist! Racist!" He continued, "Black students are again disrupting the campus. A significant number of whites, including faculty members, condone and even defend this maneuver. In other words, there are many whites who do not apply to blacks the same standards of morality and behavior as they apply to whites. This is an attitude of moral condescension that every self-respecting Negro has a right to resent, and does resent."

As a self-respecting minority himself, he felt he could speak for the Negro. And this was not the first time. In one of his many books, he devoted an entire chapter to the subject: "The Self-Image and Intercultural Understanding, or How to be Sane though Negro." The tenants of this chapter were simple. If the Negro has a self-concept of *I am a Negro* accompanied by a sense of inferiority, he will act obsequiously, and the white person he encounters may act with superiority. If the Negro has a self-concept of *I am a Negro* accompanied by a sense of defensiveness, he will act counter-defensively, and the white person may act offensively. If the Negro has a self-concept of *I am a Negro* as a simple statement of fact, then he will act naturally, and the white person may act naturally too. Therefore, the power to determine the outcome of a meeting lies with the Negro. Now the Negro might say that he *is* acting naturally, but how do you know you are acting naturally? The secret to acting naturally is exemplified in the famous person, a movie star or prime minister, who forgets he is famous and acts naturally. To act naturally, you have to forget that you are Negro. Why shouldn't this be possible—our acting president himself was able to forget he was Japanese. White people are ignorant and require psychotherapy to get over their obsession with skin color; so, the Negro must act as the white person's psychotherapist. Granted, this will be accepted in small steps, but the basis for happiness is minimum expectations. In the long struggle for equal rights and opportunities, because of the strong moral sense of the nation as well as economic and practical necessity, segregation must eventually end. This is the self-fulfilling prophecy of political democracy, and communication is the first step.

However, psychotherapy at the impasse of the current breakdown in communications was no longer possible. Didn't the faculty realize, as our acting president did, that the SDS had assumed tactics similar to those of the Nazis of the thirties, intending to disrupt democratic institutions and bring down the political structure? He characterized the BSU leadership as actuated by self-hatred, strutting about self-consciously behind dark glasses, playing Black Panther, stalking in gangs, scaring little girls. This behavior, he said, would have been simply pathetic if knuckleheaded whites didn't take them seriously. He never took them seriously. He recognized the primitive and animistic notions embedded in their language that prevented them from comprehending civilized paths to a democratic society. This was what he had characterized as the "Jim Crowing of the mind." Segregation was not a physical condition but a mental condition. He knew they were all flying high as kites on dope.

He only took this job on the condition he be allowed to call in the police. He testified to Congress that to restore proper order during campus unrest, troops should be sent in early, and lots of them. He personally addressed the police himself as they entered the campus, advising them to ignore the students' bad words and to smile. Bad words, he said to them, can't harm you, and shouting them allows the students to blow off steam. Cursing has a therapeutic effect. However, if arrests were necessary, they would not be made in vain, for he would offer no amnesty to students. He further offered his knowledge of general semantics, saying some people, as the result of a childhood experience, cannot help being frightened by the mere sight of a policeman. Similarly, some people automatically become hostile at the words *un-American, Nazi,* or *Communist*. This is the unfortunate business of being blinded by prejudice and living in the delusional world of abstractions.

Ten thousand letters came to his desk supporting his decisive actions. The governor himself saw him on television and announced to his cohort, "I think we've found our man." Our acting president was not only exhilarated by this response, but also by the confrontation itself. It was a rollercoaster he rode with the excitement of a child born again.

Although no one took his dismissal of Chen seriously, it was cited as a further example of our acting president's autocratic highhandedness. During the strike Chen used a café in North Beach as his classroom. The Brighton Express on Pacific Avenue was a popular café and hangout for the bohemian crowd. A nisei woman named Joanna ran the café. In the past, when the president enjoyed the local jazz scene, on occasion he too frequented the café. Joanna, always good-humored and friendly, called him "Professor." One supposes she called Chen "Professor" too. During the strike, they were all teaching their classes off campus somewhere, in their homes or in churches. This business with the strike was nonsense. No student wanted to lose a year of coursework. No teacher wanted to waste his time on a picket line.

Students gathered around a couple of tables, and Chen began his lecture, "Mao Tse-Tung on Literature and Art." *"Comrades!"* he both addressed the students and quoted from Mao. *"You have been invited to this forum today to exchange ideas and examine the relationship between work in the literary and artistic fields and revolutionary work in general . . .* This," he said, "is how Mao addressed the Yenan forum twenty-six years ago on May 2, 1942."

One of Chen's young protégés, Paul Wallace Lin, sat among the students with a notebook and fingered the pages of Mao's talk.

Chen moved around the tables confidently. Two or three patrons were huddled in the corners with coffee, reading their newspapers but still listening to Chen. Even Joanna was seated among the students. "It's important to consider the date of this talk. May second, two days before the May Fourth movement anniversary. As we have previously discussed, on May 4, 1919, a student uprising in Peking and Shanghai protested the Versailles Treaty. The Versailles Treaty marked the end of World War I but also relinquished previously held Chinese territory to the Japanese. This was the beginning of a Chinese nationalist movement driven by Marxist antifeudal, anti-imperialist political forces."

Paul nodded and underlined *student uprising*. His father had been a student then too.

"And 1942. The United States had just entered the war against Japan, a war the Chinese had been fighting already for five years. Mao identified the principal enemy of this period: Japanese imperialists."

Paul scribbled the dates into his notebook. Imagine Professor Chen pontificating on Mao, adding fuel to the fire already destroying our campus.

Chen continued, "Taken in this context of war, Mao continues . . . '*In our struggle for the liberation of the Chinese people, there are various fronts, among which are the fronts of the pen and of the gun, the cultural and the military fronts. To defeat the enemy we must rely primarily on the army with guns. But this army alone is not enough; we must also have a cultural army, which is absolutely indispensable for uniting our own ranks and defeating the enemy.*'" Indeed. But to be fair, Chen never had the teeth for violence. He would never have jumped on a truck and yanked out power cords and destroyed equipment. He was much too refined. He really believed in the cultural army, in liberation by means of the pen. So he continued.

"I realize, considering the violence we have sustained in recent days under the severe measures of the current administration—"such an oblique reference to our acting president—"it would seem to some that the gun might be the more appropriate tool. I want to make it clear that I am not advocating the gun. We are here to discuss contemporary Chinese literature, but we cannot examine that literature without also examining the political and social context that drives its formation during this time period."

The students loved Chen. Suddenly his knowledge of the Chinese revolution and his Marxist point of view were in vogue. They sat around him mesmerized, as if he were Confucius himself, Chinese wisdom coupled with his contemporary knowledge of revolution. They all wanted revolution, but they didn't know what revolution was. Paul, for example, wanted revolution, and he wanted this revolution packaged in the poet intellectual. But was he listening when Chen again quoted Mao? *"Many writers and artists stand aloof from the masses and lead empty lives; naturally they are unfamiliar with the language of the people."* The language of the people was exactly the language our acting president had spent his life studying. Unlike Chen, he knew this language and how the common understanding of this language controlled society.

Accordingly, what Chen was not telling his students is that any war of words will ultimately be resolved in society's decision to define those words. Art and literature. Mao Tse-Tung and the Cultural Revolution defined those words in the service of a political agenda. Poetry for the Marxist-Leninist must be written for the proletariat. Everything that Chen loved about art and literature had to be destroyed or changed. He knew this, but he didn't tell the students.

Chen's class was over. Students paid for their coffees and mud pies and wandered out, back to the picket line or to the next noon rally. Paul remained behind.

"Where's Yat Min today?" Chen queried, using Edmund's Chinese name.

"Working. Always working. He sent his apologies, and here's his paper."

Chen nodded. It was a thick treatise written entirely in Chinese. "Since he's mastered two languages, maybe he should study a third." Chen said this as if thinking to himself.

"Right. I'll let him know."

"It's not necessary. He'll figure it out for himself." He packed his papers away in his briefcase and announced, "Do you have some time for a short walk? It's just down Montgomery." As they passed out of the café, he asked, "Did you know the Brighton?"

"No."

"Maybe not. Your father used to hang out here, but then after your mother died, I guess he never came around again. Do you know Janis Joplin?"

"Not personally."

"She was here the other day. Everyone's been here. Now you too."

They walked down Montgomery to Washington and stared at a parking lot. "Remember what I said about the Monkey Block? It used to be right here. There was a huge building, four stories, occupied most of the block. Your father lived here. It's where he painted his best work. Where he met his friends. He knew everyone. William Saroyan, Diego Rivera, Kenneth Rexroth. Well, Rexroth is still around anyway. When Rivera came to paint his murals with his wife, Frida Kahlo, your father got the Chinese Revolutionary Artist Club together to host them. He was going to name you Diego, but your mother favored Paul. It was Paul for Paul Cézanne and Paul Valéry. Painter-poet. They had romantic hopes for you. You know, he knew Valéry in Paris."

"What about Wallace?"

"Wallace? Middle name? Must have been Wallace Stevens. Your mother studied him at Stanford. It was her thesis."

Paul shook his head because he didn't know any of this. Chen could have been making it all up. The building was a parking lot, gone, Chen said, for about ten years now. All Paul ever knew during his years growing up was this parking lot. And there was more history before that, including Robert Louis Stevenson, Ambrose Bierce, Bret Harte, and Mark Twain. The names read like his American literature textbook. A history of artists and writers had been swept away, and now Chen was saying his father had been the rare Chinese American artist to add his name to the Monkey Block.

"Chinatown is just over there." Chen pointed. "One day, your father went inside and closed the door."

"Why? I don't understand. I didn't even know."

Chen was silent for a moment. "I didn't consider that. Of course, nothing was ever different for you. You never saw the change."

"I feel I knew someone different. I know the paintings. Found all of them. I put them up, but I don't know the person who painted them. I found his old easel and a box of dried-up tubes, but I never saw him paint."

"You know, Valéry was a poet, then one day he quit, just like that, and never wrote a thing for the next twenty years. I think your father admired that sort of resolve to find another path. Does that make sense?"

"Maybe."

"Some of those men at the funeral know your father's past. They were in the artists' club, but they might not admit it today. People like Rexroth and the North Beach crowd didn't even know he died. For them, he disappeared."

Chen crossed the street and Paul followed. They walked in silence over to Kearny, weaving around the old Chinese and Filipino bachelors emerging from the pool halls, barber, and cigar shops. "Like this building, this International Hotel." He pointed to the sign on the central door and gestured up. "Occupied the entire block. The Monkey was taller, another story higher, and a more beautiful, stately granite structure, but like this, with businesses below, offices, restaurants, and when your father was there, the general motley crowd of bohemian types." They turned the corner at Jackson to get a sense of the size of the building.

Some Chinese kids were hanging outside a storefront, smoking in a group. "Hey, Paul," they nodded in recognition. He knew them from the Y. Now they were hanging out at Leway's, playing pool after school every day.

"Hey," he answered coolly.

"You at State now?"

"Right."

"Cool, man. Heard it's tripping there."

"Yeah."

"I could do that. Cherry bombs. Shit."

The group all simultaneously puffed into the air and laughed.

Paul shrugged and walked on. "Back to my history lesson," he prodded Chen, who had conveniently become momentarily invisible.

"I lost touch with your father for a while after your mother died. But he promised to raise you. And I suppose the Monkey Block didn't seem like a place to raise a child. Not that you were living there. He had already given up his studio. He was probably under investigation by the FBI. You were born right in the middle of those years when Joseph McCarthy was active. Remember, your father had a history in Paris with Chou En-lai, and he was friendly with all the wrong people: Rivera, the revolutionary artists' club. They had us all running scared."

So this was the avuncular role Chen took on with his friend's son, now his student, as if he could retreat into a romantic past, escape the revolution that threatened his bourgeois intellectual role. In any case, Paul was about to live his own youth.

Paul met his friend Edmund. "Are you thinking about learning a third language now that you've mastered English and Chinese?"

"I'm working on Mandarin. Does that count?" Edmund spoke with a Shanghai dialect.

"I guess so."

"Our acting president is going to be honored by the Japanese American Citizens' League at a banquet on the wharf. We're going out there to protest. Coming?"

"I've got to work that night."

"Right."

"I've started writing articles for the newspaper *East West.* If you take notes about the protest, I'll write the article. We can share the byline."

"Good idea."

As it turned out, Paul's notes were interesting but useless. Edmund Lee discovered that the banquet he was waiting tables at that evening was the very JACL banquet in question. Paul covered the one hundred protestors on the cold, wet wharf outside the restaurant that evening, and Edmund listened to the president's speech and briefly interviewed him in the kitchen as he snuck out the back and up to a waiting helicopter on the roof to avoid the angry hubbub. Only Japanese Americans would go to so much trouble to avoid conflict. Edmund thought if it were the Chinese, the Six Companies would have just hired their goons to take care of business.

Edmund listened to the president's speech with interest, scribbling notes at intervals and stuffing them into his white coat pocket. It all made beautiful sense. For example: *What kind of language we speak largely determines the kinds of thoughts we have.* He went on to explain that the informal and formal structures of our language determine the way we interpret our experiences and therefore the way we act in any given circumstance. Edmund thought about himself, his accented English and the Shanghai Chinese that ran under and around his speech and writing. How was this speech controlling his thinking and actions?

The president looked out on his Japanese American audience and gave the example of his Meiji Japanese immigrant mother. "Shikataganai," he intoned, for example. All the nisei nodded and thought about mama. "'It can't be helped.' Or, 'don't cry over spilled milk.' The sanseis who are out there rabble-rousing against me hate this idea of shikataganai. They have their points to make, but they don't understand the source of strength that this idea comes from, the ability to endure suffering and sacrifice. Our parents, the issei, interpreted it to mean endurance, but we nisei probably interpret it to mean don't cry over spilled milk, so let's get on with it and move to the next thing."

The audience murmured approval. They fancied themselves a bunch of positive pragmatists. How else could they have come so far?

"But the sanseis," he continued, "interpret shikataganai to be a show of weakness. You hear it from the students all the time. They say, 'We don't believe in shikataganai; that's why you all got sent to camp, because you gave in.' But you all know it's not so simple. Well, what is shikataganai anyway? It's just a word, or series of words, and we've got to communicate better with each other about what we mean when we say or think it. And until we have this honest exchange with our children, when we really listen to each other, we won't bridge the gap that is growing between us."

Edmund bused some abandoned dessert plates and hurried back to fill the glasses with ice water. He could sense the approval of the nisei as they stirred the cream into their coffees. They were willing to take a little browbeating from the president. After all, here was a very reasonable man who wanted communication and exchange, and they should follow his example. Obviously those sansei on bullhorns out there were incapable of listening.

Edmund did everything slowly and carefully and obsequiously, nodding graciously to every guest like an invisible immigrant. No one suspected he was a brilliant student in Chinese studies at the president's college. He was going to make himself necessary as long as possible. Meanwhile, Paul was outside chanting to keep warm, leafleting the tourists and standing next to the signs that said, "We Orientals may look alike, but we don't all think alike." Someone had created a life-sized puppet complete with tiny mustache, tam-o'-shanter, glasses, suit, and tie. The puppet was held aloft in the air with poles and entertained the crowd with foolish antics while someone screeched into a bullhorn: "Don't touch me! I'm the president!" And the crowd answered in unison: "No! You're a puppet! You're a puppet!"

Inside, the president was explaining something he called *time-binding*. "Time-binding is what distinguishes human beings from other living things. Plants," he said, "survive by their ability to energy-bind, that is, a system for taking energy from the environment to feed their organisms. Animals survive by the hunt, or their ability to move around to get their food; this is what we call space-binding. But humans are unique in that we survive by our ability to time-bind, that is, by using and controlling time."

About this time, Edmund slipped around the tables and poured coffee, as if coincidentally to nudge a few from nodding off to sleep. They gratefully brought the cups to their lips and regained their alert and interested composures. Edmund rushed back to fill his carafe with hot coffee and jotted *time-binding* into his notes.

"What are you doing?" another waiter queried.

"Getting more coffee," Edmund parried.

"We get paid by the hour for this. No tips."

"Yeah."

"It's a goddamned banquet. Relax."

"Right." Edmund rushed back to hear more about time-binding.

"Humans," the president continued, "have created language to communicate, to pass on vital information to each other and to the next generation. That's how we survive over time. This time-binding capacity is another name for our ability to create society and civilization."

One JACLer waved Edmund over and asked for an ashtray. Edmund returned with the ashtray, popped a lighter from his pocket, and lit the man's cigarette.

"For example, the JACL is a society of citizens that depends on communicating your purpose and your history. This, I agree, is the difficult task ahead." Outside, the president's puppet was going through the motions of ritual disembowelment while the crowd chanted, "Haya-kiri, haya-kiri, haya-kiri . . ."

The JACLer puffed in the air away from the half-eaten slices of apple pie and nodded appreciatively to Edmund.

The president adjusted his bifocaled vision, scrutinizing his crowd in various dispositions of alertness. "You of the Japanese American Citizens League have an important history and mission to communicate. If the youngsters outside could hear your brave history and mission, they would join your ranks and extend your proud history." This comment brought about some grunting and scattered clapping. The youngsters outside had gotten their puppet into a kneeling position with a knife stuck in his belly.

Inside, the president continued. "If you fail to communicate or become stagnant in your thinking, if you lose your ability to think toward the future, this league is doomed to pass away without change." He paused to let the doom of it all sink it.

Edmund jotted down with some glee: *Nisei dinosaurs. Extinction.*

"But"—the president wagged a telling finger—"I know that the JACL is an association that knows great change, and you have not and cannot be afraid of change. After all, you survived World War II." More grunting and clapping. "But think about one of the reasons you survived the war—"

Edmund panned the room, wondering what these second-generation Japanese Americans could be thinking.

"English," the professor announced. "As nisei you were able to speak English and communicate your concerns to the American government. The English language: a small thing we take for granted, but a key to our survival. Your ability to communicate effectively in English binds you to your American citizenship."

Outside, the poor puppet protested, "Ouch ouch!" while the crowd cried out the Japanese translation, "Itai itai! Aiyaiyaiyai, itai yoooo!"

Someone tilted his head toward Edmund, to which Edmund responded while trying to keep an ear on the president's speech. "Do you speak English?" the nisei asked Edmund.

"Pardon me, sir?" Edmund tried a British accent on the man. It was a reflexive response, a haughty survival tactic learned on the job. Edmund caught himself; maybe this guy had taken the president's words to heart and wanted to bind his English to their shared American citizenship.

But the nisei replied with controlled agitation, "Ah, the toilet, the men's room?"

"Yes sir. Right this way, sir."

Edmund ushered the man out. Beyond the doors of the banquet hall, the ruckus was a low roar. Police were stationed at the entrance, and clients slipped in and out with amused babble or testy exchanges, the din rising and falling into the foyer. Edmund thought he saw Paul with his picket sign but ran back to hear the president's closing remarks.

"Now I'm not talking about change for the sake of change, but about progress, progress that is a forward-thinking process of time-binding in which we pool all of our technical and intellectual resources and support the freest cultural exchange between all races and creeds and classes for the purpose of solving the world's problems."

At this moment, the puppet sewn from rags was splitting its guts. Long red ribbons sailed into the foggy night, flung across the wharf with spraying clouds of sparkling crimson confetti. The poor puppet heaved his entrails over the dancing protestors in a bizarre display, an Oriental Mardi Gras.

As the JACLers rose to applaud their speaker, Edmund ran into the kitchen, positioning himself at the salad bar to accost the acting president as he moved quickly along with his entourage.

"Sir, Mr. President." Edmund stood in the narrow aisle and called out like a reporter.

The voice, coming from the bins of lettuce and tomatoes, caught the president's attention. Who was this young waiter?

"I listened to your speech with great interest." He fumbled quickly with a pertinent question. "I was thinking, won't it be necessary to promote a civilization of people who speak multiple languages in order to translate and exchange ideas and technology?"

"An excellent question. Who are you?"

"Edmund Lee. I'm a student at your college."

The president nodded to his nisei bodyguards. "This is what I'm talking about. Intelligent and hardworking students like this young man. Studying by day, working by night. That's what we're about, not that minority of rabble-rousers." He patted Edmund on his padded white jacket shoulder. "Ed, come to my office and we'll talk about your question. But tell me just one thing: what did you learn tonight?" He began to walk on, pushed along by his bodyguards.

Edmund, following, ventured awkwardly, "Well, I think you said that the winning civilization will be the one that keeps its history going."

They climbed the stairs to the roof, and Edmund could hear the deafening roar of propellers. The president placed his hand over his tam-o'-shanter and looked back at Edmund, yelling something incomprehensible, his mouth a grin and a grimace at the same time, then ducking away into a whirring fog, tiny bits of crimson confetti glinting here and there.

"Fuck," Paul exclaimed. "I can't share that byline with you."

"Why not?"

"I was outside. You were inside."

"So? That's the beauty of it."

"My participation is about ten percent. The whole article is yours. And besides, who reads his work? Now you're inside his goddamned head."

"Pretty weird, huh?"

Paul read from Edmund's draft. "'To paraphrase the president, he states that conflict is essential to growth, but unresolved conflict over time results in emotional disturbance (i.e., you become crazy) as one's self-concept departs from the reality of the self. Your territory separates from your map.'" Paul looked up from his reading. "What's this map/territory thing?"

Edmund's face scrunched up. "It isn't very clear yet, is it? O.K., it's like the territory is the real land and the map is just a representation. So you got a map in your head about yourself, but there is the real you or self that is the territory. So this conflict he's talking about is when the territory is changing but the map stays the same. It's this disconnect between the two, between the abstraction and the reality, that causes one to be insane."

"That makes sense," Paul nodded. He was thinking about how he himself could be defined as insane, but he read on: "'The man's entire body of scholarship—ideas that can be said to be largely utopian—has been demolished by his actions. His *map* is that he's an effective communicator, a great scholar applying his theories to active duty. His *territory* is that of a convenient minority banana used by the white power structure. Even if that's an exaggeration, his recent displays of buffoonery and arrogant affectations take on that role. He's abandoned his principles of human dignity and self-concept to play the fool. So even by his own terms, he's insane.'"

Edmund started to pull his jacket on. "I've got to revise this for the paper. What do you want to do?"

"It's not my article, Edmund."

"Yeah, I better take full responsibility. Probably nobody will read it anyway."

"It's brilliant, really. Only you would do that sort of homework."

"I've got these photos that Professor Chen took that I'm going to use. He's got the students being handcuffed, lines of police with batons, injured students, blood on the concrete, teachers marching with armbands, paddy wagons."

"Talk about the territory," Paul scoffed.

"Exactly." Edmund stood in Paul's living room, staring for a long moment at an oil portrait of a mustachioed man in a suit and tie, his tilted head and ochre colorings against the brushstrokes of an olive green background.

"Paul Valéry, a French poet," Paul commented, mystified as Edmund that this canvas left by his father should be his personal window.

Edmund adjusted his jacket and stuffed the article into its deep pockets. He muttered a partial thought, "The winning civilization—" opened the door, and left.

3: Analects

Authors sometimes take strange liberties.
—*Charlie Chan*

I

The tradition of all the dead generations weighs like a nightmare on the brain of the living. —*Karl Marx*

1.1 She said: Who am I if not the dowager empress, called upon in modern times to weave a brocaded wisdom? Admit it: you step lightly, fearing to see my visage in the carpeted tapestry; you suspect me to be hiding in the wings of every drama; you want to believe my tiny stinking feet and painted peony lips have long decayed, chopped up with my decadent remains, but language recuperates me again and again. I am hidden in a library left behind over time, incrementally established with great care and then abandoned as if its librarian had suddenly escaped. Indeed he fled, left his great collection in this great sitting room overlooking a craggy scene of California cypress framing the stately Golden Gate, a play of red arches in the blue Pacific. Two young men—let's say his scribes—were left to tend these archives, and in offering his home for their services, they had already begun to assume the robes of their hopeful futures: poet and scholar. Truly a library is a room of dreams.

1.2 Poet: Paul Wallace Lin stretched himself out in the cushioned embrace against one end of the expansive bay window, puzzling over the mind of Monsieur Teste and his creator Paul Valéry. He wondered if his father, who had painted the French poet's portrait, had ever read *Monsieur Teste,* and if reading it himself would illuminate his father's expectations for his son. Even the man who is free of his father's will desires some direction.

1.3 Scholar: Lee Yat Min, similarly stretched at the other end of the window, did not speculate on his father's ambitions for his son. After establishing a laundry business, his father sent for the family in China, and when Yat Min arrived in California at age twelve, his father sat him down between the damp steam rising off pressing irons and the reeking shirts stained in sweat and growled very plainly that if Yat Min ever worked in a laundry like this, he'd break his son's legs. Yat Min learned that the mind can run faster than the legs. He turned the pages of Lu Hsun, running a finger down the printed characters of a story entitled "Diary of a Madman."

1.4 In such a fashion, two young men framed the sunlit entrance to the library, one seeking to decipher a Western mind and the other an Eastern, only to discover that neither was more inscrutable than the other.

1.5 Now, let us pull away from this great window as if riding the soft fog that creeps into the bay beneath the Golden Gate, and observe the stunning house against the cliffs. Professor Chen Wen-guang designed this custom-built palace for his second wife, a wealthy Austrian baroness. It's engineered in three split-levels on a hillside beneath Mount Tamalpais, great windows on every level overlooking the San Francisco Bay. On the first level, a dining and living room; on the second level, the library and bedrooms; on the third level, an artist's studio and gallery. The Baroness lived only briefly in the finished house, Europe and China meeting in cordial feng shui, before she died, leaving a comfortable stipend to her learned and beloved Chinaman.

1.6 Chen Wen-guang modestly insisted that he was but a historian, a witness to events, a chronologer, if such a title exists. In that role, predictably, he created a chronology of those days in turmoil at San Francisco State College as if such a record would create an enlightened path by which to walk through and finally leave behind disturbing events. By such chronology the puzzle of history was stretched out, one factual account stepping after another factual account, moment by moment, day by day, month by month. But upon scrutinizing his own work, he discovered but a single and continuous silken thread pulled away, unraveling at every tug the very fabric of a robe once splashed in calligraphic dreams.

II

> When dealing with a man who is capable of understanding your teaching, if you do not teach him, you waste the man. When dealing with a man who is incapable of understanding your teaching, if you do teach him, you waste your teaching. A wise teacher wastes no man and wastes no teaching. —*Confucius* (15.8)

2.1 The wise Professor Chen read with great interest a position paper on the establishment of Chinese Ethnic Studies, presented to him by the Intercollegiate Chinese Students Association. He approved of their proposed curriculum in sociology, social psychology, community counseling, and Cantonese language. He supported their argument that eighty-three percent of Chinese in America speak the Cantonese of the streets. But he could not help but notice the absence of the study of mainland China, Taiwan, and Chinese living in Southeast Asia. Even if the students had not forgotten that he was a scholar of contemporary Chinese literature and political thought, they could not see how this learning was connected to their desire to serve the people. There are situations for which a Mandarin's knowledge is not required.

2.2 Professor Chen resigned his high post as chair. It is the Confucian belief that enlightened intellectuals should naturally conduct the political life of a just government. However, the American egghead is perhaps not such an intellectual.

2.3 Professor Chen applied for his long-delayed sabbatical and accepted a scholar's invitation to the Sorbonne. In making arrangements for his house, he entrusted its financial upkeep to his student Paul Lin, who had inherited the business of overseeing his father's properties, and he hired Edmund (Yat Min) Lee as a caretaker in exchange for free rent. The teacher with trusted students is surely fortunate.

III

> See Paris, die happy. —*Charlie Chan*

3.1 Chen Wen-guang strolled the old Parisian streets where he was born and raised within the formalities and rituals of the Chinese legation in the 1920s. He was a boy of fourteen when he left; the next year, the Germans crossed the Meuse River and bombed and occupied Paris. The boy who returns as a man sees with a boy's eyes.

3.2 To Paul, he wrote: *I heard Charles Mingus at the Palais de Chaillot the other night. Marguerite Duras, whom I happened to meet there, sends her regards. "Paradoxically," she says, "the freedom of Paris is associated with a persistent belief that nothing ever changes. Paris, they say, is the city that changes least. After an absence of twenty or thirty years, one still recognizes it." And yet, I am lost in this familiarity.*

3.3 Contrary to his questionable recognition and usefulness at his own institution in the United States, Professor Chen was everywhere in Paris, and as they say, the talk of the town. Thus it was proven that a man's wisdom is rarely appreciated in his own household. His French colleagues wanted to compare student movements. They gave him an office at the Sorbonne, although the school was closed intermittently by student protests. But was this not the case the world over? This was the rise of a new Communist movement inspired by Mao and the Chinese Revolution. And what of China that had so inspired Western Marxists? What did he believe to be Chou En-lai's possibilities to succeed Mao Tse-tung? What was his analysis of the Cultural Revolution? Of the Russia/China split? How should one predict a revolutionary future? Three steps forward and two steps backwards.

IV

The best way to make your dreams come true is to wake up.

—*Paul Valéry*

4.1 It was not *Monsieur Teste* but a poem by Valéry that aroused an awakening in the spirit heart of the young poet. Paul Lin wrote enthusiastically to his mentor Chen Wen-guang at his address in Paris. He did not think it was a mere coincidence, that is, the poem's title, "Le Cimetière Marin." He knew himself to be in the same hills of California's Marin County, in a beautiful cemetery of books overlooking the salt-breathing potency, that fresh exhalation of the sea.

4.2 The poet commanded: *The wind is rising . . . We must try to live! / The huge air opens and shuts my book: the wave / Dares to explode out of the rocks in reeking / Spray. Fly away, my sun-bewildered pages!* Where, Paul asked, in France was le Cimetière Marin? Would Chen be visiting?

4.3 In Paris Chen felt a strange foreboding, as if Monsieur Valéry's ghost lurked at his sleeve, even as the memory of Paul's soft features floated over the flickering sunlight tracing the scaled surface of the Seine. The teacher embraced the exuberance of his young and awakening apprentice. "Yes, perhaps," he replied. Valéry was born in the port of Sète on the Mediterranean. He had planned anyway a trip to Provence to visit James Baldwin in the coastal village of Saint-Paul de Vence.

4.4 Edmund rolled his eyes but smiled. He asked: "How is it that our teacher knows everyone?" Scanning the shelves for Chen's American collection, they found a copy of *Giovanni's Room* signed by Baldwin: *To my dear friend Wen-guang. James.* Those who walk in the same spheres enjoy the coincidence of friendship.

V

Mind, like parachute, only function when open.
—*Charlie Chan*

5.1 Chen collected postcards of predictable sites (the Eiffel Tower) and obscure significance (a bald woman), stood in what he thought to be significant locations, and penned cryptic aphorisms to the boys at home. On the Rue de Fleurus, outside of Gertrude Stein's flat, he wrote to Yat Min in scripted Chinese characters: "*It is wonderful how a handwriting which is illegible can be read, oh yes it can.*" *So said Gertrude Stein.*

5.2 To Paul he wrote in blocky English: "*There ain't any answer, there ain't going to be an answer, there never has been an answer, that's the answer." Gertrude Stein*

5.3 The young poet wrote to his long-distance mentor: *I am collecting your postcards (please send more) along with my own reflections and jottings, nonsense, and whatnot too, in a journal I have named* Analecta. *I am adding analecta to it every day. For example, Valéry writes in his analecta: "Reality can only express itself with absurdity."*

5.4 P.S. *I met Jack Sung, as you suggested. He hangs out at Il Piccolo with some others. Edmund hangs out at Il Piccolo too, but for other reasons. Edmund calls Sung and his bunch "the Poetry Boys Club." We meet, then head out like a bunch of gangsters, rummaging around used book stores, looking for any discarded book by an Oriental. So far: Sui Sin Far and Onoto Watanna.* Youth has its purposes.

VI

> Politics is the art of preventing people from taking part in affairs that properly concern them. —*Paul Valéry*

6.1 Edmund Lee played tricks with the weekly Chinatown newspaper, published bilingually—English running left to right on one side, Chinese running right to left on the other. On the Chinese side, the Chinese Consolidated Benevolent Association, aka Six Companies, promoted the Miss Chinatown USA Pageant with a large spread and photograph of the charming Carole Yung, Miss Year of the Rooster Chinatown, crowned and smiling nervously with a live rooster in her arms, more than ready to turn over her crown, sash, and animal on February 8 at the Masonic Temple at 1111 California Street at eight p.m. to the new Miss Year of the Dog Chinatown. Above the Chinese article about someone voted the most beautiful Chinese girl in the USA, Edmund set the large headline in bold type: GALILEO STUDENTS WALK OUT!

6.2 Two hundred impetuous Galileo High School students walked out on February 5 in a demonstration to make Chinese New Year an official U.S. holiday. As they say, fat chance. Could it be that the lovely Carole Yung, like an impertinent homecoming queen with her crowned princesses in tow, also walked out? Beauty may sometimes be used for political gain.

VII

> At times I think, and at times I am.
>
> —*Paul Valéry*

7.1 Paul Lin signed up for Jack Sung's creative writing workshop at SF State. The other students in the workshop were confused by Paul's work. They said: We want to know what it is. What's this cryptic shit about? Sung said: Leave him alone. He's working it out. That was how Paul knew he had arrived in the Poetry Boys Club. The reasons for membership were not always explained.

VIII

> As for the good man: what he wishes to achieve for himself, he helps others to achieve; what he wishes to obtain for himself, he enables others to obtain—the ability to simply take one's own aspirations as a guide is the recipe for goodness.
>
> —*Confucius* (6.30)

8.1 In the same year, Edmund Lee investigated and wrote articles about the infamous Wah Ching Chinatown gang and their exploding violence. His first article was about Glen Fong, who ended his short nineteen years of life shot and killed by a rival tong on Jackson Street at one in the morning. In another few months Teddy Ta, twenty-one, was stabbed, and by the end of the year Larry Miyata, sixteen, and Raymond Leong, eighteen, were also shot and killed. Their blood smeared the sidewalks of the street the Chinese affectionately call Dupont Guy.

8.2 Edmund also wrote the obituary for Sai Gin Lew, PFC, born September 20, 1949, died in Vietnam December 5, 1970.

8.3 Edmund hung around the Il Piccolo coffee house, where he met the lost Chinatown kids he recognized to be like himself: fresh off the boat but with nothing to show for it, and no pop to bless their arrival in America with a break-your-legs warning. To see oneself in another is to learn both fate and possibility.

8.4 March Eu Fong, our crowned assemblywoman, and her political entourage visited our forbidden city—labyrinth of tourism, flaming woks, gambling dens, herb and curio shops. Something had to be done. High commissioner Fong asked who among her constituents had the talent to write. It was thus that Edmund volunteered to write the proposal to the federal department of Heath, Education, and Welfare. By the end of the Year of the Dog, to Edmund's great astonishment, the government granted one hundred thousand dollars in funding to open a Chinatown Youth Service Center. Writing can be lucrative.

IX

Ancient ancestor once say, "Words cannot cook rice."

—*Charlie Chan*

9.1 Someone said, "Edmund Lee, you wrote the proposal, now you better make it work for us. You are now the director of the Chinatown Youth Service Center, with offices in the old Hungry i in the I-Hotel." What was the responsibility of the director of the Chinatown Youth Service Center? As Edmund Lee himself had proposed, he should get jobs for the Chinatown youths. Otherwise they were going to spend their time on the streets making trouble and killing each other.

9.2 Down the street and across from Portsmouth Square, in the heart of Chinatown, the Holiday Inn was inaugurated with twenty-seven floors and 565 rooms, but there were no Chinese working there. Edmund went as the director of the CYSC, but who was he, a young skinny student with horn-rimmed glasses and some federal funding? "We are sorry," they said, "no qualified Chinese have applied." A hotel with a name like Holiday can only be a business, not a charity.

X

> Virtue is not solitary; it always has neighbors.
>
> —*Confucius* (4.25)

10.1 Edmund angrily paced Professor Chen's library in Marin overlooking the Golden Gate, reading the cruel history of celestials in America. He wrote his manifesto in the newspaper and called for a new organization: Chinese for Affirmative Action. Paul Lin said, "Remember when you were always working as a waiter and had no time to protest?" Every man must take his turn to stand out in the cold and face the riot squad.

10.2 First he and Paul Lin and about a dozen others, then fifty, then two hundred, then more and more Chinatown Chinese who now called themselves Chinese for Affirmative Action protested in front of the Holiday Inn, blocking the doors and marching around the tourists with picket signs and bullhorns. They were joined by the International Hotel Tenants Association, the Save the Kong Chow Temple Committee, and the Chinatown Cooperative Garment Factory Workers. *Gung Hay Fat Choy! Whose holiday, Holiday Inn? Holiday Out! Holiday Out!*

XI

> When nature prevails over culture, you get a savage; when culture prevails over nature, you get a pedant. When nature and culture are in balance, you get a gentleman.
>
> —*Confucius* (6.18)

11.1 Being the director was not easy, especially when the youths he was supposed to be helping walked in the next day as Red Guards, talking militant revolution, waving Mao's *Little Red Book* in his face, accusing him of reformist measures, and wanting to set up a breakfast program like the Black Panthers', for Chinatown kids. One man's program is another man's complaint.

11.2 The Six Companies yelled about how the Red Guard marched around throwing cherry bombs at tourists and yelling, "Off the Honkies!" What kind of business plan was that? And Chinatown kids don't need a breakfast program; their mothers feed them every morning. I might be a dead dowager, but I know a thing or two. This is Chinatown; did your mother ever send you to school hungry? It's an insult! What sort of son are you anyway?

11.3 Are we Yellow Panthers to mimic the blacks? We are one billion Chinese in the world, a powerful majority with a decisive role in history and the destiny of humanity. Insult your mother, and one billion Chinese will destroy you. And if it is not already clear, the Chinese are the wisest people on earth.

XII

Knowing others is intelligence; knowing yourself is true wisdom.
Mastering others is strength; mastering yourself is true power.
—*Lao Tzu*

12.1 Paul Lin wrote this poem:

I have been left to wander this
three-tiered palace
among your memories
your priceless antiquities
paintings and poetry
your hair oil scented in the cushions
and bedsheets
your spiced preferences
old canisters of herbal remedies
and aged teas and cognac.
In your absence
I practice the art
of the gentle scholar,
while across the bay
the red arches of revolution
beckon home my
Chinaman self.
On which side of the bay
does the father live?

On which side of the bay
the worthy son?
On which side of the bay
the beloved?
The yin and yang
of self
split in multiple and
prismed refractions
against the sun
that inevitably sets
in the West.

XIII

No one knows less about servants than their master.
—*Charlie Chan*

13.1 The masculinity of the man of color in America is constantly called into question. What should be done about those colored homosexuals and raging feminists whose presence undermines the full and masculine citizenship of every man of color? I ask, if your masculinity is not your own, to whom does it belong? But in the Year of the Dog, who is listening to the dowager who lived among eunuchs? Only the tough and vitriolic can survive.

13.2 Paul Lin read Chen's signed copy of Baldwin's *Giovanni's Room,* and for the first time read a literary critique that spoke plainly of it. But he also read the Panther's Minister of Information, Eldridge Cleaver, who spat his hatred of the homosexual traitor Baldwin, who displayed, he said, the most agonizing self-hatred and "the most shameful, fanatical, fawning, sycophantic love of whites." Then one of the black writers in the Poetry Boys Club came around and laughed about Baldwin, calling him that "hustler who comes on like Job." Paul remained silent. Club membership depends on keeping its pretenses.

XIV

Life is tragic simply because the earth turns and the sun inexorably rises and sets . . . —*James Baldwin*

14.1 Chen joined others at James Baldwin's eighteenth-century house nestled among arbors of hanging grapes, peach and almond orchards, and fields of strawberry and asparagus in the acreage just outside of Saint-Paul de Vence, an ancient walled village overlooking the Mediterranean Sea. He sat nursing a glass of local wine, scribbling postcards, and overheard the questions posed by a bright young black reporter to Baldwin sitting in the dappled sunlight. What did Mr. Baldwin feel about Cleaver's accusations?

14.2 Baldwin played magnanimous. He wouldn't be intimidated by this young, impressionable reporter who no doubt sided with the radicalized machismo of the current black movement. Baldwin said he was very impressed with Cleaver's writing, that he couldn't be insulted since what did Cleaver know except from his assumptions of the debased faggots he met in prisons? They'd never met. Cleaver's thinking was understandable from his life experience and also his perverse encounters with his angry sexuality. (Baldwin never mentioned the word *rape.*) No, he didn't mean to patronize Cleaver.

14.3 The reporter looked off with some distraction into the olive and pine trees, sniffed the wild rosemary and thyme perfuming the air. What is the use of a garden if not to rest the mind and to soften the heart?

14.4 But how, insisted Baldwin, were he and Cleaver so different, created out of their different but equally oppressive encounters with white society? Baldwin himself was an "odd and disreputable artist," and Cleaver an "odd and disreputable revolutionary." A pity there should be no time for them to meet. All men are brothers.

14.5 The reporter smiled. Did Mr. Baldwin know the news that Cleaver was even now just across the Mediterranean, escaped to Algiers? Baldwin said nothing but smiled over at Chen, who must have quietly made the delicate connections to allow Cleaver to travel at all and, eventually, to China. A true benefactor is surely invisible, if not coy.

14.6 The young reporter would finally leave and malign the memory of the writer, declaring Baldwin's show of magnanimity the pathetic response of the has-been writer, out of touch with his subject. Distant from hospitality, one's gratitude may disappear.

XV

A poem is never finished, only abandoned.

—*Paul Valéry*

15.1 Edmund said to Paul, "If you want to be a poet, you have to present your poetry to the public. You have to rise to the occasion and read, like Allen Ginsburg, Kenneth Rexroth, and Gary Snyder. What are you waiting for? Why should those guys be writing Asian American poetry anyway? I propose a *real* Asian American read-in. You can read here at the Chinese Youth Services, on the old stage of the Hungry i. You, like Barbra Streisand and Lenny Bruce, can make your start at the Hungry i. I'll give you top billing, and you can bring your Poetry Boys Club along as well." Oftentimes the declaration itself is one's independence.

15.2 The Poetry Boys Club called themselves CARP, like the fish.

XVI

Best place for skeleton is in family closet.

—*Charlie Chan*

16.1 In the Year of the Dog, in the month of the ninth moon, the Gay Liberation Front recognized the Black Panthers as the vanguard of the revolution. Some gifts arrive like undersized lingerie for a heavy-set woman.

16.2 Do you not know the stories told in our classical literature of the half-eaten peach or the cut sleeve? A beautiful lover offers the sweetest side of his half-eaten peach to his beloved lord. A Han emperor cuts away his silken sleeve, caught beneath his sleeping lover, rather than awaken such quiet beauty. The inscrutability of any story is to be deciphered by those intended to know the answers.

XVII

Those who have innate knowledge are the highest. Next come those who acquire knowledge through learning. Next again come those who learn through the trials of life.

—*Confucius* (16.9)

17.1 Jack Sung, the leader of the Poetry Boys Club, mischievously called the Chinatown Red Guard a Chinese minstrel show that mimicked the Black Panthers. He also presented a few choice episodes from his newest play, *Dear lo fan, fan gwai, whitey, honey babe,* with provocative lyrics like "Ching-chong Chinaman" and a monologue satirizing the proud leader of the Red Guard. After the *real* Asian American read-in on the old stage of the Hungry i, Paul rushed to see the leader of the Red Guard call out the leader of the Poetry Boys Club and punch him unceremoniously to the ground. Irony is lost on he who is satirized.

17.2 Later Jack Sung said philosophically, "I think I was beaten up kind of Western style. Maybe I was lucky in that I didn't have one of these legendary forms of Oriental self-defense used on me." In the full production of Sung's play, G.I. Joe tossed a bloody cow liver into the audience. A woman felt the slop plop into her lap. Irony is lost on she who is splattered with blood.

XVIII

Door of opportunity swing both ways.
—*Charlie Chan*

18.1 Who are the true heroes? The poets or the revolutionaries?

18.2 Who are the true men? The poets or the revolutionaries?

18.3 The answers to these questions are on page ___.

XIX

A journey of a thousand miles starts from beneath your feet.
—*Lao Tzu*

19.1 Chen bid farewell to his French Maoist colleagues, who dreamed of an intellectual Maoism championing Third World revolutions. They tested their endless theories on Chen, who tired of the pretense that he might be Chou En-lai, their very own French interpreter. One man's history is another man's imagination.

19.2 Meanwhile, Chen received news from his colleagues in San Francisco. Student and union agreements to end the strike at the college in 1969 were in fact never signed by the president, nor the board of trustees; demands were never met, agreements were never enacted. Students were punished. Professors denied tenure. The trustees failed to protect academic freedom, and the California Senate drafted over one hundred bills to suppress campus dissent. *But,* they wrote, *flowers are blooming on campus—daisies and petunias and marigolds . . .*

19.3 Chen returned to San Francisco, but not before standing on the hill of le Cimetière de Marin and penning a final postcard to Paul: "*Some have the merit of seeing clearly what all others see confusedly. Some have the merit of glimpsing confusedly what no one sees as yet. A combination of these gifts is exceptional." Paul Valéry.* But who among us is exceptional?

XX

Old man, how is it that you hear these things?
Young man, how is it that you do not?

—Kwai Chang Caine and Master Po

20.1 When Chen returned, he opened his long-closed and dusty garage, took the Siata 208s Spider coupe off its blocks, and bought new wheels for it. He made Paul, who had nothing better to do, drive it back and forth to the mechanic, replacing, testing, and cleaning parts, and polish its red body to a high luster. He had met his second wife at the Grand Prix in Monte Carlo; she was a race car enthusiast, and this was her car.

20.2 He said, "Listen to the soft purr of that engine. Can you hear it? That's the Fiat 2-liter v8. Crafted in Geneva in 1952. Nica took the prize with this at the Targa Florio in 1957." Paul and Edmund looked skeptical. When had their teacher become a mechanic? "Now listen to this." He revved it up. What else does one do with a race car? One races it.

4: My Special Island

Okinawa is vital for the security of the U.S.
Korea is vital for the security of the U.S.
Indochina is vital for the security of the U.S.
The Philippines are vital for the security of the U.S.
Taiwan is vital for the security of the U.S.
The Tiao Yu Tai islands are vital for the security of the U.S.
Tiao Yu Tai?

Two Days after the Lunar New Year of the Pig (Boar) . . .

Now don't get Maoist with me. You know I'm not a proselytizing kind of girl. Look who you're fooling with. Do I look like I'll do time with a naked face and/or nails? Not that I couldn't, but girls like me don't get starring roles in *The Good Earth.* There might be days I could do pigtails, and if you put beads and brocade on that Mao jacket, it might go over something more evocative. A red silk cheongsam slit to the hip, for goodness sake. I could substitute my bangles for some red star earrings. I'll tell you one thing: I could go for the *beret à la Che* look. I would wear that man stretched over my bosom any day. Now, honey, would that arouse you?

Now, you know where you should be. You should be out there with your friend in Saint Mary's Square next to Sun Yat-sen, protesting with five hundred others over the Tiao Yu Tai. It's quite a crowd. All riled up good and Chinese-like. And there's Father Sun presiding, looking all sun-reflective, proof that the Chinese padred California too. But no, instead here you are, humping with me in a pathetic little room in the I-Hotel. Oh no you don't. Don't come yet. I'm not finished with you.

Did you read their manifesto? What manifesto? The Tiao Yu Tai manifesto, of course. But who nowadays doesn't have a manifesto? Even I have a manifesto. But as a good Oriental citizen, I'm all for their manifesto. Think about those beautiful little islands out there in the middle of nowhere, just waiting to be grabbed up like Hawaii. Wild flowers. Flying fish.

Green and verdant. Just thinking about them makes me go paradisiac. But I hyperventilate. The Japanese and the American military need to keep their pesky hands off those islands. If anyone knows what to do with an island, it's the Chinese. What? Oh well, overpopulate it, I suppose. Fill it up with all those number-one sons, sail them out on picturesque junks, come home to honey with a big catch, and make a lot of babies. Turn it into one big happy i-land commune.

AN INTERNATIONAL CONSPIRACY!

U.S. *government succumbs to Japanese secret demands and agrees to deliver the oil-rich Tiao Yu Tai islands to Japan. The Tiao Yu Tai islands, 20 miles north of Taiwan and 240 miles south of Ryukyu, are rightfully Chinese. Chinese fishermen have used these territorial waters for centuries. The recent discovery of rich oil deposits around the islands—almost twice the deposits of California—is too attractive to the Japanese militarists. The Sato regime has secretly demanded that the islands be included in the Ryukyu group and be returned to Japan in 1972. The* U.S. *had yielded to Japanese demands and had agreed to return the islands to Japan without the consent of the Chinese people. Our Chinese people strongly protest this Tokyo-Washington plot and tell the world you may forget Pearl Harbor, but we will never give away Tiao Yu Tai.*

Chinese Six Companies
San Francisco, California

I'm here today representing the Japanese Community Youth Council, and we Japanese in America condemn the government of Japan for this act of international robbery against other Asian people. Just as we condemn the American government for its criminal acts in Southeast Asia, we condemn the Japanese militarist government of blatant pig acts against the Tiao Yu Tai islands. This pig activity, whether in the oil fields of these islands or the rice fields of Vietnam, this pig activity is called imperialism. *Down with Japanese imperialism! Down with KMT traitors! Down with U.S. imperialism! All power to the people!*

A revolutionary
Federal Building
January 29, 1971

Around noontime on April 9 . . .

I saw Ike and Tina Turner the other night at the Fillmore. Tina worked the mike, you know what I mean? She worked it, like it was her object. She tongued the machine. I was there, right there in the front watching her try to wrap her body around and get into that thing. Right, disgusting. By now you'd think it would be a cliché, the mike thing, but it's the music that gets into your system. So we're gonna pump those speakers into the floor. Take your shoes off. Now feel that. *Oye Como Va*. The floorboards are vibrating like they got a pulse.

Old Chinese guy below is probably deaf, don't you know. But he's not there anyway. He got his old Chinese brothers together to march around Portsmouth Square with Edmund and the others. Want to imagine it on KPFA? Come on. Stretch yourself out, and feel it happening like we're there. Let's do some island lovin'. Oh, we're in luck. It's Arthur Ma reporting. Listen. They're singing the Tiao Yu Tai song in Portsmouth Square.

Arthur Ma: *About fifty demonstrators, mostly students from China going to school here, are gathered today in Portsmouth Square in Chinatown to protest the U.S. and Japanese takeover of the Tiao Yu Tai islands. They have been making their speeches in Cantonese, and the student organizers of the rally urge their supporters to keep up the pressure against the oil grab of these islands. The students are showing their support by putting up their fists in power signs.*

Down with Japanese militarism!
Down with U.S. imperialism!
Down with the KMT sellouts!

Ma continues: *Now you notice in the park, there are the usual Chinese elderly folk sitting around playing checkers, reading the paper, and sunning themselves, but with these excellent speeches, some of them have begun to perk up and take notice. You can see their shy smiles and quiet claps of appreciation and approval. The speaker is saying: "Chinese must have pride and not allow foreign governments to step all over us and then allow the Chiang Kai-shek government to do nothing! It's because of this that our Chinese people have had to leave China." Now they are standing up and clapping. What the—? Who are these guys?*

Who are these guys? The Wah Ching of course, hired by the KMT sell-outs come to beat up the Communists. What did that ruffian yell? *Death to the Communist traitors!* Oh, it's kung fu time. Oh baby, come get me like a *Water Margin* outlaw. Just rough me up a bit. Oh yes.

Ma: *Eight guys dressed up in black have just rushed onto the stage! They're attacking the speakers and throwing around the sound equipment!*

Oh, the commotion! But check this out honey, the Chinese elders from the park are rushing to the stage! Oh, that's gotta be my old man downstairs. Spinning around with kung fu kicks and punches! Truth is, only real men with experience can fight like this. It's like a kung fu motion picture! Baby KMT gangsters are just no match. They're scattering like black mice. There now. There's our interlude. The rally can go on. Oh, but can you hear it now? Oh baby, it's the Tiao Yu Tai song! Nothing moves me like island patriotism.

Student speaker: *We will march as planned! We will not be intimidated! Follow the monitors in black armbands. First we will march to the KMT Chinese Consulate. Then to the Japanese Consulate. And then we will march to the Federal Building! Follow us!*

Hey hey hey!
U.S.A.!
Stay away!
From Tiao Yu Tai!

Ma: *This is Arthur Ma for KPFA signing off at one thirty p.m. from Portsmouth Square in Chinatown on April 9, 1971.*

The Ping Heard Round the World

On April 10, nine ping-pong players, four officials, and two spouses stepped across a bridge from Hong Kong to the Chinese mainland, ushering in an era of "Ping-Pong diplomacy." They were the first group of Americans allowed into China since the Communist takeover in 1949.

On the Anniversary of the May 4 Chinese Student Movement . . .

I'm just like that little Mowgli feral child in the *Jungle Book.* Can you believe I cried when I saw that cartoon? That was me: a little Asian girl raised among drag queens. Now, they've dropped me off in the forbidden city to hide my sorry ass. But who in Chinatown isn't facing the same circumstances? Look at you. We were all left here in the tribal village to fend for ourselves. Honey, pass me that pipe. I've got some forgetting to do.

Edmund's going to have to make some choices. Five hundred academic sinologists can sign off on a letter, tell Taiwan what for and so on about how to run its business, but in the end, what does it mean? You can't stir up a pot with five hundred sinologists. Honey, you need five million sinologists.

My old man downstairs explained it all to me. He was right there on the very day at the birth of the revolution. He told me that he arose a new man on that day. But I'm confused. May 4 is the birth of the revolution, but which revolution? The one for Sun Yat-sen, for Chiang Kai-shek, or for Mao Tse-tung?

The land of China can be conquered but not ceded; the people of China can be slaughtered but not bent. The nation is falling! Fellow men, rise!

Luo Jialun
Tiananmen Square, May 4, 1919

Overseas Chinese will never forget the motherland!

Well, you should know more than I. Your dear professor friend is always advising Edmund, isn't he? He's the one who suggested tying the island protest to the May 4 Chinese student movement. I'm with RG, Mr. Red Guard himself, who said who gives a shit what happened in China over fifty years ago, but obviously Professor Chen knows how history works on people's psyches. If people see history repeating itself, they get all nostalgic and riled up. I know. I was there, sitting next to Edmund in that same movie.

You know those movies. They're showing them every weekend downstairs at the Asian Community Center, like entertainment for the old folks, to give them a peek of the homeland. You see maybe millions of

Chinese in black-and-white, standing room only, in that square in Peking that looks likes it's a mile wide, red flags flapping around everywhere. They're going crazy. Now that's a rally! What's a mere one-fifty at Portsmouth Square, or even five hundred at Saint Mary's? All right, I agree. Each of those five hundred represents five hundred more. At least Chinese know how to count.

Edmund's over at Portsmouth Square again, rallying the folks. They're all making speeches in Chinese about the anniversary of the May 4 student movement. But notice that the Red Guard is doing security backstage with their Mao caps and shades, packing loaded revolvers behind their flack jackets. No one's taking any chances this time. No eight KMT gangsters dressed in black are going to disrupt this session. They've got Red Guards posted on the roofs above the square with loaded rifles. Wah Ching could only arrive to a bloody surprise. The Tiao Yu Tai college types are making their speeches in Cantonese, with translations in English for the ABC. Please be patient, darling.

ABC: American-Born Chinese
MIT: Made in Taiwan
HIP: Hong Kong Instant Product
FOB: Fresh Off the Boat
KMT: Kuomingtang
ROC: Republic of China (Taiwan)
PRC: People's Republic of China (mainland China)
MTTT: Mao Tse-tung Thought

O.K., now they're finished with their history lesson.

Here comes the ABC Red Guard with their flamboyant red flags, blasting "East is Red." RG struts his thing to the podium and makes his speech: *We of the Red Guard salute you in the Year of the People Off the Pig!*

(chanting) *People Off the Pig! People Off the Pig!*

Let it be known today, May 4 in the Year of the People Off the Pig, that we, the Red Guard, claim the territory of Portsmouth Square in the name of The People and henceforth rename it Tiao Yu Tai Park!

China in the News in 1971

July 15
After Secretary of State Henry Kissinger's secret mission to Peking, President Nixon announces he will visit China.

September
Lin Piao, understood to have been Mao Tse-tung's successor, is killed in an airplane crash in Mongolia. The official explanation is that he had been involved in a failed plot to kill Mao and was killed fleeing to the Soviet Union.

October 25
Resolution 2758 is passed by the General Assembly of the United Nations, withdrawing recognition of the ROC *as the legitimate government of China, and recognizing the* PRC *as the sole legitimate government of China.*

But, darling, as I was saying about the movies: I'm sitting next to Edmund in the dark with those millions of black-and-white Chinese flickering off our faces, and they say: THE CHINESE PEOPLE HAVE STOOD UP! And Edmund, he's wiping his tears away. O.K., I admit it: I cried too. I cried, and I'm not really Chinese. When it comes to solidarity, I'm solidarity all the way.

So right now, Edmund and his comrades are marching over to the Taiwan—or was it the Formosa?—Consulate to deliver their manifesto. Oh excuse me. The Republic of China Consulate. Listen, if you ask Edmund, he'll tell you that this is not an issue of supporting one government or another. It's not about long live Chiang or Mao. This is about the sovereignty of the Chinese people, period. You and I could be there now with the masses, yelling. The Chinese people have stood up! The Chinese people have stood up! Oh, rub me there, baby. Right there. It's time now, baby. Oh yes. The Chinese people have stood up! The Chinese people have stood up! THE CHINESE PEOPLE HAVE STOOD UP!

5: We

When we arrived, there was no Golden Gate, no Statue of Liberty. Even so, some shouted: *America! America!* And we floated into the bay like the fog at twilight. If we got here earlier than the great earthquake and fire, our first impressions of our golden city were on the Barbary Coast—loose men and women of the vintage Gay Nineties carousing in dance halls and bars, around and about in horse-drawn buggies, speculating on a future and fortunes made from California gold. If we arrived after the fires, some of us might have noticed the island of Alcatraz but were forced to dock at another prison island, the one called Angel.

In those early years, the bay's geography was traversed by ferries, fanning out from the city's great transportation hub: the Ferry Building. We ourselves fanned out across the peninsulas, congregating in cities segregated by covenants, in farmlands confined by land laws and leasing contracts, on coastal waters in small fishing boats. We worked as houseboys, cooks, pickers and stoop labor, gardeners, fishermen, and canners. We opened shops: groceries, dry goods, tailoring, restaurants, flower shops, drug stores with soda fountains. We ran boarding houses and hotels, churches, temples, newspapers, health clinics, language schools, YMCAs and YWCAs, and kenjinkais. We gave our adopted towns names like Li'l Yokohama and Nihonmachi.

By the third decade of the century, our children witnessed the great engineering feats and the openings of the stately Golden Gate and Bay bridges. Cable cars and automobiles replaced horses and ferryboats. We sent our children to school and college, only to see them return home jobless. Those were the days when you'd meet a fella with an engineering degree selling fruit on the corner. Everything changed with the bombing of Pearl Harbor. We were forced to leave our li'l towns and farming and fishing communities and were herded en mass to desert camps surrounded by barbed wire and gun towers. We looked like the enemy, but that's not the same as being the enemy.

At war's end, those of us who survived came back to our golden city and our little towns, took up our old jobs or started new ones. We rebuilt our old communities and started new families. Our youngsters turned into the third generation, what we call the sansei, and that's about the time when this story begins.

Who's to say what love is or how it starts inside each person? Who's to say what triggers the feeling, the knowing that passes from one to the other? We saw the young man walk through the tattered remains of the old ferry building. Maybe it was the old building with its ghost lovers, we can't say. We could see his footfalls avoid the scraps of trash ground into grimy crevices. Maybe it was the decay of an old place. He was wearing gold alligator cowboy boots. We could see them shuffling out from his ragged bells, scuffed and shredding at the toe. We could tell that those boots were his favorite, snug in the right places, his walk confident.

He walked out into the warm-swept sunlight, the sort of day we rarely know in our foggy city. When such a day arrives, it's like a sweet summer gift, and we know that we truly live in the most beautiful city in the world. From the hills we can see the glorious expanse of the azure bay and its bridges reaching into the picturesque vistas. All the pastel Victorians winding up and down over the hills in rows, like glittering ladies with gloved hands pressed one to the other.

We saw him remove his jeans jacket and toss it jauntily over his shoulder. Beneath the jacket he was wearing a thin shirt, so thin it was threadbare. It was sepia in tone, and perhaps it was silk or some sort of nylon imitation. We could see it flutter at the sleeves but press with the wind about his body, exposing the curve along his spine and the rise in his chest above his ribcage. The sepia of the shirt reflected off his felt fedora of the same faded sepia, which he adjusted to account for the sun.

He presented his ticket and walked the gangway into the ferry. He chose a place along the starboard railing, looking out across the bay in search of his destination. His soft features shimmered off the glinting ocean.

We weren't tourists. We lived here, but taking the ferry in those days had become unusual, like the weather on this particular day. A few of us worked on the other side, and the ferry was still the most direct way to some points. But that day, we wanted to revisit old haunts that held our memories. We'd step onto Angel Island and remember our lives as we began our American journey with detention and interrogation.

Chen was already on the ferry, seated on the top deck in his usual spot, reading a book. We knew him to be a regular on this ferry when the weather was good. Maybe our commotion bothered his reading, but when he looked up he watched the young man in his gold boots saunter across the ferry. We smiled at the man's show of casual independence, and so did Chen. The felt fedora shaded his face with a slight attitude of mystery. In that moment we sensed a longing pass from the young man, flittering like the gulls along the ferry's wake. We knew that the young man knew he was being watched by the older man. He felt that watching. Craved it. *Please see me,* his longing seemed to speak.

Chen stood and walked to the railing. He held his book before him. The young man saw the book in his hands before he saw Chen, but he knew it was he. Their shoulders touched. The threadbare shirt grazed the short-sleeved cotton bound to Chen's muscular biceps. "For your birthday," Chen said, proffering the book to the sea. "It's today, isn't it?"

"How did you remember? I'm twenty-one."

"We'll celebrate."

Every culture has its day of passage. We'd adopted this one because we believed in the law. We of all people knew the promise of law could be broken, but we doggedly struggled behind that faith.

The young man took the book from Chen and turned from the sea. He leaned his back into the railing with the open book. The pages flapped up in a salty gust as the ferry left the dock. We looked up into the sky with Chen as the ferry's horn announced its departure. But the young man was troubled with the wild pages of his new book.

"You've written another book."

"I translated the calligraphy and wrote the historic text. It's the work of an artist I've long admired. He died a few years ago in his nineties."

"When did you do this?"

"This year."

"You've been busy."

"So have you."

"I moved into the I-Hotel."

"Edmund told me."

"It's over. She left for Cuba."

Chen nodded. "Venceremos?"

"She was stripping to save the money."

"Viva Che."

The young man smiled. "The things we do for the revolution."

"And you? Why didn't you go too?"

"I guess I couldn't strip for the revolution."

"Ah, no?"

"I have bourgeois tendencies."

"Stripping is not?"

"The experiment failed."

We understood Chen's quizzical look, but he remained silent.

"I was the experiment, I think. She gave up. No, she got tired. I got tired."

Chen said nothing.

"It was all about pretending. I couldn't pretend all the time."

"Drugs help."

The young man turned to Chen with some astonishment, then embarrassment. He turned to the sea and felt his tears well uncontrollably.

Neither spoke for a long time. We felt the ferry press across the bay, chased by gulls.

Chen spoke first. He changed the direction of the conversation. "The work of the revolution is a life devoted to the people, that is to say, the public. It's a public life. A man's private life, one's deep interior, must at times be forgotten or sacrificed."

The young man shifted. We shifted too, wanting to avoid the weight of these words.

"Here." Chen retrieved the book offered as a gift, searched the pages. "This is one of my favorite paintings. Twin peaches in a small basket. Peaches represent long life, but as you know they are delicate, bruise easily. If the tree lives long, the fruit is ephemeral. Picked ripe from a tree, there is nothing sweeter or more succulent. Here twin peaches sit together, sweetly and exaggeratedly red in color for a lifetime." Chen reached up to touch the soft fuzz of the young man's felt fedora and tugged it down in jest.

If we felt confused, it was also the young man's turn to look with questioning, as well as sheepish, eyes.

Chen sighed. "Revolution is old, but older yet is the sentiment of this painting, of love and of poetry."

We studied the painting. We admired the swift brushstrokes, rapidly accomplished in a single sitting. How could such a thing seem so simple? It was a demonstration of a life of training revealed in a moment. It was unlike the Western oil painter's painstaking labor of color and light and perspective revealed over many years.

Chen continued, "I don't have an answer except for the experiment, as you say, of my own life. If it's your own experiment, how can it fail?"

The young man looked up.

"A long life might be many lives, many ephemeral lives within one life."

The ferry chugged into its slip, and we ambled onto Angel Island. Angel Island felt like it might be our island; so much of our history was here. But it was now a state park, and the authorities in control were friendly park rangers who directed hikers and picnickers. They had mostly forgotten the old history of the island.

The young man followed Chen, who walked quickly toward an old two-story building. A park ranger came forward to greet them. "Professor Chen? I'm Alexander Weiss."

We followed Ranger Weiss to the dilapidated building. "You'll excuse the mess. This building was a barrack. It's been used as storage. As you know, it's slated for demolition. I thought we should see what was in it before we tore it down. You never know. I didn't expect to find any treasure." He turned the key on the lock and shoved the door open. The light through it illuminated a cloud of dust, and we stepped inside.

"Watch your step. Upstairs. Over here." Weiss held a flashlight to a section of the wall.

Chen scrutinized the wall. Looking closely we saw the wood was carved away, inscribed in Chinese characters. We saw Chen's fingers delicately touch the wall. We thought he closed his eyes as if a blind man reading vivid Braille. He translated slowly:

Leaving behind my writing brush and removing my sword, I came to America.
Who was to know two streams of tears would flow upon arriving here?
If there comes a day when I will have attained my ambition and become successful,
I will certainly behead the barbarians and spare not a single blade of grass.

"A poem," said the young man.

"It's haunting," said Ranger Weiss. "I've searched the other walls. There are many others. Like cave paintings, I think. A record of each man's time here."

"Plans for demolition will stop?" Chen asked.

"Yes, hopefully we can stop it. I'll have this building cleared out so you can see safely."

"When?"

"In a week or two? Can you return?"

"Yes, yes!" Chen said excitedly. He stepped back to the carved wall and read the bitter, defiant poem again, this time in Chinese.

We heard the long quiet in those barracks as his recitation came to a close, standing with three men in a jubilant circle in a dusty path of light.

We left Angel Island with Chen and his young companion. They took the ferry on to the far side of the bay, to Tiburon, their conversation filled with plans and possibility.

"We'll get Edmund involved. He can help with the translations."

"But a poet's sensibility about language is necessary, to transmit the feeling of the poem into English. You should help with this."

We saw Chen's racy white Shelby Mustang GTO was parked conveniently at the ferry port.

"How about the Siata? How's it running?" the young man asked.

"I raced the Monterey Historic last week," said Chen, gunning the engine to emphasize his boast.

"Are you angry with me for disappearing?"

We tooled with the racecar up the hills to the familiar layered pavilion that was Chen's house overlooking the bay. "I've been too busy missing you to be angry."

Chen set a table on the terrace. He placed stemmed glasses, silverware, and candles in a precise pattern on the cloth. We followed him back and forth from the kitchen. "One of my specialties," he said, fussing over a complicated sauce. "I learned it from a French chef."

"Julia Child?"

"How did you know?"

We didn't argue, since Chen was the sort of person who might really know Julia.

"Julia's instructions are to grill duck breast rare."

We stared at a photograph of a woman decked out in racing gear—gloves, goggles, and helmet—and standing next to a car. "Porsche 356 Monza. I'll never forgive Nica. She gave it to a girlfriend who one day just drove it away."

We continued to stare at the photo, trying to see the woman behind the goggles while pretending to scrutinize the car. What does a baroness look like?

"Nica was a bit older than me." Chen thought for a moment. "Our marriage was happily arranged. She and I were excellent company. I cared for her when she became ill."

He popped a bottle of champagne and nudged a glass at the young man. We looked out at the island where we had passed the day, and at the city's hills. They toasted the sunset over the bay, slipping behind the Golden Gate.

The young man knew as he had craved his knowing in sepia tones on the ferry that morning. And Chen had also known the ephemeral moment that would constitute another life in a long wish for a long life. Once again they leaned out over a railing, their shoulders touching, the soft youth of a man newly twenty-one and the toned muscularity of a scholar of many lives.

Many years later we would sing the poem penned in the morning after:

Speaking of love and the revolution across the bay.
Speaking of ferrying south, that endless intent.
The ocean is wider than the sky, your grace taller than Tamalpais.
How could spring rain turn rocky cliff into soft soil?
How could sprouts grow taller than this outlook?
Wind chimes have replaced the sound of water on the roof.

I've been too busy missing you to be angry.
I've been too busy missing you to be angry.

6: Tofu Tigers

For those born after the liberation, it is necessary to attend speak-bitterness sessions and to listen to the old folks talk about the old days, what they suffered and how they were abused by the old system. The new generation does not know this past; they only know about the days after liberation. Chairman Mao says that the world and China's future belong to the youth, but because of their inexperience they cannot comprehend the hardships of the past and the struggle required to establish a happy socialist society. This must also be true of overseas Chinese people. Although they may confront hardships, their struggles have not yet led to socialism. Lately, many overseas Chinese citizens return to visit the motherland. They come in the spirit of pride and learning and are welcomed as compatriots and comrades. They are quickly infected with the energy and spirit of the people, and they acknowledge their industry and progress.

This return coincides with the visit last year of the American President Nixon to the People's Republic of China. This is a momentous event that signals a new era of exchange and equal standing between great nations. The People's Republic of China in a short time accomplishes the unification of the country. This is a long and arduous road for which millions of Chinese sacrifice their lives. Since May 4, 1919 the Chinese people fight bravely for three decades to expel the Japanese imperialists and defeat reactionary nationalists. This struggle is won through the leadership of the Chinese Communist Party and the revolutionary army it commands. Thirty years later on October 1, 1949, Chairman Mao stands on the rostrum of Tiananmen Square and announces a new era for the Chinese people. This is a great victory for the worker and peasant masses, who together bring about this great proletarian socialist revolution. Now in fewer than twenty-five years since the liberation, the Chinese people demonstrate their ability to change the social, political, and physical landscape of China by removing, one by one, the three big mountains of imperialism, feudalism, and bureaucrat-capitalism.

Chen Wen-guang and Lee Yat Min are such overseas Chinese returnees; they are traveling in China to experience for themselves the great changes that have occurred in their absence. Chen is invited to continue his study of Chinese literature since the liberation. For six months, he is actively collecting newly published books and interviewing writers. Lee, who is Chen's student, has come for a shorter period of one month with a group of Chinese American journalists. Since Lee is fluent in several dialects of the Chinese language, he is the interpreter for his group. Not all returning overseas Chinese are so fluent in the language or so knowledgeable about China. Understandably their memories of the China they left behind mix with new realities. Such a leap in time may be a shock. For Chen it is more than twenty years. For Lee it is only a decade, but for the young man as for the older, this leap in time represents almost half of their lifetimes. To accompany their new understanding and many sensations is to learn about the past and to participate in their rebirth.

Lee and his group of Chinese American journalists arrive from Hong Kong, stepping into the People's Republic at Shum Chun. The transition—crossing from a decadent colonial to a prosperous socialist society—cannot be more apparent. On the one side, a city of grimy poverty, crime, and prostitution, rich tourists ignoring children begging under the signs of Coca-Cola and Lucky Strikes. On the other, verdant hills laced with communal rice paddies, happy children playing under newly planted trees, red flags, and posters with encouraging slogans to the people.

Members of the Chinese Communist Party, specially trained as guides for foreign guests, meet Lee's group as they board the train. Everything is carefully planned; journalists like Lee will report back to their people to tell the truth about China's revolution. The guides welcome the overseas Chinese back to China, although most of them were born abroad and have never been to China. This is the feeling of brotherhood and solidarity extended to Chinese people all over the world. The excitement and pleasure of the group is evident as they choose seats near the windows to view the landscape. Lee interprets: "This train was built entirely in China by the Chinese people."

His is a group of ten, almost all of them young. They represent student newspapers and underground papers for mass organizations. One older comrade writes for a Chinese-language newspaper considered to be left-leaning. He and Lee interpret for the group, although only Lee can also speak Mandarin and, as it turns out, the dialect of Shanghai. One sister-comrade gets to work quickly and initiates a conversation with one of the train workers. Lee is called to sit between them.

The train worker says, “I graduated high school four years ago and have been working on this train since that time.”

She asks, “Did you wish to go to college?”

“I applied, but it’s my country’s wish that I work here.”

“Would you rather go to college?”

“If my work benefits the country, then I do it wholeheartedly.”

“Did you study America in school?”

“Yes, we studied the history and politics of the United States. I learned that there is a wide gap between the rich and the working people that is not right.”

“If you were an American citizen living in those conditions, what would you do?”

“Start a revolution.”

“That is not so easy.”

“I know, but we did it here. So it is possible to move such mountains.”

Lee himself asks no questions. He is trying to listen to more than the answers. He is grateful for the direct questions that he himself feels uncomfortable asking, but he tries to put himself in the train worker’s place.

The sister speaks to Lee excitedly as she copies everything down into her notebook. “Well, we’re not in Chinatown anymore,” she muses. “I know this sounds obvious, but you know when they talk about the Chinese being one-fourth of the world’s population? Well, I never really thought about it until now. That’s what we are a part of. I never really felt that way until now.”

The train is on its way to Canton, and from there, in the next few weeks, the group travels on to Peking, Nanking, and Shanghai. Before reaching Peking, walking through Tiananmen Square and the Forbidden City and the requisite trip to the Great Wall, they make an important stop at the Tachai Commune in Shansi Province.

A three-hour documentary about Tachai describes the struggles of the Tachai Production Brigade to resolutely implement Chairman Mao’s revolutionary line. Tachai is a poverty-stricken village built against a steep mountain where the people live in caves. The soil is eroded and washed out from gullies on Tiger Head Mountain, but with their bare hands, the peasants of Tachai move the soil and rock from the ridges and fill the gullies to create terraced fields. They build twenty reservoirs and dams, fertilize the soil, dig wells, and build new houses. The peasants literally move mountains to create a productive agricultural community that boasts of contributing seventy percent of their crops to the country while keeping thirty percent for their own needs. Now corn and millet grow in the terraced fields. There are hundreds of acres of conifers, nut and fruit orchards, and they have electricity and machinery as well. They raise pigs and start a noodle factory. They also build a school and a health clinic. Chairman Mao says, "In agriculture, learn from Tachai." Thousands of people visit Tachai every day from far places in the country to learn from their heroic example.

The sister-comrades in the Chinese American group ask to meet the sister-comrades of Tachai. Lee goes along as the interpreter.

This is a warm and excited meeting, the conversation going back and forth in a lively exchange.

"What is it like to be women in America?"

"We Chinese American women have to fight the oppression of both American society and the old Chinese patriarchal society." A discussion continues for a bit about the patriarchy. Chairman Mao says that men are oppressed by three systems of authority: political, clan, and religious. Women, however, are further dominated by a fourth authority: their husbands.

A Tachai sister says, "Chinese women fought in the war for liberation. Some fought with guns and others with their labor. The war may be over, but the revolution continues. So we continue to prove our strength here in the fields."

Then a Chinese American sister asks, "What do you think about your relationships with men? We struggle with the attitudes of men who we feel must share the work of the household."

The Tachai sister answers, "It is the same here, but women must be strong enough to do both—to work and fight like men and to take care of the household and the children."

The Chinese American sister replies, "If we are to change our position in society, men as well as women must change. Men must also care for children and cook. It is reactionary to think that women must be superwomen and do everything."

When Lee translates the sister's response, there is a confused murmur among the Tachai sisters. One sister rises in some distress; then all of the Tachai sisters follow her out of the room.

"What happened?" The Chinese American sisters look at Lee for an answer. "Where did they go?"

Lee shrinks down in his chair and shakes his head.

After a while, one woman returns with a tray of tea and nervously passes the cups around.

The sisters say to Lee, "Ask her where they went. Why don't they join us for tea?"

Lee translates, but the woman only smiles.

"That's so weird."

"Is it something I said?"

Lee nods. "I think so."

One of the guides assigned to the group walks in quickly and speaks with Lee. Lee nods and turns to the sisters. "He says that they said you called their thinking reactionary."

"Right."

"You can't say that!" Lee jumps up, tipping over his tea.

"Oops."

"He's right. Haven't you figured it out? Being reactionary is like being an imperialist capitalist pig."

"What did Mao say? All reactionaries are paper tigers."

"What does that have to do with anything? You insulted her."

"Oh, shit."

After about an hour, the Chinese American sisters find a way to apologize and to get the Tachai sisters back into the room.

Lee translates, choosing his words carefully. "There has been a misinterpretation. What we meant to say was that in a historical context, women in China have advanced to a stage in which they are still proving their strength, and this is also the case for us in America, but in comparison we have also reached another stage, in which our men must share the burden of the household. This we see as a progression similar to the stages that lead from capitalism to socialism to communism."

The Chinese American sisters look anxiously at the Tachai sisters, who break into smiles of relief.

"Yes, now it's clear. An unfortunate misinterpretation."

"Good job, Edmund."

While Lee is busy interpreting, his teacher Chen is in Peking, housed at the Overseas Chinese Hotel and waiting anxiously to see, after an absence of twenty-five years, his old teacher and mentor.

As soon as Chen hears the hesitant knock at his door, he springs forward excitedly. The elderly man standing in the doorway of his hotel room chuckles to see his student, now a middle-aged man. Even after so many years, the gracious formalities of greeting each other seem improbable, and Chen finds himself speechless. As if to save Chen from any unseemly emotional outburst, the old teacher smiles and simply nods, "So it is you," and walks into the room.

"I've been here for many weeks, but the process to see you has been complicated and very slow. You are the first person I asked to see," Chen complains.

"I have been in the countryside," says the old teacher. In fact, Chen's persistence must have called the old man back from the country. But it is just as well. Even though the old teacher volunteers to go, he is much too old to be useful, and the mud and damp in the winters are hard on his old bones and bad for his rheumatism. He volunteers to go in order to be closer to his wife, who is sent there to teach. Fortunately she finds a small compound for the two of them, and his duties are light.

"Where in the countryside? I should have come to visit you."

"Not too far from my own village in Hunan."

"Then you had an opportunity to write again?" Chen remembers that his teacher was known for his stories about village life in Hunan.

"I have not written in many years."

The old teacher is a well-known and celebrated writer during the days before the liberation. Chen studies his work along with other writers of this generation. They are men and women who are infused with the spirit of the May 4 movement, and urged to write a new Chinese literature that reflects the reality and future aspirations for a new China. Inspired to do their part for the revolution, they congregate with artists and other writers in Yenan, the intellectual center of the Communist revolution. They come inspired by their fellow writer Lu Hsun's *Call to Arms.* Chairman Mao calls Lu Hsun a great man of letters, a great thinker, and a great revolutionary. The work of revolutionary writers is a heady time in Yenan in those days.

Chen knows that his teacher no longer writes, but he still hopes. He goes out daily to the bazaars in Peking, standing in line at the China Books counter where books are sold cheaply and by the thousands. He buys books of every sort, but can never find any of his old teacher's, nor of any of his colleagues' of those early days.

The old teacher looks around the room and notices the piles of the small five-by-seven-inch books stacked everywhere.

"Why have you have stopped writing?" Chen questions his old mentor. Again, Chen asks an empty question for which he already knows the answer, but he wants to hear his teacher's words.

"My writing is out of touch with the people." He picks up a copy of Hao Ran's *Broad Road in Golden Light* from one of Chen's stacks and peruses the cover.

Hao Ran himself sits in the same room only a week earlier. Chen interviews the popular writer who, if it really mattered, could claim that several million copies of his new novel were sold in a matter of weeks. People are hungry to read, and these days anyone can afford the thirty-two cents it costs to buy a book. Royalties are irrelevant; Hao Ran tells Chen he is a "worker in the field of literature." He is of the generation of writers after the old teacher.

The old teacher sits on the edge of Chen's bed and removes his cap. "My writing is not what is required these days." He replaces Hao Ran's book on another tall stack. It is Hao Ran, a peasant cadre who learns to read during the war of liberation, who now represents the spirit and the realization of the Yenan Forum in 1942, where Chairman Mao declares that there is no such thing as art for art's sake—that all literature and art are for the masses of the people, for the workers, peasants, and soldiers.

Chen leans forward from his chair. "I'm reminded of the last time I saw you. I was seated on the edge of your bed in that small room you occupied near the university. In fact, the bed was covered with books. I think you slept on top of them."

The old teacher smiles. "Nothing has changed. I still sleep on a bed of books."

"I remember you joking. You said: 'The able join the revolution, the wise become government officials, but only fools want to become writers.'"

"Did I say that?" He scratches his head.

"Do you still collect antiques?" Chen recalls his teacher's extraordinary collection of jade and porcelain, but especially his collection of handmade paper dating back to the tenth-century Sung Dynasty.

"I don't have to. I work for the museum."

"And your collection?"

"I gave it to the museum. It was best to share this treasure with the people."

"Tell me about your work."

"We are the receiving center for archeological finds sent in from all over the country. As buildings and industries go up, more and more excavations are taking place. We collect and classify this material and prepare it for storage."

"Storage?"

"Yes, it's a shame we don't have more skilled students in museum work. We can hardly manage the task. Curating the material for display is next to impossible. So much is hidden away."

"Your collection included."

The old teacher nods. It is only a few years ago that the students band together as Red Guards. The People's Army protects the museum to prevent the students from looting it. Chairman Mao speaks to the students in Tiananmen Square, ordering them to smash the four olds: old ideas, old culture, old customs, old habits. The old teacher is dragged from his work classifying old objects taken from an old tomb. The objects are saved, but the old teacher takes his lessons from the Red Guards. When he cannot recite passages from Chairman Mao's writing, he is sent to stand facing the wall. He can remember the titles of hundreds of books and the dates and origins of every piece in a collection of silk, but he cannot remember what Chairman Mao says about the unity of art and politics.

"While classifying these artifacts, I have been contributing to a meticulous history, for example of Chinese silk. Do you know that we can identify the origin of the silk, the date, the dye, the weaver, and the wearer from a single strand of thread?" The old teacher's eyes light with excitement. What he describes is the collective work of research based in history, art, and science. Twelve other professors like the old teacher leave the university at the same time to devote their lives to this work.

Chen still pursues his concern about his teacher's writing. "You are now writing about silk?"

"Yes, we published a history and compilation of forty thousand illustrations." What is important is to create a record of the craft of silk, the skilled craftspeople and artisans who developed their art and techniques to the highest levels. This record also parallels the movement of people and historic change.

Chen hears the insistent tone in his teacher's voice, and remembers the same timbre in Hao Ran's words when describing how a factory worker he didn't know bicycled a hundred li to tell him what needed to be changed in his novel. "The people have a stake in our literature, and we must learn from them."

Although Hao Ran is himself a peasant farmer, he lives and works on communes to draw the most accurate portraits of the life and people. And he does not embark upon his first novel until he undergoes a thorough study of the Marxist theory of literature. "I thought finally I was ready to write, but I was told to study the communiqué issued by the 10th Plenary Central Committee of the Communist Party at the end of the 8th Session. Also the Anti-Rightist Movement and the Chairman's writing on the struggle in 1957. Then there was the material on the Second General Assembly of the Soviet Russian Communist Party on Greater Democracy, championed by Krushchev." In this study, he grasps the significance of true class struggle and its worldwide implications. Finally Hao Ran is ready to write his novel.

Chen reminisces about his days as a student under his teacher's tutelage. "I remember when your book of short stories was published. There was so much excitement. I had to fight to get a copy. Your style and approach were entirely new."

"I remember you had a wall newspaper."

"That's right. I posted it weekly on the college wall. There were a number of students who posted. I was mostly interested in poetry in those days."

"And do you still write?"

"These days my writing is mostly historical and critical, translating Chinese to English, sometimes French."

"And your poetry?"

"What there is of my poetry is in Chinese, and there is not such a market for it in America."

They are both quiet for a long moment, each thinking perhaps about their separate destinies. Chen leaves China as an interpreter for the American Army during the war. He marries and divorces his first wife and then a second wife, and eventually he cannot return.

Chen asks about the old teacher's colleagues. What happened to this or that writer?

"Oh I hear from them from time to time. They are somewhere in Manchuria. They are doing well. You need not worry about them." Some of these writers are accused of being poisonous weeds, capitalist rightists in support of individualism and leading literature backwards. He changes the subject. "What will you do with all these books?"

"I will take them with me."

"What will you say about them?"

"That is difficult to say. I hoped to learn from you."

"Every generation hopes by its literature to leave its mark. My generation is over, and we played our part. The use of literature to rebel is one thing. We thought there was the gun and the pen and that we would be the pen. Yes, the pen can be a revolutionary force and a weapon, but we did not entirely understand what that means. The pen is also used to ensure conformity and political order, and that is as old as Confucius."

"There are many ways to read."

"There are many ways to teach one to read. Remember when you lived here, most people in China could not read."

"And writing? You taught me to write."

"I taught you nothing. You made your own choices. You came to me educated already in three languages. I was myself not so educated. I am almost entirely self-taught. Do you remember this? You were an extraordinary student."

"You invited me to spend the summer writing. You admonished me to never lose the desire to write. That desire, you said, is life itself."

The old teacher withdraws his glasses and polishes the separate lenses with a fold in his shirt. He tries to kill himself in 1949. There are details about their individual lives that cannot be reconciled in a few hours of a scheduled appointment after twenty-five years.

Chen walks his old teacher to the bus stop. "I should make a visit to your home. It's only proper as your student." He does not want to end their meeting so abruptly. He wants to know what expectations his teacher has for him, the pupil; what future does he anticipate? What potential does his teacher see in him that he could not in those days see? He does not expect to return to admonish his teacher about the very things he has not accomplished. He feels ashamed.

On the other hand, his teacher has to make a reckoning of his life, to write a full accounting of himself as self-criticism. During this period of self-reflection, perhaps a year, he takes the job of cleaning the museum latrines. He laughs at Chen and even seems to hop on to the bus. "This relationship of the teacher-student is no longer relevant. Don't worry yourself about such things."

"How is it that you are so healthy?" Chen calls to him through the open window of the bus.

"Silkworms," he yells out. "Forty pupas a day. Keeps the blood pressure down." And the bus pulls away.

It is not until Lee arrives in Shanghai that he really feels he has returned to China. He can hear the sounds of his parents' voices in the people on the streets. They speak the language that is always encapsulated inside of his house. Even when he lives in Hong Kong, he lives among people who speak Cantonese, and it is the same inside of San Francisco Chinatown. At the same time, nothing in Shanghai is familiar to him. His family leaves in 1960 when he is a small boy; all he can honestly remember is being hungry. Those are the years of the great famine and the failure of the policies of the Great Leap Forward.

Lee walks around the city with one of his sister-comrades. She is the one who is always taking notes and asking forward questions. She asks Lee, "What does your father do?"

"He has a laundry business."

"Oh really?"

"You sound surprised."

"I didn't think you were working class."

"Why?"

"You're so educated. And so polite."

"Good grief."

"We all assumed you were upper class."

"We?"

"The sisters, you know. Stupid gossip."

"And you?"

"Me too. My dad's a janitor. My mother a garment worker."

"The others in our group are probably all middle class, don't you think?"

"Funny. That's probably true."

"They have a stereotype about the working class, that we're all gross and unmannered."

"That's not fair."

"Actually, it's a romantic idea about the proletariat. They want to be proletariat. That's why they pretend to act gross and unmannered."

"Sounds like you're tired and need to go home."

"I thought I was home."

"Look, one of those middle-class pretenders lent me her camera. I'm going to take pictures." She looks around for something scenic. A man is stooped on the sidewalk cranking a metal contraption over a small stove. "Look, that man's cooking something."

"Looks like a small bomb."

"Can you hear that? Firecrackers inside."

The man pries open the lid of the metal contraption and positions the opening into a small sack. There's a sudden BANG.

They jump back, and the aroma fills the air. "Oh shit. It's puffed rice!"

"Go get us some. I've got to get a picture of this thing."

Lee digs into his pockets for some change and approaches the puffed-rice vendor. The sister readies her camera to snap, then puts in down. "What's the matter?"

Lee points to the other puffed-rice clients gathering, all holding metal tins and small baskets. "We didn't bring a container."

"Doesn't he have any bags?" The sister snaps her photo.

Lee shrugs and turns around to hear a woman yelling: "Why are you taking a picture? Did you ask for permission? Do you think we are monkeys, so you can steal our pictures?"

The puffed-rice vendor looks up in confusion. Another citizen comes to join in. "Did you see her take your picture?"

Others on the street stop to hear about the incident.

"She's not from here. Maybe she's never seen a puffed-rice vendor."

"What nonsense."

"How did she get that camera? Is she a rich capitalist?"

"Ask her what her work is."

Lee waves his hands. "Please. Please." He tries to defend the bewildered sister. "She meant no harm. She's just a foolish overseas countrywoman. How could she know the correct way?"

The sister backs up into Lee. "You said I was a foolish overseas something. I understand at least that much. What's going on here?"

"That's no excuse! She needs to learn some manners!" The original accuser is now very irate and red in the face. Her yelling attracts more and more bystanders until there is a large crowd of some fifty people surrounding Lee and the sister and the puffed-rice vendor. The people in the center continue to argue, and their arguments are passed on to people at the back of the crowd.

Lee looks at the sister, usually a woman of great self-confidence. Her eyes are wild with fear. "I could give up the camera, but it's not mine," she whimpers, clutching the straps around her neck.

Suddenly the crowd seems to part for a small man in a tattered uniform. Lee realizes that he is a police officer. He says, "Follow me."

Lee and the sister follow him, but so does everyone else—the citizen accusers; the puffed-rice vendor–now with his small stove, bellows, and puffed-rice machine attached to either end of a bamboo pole; and everyone on the street. They follow the officer in a growing parade for two blocks to a traffic kiosk in the middle of the street. "Wait here," he says. "I will check with my superior."

By now there are certainly more than one hundred people surrounding them, and at every moment the crowd seems to grow. Lee notices that they are very comported, arranging themselves by height so that the shorter people are at the front of the crowd to see properly. This means that the children are in front. Even so, they are pressed up closely to the kiosk and seem to move in closer as the crowd from behind presses upon them. There will be no escape. Everyone stands there sullenly with stern faces, waiting for the police officer.

Lee can hear his own breathing and thinks he can hear the sister's heart beating furiously. He feels his sweat dripping from his chin. He doesn't dare move his arms. It is as if they are all standing together in a gigantic elevator. He looks down at a little boy who looks back up at him. The boy's eyes follow his sweat and seem to be intent on watching each drop fall. Lee smiles at the boy. He is wearing a red and blue striped T-shirt that he has already outgrown because his belly is exposed. Lee speaks to the boy in a soft Shanghaiese. The boy's belly is maybe two inches from Lee's hand; he tickles the boy.

"Do you know how to sing?" Lee asks.

The boy giggles and says, "Yes, uncle. I can sing."

"Show me what you can sing. Can you sing the 'Internationale'?"

"That's easy." And he begins to sing. His voice is squeaky and sweet. It seems to rise up like a little bell at the center of a storm. Lee sings too, and very soon hundreds of people are also singing, like the great chorus in a revolutionary opera. They sing triumphant verse after verse that Lee does not know. The sound of their voices fills the city. Lee looks up into the Shanghai sky that seems at that hour to glow pink and hears one-fourth of the world's humanity singing:

Arise, you prisoners of starvation.
Arise, you wretched of the earth.
For justice thunders condemnation,
for a better world's in birth.
No more tradition's chains shall bind us.
Arise you slaves, no more in thrall.
The earth shall rise on new foundation.
We have been naught, we shall be all.

'Tis the final conflict.
Let each stand in his place.
The Internationale unites the human race.

7: Chinatown Verité

1 CHINATOWN—NIGHT

(overheard) Forget it, Jake—it's Chinatown.

Chinese extras crowd around the cream-colored convertible Packard in the final scene. Chinese men in caps or fedoras; Chinese women with hats and purses; a white soldier and his date. More Chinese appear on the street to rubberneck the final scene, bewildered and amused. SOUND of jazz horn.

Credits roll down over the night neon and paper-littered street. Cars and an occasional bicycle pass. Chinese continue to loiter. *Butler: James Hong. Maid: Beulah Quo.*

2 SAN FRANCISCO CHINATOWN—NIGHT

The Hollywood set fades into real takes of Chinatown nightlife. Camera view alternates between drive-by views and a walking jaunt down Grant Street in the dark. Pans the neon, pagoda facades, catches tourist couples, groups of families emerging from restaurants, shops closing, and workers walking briskly home. SOUND of radio music: *Mighty Mighty* (Earth, Wind & Fire).

OPENING CREDITS

Credits superimposed on the continuing Chinatown street walk. Camera view seems to be wandering, but it's the yearly parade route. SOUND of the parade as a kind of residue only.

As the walk continues the night deepens, and the morning lights up through the fog. The streets are the same, but the traffic and passersby change from drunken tourists and bums to early-morning produce trucks, newspaper stand deliveries, shopkeepers opening up. SOUND of pedestrians, cars, restaurant noises, deliveries, music from bars and radios.

By the end of the credits it's early morning, and the camera view heads into Portsmouth Square, still in fog.

3 PORTSMOUTH SQUARE

Stills of the plaza from four angles: Grant, Kearny, Clay, and Washington streets.

4 CLOSE—CHECKER TABLES

Pool of blood drying on stool next to one of the checker tables, with a trail dripped over the cement walkway. Water from a bucket is being splashed onto the stool, and a scrub brush is scrubbing away. As the blood is washed out, the black stenciled image of Mao Tse-tung emerges on the orange stool. As the camera pulls away from the one stool, it can be seen that all the stools around the table have been stenciled with Mao's face. SOUND of scrubbing and background radio news about Watergate scandal, calls for impeachment.

5 GARDENER

Middle-aged Chinese man in his forties, in cap and uniform. He's the caretaker of the square who does gardening and janitorial work. Good-natured and earnest. He's got a portable transistor radio in his shirt pocket that he turns down before continuing his cleaning.

GARDENER

Drug addicts probably. Pool of blood downstairs too. No. No body. Maybe he got picked up. You don't know what happens at night. Knifing each other for a fix. I leave at four p.m. That's when my day's over. I'm hired to garden, but daytime, this is like a living room, see what I mean? Old guys come out of their hotel rooms and spend the entire day here, playing checkers and mah-jongg. They gonna be here soon. Got to get this shit cleaned up.

6 TRASH CANS

Cans are painted with graffiti: *Off the Pigs!* Gardener continues to work, sweeping and throwing trash into the cans. Throws more water on the tables and Mao-faced stools.

GARDENER

Radicals did this. I could order some paint, but first it's the city bureaucracy and second, the old guys say leave it alone. Old Fong said, *"It could be my imagination, but my ass's warmer these days. Why bother? More work for you."* Secretly, they don't say. They're, you know, red. Commies. You work all your life and end up with no family, alone in the park with just your best suit and hat and a social security check for $125, you gonna be a Commie too.

7 FOG LIFTS

As the fog lifts, a few men can be seen gathering in the square, their figures floating in like ghosts. SOUNDS of greetings, formalities. Some sit on benches and stare. Others settle down to read newspapers. A game of Chinese chess begins at the table where the gardener had been scrubbing.

The square fills up with business people passing, kids on their way to school, eventually employees crossing the square to lunch in Chinatown. Someone passes out leaflets. The gardener works in the background, trimming hedges, mowing. SOUND of traffic, bustle.

8 CHINESE CRAZY MAN

A Chinese man is walking around the plaza talking to himself. The camera follows him. He talks into the camera gesticulating and lecturing in Chinese. He walks over to a bench and stands on it. He continues to make his speech.

CRAZY MAN

(speaks in Cantonese with subtitles in English as follows) *Chinamen are made, not born . . . out of junk-imports, lies, railroad scrap iron, dirty jokes, broken bottles, cigar smoke, Cosquilla Indian blood, wino spit, and lots of milk of amnesia.*

*. . . in the beginning there was the Word! . . . And the Word was CHINAMAN.**

The men playing chess and reading their papers look up and look away. They ignore him, or they seem to gesture and say something to their companions and continue to play or read.

CRAZY MAN

(continuing English subtitles)

*I am the natural born ragmouth speaking the motherless bloody tongue. No real language of my own to make sense with, so out comes everybody else's trash that don't conceive. But the sound truth is that I AM THE NOTORIOUS ONE AND ONLY CHICKENCOOP CHINAMAN HIMSELF that talks in the dark heavy Midnight, the secret Chinatown Buck Buck Bagaw.**

SOUND of voice of Crazy Man continues in the background.

GARDENER

That one there. He'll talk himself out next few days. He can do some sweeping around here. I'll give him a couple of beers. Then they'll pick him up, and he'll be gone again to the mental can in San Bruno. Another thirty days, and he's back again.

CRAZY MAN

(continuing English subtitles)

*. . . I am a Chinaman! A miracle synthetic! Drip dry and machine washable.**

9 CHECKER TABLES

Men gather around the checker tables, look at camera and answer questions between turns.

OLD CHINAMEN

That one there, he's crazy, but you listen. He say something smart. Most of the crazies, they got nothing to say.

* From *Chickencoop Chinaman* by Frank Chin, from *Aiiieeeee!*, Howard University Press, 1975

This place here like a stage.

Ha ha. What they say? All world's a stage.

I tell you something. We Chinese all actors. Pretending. (smiles into camera)

There you go again. Don't listen. Go take your camera someplace else.

No really. Chinese are greatest actors. We play double roles. We got our real names and then we got our paper names. Name in lights, name in stone.

What you want to go tell them that on TV? You stupid or something?

What's it to you? I'm old. I die tomorrow, they send my check to my paper name, but they bury me with my real name. Great Chinatown secret is we all got two names.

Both names real. Paper more real—that's the one America wants. Give them what they want!

(Men argue in Chinese with the following subtitles)

Why don't you tell TV what they want to hear? Like we got an underground tunnel system. Connects gambling joints to opium dens to prostitution houses. All run by the Hock Sair Woey!

Tell them you're a fucking spy for Doctor No!

Draw them a map of the tunnels! Secret door right here underneath us. Push a button. Bingo! They can send their luk yi down there to die!

SOUNDS of laughter and continuing monologue of Crazy Man.

10 CLOSE—RICE PAPER

A hand with a flat piece of charcoal is rapidly working over the surface of rice paper tacked up on a wall. Very slowly the charcoal reveals carved Chinese characters beneath the paper. SOUND of charcoal against paper.

VOICES

(reading in Chinese overlaid by English translation)

Instead of remaining a citizen of China, I willingly became an ox.
I intended to come to America to earn a living.
The Western-styled buildings are lofty, but I have not the luck to live in them.
How was anyone to know that my dwelling place would be a prison?

11 EDMUND LEE

A young expert and translator of Chinese literature, Edmund Lee, is interviewed.

EDMUND LEE

This poem is one of more than one hundred poems inscribed by Chinese immigrants on the walls of the Angel Island barracks over a period of thirty years, from 1910 to 1940.

12 CUT TO—ANGEL ISLAND HISTORY

Photo stills of Angel Island history and Chinese detention.

EDMUND LEE

(voice-over) One hundred and seventy-five thousand Chinese immigrants passed through Angel Island, also known as the Ellis Island of the Pacific.

Immigrants were detained for medical examination, interrogation of documents, and deportation. They lived imprisoned in these barracks for months and years. Some made the long journey across the ocean never to touch the mainland.

Chinese laborers were excluded from immigration by a long history of U.S. laws beginning with the Chinese Exclusion Act of 1882. Chinese could, however, enter as merchants or as the descendants of American citizens.

13 PAUL LIN—POET IMMIGRANT

A young Chinese American poet, Paul Wallace Lin, muses about the poets and their poems.

PAUL LIN

(points to the charcoal impression of the poem he's removed from the wall)

I imagine this poet was a "paper son," bought his immigration papers from a Chinese "paper father" he never knew.

14 PHOTO STILLS—SAN FRANCISCO EARTHQUAKE

PAUL LIN

His paper father was in San Francisco at the time of the Great Earthquake in 1906. When the city records were destroyed by fire, he got himself an American birth certificate, sailed home to China, and recorded the birth of ten sons— ten paper sons who could be citizens too.

15 PHOTO STILLS—COACHING BOOK

Photo stills of coaching books used by immigrants to memorize details about their paper villages and paper homes.

PAUL LIN

So this poet had to memorize the paper details of his paper family and paper village.

16 PHOTO STILLS—VILLAGE LIFE IN CHINA

PAUL LIN

How many houses in your village?
How many rows of houses?
On which side of the village is the altar of worship, east or west?
Where is your house located? Is it near the market?
How many rooms in your house?
In which room did you sleep?
Is the floor brick or dirt?

Where is the rice bin kept?
How many steps to the well?
Did you have a dog?

17 CLOSE—PAUL LIN

Return to close head shot of Paul Lin.

PAUL LIN

Sometimes a real son is deported, but a paper son is admitted. Sometimes the paper father was himself an adopted son. Maybe this poet arrived never to see his village again.

18 PORTSMOUTH SQUARE

Return to Portsmouth Square scenes where Crazy Man in the background is still pontificating.

PAUL LIN

Paper memories replace real memories. Memories merge and fade.

19 CHINESE PLAYGROUND

Groups of young people hanging around a playground. Some have permed hair and Mao-type silk jackets. Others wear polyester shirts, bells, and platforms. One group is in T-shirts, playing basketball. One of the players bounces the ball over to the camera. The others hang back, looking wary.

TEENAGE YOUTH

Hey cuz, it's Edmund, from the Center. Yeah, I live on the Dhon side. My mom's not there now. You still better not tell her I let you in. It's not cleaned up or nothing.

Camera follows youth through Chinatown alleys and streets to Ping Yuen Housing Project. SOUND of kids playing in streets. Shots into shops: fruits and vegetables, hanging roast duck, pig snouts, fortune cookie machine, whole fish on ice, smoke shop, barbershop.

20 PING YUEN HOUSING PROJECT—PACIFIC AVENUE

Camera pans Ping Yuen apartments, picks up Chinafied details in the stylized roof and window treatments, and peeling green and red paint; follows children playing, residents laden with bags walking along the outside corridors.

TEENAGE YOUTH

My family moved here maybe five years ago. Compared to where we lived, this is the fuckin' Gum Shan! This is the projects, Chinatown style. Man, where you gonna find projects matches the tourist town?

21 PHOTO STILLS—YOUTH'S FAMILY

Stills of tenement on Stockton and Washington, plus photos of the family, portraits of mom and dad.

TEENAGE YOUTH

Before Ping Yuen, we lived on Stockton in a one-room, maybe eight by ten. It could just fit one double bed, but we had a sofa stuffed in there too. I slept with my little brother on the sofa, his head that side, my head this side, and my sisters slept with my parents on the bed. We had a card table to eat and study. We cooked everything on a hot plate, but mostly my dad brought home leftovers from the restaurant. Shit, we left, family of ten moved in.

22 INTERIOR—PING YUEN APARTMENT

Camera follows youth around the two-bedroom apartment.

An old man is slumped over asleep in a chair before the television. He awakens disoriented, and the TV's showing a news broadcast of the SLA and Patty Hearst kidnapping. SOUND and television visuals of burning house and gunfire.

Old man shuffles off and locks himself in the bathroom. SOUNDS of old man coughing, then hacking; a flush.

Bottles and boxes are stacked everywhere. Clothes are scattered. There's a sewing machine in the living room with pieces of material stacked on the floor in one corner; a table stacked with books and cluttered with papers; and food, bowls, and plates spread on newspaper.

TEENAGE YOUTH

(points to sewing machine)
My mom had her sewing machine stuffed in the old place too. She does piecework at night. Sews all day in the shop, then comes home and sews some more. It's *whir whir* all night. (He hits the peddle.)

SOUND of sewing machine.

TEENAGE YOUTH

(holds up a little girl's dress)
Hey, she does a dozen of these, she gets five dollars.

23 GARMENT FACTORY—JUNG SAI

Exterior shot of Jung Sai Garment Factory. About one hundred women march with picket signs: *Jung Sai Unfair! ILGWU Demands Just Wages! Support Childcare for Working Mothers! Boycott Plain Jane! Boycott Esprit! We Will Not be Exploited! Close the Sweatshops!* SOUND of chanting.

STRIKERS

Minimum wage is $1.65, but we are not paid even that. Jung Sai says it complies with the minimum wage law, but in fact, our time cards are falsified to meet the minimum requirement.

For years we afraid to speak up, but now all of us united to protest!

We demand back wages and fair negotiation for better working conditions!

24 CHINESE RESTAURANT—LATE EVENING

Exterior shot of Sai Yon's on Jackson Street. Teenage youth is hanging outside with a group of young men. Camera saunters in with him and others.

Interior of restaurant. It's the late-night crowd, hanging out with bowls of noodles. About twenty young men commandeer two round tables, ordering platter after platter and beers. One waiter is feverishly rushing around trying to keep up with the orders.

YOUNG MEN

Yeah, you got your Wah Ching, your Joe Boys, your Suey Sing Boys, Hop Sing Boys, John Louie's, Cookie Boys. Then there's always the babies: Baby Wah Ching, Baby Joes. Like that.

Us? No we ain't any of them. Do we look like those fei jies?

Me, I work in the area of holiday festivities. My work is seasonal, picks up around New Year's and the Fourth of July. That guy there? He's nothing but a pool shark. (laughter)

Yeah, Chinatown can be a dangerous place. It's all over the newspapers. Guys shot in the head. That baby gangster Lincoln killed. Something's got to give.

Hey, waiter. (motions to the waiter)

Let me tell you something. Tourists come to Chinatown anyway. They read the news, but they come anyway. You know why? Because the food is cheap. Tourists will risk their lives for cheap food.

(to waiter who's come over to the table) Tell him how much you make. Yeah, throw in the tips and everything. How much?

(waiter throws up his hands in disgust and leaves, cursing)

I'll tell you what he makes: what my old man makes—three fifty a month. O.K., max five hundred. He works six days a week and ten hours a day.

You wanna put down a tip, O.K. Bill's taken care of, cuz. Services rendered. (saunters out)

(no one pays, waiter yells after them)

25 EXTERIOR—JACKSON STREET

Across the street a white '66 Chevy Impala is ablaze. SOUNDS of explosion, commotion, and frantic running.

VOICES

What the fuck! Joey's car!

SOUND of gunfire. Camera swings around wildly.

VOICES

Oh my god!

Edmund! Edmund!

Edmund is staggering. Blood is splattering across the sidewalk. The camera reels around, following scattering footsteps. Swirling visuals capture parts of faces, guns, flash of neon and scuffle of dark bodies. SOUND of motors gunning away and incoherent yelling in English and Chinese.

26 UNFOCUSED—JACKSON STREET

Camera continues to run, a long-view shot parallel to the ground, stretching down the concrete along Jackson Street. Edmund's broken glasses can be seen through the viewer, and the image of a man running is framed in the glass of the unbroken lens. SOUND of gasping and labored breathing.

THE END

8: This Moment

So maybe there's this moment. It's different for everyone, but it's pivotal. It's the moment your head gets screwed off and screwed on again, and everything is changed forever. You can never see life the same way again. You can never go back. Well, you can go back, but you go back with new eyes, maybe a new brain, new ears, new mouth. It could be there's a propensity for the moment, like DNA that's planted inside you ready to catch the moment. Some folks might say it's family history. Or maybe you can trace a series of events, plot them out like a map. You remember this time in your childhood: your mother or father said this; you saw that; you got caught up in this; you read that. Then it all comes together and wham! The lights turn on. O.K., it might be more subtle, more gradual, but there's always something really significant that captures the heart and mind. And it's not to say that it might not be painful or personally devastating as well. At that moment you shed an old life to become a whole person because, you believe, your body in its actions and your mind in its spirit are wholly in sync. Your talents and possibilities exist for a purpose that is beyond yourself.

Now it's not as if this moment lasts forever, or that things don't get sticky and go back on themselves. But it's the moment you return to because it sustains meaning and empowers the lonely individual. Of course most folks never get this moment, and you who do get it are still imperfect human beings.

Witnessing Edmund's death was that sort of moment. Paul, employed to capture sound, dropped the boom and ran down the street to find a pay phone. But it was Judy Eng who found herself watching everything through the narrow hole of the camera lens. She felt her face hopelessly glued to the machine as if thus empowered to find the source of the bullet and to stop it. The camera swung about searching and recording. It was a mechanical thing, a pompous truth machine. In the aftermath, these last minutes would be replayed relentlessly, scrutinized frame by frame, used by the police and the prosecutor to identity the killer, if not his accessories. Similarly, Judy sat in a dark editing room and obsessively studied the tape over and over again.

"Stop it!" Paul yelled. "How can you keep watching that?"

Judy faced him stalwartly. Her eyes were bloodshot. "Leave me alone."

"Why are you doing this? Let the police figure this out."

"Who gives a fuck about the police!"

"You need help."

"I don't need help. I need Edmund."

"Edmund's gone," Paul said softly.

"He's there," she wept. "Look, there." She pointed at Edmund's figure collapsing on the monitor.

"No, that's not him. That's not him."

"It's my fault."

"No."

"It's true. Look. I timed the minutes from when he falls to when I stop taping. One minute and twelve seconds. Do you know how long that is? I saw him fall in my finder, and I kept on filming, like it wasn't real or like it *was* real, like fascination."

"It's just confusion."

"It's not."

"You've watched it too many times."

"I was watching him die. Like a fucking spectator!"

Running back down Jackson Street from his frantic call for help, Paul found Judy cradling Edmund's head in her lap and wailing. She was wailing again now.

One minute and twelve seconds. The time it takes to make a choice, and Judy kept watching her choice over and over again. I think it's possible at this juncture that Judy might have gone over the deep end. Paul certainly thought that might happen as he tried to drag her away from the equipment.

Chen stood in the doorway, the dark empty corridor behind him. He walked over to a table, pushed away the piles of papers, newspaper articles written by Edmund, and scattered photos, and put down the large paper sack he was carrying. "Paul," he said matter-of-factly, "I forgot to buy a newspaper, and we could use some drinks. A beer for me." He drew some bills from his pocket.

Paul loosened his grip on Judy, glanced gratefully at Chen, and walked away.

When Paul returned, Chen and Judy were hunched over Chinese take-out boxes picking out the contents with chopsticks.

"Sorry," Chen looked up. "We couldn't wait. Judy hasn't eaten in three days."

Judy had grabbed the box of rice, hoisted mein on top, and was wolfing down the contents.

Chen pulled out his pocketknife. Paul popped open a beer for himself and nursed it slowly, observing the empty boxes. He munched on an almond cookie.

"We saved some tofu for you. Your favorite." Chen pushed a box over and tossed him the chopsticks.

Paul picked out the tofu pieces and stared at a series of photographs of Edmund speaking in front of a mic at some rally. Chen puttered around him, gathered the empty cartons and rearranged the table, and finally hustled the film crew of two out of the studio.

At Judy's house, Chen said to Paul, "You stay here with Judy. Tomorrow you edit the tape with her."

"What?"

"For Edmund's memorial in two days."

"Edit? I don't know how to do that."

"She knows how. For you, it's easy. Tell a story." He spoke quietly but firmly. "Don't leave her side until it's finished. I'll see you at the memorial."

Paul fell asleep on the sofa. When he awoke he looked around and recognized all of Edmund's things, but in a domesticated setting. This had been Edmund's life since China, where he met Judy. She had arranged his practical life, become devoted to his work, learned to run a camera because he encouraged the idea. Paul thought she was stuck to him like a puppy dog. He groaned.

Two days later, Chen took his seat next to Paul at the memorial. "Nicely done," he commented.

"She did all the work."

"Where is she?"

"Behind the projector."

"Good."

"I haven't eaten for three days."

"Good."

The chief editor from the *East West* newspaper got up and spoke about Edmund. Then someone from the Chinatown Youth Services. Then from the Chinese for Affirmative Action. Guys from the Tiao Yu Tai struggle were there. A woman from the Chinese Progressive Association, aka I Wor Kuen, and a guy who ran Everybody's Bookstore for the Asian Community Center, aka Wei Min She, were also in line to speak. Old Red Guards were there too. A woman from the Health Services and even the old guys from the Laundrymen Association and the Six Companies chimed in. Wah Ching and the Joe Boys came in an uneasy truce and all the poets from CARP and Kearny. They all told the Lee family that Edmund Yat Min was a good son and exalted member of the community. It was maybe the first and last time that all these entities with competing political agendas and visions came together. In an amazing display of largess, they refrained on one side from denouncing Edmund as a reformist or on the other as a communist. Still, they all claimed some piece of Edmund to demonstrate the worthiness of their associations, shamelessly putting in a plug for Edmund's support of garment workers or bilingual education or his fight against police brutality.

I guess you could say that Edmund was our slain Chinatown Romeo, sweet prince fallen between many houses. But maybe you could also say that this event was a testimony to the kind of person Edmund had become in a few short years. He was probably not, as they exaggerated, *a man of great passion and unwavering commitment to the rights of oppressed people,* but he was a young man of uncommon intelligence who used his talents to work daily on behalf of people in need. Why did he choose to do this? There had been endless meetings, strategy sessions, leafleting, articles to write, politicians to approach, folks to interview, statistical research, funding and legal matters, speeches and debates. And Edmund did all this while nominally working on his graduate studies in Chinese political philosophy and history. Chen knew Edmund's genius and that Edmund, who alone among all his students could leave Chinatown, had chosen to stay. I am not sure if Edmund, had he lived, would not have eventually moved on, but these few years of which we speak were formative in the lives of many. A seed was planted. A moment of awakening.

Judy came over to hug Chen. "Thank you," she said.

When she walked away, Paul complained, "Hey, how come . . . ? Oh, never mind."

"Jealous?"

"Oh fuck you. That was my work too."

"I could tell."

"That wasn't easy. He was my best friend."

"I know."

Paul looked angrily at Chen, whose eyes were quietly sad. "Take me home," Paul said, shamefully. He tugged Chen's sleeve. "Please," he begged. "I'm famished."

Although the pivotal moment theory might work for some, it might be overblown. As time drags on, other events step up to the plate, and one begins to wonder why any fork in the road presented the less traveled option. Chen knew his own confused path that, upon review, could not have been changed then and certainly not now. Chen was a man who lived in several exiles. As for Paul, he was still too young to know. Thinking about Paul and Chen, maybe you couldn't exactly compare pivotal moments, but rather a single desire that united the two men: the desire to write.

The desire to write is linked to the desire to think and the desire to record. You could say it's all the same thing, but you probably favor something or another. You who think you're thinking are recording your thinking, but you who think you're writing are recording your writing. You who think you're recording are writing your record. It's all stupidly obvious except for the desire. You could say it's an obsessive trait, and once it kicks in, you're stuck with it. The desire is selfish and personal. It has nothing to do with talent or giftedness. That becomes apparent or unapparent in the act, but the desire is an enigma. You say, I want to be famous; I want to be remembered; I want to speak; I want to communicate; I want to imagine; I want to remember. But writing itself is a strange way to accomplish any of that stuff, sitting alone for hours with a pen and paper or typewriter. It's a complicated desire that becomes mixed up with the self, and Chen and Paul, if forced, would admit that it was a desire stronger than any human relationship, including the one between them.

Writing itself might be a laudable occupation, but the desire could be sinful—a lot of pretending and fakery. Mao was probably right to try to socialize writing, make it work for the people. Of course once they try to make rules about writing, you'll go off and hide somewhere and write heresy. Still, having the desire is not the same thing as having something to write. The desire has to coincide with belief and necessity at a time and place in history. So the Poetry Boys Club hung around coffee houses, mostly with their desire, and defined a belief and necessity in a time and place.

"I think we need to present ourselves professionally," Paul said. He could hear grumbling on the phone. "She doesn't know us from Adam. Truth is, we've never actually done this, never published anything."

"There's the anthology in progress, and we're going to publish her husband."

"Besides which, we're Chinese."

"What difference does that make?" Jack's voice rose.

"Did your folks wear *I'm Chinese* buttons?"

"Yeah, well—"

"We'll pick up Kamiyama in Fresno."

"Good idea."

"Listen. You agree this is important."

"John Okada publishes the first real serious novel in Asian America in 1957! It goes out of print with a couple lousy reviews. Nobody recognizes it's a classic. And we discovered it!"

"Practically in a trash bin at McDonald's." Paul patiently recounted finding the discarded hardcover at the used bookstore on Turk and Market. Heroics were all part of it.

"It means we got a history! We're yellow writers who come from a tradition of yellow writing!" Jack bellowed, then his voice got intense. "So this just in: Tuttle sent me a copy of a letter from Okada dated 1956. Okada says in the letter that he's writing another novel."

"So what happened to it?"

"It's gotta be in his papers. Maybe an unfinished manuscript. Who knows! Can you believe this? We gotta get that manuscript!"

"So we're not just asking her permission to reprint *No-No Boy*?"

"Right! We gotta get permission to ransack her house!"

Jack threw a duffel and his guitar case into the trunk of Paul's car. Then he hooked some hangers under plastic on the windows behind the driver's seat.

"What's that?" Paul turned around.

"High-school graduation suit."

"Does it still fit?"

"You want professional, this is the best I can do."

"Vintage."

"Speaking of, where'd you get this car?"

"I bought it off Chen."

"It wasn't this color."

"Right. I painted it."

"Fucking Steve McQueen. Why do I need a suit? Leather will do."

Paul laughed. "You watch too many movies." Paul twirled the '66 now-green Mustang GT out of the driveway, shot down 101 to pick up Kamiyama in Fresno, and they were on to L.A.

What happens next in L.A. at Dorothy Okada's house is history. Her husband, the writer John Okada, had died only months before, and she had burned all his papers before moving. It wasn't entirely her fault. No one seemed interested in his work or writing. Not UCLA. Not the Japanese American community. There was no affirmation of his work, and she had lived her own reality. Now these young men had driven four hundred miles of pure anticipation to her doorstep, and she could not fathom their disappointment. She did not know this desire to write and the cost of defining a belief and necessity in a time and place.

Paul looked at Jack in his high-school graduation suit. He looked like he was going to rip it off his body. Paul's look said, *Be professional or I'll kill you.* Jack was fuming, thinking that young chump Paul wasn't even born when Okada's book was published. But Kamiyama looked at Jack with a sansei look that said, *Don't make her feel bad.* So Jack said, "Well, O.K., tell us about John. Ah, what sort of guy was he? I mean, what sort of sex life did you have together?"

Paul got right to work on the book projects. Maybe he did it because he was the youngest and didn't know it was a shot in the dark. That's another thing to take into consideration, the way things happen because you are young and don't know any better. You might say it's youthful idealism, but youth doesn't really know what's ideal. It just feels right sometimes.

Paul knew how to collect rent, write up contracts, keep accounting books, carry out a will. Maybe Jack or some other poet made the contacts, but Paul followed through, got the contracts signed, deposited and signed checks, printed letterhead, licked the stamps on the envelopes. He had learned from Edmund about press releases and advertising. It was business, on the one hand. On the other, he had learned something from editing Edmund's memorial tape. It was like Chen had suggested. You tell a story. Pieces for the anthology arrived, along with interviews of the authors. A new introduction and afterword for the Okada reprint had to be written and proofed. Paul poured over the material and meticulously edited everything. He got the confidence to get Kamiyama to pull back on the nostalgia and to make Jack accept cutting out whole paragraphs of run-on blather. The whole operation looked professional, but it was just Paul, schlepping books to the post office in the back of the green Mustang.

You've got to wonder, too, about the role of teachers. The problem for Paul was that Chen had become more than a teacher. Sometimes you think the student wants to surpass or show up the teacher, but that wasn't the case for Paul. He wanted to make Chen proud. He wanted to give back something significant in return. He was busy being a member of the poetry club, of course, but he thought this was part of delivering the goods, as it were. The edited book, some of it his own writing—he wanted to give that to Chen. Of course, he didn't think about it in exactly this way until months later, so while he was busy being a singular worker in a staff of one, he failed to notice Chen's malaise.

Chen went back and forth methodically to his teaching appointment. And for days he might disappear with a car to the races.

"Where've you been?"

"Racing."

"I thought you said you were going to write this weekend."

"I couldn't."

"You say that every weekend. What are you reading?" Paul picked up the scattered papers Chen had discarded on the carpet next to the sofa. He thought they might be student papers, but he recognized the typewriter and the style. "This is Edmund's stuff."

"There's a box of it. Judy gave it all to me. For a long time I couldn't look at it." Chen rubbed his eyes. "This is the dissertation he started."

Paul slumped into the sofa.

"It's brilliant."

"Can you publish some of it?"

"Maybe." Chen shook his head sadly.

Paul tried to change the subject. "I found this artist in J-Town who does prints and silkscreens. He's perfect to do the cover for *No-No*."

"Such a loss." Chen hadn't heard Paul. He got up and walked to the large window of his study, the library where Paul and Edmund had spent so many hours reading together. Chen stared out, watching the fog slip into the bay. He didn't hear Paul leave the room.

The next weekend, Paul ran into the emergency room of the Valley Memorial Hospital in Livermore. He found Chen with a bandaged head and broken arm, rushed there from the Altamont Raceway. "You wanna kill yourself?" he barked at Chen.

"This driver cut in front. We were lucky, you know. That's skill." Chen proudly hid his embarrassment.

Confined to the house, Chen sat next to Edmund's box of writing and read and reread everything. He pulled out Edmund's translations, made corrections, and had Paul type up new drafts.

"When are you going to get that cast off?" Paul asked.

"Maybe next week. If you don't want to type for me, it can wait another week." Chen looked frustrated, shuffling through papers with his left hand.

"I can do it." Paul tapped a ream of papers on their bottom edge and said, "But I've got these transcripts to complete, then turn into bios. They want it all in a few weeks."

Chen spoke to himself. "There are another fifteen poems in this series to translate. I'll have to do that myself. But Edmund's history seems complete."

"Hey, want to hear this? This is Jack's interview of Keye Luke."

Chen looked up, but he hadn't heard Paul. He muttered, "Then there are the footnotes."

Paul got up to peruse a spread of photographs on the coffee table. He stared at a black-and-white photo of a Chinese man holding a pole balanced with two baskets filled with chickens. The man in the photo and those around him were wearing traditional jackets, slippers, and Western hats.

Chen glanced over and said, "Arnold Genthe. Took those in Chinatown before the earthquake. Tangrenbu: what they called Chinatown in those days. I've been collecting them. Thought there might be something we could use."

Paul nodded and stared a long time at a second photo, of a little girl standing in front of similar baskets. Her Chinese jacket looked soiled, torn and shredded at the sleeves; her pajama pants were wide. Perhaps she had to carry those baskets on her back.

"In that drawer over there." Chen pointed. "There may be another box of photos."

Paul pulled out a large tin box and pried open the cover. It was filled with envelopes filled with photographs. He rummaged through and pulled out a large portrait of a young Chinese man and woman. The woman was wearing a simple gown and holding a small bouquet of flowers. The man was dressed in a tux. In the can there were other photos of the same woman, standing on the Golden Gate, sitting under a tree at a picnic, standing on what seemed to be the Stanford campus. She wore a short-sleeved sweater and pleated skirt. Her hair was bobbed, her bangs cut straight against her forehead. Paul had very little memory of his mother, but the small pounding in his chest told him that these images matched the ones he knew. He looked up at Chen, who was buried in Edmund's text.

Those days Chen only thought of Edmund's work—Edmund's brilliant scholarship, Edmund's genius, the tragic loss of Edmund. Chen had realized that there would be no outlet for his own poetry, and that like his own teacher before him, his writing was *out of touch with the people.* Who were "the people"? They were young people like Paul and Jack, who had a vision for a new literature. It was now their turn. Of this new generation, only Edmund had read Chen's poetry and knew its flavor and value, but Edmund was no longer. Paul's father's newspaper was no longer. It was a limited readership in a foreign land. He could write equally well in French or English, but he did not find his creative voice there. He was not a Nabokov or a Conrad, in that sense. Out of necessity, he had become a scholar and a translator.

He hid his slight intellectual disdain of Paul's project, which seemed to him dislocated from literary history whether Western or Asian, but especially Asian. He knew that it was a breaking away and a breaking out, that someone had to stand up to American racism and to claim American English. He knew the political meaning of literary acts. He knew that if Paul and his generation of writers wanted a history, they would have to dig it up and invent it for themselves. He believed in this and accepted his small part: consulting, translating, offering historic accuracy and money. But Paul sensed what Chen would not admit: how much Chen missed Edmund and how he had thought that Edmund would eventually play out his political calling for more literary pursuits. So it's not only a question of the role of your teacher, a role that might arise from happenstance, but also your role as a student, finally chosen to succeed. Paul knew that Chen had chosen Edmund.

It shouldn't have mattered. Paul loved Chen, and Chen loved Paul. But the elegant portrait of the Chinese man and woman with the flower bouquet told Paul more than he wanted to know. Paul saw the soft features of his mother that matched his own, his own questioning eyes. And the beautiful Chinese groom was Wen-guang Chen. Paul slipped the photos back into the tin can, walked away from the house in Marin, following the winding streets down from its overhanging cliff.

After some time Chen checked his watch and turned on the evening news. Walter Cronkite presided from his desk as a frantic crowd of people scaled the walls of the American Embassy in Saigon; others fought to jam themselves against and even hang off waiting helicopters.

"Paul!" Chen ran from the room, but Paul had boarded the ferry and was crossing the bay back to Chinatown.

9: Authentic Chinese Food

How many places you gotta go before you find a decent bowl of noodles? Two? Three? Ten? Decent in this town—O.K., two, three, why not? We got standards and competition, so for decent, it's not a problem. But if you're serious, if you take your noodles seriously, you got to do your homework. Now I tell you what: true noodle connoisseur, he takes his noodles late at night. Gotta be after nine, earliest. Later the better. Midnight. You know why? It's the soup; all day long the bones and leftovers getting thrown in that pot, simmering down easy, see. Already your choices narrowed, right? Gotta be those joints open to the wee hours.

Chen, see, he's got what I call the palate. So he does the noodles tour. Not like a tourist thing, more like a quest. Not that he couldn't make quality noodles himself. It's the gritty kind he's after, the kind you can only get in a busy kitchen at the end of the day. It's a return to his bohemian days, but now he's got money. Could be it's an opera or a concert, classy event like that, or the last showing of a movie. Could be it's a smoky house of jazz and blues. That's just the set-up. Then he peels away for the noodles showdown.

So that's how I meet Chen Wen-guang. I call him Wen for short. It's one a.m., and we're at the counter side by side at the Cathay. We got the same bowl of noodles, 'cept he's dressed nice. Madison Avenue's finest. 'Course by this time of night, he's got his silk tie stretched out and thrown over his shoulder. Jacket is hanging off the stool behind him. Time was I could afford suits like that, make a killing back of Lucky M and go out and buy me the best. Pinstriped, double-breasted, silk hanky. But that was before my union days.

Wen's got his eyes closed, concentrating. Then he takes up a slurp of the noodles and gets the texture between his teeth. I look at him, and I say, "Pork neck. Could use a few more."

He says, "Snout. That would do it, too."

And I know he knows. It's the sticky cartilage that gives a soup grip. I'm impressed.

Then he says, "And some more white pepper."

He nabbed it.

And that's how it started. I say, "Have you tried Chop Suey House over on Post?" And we meet there the next week, and every week practically we're on the quest.

So one night I tell him this story:

Long long time ago in a faraway place, two lovers meet every solstice, summer and winter. That's the only time. Twice a year. You know, the gods. They control everything in those times. So those lovers they make the most of it. You bet. Having sex this way and that, like in those Indian instruction books, *Kama Sutra.* Hey, I know my stuff. Pathetic old codger like me. That's me in book six. But I been to every other book. Yeah, I been there. O.K., nowadays *Joy of Sex,* right? Like that. You use your imagination. Wet. Sticky. Hot. Rolling around. Running around. You got a chance only twice a year, you better be good. You remember your best times and then you double that. No, you triple that. Imagine that. That's probably why the gods prohibited it. They were jealous.

Then, you know, after you spend that kind of energy, you gotta eat. Now, this is the important part. This is when the lovers appease the gods, or who knows, maybe they won't let them come together next solstice. Hey, it can't be just any food, rush out and get a burger. Young people these days think porno and burgers. No, these lovers have the palate. Palate of the gods. Gotta be maybe a ten-course meal. They do the jan ken pon for who dishes up the first course, and then it's back and forth, each one trying to outdo the other, appetizer to dessert. Now this is some good cooking. Finest ingredients. Highest quality. And everything perfect like a concert. Pungent dishes followed by subtle and refreshing. Crunchy to smooth and succulent. Chicken to pork to duck to beef to fish.

So I tell Wen this story. I say to him, "You know this story? It's a classic."

He looks at me like, if anybody knows a classic, he's the one. Stuck-up son of a bitch. I can say that, you know. He's my friend, like a kid brother.

I say, "Every Asian people has a version of this very story. Japanese, Korean, Pilipino, Vietnamese. Some things different. Sometimes the sex before. Sometimes after, but basically the same story."

"And different menus."

"Now you're talking."

I get serious. "This is the great myth of Asian peoples. How can the West compare? All they got is that poison apple."

Wen laughs.

"Think about it. Innocence to knowledge. Good and evil. And *then* they get to have sex. What kind of screwed up thinking is that?"

Wen orders another beer.

"Sex is everything. Beginning of the universe. It's one big—" My gesture says it all.

Wen and I toast.

I continue, "But it's more than meets the eye. Complicated. Two cooks can't live together!"

"What do you mean?"

"It's true what they say. Too many cooks, you know? Got to be one palate at a time, but like a balancing act. You Chinese say, yin and yang. And each gonna offer the other the most delicious dish possible, but it's also competition. It gets more intense with each dish. So the gods know what they're doing. Keep the lovers apart, they get the best possible meal."

"That's the moral of the story?"

"I don't know nothing about morals. What's the moral about that apple? Don't go talking to snakes? It's already too late. It's like life. You want good sex? You want good food? You gotta go to the trouble."

"What about companionship?"

By now, I know. Wen's living in some big house all by himself.

"I'm living how many years by myself in that I-Hotel? I used to have a regular girlfriend, but then she disappeared. I never see her again. So what's left? I got food. I'm fighting this eviction thing."

Wen looks sad.

"Listen," I say, "Wen, my friend. You still young, but I tell you something they never tell you when you're young. You think you gotta have your woman. That's what you hungry for all the time. Guys like me don't have that chance. So we got that knowledge. But I tell you this. Most important thing you gotta learn is to be alone. I think I'm not cut out for this. I go back to the Philippines or something. But this is my home now after fifty years. It's my freedom. I'm gonna die free. And I'm gonna die alone. Same for everyone."

I don't see Wen for a while, then he comes around and we go look for noodles like usual. He says, "I been thinking about your story."

"Oh yeah?"

"Yeah, the part where I'm confused is the menu. You said twice a year on the solstices. That's summer and winter. How about the equinoxes? Spring and fall?"

"O.K., we can change the story. Why not? Four times a year."

"You can change the myth like that?"

"Why not? It's my myth. I change it if I want."

"Is that so?"

"This is improvement. Definitely. You got to get the variety of food in each season. Of course! Spring duck! Summer could be tropical, refreshing. Fall, big harvest. Winter gotta braise the meats, slow cooking in heavier wines." So that's when we start to make menus. I say, "At night, I'm dreaming menus. Like summer. First course: lime ceviche, try albacore."

He says, "Second course: drunken chicken in Shao-hsing wine."

I say, "Fried lobster claws."

He says, "Cold sour soup with cucumber."

I say, "Peking duck on steamed bread."

He says, "Zucchini flowers and tofu."

I say, "Barbecued spareribs."

He says, "Beef with asparagus."

I say, "Brandied scallops."

He says, "Lychee sorbet." Then he says, "The first dish, ceviche. That's not Chinese."

"Who said it has to be Chinese? What about lychee sorbet?"

"Closer than ceviche. We do South America later. For authenticity, the menu should match the Chinese version of the myth."

"O.K. Squab-stuffed mushrooms."

"Now I'm hungry."

"O.K. You buy the ingredients, I make everything. Completely authentic. You gonna think you're Nixon in China. I heard he got himself a Chinese cook, but common knowledge he's Pilipino."

"You're lying."

"Maybe not. You look around. Take the movies. Pilipinos stand in for everything: Indian, Mexican, Chinese, Egyptian, Hawaiian. That's what good coloring does for you."

"What's the movies got to do with this?"

"Hey, I cook you any kind of cooking. Doesn't matter. People come peek in the kitchen to see who the chef is. Ask me, when did you come here from Japan? Or, you must be French Vietnamese. Did you get your training in France? I always say, that's right. How did you know?"

So that's how every once in a while I go to Wen's place, put on my chef hat, and cook. Always a crowd there testing the palate. Like I said. At night, I'm dreaming menus. O.K., I'm dreaming beautiful women too, but all I remember in the morning is the menu. Think about it. Beautiful menu like a beautiful woman: refreshing, delicate, sophisticated, succulent, juicy, spicy. Takes your breath away. You die happy. So if I give the menu to Wen, one day we go shopping. Half of my dream comes true. What you think? Fifty percent is pretty good for old guy like me.

People say, you gonna give us cooking lessons. Pass on the traditions. Pass on the secrets. I say sure. I pass on everything. Some say, what is it? The ingredients? You get this stuff imported? I say, I don't know. Most of it hundred percent American ingredients. Made in America. Where you think we are? Some stuff you improvise. Make your own. Then there's bird nests and shark fins. Ube and taro. If you get your hands on the exotic stuff, they all go wild. They can't believe their taste buds. But from my point of view, it's only fifty percent ingredients. Other fifty percent is technique. Every cuisine got technique. You got to know the way. For Chinese, it's the way of fire.

So Wen's got a celebration going, and three of us taking turns with the dishes. Wen, he got a duck smoked in tea, red peppers, cinnamon, and star anise. Then Jack Sung's making lobster Cantonese with black beans. But I got the piece of resistance.

Jack says, "Hey, manong. You starting to sound like Master Po."

"That's me. Kung fu cooking master."

"What's that dish you got there?"

"You know this dish? Mrs. Nixon's favorite."

"Mrs. Watergate herself?"

"Serious. I made it for her in the Great Hall when she visited China in 1972."

Wen laughs. "Another true story."

I take out the *Life* magazine and show Jack the pictures. "Here it is. You call this dish, 'lady's quivering buttocks.'"

"No fucking shit!"

"Dongpo pork," says Wen. "It's a Song Dynasty recipe named after the poet Su Dongpo. Dongpo wrote a poem for this dish: 'In Praise of Pork.'"

"He compares it to a lady's quivering buttocks?"

"Why not?"

"Oh, mama!"

The pork belly melts between your teeth. Like I said, it's a piece of resistance.

"What else you cook up for Pat?"

"Oh, jasmine chicken soup, three-colored sharks fins, smoked duck in tea."

"And they say I'm bourgeois."

"You convert to Mao, we let you eat like this too. By the way, this was Mao's favorite too. That's why I make it. To honor Mao."

"End of an era."

We toast to Mao, who just died. We toast to Chou En-lai, died in January. "To the end of the Long March."

"That's it," Jack says. "You should write a cookbook."

"I been thinking the same thing. I base it on the classic Asian myth of the two separated lovers."

"What's that?"

I tell him the tragic story of the lovers that all Asians should know.

"Chen, this guy's a real bullshitter."

"You look it up. All Asian people know this myth."

Wen winks. "Look it up."

I say, "My idea for the cookbook is simple. We do Asian American cuisine. American because we use ingredients found in America. Imported is O.K. Ajinomoto. Soy sauce. Wonton wrappers. Then we do ten-course menus in Chinese, Japanese, Pilipino, Korean, you name your Asian American. Only problem is I can't write."

Jack says, "You leave that to me."

"You got to tell the classic myth. That's the key."

"If you insist."

Wen knows better. "And we have to test all the recipes."

"No problem. I volunteer."

I say, "After Nixon in China, you see all these Chinese cookbooks. Problem I see is no pictures. I gotta have pictures in my cookbook."

So after this, I'm telling Jack the menus and the recipes, and Wen is painting pictures of the food. He's also got poems in Chinese next to the pictures. How do I know what they say? I say to him he better have sex in those poems, like "quivering buttocks."

He says, "Don't worry." Up in his studio, he's painting every day. I find out he quits teaching. Quits writing his books. It's just painting and cooking and writing poetry.

I say, "Maybe you taking this thing too far. After all, just a cookbook. Me, I still got to go out and protest, argue with the mayor. Stop this eviction. If I don't do that, I got no place to live. What's a cookbook?"

"Not just any cookbook," he says. I can see he's fighting loneliness. Working out his freedom. He makes arrangements of food and paint. We go to the markets and he sketches everything. When we cook, he's got his paintbrush right there in the kitchen, and he gets the inspiration. Quick brush work. He's painting everything. Knives and woks, ducks and bamboo, lobsters and mangos. Step by step and more poems. It's all there. Pretty soon, you see a whole world.

Meantime, I'm telling my story to Jack, who's taking it all down on his typewriter. He's always arguing, "We can't say you cooked in the Great Hall for Nixon. It never happened."

"So what? In my mind, it happened."

"What about this story about you and Ho Chi Minh in Paris?"

"That's one of the best stories."

"And this one, cooking for Imelda?"

"She goes wild for my pancit. She goes so wild, she worked it into her love cosmology."

"When were you in Yokohama?"

"That's really true. I docked there with the merchant marines. I got a girlfriend there. Wanna see her picture? Yoko like Yoko Ono."

"Like Yoko-hama."

"Hey, I forget to tell you all my girlfriends. We got to put them in."

"You got a girl at every port, right?"

"You know it."

"I give up."

"In my long life, there's no work I don't do. I do everything. I been everywhere. If I don't do it with my own two hands and my back, stooping with my legs, walking with these old feet, I do it with my head. I fish up in Alaska. I do canning work. I do stoop labor and cut asparagus, artichokes. Pick tomatoes, strawberries, grapes. I carry a gun for the U.S. military. I build houses. I plant flowers. I build bridges. I sell grocery. I'm a bartender. I work the dock. I organize for the union. I gamble. I bust some butts in my time. Short time I do acting jobs in Hollywood. Dance with Fred Astaire. I play the ukulele in Honolulu with Don Ho. And all the time, I got the women. You write that down."

"Where's Paul? Let him do this. Hey, Chen, I got a postcard from Paul. He's in Taiwan. When's he coming back?"

Wen shrugs. "Haven't heard."

"The Okada book came out and he left. I think we worked him too hard." He shakes his head, then looks at me. "Is this a cookbook or a fake autobiography?"

"Nothing fake here. I'm for real. I'm your real Makoi."

"What?"

"Makoi. Makoi. You don't know?"

"I'm not ghostwriting no imaginary autobiography, McCoy or not."

"Why not? All the recipes I give you: authentic. This one goes back to Song Dynasty, original recipe with original poem. Taste travels to you from eight centuries."

Wen says, "He's right. Anyway, you've been doing the research. You should know. A whole history of civilization in a single dish. In time, everything else vanishes, but the dish can be recreated."

"Food is made in America, but the recipe is guaranteed authentic, put your mark of good housekeeping. O.K., sometimes I change something here and there. Working to perfection, but I'm like the artist. Add my signature. But my life? My life is a dream. It's what I got. What you want? Take it away?"

Wen's got his brush out, splashing color. Dark red plump chunks of lady's buttocks. Almost feel the quiver. Then the poem. Brush goes in quick flashes. *Swish. Swish.* Poem's like cuisine. Makes the world sensible. Ingredients in the head, then apply fire. Have you eaten today?

10: All the Things You Are

What thoughts I have for you tonight, for I walked down Kearny under the shadow of an invisible hotel with a piano improvisation: all the things you are. Sweet poet. Sweet lover. Monk of the Tenderloin. Master Konnyaku. Fillmore Pilipino priest of ten thousand pianos. Play a song for former lovers meeting in the howling rain.

A drenched, unshaven man disappears in a steamy cloud behind the glass of a telephone booth.

Paul?

Wen-guang? It's been a long time.

Yes. I need a favor.

Where are you? Bad connection.

It's the rain. Did you hear that? Thunder. I'm at the gas station. Bottom of the hill. You know the one?

Car trouble?

No. They've condemned my house.

What?

All this rain. The foundation is slipping. They've cordoned it off.

Shit.

I've removed your things. What you left. And there's more. Could you come? I borrowed a truck. I've been filling it up.

Shit! I heard that one.

That was close.

I'll be there.

Sitting in your teahouse made from the refuse of the demolished Fillmore, the rain is softer, drenching the hydrangea along the bamboo wall. The spirits of those old Victorians seep through the wood and curl around your tea. Some are raucous spirits, dark panels pulled from dance floors and smoky bars, titillating tunes of blues and bebop. Some are cloistered spirits set in dark hardwood cherry, hoarding precious leathered first editions. What of those books? The music and the words now silent.

Konnyaku, the three-legged, one-eyed cat, curled in a disheveled ball next to a warm teapot.

Meanwhile, the rain crashes in great waves across the Golden Gate. Cars slither precariously, headlights groping forward. Up the winding hill, two small rivers of mud and debris rush past on either side of the traffic parade. At the top of the hill, the cypress point to the ocean in the direction of the windswept storm.

A drenched man is running from his house with an armful of books.

Your stuff. It's all in the Siata. There's more. I threw in what I could. I filled the trunk, the backseat. Car's too small. It's a mess, but they didn't give me any time.

I don't need my stuff. I haven't needed it all year.

I need to tell you something.

It doesn't matter.

Your mother and I met at Stanford. She was a brilliant student of English literature.

Can't this wait? You're soaked!

We were great friends, so we got married, but I could never be faithful. We were married only a year, and she left. But we were always friends. It's really true I introduced her to your father. They were very happy together.

Why didn't you tell me before?

When your father died it didn't seem appropriate, and later, it felt very strange. I thought you would be repulsed, and you were.

I thought you might be my father.

No! That's not true! That could never be true. Is that why you left? Why didn't you tell me?

Why didn't you tell me?"

I've missed you.

It hurts, Wen-guang. It hurts badly.

Konnyaku, with a dingy spotted coat the color of konnyaku, a tail hairless in spots, a dark socket for the lost eye. That must have been some fierce fighting, screeching yowling dissonance, claws and teeth ripping and tearing. Two crazy cats in a fight to the finish. How did you come by this ugly old soldier, this war-torn survivor?

The relentless rain washes across their faces, dribbles from nose to chin to chest to stomach to crotch. The clothing has to be peeled off, layer by layer, abandoned with boots in sloppy piles in the dark entryway. Naked, shivering.

They've turned off the gas and electricity.

What did they say? Can they save the house?

Too precarious to know. They told me to leave immediately.

Immediately. Then—

You're shivering.

Get under. Hurry.

Hurry.

Whip me up some frothy tea from boiled rainwater and tell me about all the women you have ever loved, all the serenading and sweet-talking, all the tender tunes you played. Or better yet, toss a fish head in the boiling rainwater and tend the roiling pot, replay the minor keys along the spine, the major keys across the hips, the soft and frantic melodies that brush the lips. Or better yet, throw in bulbs and tubers, roots and leaves, seeds and bark, algae and fungus, and stir the moaning moaning in the pot.

It was as if the thunder of the ocean's waves engulfed the house, crested in white sheets against the windows, pounded the roof.

Wait. Listen. Hear that?

Rain. Never stops.

No. Get up.

I can feel it. Do you feel that?

Here. Put this on. Quickly.

Like a small earthquake.

Hurry! Get out!

Take the Siata. I'll follow in the truck.

Where are you going?

One last thing. I just remembered.

Forget it. We can come back later.

It's too valuable.

It's too dangerous.

You're getting wet again. Get in the car.

Fuck it! Just hurry.

I'll meet you at the bottom.

The hot pot sits between us, steam and fragrance curling up to the dark underbelly of your Fillmore roof. We fish with long chopsticks for the tender and shared sustenance. You pick out a bulb. I pick out a tuber. You pick out a root. I a leaf. You a seed. I a piece of bark. You algae. Me fungus. The fish head cools in a bowl for Konnyaku.

The Siata pulls away, its wipers flapping, wildly banging at the splatter. Headlights search the road, chasing the water to the bottom. She pulls herself around the hairpin curve, tires slipping, skimming a slick skin of water. She skids to a stop, backing away from a torrent of mud and uprooted trees. Within, she holds a small treasure and the unrequited future: a pink slip; two unfinished manuscripts, one of translated poems, songs of Gold Mountain, and another, an illustrated cookbook; a tin can of old photographs.

Light flashes a sudden blast, illuminating the falling house, but the thunder that follows is the thunder of its crashing: groan and slippage of parting concrete, shattering glass, crossbeams of weighted timber caving in on three tiered floors of gracious elegance, living room falling into library falling into studio, falling.

1969: I Spy Hotel

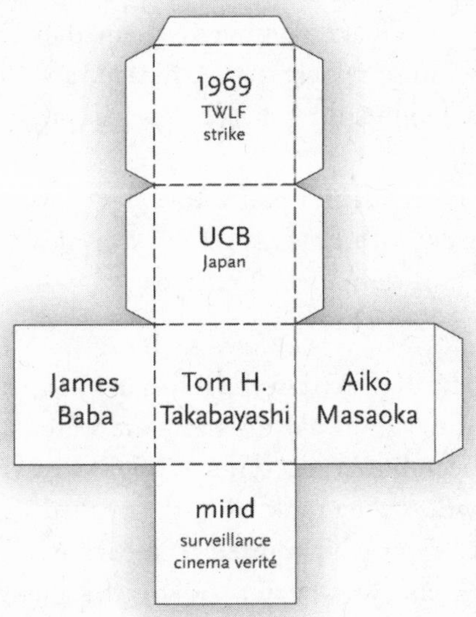

1: Dossier #9066

CONFIDENTIAL:

1 PROFESSOR THOMAS HISAJI TAKABAYASHI

Photographic stills of Tom Takabayashi. Large portrait photo of young nisei professor, followed by Takabayashi family photos and Tule Lake Relocation Camp. Voice-over is white male.

VOICE-OVER

Professor Tom Hisaji Takabayashi, nisei, second-generation Japanese-American, born in a rural community outside of Seattle, Washington, on February 28, 1926. At age sixteen, in 1942, he is interned with his family at Tule Lake Relocation Camp. His older brother is imprisoned separately in an Arizona prison camp for disobeying the curfew imposed on Japanese. Takabayashi leaves Tule Lake with his father to work on a potato farm in Idaho. He requests CO draft status, self-identifying as a Quaker. 4F status is granted in lieu of CO. Takabayashi's family relocates to Chicago, and he enters the University of Illinois in Chicago at war's end, in 1945.

2 UNIVERSITY OF ILLINOIS—CHICAGO

Taped interview with Professor Takabayashi with stills of the University of Illinois campus in Chicago.

TAKABAYASHI

At Tule Lake, I worked in the infirmary as an aid. I was just a kid. I had to stay awake all night and watch over this man who had been beaten up. They brought him over from the stockade where they took what they called "incorrigibles," the No-No guys who wanted to repatriate. To this day, I believe that he was beaten up by the guards, but they accused some other nisei. My job was to watch him through the night. He groaned all night, in and out of sleep or unconsciousness, the blood caked up under his head bandages. I thought they might come to finish him off. It was cold, and I was really afraid.

I wrote about this for a rhetoric class at the U, and the paper came back with a C for writing and a D for content, with the comment: *What about Bataan?* I went to ask the professor what this meant, and he said, "Exactly what it says." I sat down on the steps of that building and looked out over the lawns and that sea of white students. My father had already died in Chicago; my mother died a few weeks later. I left, took the train for Berkeley.

3 UNIVERSITY OF CALIFORNIA, BERKELEY

Still photographs of UCB, circa late 1940s. Photographs of Takabayashi as a student, with Berkeley friends, working as a probation officer.

VOICE-OVER

Takabayashi enrolls at UC Berkeley in 1947. During these years at Berkeley, he supports himself by working for the Alameda County Probation Board, handling probation cases for petty crimes. He attains his BA in psychology in 1951. In 1952 he receives a Fulbright to study in Japan.

4 JAPAN

Still photographs and film footage of postwar Japan. Copy of Fulbright proposal, title page with abstract. Photographs of Takabayashi in Japan.

VOICE-OVER

Takabayashi pursues a research project to examine the prison system in Japan. He cites his personal experience in the American parole system, but focuses on the Meiji era, pre-1900 Japanese adoption of the penitentiary model.

5 LOS ANGELES

Footage of Los Angeles in the 1950s: Little Tokyo Japanese-American community, Hollywood movie star scene on Sunset Boulevard.

VOICE-OVER

Completing his Fulbright Fellowship, Takabayashi returns to the United States and takes a job in Los Angeles as a parole officer in Hollywood. His parole cases involve celebrities and jazz artists who include ██ ████, █████ ███, ██ ███, ██ ██, and ████ ██ ██, many of them working off heroin or marijuana charges.

TAKABAYASHI

Occasionally I did investigative work for the parole board, traveled up and down the state. I began to have questions about the people paroled, about the judges who made these decisions. You might have a three-to-six or a four-to-five split, and what about this split? What made them decide on the same factual evidence? If the facts were the same, then justice should be the same, but this wasn't the case. Why?

VOICE-OVER

During this time Takabayashi meets Jean Sakai, the daughter of a successful Japanese restaurant owner on Sunset Boulevard, frequented by the movie crowd.

6 JEAN SAKAI AND TOM TAKABAYASHI

Photographic stills in Los Angeles of Takabayashi wedding and young married couple with new baby.

7 STANFORD UNIVERSITY—PALO ALTO

Footage of Stanford University in the early 1960s. Still photographs of house in San Francisco, wife and growing young son. Takabayashi interview continues.

TAKABAYASHI

I applied to Stanford and was accepted. I did my dissertation on that question of the justices. I took actual parole cases and crossed out the names and decisions, sent them to justices around the state, and had them retry the cases on paper. In all cases, the results were different. Some counties were more stringent, others less. The decisions were ultimately preferential, personal, and ideological.

VOICE-OVER

While Takabayashi does his doctoral research, his wife Jean works as a secretary for the attorney Wayne M. Collins, known for his defense of Iva Toguri, also known as "Tokyo Rose." During these years, renegade attorney Collins fights to reinstate Japanese Americans who renounced their citizenship during the war.

8 HAVILAND HALL—SCHOOL OF CRIMINOLOGY—UNIVERSITY OF CALIFORNIA, BERKELEY

Typical 1960s footage of UC Berkeley, Sather Gate, President Kerr, the Free Speech Movement in 1964, students protesting the Vietnam War. Photographic stills of the School of Criminology at Haviland Hall, catalog copy of the curriculum, Professor Takabayashi lecturing.

VOICE-OVER

The UC Berkeley School of Criminology was founded in 1950 to instruct policemen. In the fall of 1964, when Professor Takabayashi joined the school, there were one hundred and nineteen undergraduate and seventy-five graduate students. The teaching complement numbered approximately thirty. There were forty-five upper-division criminology courses ranging from general introduction to field studies and individual research. The twenty-five graduate courses covered crime and the political process, prediction methods in probation and parole, and seminars in psychologic theory of criminality and problems of criminal responsibility.

Footage of Black Panthers: marches on Sacramento; Huey Newton arrest, trials, and *Free Huey!* rallies; Bobby Hutton death; Eldridge Cleaver arrest and escape into hiding; Bobby Seale arrest and trials after Chicago Democratic Convention.

VOICE-OVER

Professor Takabayashi won tenure in the next years but also became associated with a group of Marxist infiltrators who called themselves radical criminologists. Key members of the group were ██ ████, █████ ███ ██, ██ ██████, ██ █████, and ████ ██████.

Slide stills of individual associates: scholars and lawyers, all white, all male, one Jew. SOUND of projector clicking with successive shots.

9 THIRD WORLD LIBERATION FRONT—UC BERKELEY

Footage of TWLF strike: Asian American contingent circling Sather Gate, student leaders making statement of demands before microphones.

TAKABAYASHI

██ ██████ was a grad student who asked me to be on a seminar panel. He was in the process of founding AAPA in those days. I think they billed it as the Yellow Identity Conference. Maybe nine hundred came from across the state. The Berkeley folks spoke first. I did a talk on international issues in Asia and how we're affected here. I could see the Berkeley people were upset when we let this contingent from SF State College speak. Two fiery speakers, ████ ██ and ██ ██████, spoke about their strike. There were maybe two hundred officially at the talk. Ten days later a core group of about a dozen or more formed, joined forces with the Blacks, Chicanos, and Indians, and called for the strike.

Still photographs of the front of Takabayashi home in Oakland with telescopic shots of individual students entering premises. SOUND of camera shutter in successive shots.

VOICE-OVER

Of the few tenured Oriental faculty at Berkeley, only Takabayashi agreed to support student agitators, opening his own home for frequent meetings.

Return to footage of student strikers in Sproul Plaza.

TAKABAYASHI

The Asians had the eight a.m. picketing shift. Jean drove out in the mornings to Bancroft and Telegraph and brought them coffee and doughnuts. They'd say, *Mrs. Takabayashi, what are you doing here? It isn't safe!* (laughs)

Slides of Mrs. Takabayashi distributing doughnuts. Photograph of her car, a white Dodge Dart, license plate BCU442. SOUND of camera shutter in successive shots.

VOICE-OVER

In addition, Takabayashi also agreed to sponsor an experimental course titled 100X: The Asian American Experience.

Footage and stills of students, teaching assistants, lectures, and meetings. SOUND of camera shutter. Also stills of course syllabus, copies of articles, reading list, associated fliers and articles, and list of registered students.

TAKABAYASHI

The students pretty much took care of that class themselves. You could say they invented it and owned it. Heck, they invented a new political category: Asian American. Then they took on Third World politics. It was a first. They stood next to the podium, sat around on the platform. ██████ ████, ███ ███████, and █████ ███ ██████ were the TAs. For example, I invited this white anthropologist who did work on Japan to lecture. I thought his work might be interesting, but they called him a racist. They stood up and confronted him and finally removed him from the podium.

Stills of white professor being escorted by Asian students in fatigues and dark glasses out of course 100X. SOUND of camera shutter.

10 PINE METHODIST CHURCH—CENTER FOR JAPANESE AMERICAN STUDIES (CJAS)—SAN FRANCISCO JAPANTOWN

Photographs of the Pine Methodist Church in J-Town, San Francisco.

VOICE-OVER

Takabayashi helps to found the CJAS, a group that meets monthly at the Pine Methodist Church in Japantown. This group's purpose is ostensibly to build educational support for the study of Japanese in America.

Still copies of pamphlets, book lists, curriculum proposals, and meeting minutes. Slides of CJAS members and roster. SOUND of camera shutter.

VOICE-OVER

The membership, suggesting the group's possible "umbrella" status, consists of antiestablishment-leaning K through twelve school teachers and college instructors, librarians, amateur historians, one playwright, one bookseller/collector, an occasional poet, a Japanese-vernacular newspaper editor, a known radical JACL member, a church pastor known for his militancy, and student radicals.

TAKABAYASHI

Suddenly the students got what they asked for: Asian American Studies, but we had to find out what that was. We had to find the books, hire the teachers, create a system of knowledge building. And I had to juggle two hats: the Crim curriculum and the Asian American.

Footage of civil rights protests, atomic bomb mushrooms, and Japanese Americans leaving by train for internment camps.

TAKABAYASHI

I didn't think they were necessarily at odds. I believed there were two issues that had to be addressed: civil rights and war. What if you practice civil disobedience and are arrested? Is this a crime, and how should it be prosecuted? What about crimes against humanity? Hiroshima and Nagasaki? War crimes? What about the internment of Japanese American citizens during the war?

11 PRISON DAY SEMINAR—NEWMAN HALL, BERKELEY

Footage and photographic stills of participating professors and students at the School of Criminology in 1971.

VOICE-OVER

Professor Takabayashi and his contingent of radical colleagues in the Crim School sponsor a Prison Day seminar on prisoner humanity and justice.

Stills of the covers of journals and books edited by Takabayashi. Eighteenth- and nineteenth-century etchings of prisons, such as the Walnut Street Jail and the Eastern State Penitentiary in Philadelphia.

VOICE-OVER

Takabayashi presents a paper entitled *The Walnut Street Jail: A Penal Reform to Centralize the Powers of the State.* His colleagues report on such subjects as alleged police brutality, police surveillance technology, and the federal Law Enforcement Assistance Administration, acronym LEAA, no doubt a funder of the school.

Photographs of FBI director J. Edgar Hoover, George Jackson, the Soledad Brothers, and footage of the Attica Prison revolt.

VOICE-OVER

Coincidentally, in the following months COINTELPRO documents are stolen from the FBI office in Media, Pennsylvania; George Jackson is killed in San Quentin; and the Attica Prison in New York explodes in riots. These events were preceded by numerous and well-organized prison protests at San Quentin and Soledad, a shoot-out instigated by Jackson's brother in the Marin County court, and the deaths of guards and prisoners at Soledad.

12 ASIAN LAW CAUCUS—BOALT HALL, UC BERKELEY

Stills of Boalt Hall and slides of founding members of the Asian Law Caucus. SOUND of camera shutter. Footage of student arrests during strike. Front-page articles from the *Daily Californian* with names and photographs of arrested students.

VOICE-OVER

Takabayashi supports the founding of the Asian Law Caucus in 1972. These young militant Asian attorneys, notably █████ ███████ and █████ ███, just out of Boalt Hall and Hastings Law School, intern at Takabayashi's instigation with the known-progressive nisei lawyer ███████ ██, who was the principle attorney for dissident students arrested during the Third World strike.

13 WENDY YOSHIMURA

Symbionese Liberation Army newsreel, kidnapping of Patty Hearst, and final arrest of Hearst, accompanied by Wendy Yoshimura, in San

Francisco. Photographs of the Japanese-American woman accompanied by her attorneys from the Asian Law Caucus.

VOICE-OVER

Wendy Yoshimura, who emerged with Patricia Hearst, heiress of the Hearst fortune, was released on bail to be housed at Takabayashi's house in Oakland. Presumably this was because Takabayashi was a former probation officer. As a small child, Yoshimura was also interned with her family at the Tule Lake Internment Camp during World War II, and her parents were alleged renunciants of American citizenship.

14 HAVILAND HALL TAKEOVER AND SPROUL PLAZA RALLY— UC BERKELEY

Photograph of UC Berkeley Chancellor Albert Bowker. Portrait stills of criminology faculty. SOUND of camera shutter in successive shots.

VOICE-OVER

In June of 1974, Chancellor Albert Bowker announces his decision to close down the Berkeley School of Criminology. The conservative faculty of the school blames Takabayashi and his cohorts. They also criticize his association with Ethnic Studies. One colleague characterized it as an invented racial science. Prior to this announcement, two assistant professors, ████ ██ ████ and ████ ██████ of the radical Crim contingent, are fired; another, ██ █████, a proclaimed Marxist and member of the Union of Radical Criminologists, acronym URC, is denied tenure; and the subversive lawyers in the group are sent back to Boalt Hall.

Footage of occupation of second floor of Haviland Hall, School of Criminology, and stills of arrests of the Haviland Twenty. SOUND of camera shutter in successive shots. Next-day footage in Sproul Plaza of protest crowd estimated at thirty-five hundred, Professor Takabayashi and others at the mic.

VOICE-OVER

In a fruitless effort to "Save Crim," twenty students occupy the second floor of Haviland Hall for almost twenty-four hours before their arrest and expulsion. The following day a sizable crowd demonstrates in Sproul Plaza.

15 OLD CAMPUS BUILDING SLATED FOR DEMOLITION—UC BERKELEY

Photographs of empty building.

VOICE-OVER

Stripped of his association with any school, Takabayashi is banned to an office in an empty campus building slated for demolition, where he meets remaining students who are allowed to finish their degrees.

SOUND of wiretapped phone voice: "Who is this? Who is this?"

VOICE-OVER

After a series of anonymous phone calls and a letter signed by "a friend," Jean Takabayashi moves out of the house, leaving her husband.

TAKABAYASHI

I learned the hard way that whether it's the prison community or the Asian American community, the academy will close ranks to keep that experiment with reality out. In a short period of time, we saw the politicization of prisoners and the criminalization of students. And this scared folks. Students saw three choices: go to school, go to prison, go to war. We challenged the idea that society, and therefore education, should be controlled by the threat of punishment and the history of race.

DOSSIER CLOSED: JUNE 15, 1976

2: Recorded Live in Your Face

1 1969: 100X: THE ASIAN AMERICAN EXPERIENCE—DWINELLE HALL, UC BERKELEY

Pan of lecture hall, two hundred STUDENTS crowded into presidium seating, some in the aisles. The majority, if not all, of the STUDENTS are of Asian descent. On the platform, STUDENTS are also sitting on tables or standing before the long blackboard like guards. A few of the STUDENTS are dressed in fatigues and berets, sporting dark glasses, but most are conservatively dressed, men in plain shirts and slacks, women in skirts and knit sweaters. Women have short bubble cuts or long straight hair; the men, short cuts that are beginning to straggle or bush out. Horn-rimmed glasses for the men, more stylish glasses on the women. Some slump in their seats, their feet hung over the backs of chairs; others sit at attention with pens and notebooks.

One STUDENT speaks from the podium.

STUDENT ORGANIZER

O.K.! First order of business. (points in the aisle) JB, that's James Baba. James, wave your hand.

JAMES BABA is in the aisle passing out issues of the AAPA newspaper. Waves.

STUDENT ORGANIZER

Right on. We call him JB because his other life is being James Brown. (laughter) I'm serious, the man can move! But right now, he's moving to hand you important information.

Another STUDENT approaches the podium and whispers something into the speaker's ear.

STUDENT ORGANIZER

Oh yeah. (nods to other STUDENT) Right. Professor Takabayashi, respectfully, we are going to ask you to leave the room for just a few minutes. We have business to conduct, and we don't want to compromise your position in any way.

PROFESSOR TAKABAYASHI nods and walks up the aisle out of the room.

STUDENT ORGANIZER

Number one: we want you to check out page three of the AAPA paper, *Revolutionary First Aid.* Review this material. By now you've heard the news that Cordell Abercrombie, an Afro-American Student Union member, was seized by six plainclothes pigs and beaten up in the basement of Sproul Hall, then charged with felonious assault. That was Thursday. And you know that the day prior, Wednesday, Reagan declared a state of extreme emergency, so that Chief Madigan and his Alameda sheriff pigs could have the excuse to beat us up. So this is serious. Do your homework and come prepared.

ANOTHER STUDENT ORGANIZER

Right. Check out what it says about mace and tear gas. Also important, protecting your collarbone. Get some padding in that area. Wear a helmet and get yourself some goggles. Don't bring anything with you except your ID, nothing the pigs could use to get information from you, and no dope, no weapons, and no big pockets they can fill to plant shit on you. And memorize our central command telephone number. You get arrested, you have a right to a phone call. Write the number on your arm. Hey, JB, what's that number?

JAMES BABA writes a telephone number on the chalkboard.

STUDENT ORGANIZER

So the word is: Tomorrow, meet at Wheeler Oak, eleven a.m. sharp. Got that? And right after this class, strike captains stay for an emergency meeting. If you have any questions, talk to your strike captain.

STUDENT ORGANIZER

(runs up to the podium) I just wanted to make an announcement. We're organizing a community field component for this course at the I-Hotel in the City. That's 848 Kearny Street in Manilatown-Chinatown. This weekend we're doing painting and repairs. If you're interested in joining, see me after class.

PROFESSOR TAKABAYASHI is ushered back into the room and takes the podium. A WHITE PROFESSOR accompanies him.

PROFESSOR TAKABAYASHI

Today, I'm going to turn this over to my colleague in anthropology, Professor Harold Hass. You've had a chance to read his article on Japanese psychology and should be prepared with your questions. Professor?

PROFESSOR HASS

Assuming that you've read my work, let me entertain some questions first. Yes? (points into audience)

STUDENT

A question came up in discussion about the work of Ruth Benedict, *The Chrysanthemum and the Sword,* that in the first place she never went to Japan, and in the second, she studied Japanese Americans in the internment camps to get her material. So how does she justify using people in prison as her subject matter then applying it to people who were defeated in war?

PROFESSOR HASS

Interesting question. Japanese communities have been ghettoized in the United States, duplicating and sustaining to a high degree cultural traditions, language, family constructions, et cetera, so it's not entirely impossible to draw conclusions from this minority that cross over, but I agree, there are differences.

STUDENT

Aren't you in danger of making the same mistake as Benedict? I mean, you go to Japan and study the Japanese and say they are socialized for achievement, then this sort of argument is used on Asian Americans here.

STUDENT

(speaking before the PROFESSOR can respond)
It's a stereotype to say we are all high achievers who are playing the assimilation game the right way and getting ahead, so racism in America isn't a factor in our oppression. What's your excuse for teaching about Japan instead of about Japanese Americans?

STUDENT

(yelling from the back)
Why doesn't our history count?

PROFESSOR HASS

I think you've jumped to conclusions that I don't claim in my work. I don't claim to be speaking about American Japanese per se.

JAMES BABA

I understand you were on the committee to recommend Ethnic Studies to the chancellor but that your committee excludes student members in the planning.

PROFESSOR HASS

Now that's another matter entirely. I didn't come here to discuss administrative matters.

STUDENTS

(standing up and becoming disruptive, speaking in succession)
What do you mean? It's all the same thing. It's about our right to determine our own educational needs.

You want to whitewash it!
This is an example of why we need our own department of

Asian American Studies. We need the folks from our own communities to speak. Not this racist shit.

Who is this guy anyway?

JAMES BABA

(yells out)
WHADDA WE WANT?

STUDENTS

(chanting)
SELF-DETERMINATION!

JAMES BABA

WHEN DO WE WANT IT?

STUDENTS

NOW!

STUDENTS move forward down the aisles toward the podium, chanting. *Whadda we want? Self-determination! When do we want it? Now!* STUDENTS crowd around the professor and usher him out of the lecture hall. STUDENTS jeer and chant.

Rising SOUND of music: James Brown: *Say it loud: I'm black and I'm proud! . . . Uh! Put your pants up!*

2 SATHER GATE—UC BERKELEY
Camera captures wide angle of street moving up Telegraph Avenue toward the university. Cars, buses, vendors, students walking and crossing. Camera crosses Bancroft Avenue, pauses on a group of a dozen STUDENTS, a mix of mostly black, Asian, Mexican, and Native Americans, passing out flyers. One STUDENT holds up a flyer in front of the camera. The camera focuses on the TEXT.

FLYER

SUPPORT THE SELF-DETERMINATION
OF THIRD WORLD PEOPLE!!!

THIRD WORLD LIBERATION FRONT
STRIKE DEMANDS:

1. **Establish a Third World College**
2. **Recruit Third World people to positions of power**
3. **Special admissions, financial aid, & work studies for Third World students**
4. **Third World control of Third World programs**
5. **No disciplinary actions against any student, faculty, or staff supporting strike**

THESE DEMANDS SUPERCEDE ALL OTHER
PREVIOUS DEMANDS

Camera continues a wide-angle approach, moving toward Sather Gate across Sproul Plaza, past makeshift tables set up by various organizations, along the Dr. Seuss-style lopped-off sycamores that line the plaza. Camera arrives at Sather Gate with a growing crowd of third world students, many carrying posters: *Third World Power Now!* TWLF *Fights For Unity!* AFT *Local 570 Supports* TWLF *Strike! Close It Down! Stop Racism! Dig It!* Focus on STUDENT with a bullhorn. SOUND of voice echoing across the plaza.

STUDENT ORGANIZER

(through bullhorn) O.K.! We gotta let everyone know we're here! We are the Third World Liberation Front, and we wanna let this university know who we are. We are a coalition of black, brown, yellow, and red brothers and sisters. We come here together in solidarity, so all you brothers and sisters, say it loud: I'm black and I'm proud!

CROWD

I'M BLACK AND I'M PROUD!

STUDENT ORGANIZER

I can't hear you! If I can't hear you, the chancellor can't hear you! The Regents can't hear you! Raay-Gun can't hear you! Try this for La Raza: I'm brown and I'm proud!

CROWD

I'M BROWN AND I'M PROUD!

STUDENT ORGANIZER

That's better. So now I wanna hear it the loudest for the real Americans: I'm red and I'm proud!

CROWD

I'M RED AND I'M PROUD!

STUDENT ORGANIZER

Now we got you worked up good. So let's hear it for my people! I'm yellow and I'm proud!

CROWD

I'M YELLOW AND I'M PROUD!

STUDENT ORGANIZER

I'm white and I'm proud!

CROWD

I'M WHITE AND I'M PROUD!

(someone) Uh uh, man, I ain't white. Do I look white?

(another) One drop, man, one drop's all it takes. You got a drop. Don't say you don't.

STUDENT ORGANIZER

I'm bourgeoisie and I'm proud!

CROWD

(laughter with sporadic yells and hoots) I'M BOURGEOISIE AND I'M PROUD!

As the chanting continues, PICKETERS line up in front of Sather Gate, shoulder to shoulder, arms crossed or holding signs, and feet spread to stand their ground, blocking access across the bridge. Incoming STUDENTS congregate at the impasse unable to cross, forming a traffic jam.

Camera swings to focus on two UNDERCOVER POLICEMEN posing as students, who rush forward to argue with and then accost protesting STUDENTS.

UNDERCOVER POLICE

You're under arrest for blocking a public entrance!

STUDENTS

He's a pig!

That one, he's a fucking spy!

STUDENTS protest and resist arrest, locking arms to maintain the line. This initial confrontation results in calling in a waiting contingent of fifty CAMPUS POLICE and ALAMEDA COUNTY SHERIFFS in leather jackets with fur collars, face masks, helmets, and billy clubs. Camera bounces around and runs after police actions: clubs pushing bodies and cracking bones, STUDENTS chased across the plaza, shoved into paddy wagons, dragged into the basement of Sproul Hall.

3 SPROUL HALL BASEMENT—UC BERKELEY

Camera chases behind POLICEMEN dragging a STUDENT dressed in fatigues and wearing horn-rimmed glasses down the stairs to the basement.

POLICEMAN I

We got him! This is him, the leader of the Orientals. The guy talking to the press. James Baba.

STUDENT

That's not me. You got the wrong guy!

POLICEMAN 1

(Punches STUDENT in stomach with his club, then pulls him up by the hair and looks at his face. STUDENT drops to the ground, trying to retrieve his fallen, broken glasses.)

They all got glasses.

POLICEMAN 2

They all got black hair and brown eyes. You sure this is him? (punches STUDENT's face) This is not him.

POLICEMAN 1

They all look alike. (jabs club into the STUDENT's side) S'gotta be him. (kicks STUDENT)

POLICEMAN 2

It's not him.

POLICEMAN 1

Book him anyway. Resisting arrest. Assaulting a policeman. Obstructing entrance to a public place.

4 SPROUL PLAZA

Outside, a visible force of three hundred POLICE, HIGHWAY PATROLMEN, and SHERIFFS line the steps of Sproul Hall and the plaza. NATIONAL GUARDSMEN in military garb with rifles are stationed near a contingent of jeeps and camouflaged trucks along Bancroft Avenue. An Eyewitness News station wagon is parked on Bancroft. Canisters fly across the plaza, jet streams of tear gas propelled into the sky. STUDENTS scream and run in every direction, covering their faces. Walking slowly but with determination across the plaza, a BLIND WOMAN in dark glasses with a white cane leads ANOTHER WOMAN, who is overcome by the tear gas. ASIAN AMERICAN STUDENTS have formed themselves into a linked line—a snake dance— scurrying and chanting, in and out and around trees and pillars. Chanting: *Third World Power Now! Yellow Power Now!* They emerge from the smoke and then disappear into it, passing through Sather Gate. SOUND of chanting growing faint. A helicopter circles overhead.

SOUND of helicopter fades into SOUND of James Brown: "Mother Popcorn."

5 1970: JACL CONVENTION—MIKE MASAOKA TESTIMONIAL DINNER—CONRAD HILTON HOTEL—CHICAGO

Eight hundred capacity ballroom of round tables decorated with tablecloths and flowers and surrounded by well-dressed Japanese American Citizens League delegates. Waiters run around removing plates and pouring coffee and water, passing out desserts, etc. Speeches resound from the podium and then clapping from all around as the honoree, Mike Masaoka, steps to the podium. A group of FOUR SANSEI MEN excuse themselves from their table in the back of the room and leave as the crowd rises to their feet in a standing ovation.

FOUR SANSEI MEN walk powerfully into the Chicago night, four abreast along Michigan Avenue. SOUND of James Brown: "Try Me."

6 1970: JACL CONVENTION—LIBERATION CAUCUS MEETING—PALMER HOUSE—CHICAGO

Inside the Palmer House Hotel, room 826. Clothing and suitcases strewn around the room and on the beds and sofas. SANSEI in their late teens to early twenties come and go. Three women come in with ice cream cones, talk and banter with the FOUR SANSEI MEN, who arrive from their walk. Camera follows the group, who leave for a caucus meeting in Parlor A on the sixth floor. Gradually others join the meeting. At some point, a woman bursts into the meeting screaming. Camera follows her with others to room 725. Others are already there, trying to assist two bleeding women. One woman seems to be alive, bleeding from her throat. The other is lifeless on the floor.

SANSEI (scattered voices)

Somebody call an ambulance!

It's done. Security should be here. What's taking them so long?

JB, come with me. Maybe the guy's still in the hotel! Check the stairwells!

Right! Someone should go and secure the doors.

We're on it. Let's go!

Camera follows SANSEI down stairwells and through the exits. Ambulance and paramedics arrive at the front and move quickly to the seventh floor to move two women out. Flashing lights leaving hotel and SOUND of moaning siren move out into the Chicago night. Commotion of SANSEI entering a taxi and following.

SANSEI (scattered voices)

Where's the hospital?

Some place called the Henrotin. Is that for real? The driver should know.

When we get there, we need to set up security. She's a witness. She left a note. Did you take it?

I'm going to lose it. Oh shit.

Not now. Not now!

O.K., O.K. I'm O.K.

7 HOUSE AT PINE AND BUCHANAN STREET—SAN FRANCISCO J-TOWN

Camera wanders to street corner, observes the Victorian house, an unpainted, slightly dilapidated place. Panning up to the second-floor window, we see a peace sign, and in another window, a poster of Malcolm X. Camera moves up the stairs and into the house. Living room is strewn with pillows against the bay window. Walls are plastered with various posters of Mao, Che, Malcolm X, Ho Chi Minh, protests, and announcements of concerts and political and cultural events. A GROUP OF MOSTLY SANSEI are sitting around on the sofa and floor, listening to RIA ISHII talk.

RIA ISHII

We went to the hospital with the ambulance and did security there until the police came. When we got back to the Palmer House, no one wanted to go back to their rooms. So everyone stayed in one of the conference rooms with pillows and blankets and security at the door. I never slept. Next day, the JACL flew us all home.

SANSEI I

Makes you wonder why they had to have the convention in Chicago. Fred Hampton was killed last year. Chicago's the worst. Those pigs will never find the killer. It's all bad news. Now this.

SANSEI II

Yellow Brotherhood drove up from L.A., picked up those Yellow Seed folks in Stockton. Those Stockton girls got in that caravan to Chicago. They were saying stuff like, *it's gonna be the Yellow Summer of Love.* Now the Stockton brothers are talking about going to Chicago and settling.

RIA ISHII

That's the kind of shit the media wants to hear. So far they've tried to put the blame on the Panthers and the Young Lords, since we went to visit their operations. Media said shit like the girls were flirtatious, suggested that they invited trouble.

JAMES BABA

We've got to step in quickly to counter the media stereotypes and racism and to make our position about this clear.

SOUND of commotion. Camera swings around, captures RIA's surprised face, then zooms in to catch an arm attached to a gun. Tough sansei dude, MO AKAGI, struts into focus in black beret, shades, and leather gloves and jacket.

MO AKAGI

Where the fuck is he? I'm gonna kill him! Where is he? Is it you, you fucker? (points gun at JAMES BABA) Ria! (points at RIA) Who is he, Ria? You think you can go to Chicago and come back with another man? Who is he? I'm gonna blow his brains out!

RIA ISHII

Mo, stop it! You're drunk! Put it down! Are you crazy?

JAMES BABA

Hey man, cool it, brother. Take it easy!

MO AKAGI

(points around the room at each of the men) You? You? Who's fucking my woman? (staggers forward)

Someone grabs AKAGI's pistol arm and pulls it back. Another jumps him from behind and grabs his neck, pulling him backwards. Everyone topples over. AKAGI flails on the floor and is covered by more men. The gun is thrown across the room; RIA runs over to grab it.

SANSEI I

It's cool, man. It's cool. Get him out of here. Wait, check him out. He's got some kind of armory. (feels him over, checks pockets, boots)

MO AKAGI

Shit. Take your hands off me.

SANSEI II

I'll take care of it, man. Come on, Mo. Let's go. We're going. We're going.

MO AKAGI

Hey, where's my piece?

SANSEI II

Forget it man. (shoves AKAGI out)

AKAGI is hustled out by several men, just as another GROUP OF SANSEI begins to arrive.

SANSEI III (from arriving group)

Hey Mo, you leaving already? We haven't even been to this party yet.

MO AKAGI

Gimme back my piece!

SOUND of AKAGI shouting obscenities down Buchanan as more people begin to arrive at the house. Dusk follows and the street darkens. Camera follows GROUPS into every corner of the house. A couple of GUYS pop reds. A joint and beers are passed around in the kitchen.

SANSEI I

Pass that thing. I need that. (sucks deeply on the joint) I thought it was all over. I thought that was going to be it. I turned white. Now I know what it feels like to be white.

SANSEI III

Feels like shit. Where's James?

SANSEI I

You mean JB? Double personality. Mild-mannered genius by day, but the light goes out, and he's James Baba Brown. Chain-smokes, too. Night smoker.

SANSEI III

So Ria got it on for which personality? James Baba by day or JB by night?

SANSEI IV

Guy's like superman. Mo never had a chance.

SANSEI I

(mimicking AKAGI) Where's my piece? Where's my piece? Gimme back my piece! (RIA appears and gives him a look) Oh Ria, peace. (makes a peace sign with fingers)

RIA walks out. Raucous laughter. SOUND of James Brown: "Like a Sex Machine." Camera follows SOUND into living room, now darkened with red lamps and bouncing bodies. JAMES BABA has a beer in one hand and a cigarette in the other, feet twisting and torso pumping. RIA dances into the crowd of sweaty bodies and he moves toward her, smoking and gyrating. *Get up. Get on up.*

8 1971: J-TOWN COLLECTIVE—J-TOWN

Inside an unidentified house, sitting around a kitchen table. An array of weapons are on the table. The faces of the participants are never shown on camera, only the guns and the hands manipulating them.

MINISTER OF DEFENSE

We're gonna take this step by step. Today, lesson number one, we're gonna get some basics covered. Identification. What we got here are your basic handguns. This one here is a Browning automatic with a three-shot magazine. Safety features: you need the magazine to fire it; see how that works? (clicks in the magazine) It weighs thirty-two ounces. Compare that to this one here, a Colt Commander that weighs twenty-six ounces. It uses a seven-shot magazine. Notice the difference with this heavy-duty Colt with a revolver. (spins the barrel) It packs six shots in the cylinder. It's an official police revolver. Here's another pistol they make for the pigs. It's a Llama model 8 automatic. Comes point-38 or point-45. Notice that we don't have any point-22s or point-25s. The difference is in the range. Not to be chauvinist or nothing, but the 22's a lady's gun, the kind she pulls out of her little purse. Not that it won't put you away, but you gotta get close, see.

WOMAN MEMBER

Yeah, I see. (her hand forms a gun and punches the speaker in his stomach)

MINISTER OF DEFENSE

Ow! Shit. O.K. I'm joking. (laughter) All right. So let's take a look at the slugs, what you call bullets. Depending on the caliber, you got different types for each weapon. Here you have the round nose (passes each one around), a flat point, spire point, and a soft point. And you load your magazine like this. (demonstrates) Or you load the revolver like this. O.K., everyone try this. Load and unload.

Guns are passed around the table and hands can be seen turning the guns, holding them for heft, loading and unloading, spinning the barrels, snapping in the magazines, etc.

MINISTER OF DEFENSE

So now, everyone get yourself one of these pieces, and we're gonna take them apart, learn how they're put together, and clean 'em. (puts some screwdrivers and rags on the table) Take this Browning. Comes apart easy, see. (pulls the pieces apart and spreads them on the table) You take the pieces and clean them like this. Little oil helps. Now, what you got to learn (mixes the pieces up) is how to put it all back together. Next, lesson number two. I time you doing this, O.K.?

MEMBER I

(to MEMBER II) Hey, don't get your parts mixed up with mine. (something pops up) What's that?

MEMBER II

It's the spring. Don't lose it. Hey, where'd it go? (camera watches spring roll off the table)

Camera observes the different guns coming apart and then the fingers trying to remount them. Some MEMBERS work quickly while others struggle with one thing or another.

MEMBER I

How's it coming?

MEMBER II

Shit. Where's the trigger?

MINISTER OF DEFENSE

You put it together without the trigger?

MEMBER II

I think I lost it. (gesturing to MEMBER I) Maybe you put my trigger on your gun.

MEMBER I

No way.

MEMBER II

Is this it?

MINISTER OF DEFENSE

Shit. What are you doing? (disgusted) Gimme that thing.

MEMBER II

I got to tell you, man: I failed metal shop. (laughter)

9 SOMEWHERE IN SONOMA COUNTY

Camera follows a gray Oldsmobile down a country road, farmland passing on either side. Oldsmobile pulls onto a gravel road and parks in front of a barn. SIX FIGURES climb out of the car. They are variously dressed in T-shirts and jeans, denim or camouflage military-surplus jackets. The DRIVER opens the trunk and distributes a rifle to each passenger. Boxes of ammunition are passed around. The FIGURES lean against the car or the barn and work at loading the rifles. Meanwhile, one FIGURE walks into the distance and hammers a target onto the trunk of a tree. He counts out paces from the tree and rubs a line in the dirt with the heel of his boot.

MINISTER OF DEFENSE

So your mark is there. Who's up first?

MEMBER I

O.K.

MINISTER OF DEFENSE

(noticing MEMBER I's stance) That's good. Cup your left hand here. The heel goes here against your shoulder. Get comfortable. You're sighting through with your right eye. Watch it line up. Take your time.

MEMBER I shoots. SOUND of gunfire.

MEMBER I

Ow! That burns. (looks down at the ground where the shell has fallen)

MINISTER OF DEFENSE

I warned you about that .30 carbine. You'll get used to it.

Everyone takes turns shooting at the tree. SOUND of successive shots. Then they line up and practice shooting all at once. At some point everyone stops and walks up to the tree.

MEMBERS

Hey, someone made a bull's-eye!

Lucky shot.

Count how many hit the target. (counts)

All that shooting and this is all we did?

We couldn't hit a cow if we tried.

When the revolution comes, we're dead meat.

What kind of tree is this?

Cherry? Looks like cherry.

Or kaki. Yeah, winter persimmon.

MINISTER OF DEFENSE

(walking from the Oldsmobile with two large weapons) O.K., now I'm going to show you something else. These are semiautomatic. (hands one of the rifles to one member)

SOUND of automatic weapons blasting. At some moment the tree, which is not very large, begins to waver and creak and falls over. As the tree topples, SOUND of James Brown: "Super Bad."

10 1972: PINE METHODIST CHURCH—SAN FRANCISCO J-TOWN

Growing crowd of mostly JAPANESE AMERICAN people—a mixed group of nisei and sansei and a few issei—slowly filling the social hall of the Pine Methodist Church. Metal folding chairs are arranged on linoleum flooring in front of another projector screen on tripod feet at one end of the hall. In the middle of an aisle created by the arranged chairs is a large film projector on a table, wires running via extension cords to the back of the hall. At the front there is a standing mike with a cord trailing back to a wall. A JTC REP, a young man, struts up to the mike.

JTC REP

Hi. I'm here to welcome you on behalf of the JTC. That stands for the J-Town Collective. We organized ourselves last year in August, coming together to defend the Japanese in our community. Our offices are on the corner of Post and Octavia, and we're open every day from seven a.m. to seven thirty p.m., so come check us out. We're working to build programs to serve the needs of our people: women's health, high school education, and legal services. If you want to know more about us, pick up a copy of our paper, *New Dawn.* Hey, JB! (motions to JAMES BABA, who is passing out a stack of issues) Our last issue here (holds up a copy) is dedicated to George Jackson and the Attica Brothers. You know, the JTC was founded on August 8 last year, and three days later George Jackson was gunned down at San Quentin, and three weeks later Attica prisoners took a stand and were slaughtered. Our dedication to these black brothers is to continue the struggle, to wage a war to defeat U.S. imperialism and to unite oppressed people. Part of our effort is to bring the truth to the people, and this film tonight documents the struggle going on now by Japanese farmers to keep the government from taking their ancestral land for an international airport.

Tonight is our first film show. Our next film will be . . . what is it, JB?

JAMES BABA

Battle of Algiers. Here at Pine Church again next month, but we haven't set a date.

JTC REP

Battle of Algiers. Look for our posters for the date or pick up the next copy of *New Dawn.*

Now I wanna introduce Kaz Ono from the East Wind Collective, who's come up from L.A. with these brothers from Japan.

KAZ ONO

For those Japanese-speaking folks here tonight (speaks in Japanese) (SOUND of laughter and agreement from those who understand Japanese) (back to English) Tonight we have two guests from Japan, Tamura-san (gestures to TAMURA-SAN, who makes a slight bow), a member of the film crew from Ogawa Productions, who made this film, and Atari-san (also bows) of the Zengakuren student organization, who have been fighting with the Narita farmers against the government and corporate takeover of their land to build the New Tokyo International Airport.

TAMURA-SAN

(speaks in Japanese, which ONO translates) Our director, Ogawa Shinsuke, regrets he could not be here to speak about this film. Although Ogawa Productions is a communal project of fourteen people, we have a philosophy of being an invisible camera presence at the front lines. In 1966, the farmers of Sanrizuka in Narita City formed the Anti-Airport League to fight the construction of the airport. Our film, *Sanrizuka: The Peasants of the Second Fortress,* was filmed last year when the farmers had already been fighting for five years. We have been screening everywhere in Japan and now the world. We are also working with the Newsreel cooperative here in San Francisco.

KAZ ONO

We will be passing a basket around for your contributions. This is the only way that Ogawa Productions can continue their work. (JAMES BABA can be seen holding up and starting the basket around from the front row) Now, Atari-san from the Zengakuren.

ATARI-SAN

(speaks in Japanese, followed by ONO's translation) After I saw Ogawa Production's first films, I had a complete change of mind. Not only I, but many students who joined the movement, were influenced by Ogawa's films. Thousands have joined the fight against the airport. Twelve hundred people were arrested and five thousand injured. The farmers built a lookout tower, trenches, and barricades. We in the Zengakuren came from different universities to support the farmers' struggle. We have been living with the farmers, helping to dig pits and carve spears, for example. We have been on the front line of defense against the police, and so many of us have been beat up and arrested. You will see how bravely the farmers have been fighting. We ask for your support in our struggle. You must protest the Japanese militarism that your U.S. government is promoting.

JTC REP

Just to let you know, we'll have a question-and-answer period after the film. So JB, can you get the lights?

Hall darkens as black-and-white film flickers on projection screen. Titles in Japanese with subtitles in English: *Sanrizuka: The Peasants of the Second Fortress.*

SCENES

Shot of wooden lookout tower and emanating SOUND of voice announcing the arrival of the police.

FARMING WOMEN in padded peasant garb and headscarves wind chains around their necks and torsos and then around a barricade of trees. They use large combination locks to secure their bodies.

As the POLICE approach, gasoline fires flare up in the trenches surrounding the barricades.

MOTHERS block POLICE in the first line of defense. One woman is yelling: "How can you do this? Aren't you ashamed? You don't have to do this kind of work. You could leave. Who is your mother? Does she know you are here?"

Camera sweeps over an immense field, presumably the airport runway under construction. As the camera pans lines of STUDENTS and troops of POLICE, the runway looks like an enormous battlefield. CADRES OF YOUTHS with helmets and towels covering their faces move with bamboo spears and flags across a muddy field. SOUND of whistles blowing at intervals to create the cadence of marching, much like pushing an omikoshi in a festival parade. Other CADRES move with their arms locked. It's raining, very muddy, and very cold. Everyone, although in layers of clothing and jackets, looks wet and miserable.

Scene of POLICE and AIRPORT EMPLOYEES roping trees, using bulldozers to pull them down, cutting chains, and dragging yelling women away.

Bloodied STUDENTS and FARMERS sitting in group, smoking and discussing strategy. Someone complains: "Nonviolent resistance doesn't work." A WOMAN says: "We should gouge out their eyes!" ANOTHER WOMAN: "Molotov cocktails and stones are called criminal weapons, but how else can we defend ourselves?"

Camera follows a FARMER into an underground tunnel. FARMER describes the work done to carve out the tunnel. Shows the room that has been created, where he has been living. "This," he says, "will be the last line of defense."

The camera on the meeting room slowly pulls away from the film on the screen, revealing the dark heads of the audience and the light from the projector flickering across JAMES BABA's horn-rimmed glasses as he operates the machine. SOUND of *Sanrizuka* fades into SOUND of James Brown: "Hot Pants."

11 1973: CANE OFFICES—SAN FRANCISCO J-TOWN

Pan of J-town streets, pausing on passing people and particularly on businesses and houses marked for removal or demolition: Wong's Bait Shop, Yamato Garage, Spear's Barbershop, Roy's Barbershop,

Weldon's Grocery, Kintoki Restaurant. Camera moves along both sides of the streets of Japantown: Laguna, Post, Webster, Sutter, Octavia, Bush, Pine, Buchanan. Camera scans the Miyako Hotel and Japan Trade Center, follows the Peace Pagoda up to its spire, captures various old business establishments: Uoki Fish Market, Benkyo-do Sweet Shop, Soko Hardware, and passes along institutions such as the *Nichibei Times, Hokubei Mainichi,* the YWCA, the Pine Methodist Church, and the Buddhist Temple.

Enter CANE offices on Sutter. Close-up of CANE sign: *CITIZENS AGAINST NIHONMACHI EVICTION.* Camera follows TWO PEOPLE, one of them SEN HAMA, who are carrying SEN's disabled brother, HARRY HAMA, up the stairs, leaving his wheelchair at the bottom. Entering the upstairs offices, a GROUP of perhaps a dozen have already gathered. They are scrutinizing a series of photos and graphics arranged on poster boards.

SEN HAMA

(walks forward and holds up posters) So this is a map of Nihonmachi as it exists today. We've drawn it to scale to show each business and residence. You folks have been canvassing every street, so if you see something that's not accurate, let us know.

CANE MEMBER I

Well, since you asked, I'm on the residents' committee for Laguna, and you switched the tackle shop with the barbershop.

SEN HAMA

Oh, right. Remind me after the meeting. Now this (points to second poster) is a pre-1951, pre-Western addition demolition map, and you can see all the businesses and houses that used to be and are no more. And here are aerial photographs of the demolition to widen Geary. A twenty-six-block area of housing and business was razed for a thoroughfare. The folks living here were mostly black, Japanese, and poor. All were bought and moved out by the RDA.

JAMES BABA

Buchanan used to run into Geary right here (points), and both sides of the street were Japanese businesses. And all along Post were black and Japanese businesses. Promises were made that these businesses would move into the Trade Center, but mostly these folks sold their businesses and left. They couldn't afford the higher leases.

SEN HAMA

We're thirteen years too late. They started talks to build the Trade Center back in 1960. By '68 and five million dollars later, you got your Trade Center.

AIKO MASAOKA

O.K., we know we're thirteen years too late for those folks who got bought out cheap, but we're not too late for the rest of Nihonmachi.

SEN HAMA

Exactly.

HARRY HAMA

So what about the Nihonmachi Terrace? That's housing for issei, right?

JAMES BABA

We also put together a timeline so we can all be conversant in the history. (points to another poster) So here you can see the Terrace is projected to be a thirteen-story highrise. They broke ground but haven't started construction. They say they'll start next year.

SEN HAMA

Our position is to support their project to relocate residents. There's projected to be 255 apartments in the Terrace. What we can do is canvas the issei and make sure they fill out the paperwork to get a place.

CANE MEMBER 1

What about the NCDC? What's our position on them?

JAMES BABA

The Nihonmachi Community Development Corporation is a group of eighty shareholders, sixty percent residential or business owners. They got together and purchased four blocks, this area here (points) that includes Buchanan. Sam Tezawa is the president.

CANE MEMBER II

Someone suggested that those guys on the NCDC got together and made a separate deal with the city.

CANE MEMBER III

We went to their meeting, and they don't want to listen to us. They're like the Chinatown Six Companies. They control everything.

SEN HAMA

It's not productive to make that comparison. It's better to go after the city Redevelopment Agency. Look, they razed the Western Addition block by block, then left it like a bombed-out area for how many years? Eight years. Then what do they do? They get these corporations with no vested interest in the old neighborhoods to rebuild for them. It's just an investment. The poor who are struggling to survive get kicked out first.

JAMES BABA

Really, we should go after Gintetsu. It's the real enemy. It's the corporation that now controls twenty-five percent of Nihonmachi, that being half of the Japan Trade Center plus the Miyako Hotel. Gintetsu is an extension of the Gintetsu Nippon Railway Company that has a monopoly on the Japan Railroad. It also owns Japan's bus services and taxi cabs, eleven department stores, fifty supermarkets, land and housing developments, nine hotels, travel agencies, recreation centers like baseball parks and bowling alleys. Manages all the Ford dealerships in Japan, plus Ford's air cargo.

CANE MEMBER I

Shit. What's Nihonmachi to them?

SEN HAMA

Precisely.

JAMES BABA

Gintetsu actually posted a loss on the Trade Center in 1968. Can you imagine? Said they lost two million, but I looked up their records last year. They made three million in the first quarter.

CANE MEMBER II

Where does all that money go?

JAMES BABA

Stockholders. New investments.

HARRY HAMA

We need to get a commitment from these guys to put these profits back into Nihonmachi. It should be part of the contract.

CANE MEMBER III

Gintetsu and the others, the NCDC, are already here. There's got to be a way to get them to share.

AIKO MASAOKA

That's so naïve. Corporations don't get together to share, they get together to make money. It's capitalism. Liberals always want to make concessions that buy into a continuing system of oppression.

CANE MEMBER III

That's why I think we need a position on the NCDC. These guys are saying they are insiders protecting Nihonmachi interests, but all they want is a tourist town, to bring in business.

CANE MEMBER II

They need to feel the heat. These guys are enemies of the people. (holds up a cartoon he's been scribbling)

Cartoon of Sam Tezawa, president of the NCDC with the caption: *Enemy of the People.* (laughter)

CANE MEMBER I

Shit, it's almost one a.m. I gotta get up and work my shift at the tofu factory in a few hours.

Meeting begins to break up. Members disburse and leave.

12 J-TOWN COLLECTIVE—SAME NIGHT

As the CANE crowd leaves, SIX JTC MEMBERS peel away to the J-Town Collective office in the next room, and sit around on its desks and chairs.

JTC MEMBER I

JB, that was great work on the timeline and the maps. You been doing that all week, keeping late hours here?

JAMES BABA

I didn't do it all. It was Sen. He did the research and found the photos.

JTC MEMBER II

Can he be recruited?

JTC MEMBER III

We're working on him. He's coming to the Wednesday night study group.

AIKO MASAOKA

You know, we shouldn't just have that poster information in the CANE office; we should get it out to the public.

JTC MEMBER IV

Who's on the publicity committee? JB? You should be the one to make that suggestion. Also, write another article for the *Hokubei*.

JTC MEMBER I

What was that all about in there, trying to bring up the NCDC?

AIKO MASAOKA

Isn't that what we agreed? We need to push to get folks to take on the NCDC. It's just another capitalist configuration.

JTC MEMBER II

No one seemed to go for it.

JTC MEMBER III

But they liked Sam Tezawa, *Enemy of the People.*

JTC MEMBER I

You're going to cause problems for at least one of the members. Bob's father is best friends with Sam. We need Bob's support. More importantly, we need his dad's support.

JAMES BABA

Moving on, guys—we were going to discuss the first anniversary of Okinawan reversion to Japan last year. Nixon and Sato want to renew the U.S.-Japan Security Treaty because of the strategic military necessity of U.S. bases on Okinawa. Did you know there are 117 military installations on Okinawa?

JTC MEMBER IV

O.K., just let's strategize. JB's on publicity as usual. He should write something for *New Dawn.* Aiko, dream up an action, like maybe we picket some Japanese dignitary coming through.

AIKO MASAOKA

We should also think about a tie-in to CANE. It's the same shit after all, imperialist military and corporate takeover of land that belongs to the people. Okinawans suffer from dual-repression: by the U.S. military and the so-called Japan Self-Defense Forces. It's an imperialist partnership. Same thing could be said for Gintetsu and the NCDC.

JTC MEMBER I

What time is it? Shit. It's two a.m.

Scuffle of chairs and coats as the MEMBERS clamber out of the office, down the stairs, and walk out together into the J-Town night. The fog shimmers against an occasionally neon light from a bar or CLOSED sign. JTC MEMBERS walk silently, following the red char of JAMES BABA's constant cigarette. Suddenly, he stops in the middle of the street and does a jig, twirls around, and whoops. Someone says: *There he goes.* Another: *Shit, it's fuckin' two a.m.* JAMES BABA's steps pick up speed, dancing across wet streets and through fog. SOUND of James Brown: "Get On the Good Foot."

13 1974: HAVILAND HALL—SCHOOL OF CRIMINOLOGY—UC BERKELEY

Camera circles Haviland Hall. From one window on the second floor, TWO STUDENTS appear and a banner unfurls: *Defend Criminology!* In a second window, another banner: *Hands Off Crim!* As the banners appear, SOUND of cheers from CROWD below. TWENTY STUDENTS appear at various windows and wave at and show fists to the CROWD below. Among the students are RIA ISHII and WAYNE TAKABAYASHI, Professor Tom Takabayashi's son. A rope is thrown down, and the CROWD rushes forward with bundles in bags. These bundles are hoisted up through the windows.

VOICE

What's going on here?

REP FOR HAVILAND TWENTY

Twenty protestors have succeeded in occupying the second floor of Haviland Hall and the offices of the School of Criminology. They've done this to protest the order by the Regents to close the school.

VOICE

What do you mean "occupied?"

REP FOR HAVILAND TWENTY

They've locked themselves in the offices on the second floor.

They won't leave until our demands to keep the school open are met.

VOICE

What are those bundles being pulled up on ropes?

REP FOR HAVILAND TWENTY

Those are blankets and food supplies. We in Ethnic Studies have organized a united front to support this effort. We've also sent up a bullhorn.

STUDENT appears at window on a bullhorn.

STUDENT

ALL POWER TO THE PEOPLE!

CROWD

ALL POWER TO THE PEOPLE!

STUDENT

Haviland Hall is now under occupation by the students of the School of Criminology! (CROWD cheers) We have not taken this action lightly. All of us have put our lives on the line to make a statement to the Regents and the chancellor. Traditionally, this school has been a technical school to train police in things like police science forensics, but times have changed, and to meet these changes, we need to study the true nature of crime, punishment, and justice, and of rehabilitation in our society.

Camera fixes on speeches and events at Haviland into the night. A small crowd of vigilant PROTESTORS remains at the base of the building, wrapped in blankets. At around three in the morning, a contingent of POLICE run into the building. The camera follows them as they bust through doors, throwing off the barricades of chairs and tables. They grab the STUDENTS, cuff and arrest them, and haul them out into the dark in a line. PROTESTORS jeer the POLICE and cheer THE HAVILAND TWENTY as they are pushed into paddy wagons and driven away. Meanwhile, POLICE push PROTESTORS away from the building and set up barricades with sawhorses and tape.

As light rises on the campus, the camera follows a second group of PROTESTORS jumping the barricades and rushing toward the building. These STUDENTS chain themselves together and to the doors. The POLICE beat the STUDENTS with their clubs, saw off the chains, and drag them off. By late day, there are thousands of PROTESTORS surrounding Haviland Hall, marching and chanting: FREE THE HAVILAND TWENTY!

SOUND of James Brown: "Papa Don't Take No Mess"

14 1975: WESTERN ADDITION REDEVELOPMENT ADMINISTRATION OFFICE—SAN FRANCISCO

Camera marches behind a delegation of TEN MEMBERS OF CANE, or Citizens Against Nihonmachi Evictions, following them into the office of the DIRECTOR of the Western Addition Redevelopment Administration. One of the members, HARRY HAMA, is pushed in a wheelchair. All are in their twenties except for one man who could be their father. One young man is black. JAMES BABA pulls a statement from his pocket and reads it.

JAMES BABA

We are CANE, representing the residents of Japantown at 1772 Sutter and other locations. We demand, one, that the RDA stop the demolition of 1772 Sutter; two, that the RDA repair 1772 Sutter for low-rent housing; and three, that the RDA repair other affected buildings, such as 1622 Laguna. We will not leave until our demands are met.

DIRECTOR

Your community has been aware of the plans for Sutter Street for many months now. These plans were agreed upon by the Nihonmachi Community Development Corporation, which legally represents the Japantown business community.

JAMES BABA

The NCDC does not represent the people of our community. It is a conglomerate of well-to-do property owners and business interests in collaboration with the Gintetsu Corporation. Their aims are selfish and do not account for the lives of longtime renters who have lived and operated their businesses in Nihonmachi for generations.

DIRECTOR

Well, perhaps what we should do is schedule a meeting with all of the parties concerned to resolve this question.

AIKO MASAOKA

A meeting can be agreed on, but first we have to be assured that 1772 Sutter will not be demolished. Your people have been harassing the residents with evictions. They have nowhere to go or live.

DIRECTOR

They've been informed properly for a long time. Your group has been tearing down our notices and disrupting the process.

AIKO MASAOKA

Your process, as you call it, is causing the breakup of our community. The people you are evicting have already suffered evacuation and internment in concentration camps.

DIRECTOR

My understanding from canvassing the Japantown businesses is that the majority supports the current redevelopment project. Your group is creating unnecessary confusion and divisiveness. Let me make some calls—

The RDA DIRECTOR reaches for the phone. HARRY HAMA pulls out a chain hidden on his lap under his jacket, and NINE PROTESTORS quickly chain and lock their arms together. The TENTH PROTESTOR, another woman, rushes to the door, locks it from the inside, and runs out. The RDA DIRECTOR puts down the phone and nervously looks at the NINE PROTESTORS blocking his door.

JAMES BABA

(starts chanting) THE PEOPLE UNITED WILL NEVER BE DEFEATED!

CANE PROTESTORS

THE PEOPLE UNITED WILL NEVER BE DEFEATED! THE PEOPLE UNITED WILL NEVER BE DEFEATED! THE PEOPLE UNITED WILL NEVER BE DEFEATED!

Meanwhile, on the street outside the RDA offices, one hundred PROTESTORS picket with signs in Japanese and English: *STOP EVICTION NOW! SAVE NIHONMACHI FROM THE RDA! J-TOWN FOR THE PEOPLE, NOT THE TOURISTS!*

Two hours later, the chained protestors in the RDA DIRECTOR's office are still chanting. They are also sweating under their heavy coats, worn in anticipation of holding forth through the night.

SOUND of POLICE banging at the door, forcing it open. Police rush in, apply gigantic cutters to the chain, and drag eight of the protestors away. The RDA DIRECTOR stands up and leaves, but the last protestor, HARRY HAMA, remains in his wheelchair, waiting to be arrested. SOUND of PROTESTORS chanting as they are dragged away: ALL POWER TO THE PEOPLE! STOP EVICTION NOW!

HARRY HAMA

Hey! Hey! (SOUND of commotion and chanting fading into quiet. No one answers. HARRY HAMA finally shrugs in frustration and wheels himself out.)

Camera follows HARRY HAMA to elevator and out of the building to the jeering and chanting of the picketing crowd outside. He gives the power sign to loud cheering. KEN, a young attorney, meets the PROTESTORS as they are taken away in a paddy wagon. HARRY rolls forward, wanting to get in too.

KEN

Harry, forget it. You've done enough. I'll take you home, O.K.?

HARRY HAMA

Ken, it's discrimination, you know.

KEN

I know. Come on.

HARRY sighs. Rising SOUND of James Brown: "The Payback." PICKETERS continue their commotion as KEN and HARRY watch the paddy wagon doors close and the vehicle pull out into traffic. Everyone raises their fists in power signs.

15 1976: J-TOWN COLLECTIVE/CANE—OFFICES ON SUTTER STREET
Meeting is already in session in the CANE offices. Camera pans faces and captures a sense of rising tension.

MEMBERS (speaking variously)

So, we've called this meeting because we think there is a growing number of our members who are worried about the direction we've been taking. We're being seen by the community as a radical organization of outsider students.

This perception is definitely hindering our work. We need to grow our membership and support. People are afraid to join us even if they agree with our position.

For example, when certain members blocked the merchants' plan for a low-cost housing and retail space. Supporters were criticized for promoting capitalism. Has anybody considered that the merchants need their businesses to survive?

But we've been working to close this gap between CANE activists and the general membership.

Activists are fine, but provocateurs?

What?

I think, and I don't want to point fingers, but I think some of our membership has double interests. I don't say they are manipulating things, but—

I disagree. I think some of our committees have been coerced into committing actions that we don't all agree on. For example, that campaign against the NCDC, calling their leadership *Enemies of the People.* Who decided we should plaster Nihonmachi with those flyers of their faces everywhere?

That was really damaging. We lost a lot of support. It was really poor judgment.

I think we all know who's been responsible for this trend all along, and we need to recognize that we've been too quiet. We know these people have done a lot of groundwork, but that doesn't mean we go along with everything they say.

One of our catchwords is *unity*. But what's happening is undermining the trust of our members.

Why don't you just say it? The JTC has been planning everything in those offices next door and then implementing their plans at CANE. CANE is not a Maoist-Marxist organization. It's a community organization fighting for the people.

I don't see how the JTC's politics is involved in this. The hardest workers in CANE are also members of JTC.

But CANE is not an arm of the JTC.

Who do you think started CANE in the first place?

Oh no, we're not your fuckin' mass organization. It's not like that. Either you play by our rules or you leave.

Fuckin' shit! (jumps up)

Hey, cool it.

You guys don't want community. You just want to bring it down. Fuckin' anarchists is what you are.

You don't know what you're talking about. We've been trying to raise a critical question: What is Nihonmachi? Is it a Japanese ghetto or an all-races, low-income neighborhood? We've got Clarence Spear's barbershop and Weldon's Grocery. Can we afford to be narrow nationalists? This has got to be struggled with.

What's "narrow nationalist"?

It's just talk to confuse the issues.

Fuck it. I got better things to do.

JTC MEMBERS stand up and leave the meeting.

16 GENERAL MEETING—MORNING STAR SCHOOL, NIHONMACHI

General meeting of CANE held in the lunch hall of the Morning Star School. The CROWD of two hundred is very mixed: Japanese sansei and nisei, some issei, a sprinkling of African Americans and Chinese Americans. Children are running about and around the tables. They are all coming from a potluck line of food, their paper plates piled with chicken teriyaki, salads, musubis, cupcakes, Jell-O, etc. They sit along the low benches of the lunch tables and start in with plastic forks and wooden chopsticks. A woman comes around with a brass pot of hot tea and pours it into Styrofoam cups. A nisei man, CANE'S PRESIDENT, walks to a standing microphone at the front of the hall.

CANE PRESIDENT

Thank you for coming out tonight. This is CANE's third anniversary dinner. I don't think any of us knew what was ahead when we started, that we'd even still be here after three years. I guess I'd have to say that, unfortunately, we've had to be here this long. It's been a lot of hard work and there's more work to come. We've had some successes, and the committees want to share this with you tonight. Then we want to open a forum to talk about what's ahead for CANE.

17 J-TOWN COLLECTIVE OFFICE ON SUTTER

Meanwhile, JTC MEMBERS are moving up and down the stairs with office furniture, desks, file cabinets, shelves, books, papers, lamps, chairs, mimeograph machines, telephones. Everything is hauled off into a waiting truck on the street. It's dark, no one else in sight on Sutter Street. The camera takes a last look into the old offices before the light is turned off. All the posters have been ripped off; nothing remains. JAMES BABA uses the claw of a hammer and yanks out the J-Town Collective plaque on the door. He runs down the stairs and jumps into the back of the truck, slapping the side of truck to signal O.K., and it pulls out in the dark. Truck passes the camera as JAMES BABA lights a cigarette and blows smoke into the night. SOUND of James Brown: "Get Up Offa That Thing."

CREDITS rise over the San Francisco Nihonmachi night.

CREDITS

This film is a collaboration of YELLOW PEACE and CAMERA AS WEAPON PRODUCTIONS.

DIRECTOR/FILMMAKER: Judy Eng

FINAL STATEMENT

This film is dedicated to the memory of Edmund Yat Min Lee.

3: A Need to Know Basis

If you or any member of your IM *Force are caught or killed, the secretary will disavow any knowledge of your actions. As usual, this recording will decompose after the breaking of the seal . . .*

—*Mission: Impossible*

. . . to expose, disrupt, misdirect, discredit or otherwise neutralize such groups and their leadership, spokespersons, members and supporters; counter their propensity for violence; frustrate their efforts to consolidate their forces or to recruit new or youthful adherents; exploit conflicts within and between groups; use news media contacts to ridicule and otherwise discredit groups; prevent groups from spreading their philosophy publicly; and gather information on backgrounds of group leaders for use against them.

—J. Edgar Hoover
COINTELPRO memo
February 29, 1968

This is made from stray sea kelp and ground eye of octopus. Drink it, Mr. Robinson. You'll feel better immediately.

—*I Spy*

A review of FBI *files ordered by the attorney general indicates that you may have been affected by an* FBI *counterintelligence program in (date). If you would like to receive more information concerning this matter, please send a written request specifying the address to which you want this material mailed.*

—Office of Professional Responsibility
Justice Department
Delivered by U.S. Marshals
April 1, 1976

PICTURE:	VOICE-OVER:
San Francisco Golden Gate Bridge, sunset, slow walking across bridge, with cars rushing past.	Q: Were you surprised to learn about the FBI's counterintelligence operation? A: With the stuff that's come down, we know these guys are operating but probably not to what extent. Q: Have you requested your files under the Freedom of Information Act?
Memo pages with official stamps, most of the text blacked out. Camera moves into black text until the screen is black.	A: We have, but it's like pages of, what they call *redacted,* blacked-out text.

1 MIDNIGHT—SUTTER STREET—J-TOWN

Footsteps down the empty street. A FIGURE is moving quietly from parked car to parked car, trying the doors to find an open one. The cars are wet and frosted in the fog, their interiors a dark secret. The figure pulls on the handle of a Volkswagen Bug—to his delight it's unlocked, but to his dismay a HEAD of straight black hair leaning against the door falls out, followed by its attached body, as he opens it.

AIKO MASAOKA

Goddamn it!

NELSON LOPEZ

Oh, shit.

AIKO

(half asleep and waking) What time is it? Is it that time? You fuckin' scared me. JB (she gets out of the car to confront a figure she thinks is JAMES BABA), don't do that again! (scrutinizing the figure in the dark and realizing her mistake) Who are you? Where's JB?

NELSON

I dunno. Can I have your car?

AIKO

What?

NELSON

Gimme the keys. (puts his hand in his coat pocket and points it like a gun at her)

AIKO

That's the oldest trick in the book. (pushes him away) Get out of here! (gets back in the car and tries to close the door)

NELSON

(shoves the door back open and grabs her, pulling her out of the car) I said, gimme the keys!

AIKO

(pulls a gun around and points it) Can you say, "please"?

NELSON

(puts his hands up) O.K., please.

AIKO

Do I know you?

NELSON

Can I just go? Just forget it.

SOUND of footsteps walking up the street. JAMES BABA is sauntering over, puffing on a cigarette. When he sees AIKO pointing her gun, he flicks his cigarette away and starts to run.

JAMES BABA

Hey! What's going on?

AIKO

(shrugs) This guy was trying to steal the car.

JAMES

Nelson?

NELSON

Hey, brother. James Brown, JB, right?

JAMES

Right.

NELSON

Hey, right on.

JAMES

So—

NELSON

So, whatchu guys doing out here this time of night?

JAMES

Surveillance, man. We got to keep a twenty-four-hour watch on that apartment there (points) or Redevelopment might come and evict those folks.

NELSON

Oh yeah, I heard about that. (points to AIKO, who is still pointing her gun) Could you tell her to put that thing down?

JAMES

(nods at AIKO) Nelson, this is Aiko. Don't mess with her. I'm serious. She's a crim student.

NELSON

Shit, she was sleeping on the job. I coulda gone in there and busted those poor folks myself.

AIKO

JB! He was going to steal the car!

NELSON

Keep your voice down, would you?

JAMES

(looks down the street) Wait. Aiko, shut up. Get in the car. Nelson, get in the car. In the back. Quick!

POLICE car patrols street and passes by. NELSON looks out the back window then scrunches back down in the seat.

JAMES

(to NELSON in the back) They're looking for you.

NELSON

I ain't going back. That cop killed his own partner. I didn't kill him! Who's gonna believe that?

AIKO

You're one of them from the Mission? Los Settay?

NELSON

Los Si-e-te. Please.

JAMES

(starts the car and pulls away from the curb) Aiko, we'll take Nelson to your place.

AIKO

What? No way!

NELSON

Yeah, no way.

JAMES

Just for a few days. Until we figure it out.

PICTURE:	VOICE-OVER:
Asian children in a park playing, running around in circles, playing in the sandbox, moving hand over hand across on the rings, skipping rope, throwing balls, waddling around aimlessly.	Q: How about wiretapping? RS: We figure the phones could be tapped. If it's important, we use pay phones. Usually we turn on a radio to create interference but I don't know if it works. DT: We suspect the offices are bugged, so we move our strategy meetings around to other locations.

2 KITCHEN IN APARTMENT IN J-TOWN

NELSON and AIKO are sitting at the kitchen table staring at each other.

NELSON

What did he mean, you're a "crim" student?

AIKO

I study criminology at Berkeley.

NELSON

No shit. You study guys like me. Hey, you're studying to be a cop! (gets up to leave)

AIKO

Sit down. It's not like that. Anyway, my school is being phased out.

NELSON

What you looking at me like that for?

AIKO

Just thinking. You could pass.

NELSON

Pass?

AIKO

Well yeah, for Asian. So which of those Los Siete guys are you? Uno? Dos? Tres? Cuatro—

NELSON

Who the fuck knows? Maybe I'm cinco.

AIKO

O.K. That's go. You know, Japanese numbers: ichi, ni, san, shi, go. You can be Goro.

NELSON

Whaddya mean, Goro?

AIKO

(gets up to check a pot of rice on the stove)
We got to get you a Japanese name.

NELSON

Do I look Japanese?

AIKO

(starts to fry a couple of eggs)
We just say you're hapa. Mixed. You can be Nelson Goro Tanaka. Your mom was Mexican. No, Filipino. Or maybe Hawaiian. That could work.

NELSON

My mom is Salvadoran. I ain't no Mexican.

AIKO

(looks back from the stove)
Details.

NELSON

It's different, O.K. We're not MEChA. None of that Chicano shit, see?

AIKO

I get it, different like Chinese and Japanese. (dishes out the eggs on top of a pile of rice and serves them to NELSON) But now you gotta be Japanese. First off, you gotta keep your mouth shut. Japanese don't talk, especially the guys. You got to be low-key and shy and boring. (hands him a pair of chopsticks)

NELSON

(holds up the chopsticks)
Shit. You're crazy!

AIKO

Hey, you want me to hide you or not? (walks over to reach for the phone)

NELSON

O.K., O.K.!

AIKO sits down with a chawan of rice, cracks a raw egg over the hot rice, pours shoyu over that, and whips it all up. NELSON looks on, picks at his fried eggs with the tips of his chopsticks.

AIKO

(slurping up some of the egg-rice, looks up and snaps the chopsticks at NELSON) This time you get off easy. Next time you do it raw.

PICTURE:	VOICE-OVER:
Pond of koi swimming languidly and swirling around, their red and white patterns seen skimming along the surface of the water and disappearing beneath water lilies.	Z: Infiltration is like this. It isn't just spying—it's about undermining trust. So you have a real idealist-activist type, but the infiltrator goes in there and spreads shit so his cohort suspects him to be an agent. His own people do him in themselves. It's not pretty.

3 NEW DAWN—J-TOWN COLLECTIVE BOOKSTORE—J-TOWN

JAY, a man in his later twenties, is shelving books. Bobby Seale's *Seize the Time,* Edgar Snow's *Red Star over China,* Frantz Fanon's *Wretched of the Earth,* and *Roots: An Asian American Reader.* There are stacks of newspapers: *Gidra, New Dawn, Getting Together.* Also stacks of *Mao's Little Red Book.* AIKO walks in with NELSON.

AIKO

Hey Jay.

JAY

Aiko.

AIKO

This is Nelson. Nelson Tanaka.

JAY

Brother. (guys do handshake)

AIKO

His dad and mine go back. 442nd.

JAY

Oh yeah? You from Hawaii?

AIKO

He was just born there. Brought up down south, L.A.

JAY

Right on, Nelson.

NELSON

You can call me Goro. Folks call me Goro.

AIKO

(flashes NELSON a look; he looks down pretending to be shy)
Goro wants to help out here. You got some work for him?

NELSON moves away and peruses books along the shelves while AIKO takes JAY aside.

AIKO

Jay, he's, you know, hapa. His mom was Filipino or Hawaiian. But then they came here, and he got stuck with the Mexicans back in L.A. Anyway, he's like, in that stage, getting back into his roots. So I thought maybe if he hung out here, he could read and learn some stuff.

JAY

No problem.

AIKO

(walks over to NELSON) So can you help out here? I gotta go to work. My shift starts in an hour.

NELSON

Hey, (speaking softly) what's 442nd? Your dad? My dad?

AIKO

(grabs a book from the shelf) Here, read this. Study up. I'll see you tonight.

PICTURE:	VOICE-OVER:
Moves across the window pane of a Japanese restaurant displaying food selections in plastic. There's noodles with shrimp tempura, an oyako donburi, a tonkatsu plate, a sushi plate, etc.	Z: Another job for the infiltrator: create dissension to prevent unity between groups. Say a white group and a colored group want to align themselves for power purposes. It's easy. Pull the race card, shit about their "national" position, see what I mean? No way they see eye to eye.

4 AIKO'S KITCHEN

Couple weeks later, NELSON has grown a goatee and his hair. He is trying to eat noodles in a bowl of soup with chopsticks.

NELSON

How's work?

AIKO

I'm learning. We're thinking of organizing a co-op, open our own garment factory. That way the women will have control:

hours, piecework, work conditions, everything. We could include childcare. (watching NELSON eat) Just get down and slurp it up. (demonstrates noisily) You're a guy, after all. You can be sloppy.

NELSON

My dad was a hero, you know.

AIKO

Oh yeah?

NELSON

The 442nd Regimental Combat Team. Saved a bunch of Texans. More of us died to save a few of them. He was lucky to get out alive. (pauses) Do you think he should've lost an arm or a leg or something?

AIKO

Don't go around exaggerating.

NELSON

Maybe he died in the war.

AIKO

You have to be born, stupid.

NELSON

Oh, right. My grandparents were in camp, meanwhile. What camp?

AIKO

Tule Lake. Grandparents are issei. Your dad was nisei, and you're sansei. Ichi, ni, san. Get it?

NELSON

You folks always counting. Jay asked if I had other brothers. I told him I was named after my dad's buddy who died in Italy.

AIKO

Quick thinking.

NELSON

You know, there's this guy who comes in and asks questions.

AIKO

What questions?

NELSON

One time he bought a *New Dawn* and asked about meetings. When did the editorial staff meet? Today he asked if I knew JB, if I have a number for him. He has to get in touch with him, has some shit to tell him.

AIKO

Hakujin?

NELSON

Who?

AIKO

White?

NELSON

(shakes head) Uh-uh. A real Asian. He could still be an agent. Hispanics must get recruited all the time. Why else we're so fucked up?

AIKO

What did you say to him?

NELSON

Said I was new. Talk to Jay.

AIKO

What did Jay say?

NELSON

He's never there when this dude comes in. It's a vibe, you know. Could be a setup. I'm screwed.

AIKO

Let me talk to JB.

PICTURE:	VOICE-OVER:
Follows an old lady holding a bag full of groceries in one hand and a small child in the other. Follows them moving slowly up a hill. The kid is eating something, maybe a manju. When he's finished, the kid stops to pick up something on the sidewalk. They argue a bit, then continue to walk on. Then the kid's hat falls off, and they have to stop again. The woman puts her bag down, adjusts the hat on the child's head, then gathers up everything and continues walking slowly up. The camera stays back and the figures move away, becoming smaller and smaller.	Z: "So then you got what they call "psychological warfare." It's like this fake stuff. Flyers with the group's name printed with shit they never wrote plastered all over the place. They have to run around and do triage, tear the things down, and then ask who did it. Fingers get pointed. Fights break out. SL: Or someone sets up some meeting that someone important's supposed to come to. Folks show up, but the VIP never shows so they look like flakes. Z: Anonymous letters. Send a letter to a funder, could be the nice corner church. Suddenly they stop giving money for the breakfast program. SL: Anonymous phone calls. Someone calls with a tip. Same tip for another guy on the other guy. Could be regarding a woman or money. Either will do. Starts a fuckin' war.

5 BAACAW—BAY AREA ASIAN COALITION AGAINST THE WAR—MEETING—PINE METHODIST CHURCH

The meeting is already convened, and people are sitting around on metal folding chairs listening to a speaker. AIKO is sitting in a row toward the back of the room. NELSON arrives to sit next to her.

AIKO

You're late.

NELSON

Gomen nasai. My Japanese class got out late. Sensei is strict. You can't just leave. Gotta be dismissed.

AIKO

Aren't you taking this a bit too far?

NELSON

I'm digging it. Getting my identity, man. So now, I'm getting me a Japanese girlfriend, too. (snuggles up to AIKO)

AIKO

(growls softly) Get off of me. (changes subject) Did you change jobs again? Mama Kintoki was calling for you.

NELSON

No. I still bus tables for her at noon. JB got me a job at the *Hokubei* doing the paper run.

AIKO

Damn. You've become Mr. J-Town himself.

NELSON

Nihonmachi-san, that's me. (looks around) Hey, that's him.

AIKO

Who?

NELSON

Guy who showed up at the bookstore. You know, the inu.

AIKO

Inu?

NELSON

Do I have to spell it out? (whispers) Dog. Spy. It's what we called those traitors in camp.

AIKO

(rolls her eyes but stays serious about the stranger) Never seen him before.

NELSON

See?

AIKO gets up and quietly walks to the back to talk to JAMES BABA, who is doing security at the door. He nods. Meanwhile, the meeting breaks up and JAY can be seen walking across the room to greet NELSON.

JAY

Hey, Goro. Where you been?

NELSON

Around. Working for Kintoki and taking Japanese lessons. So I can talk to the customers.

JAY

Cool. So, what's your status, man?

NELSON

Number's up there, but they're not going to find me. No forwarding address. What about you?

JAY

I did my time. Went to DC and threw my medals away. Nam's a racist war.

NELSON'S GUY comes over and puts his hand out.

GUY

Hey, man. How's it going?

NELSON

(looks at JAY)

GUY

You're Goro, right? I met you at the bookstore. Remember?

NELSON

Don't remember. Sorry, man.

GUY

Great bookstore you got going. Great stuff. Better than that one in the I-Hotel—what's it called? Everybody's Books? Hey, better than China Books even. Don't tell anyone I said so, but those Wei Min folks need to get their shit together better.

JAY

(shrugs) Different stuff.

AIKO

(interrupts) You walking me home?

NELSON

Yeah. (to JAY) Catch you later.

PICTURE:	VOICE-OVER:
A chubby woman with a smiling face is behind a counter at the fish market. She's pulling up a slimy octopus, showing it to the kids standing at the counter, pulling on its long tentacles as they look with funny faces. She laughs and teases the kids, who jump around in delight.	Z: Actually, all you have to do is follow someone around. Every time he looks, you're following him. Pretty soon, everybody notices he's being tailed. Everyone gets the jitters, starts to act like criminals. Combine that with other shit, and before you know it, got him for graft and corruption.

6 KIMOCHI—SAN FRANCISCO J-TOWN

Front of the Kimochi offices. Sign in front says: *Kimochi means "caring for the elderly."* NELSON is helping an ELDERLY ISSEI WOMAN up the steps.

NELSON

Obasan, iidesuka?

ISSEI WOMAN

Nihongo joozu desu ne.

NELSON looks up and sees AIKO running toward him.

AIKO

Goro. Did you hear? Bookstore was broken into last night. Jay just called.

PICTURE:	VOICE-OVER:
Small children and issei grandparents are sitting at a table folding origami paper. They are making paper cranes. The issei ladies move around the table, helping the children and laughing softly.	RS: Worst thing is when they go around and ask questions. They show up at your parents' house or maybe your girlfriend's parents' house. They show up at your school or landlord's and ask questions. That's all they have to do, ask questions, and you're screwed.

7 NEW DAWN

Windows are broken. Books and papers are strewn everywhere. Shelves have been pulled down. Posters torn off walls. Lighting smashed. JAY is picking through the debris.

AIKO

Didn't anyone hear them do this?

JAY

Should have paid attention to those calls.

AIKO

Calls?

JAY

Yeah, some jerk was calling, threatening to close us down. Yelled stuff like, *You yellow Commies go back to where you came from—*

NELSON

What'd they take?

JAY

Week's receipts. Maybe two hundred dollars. I was going to go to the bank this morning. Maybe we can sell this damaged stuff for fifty percent off, get some money back. Good thing we don't pay any rent.

NELSON

Why's that?

JAY

Building's condemned for redevelopment.

NELSON

Shelves are trash.

JAY

Shit, I liberated those myself. Nearly got caught doing it, too.

8 NIHONMACHI FAIR

Buchanan Street between Post and Sutter is closed to traffic. Booths and tables are set up along the street. NELSON is standing in one booth underneath a sign that says *Kimochi*. He's got on a happi coat and sports a hachimaki with a red sun around his forehead. In the middle of his booth is a low table filled with little goldfish bowls. He's handing out Ping-Pong balls to kids, three balls for a ticket.

PICTURE:	VOICE-OVER:
An issei couple is sitting on a bench. He's reading a paper and she's crocheting a blanket. Pretty soon he's nodding off and leaning against her. His mouth is open and the paper falls from his lap. His head falls off her shoulder. She pushes him, slaps his knee, and laughs.	DT: Some people say that black cat who killed that sansei girl in Chicago at the JACL convention was sent in to start a race war. The media picked up on the Panther connection and tried to smear the girl's reputation. They never found the guy. Why is that? RS: The law owns itself. That is, they make their own rules; so they do break-ins, vandalism, assault, assassinations, all this to serve and protect. So what are they protecting? The American Way of Life? From what? Communism? Red China? Mao? Uncle Ho? The Yellow Peril?

NELSON

(little kid throws first Ping-Pong ball and gets lucky) Hey, we got a winner! (picks up the bowl and pours the goldfish into a plastic bag, hands it to the kid) O.K., there you go.

AIKO

(comes by with a snow cone) Poor fish. They'll all be dead in a week.

NELSON

Hey, where's my snow cone?

AIKO

You want this one?

NELSON

It's rainbow.

AIKO

Yeah.

NELSON

I want one with sweet beans.

AIKO

(smirks) I shoulda shot you that night.

NELSON

(smiles) Shoulda given me the keys.

AIKO

You got 'em anyway.

PICTURE:	VOICE-OVER:
Ladies are standing around tables strewn with vases, flowers, branches, and grasses, working to arrange flowers this way and that. Vases are chosen, flowers examined. Close view of a woman's hands placing irises at different lengths and angles.	DT: Drugs are just around. I don't know where they come from, and if I did, I wouldn't tell you. You have to figure they're planting them, too. RS: What's-his-name who does security checks on these guys. He gets down and drinks with them. He can drink anyone under the table. Loosen the tongues, that way. Then he'll suggest pot, and then acid. He figures, if the suspect will go down with acid, he's not a pig.

9 TULE LAKE PILGRIMAGE

Caravan of cars drive up a dirt road to what appears to be an abandoned building out in the middle of nowhere. Cars park along the road and people get out, stretch, and wander toward the building.

NELSON

This is it?

AIKO

Yeah, I guess so. JB said that's the stockade. It's all that's left. No barracks. No lake. No evidence.

NELSON

Tule Lake's a dry lake bed. Hey, look at this: seashells. (picks up tiny shells from the dirt) See what I mean?

NISEI MAN (MIYAKI)

(notices the shells) Ladies used to gather those shells and make necklaces.

AIKO

Mr. Miyaki, I heard you built that stockade.

MIYAKI

I was on the construction crew. Goro, your folks were here?

NELSON

My dad's family.

MIYAKI

You know which block?

NELSON

No, I don't.

MIYAKI

Did you say your dad was 442nd?

NELSON

Yeah—

MIYAKI

Maybe he was here with his family when he was younger and left earlier. If he's 442nd, maybe he left for another camp.

AIKO

That's probably what happened.

MIYAKI

You know the history of Tule? This is where they sent the No-No folks, the ones who refused to fight. That's the reason for this stockade. Jailed the guys who got in fights over it. Some were what you call conscientious objectors. Others were pro-Japan. We had all kinds. Yes-No. No-Yes. Maybe No-Maybe Yes. No-No. What's your dad's name? You know the name of your grandfather?

NELSON

No, I guess he died before I was born, but my dad is Joe. Joe Tanaka.

MIYAKI

The WRA has old lists. Let me look it up for you. Where were your folks from originally?

NELSON

L.A.?

MIYAKI

You sure? Those folks went to Manzanar. So after the war, he went to Hawaii?

NELSON

Right. He went to bring back his buddy's things, and then he married my mom.

AIKO

It's a good story, isn't it, Mr. Miyaki?

MIYAKI

That's the thing. Lots of stories. We've been silent all these years. You kids are right to make us talk about this again. Shouldn't forget as if it never happened.

NELSON looks over, then nods to AIKO, who also notices a GUY hanging around near their conversation.

AIKO

Goro, where's my camera? (she moves toward the road)

NELSON

I'll get it. Probably in the trunk of the car. (pulls out the keys and walks with AIKO; after a distance, to AIKO) Shit, there he is again.

AIKO

Bad vibes.

NELSON

So, where did my folks come from to Tule?

AIKO

Let's research it. Maybe it's Washington, like Seattle or Tacoma or something.

NELSON

I think my jig's up. I just have this feeling.

AIKO

Ssshhh. (pecks him on the cheek)

PICTURE:	VOICE-OVER:
Multidenominational, that is to say a Buddhist and Christian shared service, staged next to the stockade at the former Tule Lake Internment Camp. A Buddhist priest and Christian pastor preside in a ceremony of remembrance. A small group of young and old Japanese Americans hold hands and pray. The flat, dry lake bed spreads into the distance against a rocky outcrop that reaches into a blue sky. It's July 4, 1974.	RS: It's come to this. Who can you trust? Nobody. DT: Information is given out on a need to know basis. Does this individual need to know this in order to do his job? If not, he doesn't need to know. It's for his own protection.

10 KINTOKI RESTAURANT—NOON—SAN FRANCISCO J-TOWN

AIKO and JAMES BABA are having lunch at Kintoki's on Laguna Street.

MAMA KINTOKI

What happened to Goro? One day he's gone. He's a good boy, good worker. More dependable than you radicals. (chuckles)

JAMES

What's that supposed to mean?

MAMA KINTOKI

You know, go off, get arrested, and don't come back several days.

JAMES

(teasing) That's the thanks we get?

MAMA KINTOKI

Just kidding. So far I still in business. I thanks to you. (pauses) How come Goro never tell me he's going to leave?

JAMES

His father has cancer. He had to go home. It was really sudden.

MAMA KINTOKI

Oh, that's terrible. You tell him I understand, but don't forget we're his friends. Aiko, you look so sad. Don't worry. He loves you. He'll be back.

AIKO

(hiding behind her tea, trying not to cry)
Yeah, Mama.

Everyone looks up as JAY comes into the restaurant. He's got a stack of *New Dawn* papers. He joins JAMES BABA and AIKO at their table.

JAY

Hot off the press. (passes out copies) Take a look. We outed that agent. (he points to an article with a photograph)

HEADLINE

FBI Agent Sanford Miike Snooping around J-Town

JAY

And check this out. Remember that guy they never found, who was one of the Los Siete? So get this, he hijacked a plane to Cuba. Man, one of these days, when the revolution comes, I'm going to Cuba to shake that man's hand. He made it out!

PICTURE:	VOICE-OVER:
Picnic in Golden Gate Park. People are gathered on mats, eating teriyaki chicken and musubi. Beyond, a couple is tossing a Frisbee, and nearby under a tree, someone is strumming a guitar, a group singing along in the shade.	Z: What kind of person could be a spy on his own people? You make choices among your own skin, your parole, feeding your habits. It's not about ideals; it's about *I-deals.* SL: Think about it like this: The Crim School at Berkeley, right? They shut it down, but it was a contradiction. One side, you got your radicals doing social sciences, but the other side, they're doing the forensics stuff like Q-Branch inventing double-oh-seven-type weapons and mind-control shit. What do you choose to do? Join the radicals or Q-Branch? Z: What I found out is that the conspiracy is real. Personally, I want to be in control.

1970: "I" Hotel

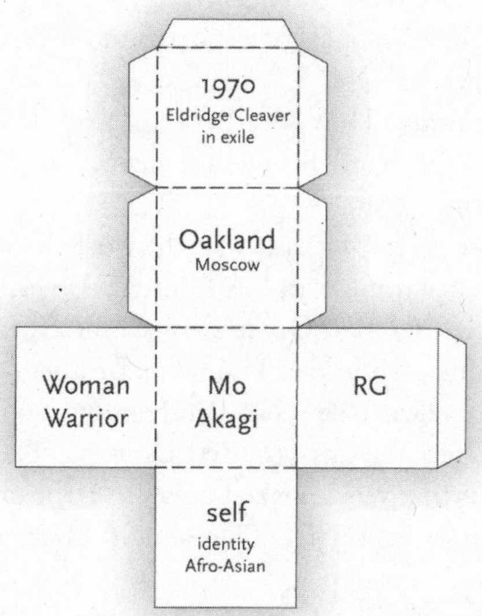

1: I Am Hip

Freedom is just another word for nothing left to lose
Nothing don't mean nothing honey if it ain't free, now now
—*Janis Joplin*

So I am hip, dig, and it's Moscow in 1970. Communism is alive and well. Kremlin's down the street, and you're in for a treat. The honorable ministers of information of the Black Panther Party and the Red Guard Party are holed up in a hotel room resting their feet and contemplating their next moves.

"What time is it?"

"Midnight."

"Shit. Can't sleep."

"Everybody else sleeping."

"Sleeping sweet like Lenin over there in Red Square."

"Might as well be in Podunski, Nebraska."

"Where are all the vodka bars?"

"This is why colored people got to be part of the revolution. Make sure we get our nightlife."

"You were in Havana. How was that?"

"I had to go after them for their racism, but they do have their nightlife. Grant them that."

Conversation goes on like that. Now, the world knows who wrote *Soul On Ice,* but the other young cat, he's Chinese. I mean to say, he's Asian American, representing. Red Guard's not Chinese per se; it's a new formation outta Chinatown in San Francisco. Brothers there got together, wanted to be Panthers, maybe Asian Panthers, but Bobby said no, you got to be your own thing. First it was Red Dragons, like they was kung fu Shaolin types, but that was knocked down in favor of the political: Red Guard Party. Got to be a party. That should catch some notice in the next few months.

Ministers are part of the U.S. People's Anti-Imperialist Delegation traveling to the Red East: Democratic People's Republic of Korea, People's Republic of China, and Democratic Republic of Vietnam. Moscow's their introductory point, but it's touchy. Sino-Soviet split, know what I mean? So first you ask for an introduction to Korea, then from there you ask for China, then you hop the border to Vietnam. That's the plan. Delegation's investigating the international situation; it's not taking sides. Let's agree that the principal enemy is U.S. imperialism. Indirect path to the man: Mao.

Meanwhile, sleepless revolutionaries got to pass the time. Drink that salty mineral water and swap stories.

"How come you didn't get caught by the draft? You don't look like the college type."

Red Guard kicks off his boots. He says, "It's all because of Janis Joplin."

"No shit. Take a piece of my heart, baby."

"I was saved by the Summer of Love."

Everybody knows Janis, white baby girl birthed out the mouth of Big Mama Thornton, but truth be told, Red Guard is saved by his own papa. Chinese dad was a Vaudeville magic act. Did Barnum & Bailey, Las Vegas, and Forbidden City. Used to make a Chinese doll turn into a real China woman; turns out this is RG's mama. Vaudeville was over, but the old man can't do anything else. Makes ends meet by opening for Jefferson Airplane and the Doors. That's how Chinese magic makes it happen. Old man opens for Big Brother and the Holding Company at the Avalon. Janis makes her debut, and RG is there.

"So you took up with Janis? Son of a bitch."

"Not exactly." Turns out RG is a stagehand for his papa and follows Joplin's shows around. Avalon Ballroom, Winterland, Matrix, Fillmore Auditorium. He asks, "You heard about the Trips Festival at the Longshoremen's?"

"Do I look like some hippy? Either I was doing time at Folsom or in Oakland putting out the Panther paper."

"Missed your acid test." RG shakes his head. Ken Kesey's Pranksters wired Longshoremen's with speakers, every kind of gadget, projections and strobes, crazy-assed climb-in sculptures—the total psychodelic experience. "You didn't need it, but just in case, they were passing around a shopping bag of acid."

"I'm hip. You were grateful dead."

But there's more: thanks to RG's magic papa, Trips Festival brings in the Chinese Drum and Bugle Corps. Corps blasts their way in, parading through the crowd, followed by colorful Chinese New Year lion dancers.

"Get this." RG leans over. "I was a lion dancer."

"One stoned lion dancer."

"You know it." RG takes his half of the lion into the hippie revelry. Gets lost and found. Discards the giant headdress with that big furry do and those gigantic flapping teeth and goes home with a girl from the Haight. She's one of those red diaper babies, hanging out with the Russian émigrés.

Panther nods. "I bet you took that red diaper off."

"Rolled around in the good stuff for days."

"We surrounded by red diapers and Russians. If only this Moscow were a bigger Haight."

RG looks out the hotel window into the dark Moscow night, contemplates those immaculate streets below. These Russians don't know what they're missing. "That's how I got my education." It was a total deal: social, sexual, and political. Sex and Marx. Acid and Lenin. Ganja and Guns.

"College of the Haight. But that don't get you no deferment."

"Nope. Signed up with the guerillas."

"You jiving."

"For real: guerilla theater. Figured I had acting genes."

Panther minister kicks off his shoes. It's gonna be a long story.

"So I trained for the theater. Took it to the streets. I trained to be crazy."

"You already crazy."

Guerilla theater frolics down the Haight for festivities on the Panhandle. Does the prankster thing twenty-four hours a day with music, drums, and dancing in the street. It's political theater at Union Square, from the Embarcadero down Market Street. It's theater warfare in front of the Federal Building, in the city council meetings, making fools of the politicians on TV. It's happening at the Fisherman's Wharf, carrying on on the cable cars, making points with the tourists. If you come to the tripping city, you got to get your money's worth. A visit with no run-ins with live, love-in be-in antiwar hippies can't be a true visit. It's all about spreading the flower power, ending the war, and getting high.

One day, RG gets off the bus around Masonic and sees this guy who is genuinely crazy. He follows the cat to make a study. Mimes the cat's moves. Repetitive jerking and twisting. Then sits down on a bench for some chitchat, just to get a sense of the speech patterns.

He asks, "What's your secret, man? What keeps you going this way?" Turns out it's meth. Keeps you awake forever until you die with your eyes open.

RG puts an order in, kicks off the habit of sleep for a week. Plays Janis over and over like a mantra till her voice permeates his skin and he's picking at it. One minute he's sweet as honey; next he's a monster. Eyes get dilated out to the rims. Practices his mimes and jerky moves to match the crazy cat. Makes his way into the nearest military recruitment office. Time to test out this guerilla's answer to meth-od acting. Gonna scare the shit outta those military fuckers. You want My Lai? You want a gook infiltrator? I'm hip! Here I come! I'M YOUR MAN! I'M YOUR SOLDIER! I'M YOUR G.I. JOE! I'M YOUR GREEN BERET! I'M YOUR KILLER!

The Black Panther Party hereby offers to the National Liberation Front and Provisional Revolutionary Government of South Vietnam an undetermined number of troops to assist you in your fight against American imperialism.

—Huey P. Newton
August 29, 1970

2: I Am a Brother

If you see me walking down the street
And I start to cry each time we meet
Walk on by, walk on by

—*Dionne Warwick*

"What am I doing in the heart of the Soviet with a mad-assed Chinaman like you?"

Good question. RG could be the firecracker that kicks off the war, unhinges the split. Causes an international malfunction. But shit, don't let it happen until they're on the right side of the line. Didn't they agree to go with Albania?

Panther fiddles with the stickers on a pack of Russian cigarettes. Manages to coax one up for himself, then offers up another to RG.

What does RG know about Russian revisionism? "I don't know what's Albania. Where the hell is it? That shit confuses me. We got our own problems to take care of in the belly of the beast: Chinatown, Amerika."

But isn't that the point? It's the spark thing. RG produces the match, but Panther wants to be the spark. What was he doing two days after MLK was shot? He was trying to trigger the revolution. Now he's wandering the international scene in exile, aiming for the spark long distance. When he gets to Vietnam, he'll arrange to free American POWs in exchange for Panther POWs: Huey P. Newton and Bobby Seale.

He rubs his pharaoh's chin. "Supposed to be Akagi here."

Now Akagi, he knows his political shit, the correct line through Albania and so forth, but he's caught up with the bullshit trying to free Huey. Taking care of business. How long Akagi been corresponding with Robert F. Williams? First from Cuba, then from Peking. It was Akagi said it was too bad the ministers were going to miss Brother Robert, who's gone from China by the time they arrive.

Panther points at RG. "Akagi recommended you. Said Asians got to go to China. If we don't bring you, we got no credibility."

"How come you let that Japanese Akagi into the Black Panthers? You didn't let us in."

Now that's a story.

This story's got to be told with Dionne's mellifluous voice wafting through those uneven teeth and walking on by. Get you in the mood for growing up in West Oakland. How many kids like little Mo Akagi walk with their folks out past the barbed wire of American concentration camps like the one at Tule Lake in 1945? Walk into the can at age five and get paroled at age nine. Find themselves on the other side, but it's still the desert. Got to trek on back to the cities to find out if there's still a house, still a business, still some possibility for a future in the American landscape. West Oakland's still the same ghetto. Before the war Akagi family had a noodle shop, but that's all gone. Old man died a broken heart in Topaz when his son went No-No and left for Tule. Future dried up in the desert. Mo's the grandson, but what does he know of that? Raised in his early years in dusty wooden barracks, shitting on communal pots and running free between guard towers. What's West Oakland but another concentration camp? Covenants don't let you out. Difference is that Mo leaves his house on Twenty-sixth and Poplar, he's got to fight his way back and forth to school. Gets in a fight with this punk kid.

What kinda name is Mo?

How's he gonna explain? If he's at the Buddhist Japanese school, he's Momotaro. If he's going for jujitsu, maybe it's Mo-kun or Mochi. If he's at the West Tenth Methodist for Sunday school, he's Moses.

Punk kid and Mo work their baby fists into battering machines. Go at it like fools. Turns out punk kid's name is Huey Percival. Huey P. Newton. Like Alfred E. Neuman. Shit. Who you boxing for the worst name on the block? This here's Mo Bettah. Both live on the wrong side of the tracks. Got to stick together. In time, got to run with gangsters, get their reversible silk jackets, and fight over the ladies. Line up with bats and knives and go at it. Goddamn bloody mess. Turn eighteen and it's time to use those fighting skills against a real enemy: Communism. Hey Mo, the buddies come around to send him off to the army. Kill a Commie for me, will ya? Akagi was going to set the family story straight; real heroes were the 442nd, not the No-No kind like his dad. Got to do right by the nation. But Korean War is over, and Vietnam hasn't started. Training for the war that was and could be. Who'da thought it was going to be back in his own backyard? West Oakland.

"So they go back. So what?" RG shakes off Dionne's reverie and acts miffed.

But back up, brother. There's more. So Akagi gets out of the army and takes his G.I. points to college. It's 1964. Free Speech at Berkeley. Starts reading. Everybody's reading Marx. What's this communism he's been fighting to protect the homeland? Meets up with another old buddy from the days who's back from the same stint in the military. He's making use of the G.I. bill too. It's Bobby Seale. Then there's David Hilliard. Lived two blocks down. Huey was around Thirty-fourth.

"No shit." Puffs a donut into the air.

One day, they all check into the Muslim Temple around Third Street and get ready to join up with Elijah Muhammad. But wait, you got to give up smoking, drinking, and women. Can you live on sweet potato pies? Someone says: I could give up women, but not smoking! Brothers reconnoiter. News is, Malcolm's moving out anyway. Do the Muslim thing minus the religion plus the politics.

Akagi's at UC Berkeley, so he's the minister of education. Builds a curriculum. They all got to study up. It's Marx, Frantz Fanon, Malcolm X, Che Guevara, and Robert F. Williams. But what's this Cultural Revolution People of China thing? If there's a black thing, what about a yellow thing? That's a lotta colored people marching to the revolution. Akagi checks out China Books in San Francisco for some research.

He's remembering the army with these little easy-to-read books with everything you need to know: your rank, your duties, the Geneva Convention. Keep that baby in your breast pocket. Could be it'll even stop a bullet to your American heart. This little red book: *Quotations from Chairman Mao Tsetung* looks just like it. Buys out China Books. Then goes looking for a wholesale distributor. Finds out Canada has diplomatic relations with the PRC. Sends a Canadian friend to the Vancouver dock to pick up the shipments and smuggles them into Berkeley.

You know the rest. Sell those thirty-cent red puppies for a dollar each to the boujwah Berkeley students at Sather Gate. Get your *Little Red Book*! Pretty soon the whole campus walking on by with their pocket-sized Maos.

And the brothers? Making their money to finance the Party. First off, it's a business proposition, but hey, check this out! Page 88: *The People's War.* Page 99: *The People's Army.* Page 170: *Serving the People.*

Armed with Mao's Thought, Chinese People are Invincible—
Down with Soviet Revisionist Social-Imperialism!

—Eldridge Cleaver
The Black Panther
March 23, 1969

3: I Am a Warrior

There's not a man today
Who could take me away from my guy
(whatchu say?)

—*Mary Wells*

To make a long story short, that's why Brother Akagi's bonafide.

"How come nobody knows that story?"

"We keep our network confidential."

"That's not it. It's because the yellow brother's invisible."

Panther shrugs. Could be good. Kung fu invisible. Could be bad. Fuk fu invisible. "Days I wish I was invisible."

Goes into his suitcase, pulls out his tape recorder. Pries open the battery door and pulls out an alternative battery. He's been saving this, but now's the time for some relaxation. This shit's cultivated by farmers with turbans on rocky mountainsides and transported along a Mediterranean trade route, the old spice road, know what I mean? Exile in Algiers has to come with appropriate medication.

Panther continues the storytelling. "If I recall, you never read Mao before the Panthers turned you on."

RG grins. "We were just street gangsters. Yellow kids with no math genes."

"How did you hook up with the Panthers anyway?"

Now that's another story.

Black-yellow connections go back. Deeper than Mao. Some Asians got a little red book; others got Little Red Riding Hood. Now she's been serving the people for some time.

"Hmmm." Panther takes a Swiss knife and commences to extract some shavings.

How many Chinatown girlfriends got themselves Panther dates? Whole group of them: Leway Girls. Legitimate Way. Girls cross the bridge to Oakland, and the brothers reciprocate and go Leway. Hang out on Jackson under the shadow of the I-Hotel at their Chinatown pool hall, swapping looks over the soda fountain of long life and trying to beat the odds at pinball. It's about broadening horizons, taking the Third World to heart. International understanding while they get some sweet satisfaction from those black boys in their black turtlenecks and black jackets. Got to push the fingers through those spongy naturals. Pull away the heavy leather with those *Free Huey* fist buttons and set aside the weapons. Sweet satisfaction from those radical sisters who set you straight about the Suzie Wong stereotype. Oh yeah, set you real straight. Are you ready to mess with such sweetness? Gingerly. Don't you know? You dancing slow to "My Guy," but turns out she's packing.

Takes you to a basement trapdoor in the linoleum floor, leads to the Chinatown underground. You thought it was a myth, but Leway's taken the myth down to a new level. Cold shock of turned earth and rat piss and something acrid, like it's smoldering. It's deep enough you can stand upright. She pulls the string on a measly lightbulb. You in a long tunnel grave that stretches into a shooting range. You see the shovels discarded on one end. Beer bottles and cigarette butts, discarded bits of joints, moldy cartons emptied of their chop suey contents, chopsticks and shit. Who'd come down here to eat? Then you see the arsenal that's lined up against the wall. Pistols and rifles of every carbine and caliber. Bolt-action, high-power, semiautomatic, automatic, ultra-automatic, rapid-fire, military.

She picks up a shotgun, cocks the goddamn thing, points down the long corridor, and *bam!* You look down to the dim end and see Emory's cartoon rendition of a pig blown up to full size, now full of holes. Pick up your own choice of weapon and swap shots with woman warrior. *Bam! Bam! Bam! Bam!* Upstairs the pinballs and pool balls clacking, but floor's so thick, nobody can hear your action below. You raise some smoke and as it settles, she pushes you up to the wall, hikes up her skirt, and you jimmy into her. She rides. Oh, oh. *Bam! Bam!* You say, *baby one more time,* and she says, *no no, got to pick my kid up from the sitter's.* Your hand passes her breasts, and you lick sweet fingers that come away wet. Mama's milk. Gun-toting mama with a babe at her breast.

Woman warrior comes to West Oakland and takes up residence some evenings on Shattuck and Alcatraz with the Panther collective. Nights she's there, she's got to do security—night watch—like everyone else. Put her on the schedule from midnight to four a.m., when nothing's happening. You catch some winks and leave her at the door toting her rifle and doing the rounds every half hour. You sleep pretty because you know this sister's reliable.

Then, it's the day before Thanksgiving in 1968. Pine Street house is a holdout. Entire San Francisco Police Department plus California Highway Patrol stationed outside. Word is, the minister of information is holed up inside. He's not returning to San Quentin. It's not an option. Woman warrior's next to the sisters in the second tier of defense. It's a twenty-four-hour vigil. Guns pointed out at the guns pointed in.

Is America going to have a Class War or a Race War? The fascists have already declared war upon the people. Will the people as a whole rise up to meet this challenge with a righteous People's War against those fascist pigs, or will Black people have to go it alone, thus transforming a dream of interracial solidarity into the nightmare of a Race War?

—Eldridge Cleaver
International Section, B.P.P.
Algiers, Algeria
March 2, 1970

4: I Am a Crusader

Stop! in the name of love
Before you break my heart
Think it over
Think it over

—*Diana Ross*

That's the night the Panther makes his escape. He does not stop in the name of love. He does not have to think it over. He is never there on Pine Street. Never does his scheduled talk at UC Berkeley. Long gone. Standoff was a sitting decoy. When word comes down he's across the border, West Oakland breathes a long sigh. How did RG know for sure the yellow sister was there risking her neck? Who can be sure? Think it over. Down the line, who will be left to tell the story?

Panther's stuffing a pipe with a sweet concoction. Gives it a light. Ooowee! That's potent product. Put it out before the KGB gets here! RG jumps up, fans the air. Too bad they're not Cuban cigars. Castro's finest might be justifiable. Speaking of which . . .

Everyone was reading Robert F. Williams's *Negroes with Guns.* He's the man. He's in Cuba transmitting *Radio Free Dixie.* Akagi finds a postal system to his box in Havana. It's complicated, but he gets the word to Brother Robert: Salutations! The Black Panthers for Self-Defense are opening for business. Then one day, Akagi gets a package by way of Peking: 1 Tai Chi Chang, Peking, China. Got a stamp of a Vietnamese shooting down a U.S. warplane. It's *The Crusader,* Williams's newsletter. Do you know how many copies you can smuggle if they're printed on rice paper? Slip a hundred of those papers under your jacket and distribute them on the Third World picket line at UC Berkeley. Check it out. Brother Robert's in China, sitting at the left hand of Mao.

Fifty percent Malcolm. Fifty percent Williams. Mix and stir into a magic brew. Poof. You got a Black Panther. Huey's got the plan and the ten points, but who knows about guns? Bobby and Akagi. They turn the thing into a military operation. It's better than religion. Akagi can identify any weapon through his binoculars, take apart an M-1 blindfolded. He's got a Chinatown supplier with a good price. It's like shopping in another country—access to every kind of gun, shape, and caliber. Pretty soon he's Field Marshal. You gotta train with Akagi, or you don't get your weapon. Think it over. Trains the brothers who die.

Panthers walk on Sacramento; it's national news on prime time, and overnight there's forty-three Black Panther Party chapters nationwide. Telegrams come in daily; this one's from this place called Reed College, wants to form a chapter.

Huey asks, "Akagi, you're a college man. What's this Reed College?"

Akagi thinks about it. "College for geniuses, but the crazy John Reed kind."

"Check it out."

Reed is honky territory out in Portland, Oregon. Shit. Could be a bunch of black brothers infiltrated behind the lines. How'd they get into Reed? They're letting colored people into fancy places everywhere. Affirmative action my ass! Could be a hoax. A trap! Akagi gets three of his best men. Drive up to Oregon and do calisthenics and shoot up the desert on the way. Take a pilgrimage detour to Tule Lake and shoot at the leftover guard towers. Get to Reed in prime condition—trained and mean and looking sharp. Field jackets, black berets, shades, rifles. March into the designated coffee shop for the meeting. At attention.

Who walks in? It's one black dude. Just one.

"Where're the others?"

"It's just me."

"Just you?"

"Just me."

It's a chapter of one! A fucking chapter of one! Break my heart!

Akagi could lose it, but stop! He tugs nervously at his leather gloves, then faces Reed off and says, "Name the ten-point program!"

I call upon the workers, peasants, revolutionary intellectuals, enlightened elements of the bourgeoisie and other enlightened personages of all colours in the world, white, black, yellow, brown, and so forth, to unite against the racial discrimination practiced by U.S. imperialism and to support the American Negroes in their struggle against racial discrimination.

—Mao Tse-tung
August 8, 1963

5: I Am a Martial Artist

R-E-S-P-E-C-T
Find out what it means to me
—*Aretha Franklin*

"So, what you're saying is we shoulda sent a telegram saying we set up a chapter in Chinatown."

"Right on. Coulda sent a field marshal and three guards around to test your knowledge. Saved everybody some time."

Instead, Legitimate Way girls take up with some Panther brothers, slip into the Great Star Theater across the street on Jackson, and do some serious necking and feeling during the kung fu features. *Wap. Eeow. Aiiieeeee!* Now, between the kissing sweeter than honey, it must have occurred to the brothers that the Legitimate guys, not to mention the girls, might be hiding some serious talents. Whip out fists of fire, deadly kicking. Rip off the shirts and start swinging nunchukus and spitting poison darts and daggers. Shit. Whose sister are you, anyway? You get those dirty looks from the villagers on the street. Leways are bold, showing their rebel colors, doing it to piss off their families, shock the old guys from the Six Companies. Same sisters with crushes on the cable car drivers, riding the cars to draw attention from those big black men in uniform.

Turns out Legitimate Ways is made of mostly the Chinatown-born kids who are getting their butts kicked by the foreign-born. Call them FOBS, Fresh Off the Boat, but they call themselves the Wah Ching. Gangster kids hanging out doing the dirty shit for the tongs, petty extortion, illegal fireworks, gambling, drugs. Wah Ching working their territory, doing their hustle, training with their sifu. Independent of their origins, both Leways and Wah Ching in and out of juvie and the Log Cabin. Some Wah Ching move over to Legitimate, push cues at the pool hall. Pool hall is a legitimate business. Give the gangsters jobs to keep them outta trouble. War on Poverty money forked over to lease the place. But twice a day, police raid the hall, take down names and descriptions. Stop the brothers with their fucking warrants for *someone on the street between the movie house and the pool hall.* Is it you? You all look the same, anyway. Depending, "protect and serve" can mean to trip, kick, box, and club. Part of their gangster control program, they say. It's pure harassment. Liberal capitalist venture is screwed from the start.

White Russian kid from the Potrero hangs out with Leways like he's Chinese. Maybe he is. Speaks more Chinese than the ABCs. Friend of RG from his hippy days. Crosses the Broadway/Columbus border daily. Supplies the brothers with sources for quality drugs. Parks his hopped-up 'Cuda on the street and works in the stolen parts. Mechanical genius. Political genius, too. He's saying, take note, police brutality is under control in Oakland. Got to follow the path of the Panthers. Got to get the police off their backs. Running out of fooling. It's not about give the lumpen jobs. It's about organize the lumpen. RG and the Russian put together a plan. Notice when the black brothers come around, the Wah Ching stay at bay. That's what we gotta do; we gotta join up. It's a war, anyway. Got to get some R-E-S-P-E-C-T.

Not enough to be Wuxia heroes. One-armed swordsmen. One-armed boxers. Fighting at a disadvantage. And it's just a lost arm! Check out a history of disadvantages. How many Wuxia heroes promise themselves to a life of nonviolence and have to give it up? It's an impossible dream. Brutality on the street. The only thing the brothers know is how to fight their way through. The Wuxia got one thing. Got a philosophy about fighting. That's what the Panthers offer. Study up. Revolution's coming. Pick up the gun.

Panther's getting antsy. What he wants. What he needs. Needs what's in that pipe. Goes to the door and peeks down the hall. Nobody there at this hour. It's dead.

RG looks skeptical. Aren't they used to surveillance? Aren't these the Stalinists who invented it?

Panther's got an idea. He's got a bottle of perfume for his honey, bought in Paris. "Smell this stuff."

Oof.

That's why women use just a little bit on the wrist. Molecules move through the air and whip it to you. Yeah, it was expensive; bought it to impress the French lady at the glass counter. Revolutionaries have style, why not? O.K., let's sacrifice this boujwah shit. Buy the baby something else along the way. Give her her profits when he gets home. Empty out that silver caviar bowl and pour this potion out. Set it up near the door for full effect. "Gimme your lighter." That's the spark. Test the alcohol content like it was a Molotov cocktail. Hey, who was this cat, Molotov? We setting a new standard for his invention. Bringing it back home.

Silver bowl is burning like the eternal flame, set up next to the slit under the door. "O.K., hippie, we got some incense going."

Panther and RG settle back in their chairs, ready to puff up some full flavors.

Meanwhile, the eternal flame is growing. Some of that sweet honey spilled over onto the carpet. Burning up the carpet. Spreading to the door. Flames rising up like it's a tinderbox, and they ain't even holding out against hostile forces. RG sees it from his direction. Spits out his smoke. "Oh, fuck! We got a situation!"

The Lumpen has no choice but to manifest its rebellion in the Universities of the Streets.

—Eldridge Cleaver
The Black Panther
June 27, 1970

6: I Am the Third World

I left a good job in the city
Working for the man every night and day
. . .
Big wheel keep on turning
Proud Mary keep on burning
—*Tina Turner*

But let's leave those brothers in their smoking Moscow hotel room and check out what's happening back in the States.

Listen to the story. It's rolling.

Like I say, Akagi stays behind to take care of business. After three years Huey gets free, but there're dead brothers all across the country. Police raids and shootouts in Oakland, Chicago, L.A., and the Marin County Courthouse. Repression, provocation, conspiracy, purges. Head of the Panthers incarcerated, but the body struggles. By the time it's over, there're thirty-four killed and hundreds imprisoned.

Rally round Bryant and Seventh, Hall of Justice and the San Francisco Jail. Everybody represents: Panthers, La Raza, Venceremos, Los Siete, Soledad, Patriot Party, National Committee to Combat Fascism, plus the significant attorneys for the defendants. But back up: Asian American Community is also represented. Hey, where's the fancy name? Mothers for Mao, Uncle Ho's Nephews, Godzillas, or East is Red? Where's the Red Guard Party? RG missing an historic event. Who comes forward? It's Akagi, surrounded by his guards. Underneath he's a Panther, but if necessary, he's the Asian American Community.

He gets introduced, and the crowd claps. Can he get a rise outta this crowd?

He comes on easy. "Good afternoon, brothers and sisters." Makes adjustments to the microphone.

He looks around at his four guards, nodding at these Asian brothers dressed in fatigues, headbands, sporting shades so you can't tell what's in their sight, folded arms across their chests, ready for any eventuality. No doubt, they're packing. It's a show of force, but he says, reassuring-like, "Ah, don't let the other brothers on the stand put you on any trip. Usually people think that when other brothers come up on the stand, these brothers are here to protect me. Well this is all false, because every brother up here, just like every one of you out there, is so important for our struggle." Some kind of apology because these cats with their fu manchus look mean.

Then he goes into his talk, starting nice and easy. Talks about the Los Siete cats who are in prison awaiting trial for the shooting of a policeman. Talks about the Soledad Brothers on trial for the same shit. Talks about Panthers in the same situation.

Then he says, "See, understand that the Los Siete trial and what's happening to the Soledad Brothers are not isolated incidents. They're just like the practicing of a theory. And dig, this theory is a theory of genocide by the United States government and all their lackeys domestically and internationally. Understand that this theory is not an academic one, dig. It's not even really very heavy, but if I was to articulate this theory it would go like this: *The only good one is a dead one.*"

Lots of grunts of approval on this statement.

He goes on, "We have to understand that this theory is no new thing, see. I think it was this one cat name General Custer, in one of his more sensitive moments, said this in reference to the Native Americans." This is where we get our history lesson. "Now, Goldilocks may have coined this phrase, but see, it was practiced long before he was on the scene. It was like when the first invaders from Europe came and, in quotes, 'discovered' America. Understand, when they first discovered America, they immediately started practicing this theory. Initially it was focused against the Native Americans, then finally against the Mexican people on the West Coast, and they disguised this theory of genocide as 'manifest destiny,' dig. And toward the black people in the United States, they disguised it as a racist stereotype portraying the black man and the black sister as subhuman persons, and this was the rationale for slavery and their subhuman treatment. Once again, an example of the theory of genocide of the United States."

But he don't stop there with his theorizing. He keeps going, and this next part brings the Asians into the general picture. He's got to do that, so he continues, "Now toward the Chinese people, see, this theory was disguised another way. It was called 'Yellow Peril,' and that was the rationale for exclusion acts. That was the rationale for forcing Chinese people to group together into Chinatowns, and the reason they did that was for self-defense, if you can dig that. And understand, against the Japanese people in more contemporary history, they had the same theory of genocide, and the game they ran on the Japanese people, when they put over a hundred thousand Japanese Americans into camps, was that they put them in camps 'for their own protection,' if you can relate to that." This is where he gets some heavy applause and shouts of encouragement from the crowd.

He pauses, then says, "Now see, understand, what we have to realize is that this same theory is being practiced today. Man, the same theory is happening in Chicago, San Francisco, Kent State, Jackson State, and definitely internationally in terms of the Indochina War and the genocide over there. And understand that the sheep's clothing for this theory now is the disguise of 'law and order.'"

"See, what people need to understand is that we come together today to show Third World solidarity and unity for political prisoners within the United States. Now, I can dig that's why we're here, but you have to understand that when Los Siete walks free of the San Francisco County Jail, when the Soledad Brothers leave the 'gladiator school' (what it's more affectionately called), then we will be free. See, because when the political prisoners walk free of the institutions that bind them, then we will walk free of the institutions that bind us, institutions like the credit agency our parents owe money to, institutions like the Bank of America, institutions like the system that asks us to give six years of our lives to Uncle Sam." Twist your mind around that: we're all some kind of prisoner.

So he's tying it up see, but he's got to include the women, the feminist position. So he continues with, "the same institution that perpetuates the thought that builds and works on male chauvinism," but then he wants to make the big point, so he points back to the jail behind him and he says, "the same institution that built that motherfuckin' piece of shit!" Now this brings the roar of approval from the crowd because finally he's rolling his nice and easy talk around to the hard and rough. And that's what the crowd is wanting. They are motherfuckin' mad.

When they calm down a bit, he goes into his denouement: "Now in order to change this thing, brothers and sisters, in order to make things right, we have to do something, make a real big change."

Now this is where he's going to show off his Marxist take, but he wants to bring it down to the level of common understanding. Make it plain to the people. "Now I'm not too intellectual or academic, but I heard that this thing is like where the quantitative change turns into the qualitative change, or where the thesis and the antithesis struggle and therefore make the synthesis."

But the brother's got to show his Asian colors, where it's going to relate to yellow folks. So he says, "Now, philosophically, dig, I just put it one way: when this change comes, it will be when the yin turns into the yang."

And for the final touches, to prove he's into Malcolm: "And to put it into the words of the people, dig, this is when we will return the power to its rightful owner, and that rightful owner is the people, and we will get that power by any means necessary! ALL POWER TO THE PEOPLE!"

Asian guard-brothers on stage know the grand finale, and all the fists pump up.

On the subject of racism, Marxism-Leninism offers us very little assistance. In fact, there is much evidence that Marx and Engels were themselves racists.

—Eldridge Cleaver
The Black Panther
June 6, 1970

7: I Am a Revolutionary

I know you're no good for me
But free of you I'll never be
Nowhere to run to, baby
Nowhere to hide

—*Martha & The Vandellas*

RG and the Panther running around pulling the blankets off the beds, throwing them at the door to snuff that fire out. Flames flying off that door like it's tinder wood. When they get the flames down, RG gets some glasses of water and tosses them to cool down the egress. Outta curiosity, opens the door and checks the hallway. It's still the same empty hallway, somewhat smoked up, but no one's running out trying to save their lives. Coulda been a major disaster. Shit, coulda been the spark. But all the Moscovites tucked in and sleeping pretty.

"What're we going to say about the door?"

"Damn cigarettes. Need to quit the habit."

"Shitload of smoke in here."

"Windows don't open."

"Where's that pipe?"

"Yeah, after that, we got to relax."

Pipe lights up with its customary stink. If a fire don't arouse nobody, what's a little stink?

RG takes a drag and speculates. "Never thought I'd ever come to Russia."

"That's a fact."

"Used to think the whole world existed inside Chinatown."

"I never had that problem. Whole world was always out there." Panther grabs the air like there's bars and juts his chin forward.

RG and the Panther hold their breaths, then pause to consider how this thing—the whole world—works. How you gonna catch a thing like that in your mind? Che got on his motorcycle. Mao did his Long March. Malcolm did his hajj to Mecca. Now RG and the Panther doing it by socialized modern transportation. In search of the Third World. Could practically fly into every Third World war zone and get a handle on the national question. What's it gonna come to? Revelation on the revolution at the end of the road.

RG walks to a window you can't pry open. Looks out on that dark sky and observes the moon over the USSR. Moon this side of the Earth should be red, but it's all the same. What about that sputnik dog circling around? What kind of dog conclusions does he come up with? How do Russian dogs say *bow-wow*? Or Neil Armstrong putting his big boot into the moon for mankind? Shit. They're always trying to colonize someplace. Colonize the moon, if anybody was there. Get this, same day Neil and Buzz walk the moon, Panthers're in a revolutionary conference to build a united front to combat fascism. Advocate the revolutionary struggle to abolish capitalism and introduce socialism to the USA. Stepping and leaping for mankind.

But let's get back to the storytelling about how some Chinatown street gang makes a radical turn. Back to the revolutionary war front at home. Pass the pipe, and hunker down with jet lag.

RG obliges. "So everything changes in the year of the rooster." Meaning last year, 1969. Leway brothers come to the realization that the liberal capitalist venture is jive. What's legitimate if you still get beat up by the pigs? What's legitimate if the charges are trumped up? You got nowhere to run, unless it's Vietnam. Time to stand up to the bastards. Become the defending force at home.

Come Chinese New Year, Leway contingent splits off to become the Red Guards. Set themselves up to do security for the youth festival on Waverly. Waverly's the heart of Chinatown. Every year, some white carnival comes in, closes off Waverly, and takes it over. This year, Red Guards get smart. Put out a call for every Chinatown group to put up a booth, make your own money, and keep it in Chinatown.

Red Guard security duty is serious. Brothers on watch on the roofs and off the balconies. Their commander is the minister of defense; he got his position by virtue of his size. You know Goldfinger's Oddjob? Big Oriental cat with the steel hat? Yeah, that's him. He's the biggest, baddest brother among them. You see him patrolling the fair and watch the crowd part around him.

Some drunk tourist is playing with firecrackers. Like he's in a foreign country whooping it up. Frolicking idiot's tossing packs into the crowd like popcorn and watching the folks disperse. A little kid is crouching to pick up a fallen toy when the crackers hit the pavement near her face. Suddenly her face is singed in soot. She screams. Her mother screams.

Oddjob Minister rushes over, picks the tourist off the ground and throws him. Pigs patrolling the event as well, looking for an incident. This is it. Two of them come to the rescue to protect and serve the drunken tourist. Ignore the mother and her child screaming for help. Trounce on Oddjob, pulling him away from the tourist, try to get him down. Try to get Oddjob down? That's a fucking job for twenty! Tosses them off like flies. By now the rest of brothers are alerted. Red Guard comes out of everywhere with every sort of rifle and pistol you can imagine. It's a red army. Pigs are smart. They're outnumbered. They run. They got nowhere to hide.

That night, expecting reprisal, Red Guards station themselves up and down Jackson Street and throw their anti-personnel arsenal—firecrackers and cherry bombs—into the street all night. You know what is all night? Long line of Guards must set off every available firecracker in Chinatown. How many bricks does it take? It's the Great Wall! Who knew you could sustain a battle as long as a celebration? Street's a smoke screen, and the crackling and popping never let up.

Revolutionaries are Monkey Kings; their golden rods are powerful, their supernatural powers far-reaching and their magic omnipotent, for they possess Mao Tse-tung's great invincible thought. We wield our golden rods, display our supernatural powers and use our magic to turn the old world upside down, smash it to pieces, pulverize it, create chaos and make a tremendous mess, the bigger the better!

—Red Guards
Tsinghua University
June 24, 1966

8: I Am the Vanguard

I heard it through the grapevine
Not much longer would you be mine
. . .
People say, believe half of what you see
Oh, and none of what you hear

—*Gladys Knight*

Smoke screen in the Moscow hotel room like a great cloud. RG and Panther sitting in that cloud hearing the past and present converge through a wispy grapevine. Everything gets that clarity when sitting in silence. Smoke thickens to a marbleized liquid substance, and the mind wanders into the future.

The dope proposes the inevitable possibility of change. Everything changing. Everything in flux. Moving on. Supposed to change inevitably from this ism to that ism. Are you going to be there for the revolution? Are you going to be there kicking ass with the vanguard?

These are the days when we get the women to love their lumpen. That's the truth. Panther's today's number one lovin' lumpen. RG could be a fast second. Jail's a badge of courage. You could be Malcolm in the Charleston State Prison or MLK in the Birmingham Jail. How many women fall in love with those prison letters? Baby, baby. Get her one of those prisoners who dream about her every night. Enough to make her lose her mind. Next thing you know, she's toting a gun for you. She's your Mata Hari in a miniskirt with a .22 in her purse. She's the chorus backup for the revolutionary chanting. How come all of Chinatown's plastered with *Free Huey* flyers? She's tacked up every corner of the Chinese ghetto with his face, but what Chinese can relate to that? Still, you got to appreciate that she loves you more.

She's working the telephones at the office, waking up early to cook for the breakfast program, distributing the paper, running day care during the morning and a free school in the afternoons, lifting shit and raising money for the programs, doing political study in the evenings and basic training on the weekends. In between, she's got to be giving you honey, even though you might be getting several honeys. Even though from time to time you lose your mind and put your revolutionary fist in her face. She accepts your weeping apologies because what lumpen can be perfect? Takes time to get your freedom. She's gonna bear it for you. Gonna prove her mama's wrong about you. After all, she's got your babies and another one coming. Producing those power children for the next generation. For the protracted struggle.

But how long's this gonna last? Dope offers up the future: funk wears off. What else you got to offer? By the time it takes you by surprise, you know she's found it all out yesterday. Oh, yes.

So while we're in the purple haze, let's do some storytelling.

Akagi has himself one righteous woman. It's those righteous women you gotta hang on to, but it might not be possible after all. Maybe he met her in a more innocent state, but she's a fast learner. Catches on. Figures out she's got a place in the scheme of things.

Every night, field marshal takes his ratty briefcase with his personal arsenal out someplace. Leaves her nursing the baby on the home front. She's taking in the situation, and she knows this can't be good, in the final analysis. She's not fooled anymore by all that strutting machismo. She asks, "Where're you going?" Quips, "Going to kill someone?"

He grumbles like, what's this woman know about taking care of business? "Tonight we're packing. That's all. We're packing."

She gives him the eye with the smirk, and he leaves in a huff.

Comes home at night with the same ratty briefcase. She asks like she's distracted from her knitting, "Killed someone tonight?"

He gives her the look. "We was packing is all. Everyone packing."

How many nights she's got to sit home with the baby waiting for the field marshal to return with his ratty briefcase? One night he comes home, finds the door ajar. First time he has to really draw his weapon, kick the door aside, and jump around with his heart in his throat, thinking, what's the door open for? She'd never leave it open in this neighborhood, not at this time of night, not with what's been going down. He searches the house, kicking in the doors, checking every room like he's in enemy territory, snuffing out a sniper. But it's empty, and she's gone.

O.K., so much for the future you could predict. What happens next, and over time? Hasn't happened yet, but you gonna find Akagi renting a room in the I-Hotel with the old Filipino and Chinese bachelors. Nothing strange about that. He's a bachelor too. He's like all the other activists down home with the tenants, working for their rights. Even though he's been purged from the Party, he's not like others to go wash his hands of everything, reject his beliefs. Where's he gonna go anyway? Gonna keep working for the people.

Things take their turn, but the mind is always helped by a little dust. Twinkle dust makes you fly. Steps out on the window ledge of his room on the second floor of the I-Hotel. Believes half of what he sees and none of what he hears. Trouble is, which half, and what does he hear? Looks out on the crowd moving slow and incrementally below. Traffic passing easy on Kearny. Across the street, familiar haunts—liquor store, pool hall, café with the gravy on the rice. Honk of cars and honk of old men coughing up yellow phlegm onto the sidewalk. Ukulele tunes waft up from Tino's Barbershop just below his feet. Muffled sounds from the pool hall—soft clack of the cue balls hitting their mark. Go on, Akagi, take the next step. How much longer would you be mine? Windowsill's a launching pad. Oooweee! This is it. The yin becoming the yang. Take it to next level.

RG's got his mind embracing the yin/yang, but he's gotta admit, "Future looks bleak."

"You forget one thing." Panther wags his finger. "Woman warrior."

All's said and done, women of the lumpen don't come away with nothing. Survivors. They catch their licks, but they're gonna give 'em out too. For the protracted struggle.

Tom: Today's top story: Twenty-six-year-old Angela Davis, the once political philosopher at UCLA who was fired because of her affiliation with the Communist Party USA, was linked to the Marin County Courthouse shootout earlier this week. . . . We have Lisa Cornwaller in California with Governor Reagan. Lisa. . . . Lisa: Thanks, Tom. Governor Reagan, would you consider Angela Davis dangerous?
Reagan: Yes, she is a Communist.

—Channel 45, 6:00 PM News
August 24, 1970

1971: Aiiieeeee! Hotel

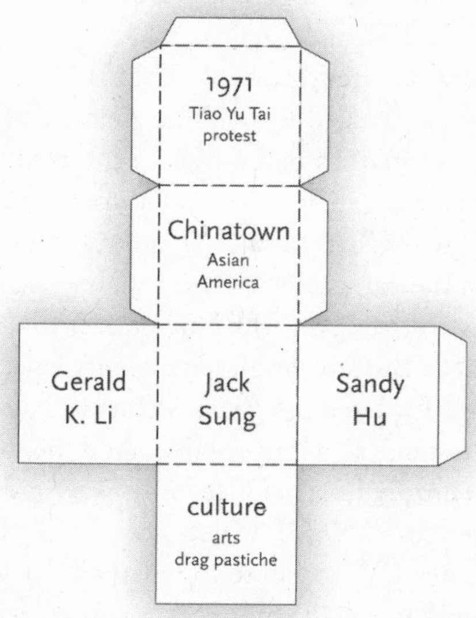

1: Outlaws

Honey, there are *in*laws and there are *out*laws. I will always be an outlaw. How I love my outlaws, all 108 of them. Go skinny dipping with the merry men in the *Water Margin*. Some women look for their men in the zodiac, but I can't work with those limitations: twelve lunar months, twelve-year cycles. What's that? I'm looking at 108 incarnations of the stars. I'm working my way through the first set of thirty-six heavenly heroes right now. After that, there are seventy-two earthly fiends to go. Sure, you get bravery and wealth, but then you get ravage and machinations. Then it's madness and penetration. Give me slaughter, crime, disaster. Give me murder. Swords and axes. Whips and daggers. Give me liberty or give me death!

But let me set up the backdrop for a little talk story as they say. Lately everyone's into this talk story, like the fairy tale was reinvented yesterday.

You know, the Slanted Eye does the light shows for all the Asian troubadours. They infiltrated the Fillmore and got away with psychedelic's secrets: oil and colored water in glass bowls on overhead projectors. Now they project Ho Chi Minh and Chairman Mao over what looks like lava lamps. Do this to a jazz rendition of "East is Red." They have their Kodak slide carousels stacked up with all manner of Asian American photographic subject matter: barbed wired internment camps (sacred shakuhachi accompanying), Chinatown playground (Chinese lute plucking), manongs at the I-Hotel (ukuleles). Now, that's the tame stuff.

So now I slip in the carousel with the outlaws, my Chinese banditos, those killer men with their powerful bare chests, wild hair, fu manchus, and painted grimaces. But stop at number twenty-one. He's the Iron Ox. They call him the Murderer, the Black Whirlwind, with his double-ax action. He's iron, but he's also irrepressible. And the more he drinks, the meaner and more unruly he gets. Get in his way, and he'll hack you to pieces for no reason at all. Once he gets going with the axing, he won't stop till everyone's dead. Who can resist? Slanted Eye gives the oil/blood water combination some pulsating action, and the Black Whirlwind appears and disappears like a bad dream.

Once upon a time . . .

Iron Ox has joined the outlaws up in the mountains. He is a trusted and loyal member of the outlaw band. One day the chief outlaw, Timely Rain, finds Iron Ox at the main gate crying loudly. That's right. A grown man who is also a known for hacking folks in half with his ax is bawling like a baby. It's the thirteenth century. He can cry all he wants.

What is the matter? Iron Ox complains to Timely Rain, "Other outlaws can bring their fathers to our mountain hideout, and some are given permission to visit their mothers. Only I, Iron Ox, am not allowed to see my poor mother, who lives in poverty." Now, I could be wrong, but I see an Oedipal message here, but then these guys are Chinese, not Greek. Let's not get our psychoanalyses and cultures confused, shall we?

Timely Rain thinks about this. "O.K., you can travel to see your mother, on three conditions. One, you must not drink wine along the way. Two, you must go alone, because you always get your companions in trouble. Three, you must not take your axes. Don't get into any trouble, and come back quickly."

Iron Ox doesn't take his trusty axes, but he does arm himself with two swords. Axes? Swords? And you thought these outlaws only used their bare hands!

Along the way he meets a common brigand in a red silk turban with two axes. "Stop!" shouts the brigand, raising his axes. "I am the feared outlaw, the Black Whirlwind. Pay a toll, or I will hack you to pieces!"

Iron Ox scratches his head. *Who is this guy? I am Iron Ox, also known as the Black Whirlwind. Are there two of us?* He looks at his double and shakes his head. It's very confusing. Maybe it's the stupid red turban. He'd better settle this matter. He slaps the fake Black Whirlwind down with his sword and gets ready to kill him. *There, that's better. I must be authentic. That one is fake.*

The fake outlaw trembles and pleads for his life. "Don't kill me! If you kill me, you will kill two of us. I am only impersonating the Black Whirlwind in order to get money to support my poor mother. If I die, so does she!"

"What's this about impersonating me?"

"Normally people run away at the very sound of your terrible name." The fake outlaw trembles, and Iron Ox thinks about this. This sniveling faker could ruin his reputation. He should kill him now. But it's a good thing for the faker that Iron Ox isn't drinking. He thinks about this two-for-one proposition. This fake Black Whirlwind still has some things in common with the real Black Whirlwind. They both have poor mothers. Such a coincidence. Iron Ox lets the fake outlaw go. He says, "Take this money and start a new life with your poor mother." He's feeling generous and nostalgic for his own mother as he watches his fake self run away.

Now he's hungry. Actually he's always hungry. So he continues his travels, finding a farmhouse along the way. He announces to the woman living there, "How about some food?" O.K., no wine. He promised.

She says, "Will a peck of rice do?"

He says, "Three pecks would be better." Look at his size. He's a big guy.

She goes off to cook the rice, and he goes off to the privy to relieve himself. Sitting in the privy, he hears the conversation between the woman and her husband.

"Pssst!" The husband calls her over. He's the fake outlaw who ran away! He tells his wife what's happened, that he lied about a poor mother in order to save his life. Why couldn't he have lied about a poor wife? That would have been closer to the truth.

That's it, thinks Iron Ox. *I've been lied to.* He pulls up his drawers, or whatever Chinese bandits use, stomps out of the privy, draws his sword, and cuts off the faker's head, red silk turban and all.

Meanwhile the wife runs away, but thankfully the rice is cooked. Where're the vegetables and meat? Oh well. Iron Ox settles down and eats three pecks. Then he drags the bloody, headless corpse of the fake outlaw into the farmhouse and torches the whole thing. The fire rages behind him as he walks off.

We could say he walks off into the sunset, but the day's not over. Around five o'clock, Iron Ox comes to his old village and pushes in the door of his old home. There's his impoverished mother. Ma! She says, "Where have you been, my Iron Ox? I have wept so long for you, I have become blind with my weeping." Now that's a guilt trip.

Next thing you know, he scoops up his ma and puts her on his back. It's decided. He's taking this blind woman back to the mountain hideout to live in peace with a band of 108 criminals. He carries her through the back mountain roads until she complains, "I'm dying of thirst."

O.K. Ma. He sets her down by a green boulder in the shade along with his swords and goes off to find water. He finds a stream next to a temple, but the problem is how to bring water back to Ma. This is where being strong and dumb comes in handy. What about that stone incense urn in front of the temple? It should hold a load of water. But first he's got to rip it out of the earth, breaking it from its mortar base. Then after he rips it out, he's got a five-hundred-pound urn to drag to the stream to fill with water, and by the time he gets it filled, he's got a thousand-pound urn to drag back to Ma.

When he gets back to the green boulder, where's Ma? His swords are resting quietly in the grass. It's a little too quiet, and there's a trickle of blood dribbling away from the boulder. Ma! He follows the dribble of blood to the mouth of a cave, where he finds two tiger cubs gnawing on a human leg. Ma's leg! Ma's ripped up, spread out all over the place. Her old clothes and bones and white hair shredded in grotesque pieces everywhere. Ma! Her Iron Ox goes crazy. You've never seen him this mad or this fierce, even in battle. The hairs of his mustache stand out like porcupine quills. He picks up the tiger cubs and slashes them to pieces. But that's the easy part. Now he has to fight the tigress and the tiger. He brings her down with his dagger and him with his sword. Now there are human parts and bloody tiger all over. He wanders around weeping, trying to figure out what's Ma and what's not. He gathers up her pieces and buries them behind the temple. Exhausted, he finally falls asleep at her grave. Maybe there's a lesson in this, but it's difficult to say.

O.K., you think the story ends there, but it doesn't. So the next day Iron Ox wakes up. Ma's dead, but he's still her Iron Ox with a big appetite. He's got to find himself some food. He runs into five hunters who wonder about the blood on him. "What happened to you?"

"I had to kill four tigers who killed my ma."

The hunters are really impressed. Four tigers? "We've been trying to kill those beasts without success for years." Who is this guy? They bring him to the house of an unscrupulously wealthy bureaucrat to get some food and a change of clothing. They celebrate the heroic killing of the four tigers and eat and drink and eat and drink. Iron Ox has forgotten his promise to Timely Rain not to drink wine. But then, poor Ma is dead anyway. Pretty soon he's one drunk whirlwind. As he falls into a stupor, he doesn't see the wife of the fake outlaw he beheaded hiding in the wings.

So of course when he wakes up, he's a captive. A brave police captain with fifty policemen have come to make his arrest. They bind him up in ropes and take him away. It looks like the end of the line for the Black Whirlwind. The real one, this time.

Meanwhile, Timely Rain has foreseen possible mishaps in Iron Ox's plan to visit his mother. He's sent an outlaw scout to tail him. Sure enough, Iron Ox, guarded by fifty police, led by a valiant and courageous police captain, is marched into town. What a commotion! What to do?

The outlaw scout rushes to greet the captain and his police with a contingent of servile servants and gifts of meat and wine—just a small token of local appreciation for their gallantry. The brave captain dismounts his horse. He is much too polite to refuse a small toast, but sips only a drop. Now there's a man on duty.

"Please," the outlaw scout plies the captain. "Your men are hungry. Let them enjoy the wine and drink."

Iron Ox can't help himself. He ate and drank last night, but this is the next day. "Hey," he roars, struggling behind his ropes. "What about me?

Don't I get some wine and meat? What are you feeding them for?" *Furthermore,* he begins to say, *why aren't you saving me? You are one of us, an outlaw like me.*

But the outlaw scout cuts him off. "You," he sneers, "are a mere criminal who will soon be dead!"

At that moment, the policemen begin to fall limply to the ground, tossing their cups of wine and bowls of meat. All fifty of them pass out. The brave captain falls away too. It's a trick as old as the thirteenth century.

Iron Ox bursts from his ropes and grabs the nearest sword. First he kills the unscrupulously wealthy bureaucrat. That's a messy but deserved death for a man who's spent his career extorting the people. This must be why Chairman Mao loves the outlaws. Then Iron Ox cuts open the stomachs of the five hunters who couldn't kill the four tigers in the first place. Then he slashes the throat of the wife of the fake outlaw. Worthless woman who couldn't provide vegetables and meat with three pecks of rice, and then has the audacity to turn him in for beheading her husband. Finally, he battles all fifty policemen, even though they are drugged and useless fighters. He cuts them all down in the prime of their youth. Everyone is lying dead in big pools of blood and gore by the roadside.

Only the brave police captain remains. He is known as the Black-Eyed Tiger. He wakes up to battle the Black Whirlwind. They fight for hours in seven bouts. Finally, the Black-Eyed Tiger is convinced that his career in the police force is ended. The spectacle of carnage is all around him. He joins the outlaws, marching away with Iron Ox toward a destiny mandated by the heavens.

And honey, that's just one outlaw story. There're 107 more.

2: Theater of the Double Ax

So honey, what's all this boohooing over masculinity? Boohoo. I've been weeping so long, I'm going to go blind. A lot of good that will do. You'll probably leave me dehydrated next to some green boulder and let mad tigers gnaw on my private parts and eat out my heart. Eat my heart out! But baby, I'm by your side, questing the same quest for the Asian outlaw. Any man who can kill fifty policemen, five tiger hunters, one lousy bureaucrat, and one tossed-in woman in one paragraph has my congratulations. Now that's literary massacre.

Oh, I'm in perfect agreement. This is a war. You've made your declaration. The pen is mightier than the sword. It's your hatchet, your ax, and you've got two of them, one in each hand. You're ambidextrous. Oooo, ambidextrous. I should know. You want to grind this ax. I'll grind it for you. Oh no, don't you let them talk about how poetry is for faggots. You might have long nails, but they're for playing your guitar. O.K., you might be a faggot, doing flamenco with Lorca, but this is still a man's job. Most importantly, let's get some tongue action in there. Since when did they lop it off too? That's right, they never did. It's all metaphorically speaking, and only you can lick those metaphors. Time to wag that thick honey tongue of yours, translate all those grunts and gutturals to the page. Aiiieeeee!

AX I

Characters

PA (paper name: AH GEE; real name: SUNG CHIANG), *owner of a Chinese delicatessen and father of five sets of Siamese twins:*

CHARLIE CHAN and #1 SON
MAO and CONFUCIUS
GREEN HORNET and KATO
CAPTAIN KIRK and MR. ZULU
FU MANCHU and DRAGON LADY

Place

Asian America (where's that?)

Time

1971

Now, it's just possible you'd prefer to read the original dramatic play in all its scenes and acts, hack out the middlewoman as it were, and you are perfectly free to do so. But I'm all for reading the reviews and the CliffNotes, watching the trailers, and making use of any shortcuts available. If a play is any good, my opinion is that you ought to be able to strip it down and dress it all back up. So let me strip this down for you.

Pa is a longtime Californ. That's right. This great general of the outlaws is really Sung Chiang, hiding out in America using a paper name. This is the great conspiracy: 108 outlaws snuck through Angel Island using paper names. Pa's Ah Gee cover is that he's the owner of a third-generation delicatessen that's been hanging slabs of red barbequed pork, roasted ducks, and soy sauce chickens from their necks for almost a century. Similarly, his band of outlaws is scattered across Gold Mountain pretending to be hardworking laborers—pressing laundry, firing up woks, busing tables, picking asparagus, shifting locks on railroad tracks. Any day now they'll be called to their heavenly duties, but in the meantime, it looks like they're becoming a gang of old farts.

In Pa's case, he's got a load of kids, a pretty good count—nine sons and one helluva daughter, but this scenario's not without complications. His long-suffering wife gave birth to five sets of twins and finally gave up the ghost with the last labor of love. Discovering that she'd finally produced a daughter was a brief moment of joy followed by a broken heart upon learning that, once again, she'd birthed an attached set. Pa doesn't mince his words; he says, "My beautiful wife, your ma. You *(points at Fu Manchu and Dragon Lady)* born. She take a second look, scream *AIYA!* And die." A widower with five sets of American-born twins. My my. He's in deep cover, but is it worth the quintuple headache?

The stage directions for representing Siamese twins are vague. Actors might share a pant leg or be drawn together in a constant embrace with appropriate costuming. Clever use of acrobatics might produce grotesquely comic attachments. This might be a director's nightmare, but the playwright insists on the visual possibilities of the circus—an Asian freak show. As I always say, it's best to use your imagination.

But use your imagination to what end? What's the point of this circus of Siamese twins fathered by a hapless outlaw? Come to America, and your children all come out hyphenated. Half this–half that. Nothing whole. Everything half-assed. And it's more complicated than that. One half trying to be the other half and vice versa. As they say, duking out the dialectics. Working through schizophrenia and assimilation. Poor man. These kids drive him nuts. He's taught them everything they know, but still they have no respect. They think they're supposed to be free in Asian America.

Pa commiserates with a customer.

CUSTOMER. These kids all sneaking around with split personalities. What they call it? Identity crisis.

PA. Ha! *(unhooks skewered roast duck and tosses it on the chop block)* Think you got problems!

CUSTOMER. Where did this second personality come from?

PA. What? *(picks up cleaver, slits open duck, and dumps out soy sauce marinade)* Who not split? Every paper son split in two memories. Now whose fault that?

CUSTOMER. Who knows who is fault? But they blaming us.

PA. *(brings cleaver down on duck neck;* shwack!) Who?

CUSTOMER. Kids. Blaming us. We don't set good example. Continue to live like Chinese in America.

PA. Whatsa matter that? *(cleaves duck in half;* shwack!)

CUSTOMER. Gets them confused. Don't know if they coming or going.

PA. That's it! *(waves cleaver around)* I get them coming and going. *(leaves, marching off with cleaver)*

CUSTOMER. Hey, where you going? What about my duck?

Now I wouldn't want to spoil the end for you. But just think about this lot of thankless sons wallowing in their duplicity. Our hero Pa goes off with his cleaver in search of each paired progeny, and that in itself is a search for Asian America (where's that?).

AX INTERLUDE

Il Piccolo. Coffee house in Chinatown. Council of the Third World Liberation Front. Various representatives of the colonized arrive: blacks, Mexicans, Native Americans, Pilipinos, Chinese, and Japanese. There's some jockeying for position, but they all settle down in chairs around the small tables, adjusting their attitudes for a powwow.

BSU REP. Let's get this meeting started. *(general agreement)* Now what we need to negotiate here is what our demands are in terms of getting faculty for our programs. The way the BSU sees it, each group should propose a number of positions.

LA RAZA REP. Each group should get an equal number of positions.

NATIVE AMERICAN REP. I agree.

LA RAZA REP. It's like, if it's five positions, it's five for blacks, five for Native Americans, five for us, and five for the Asians. That's five times four, twenty positions.

BSU REP. Seems like we should be working from a question of need, dig? Who needs more faculty?

JAPANESE REP. What does that mean? How do you determine need?

NATIVE AMERICAN REP. That's right. We're starting from nothing.

CHINESE REP. I think you miscounted the groups. Look at who's represented here. *(points)* BSU, La Raza, Pilipinos, Chinese, Native Americans, and Japanese. I count six groups. On that plan, we gotta ask for thirty positions.

BSU REP. Now aren't you overstating your presence? I mean, I take it you are all Asians, right? You constitute one group.

Suddenly, a young Chinese Wah Ching gangster type saunters in. He looks around at the strangers congregated and spits out his cigarette.

WAH CHING. What the fuck! Who are these guys? *(He rushes over to a table and pulls out an ax, which is taped to the underside of the table for some reason. Raises the ax and brings it down violently on the table. Proceeds to chop up the table. Everyone jumps out of their seats and backs off.)*

OWNER. Hey, hey! Stop! Stop!

WAH CHING. Fucking! Fucking! Fucking! *(throws the ax into the pile of table pieces and runs off)*

CHINESE REP. *(takes the ax and hands it to the owner)* Don't worry, uncle. We'll pay you back for the table.

OWNER. *(shakes his head and walks away with the ax)*

BSU REP. Shit. Who was that?

PILIPINO REP. Let's get back to this meeting before he comes back.

LA RAZA REP. Comes back?

CHINESE REP. Yeah, comes back with the others.

BSU REP. Others?

CHINESE REP. Don't worry. We'll take care of it.

JAPANESE REP. Where were we?

PILIPINO REP. Remember? We have to ask for positions for six groups.

JAPANESE REP. Who's writing this down?

Now, I always maintain that if you're gonna go to war, you've got to level the playing field. That's the power of theater. That's the theater of war.

What's Il Piccolo? Is it a coffee house? A doughnut shop? A Chinese cake and tea shop that plays Italian opera? Honey it's a stage, a dais for the imagination. It's reproduced in every city on every continent. Gather the intellectuals, the politicos, and the surrounding lowlifes to exchange the necessary drugs that fuel the imagination: caffeine, nicotine, absinthe, opium. So on the one hand, you have the revolutionaries staging their purposeful antics, and on the other, you've got the outlaw literati. Whose idea was that ax conveniently duct-taped to the bottom of the table anyway? What else are they hiding under the table?

As you might know, Jack Sung hangs out at Il Piccolo. He's got his outlaw literati thing going, but it's all boys. Sandy Hu and I come around occasionally with our entourage, strut some femininity into the scene, make eye contact, and leave. We do it to get a rise out of the boys, let them know that we just might be out of their league.

AX II

Characters

SANDY HU *(paper name)*, aka HU SAN *(real name), a Chinese American poetess, actress, and chanteuse who in her other life is the outlaw swordswoman of double swords, the woman of ten feet of steel (two swords, five feet each)*

NARRATOR *(paper name)*, aka LADY MURASAKI *(real name), an Asian American who as a little girl was raised by drag queens and left to fend for herself in the Forbidden City and who sometimes poses as the great novelist who wrote her memoirs of Japanese court life recounting the poetic trysts of the Japanese Casanova, Prince Genji.*

Place

Il Piccolo, Chinatown, Asian America (where's that?)

Time

Twilight, 1971

Sandy Hu and I make our entrance. I should say en-*trance.*

For Sandy: stilettos that puncture the floor with every step. For me: spiked boots. I start with the feet because first you hear us coming. You look for the footfalls and get a load of Sandy's net stockings with dragons running up her thighs, a leather miniskirt that almost reveals her embroidered bikini panties, and a tight-fitting knit turtleneck under an orange brocade Chinois jacket.

Me: sleek leather pants and a low-cut silk blouse just barely covering black lace lingerie, topped with an Argentine fedora with matching ribbon and pheasant panache. Lots of bangles and silver and gold dangling, eyelashes flashing, and lips glossed into a deep shimmer.

Every other woman is looking for the Japonified Pre-Raphaelite Dante Gabriel Rossetti look, but Sandy and I have already been through that stage. Our wardrobe is constantly evolving. Besides, we hate folk singing. All right, so this is an overstatement, but if not us, who?

We survey the scene while our ensemble sets up: bongos, electronic keyboard, and tenor sax. Minimal. Sandy and I sing a capella into the mike to warm up. She does the upper melodies and I provide the alto. We exchange song for breathless poetry, snarls, uhuh uhuh, ouou, and massage the crowd with our jazz voice renditions. Meanwhile the communal jug passes, everybody's lips partaking of a purple swig of Christian Brothers. Blessed be in the name of the Mother, the Daughter, the Sister, and the Lunar Spirit.

> *Enter* HU SAN *and* LADY MURASAKI *from opposite ends of the stage, with enormous matching bags filled with appropriate paraphernalia. They approach a large, empty frame midstage that represents a giant looking glass. Although they are not attired in the same fashion, their steps and movements mirror each other. They spend some time removing and applying lipstick and other makeup, donning various wigs and headgear, stepping into footwear, and shedding and slinking into a variety of silk garments from cheongsam to flowing kimono. This carefully choreographed dance with accompanying music recalls the women of various films and musicals:* Shanghai Express, Flower Drum Song, The World of Suzie Wong, Teahouse of the August Moon, Sayonara, etc.

SUB-SCENE/DANCE I:

HU SAN *and* LADY MURASAKI *dance while wielding thick sabers, taunting and menacing the audience.* HU SAN *and* LADY MURASAKI *move into the audience, and at the point of their sabers, each takes a man hostage. They pull their hostages to the stage and demand that the men lie down on the floor. Perhaps pillows are provided for the heads.* HU SAN *and* LADY MURASAKI *kneel ritualistically to the side and "perform" koto music over their hostages' male bodies.* Pluck. Pluck. Pluck.

SUB-SCENE/DANCE 2:

HU SAN *and* LADY MURASAKI *dance while wielding daggers, again taunting and menacing the audience.* HU SAN *and* LADY MURASAKI *move into the audience, and at the point of their daggers, each takes a second man hostage. They pull their hostages to the stage and demand that they lie facedown on the floor. Perhaps mats and pillows are provided.* HU SAN *and* LADY MURASAKI *remove their footwear—possibly stilettos or tall lacquered clogs—and walk in tiny steps with bare feet over the backs of the hostages' male bodies.* Step. Step. Step.

SUB-SCENE/DANCE 3:

HU SAN *and* LADY MURASAKI *dance a final dance with long samurai swords, taunting and menacing the audience.* HU SAN *and* LADY MURASAKI *swagger into the audience, and at the point of their swords, each takes a third man hostage. They pull their hostages to the stage and demand that they lie down on the floor. Again, perhaps a pillow is provided. Perhaps a quilt. Cutting boards are ritualistically placed on top of each man, perhaps on his chest or stomach or . . . A porcelain plate is placed in the upraised palm of the man's hand. On each cutting board is a slab of raw tuna. In a final dramatic dance with swordplay,* HU SAN *and* LADY MURASAKI *bring down their swords to cut the fish.* Slice! Slice! Slice!

And honey, don't forget the drumroll and the clanging cymbals. *Hyah! Hyah! Hyoooooouh!* Of course I always whisper into my man's ear to keep him calm through the whole ordeal: *It's all right, baby. You know I'd never really hurt you.* And at the end, it's *scoop!* with the tip of my samurai sword to his proffered plate. Like Benihana: *shwap!* A subtle splash of soy sauce and a dab of hot wasabi. You know, I always feed my man oh so delicately with a piece of that raw business. I might use chopsticks, or I just might use my bare fingers.

3: Liang Shan Po, California

Now, as Pearl Buck tried to make clear, all men are brothers once they are orphaned. And once a man is orphaned, he is free to create himself, to be self-made. Orphaned brothers are free to reformulate their loyalties, wresting brotherly power and territory from emperors, usurpers, usurers, priests, and bureaucrats. And while they're at it, they've taken Gold Mountain. Let La Raza have Aztlán; we've taken the entire mother lode, crisscrossed by transcontinental railroads.

The following story takes place in the Gold Mountain hideout of Liang Shan Po, California, where a boy, one day to become the great outlaw leader, is being raised by a poor white couple.

The boy saw the lizard slide from the shadows beneath a clump of brush and scamper across the road, making a swishing trail across the dusty surface. He ran forward and pounced like a cat and missed, his chin hitting the dirt. He spit away the grit stuck to his lower lip and continued his pursuit, scuttling like the lizard and pushing off from his bare toes. The lizard was headed for a higher perch in the old pine. On the third try, he grasped at the tail before the lizard scaled the tree, snatching hard. He felt the wiggling tail between his fingers and excitedly drew his prey to eye level, the eye level of a five-year-old. The appendage twitched, then hung there, eventually lifeless without its body. He looked up to see the attenuated lizard scamper higher into the knotty bark and dark evergreens.

"Chinaboy!" She called from the open door of the house that was more a lean-to that seemed to have lost what it had been leaning into. Perhaps it had been a barracks for migrant workers long moved on to other labors.

He saw her through a pillow of dust and hair that she swept off the steps from the worn timber floor, and he ran with his catch. Her graying brown hair was pulled back into a low ponytail. She pulled a handkerchief from her apron pocket and sneezed.

"Chasing varmint again?" She waved the broom around. "What you got there?" She snatched the lizard tail from his hand and tossed it away into the dirt. "Don't you bring that in here, you hear?"

The boy ran back to retrieve his tail.

She continued to sweep and gesticulate. "You bring that in, and you'll see. I'll cook it and make you eat it."

He picked up the tail and patted it in the palm of his hand. "Mama, it's my pet."

She glanced around but hid her amusement. "Half a pet, Chinaboy. That's what you got. Just half."

The sound of a motor and the crunch of tires against the gravel turn-in grumbled from past the pine tree. Both looked over to see the old green truck, paint flaking from rusty patches, grind to a halt. The man stepped out, his boot hitting the ground with a thud. The other leg was lame, and he pushed it out and limped around to the back of the truck, heaving out a bag of groceries and a box of supplies.

"You get paid?" the woman queried.

"Nope, but his money came." He patted the boy on the head. "Yes, Chinaboy, you are our little golden goose. Your egg comes like clockwork every month. Not much, but that you can depend on."

"You'd think by now they'd forgotten him. Never come once to see him."

"Got other ways, those Chinese."

"Gave away all the good factory jobs to the Chinese and the coloreds."

"We coulda gone too, so don't start."

"How many years it's been?"

"Four since the war started."

"Speaking of which, today's his birthday."

"Is that so? How about that." He looked at her significantly and placed his hand momentarily on her shoulder.

She looked away. "That's why I asked for the flour. I'm baking him a cake."

The man followed the woman into the house and set the bag on the table. He bent down and scooped the boy into his arms. "Hey there, Chinaboy," he bellowed. "How old are you today?"

"Five, Papa." He showed his full set of grimy fingers on one hand.

"Five big ones. Yes, you are."

In his other hand, the boy grasped the lizard tail.

"What you got there?" The man pointed.

"My pet."

The woman pulled out the sack of flour from the purchases and turned around. "I told you not to bring that thing in here."

The man smiled. "You only got the tail, Chinaboy."

The boy pulled the tail to his chest protectively. "I'll get the rest tomorrow," he said decisively.

"I bet you will," the man laughed and put the boy down. He gestured to the woman. "Let him keep it. It's his birthday."

"I'll cook it in his cake," she threatened.

But the boy had run off. He would hide it somewhere safe, and she'd never know.

The man chuckled. He drew a tiny red envelope from his pocket and handed it to the woman. "They sent another one this year."

She hefted the coin in the red envelope and added it to the other three sitting on the shelf next to Jimmy's photograph. "Devil money, do you think?" she asked.

The rest of the day, the boy hung around the house, occasionally sneaking off to check his lizard tail, then standing near the stove where he could smell the sweet scent of vanilla and sugar that spread magically from one end of the house to the other. He watched with attention as the woman whipped up the frosting and spread it carefully layer upon layer. She noticed his interest with amusement. "Where were you last year?" she asked. "I don't remember you underfoot like this."

"I don't know," he said, propping himself up on a chair to see her work.

"I haven't missed a year since you come here," she remarked. She pressed her hand over his forehead and pushed back the black bangs from his brows. "Time we cut your hair again. Not a curl on this China hair of yours. Not like Jimmy."

"Jimmy." The boy nodded.

"Remember Jimmy?"

"Yeah." He pointed at a photograph on a small shelf.

"Just as you came, he was leaving." She paused, looking out to nowhere in particular. "Has it been that long? Hey!" She slapped his hand away.

His hands were woven in crevices of dirt. "What did I tell you about washing up?" She grabbed him by the chest and held him over the sink, slathering a slippery bar of soap over his hands and wiping them on her apron. "Here, now." She set him down in the chair with the frosting bowl and a wooden spoon in his small lap. "You lick this clean. Make sure you do a good job. I'll be checking."

He grinned big at her.

"What do you say now?"

"Yes, Mama."

Later that evening he could hardly eat, and she had to coax him. "You eat up. Your cake's not walking anywhere."

"Five years old, Chinaboy." The man pushed his spoon across the plate and smiled.

"Got to get some schooling next year," the woman commented. "Wonder if his people have thought of that?"

The man nodded.

"He'll be needing a new set of clothing. Should ask for more. He'll be eating more too."

"You getting pretty attached to the boy." The man looked down at his plate. "In the beginning, I recall . . ." His voice trailed off.

She bit her lip and said, "Like you said, it's four years I been his mama. Did all the hard part, changed his diapers, bottle-fed him, helped him with his first steps. What his Chinese mama do for him?"

"Don't talk like that in front of him. He don't understand none of this."

She stood up to clear the table. "I'm not attached like that, you know. He's just a kid. I'm doing my job."

The man touched her elbow as she took his plate. "You doing a fine job."

She stood sadly with the plates in both hands and stared at the photograph of Jimmy on the shelf. It was a portrait of a smiling young man in uniform, an army cap hugging his shaved head. "He'd be twenty-one today," she whispered. "I can't forget it."

A knocking came from the door. The man was quiet, but she said, "That'd be Sam and Martha. I asked them over for cake."

"Cake!" smiled the boy.

"Go on and get the door." She nudged the boy. "You got company."

When they'd settled around the table with pieces of cake, the men talked about the war. Sam said, "I'm hearing the war could end this year."

"Europe maybe."

"Boys'll come home."

"Turn right around and go on and fight the Japs."

"Our boys done their time."

Martha interrupted, looking at her friend. "Oh, that's all you men talk about, the war. Can't talk about nothing else." She patted the boy who sat next to her, frosting smeared over his cheeks. "Hey, Jackie, how's that cake, hon?"

Several months passed, but by the end of the year, a shiny blue sedan pulled up to the old pine tree. The boy saw a couple emerge from the car. They were nicely dressed, like city folks—he in a suit with a felt hat and she in a blue suit dress, stockings, and soft leather heels. He looked on with curiosity at these strangers, their black hair and Oriental features. He heard the sound of their voices chopping the air with punctuated speech he could not understand. When the woman saw him, she uttered an exclamation and hurried toward him. He ran away to hide.

Eventually the man came with his limping gait to find him. "Come on, Chinaboy. You got some visitors." He took the boy by the hand and walked slowly to the front of the house.

The woman was already there with a small bundle of his things. She said to the couple, "I kept his baby clothes. I couldn't bear to part with them. He was so cute in them. There's a change of clothes in there that fits him, though. But he's growing fast these days. Gonna be a tall fellow."

The Chinese woman pointed to the boy's head, noticing it was completely shaved.

"Oh, that. Lice. We had to shave his head a week ago. Infestation, you know. But he's rid of it now. He's been healthy all through. Only once we went to town for a fever. With all his antics, he never broke a bone."

"Yep," the man added. "He's one strong kid. Good disposition, too."

The woman pushed a few strands of her graying hair back and said, "Wish we could've had more warning you were coming. Got him cleaned up and ready."

The man said to the other man, "Hey, Sung, you know the life here. It's country, wide open. Air makes you strong. Dirt keeps you strong." He pounded his chest for effect. He nodded at the boy. "Right, boy?"

The boy pounded his chest too, and everyone laughed.

"Chinaboy, you gonna get to ride in that pretty car there."

The boy balked and stepped back. He watched the strange woman take the bundle from Mama and put it in the car.

"Just a little trip, Chinaboy."

"You going too?"

"Nope. Not today."

"Mama?"

"You know I got work to do."

"I got work to do too," replied the boy.

"Not today. You go on. Go take your ride."

"We'll be waiting here for you just the same."

Mama took the boy's hand and led him to the car. "You be good, now. Don't be giving your folks trouble. You show them I raised you right." She slipped four faded red envelopes into his pants pocket. "These are yours. Been saving them all this time." She leaned into the backseat, where he seemed engulfed by the big leather seat, hugged him hard and kissed his cheek, then rushed to close the door.

He looked up, trying to see out the window, a wide portal above his head, but her back was turned. The car backed slowly away from the old pine. He stared at the backs of the couple's heads, animated in foreign conversation, and watched the tree and the lean-to house recede into the distance forever. One by one, he pulled out each tiny envelope she had tucked away. Then he remembered; pushing his hand deeper into the pocket, he pressed his small palm around a desiccated piece of lizard tail.

All right, you're not impressed. It's just one of those best American short stories reprinted again and again in every literary magazine and Chinese American, Asian American, minority writers, new and promising American writers anthology you've seen lately. The story has appeared so many times that some reviewer said *ho hum, another mother-son story,* but it's actually the same story. How many Chinaboys farmed out to whites so that Chinamamas can get the benefits of wartime factory work? Maybe those white trash Okie folks are abusive and not God-fearing. Maybe they're dishonest and bigoted, and they kidnap and enslave the kid. But every outlaw hero bound for glory, whether he is Moses or Abraham Lincoln or Tripmaster Monkey, has got to have his start.

4: War & Peace

Son

Daughter

Sister

Brother

Wittman Ah Sing
Fake

Pandora Toy
Fake

Fa Mulan
Real

Kwan Kung
Real

Chinaman

男

Chinawoman

Dragon
Ba

父

Dragon
Ma

Patriarch Matriarch

5: Sax & Violence

If it's Il Piccolo by day, it's Jigoku by night and into the wee hours. Say you're in the mood to descend into a little hell. The J-Town version is underground, on the corner of Post and Buchanan. Imagine you got those cold stone demons leering at the gate as you make your way into the bowels. Every step down says you are bad, you are so so bad. You feel the heat of your descent, but the sound emanating at the bottom draws you down. It's the sinful sound of the double ax. The man under the dusty lights is blasting through both sides of his mouth—two saxophones in a one-man duet. You fall in love at once, but Gerald K. Li is Sandy Hu's new boyfriend, though soon to be her ex. But while he's hers, she loves him so. As I was saying, he's outlaw number twenty-one, just released on probation after doing four months at San Bruno County Jail. Even though they got him for assault and battery and resisting arrest, Sandy maintains that her honey did time as a political prisoner, protesting the fascist administration at San Francisco State College.

But let's return to the wee hours down in Jigoku. By this time, Flip at his keyboard has run down all the standbys, and the crowd is too drunk to notice the music changing, and the musicians are so gone to mellow that their instruments are playing on automatic. The sounds are moaning through the smoke and slapping together like humping bodies in rising and falling intensity like there is no tomorrow, and in Jigoku, maybe there is not.

So, there's Gerald wailing on his instruments: an alto to one side, a tenor to the other. Oh, he could do soprano, baby soprano, or any number of wind instruments. He's got a whole collection back home, antique reed pieces that don't exist anymore, flutes of every ethnic persuasion, nose flutes from the Philippines and such. He could abandon his saxophones for a shakuhachi if you like. It's all part of his extensive repertoire, understand? But tonight it's the twin saxophones that are in command. They hang from his lips like golden dragons blowing fire. Now, one thing you need to know: nobody makes music like this without tasting some form of peyote; every shaman knows the sacrifice of the body for a higher knowledge.

* * *

But speaking of higher knowledge, it's only been a couple of days since Gerald had a run-in with the acting president of San Francisco State College. Not only was Gerald high (he's never not high), but he met the president high up in the sky going PSA from LAX to SFO. Imagine Gerald's surprise to find the president-professor in the aisle seat next to him, snapping together the metal pieces of his seatbelt over his middle-aged belly in clear obedience to the sweet tinkling voice of the stewardess in a shocking pink miniskirt with matching polka-dot blouse, scarf, and cap. Aye-aye, Captain!

So Gerald said, "Hey, don't I know you?" This is a completely rhetorical question; who wouldn't recognize the Japanese under the tam-o'-shanter with the pom-pom and the little mustache pasted to his upper lip?

"Oh, hello. Why yes, I'm president of San Francisco State College." Indeed.

"I'm Gerald. I go to State." He should have said he goes there occasionally, but why go into details.

"Excuse my curiosity, but weren't you the young man in line ahead of me with the saxophones?"

"That's me. They're up there." He pointed to the overhead baggage compartments. "How'd you know?"

"The shape of the cases. It's unusual to see someone carrying two. Are you studying music at our fine college?"

"You might say that."

"What's your persuasion?"

"What do you mean?"

"Classical? Bandstand? Rock?"

"Jazz."

The professor smiled approvingly. "You have a lot of luggage. I'm easy, you see." He pulled a harmonica out of his breast pocket. Now he must have thought he'd impress Gerald. "Sonny Boy Williamson, know him? He's my model."

"Cool. Plays with Muddy Waters."

"No, that's another Sonny Boy. I mean the original. There were two, you know. I knew the original Sonny Boy in Chicago before he died tragically in 1948."

He tossed this one to Gerald like a throwaway thought: "Then there's the Belgian Toots Thielemans. Once I saws Toots play with the Bird. I can't play sax like you, but that's when I thought maybe I might press my luck with the harp."

"You saw Bird play?" Oh my, now Gerald was trapped. All the president had to say next was he knew Trane, and Gerald was gone over to the other side.

"In Chicago in the forties. You weren't born yet."

"How about Coltrane?"

"I know his work. But I'll admit I'm still back with the old bebop. 'My Favorite Things,' though," he mentioned Coltrane's rendition. "I like that."

Gerald nodded.

The pink stewardess rolled up with her cart of goodies. "Gentlemen? Can I interest you in our drinks?"

The professor said, "I'll have scotch on the rocks. You?" he asked Gerald. "Don't worry. It's on me."

"Make that two," said Gerald, and Miss PSA passed over the little bottles of J&B that got poured over ice in glasses. They could have been cozy in a nightclub somewhere in old prewar Fillmore.

The professor imbibed casually. "Before I came to San Francisco, I used to do a jazz radio show in Chicago. I'm most familiar with the Chicago scene in the forties and fifties."

"Oh, interesting." Gerald thought about all of this. If the students knew, would it change anything? He wondered.

"That's when bebop made its appearance. Like anything new, folks hated it at first. It was the same reaction to modern art and Picasso."

"So, what do you think of guys like Cecil Taylor and Archie Shepp?"

"That's what I mean. Frankly, I feel they've gone over the edge. Like that fellow Jackson Pollack. I don't like it much at all."

Gerald thought he should test the professor with some other questions that students would like to know. "Do you listen to rock?"

"I have nothing against it. My children listen to it. Let me put it this way: the only electric guitar put to good use was Charlie Christian's."

"Christian played with Miles."

"And Parker and Thelonious Monk. I have a recording of them at Minton's. Do you know it's said that Christian coined the word *bebop*?"

Gerald took a swig of his J&B and let the rocks settle in small clunks. He knew the protocol, the way a knowledge of jazz, or just any music, could be a test of your masculinity. Honey, now how did that happen? In any case, he had better even up the score, so he said, "It's the way Christian used the electric guitar that changed the music, used it to augment and diminish chords."

Now the professor nodded in approval. As the French say, *formidable.*

"So," continued Gerald, "you can see how the guitar is used by guys like Hendrix." He was showing he didn't have any musical prejudices, though he probably does.

The professor changed the subject, probably because he hates rock anyway. "When you have time, come by my office. I've got a collection of LPs and a turntable there."

"Thanks."

"By the way, I've been talking to Duke Ellington, and it's almost settled. I'm bringing Ellington and his band to our college. What do you think?" And this was the same guy who sent the TAC squad in to beat up black students? If only those Negroes would listen to jazz instead of James Brown.

But Gerald kept it mellow and uncomplicated, as if he could hear the indifference of Monk's cool piano over the plane's loudspeakers. Another J&B on the professor almost swindled his mind.

The conversation went on amiably and maturely like that for the duration of the short flight, until the pink stewardess came by with her sweet suggestions to store their tray tables and to reposition their seats to their upright and proper positions. Stiff-backed, Gerald and the professor braced themselves for the landing. The pink stewardess took her own seat, perky and at attention, and PSA dipped into and caressed the fog. Gerald practiced his circular breathing and heard a high C blow in his mind forever, heading for SFO's spreading tarmac.

* * *

The crowd at Jigoku goes through a kind of metamorphosis so that by the wee hours there's new blood looking for the *out there* sound but can't afford the price of the cover. They are the lost souls who stand outside in the cold, smoking and hoping to catch a whiff of the music through the open doors, and then slipping in for the second set on a nod from the bouncer who figures, what the hell. Then there are those who nuzzle in for a quick transaction to keep the buzz constant. We cozy around those little ashtrays on their circular pedestals with our elbows and palms propped to hold up our chins and that stub of cigarette, its forgotten ash trailing over because we're caught in Gerald's relentless trill and groan. Honey, you think you are dying, dying with every note.

* * *

So when Gerald and the professor landed at SFO, the jazz aficionados were in a good mood, and the professor said, "Do you need a ride into the city?"

"Hey, man. I'll take you up on that," said Gerald, grabbing his horns and slinging the straps over his shoulders. "I got these, plus I got to lug a suitcase of my stuff."

Gerald's suitcase went with the professor's briefcase into the trunk of a silver Oldsmobile, and they headed north into the city.

The professor asked, "Where do you live?"

"J-Town, on Laguna."

"Your family from here?"

"No. L.A."

"Visiting?"

"Yeah, thought I'd better see my mom."

"Has it been a while?"

"Four months."

"Studying, I hope."

Gerald paused, but thought, what the hell. "Not really."

"The strike interrupted your studies."

"You can say that again."

"Well, things have almost returned to normal." The professor was referring to the new semester.

"My mother would like that."

"I get letters all the time from your parents. They are all in agreement with me about this situation. They're the silent majority."

Gerald thought maybe this was a window of opportunity. At least he would do it for his mom, the silent majority.

"I wonder if you would consider a favor on my behalf," he opened up. "I mean as a student at State. It's not every day you talk to the president himself."

The professor pulled onto the freeway and grinned. "It depends. What are you asking?"

"Well, see, I'm on probation, and I need to be reinstated to continue my classes."

"Probation?"

"Yeah."

"Why?"

"See, I just got out of San Bruno a couple of weeks ago."

The professor's eyebrows raised in alarm. "You were in jail? May I ask why?"

"Well, I could have copped a plea, but I went to court. My mom said, 'See that woman who holds the scales? Well, they're tipped in favor of the money,' but I said, 'No, this is America. We can get justice.' What did I know?"

"What happened?"

"The jury was a bunch of old women. They found me guilty."

"Guilty of what?"

"Of defending this white girl. She was passing out these flyers, and this white guy pushed her over, grabbed her flyers, and threw them all over. So I went after him and tried to get the flyers back, and it got messy."

"Messy?"

"Yeah, he punched me, and nobody punches me." Gerald paused, and the professor waited. "I was defending myself, see."

"So the police arrested you."

"Well, the white guy took off in one direction, and I took off running down Holloway in the other. They didn't go after the white guy. They came after me."

"What were you doing on Holloway?"

"Protesting, like everyone else."

"You were striking? Then you deserved to be arrested."

"How did I deserve it? What about that white guy with the blue armband?"

The professor said, "Blue armband? Those students were showing their support for the college."

"By attacking a girl with flyers? If she'd been around to be my witness, I would have gotten off."

"She should have been arrested with you. You were blocking the entrance to a public institution and denying the right of other students to their educations. You were disturbing the peace. Being in jail should have given you time to reflect on this."

"Reflect?"

* * *

Gerald comes away from his solo, and the band pulls through on intuition. Flip takes over for a while, then Makoto, then Eiji, then Kamau. Keyboards to guitar to bass to drums and back, the improvisations circling like sweet magic. That's reflection. That's what Gerald has been missing while being locked up.

Gerald looks into the crowd and sees a familiar face waving him down. It's LaVan. Gerald shakes his head, and LaVan smiles. Gerald gives him a look like, who let you out? He can still see in his mind the piles of stolen electronic goods in the back of the house and the arguments going around about how LaVan's heist was a liability to the revolution, but when it all came around, who should be in the San Bruno County Jail doing time at the same time but LaVan.

LaVan had said, "What you doing here?"

"SF State sent me," Gerald smirked. "Field studies."

"No shit."

"You?"

"Man, it's cold out there this time of year. I get time for petty vagrancy, and I get a meal and a warm bed."

Gerald wondered if the trade-off was worth it.

LaVan said, "You got some smokes on you?"

"Yeah, man." Gerald handed LaVan a Kool.

"I noticed you rooming with the monster." LaVan referred to Gerald's cellmate, for whom everyone parted like the Red Sea.

"I give up my oatmeal for him every morning."

LaVan guffawed.

"I hate that mush shit," said Gerald.

"Monster leaving you alone?"

"So far. And some folks out there think I'm a monster."

LaVan chuckled. "Can you come up with a couple cartons?" LaVan pointed at the cigarettes.

"My mom is visiting in a week. What do they say? Visitors every twenty days?"

"Right. Come up with the smokes. I'll see what I can do."

Gerald never knew how it worked, but LaVan got him a private cell, as it were.

* * *

Back in the silver Oldsmobile, flying down One-oh-one to the city, Gerald turned to the president, who was gripping his power steering. "Reflect?" he repeated. The word stuck in his throat, a huge hungry lump. "You don't know what you're saying."

"The police were just doing their job," said the professor. The Oldsmobile squealed around the off-ramp a little too fast.

"The police didn't have to be there doing their job. You invited them in. See this?" Gerald pointed at the scar over his brow. He practically moved his head in front of the professor's view. "What sort of job is that, bashing an unarmed person?"

"Can you fault the police?" The professor's voice rose in pitch, and it was already high. "How many of you hooligans were throwing rocks?"

"Hooligans?" Gerald jumped in his seat.

"Right, hooligans. You were out there breaking windows!"

"I was not!"

"Starting fires!" The professor waved his fist around at the traffic. "Flushing books down the toilets!" That was unforgivable, and the professor looked like he was going to cry. "We had to tear out the plumbing system in the entire library! Do you know what that cost?"

"Who you blaming here? Who didn't want to negotiate?"

"Negotiate? What was there to negotiate? All you wanted was to destroy the college!"

"We were trying to build a Third World college. Build, not destroy!"

"Admit it," the professor continued his diatribe, "you were there with the rest of them, out to make trouble. And what for? You were being led around by the nose by your fascination with a small gang of Negro students, bunch of conmen, neo-Nazis, and common thieves!"

Every time the professor looked at Gerald to make his point, he pushed the wheel to the right, and the car swerved in and out of the lane.

"Shit, watch your driving, old man!"

"Who you calling an old man?"

"You. And who you calling conmen and neo-Nazis? You're the Nazi. You're a fucking fascist pig!" Gerald watched the car run the red light and heard the honking from the cross street.

"You're the fascist!" The professor was screaming now.

By now Gerald was needing a smoke, so he pulled out the toke he was saving under his jacket and lighted up. As he puffed urgently, he yelled, "Fucking fascist pig uncle Tom pig banana!"

"What's that you're doing?" Even the professor recognized the smell of cannabis. Now, wouldn't that be the scandal. If he would just keep running those red lights, maybe they'd be stopped by a cop, and the president of SFSC would be caught red-handed for possession. What did Gerald care as long as he didn't have to share a cell with him. "That's it!" The professor hit the brakes, and the car screeched into the curb. "Get out! Get out!"

Gerald jumped for his horn cases in the backseat, yanking them away, and kept up his yelling, trying to overcome the litany of *GODDAMN! STUPID! DRUG ADDICT! WORTHLESS! KID! JAIL BIRD! GO TO HELL! GO TO HELL!:* "UNCLE TOJO! FASCIST PIG! PUPPET! PIG BANANA!" Gerald tumbled out of the car. He ran and yelled after it like some kind of maniac. "FUCKING BANANA! FUCKING BANANA!"

Suddenly he stopped and looked around. There he was on the corner of Post and Buchanan. Maybe the Olds had an old directional memory of Jimbo's Bop City on the same street, gone for the last five, maybe six years. Gerald shrugged and took his instruments from their cases, hooked them to the straps around his neck, and started to blow, right there on Post Street. It was all he'd wanted to do these past four months. He wanted to shake the memory of his mother standing there behind the glass, tears freefalling, showing him the cartons of cigarettes she brought in a bag. She had looked so small and weary, but she still forgave him. She told everyone in the family that he wasn't a criminal like the others in there; he was just protesting, and everyone had a right to protest. Everyone had a right to protest.

He could hear the chaos of Coltrane's "Ascension," and that would be his fuck-off—it was everything a president was beyond understanding or knowing. It was Gerald's invisibility, the musician behind and beyond the music, the spirit of the man that blew through the horn, past his yellow skin, past all expectations. It would be everything he couldn't say because he wasn't a man of words. It would be his revolution.

* * *

Gerald gives LaVan the nod and takes his cue to pull in back to the melody. Sandy Hu struts up, throws Gerald a kiss, and takes a bow. She presses her lips to the microphone and intones that low honey voice of hers. She could say anything with that voice, and a man's heart would melt, his mind turn to jelly. She speaks her poem. "Don't do me like that," she says. "I will kill you." And we all want to be killed, drawn and quartered, molested by her voice. Don't do her like that. Lullaby. Dragon Lady. Her poetry goes on like that, gravelly and urgent. And the band holds an amorphous rhythm beneath, like holding its breath for her instrument. Finally she steps down, and the music hiccups back to loudness.

The fat guys who own Jigoku will keep hell open until daylight, as long as the bar keeps making its receipts. They'll send the waitresses home and bus the tables themselves. The musicians aren't going to make more; they just get time to do their own thing. When they quit, Jigoku goes to sleep. No one to complain about the noise and the commotion of folks high on legal and illegal remedies for whatever the spirit is suffering.

Gerald moves the melody to some kind of rapid perpetual motion, and the dream opens up like time is forever. Each musician follows suit, taking the rhythms out in multiple directions. And the individual instruments howl and scream, distinct and dissonant, pull at your genitals, rip at your heart, stroke everything until you're shaking and dripping from tears and sweat and all that funk.

* * *

Maybe it was five minutes or maybe it was an hour later. Gerald would never know because he was lost in his sound. The silver Oldsmobile pulled up abruptly with an angry squeal. The old man and his tam jumped from the driver's seat, popped the cavernous trunk, and threw out Gerald's suitcase. The hard thing hit the side of the curb and popped open. All those shirts and pants so lovingly pressed and folded by Gerald's mother, along with boxers and what-have-you, flew up in a tangled mess as the suitcase bounced over the sidewalk. Gerald played the screech of the wheels and the rumble of the revving engine pushing off, the shock of the grandmothers and other passersby gawking at a man's wardrobe strewn in a scattered path to Jigoku.

6: Chiquita Banana

HER DAUGHTERS COME TO COMPLAIN TO CHIQUITA...

THAT ANNA MAY IS LOSING HER HARD EDGE FROM MODEL As.
I'M WASTING MY HIGH ON SOMEONE WHO'LL APPRECIATE IT!

AND POOR LI'L SUZIE IS GETTING HIGH FROM ALL OF ANNA MAY'S REDS...

CHIQUITA FIGURES IT ALL OUT (THEY ARE ATTACHED SO WHAT ONE TAKES AFFECTS THE OTHER)
THIS IS SO SCREWY.

CHIQUITA INVITES DON JUAN OVER AND TRICKS HIM INTO THINKING HE'LL GET SOME...
ALL RIGHT!
OOOOH

YIPES
THEN JUST LIKE THAT, SHE PULLS A GUN ON DON JUAN.

BUT HE TURNS IT ON HER
SMACK
AND KILLS HER.
BAM!
JUST AS THIS OCCURS, MULAN ROUGE, CHIQUITA'S SISTER FROM CHINA, ARRIVES AND SEES EVERYTHING.
I'M FRESH OFF THE BOAT FOR FIVE MINUTES AND ALREADY IN TROUBLE!
MULAN PULLS OUT HER TWO FIVE-FOOT SWORDS...
KILLS DON JUAN WITH ONE
THWOK
AND SPLITS THE TWINS WITH THE OTHER.
NOW WHAT?
—THE END—

7: Doppelgangsters

Honey, you might be an orphaned brother, but what happens when you meet your orphaned double? In the case of the doppelganger, who is who? Who is real and who is fake?

Gerald K. Li says to Jack Sung, "Boss, I'm giving up women. I'm giving up drugs. I'm giving up booze. I'm giving up my wayward life. I'm turning over a new leaf for the revolution."

Jack Sung replies, "Give up women, drugs, and booze, O.K. But a wayward life? What's a revolution if we're not fighting for the wayward life?"

Gerald says, "You got a point." After all, he can't give up his axes. "I'll be honest with you. I'm doing it for my mother. She's suffered enough on my behalf."

Jack says, "Don't you have a sister who can do the sacrificing?"

Gerald says, "I got a model minority brother, but I'm the prodigal one."

Jack says, "Mothers always go soft for the prodigals. Don't they ever learn?"

Gerald says,."I gotta take that journey to make it up to my mother. Gotta take Highway Ninety-nine and make my amends."

So that's how the journey begins.

Sandy Hu has a sweet little red VW Bug. Gerald's on the outs with his honey, so he might as well get something for his time. He pays her a last honeyed visit and works on her in every kama sutra direction. Baby, it takes hours, but she finally gets her satisfaction and falls asleep in deep fatigue, at which point he sneaks off, packs his twin axes, and rolls that shiny red Beetle down the driveway. Admittedly, he has a momentary thought about the Jack Daniels on top of the TV console and that fat little joint in the back kitchen drawer, but he's made his promises. Instead, he draws himself a generous loan from Sandy's secret stash of cash. Oh she'd appreciate his discretionary choices, but no time now for promissory notes. Highway Ninety-nine is waiting.

So the sun is peeking out from the East, beaming off the Beetle's red polish in the sweet early morning hours, and Gerald remembers he never had breakfast, and it's been a long and arduous night to satisfy a woman out of her particular vehicular needs. He's got to get himself some grub, as it were. But first he pulls over to the side of the road, choosing a pretty picket fence with a creeping vine of thorny roses and proceeds to pee. Looking down the road, he sees a man approaching with two black cases, one it each hand. The man stops near him, puts his cases down, and takes a pack of cigarettes from his pocket.

"Smoke?" he offers Gerald.

Gerald helps himself. "Where is this place?" he asks.

"Lodi," says the man with the two black cases.

"You coming home from a gig?" he asks, recognizing the cases that have to hold some kind of wind instruments.

"How'd you know?"

Gerald nods at the cases.

"My axes," he says.

"Oh yeah?"

"Let me introduce myself," says the man. "I'm Gerald K. Li."

"What do you mean you're Gerald K. Li?"

"You don't know Gerald K. Li, the great Chinese saxophonist?"

"Well, yeah, but you're not even Chinese."

"How do you know?"

"Cuz I'm Chinese, and you're a white man."

"A white man can be Chinese. It's easy. We do it all the time."

Gerald looks hard at the white guy and thinks it could be true. This guy could be the white version of his Chinese self.

The white man puffs into the air. "It just can't happen the other way around. A Chinese can never be a white man."

Gerald thinks about this. "What do you play?"

"I do those riffs with an Oriental chinkified sound. Crowd loves it."

"Oh yeah?" Gerald asks, "How much did Gerald K. Li make last night from that gig of yours?"

"Not bad for Lodi. Hundred bucks."

"No shit." Gerald has never received a hundred for being himself. He reasons that amount of money could be substantial supplemental income for the journey. He steps onto his smoked-out cigarette butt and says, "I'm going to be needing that hundred."

HUNG GAR PA KWA

Strike in 5 animal forms
matched with
5 elemental forms:
tiger with metal
crane with wood
dragon with fire
leopard with water
snake with earth

Strike in the 8 directions of the I Ching:
heaven-earth
wind-thunder
water-fire
mountain-lake

animal spirit
tiger fists

Walk the circle
from winter to autumn

day to night
north to south
head to mouth
father to mother

elemental power
iron threads

64 combinations

25 combinations

Breathe

Breathe

Yin

Yang

"Yellow-faced son of a bitch," mutters Gerald and picks the man's pockets for his hundred dollars. As it turns out, there's only ten. *Must have had some debts to pay,* reasons Gerald to himself. *I'll have to take these instruments for collateral.* He throws the cases into Sandy's VDub and drives out of Lodi in a hurry.

About an hour later, the hunger is unbearable, and he's really feeling the need for a couple of burgers and a milkshake. Just outside of Stockton, he saunters into a greasy diner and finds himself seated next to another Chinese American.

"Hey, man," Gerald says.

"Hey, man," the Chinese American local replies and does a double take. He points at Gerald and exclaims, "I know you! You're Gerald K. Li, the great Chinese American saxophonist."

"How'd you know?" Gerald asks.

"Who doesn't know? You're famous!" He puts out his hand. "I gotta shake your hand. This is amazing! I've been wanting to meet you for years."

"Yeah, well, nice to meet you, man," says Gerald.

"What you having? It's on me."

"Really?"

"Really, man. What brings you to these parts? I got to drive into the City to catch you playing, but hey, are you doing Stockton? Where's it gonna be?"

Gerald's stomach is grumbling, and he's got that anxious feeling he gets when he needs to eat. He cuts into his admirer's enthusiasm. "I've been driving since dawn, and I got to eat, man."

"Sure. I understand that life. You must have played Jigoku last night."

"You might say that." Gerald nods.

"What you want to eat? A burger?"

"Make that three burgers."

"What else?"

"And three milkshakes."

"Fries?"

"Large side of fries."

As you might already understand, Gerald K. Li is an outlaw who expresses himself via his instruments. Also, over time, in his association with the African American masters of the art, he's cultivated an attitude. Those fine mentors always had the least to say about anything except when acknowledging another's possible musical existence. But the enthusiastic Chinese American goes flapping on and on at the mouth while Gerald concentrates on devouring three burgers, three milkshakes, and a load of fries slathered with ketchup.

"I can't believe it. Gerald K. Li in Stockton. Hey man, we've got a club here. Nothing like in SF, but still, it's something. I play there on a regular basis. Maybe you could show up and play with us. I've been studying your style for years. I'm nothing in comparison, but well, it's embarrassing to say, but in Stockton, they call me the Gerald K. Li of Stockton. I mean, I'll never be as good, but it's like a tribute to your talents. Man, you could show up tonight, and that'd be something. Blow everyone away! It'd be an honor. I could work up a crowd. Get you some good returns. We'll pack 'em in. It'll be a major event. What do you say?"

"I could eat another burger."

"Yeah, no problem, man. No problem."

That night, Gerald K. Li shows up at the indicated Stockton club. It's a darkened joint that reeks of smoke. Maybe there are a half-dozen folks in the audience nursing J&Bs on the rocks. The Gerald K. Li of Stockton apologizes. "I been telephoning everyone, but it looks like a caravan of cars and a busload left for the City to hear Miles. Hard to compete with Miles."

"Do tell."

EAGLE CLAW	MONKEY
108 points of attack 36 are secret (lethal) 72 will not kill or cripple	
	5 monkey types: drunken stone lost standing wooden
claw hand to lock joints	

muscles
pressure points

5 principals:
be sly
be poisonous
be evasive
be bluffing
be unpredictable

immobilize

roll and tumble
relentless attack

finish

"I'm gonna cut you some slack," says Gerald to the Stockton Gerald. "I got this extra ax I picked up in Lodi. It's yours." He's feeling generous with his collateral since, after all, there are two of them, and besides, his imitation is never gonna be able to blow out of both sides of his mouth.

Gerald is back on Ninety-nine headed toward Modesto. After that, it's Turlock, Atwater, and Merced. You'd think an outlaw taking the backroads would be safe, but there are more adventures to come. For example, he finds a cheap motel near Merced and decides to check out the extra ax he's come by. When he opens the case, it's a terrible surprise for a man who's made his kind of promises. It's filled with little bags of white powder. Oh my! In a few days, the Gerald K. Li of Stockton will get busted for possession and assaulting a pathetic white saxophone player on a Lodi roadside.

Gerald shoves the imaginary saxophone in its case under the bed and whistles out the room. At this point, Gerald could really use a drink. He heads for the corner bar under neon lights and saunters in.

"What'll it be?" asks the bartender.

Gerald thinks about his promise and says, "I'll have a Coke."

The bartender looks at Gerald significantly, and when Gerald bothers to look back, he freezes in shock. He's staring at his twin, his spitting image, his actual doppelganger. "Goddamn," he mutters.

"I've been expecting you," says the bartender, pouring the Coke.

"That so?"

"That's right."

"Who do you think I am?"

"You're my twin brother, Jack."

"Jack?"

"Jack, it's you, right? Jack Sung."

"Jack Sung, the poet?"

"Don't you recognize me? I'm Joe."

"Yeah, I recognize you, but—"

"I know all about you. I've read all your poetry."

"You like poetry?"

"I don't understand poetry."

"But you read Jack's, I mean, my poetry?" Gerald scratches his head. He might as well go along with this. The way this journey's going, he couldn't be Jack, or could he?

The bartender pulls out dog-eared copies of Jack Sung's books: *Cooking with Chinamen, Water Margin Memoirs, Mao and Me.* He points to *Mao and Me.* "I don't know about the others, but I object to this one."

"Why is that?"

"That's the trouble with poets. You can't understand the work of the revolution."

Gerald remembers what Jack said when he told him he was turning over a new leaf for the revolution. "Look," he tries to explain. "I've given up women, booze, and drugs, but not my wayward ways."

The bartender doppelganger laughs. "Always trying to be rebels but ultimately you and your kind are a bunch of bourgeois intellectuals patronized by the capitalists."

Gerald shakes his head, trying to think of what Jack would say, but he can't think about any of this at all. Still, it sounds like maybe he should fight the guy.

HSING-I WHITE CRANE

5 elements:
earth
metal
water
wood
fire

4 fists:
fast punch
block strike
circular strike
roundhouse punch

12 animals:
dragon
tiger
monkey
horse
chicken
falcon
snake

phoenix
lizard
swallow
eagle
bear

always defensive
circling, elusive

stance:
sink to one's center of strength
30% front leg
70% rear leg

one hand lies
one hand tells the truth

shape of mind

force of opponent
against himself

end fight
quickly as started

The bartender says, "You didn't come here to fight me, you came here to help."

Gerald says, "I did?"

"You may not be a true revolutionary, but fundamentally you believe in it."

"Maybe I do." Gerald nods.

"Don't get me wrong. You and I don't see eye to eye. Only in one thing are we alike."

"You do look like me." Gerald is still amazed at the mirror image.

"We both believe in the passionate pursuit of our ideals."

Gerald needs more time to twist his mind around this idea, but the bartender is impatient, pushes his face across the counter and growls a whisper toward Gerald's ear, "I've been hiding out here since that bank heist."

"Heist?"

"Yeah, we pulled a heist to finance the revolution."

"Oh."

"I'm prepared to take on your identity as a poet."

"We're switching?"

The bartender removes his apron and hands it to Gerald. "Wait a few days, until the coast is clear."

Gerald puts on the apron. Anything to help Jack's twin brother. He hands the bartender his motel key. "Room Twenty-one," he says. "You might take a look under the bed. Think of it as my contribution to the revolution."

"Thanks," says the former bartender, now undercover poet revolutionary.

For the next few weeks, Gerald maintains the bar under the neon sign somewhere around Merced. Big bully truckers come through. Tattooed Hell's Angels tear up the place. FBI agents try to make like they're inconspicuous. Revolutionaries posing as hippies and hippies posing as revolutionaries all try to test Gerald with the correct line. He pulls out Jack's books and reads them passages from *Mao and Me.*

One day, a masked stranger walks in. "Gerald K. Li," the stranger laughs. "You never even made it to Fresno, much less Bakersfield."

"Who are you?" Gerald asks cautiously.

"I'm the one who's come to take back what's mine," says the stranger.

Gerald looks closely. Is it the Lodi imposter?

"If you want your axes, they are long gone."

"Your journey down Ninety-nine has ended," says the masked stranger.

PRAYING MANTIS WHITE EYEBROW

Hand moves:
mantis claw
gou
lau
tsai
qua

soft hand
Phoenix eye fist

Ferocious self-defense

5 external forms:
eyes
mind
hands
waist
stance

block punch
pull in

5 internal forms:
thrust
sink ball into water
spring forward
neutralize softly
rip shark-like

off balance, strike

wit

no mercy

Sandy Hu removes her mask, pushes her hand deep into Gerald's pockets, slips away the keys to her shiny red VDub. "Honey," she says. "I've come here to practice my imagination. Truth is beauty, and beauty is truth, and that, honey, is all you have to know. And," she continues as she turns on her heels, "this is my revolution, and don't you forget it." Like I've said, you hear us coming before you see us, and *click click click,* she walks out, takes her seat in the cool black leather inside that red, red exterior, and completes that journey down the rest of Highway Ninety-nine.

8: Dance

the substance I am made of.
a river that carries me away, but I am the river;
iger that mangles me, but I am the tiger;
fire that consumes me, but I am the fire.
Jorge Luis Borges

Now honey, not to confuse you or anything, but some of us are reading Borges instead of Mao. As far as Sandy Hu can tell, that blind old Argentine has something to say about dance, her dance. Accordingly, she choreographs the following piece based on the story of the outlaw Li K'wei reuniting with his blind mother. Sandy has this idea to combine Peking Opera with what Gerald is calling avant-garde jazz, as long as he throws in a little tango, her nod to Borges, of course. It's the Chinese butterfly harp, lute, and cymbals, plus avant-garde jazz from Gerald's double saxes. She's got Gerald in leotards and trussed up in something that's her version of a Chinese minstrel, trudging along the periphery of the stage for the duration of the dance. Maybe it's love. Most likely masochism. But Gerald is insisting that it's all about Archie Shepp's rendition of Mama Rose. Li K'wei's blind mom is Gerald's mama Rose. Isn't that sweet?

The dance is performed beneath the I-Hotel in the site of the old Hungry i nightclub, abandoned now to a bunch of Asian American artists who call themselves the Kearny Street Workshop. They say architecture is frozen music, and as architecture goes, this hotel's been long frozen, along with all the songs and comedy routines that came and went out of the little i. You have to imagine the molecules of Hungry's music rocking around between the old bricks, sliding across the dance floor, slipping around the stage, and wafting in a smoky trail across the bar. Now the old molecules are being pushed around by this new music. And this new music is pushing Gerald down one side of the stage when Sandy's two dancers appear from the back wings. The frozen becomes fluid in the form of dance.

But what is Asian American dance? Sandy wants to know. Does the body have a memory? What's the memory of the Asian American body? She says she choreographs as if blind. Choreographs as if deaf. Choreographs in silence. Sandy says you got to feel the body's energy. Watch for texture and density and intensity. Fill the space like pictographs splashed across rice paper. Now, listen to the bodies' movements.

body of music [music] body of musician

Peking Opera **[Chinese]** Gerald K. Li

Li K'wei **[butterfly harp]** back stage left

Returns **[viola]** strolling minstrel

to His **[lute]** double saxophones

Blind **[cymbols]** alto and tenor

Mother **[high-pitched]** riffing to

avant- **[singing voices]** recorded

garde **[saxophones]** opera

jazz **[improv-]** left stage edge

Asian **[i-sation]** walk pause

American **[fusion]** slowly forward

[sax]

[sax]

[sax] **body of dancer [dance]** ***body of dance***

[sax] father/mother **[back]** *ancient*

[sax] arranged marriage **[stage left]** *body woman*

[sax] born 1941 **[silent]** *woman*

[sax] Pearl Harbor **[unseen]** *tattered robes*

[sax] raised in camp **[undirected light]** *hair in knots*

[sax] brother **[appearance]** *bald in places*

[sax] born in camp **[minute]** *mother*

[sax] postwar **[almost]** *of Li K'wei*

[sax] Seabrook, Mass **[imperceivable]** *I had a*

[sax] 1959 **[movements]** *son*

[sax] return **[Noh-like]** *where is he?*

[sax] to the West **[creeping]** *is he yet alive?*

[sax] Oakland **[diagonally]** *will I see him*

[sax] shoe repair **[interminably]** *before I die?*

[sax] Grove Street **[slow]** *live one more day*

[sax] by day **[painfully]** *to see my son*
[sax] mother ran shop **[slow]** *but she is blind*
[sax] by day **[fingers]** *weeping weeping*
[sax] father gardener **[crooked]** *so many years* ***body of dance*** **[dance] body of dancer**
[sax] by night **[arms inching out]** *dried her eyes* *bold* **[back]** father Filipino
[sax] father repaired shoes **[hunched]** *to sightless stones* *brash* **[stage right]** mother Irish German
[sax] good business **[back hunched]** *my son left* *middle-aged* **[sudden]** Watsonville
[sax] until **[neck strained]** *a young boy* *muscular* **[bombastic]** she sitting on porch
[sax] tennis shoe **[chin forward]** *will he return* *Li K'wei* **[appearance]** he migrant worker
[sax] mother bilingual **[head tilted left]** *an old man?* *Black* **[pose]** came by everyday
[sax] tough **[strain]** *how will she know* *Whirlwind* **[grimace]** one day church
[sax] piano **[legs crouched]** *her son?* *feared* **[heroic]** asked her out
[sax] lessons with **[right foot inching]** *I will live* *outlaw* **[stance]** family said
[sax] Huey Newton **[heels and toes]** *100 years* *but his mother's* **[expansive]** you can't see
[sax] who wore a **[rocking forward]** *but I will know* *Iron Ox* **[movements]** that man
[sax] bowtie **[transfer weight]** *my son* *wield 2* **[fill space]** sent her away
[sax] Grove **[left foot inching]** *old woman* *huge axes* **[heavy footfalls]** live with aunt
[sax] Elementary **[heels and toes]** *you may be fooled* *Chinese gladiator* **[struts forward]** found out
[sax] Westlake HS **[rocking forward]** *any man might* *painted mask* **[lifts axes]** eloped
[sax] Free Methodist **[arms inching forward]** *fake your son* *bearded face* **[circling axes]** SF
[sax] Wesley Methodist **[hands searching]** *a fake son* *big black brows* **[circle out]** family came after
[sax] United Methodist **[eyes fixed]** *might be* *broad bare chest* **[circle forward]** mother 16
[sax] no friends **[eyes]** *better than none* *wild top* knot **[hold above]** miscegenation
[sax] wanted **[always]** *what imposter* *powerful giant* **[heroic V]** laws
[sax] ballet lessons **[fixed]** *would want* *but also a son* **[pose]** arrested dad
[sax] too expensive **[blank]** *a poor old hag?* *many battles fought* **[muscular]** leave him
[sax] traded **[stare]** *I will know my son* *many lawless deeds* **[stomp feet]** said no
[sax] house cleaning **[as blind]** *foolish woman* *yet memories* **[twist side]** disowned her family
[sax] for **[every]** *a huge and ugly man* *loving mother* **[to side]** hard life
[sax] dance lessons **[movement]** *is at your door* *playful boyhood* **[crook elbows]** raised family
[sax] mother discovered **[expresses]** *he will take* *mischievous* **[slice air]** father
[sax] angry **[heightened]** *your last bit of food* *how will my mother* **[pull blades]** couldn't get jobs
[sax] yelled at teacher **[sense]** *he will kill you* *receive me?* **[before face]** support 5 kids
[sax] Oakland Tech HS **[of hearing]** *on a whim* *a prodigal son* **[open blades]** Fillmore
[sax] Miss Versatility **[of touching]** *he is the infamous* *foolish son* **[scowl]** vibrant place
[sax] dance teacher **[of smelling]** *Black Whirlwind* *certainly* **[between blades]** black culture
[sax] film of **[ears poised]** *his footfall is heavy* *your mother* **[growl]** jazz at Bebop City
[sax] Martha Graham **[react]** *but familiar* *is dead* **[pause]** music everywhere

[sax] dancer Yuriko **[turn head]** *I know his gait* *so many years gone* **[listen]** part of our lives
[sax] I can be her **[concentrate]** *the rhythm* *you may find* **[soften face]** took for granted
[sax] married **[every sound]** *the step* *an empty house* **[close eyes]** not romantic vision
[sax] h.s. sweetheart **[fingers bristle]** *upon the earth* *a cold grave* **[tilt head]** beauty of it
[sax] Peace & Freedom **[tingle]** *playful* *see? no smoke* **[seem to dream]** always worked
[sax] union work **[to touch]** *bowlegged steps* *no hearth within* **[lower axes]** worked with dad
[sax] 1963 UCB **[skin breathes in]** *memory of steps* *too poor* **[lift feet]** kitchen, fourteen years old
[sax] from Oriental **[light]** *door creaks* *to light a fire* **[lightly]** helped at banquets
[sax] to Asian American **[heat/cold]** *pushes open* *cross the threshold* **[jig]** overheard
[sax] Political Alliance **[air]** *who is there?* *who is there?* **[pause]** wouldn't pay dad
[sax] Oakland Courthouse **[nose]** *a figure waiting* **[squint]** told him: don't work
[sax] Free Huey! **[follows]** *waiting in the dark* **[tilt head]** not going to pay you
[sax] move to **[scents]** *who is there?* **[slightly left]** dad said: shut up
[sax] LA/USC **[body]** *I know the voice* **[and up]** walked home upset
[sax] UCLA/LAUSD **[follows]** *deeper though* **[slightly right]** you don't know
[sax] teaching credentials **[sensations]** *a voice from the past* **[and up]** kind of shit
[sax] Westside Trucking **[follows ears]** *is that you?* **[bring chin in]** had to take
[sax] [sax]
sensitivity training **[follows nose]** *do you remember* **[stoop]** to raise you **[sax]**
Gidra **[follows skin]** *me?* **[fall to knees]** married **[sax]**
moved to **[arthritic]** *do you know* **[press hands]** h.s girlfriend **[sax]**
Ann Arbor **[groping]** *who I am?* **[to ground]** three kids **[sax]**
women's studies **[curiosity]** *come closer* **[crawl forward]** separated **[sax]**
rice dance pieces **[innocent]** *let me touch your face* **[face extended]** she two kids **[sax]**
raw **[childlike]** *let me smell your hair* **[eyes closing]** we another one **[sax]**
cooked **[caress]** *this is the curve of your ear* **[head turning]** love those kids, my own **[sax]**
clothing/props **[twitch]** *this is the curve of your brow* **[right]** working warehouse **[sax]**
landscapes **[right hand]** *this is the scar where you fell* **[left]** shipping goods **[sax]**
1967 San José State **[swirl right]** *this is the dimple in your elbow* **[elbow]** YMCA dance show **[sax]**
MA dance **[swirl left]** *this is the smell of your hair* **[extended]** blown away **[sax]**
Afro-Haitian dance **[left hand]** *this is the beating* **[chest]** wanted to dance **[sax]**
racism in dance **[swirl left]** *of your heart* **[puffed]** black leotards **[sax]**
Food Fantasy **[swirl right]** *this is you* **[forward]** hung to dry **[sax]**
sushi **[shaking hands]** *you are home/I am home* **[arms]** in warehouse **[sax]**
sweet-and-sour chicken wings **[groping]** *do you forgive me?* **[extended]** on purpose **[sax]**
tempura **[knees fold]** *what is there to forgive?* **[fall]** guys looked, what's that? **[sax]**
tomato beef chow fun **[beneath]** *but you are blind* **[to knees]** my tights & leotards **[sax]**
yokan **[crumbling]** *it is my fault* **[close fists]** think about it **[sax]**

fuse tape theater jazz **[body]** *young men leave home* **[beat floor]** later, what they for? **[sax]**
teach at SFSC **[struggle]** *what can a mother do?* **[beat chest]** dancing **[sax]**
work Keystone Corner **[to rise]** *if I were not blind* **[hang head]** think about that **[sax]**
North Beach **[from heels]** *I would not know you today* **[grovel]** invited guys **[sax]**
sell bagels 6 to 2 a.m. **[precarious]** *my blindness* **[crawl around]** sitting in front row **[sax]**
Sun Ra **[balance]** *is a blessing* **[roll]** mouths dropped **[sax]**
LSD marijuana **[fall back]** *I am full of sadness* **[fall back]** hey you shoulda seen it, man **[sax]**
but dance in control **[roll]** *for our time together lost* **[roll up]** really cool **[sax]**
dancers into health **[feet crooked]** *now I will care for you* **[right hand to chest]** change opinions **[sax]**
actors into drugs **[crawl]** *I will take you from this poor place* **[declamation]** not a sissy thing **[sax]**
writers into booze **[embrace]** *come live with me* **[embrace]** a trip **[sax]**
Kearny Street Workshop **[press hands]** *in Liang Shan Po* **[press hands]** really want to dance **[sax]**
Hungry i basement **[to hands]** *I promise you a better life* **[to hands]** Meredith Monk **[sax]**
dance to poetry **[go limp]** *may we grow old together* **[open arms]** Alvin Ailey **[sax]**
proper wife **[struggle up]** *my son I am more than old* **[rise]** his walk so beautiful **[sax]**
divorce **[crawl]** *I cannot go away with you* **[step back]** doesn't even know **[sax]**
Asian Media **[on four]** *leave me here to die* **[step forward]** so natural **[sax]**
move to Noe Valley **[precariously]** *it is enough to see you* **[turn]** hey, go to Cuba to dance **[sax]**
Asian American Theater Co. **[lose]** *once again* **[turn again]** yeah, Second Brigada Venceremos **[sax]**
always cast as mother **[balance]** *now I can die happily* **[leap]** grown man, but **[sax]**
Gold Watch **[crumble]** *knowing that you live* **[leap]** tell my mother **[sax]**
Soul Shall Dance **[push up]** *I can no longer travel* **[circle]** she's sewing stuff **[sax]**
dancer not actress **[pull at]** *my legs are weak* **[scoop]** mama, I'm going to Cuba **[sax]**
bad reviews **[imaginary]** *and I am blind* **[pull]** you are having an interesting **[sax]**
Year of the Dragon **[support]** *mother I am strong* **[arms akimbo]** life **[sax]**
fear of director **[pull up]** *feel my muscles* **[show]** blessing like that **[sax]**
crazy erratic aggressive **[incrementally]** *my great arms* **[muscles]** is it dangerous? **[sax]**
kicked director out **[hoisted]** *I will carry you* **[handstand]** maybe **[sax]**
Eugene McCarthy **[up]** *on my back* **[cartwheel]** she says **[sax]**
Democratic Convention **[small]** *you are as light* **[crouch]** the generation **[sax]**
delegate **[package]** *as a bird* **[backward]** that doesn't believe **[sax]**
1969 DC antiwar rally **[tiny]** *see how easy* **[pull to back]** in its children **[sax]**
San José Peace Center **[tattered]** *you are riding* **[draw arms]** is in trouble **[sax]**
first mochi-tsuki **[bundle]** *on your Iron Ox* **[forward]** always remember that **[sax]**
Yu Ai Kai senior services **[hanging]** *come away with me* **[bend forward]** FBI watching **[sax]**
San José Taiko **[on]** *the day is bright* **[retrieve]** two ways to go: **[sax]**
SFPerforming Arts Workshop **[bare]** *my step is light and quick* **[axes]** Canada ship **[sax]**
Yellow Peril **[feet]** *soon we will be* **[one]** Mexico City Air Cuba **[sax]**

entangled in long white cloth **[protruding]** *at home* **[in each]** be ready anytime **[sax]**

running monologue **[neck]** *in Liang Shan Po* **[hand]** no time to wash **[sax]**

automobile statistics: **[straining]** *mother riding* **[small circles]** dirty clothes, throw in **[sax]**

specs & calibrations **[forward]** *on the back of the son* **[large circle]** suitcase **[sax]**

Asian women stereotypes **[sightless]** *they sing together* **[concentric]** at bus, name not on list **[sax]**

1974 Asian American **[eyes]** *as they hike* **[slow]** could jeopardize trip **[sax]**

Dance Collective **[turning]** *these mountain trails* **[climbing]** leave bus, but **[sax]**

expectations: **[ears]** *many hours* **[slow]** picked up wrong suitcase **[sax]**

use Asian traditions **[twitching]** *yet the son never tires* **[motion]** nicely stacked bras, etc. **[sax]**

but what's **[nose]** *his mother pleads* **[time]** leave later **[sax]**

Asian American? **[slips]** *are you not weary?* **[passing]** via Mexico **[sax]**

go to Japan **[down]** *am I not heavy?* **[bends]** get to Cuba **[sax]**

Shiro Nomura master of Noh **[slumps]** *we should stop to rest* **[axes down]** woman waiting **[sax]**

Kyogen **[a lump]** *stop for I am thirsty* **[swing]** with my suitcase **[sax]**

Theater Yugen **[of rags]** *here is a green boulder* **[mother down]** with my life **[sax]**

go to Hawaii **[left arm]** *in the shade of pines* **[breathes]** changes **[sax]**

Okinawan classical dance **[stretches]** *let me rest here* **[stretches]** three months **[sax]**

perform Choson-ji **[forward]** *while you find a stream* **[sits]** different way of life **[sax]**

Tsukuba World Expo **[right arm]** *to quench our thirst* **[rests]** quiet watching, listening **[sax]**

multimedia theatrical **[stretches]** *mother you are thirsty* **[jumps up]** others smarter than me **[sax]**

SoundSeen **[forward]** *I will bring you water* **[paces]** return but to NY **[sax]**

Land of 'Ooz' & Ahs **[curved arms]** *rest here quietly* **[circles]** dance scene there **[sax]**

Type O **[rotate]** *until I return* **[circles]** elitist competitive **[sax]**

Seven Steps to Go **[torso]** *my son take your time* **[turns]** return home to SF **[sax]**

collect water **[rotate]** *there is no hurry* **[turns]** check into I-Hotel **[sax]**

[sax] [sax] [sax] [sax] [sax] [sax] [sax] [sax] [sax] [sax] [sax]

worldwide mud **[arms hang]** *a quiet moment in the shade* **[sax]** *place the axes* **[retrieves]** hotel built in 1920s

dancers in mud **[head rotates]** *smell the pine* **[sax]** *next to mother* **[axes]** traveling men

everyone in same color mud **[left round]** *smell the mud* **[sax]** *she cannot see* **[draws axes]** followed labor

Marxist students **[torso follows]** *a stream is very near* **[sax]** *or fear* **[up]** by 1960s

ideology vs. open path **[to left]** *but there is another scent* **[sax]** *these terrible weapons* **[forward]** seedy skid row

in the mind only **[face rises]** *that of a cool breeze* **[sax]** *useless to find* **[overhead]** loss of SROs

can't dance **[to right]** *in that direction* **[sax]** *or carry water* **[v]** homelessness

study paleontology and **[to light]** *the cool air* **[sax]** *the sound* **[poses]** drugs & prostitution

cell structures **[air]** *from a cave* **[sax]** *of trickling water* **[bombast]** build loft in hotel room

more interesting **[mouth]** *and with that cool air* **[sax]** *over rocks* **[sets axes down]** people in and out

than Marx **[opens]** *the scent of the animals* **[sax]** *behind this* **[strolls away]** learn to cook

film: **[closes]** *that live within* **[sax]** *mountain shrine* **[bowlegged]** manongs & Chinese

Hot Summer Wind **[breathe]** *I know this scent* **[sax]** *down this path* **[steps]** know their stuff
Eat a Bowl of Tea **[in]** *I am born in the year* **[sax]** *it is many hours* **[circles]** correct way
dance with text **[out]** *of the tiger* **[sax]** *without rest* **[circles]** to cut vegetables
satire **[lift arms]** *it is a tigers' den nearby* **[sax]** *my mother* **[lightly]** smell the cooking break
stereotypes **[up]** *listen to the soft step* **[sax]** *knew my thirst* **[leaps]** two stoves, no fridge, sink
body types **[struggle]** *of the tigress* **[sax]** *I guzzle a gallon* **[push-ups]** amazing food
dance sculpture **[to rise]** *she approaches silently* **[sax]** *spring water* **[push-ups]** my boy and girl
self-learner **[outstretched]** *we are mothers both* **[sax]** *clear and cool* **[push-ups]** live with me at hotel
intuitive **[arms]** *I know her need and purpose* **[sax]** *soon we will be* **[long]** run up and down the halls
funny **[step]** *ah she leaps!* **[sax]** *home together* **[leaps]** sleep on floor
[sax] *I will become* **[diagonally]** manongs care for them
[sax] *a good son* **[heroic]** feed them
[sax] *a worthy and dutiful son* **[ballet]** remarry in hotel
[sax] *at long last* **[heavy-]** woman with the suitcase
[sax] *my mother will live* **[footed]** everyone cooks
[sax] *in peace* **[but high kicks]** people off streets
[sax] *and comfort* **[jumps]** come to wedding
[sax] *but how now to bring* **[acrobatic]** music great mix:
[sax] *water* **[spins]** Chinese gongs
[sax] *to my poor* **[tumbles]** Filipino love songs
[sax] *thirsty mother* **[scratches]** swing
[sax] *cup my hands* **[head]** 1972 Martial Law
[sax] *carefully now* **[cups]** mentored by old CP
[sax] *the water seeps* **[hands]** came from working class
[sax] *through my fingers* **[clawed]** sectarianism
[sax] *no cup or flask* **[fingers]** too young to know
[sax] *brutish outlaw* **[rushes forward]** no right line
[sax] *see the temple urn* **[grasps]** if you think you know
[sax] *rip it* **[urn]** the answer, in trouble
[sax] *from its peaceful post* **[struggles]** wife pregnant
[sax] *drag it* **[bursting effort]** leave I-Hotel
[sax] *to the stream* **[grimace]** Bernal Heights
[sax] *fill this sacred urn* **[scowl]** job iron union
[sax] *with precious water* **[hugging]** first Filipino to join
[sax] *powerful giant* **[weight]** start ethnic group
[sax] *great Li K'wei* **[legs trembling]** within union
[sax] *your dear* **[each step]** organize
[sax] *mother awaits* **[torture]** hello brother
[sax] *with thirst* **[another step]** what's up, man?

9: Yellow Peril

Testing. Testing? *(Screech. Crackle. Crackle.)* Testing. Testing. TESTING. Oh. Ouch. Honey, can you hear me? *(We can hear you!)* Brothers and Sisters, welcome to the second annual picnic for the Bay Area Asian American Coalition Against the War. *(Right on!)* How are you all doing? *(Yeah!)* It's marvelous to see this kind of turnout. Now those of you who are still arriving, James and Goro are setting up more tables for your potluck. And those of you who haven't already been chowing down, get over there before the chashu baos and musubis get gobbled up. Now if there aren't enough plates, just pile that food up on those Frisbees. And you know Mrs. Takabayashi made her famous teriyaki chicken again this year, and I already got my drumstick, *(waves it around)* so go on now and get yours.

Oh yeah, and we're passing around the bucket today. We're asking for your generous contributions for the I-Hotel, which is needing your assistance for repairs and to paint it with a big mural. Hey, Sen! Did I get that right? And you all know I live in that hotel, so you better make it pretty.

Now to open our program today, I'd like you to welcome, at your peril, Jack, Stony, and Aiko of the Yellow Pearl! *(scattered applause, sound of clomping feet on the risers, adjustments to microphones as three performers step up—Jack Sung and Aiko Masaoka, with acoustic guitars, and Stony Ima with taiko and shakuhachi)*

Someone yells: Hey Jack! You gonna sing us a folk song or what?

Jack: That's right. I'm gonna sing you a folk song! Aiko, Stony, you know that poem about two roads diverging in the woods?

Stony: And you took the one less traveled by?

Jack: Not me. I took the train!

Someone: Fuckin' chonk Chinaman!

Jack: Who said that?

Someone: I did!

Jack: Gerald? What are you doing here?

Gerald (the someone): What do you think? I'm eating!

Jack: Hey Pearls, that's him. He's the one who took the road less traveled.

Aiko: You mean Li K'wei, who took revenge for his mother's death by killing four tigers?

Jack: Yeah, that's him.

Stony: I don't believe it.

Gerald: You talking about me?

Jack: Gerald, shut up and get yourself another beer. We're going to serenade you with a folk song.

Aiko: Before we start, I want to dedicate our song in solidarity to the Vietnamese people and their struggle for liberation. *(nods at Stony Ima, who starts up the song with a plaintive shakuhachi)*

(guitar chords)
(slow to vigorous taiko)

(chorus)
Big bad Li K'wei
Bold and brutal
Iron-fisted
Godzilla of a man
Feed him fifty bowls of rice
(feed him fifty bowls of rice!)
Feed him fifty bowls of wine
(feed him fifty bowls of wine!)
Then turn him loose
A revolutionary wind
A revolutionary fire

Warrior bandit with your battleaxes
Spin your weapons into whirling wind *(extended shakuhachi)*
Avenge the slaughter of your motherland
Scatter mountains into sand

(chorus)

(taiko interlude)
Warrior bandit with your battleaxes
Maligned today and called a simple thief
Struggle for the righteous and the quest
Defeat the paper tigers of the west

A revolutionary wind
(feed the hungry bandit
Fifty bowls of rice!)
(taiko)

A revolutionary fire
(feed the hungry bandit
fifty bowls of wine!)
(taiko)

Warrior bandit with your battleaxes
In the darkest forests of the night
Search out the tiger's cruelest bluest eye
And split its fearful symmetry
(shrill shakuhachi)

(chorus)
(wild taiko finish)
(applause)

Gerald: Who wrote that fuckin' folk song? Shit.

10: Iron Ox

So the other night, that radical leftist group the JTC (stands for the Japantown Collective) closed shop, just up and moved all their stuff out of that old Victorian on Sutter Street in the dead of night and hauled away every last piece of radical business and furniture. It isn't that they're giving up the radical life, mind you, or at least that's what folks are saying. Maybe they are going underground or merging with another radical formation. It's like that these days. You don't know which radical alphabet to pay attention to anymore. They come, give you a line, then join some other line. But not that they're looking to recruit the likes of moi.

Anyway, Sen Hama, who always pays attention to what's happening, gets this idea to start an art collective and to move into that emptiness left by the disappearance of the JTC. Move over revolutionaries! Here come the artists!

At first it's just Sen up there late into the night, building a studio for silkscreening, plus a light table, and setting up a darkroom for photography. One night Gerald K. Li wanders out of Jigoku and sees the light on upstairs at the Sutter place. He thinks maybe there's some action up there he's been missing and hunkers up the stairs with his axes. He finds Sen hard at work.

"Hey, Sen," Gerald growls, "what you got going here? Where's the party?"

"Just me, Gerald."

"Shit. I've been blowing all night, giving it up for others. Where's the payback?"

"I don't know, Gerald. Funny you should be here. You wanna help me set up for the next color?"

"Next color?" Gerald looks at the project at hand. "Hey, what's this?"

"That's you. It's the poster for your show."

"Me? Hey, it's me." Gerald nods. "Missing my axes."

"That's what we gotta do next. They go in here." Sen points to the blank area. "In gold."

"Nice." Gerald nods. "You did this, huh?"

"Yeah."

"It'll be my last show." Gerald grumbles.

"What do you mean?"

"They want me to play some other shit. My music is changing. I gotta go with the change. You know what I mean?"

"I understand. But don't stop playing."

"I'm not stopping. Just not playing for them."

So that's how it happens that Gerald quits Jigoku and starts hanging out with Sen at the arts collective. After they've run the next color, Gerald and Sen share a joint, which suddenly makes Sen loquacious, and he gets that fetid smoke to wander around the empty rooms and paints a graphic vision of his plan for this art studio. And Gerald sees the vision and gets excited and says, "Yeah, man, I hear you. And you could tear out this wall and put in a skylight to get some natural light. See, I know something about artists. It's all about light for you. For us, we can compose in the goddamn dark." He nudges Sen. "Different kind of sex, eh. With light. Without light."

Sen rolls his eyes.

And Gerald continues, "And over here is storage. And as for that darkroom plan, you got to put in some sinks and counters."

Sen says, "Yeah, I wanna tear out that old bathtub and wall off this area for a darkroom." They both stare at the curved iron tub with its rusting places in the white porcelain standing on its toes in the middle of dingy pink and cracked linoleum.

"No problem, let's do it."

"You know how much that iron ox weighs? We got to get some help to carry it out and down the stairs, don't forget. You drop it, and it'll put a hole in the floor."

"Hey, gimme a hand," says Gerald. He starts to tug at the thing.

"Stop!" Sen shouts. "We got to unhook the plumbing. You wanna flood the place?"

"Oh shit, yeah."

Sen comes back with tools, but meanwhile Gerald has opened and is hanging out the bathroom window looking out. Moon is full over the San Francisco night, one of those rare nights of no fog.

Sen joins him at the window. He points at the empty lot below. "Hauled away the Victorian next door on truck beds. I don't know where they took it. This one is next, but they might just bust it down with a ball. Fucking redevelopment." They finish off the joint in silence. Empty lot is strewn with rubbish, broken boards and glass, slabs of leftover concrete and stairs to nowhere, weeds flourishing in mud and garbage. Then Sen says, "You know People's Park, right?"

"Yeah, hippies on the Eastside."

"Yeah, well, when I get this studio running, my next plan is to start a garden down there. Mix it up. Japanese garden and bok choy. Put in a koi pond, benches, picnic area, maple coming up that way, bamboo. Rock garden over there."

Maybe it's the colors in the silkscreening. Maybe it's a combination of the exhaustion of playing music all night and the sweet watery clarity of the marijuana, but Gerald sees everything. The energy of the art studio presses behind him and the evening air breathes the garbage and detritus strewn below into a paradise. "I never thought about it, but maybe I need light to play."

"Moonlight?" asks Sen, observing the moon.

"All kinds of light," says Gerald. "Hey, I got an idea. A shortcut. Give me a hand here."

Mostly it's Gerald with Sen providing some stabilization, but they lift that iron ox from its pointed toes and shove it forward and out the open window. "Ouweeeeeeeee!" At that moment, if you were high, you saw it tumble and twist in a ballet of slow motion down two stories—a fat white ox flying over and over and over the moon.

After that evening, Gerald pays a visit to the empty lot to see how deep a hole a bathtub might create falling from two stories up. He looks up. He looks down. "Damn. We didn't even check to see if someone was down here." He tugs at the thing wedged in the dirt. And from that moment on, he's a gardener. Who knows why? Maybe because he got the whole vision that night from above. The tub's gotta go over there under that lone tree, has got to be filled with water and a filter system, rocks and aquatic plants and goldfish. Then there's the path from the tub to a mossy area over here, cut a path with rocks and flowing water, build up this area here to create the illusion of depth, bonsai here, a hedge of azalea here, and don't forget Sen's vegetable garden in this sunny area here. Pretty soon, the old folks are coming by, doing the weeding and planting green onions, napa, bok choy, tomatoes, zucchini, eggplant, cucumbers, mustard greens, chiso, wasabi, daikon, parsley, chrysanthemums, you name it. On the side, against the house, Gerald has a greenhouse going for the small shoots, orchids, and ferns. And some lady has her ceramic pots in there for pickling the vegetables.

Overlooking the garden, Sen paints a mural over the entire side of the house. Folks are up on the scaffolds for days painting in the numbers. One day Sen is putting in the finishing touches at the top of the house. He can hear Gerald wandering around the garden below, over the bridge and under the pines and maples, blowing on his sax. Nowadays, if you want to hear Gerald K. Li play, you have to pay a visit to the garden. If the old garde from Jigoku comes by and asks why, Gerald says, "I'm doing my thing." Sen listens for Gerald's thing. Then suddenly it's quiet. Hours later, Sen descends with his paintbrush, trying to remember where, from his high perch, he last saw Gerald in the garden. Under a maple in a grassy patch of filtered sunlight, he finds Gerald sitting closed-eyed in meditation, cross-legged and hugging his saxophones to either side. "Gerald," he whispers, but even then he knows. "Gerald," he asks again, even as he lightly touches the fingers wrapped around the sax, as cold to the touch as the brassy metal itself.

Oh sweetheart, my train's here. My Iron Moonhunter's arriving, pushing itself out like a giant dark dick smoking out of the foggy night. It's loaded with my outlaws. Are you making this trip or what?

1972: Inter-national Hotel

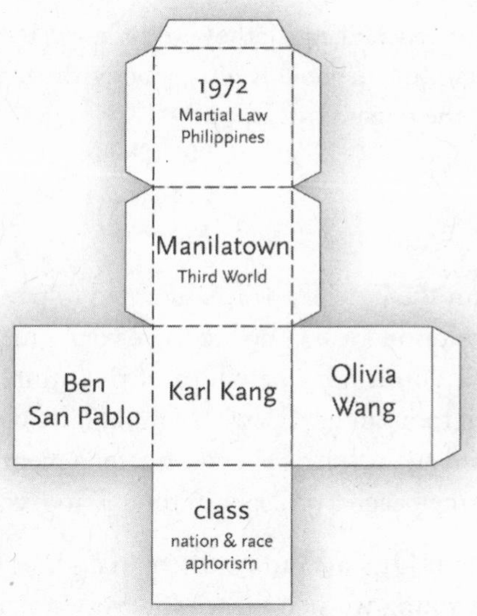

1: The Art of War

I came here with many friends
and remember those fabled months and years
  of study.
We were young,
sharp as flower wind, ripe,
candid with a scholar's bright blade
  and unafraid.
We pointed our finger at China.
—Mao Tse-tung *(Changsha)*

People who come out of prison can build up the country.
Misfortune is a test of people's fidelity.
Those who protest at injustice are people of true merit.
When the prison doors are opened, the real dragon will fly out.
—Ho Chi Minh, *Word-Play*

I

> All men are created equal; they are endowed by their Creator with certain unalienable Rights; among these are Life, Liberty, and the pursuit of Happiness.
>
> —Ho Chi Minh, *Declaration of Independence of the Democratic Republic of Viet-Nam*

1.1 She said: I am the indelible voice, returned to pay tribute to the lives of young revolutionaries. Who are these young men and women who sacrifice their youth for a new idea of the future? New idea of the future? In ten thousand years, what futures have blossomed and withered again and again, with generation after generation, each as hopeful as the former, each a whisper in time. I, too, was once so young.

1.2 Young woman: Olivia Wang was the daughter of a high-ranking family and a young woman for whom every consideration had been carefully measured. Her grandfather, a failed generalissimo, believed fervently in the promise of his progeny, fed his children with the ire of his misfortune, the fall of a great lord who could only pass the legacy of a family history that would not simply end with his escape. Every child, then, must be raised as a potential weapon, their minds honed to steel swords, their bodies made muscular beneath the graceful inscrutability of a skillful diplomat. So tutored, Olivia moved through any space with the glint of her privilege cast from her shoulders like sharp stings, but perhaps this was but a shallow performance for, in truth, the generalissimo escaped to exile, but his children escaped to freedom.

1.3 Young man: Bienvenido San Pablo, known simply as Ben San Pablo, was the grandson of a manong. It is true that to attain the honored status of a manong meant many years of struggle and survival, the plodding trek that followed the long Pacific coast from the Imperial Valley, stooping under a savage desert sun to pick fields of netted cantaloupe, to the shadow of Mount McKinley, gripping the frozen handle of a knife to slash the pink bellies of a thousand wild salmon. Ben knew that the life of his grandfather had been passed to his father, who would also one day be known as manong. But if manong is a title given to an honored elder, must it also be accompanied by the same passage through years of hardship and backbreaking labor? If Ben could find another path across his future, must he then relinquish this honored title?

II

The art of war is of vital importance to the State.
—Sun Tzu

2.1 An unlikely pair these two, Olivia and Ben, or as they were known, Olie and Benny, who in time met, found love, and joined their destinies one to the other. In another time and place, such a union would have been impossible, for such mixing of class and tribal identities should have been taboo. But these were times of war, and in war, the impossible becomes possible if only because the stakes are higher and there is nothing to lose.

2.2 Love in service of the revolution is a great love indeed.

III

All warfare is based on deception.
—Sun Tzu

3.1 If war brought Olivia and Ben together, would peace then pull them apart? For the young, seven years might seem an eternity, but for those who live seven years, it is finally only a beginning, and the promises of seven years stretch out into multiples of seven until youth crumbles into age, grasping for a reevaluation that desires once again a blank slate, the sloughing of cares piled one upon the other, the emptiness of freedom.

3.2 Ben pondered the constant warfare within his mind, the hidden mines that seemed to explode at every venture made through that dark labyrinth. Had not his heroes, Lenin and Marx, already cleared a path to light? Why was it, then, that his vision could only navigate through the clarity of a white opiate?

3.3 Nightly, Olivia dreamed about the floating child within her, its features morphing from those of Benny with his bright burning eyes, to a fat baby-face of Chairman Mao, to the stern features of her grandfather, the generalissimo. She woke in a frantic sweat and stumbled with her full belly from her bed to relieve her heavy bladder.

3.4 The political training of the mind wars constantly with its psychological training, pushing it to one side or the other but never replacing it completely. The mind is a vessel of wisdom, deception, and dreams.

IV

> Investigation may be likened to the long months of pregnancy, and solving a problem to the day of birth.
>
> —Mao Tse-tung

4.1 On the contrary, pregnancy cannot be likened to investigation, and no problem is solved on the day of birth.

4.2 Olivia drew her small bundle to her breast—his miniature fists pumping, his tiny open mouth searching for its beacon. She felt the glands within her release, gushing forth, seeming at first to drown the baby, but then, their bodies united. They gave and took in unison, the greedy baby, the provident breast.

4.3 Ben observed this world closed on itself, completely self-satisfied, and grasped at a meaning of his son's hunger and survival. The more the baby fed, the more Olivia would produce. Benny smiled and announced gleefully: *This is a clear example of controlling the means of production.*

4.4 Olivia sneered, *What bullshit.*

V

> Learn to "play the piano."
>
> —Mao Tse-tung

5.1 When the boy, whom they named Malcolm, was one year old, Ben sat with him on his lap at the piano, pressing the keys one by one. *This is the center of the keyboard,* he said. *This is the middle C. This is the scale up and down, up and down. You must learn to play with all ten fingers.*

5.2 Of course, the Chairman had something else in mind when he opined that one should learn to play the piano, but Ben also heard the old melodies that he had abandoned for the revolution, and he felt them pushing through his very fingers toward the keys, a dormant life awaking in the realization of his son.

5.3 A man may teach the revolution to a people, but what revolution must he teach to his own son?

VI

> A revolution is not a dinner party, or writing an essay, or painting a picture, or doing embroidery; it cannot be so refined, so leisurely and gentle, so temperate, kind, courteous, restrained and magnanimous. A revolution is an insurrection, an act of violence by which one class overthrows another.
>
> —Mao Tse-tung

6.1 An unmarked car with four men inside rolled slowly down the street. Olivia could feel the eyes of the men mark her gait along the sidewalk. She turned to look and thought she saw the tip of a gun resting across the window. Suddenly, two of the men charged out of the car from the backseat, but she screamed the scream she had trained her voice to throw, the terrorized voice of a woman in dire straits. The voice alone paralyzed the men, but she threw a back punch into the throat of one and slipped from their grip, a slimy fish, racing away down the street screaming, escaping.

6.2 Unfortunately, the same men succeeded in grabbing another of their cadre, accused her of possession of an unregistered weapon, rifled through her purse, confiscating an address book. *Who are Benny and Olie?* the police of the Red Squad questioned. Later, this cadre phoned from jail and warned Ben at home, who at the same moment heard the knock on the door, grabbed Malcolm, and escaped through the backyard, scaling a fence with a clinging toddler at his hip.

6.3 Olivia phoned home from a booth on the street and heard the answering voice of a strange man. She asked coolly, *Is Malcolm there?*

The voice answered, *No, he's at work. Can you leave a message? That won't be necessary,* she replied.

VII

> Individualism spawns hundreds of dangerous diseases: bureaucratism, commandism, sectarianism, subjectiveness, corruption, waste. . . . Individualism is the cruel enemy of socialism. The revolutionary must do away with it.
>
> —Ho Chi Minh

7.1 It was Ben who noticed the change. *What is it, Olie? You need to eat. You're losing weight. You need to quit that kung fu stuff.*

7.2 *It's not kung fu, Benny. I don't have time for that. My back just hurts, and I'm bloated. Maybe I'm lactose intolerant.*

7.3 *Getting to be an old lady,* he snickered.

7.4 *I can't go to that meeting tonight. I'm so tired.*

7.5 *Burned out?* he taunted.

7.6 *Bullshit.*

7.7 *You have a fever,* he worried.

VIII

> If you know the enemy and know yourself, you need not fear the result of a hundred battles.
>
> —Sun Tzu

8.1 Olivia said plainly, *My sister told my parents, and they paid for the tests.*

8.2 *What tests?* asked Ben.

8.3 *Blood tests. Other tests that say I have ovarian cancer.*

IX

> The intellectuals can overcome their shortcomings only in mass struggles over a long period.
>
> —Mao Tse-tung

9.1 *Benny,* she said from her bed, *you're a lousy revolutionary, and only I know it. I should bring it up before the central committee and have your ass blasted.*

9.2 He laughed, looked up from his book. *You know I'm only in this because I like to read.*

9.3 *You love the idea of the revolutionary.*

9.4 *It's a good idea. A very good idea, you know.*

9.5 *Like hell it is,* she said.

X

> If you want knowledge, you must take part in the practice of changing reality. If you want to know the taste of a pear, you must change the pear by eating it yourself.
>
> —Mao Tse-tung

10.1 Ben did not reply because he feared what was to come, the absence of his partner in revolution, the woman at his side who offered her energy and her skills as the practitioner of his theorizing. What sort of ideologue would he become without his intelligent and practicing believer?

10.2 For every Marx, there must be a Lenin, or a Che, or a Ho, or a Mao.

XI

> . . . the East Wind is prevailing over the West Wind.
>
> —Mao Tse-tung

11.1 But she said: I have anticipated the end of the story without first imparting the beginning. Knowing the story's end does not necessarily imply completion or knowledge, for if many endings are possible, so also are many beginnings. History may proceed sequentially or, as they say, *must* proceed sequentially, but stories may turn and turn again—the knowing end kissing the innocent beginning, the innocent end kissing the knowing beginning.

2: Malcolm X at Bandung

Bandung was a decisive moment in the consciousness of sixty-five percent of the human race, and that moment meant: HOW SHALL THE HUMAN RACE BE ORGANIZED?

—Richard Wright: *The Color Curtain: A Report on the Bandung Conference*, 1956

At Bandung all the nations came together, the dark nations of Africa and Asia. Some of them were Buddhists, some of them were Muslims, some of them were Christians, some of then were Confucianists, some were atheist. Despite their religious differences, they came together. Some were communist, some were socialists, some were capitalists—despite their economic and political differences they came together. All of them were black, brown, red or yellow.

The number-one thing that was not allowed to attend at the Bandung conference was the white man. He couldn't come. . . . And these people who came together didn't have nuclear weapons, they didn't have jet planes, they didn't have all the heavy armaments that the white man has. But they had unity. . . .

They realized that all over the world where the dark man was being oppressed, he was being oppressed by the white man; where the dark man was being exploited, he was being exploited by the white man. So they got together on this basis—that they had a common enemy.

—Malcolm X, *Message to the Grass Roots*, 1963

1

1. Respect for fundamental human rights and for the purposes and principles of the charter of the United Nations.

—Final Communiqué, Bandung Conference, April 1955

> We declare our right on this earth . . . to be a human being, to be respected as a human being, to be given the rights of a human being in this society, on this earth, in this day, which we intend to bring into existence by any means necessary.
>
> —Malcolm X

1.1 Make no mistake: El Hajj Malik Shabazz, the man we knew as Malcolm X, was not at the Bandung Conference in Indonesia in 1955. Neither was he the first African American man to set foot on Africa, nor to make his hajj to Mecca. And yet it was as if his spirit permeated these actions and events, such that others to come might measure personal accomplishments and commitments with added significance.

1.2 Similarly, Bienvenido San Pablo was, of course, not the only Filipino American to participate in 1969 in the Third World Strike at the University of California at Berkeley, nor was he the first Filipino American to travel to Havana with the Brigada Venceremos.

1.3 And Olivia Wang knew nothing of poverty or racial prejudice before she, a mere high-school student of sixteen years, volunteered to work one summer in Mississippi for the Student Nonviolent Coordinating Committee. Again, she was neither the first nor the only Asian American to travel into the deep South to discover another country and another purpose in life.

1.4 The particulars of any event may recede to favor the idea of the event.

II

> 2. Respect for the sovereignty and territorial integrity of all nations.
>
> *—Final Communiqué, Bandung Conference,* April 1955

> It is incorrect to classify the revolt of the Negro as simply a radical conflict of black against white or as a purely American problem. Rather, we are today seeing a global rebellion of the oppressed against the oppressor, the exploited against the exploiter. —Malcolm X

2.1 Ben sat in the audience and marveled at the confidence of the young woman who marched to the microphone and spoke without notes, in complete sentences, with casual but forceful articulateness. She recounted her journey, her work, and the significance of her meetings and discussions with those personages of high repute: H. Rap Brown and Stokely Carmichael. She could not have been more than twenty. He noted the sheen of her hair curled behind her ear, the elegant gestures of her hands and long fingers, the sense of her stature despite her height.

2.2 At another event, Olivia heard the intensity in the voice of the young man who introduced the labor organizer from the farmworkers' movement, Philip Vera Cruz. She heard his voice, but she watched his eyes, which seemed to her almost stunning in their bright beauty, the way his look across the crowd sparkled with both kindness and fury.

2.3 First impressions may both deceive and perceive.

III

> 3. Recognition of the equality of all races and of the equality of all nations large and small.
>
> —*Final Communiqué, Bandung Conference,* April 1955

> If violence is wrong in America, violence is wrong abroad. If it is wrong to be violent defending black women and black children and black babies and black men, then it is wrong for America to draft us, and make us violent abroad in defense of her. And if it is right for America to draft us, and teach us how to be violent in defense of her, then it is right for you

and me to do whatever is necessary to defend our own people right here in this country.

—Malcolm X

3.1 Ben read the picket sign ahead of him. *Stop the Genocide of Asian People!* Below the sign, he could not mistake the flounce of her shimmering hair and that walk of almost haughty confidence.

3.2 Perhaps she felt the attention of his eyes behind her, heard them speaking to her forward movement along the street. She turned ever so slightly to acknowledge his gaze, a flash of recognition, not without a coy smile.

IV

4. Abstention from intervention or interference in the internal affairs of another country.

—*Final Communiqué, Bandung Conference,* April 1955

You can't separate the militancy that's displayed on the African continent from the militancy that's displayed right here among American blacks. . . . [Y]ou can't separate the African revolution from the mood of the black man in America.

—Malcolm X

4.1 Marching on the picket line at the famous Sather Gate on the University of California at Berkeley, Ben thought he saw her figure passing under Wheeler Oak, the giant oak tree whose branches spread out in thick dark arms across the cold concrete. He rushed away from his duties, his sign flapping above on its stick like a blown-out umbrella. He ran after the long hair dancing at her back, weaving through the scatter of students. He could see his breath puff into the cold morning air, calling her silently, but when he reached a certain distance, he realized it was not her.

4.2 The woman turned to see the picketer following her and abruptly turned away, perhaps in embarrassment, perhaps in fear that he would accost her and force her to join his protest. Her steps quickened, and he let her figure recede into the distance with the rising campanile.

4.3 He who forsakes his duties for the curiosity of a woman's hair may find himself holding a wig.

V

> 5. Respect for the right of each nation to defend itself singly or collectively, in conformity with the charter of the United Nations. —*Final Communiqué, Bandung Conference,* April 1955

> The thing that I would like to impress upon every Afro-American leader is that no kind of action in this country is ever going to bear fruit unless that action is tied in with the overall international struggle. —Malcolm X

5.1 At yet another political event, this time a rally in Chinatown to commemorate the fiftieth anniversary of the May 4, 1919, student movement, they found themselves standing side by side.

5.2 *Hey,* he said. *Don't I know you?* His eyes twinkled, almost mischievously.

5.3 *I've seen you before,* she said. Her black hair swayed, back and forth. She spoke mockingly, *One of those, I suppose?*

5.4 *One of what?* he queried.

5.5 *Political tourists,* she sneered and walked away.

5.6 He watched her hair disappear in a swirl of red flags and the heroic fanfare of the "East is Red," the sting of her verbal jab piercing his heart in a flutter of pain and desire.

5.7 As the true intention of an act of hostility may be unknown to its perpetrator, the victim may misinterpret that act as he wishes. Flirting has its fashions.

VI

> 6. (a) Abstention from the use of arrangements of collective defense to serve any particular interests of the big powers.
> (b) Abstention by any country from exerting pressures on other countries. —*Final Communiqué, Bandung Conference*, April 1955

> The white man knows what a revolution is. He knows that the Black Revolution is worldwide in scope and in nature. The Black Revolution is sweeping Asia, is sweeping Africa, is rearing its head in Latin America. The Cuban Revolution—that's a revolution. They overturned the system. Revolution is in Asia, revolution is in Africa, and the white man is screaming because he sees revolution in Latin America. How do you think he'll react to you when you learn what a real revolution is? —Malcolm X

6.1 Ben wisely consulted the resourceful underground network of the resistance, combing through a web of rumors, layers of acquaintances, and the happenstance of knowing a fact or two. In simple truth, he confessed to his roommate: *I see this girl everywhere with this incredible hair.*

6.2 And his roommate said, *First off, you got to call them* women *now.*

6.3 *When I find her,* said Benny, *I'll call her* woman.

6.4 *O.K.,* his roommate said, *I'll put out an* APB *on her, but I need more than hair.*

6.5 *I think she's Chinese, and she's got one helluva attitude.*

6.6 When the all-points came in, his roommate said, *Benny, trust me on this one. Stay away. Far away. She's way outta your league, man.*

6.7 The man who sends a query to all points should not expect a unanimous or even auspicious answer from all points.

VII

> 7. Refraining from acts or threats of aggression or the use of force against the territorial integrity or political independence of any country. —*Final Communiqué, Bandung Conference,* April 1955

> The same rebellion, the same impatience, the same anger that exists in the hearts of the dark people in Africa and Asia is existing in the hearts and minds of 20 million black people in this country who have been just as thoroughly colonized as the people in Africa and Asia.
>
> —Malcolm X

7.1 Fluorescent lights flickered on suddenly with the closing credits of the film: *One-Fourth of Humanity: The China Story* by Edgar Snow, who wrote the seminal work on Red China entitled *Red Star Over China.*

7.2 Ben rubbed his eyes and looked around at the students in the Le Conte Hall classroom at Berkeley. He had arrived during the film, groping his way in the dark among the chairs to find an empty seat. The black-and-white footage of Edgar Snow conversing with Mao Tse-tung, both seated formally in those sofa chairs—the former a white-haired man leaning intently and the latter plumply jovial—seemed impressed on his tired retinas. Thus, when he turned to see her rising in the adjacent seat, he had a strange impression of her real presence against the ghostly flicker of the documentary.

7.3 *Leaving?* he asked.

7.4 *Yes, if you don't mind.*

7.5 *You should stay for the discussion.*

7.6 *Believe me, there is nothing you'll be discussing that I don't already know.*

7.7 *How can you be so sure, Olivia?*

7.8 At the sound of her name, she glared at him. *This film is a watered-down version of his book. Perhaps you should read it.* She pulled the book from a small stack in her arms and shoved it at him. *Now, if you'll excuse me.*

7.9 Ben held the book aloft like a trophy as she exited the room, his star over China.

VIII

8. Settlement of all international disputes by peaceful means, such as negotiation, conciliation, arbitration or judicial settlement as well as other peaceful means of the parties own choice, in conformity with the charter of the United Nations.

—*Final Communiqué, Bandung Conference,* April 1955

They don't stand for anything different in South Africa than America stands for. The only difference is over there they preach as well as practice apartheid. America preaches freedom and practices slavery.

—Malcolm X

8.1 At a meeting of the Asian American Political Alliance, Olivia stood to make her announcement. The Director of the Federal Bureau of Investigations, an officious but powerful bureaucrat named J. Edgar Hoover, had testified in Congress at the House Committee on Appropriations, declaring red China to be the number-one enemy of the United States. Furthermore, three hundred thousand Chinese Americans currently living in the United States were in his view suspicious and could be involved in espionage. Their numbers were escalating yearly, to the tune of twenty thousand Chinese immigrants sent to America, no doubt as illegal agents.

8.2 Karl Kang, self-appointed to run the meeting, added comments to the effect that this sort of red scare tactic was racist and similar to the justifications for the internment of Japanese American citizens during World War II.

8.3 Olivia continued: a protest was being organized in New York at the headquarters of the FBI on East Sixty-ninth and Third Avenue. Just in case anyone was going to New York over the fall break.

8.4 After the meeting, which included a short presentation about the peasants, students, and workers in China, Ben stopped Olivia at the door, her copy of Snow's book in his hand.

8.5 *Did you read it?* she snapped.

8.6 *To be honest, I had already read it.*

8.7 *Then why did you take it?*

8.8 *To read it again with all your notes and underlining.*

8.9 She grabbed Snow's book with a kind of dismay and shock, as if her mind and thoughts had been violated, as if an intricate diary of her life had been revealed in her scribbling in the reader's margins. The reader's life, captured invisibly in the dust between each turning page, is a secret.

8.10 *I hope you don't mind,* Ben said. *I added my notes to your notes.* It was Ben's turn to smile coyly and to flash his mischievous look. Where else may there be a true meeting of minds but within a book?

IX

9. Promotion of mutual interests and cooperation.
—*Final Communiqué, Bandung Conference,* April 1955

Expand the civil-rights struggle to the level of human rights, take it into the United Nations, where our African brothers can throw their weight on our side, where our Asian brothers can throw their weight on our side, where our Latin-American brothers can throw their weight on our side, and where 800 million Chinamen are sitting there waiting to throw their weight on our side.
—Malcolm X

9.1 Ben double-parked the pickup on Kearny Street in front of the main door into the I-Hotel. He ran around to the back of the truck and yanked the gate down, exposing a load of supplies: cans of paint, rollers and brushes, tarps, coils of wire, bags of plaster, and trowels. A crew of volunteers rushed to unload the truck. Several weeks ago, there had been a fire in the hotel, and if the hotel could not be brought up to public building standards, the city had threatened to condemn the building and to evict its elderly tenants—mostly old manongs to whose lives Ben knew himself tied.

9.2 Trudging up the stairs with fresh supplies, he found Olivia on the landing, rolling swaths of bright white paint over the walls. He stood at the bottom of the steps for a moment, appreciating the red baseball cap pushed back over her hair, this time in a long, smooth ponytail, and the smudges like war paint across her forehead and cheeks.

9.3 *Well,* he chortled, *if it isn't Miss Know-it-all.*

9.4 She ignored him, as if he were a mere working peon. *It's about time you arrived. We're running out of paint, and I could use a ladder and some brushes for the detail work.*

9.5 He pulled a screwdriver from his back pocket and pried open a fresh can of paint, stirred, and poured its contents into her waiting tray. He left and returned with a ladder and a small paintbrush and mustered his most degrading imitation: *Will da missus be needin' anytang else?*

9.6 When Olivia had climbed to the top of the ladder, he silently walked past, nudging the paint tray with his foot to position it strategically next to the bottom step of the ladder while advising her to use the wider motion of a fan to accomplish her job. *Are you trying to tell me how to do my job?*

9.7 *No, ma'am. Uh-uh. No sirree.*

9.8 Later, he smiled with pleasure, noting her left Ked, previously matching her right's red, soaked in white paint, such that it seemed glued to her sock.

9.9 One may ascend a ladder to volunteer but in descending discover the true nature of one's altruism.

X

10. Respect for justice and international obligations.
—*Final Communiqué, Bandung Conference,* April 1955

You can't separate peace from freedom because no one can be at peace unless he has his freedom. If you're not ready to die for it, put the word "freedom" out of your vocabulary. Truth is on the side of the oppressed.
—Malcolm X

10.1 A car drove up to the house and honked several times. Ben looked from his window at the gold Mercedes Benz below, shrugged, and returned to his packing. When had he ever known anyone who owned such a vehicle? Janis Joplin might croon about it, but what lord would ever provide? But then came the loud pounding at his door. *Ben, we're here. Let's hit the road.* Ben swung open the door and ran back to the window to make sure. *Shit,* he said, *when did you get a Benz?*

10.2 His comrade, Macario Amado, explained it was the ride he'd arranged. *Think of it this way, like we confiscated it from the bourgeoisie. It's like we're undercover, but shit, you still have to pay for the gas.*

10.3 Ben threw his duffel and sleeping bag into the trunk and slid onto the slippery leather of the backseat. He could not mistake the silky swish of the hair or the haughty attitude of the driver who turned to greet him in dismay. *You,* she huffed.

10.4 *What the?*

10.5 *You guys know each other?*

10.6 There are twenty-five hundred miles between Berkeley, California, and Montreal, Canada, and traveling approximately five hundred miles per day would mean a trip of perhaps five days across the great terrain of the North American continent. Ben and Olivia may have contemplated their separate anticipations, trapped with one's nemesis over five days on a road trip of twenty-five hundred miles but, after all, headed for the Hemispheric Conference to End the Vietnam War. The South Vietnamese National Liberation Front and the Democratic Republic of Vietnam would send their representatives. Their alliance must also be present to align itself with the nonaligned Third World.

10.7 The personal must be put aside for the political.

3: What Is to Be Done?

I

> The history of all hitherto existing society is the history of class struggle. —Karl Marx and Friedrich Engels, *Communist Manifesto*

1.1 Study Group #1: What is class struggle?

1.2 Indeed. Are you rich, or are you poor? Do you command great armies and oversee great territories, or are you the fodder of stinking bodies sacrificed at the front? Do you rule by the will of God or the Mandate of Heaven, or do you grovel in the dirt for your subsistence and share your food with animals? Do you stand at the pinnacle of power, however precariously protecting, with the great umbrella of your powerful arms and silken sleeves, a hierarchy of hapless fools and ungrateful subjects, or are you a struggling peon of unfortunate birth? Ah, but I have but described the peaking ascendance of only one period in the struggle of human history. Now you shall hear of the next and the next. The rise and fall of civilizations held in dusty monuments for thousands of years may suddenly be compressed in no doubt brilliant minds to explain the present moment.

1.3 Karl Kang, such a mind of brilliance, a graduate student of political economy who spoke and read in Korean, Chinese, Japanese, French, a bit of Russian, and of course English, was a mentor whose teaching was indispensable to youth desirous of answers.

1.4 They met in Kang's apartment on Dwight, blocks from the university, arriving with their copies of *Capital, The State and Revolution, What Is to Be Done?*

1.5 Kang opened the discussion. *We're going to take this slowly and build our knowledge. What I realize is that this is a body of knowledge that has been censored out of your education, whereas to think in Marxist terms outside of America is common practice.* Marxism is a way of thinking.

1.6 Ben spoke enthusiastically: *For the first time I feel as if I am reading about my own condition, about the condition of my parents as workers, and I finally understand my father's alienation.* Although he did not admit it here, it was the case that as Ben read, he came to passages in Marx where he could not help but to kiss the pages and to whoop and dance about his room.

1.7 Olivia rolled her eyes at what she interpreted to be an excessive emotional display and asked for clarification about the differences and similarities between the peasant and the industrial worker.

> Without a revolutionary theory there can be no revolutionary movement. —V. I. Lenin, *What Is to Be Done?*

II

> The discovery of America, the rounding of the Cape, opened up fresh ground for the bourgeoisie. The East-Indian and Chinese markets, the colonization of America, trade with the colonies, the increase in the means of exchange and in the commodities generally, gave to commerce, to navigation, to industry, an impulse never before known. . . .
>
> —Karl Marx and Friedrich Engels, *Communist Manifesto*

2.1 The gold Mercedes Benz drove their hostility in silence across the border of California, only Macario waking from time to time to comment on the passing scenery, the discovered America flying past their windows, the West slowly passing into the East.

2.2 Olivia turned from her driving occasionally to observe Ben's sleeping body sprawled generously across the backseat. Somewhere in the Nevada desert, he reached over and rolled down the window, allowing a gust of cold dust to rush into the leather interior. *Excuse me,* she said, *would you roll that window back up? I can put on the air conditioning for you, if you wish.*

2.3 *Wow,* he exclaimed with forced excitement. *This is the first time I've been in an air-conditioned car!* But he held out for a long moment before he rolled up the window, watching the black threads of her hair swish around the car, flying up and around and forward, her angry gestures pulling the strands away from her vision.

2.4 *So,* asked Ben, slowly squeezing the Nevada air out of their private conveyance, *how much does a car like this cost?*

2.5 *I wouldn't know. Would you like to sell it and find out?*

2.6 *Hey,* said Macario, *can we get to Montreal first?*

> . . . the role of the vanguard fighter can be fulfilled only by a party that is guided by the most advanced theory.
>
> —V. I. Lenin, *What Is to Be Done?*

III

> Modern industry has established the world market, for which the discovery of America paved the way.
>
> —Karl Marx and Friedrich Engels, *Communist Manifesto*

3.1 Study Group #2: Who is the vanguard?

3.2 How shall the people be organized, those huddled masses, that wretched refuse? Who will teach them how to breathe free? Who will show them the way to the lamp beside the golden door?

3.3 Olivia spoke first: *I find this reading more useful because Lenin outlines an organizational path. You read what is working as it is in progress. He shows how a vanguard can be in place while supporting a national war, then move in to influence and control the new state.*

3.4 Ben said, *I feel skeptical because he's saying that the vanguard is a small, conspiratorial, professional, and intellectual elite. It seems contradictory. To create an equal state, doesn't the system itself need to be equal?*

3.5 Olivia sneered, *Utopian bullshit.*

3.6 Karl Kang corrected the possibly volatile but useless direction of their discussion by intervening: *If you read further, you should understand the context in which this is stated, that of a hostile and oppressive system that at any moment may imprison and kill Lenin and his comrades. You should be reminded that this is a war, and the formation of a vanguard is a strategy necessary to waging war.*

> . . . it is not enough to call ourselves the "vanguard," the advanced detachment; we must act like one; we must act in such a way that all other detachments shall see us, and be obliged to admit, that we are marching in the vanguard.
>
> —V. I. Lenin, *What Is to Be Done?*

IV

> The need of a constantly expanding market for its products chases the bourgeoisie over the whole surface of the globe. It must nestle everywhere, settle everywhere, establish connexions everywhere. —Karl Marx and Friedrich Engels, *Communist Manifesto*

4.1 Chicago, the great city of the American Midwest, was their midpoint destination. Standing on the shores of the great Lake Michigan, a wall of skyscrapers looming behind, and autumn winds whipping up a red and brown flurry of deciduous leaves, Ben said, *I think it's time to sell the Benz. Who's got the cash to stay in this town?*

4.2 Macario suggested, *Maybe we could check into a hospital and hang out with the Pilipino nurses.*

4.3 But Olivia sauntered from the telephone box at the corner and announced, *I've found us a place. They'll caravan with us to New York, then Montreal.* Her old connections with the Student Nonviolent Coordinating Committee proved useful. She slapped a map into Ben's hands. *It's on Monroe Street off the Eisenhower Expressway. Think you can handle that?*

4.4 A year later, a Cook County tactical unit would charge into the same Monroe apartment and gun down two young Black Panthers, Mark Clark and Fred Hampton, wounding others, arresting all. An investigation would show that the police had fired a hundred shots to a miserly one shot from a single Panther rifle. Olivia then remembered the living room sofa where she had slept, watching over Ben on the floor, bundled in unconscious torpor in the clumsy cocoon of his blue sleeping bag.

> . . . our task is to utilize every manifestation of discontent, and to collect and make the best of every grain of even rudimentary protest. —V. I. Lenin, *What Is to Be Done?*

V

> The bourgeoisie, by the rapid improvement of all instruments of production, by the immensely facilitated means of communication, draws all, even the most barbarian, nations into civilization. The cheap prices of its commodities are the heavy artillery with which it batters down all Chinese walls . . .
>
> —Karl Marx and Friedrich Engels,
> *Communist Manifesto*

5.1 Study Group #3: On Colonialism

5.2 Let us speak then of opium, arriving by the chestloads via the Ganges River basin, transported on the ships of the great British Empire's East India Company, then blown into the Chinese atmosphere, lacing every pipe, befuddling every citizen, every worker, every class, creeping into every household, nestling everywhere, battering down our Chinese walls, a gunpowder without a sound. What is this invasive market but a necessary stage on the road from the barbarian to the civilized, from celestial despotism to useful history?

5.3 Olivia said, *Lenin makes a declaration of an international vision against colonialism, but Marx's ideas, especially about China, show his ignorance of China.*

5.4 *Isn't his example really India?* Ben chided, *Aren't you just pissed because he refers to the Chinese as barbarians?*

5.5 *We were never barbarians.*

5.6 Again Karl Kang made corrections. *You need to think of these writings as building blocks—Lenin building on Marx in terms of a Russian state, then Mao building on Marx in terms of the Chinese.*

5.7 *Yes,* said Olivia, *and next we think in terms of the U.S. imperial state. So on that note, what do you think about Lenin's insistence on the* Iskra, *the national paper, as a mobilizing entity? Think about it, every group out there has their rag, but it's about communications, right? We need to get ahold of other means of communication, like radio and* TV.

5.8 Ben quipped, *There you go again. Can we stick to the reading for a change?*

5.9 Karl sighed.

> Only a party that will organize really nation-wide exposures can become the vanguard of the revolutionary forces in our time. —V. I. Lenin, *What Is to Be Done?*

VI

> [The bourgeoisie] compels all nations, on pain of extinction, to adopt the bourgeois mode of production; it compels them to introduce what it calls civilization in their midst, i.e., to become bourgeois themselves. In a word, it creates a world after its own image. —Karl Marx and Friedrich Engels, *Communist Manifesto*

6.1 Traveling from the island city of New York to the island city of Montreal, Ben lost the spacious backseat to two more travelers. As circumstances would have it, the driving rotated along with the seating arrangement such that Ben finally finagled a way to sit alongside Olivia, who fought for hours the sleepy urge to nod off, then succumbing, awoke with the sudden disgust of finding her head propped against Ben's willing shoulder.

6.2 *Oh.* She pulled herself up.

6.3 Ben turned his head and observed the shoulder of his sweatshirt. *Is that your drool?*

6.4 At the Canadian border, where they presented their identifications, Olivia spoke pleasantly with the authorities in French.

6.5 One of the Panther travelers said, *Olivia, teach me some of those French fries so I can be cool too.*

6.6 Ben retorted, *Cool or stuck up?*

> . . . to concentrate all secret functions in the hands of as small a number of professional revolutionaries as possible does not mean that the latter will "do the thinking for all" and that the crowd will not take an active part in the movement.
>
> —V. I. Lenin, *What Is to Be Done?*

VII

> Just as it has made the country dependent on the towns, so it has made barbarian and semi-barbarian countries dependent on the civilized ones, nations of peasants on nations of bourgeois, the East on the West.
>
> —Karl Marx and Friedrich Engels,
> *Communist Manifesto*

7.1 Study Group #4: What is the national question?

7.2 We assume that the creation of a nation, the unification of one people of common origin, language, and traditions is a political given, a right that accompanies power, protection, and territorial sovereignty, but such a nation is subject to the whims of trade and exchange, both material and intellectual, that seep through and in time overtake the formalities of borders so carefully guarded by armies, navies, and stone fortresses. Great warlords have amassed great territories subjugating nations within nations and have discovered in time the unwieldiness of such ambitions. On the other hand, great nations have dispersed their people to every corner of the earth and may thereby subjugate the nation from within.

7.3 Ben asked, *When did we become Asian American?*

7.4 Olivia answered, *What sort of question is that?*

7.5 Karl interrupted. *Wait, it's not a stupid question. Ninteen sixty-six. There's a magazine article about the Japanese American model minority, a kind of American. Before that, Japanese are racially identified as Japanese—otherwise how could they all be interned during the war? After sixty-six, we all get racially identified as hyphenated Americans.*

7.6 Olivia posed, *But Asian American is a political designation.*

7.7 Karl answered, *It's political, racial, and national. Look, you are organizing around this designation, and that's useful, but you are going to have to scrutinize it through a Marxist analysis that includes class. Hey, trust me. This is going to make or break you.*

7.8 Ben asked, *You mean we have to move away from race and organize based on class?*

7.9 Karl shook his head. *Don't think it's that easy.*

> The centralization of the most secret functions in an organization of revolutionaries will not diminish, but rather increase the extent and quality of the activity of a large number of other organizations which are intended for a broad public and are therefore as loose and as non-secret as possible.
>
> —V. I. Lenin, *What Is to Be Done?*

VIII

> Of all the classes that stand face to face with the bourgeoisie today, the proletariat alone is a really revolutionary class.
>
> —Karl Marx and Friedrich Engels, *Communist Manifesto*

8.1 The gold Mercedes Benz arrived in Montreal in time for the opening ceremonies and remarks for the Hemispheric Conference to End the Vietnam War. Which hemisphere? you may ask. The world has been cut in half.

8.2 Twenty delegates, among them Olivia, Ben, Macario, and their Black Panther travelers, stormed to the podium in protest of the format and organizing principals of the conference and demanded that members of their radical caucus be included in the ongoing planning, assuming that significant changes in the format should be instituted, and that workshop discussion topics should be reformulated. To wit: change the conference theme from *Peace in Vietnam* to *Stop U.S. imperialism!*

8.3 A Panther spoke: *We demand that funds be immediately raised to bring Black Panther Party Chairman Bobby Seale to address this conference. The oppression of the Vietnamese people is the same oppression of Third World people in Africa, Asia, Latin America, and the U.S. of America.*

8.4 Ben San Pablo spoke: *America is conducting a war of technological genocide in Vietnam. It's not enough to make a plea for peace. We've got to begin to organize a strategic front to actively dismantle the military industrial complex that supports this genocide.*

8.5 Olivia Wang spoke: *We salute those representatives from the Democratic Republic of Vietnam and the National Liberation Front in their long struggle for self-determination and one Vietnam against the weaponry and might of u.s. imperialism!*

8.6 Later it was reported that peaceniks, white liberals, and old Communists, hooted, *Boo! Hiss!*

8.7 The politics of peace may be anything but peaceful.

> . . . in order to "serve" the mass of movement we must have people who will devote themselves exclusively to Social-Democratic activities, and that such people must train themselves patiently and steadfastly to be professional revolutionaries. —V. I. Lenin, *What Is to Be Done?*

IX

> What the bourgeoisie therefore produces, above all, are its own grave-diggers. Its fall and the victory of the proletariat are equally inevitable. —Karl Marx and Friedrich Engels, *Communist Manifesto*

9.1 Study Group #5: The Science of History

9.2 In ancient times, the whim of the gods and the stars told and foretold the unfolding of events. We have relied on prophets, clairvoyants, religious belief, philosophy, and ideology from one side or another of the globe to decipher, to instruct, and to remember the great panoply of our civilizations, but to what end? Only to discover that the exchange of one's labor in the form of a coin is at the center of the meaning of our lives.

9.3 Karl Kang introduced the reading for the week: *The fundamental idea that you need to understand here is Marx's materialist interpretation of history, that human institutions and development are rooted in economic activities, not in any mysticism or ideas controlled by the ruling class. Economic change is the driving force of history.*

9.4 Olivia said, *I see it like the scientific method, that you analyze empirical data and actual phenomena. It's a technique to observe the real world and real people.*

9.5 Ben asked, *If you follow that idea, then Marxist ideas would be like hypotheses.*

9.6 Karl Kang said, *Marx worked out a theory of history that should embody social experiments or, as you say, proposed hypotheses.*

9.7 Olivia said, *In other words, we should be able to create an experiment to test the theory with predictable results.*

9.8 Ben said, *I'm worried about the predictable part.*

9.9 Olivia gritted her teeth.

9.10 Karl said, *Marx said that men make their own history but not necessarily as they please. He predicted the inevitability of the failure of the capitalist mode of production, and you yourselves can see the contradictions that make continuous acquisition of the earth's resources and the exploitation of everyone to do so a finite proposition, but when it will fail and how, that's—*

9.11 Olivia inserted, *Up to us.*

> The smaller each separate "operation" in our common cause, the more people can we find capable of carrying out such operations, the more difficult will it be for the police to "net" all these "detail workers" . . .
>
> —V. I. Lenin, *What Is to Be Done?*

x

> The working men have no country. We cannot take from them what they have not got.
>
> —Karl Marx and Friedrich Engels,
> *Communist Manifesto*

10.1 Macario stayed behind in Montreal to scope out the scene, as he justified, but really to hang out with a Québécois woman who invited him to her collective in the Canadian backwoods. Thus, he sent Ben and Olivia back on the long trek to Berkeley alone but together.

10.2 The only thing that Ben and Olivia could agree upon was that they would take a different route on their trip home, but at every fork in the road they argued vociferously about the consequences and advantages of taking one road or the other.

10.3 *Let's head way south where it's warmer, get a load of the Bible Belt,* suggested Ben.

10.4 *First of all, I've already been down there, and just because you missed the Freedom Ride doesn't mean we need to do it this week. I say, since we're here in Canada, let's drive across and see it.*

10.5 *Good thing we've got this Benz with its deluxe heating system,* he muttered.

10.6 But when the Benz drove off the icy road into a snowdrift in the middle of the night, they sat in the car on that empty road screaming at each other until Olivia ran from the car down the highway, the imprint of her boots trailing behind. Ben watched her figure growing distant and dark in the steamy rearview mirror, then tore out after her, catching up to grab her angry body and struggling to drag her back to the car. *Fuck you! Let go of me! You goddamn bastard. Let go!* The packed snow, a rising wall along the highway, punched back the impact of their flailing bodies, bouncing, kicking, and falling. *Fucking bitch! You know how far the last town behind us is? You'll fucking freeze!* Finally he held her in the cold embrace of the Canadian snow, their bodies wedged in a miraculous bed of billions of individual flakes, every hot breath melting a thousand flakes, every angry tear reproducing another thousand.

10.7 Olivia gasped, *Look,* and he followed her gaze into the northern skies, saw the distant and heavenly fireworks of the aurora borealis.

> The only serious organizational principle for the active workers of our movement should be the strictest secrecy, the strictest selection of members and the training of professional revolutionaries. Given these qualities, something even more than "democracy" would be guaranteed to us, namely, complete, comradely, mutual confidence among revolutionaries.
>
> —V. I. Lenin, *What Is to Be Done?*

XI

> The ruling ideas of each age have ever been the ideas of its ruling class.
>
> —Karl Marx and Friedrich Engels, *Communist Manifesto*

11.1 Study Group #6: On Dialectical Materialism

11.2 The ancients have long known the secrets of the universe as a cosmic and eternal whole in which everything is interconnected and interdependent, a push and pull of life forces, eternally dynamic and in motion, eternally changing, becoming and unbecoming, a cycle of oppositions that leap from one state to another, from water to steam, seed to rooted plant, life embedded in the death of the thing itself, and death embedded in the life of the thing itself.

11.3 Karl Kang said: *A Marxist way of thinking can empower you by offering a way to see the internal contradiction of any situation.*

11.4 Ben said, *Olie needs a practical example.*

11.5 *Oh shut up, Benny,* Olivia snapped, then after a pause: *Karl, I need a practical example.*

11.6 Karl thought and suggested: *This is simple: the relationship of the slave to the master. You are a slave in that you must give your labor to the master, but the master is also slave to you in that he cannot be a master without your labor. Once you understand this contradiction, it is the beginning of your freedom.*

11.7 *O.K.,* said Olivia, *so I get thinking to change my situation.*

11.8 *Right, dialectics is a logic of change, and change is embedded in every situation. It's a logic that provides not only hope but real possibility.*

11.9 Ben offered, *The next step is that we slaves strategize how to create the conditions for change.*

11.10 Olivia continued, *We plan the uprising.*

11.11 So it is that in times of despotism, the seed of revolution exists, waiting only to be planted and watered. Strange how barbarian people can hold such secrets for centuries until a moment of appropriation, a great leap into an opposing future.

> Only a centralized, militant organization that consistently carries out a Social-Democratic policy, that satisfies, so to speak, all revolutionary instincts and strivings, can safeguard the movement against making thoughtless attacks and prepare attacks that hold out the promise of success.
>
> —V. I. Lenin, *What Is to Be Done?*

XII

> Political power, properly so called, is merely the organized power of one class for oppressing another.
>
> —Karl Marx and Friedrich Engels, *Communist Manifesto*

12.1 They drove south out of snow country, still keeping to the solitary roads, watching the asphalt stretch beyond and disappear beneath the gold Benz, sometimes quiet in their separate reveries, sometimes resuming their old arguments, but now with the soft bantering of a knowing that was of brother and sister, friend and friend. *You're such a bullshitter,* she said. *You always liked me,* she added. *You're such a bitch,* he smiled.

12.2 Back and forth, she sang Chinese folk songs and he, of course, Filipino love songs.

12.3 Driving in the night, he looked over at her dozing figure, her head resting against the window and the cloud of steam that obscured the dark window around her nose. He wanted to wake her to take notice of the horizon's starry expanse beyond the windshield before them, to tell her he had never seen so many stars. Instead, he pulled the car over into an open meadow, stopped, and killed the headlights. He rolled down the window and tested the air outside.

12.4 *Olie,* he nudged her. *Quick.* He pulled the sleeping bags from the trunk and spread them over the hot hood of the car. They removed every piece of their clothing and climbed onto the hood, lying over that sweet residue of heat and staring into the starry night, naked to the night air, pressing the hard and soft parts of their bodies into a soft rhythm, sparks and pistons for the silent motor, purring and traveling.

> . . . an organization of real revolutionaries will stop at nothing to rid itself of an undesirable member.
>
> —V. I. Lenin, *What Is to Be Done?*

XIII

Let the ruling classes tremble at a Communistic revolution. The proletarians have nothing to lose but their chains. They have a world to win.

Working men of all countries, unite!

—Karl Marx and Friedrich Engels,
Communist Manifesto

13.1 Study Group #7: On Practice

13.2 There are those whose fortune it is to dream of their futures and to live those dreams, to discover and to cultivate their innate talents and to realize and use those same talents, to live by their individual gifts and to be granted the blessings of praise and home among their people. And there are those who find a purpose for their talents and find that all their struggles and preparations are tested and given meaning in this purpose. There are those for whom the dream of their lives is also its practice, their practice fuel for their dreaming. But who among those favored also live in times of turmoil, in times of war, in exile and destitution, with the constant fear of prison, torture, and death? And what then is the nature of their dreaming practice, their practical dreaming?

13.3 Karl said, *Theory must be connected to revolutionary practice. Practice is the way to knowledge and the development of theory. It's not practice versus theory, but to theorize practice and to practice theory.*

13.4 *A dialectical unity,* suggested Ben.

13.5 *A qualitative leap from theory to practice,* said Olivia.

13.6 Ben announced, *There's an empty storefront in the I-Hotel.*

13.7 Olivia answered, *Hook up the phone, and we're in business.*

. . . we firmly believe that the fourth period will lead to the consolidation of militant Marxism, that Russian Social-Democracy will emerge from the crisis in the full strength of manhood, that the opportunist rearguard will be "replaced" by the genuine vanguard of the most revolutionary class . . . What is to be done?: Liquidate the Third Period.

—V. I. Lenin, *What Is to Be Done?*

4: In Practice

I

... as Asian people, if we seek to explain the problems of ourselves, our community and all poor and oppressed peoples in the United States, we come to the conclusion that revolution is the only answer. —Pat Sumi

1.1 Who, then, is the revolutionary woman? In these days she is a barefoot peasant, a child on her back, wielding an AK-47. Of course, she may be uniformed in cotton pajama trousers, batik sarong, sari, Mao jacket, jilbab, miniskirt, or Levi jeans; covered in straw hat, veil, hijab, worker's cap, or helmet. In every case, the winds of liberation blow through her fingers.

1.2 But to continue: Olivia Wang had ventured from her rarified and privileged existence, her private schooling, onto a bus traveling into Mississippi, and returned with a Negro boyfriend. These events were not in the auspicious plans of the Wang clan, who in fact had betrothed their youngest daughter into a mercantile dynasty whose assets might fund an entire army. One day, Olivia borrowed the key to her father's car, a gold Mercedes Benz, the starred icon on its hood pressing its silver nose through the Manhattan traffic, and drove away forever.

1.3 Patriarchy, as with other forms of oppression, may hold the key to its own demise.

II

The black woman lives in a society that discriminates against her on two counts . . . the twin jeopardy of race and sex . . . To date, neither the black movement nor women's liberation succinctly addresses itself to the dilemma confronting the black who is female. And as a consequence . . . black women themselves are now becoming socially and politically active.

—Shirley Chisholm

2.1 So it was that Third World revolutionary women converged on the city of Vancouver for the Indochinese Women's Conference. It was there that a third of the women proposed a third jeopardy to the twin of racism and sexism: imperialism.

2.2 Friedrich Engels argued that in the context of the family, a woman's relationship to her husband is as the proletariat to the bourgeoisie. Or as Mao Tse-tung said, a woman is obedient first to her father, then to her husband, and finally to her son. Triple jeopardies abound. How, under such conditions, may half of the people rise from their oppression?

2.3 Third World revolutionary women rose to the occasion with such speechmaking: *Black people and Vietnamese people have exposed the weakness of white Western dominance, revealing that the weak and oppressed can struggle against a powerful enemy. Our feminist liberation movement must be viewed within this context of an international social revolution and the struggle by women for our human rights.*

2.4 And further: *In the fight for national liberation in Asia, Africa, and Latin America, women have not waited, first, "to give their men their manhood," and second, to wage the war; they have first and foremost taken arms and gone to war.*

III

> Revolution is a serious thing, the most serious thing about a revolutionary's life. When one commits oneself to the struggle, it must be for a lifetime. —Angela Davis

3.1 Revolutionary Woman #1—Code Name: Angela

3.2 Angela Woo was one of those very competitive, highly competent, achievement-oriented young women, valedictorian of her graduating class who went on to get her MBA and consequently placement in a large multinational corporation. Year after year, she worked diligently as a team member in middle management, observing gradually younger and younger white men bumped up to higher positions.

Finally, perhaps as a crude test, she was called in to help negotiate union contractual terms for factory workers in one of several corporate subsidiaries. When negotiations came to a halt, the workers voted to strike for an increase in pay and benefits that by Angela's forecasts were probably reasonable. But being a team member, she remained silent, until she walked onto the factory floor and discovered that many of the strikebreakers were poor Chinese immigrant women much like her own mother.

3.3 To live in the colonized world is to know an international caste system; at the top, the white male ruling class, and at the bottom, your colored mother.

IV

> "The Price of My Soul" refers not to the price for which I would be prepared to sell out, but rather to the price we all must pay in life to preserve our own integrity. To gain that which is worth having, it may be necessary to lose everything else.
>
> —Bernadette Devlin

4.1 Revolutionary Woman #2—Code Name: Bernadette

4.2 Bernadette Kim ran away from an abusive husband who flung her from the kitchen wall, crashing her against the Frigidaire, hurtling her headfirst into the grill of the hot stove, shattering a warm casserole, breaking her arm, and exacting on her a purple bruise that swept across the soft features of her young face. Hidden away from the man who had become a policeman over her life, she found work to support herself and the baby growing within her. But as she came into the sixth month of pregnancy, she was promptly given notice with the justification: *We thought you were just gaining a little weight.*

4.3 For the woman, the consequences of gaining a little weight are multiple.

V

> Among poor people, there's not any question about women being strong—even stronger than men—they work in the fields right along with the men. When your survival is at stake, you don't have these questions about yourself like middle-class women do. —Dolores Huerta

5.1 Revolutionary Woman #3—Code Name: Dolores

5.2 Dolores Tadiar lived the suburban middle-class housewife life in a three-bedroom house with her three children, a dog, a petunia garden, and a salaried husband—the very paradigm of the perfect American family. One day, the salaried husband lost his job, became an alcoholic, and disappeared with another woman. Unable to make the mortgage payments, Dolores lost the house, squished her three kids into a cheap one-room apartment, carted the smallest from babysitter to babysitter, and got a job as a waitress. At the end of the month, she partitioned her meager wage and tips into rent, food, and child care.

5.3 The emulation of the American Dream is a great hoax.

VI

> Can I shake your hand?
> What for?
> I want to congratulate you.
> For what?
> For what you are doing for your people.
> What's that?
> For giving them direction.
> —Yuri Kochiyama (conversation with Malcolm X)

6.1 Revolutionary Woman #4—Code Name: Yuri

6.2 Kicked out of the house by a traditionally rigid and God-fearing father for losing her virginity to her then-boyfriend and becoming pregnant out of holy wedlock, Susan Sakai cast about for another family, another tradition, another identity. Joining a so-called radical collective, she discovered in time that the collective had no expectations for the care of her child, and that if she refused to bed down with any of the collective men, she was not fulfilling her familial duties to their collective welfare, to the greater good of the Asian American nation. *Baby,* they purred, *you are beautiful, but you got to stay back to push your man forward.* At which point, she left with her child, her lesbian lover, and a new name: Yuri.

6.3 It may indeed be impossible to escape traditions embedded over many centuries and many civilizations, falling into the mistake of reenactment of one entrenched belief or another. The immediate answer is rebellion.

VII

Better Red than Dead

—La Nada Means, on Alcatraz

7.1 Revolutionary Woman #5—Code Name: La Nada

7.2 La Nada Hayes, a mixed child—black, Chicano, and Asian—found herself unaccepted by any community—black, brown, or yellow. Her dark olive skin tone, her braided auburn hair, her Oriental eyes, all conspired to confuse. Thus rejected, she became an Oreo, a coconut, a banana, and joined a white women's lib group to demand a woman's right to education and equal job opportunities, pretending that she too suffered the boredom of the suburban bedroom, until one day she found herself employed and managed by one of the group's women, who spoke in a mincing and patronizing voice about how dating a white male colleague in the same company —who was in any case the enemy—was calling attention to herself as a black woman and creating an un-sisterly feeling among other women and that this situation might—and this was completely confidential but revealed in consideration of their long association as feminists—just might cost her her job.

7.3 Male chauvinism can be perceived as a form of racism based on a false belief in the biological inferiority of women. However, the oppression of the colored woman and the oppression of the white American housewife are not to be confused.

VIII

> So I tell people I don't want no equal rights anymore. I'm fighting for human rights. I don't want to become equal to men like them that beat us. I don't want to become the kind of person that would kill you because of your color.
>
> —Fannie Lou Hamer

8.1 Revolutionary Woman #6—Code Name: Fannie

8.2 Fannie Chow came from a long and respectable line of Chinese matriarchs. This history was not a consequence of the transgression of Confucian laws of the proper hierarchy by men over women, but a consequence of abandonment, abandonment by men who traveled off in search of the Gold Mountain, first sending home pieces of the mythic mountain and finally sending nothing. This pattern of abandonment was repeated generation after generation, each husband lost to the brutality and submission of the coolies' labor—laying tracks, mining borax, laundering shirts. This one blown to bits by dynamite. That one starved by vermin. This one convulsed by tuberculosis. That one lynched from his own queue. Fannie's father was knifed in a gambling dispute. Who was to blame for these lost men?

8.3 Do you really believe in the bitter myth of the imperious matriarch who keeps her man's testicles in a silver box under her silken pillow, removing the box from time to time to hear their soft tingle and toss?

IX

> Woman is the nigger of the world.
>
> —Yoko Ono

9.1 Revolutionary Woman #7—Code Name: Yoko

9.2 Yoko Smith married her high-school boyfriend, Jack, right out of high school and just before he was drafted and shipped out, Private Jack Smith, to defend American freedom in Vietnam. In a period of less than three months, she changed from Miss Yoko Sakamoto to Mrs. Jack Smith to Mrs. Yoko Smith, widow. A photograph in the high-school yearbook shows Yoko as homecoming queen in gold crown and pink gown, a reclining odalisque held aloft by the entire football team. After Jack's final salute into the patriotic heavens, each of his team buddies came around to console his grieving widow and to get some piece of the action that Jack had once kept for himself all senior year. By the time Yoko woke from her grief, she had tried to commit suicide, self-inflict an abortion that resulted in a miscarriage with permanent damage to her uterus, and was working through a drug rehabilitation program. Propped up on white sheets in a sterile hospital room, she flipped through *Life* magazine and stared in horror, humiliation, and self-recognition at the running figure of a naked weeping girl stripped by napalm.

9.3 If beauty is in the eye of the beholder, so too the ugly, but what of terror and atrocity?

X

> There are well over 600 million workers, peasants and soldiers in our country, whereas there are only a handful of landlords, rich peasants, counter-revolutionaries, bad elements, rightists, and bourgeois elements. Shall we serve this handful, or the 600 million? —Chiang Ching

10.1 Revolutionary sisters, like interchanging stars, floated into a small but growing constellation, tugged into variable patterns of revolutionary commitment: health care, child care, bilingual education, shelters, drug rehabilitation, counseling, co-ops, labor unions, political organization, party formation. Olivia was at the head of the phone tree. The meetings were nightly. The work was urgent.

10.2 Revolutionaries are not determined by sex.

5: On Colonialism

I

Then they put a treacherous big viper on your chest:
On your neck they laid the yoke of fire-water,
They took your sweet wife for glitter and cheap pearls,
Your incredible riches that nobody could measure.

—Patrice Lumumba, *Dawn in the Heart of Africa*

1.1 Ben San Pablo was named after his father, Bienvenido San Pablo, Sr., a strong muscular man of broad shoulders and deep voice, a tough, bold exterior fortified nightly by the golden flame lit within an amber bottle of whiskey. There was no earthly weight that Bienvenido Senior could not lift, no woman he could not charm, no comrade from whom he did not receive respect. And yet a great weight surrounded his heart like a lead suitcase, an unattainable woman sneered blue cat eyes in his dreams, a great white father reminded him constantly of his place. Thus a great man was a cripple in his own mind, uncontrollably jealous of the women with whom he became attached such that his paranoia and self-doubt eventually drove each of them away, and though a respected foreman at his job, he spent all his additional pay buying drinks and loaning money to his working crew to assure himself of their friendship and continued loyalty.

1.2 A man's self-worth can only be measured by himself.

II

Raving mad I greet you with my ravings whiter than death.

—Aimé Césaire, *Raving Mad*

2.1 Ben San Pablo, Jr., spent his teenage years running with a white crowd. After all, was not his mother, the second wife of Bienvenido

Senior, a white woman, whose marriage to a Filipino man had cast her from her family? By his senior year in high school, Ben realized that no manner of assimilation or integration would erase his dark features, which were smuggled in with those of his mother. He began to see himself mirrored in disinterest, curiosity, rejection, or patronizing humor, but nothing that a couple of beers or a whiff of pot couldn't resolve for the time being.

2.2 Yet he argued with his mother who, when Bienvenido Senior's third wife up and left him, began to bring her ex-husband his evening meals. *Why are you doing this for that Filipino drunkard?* Ben yelled at his mother. *Because,* she said, *that Filipino is your father.* At that moment, Ben recognized in himself his father's self-hate and his own deep shame.

2.3 It is possible to destroy or avoid all mirrors, but only the blinding of one's own vision may destroy the seeing reflection of another.

III

Long, long have you held between your hands the
black face of the warrior
Held as if already there fell on it a twilight of death.
From the hill I have seen the sun set in the bays of
your eyes.
When shall I see again, my country, the pure
horizon of your face?
When shall I sit down once more at the dark table
of your breast? —Léopold Sédar Senghor, *Songs for Signare*

3.1 Karl Kang, our mentor, who would father a new generation of revolutionaries, was himself a rebellious son in exile, a philosophical genius, married to a black American who skillfully made his graduate research, teaching, and revolutionary thinking possible by her impeccable household, her careful planning and budgeting, her excellent cooking, her sweet Southern mothering, and her steady secretarial salary.

3.2 One day, the study group arrived at the Berkeley apartment to find that the hot pot of coffee had not been brewed, nor was there a plate of homemade cookies on the coffee table. Instead, dirty clothes were strewn about the apartment, along with Kang's papers and books and piles of cigarette butts in scattered ashtrays. *Delia's taken a vacation,* Karl apologized, but then, her vacation seemed to linger on and on for weeks and months and then years.

3.3 Delia used to joke that she had married North Korea, and Karl, that he had married Africa. What sort of marriage was that? Delia wanted Asian contemplation. Karl wanted negritude. Marriage was a new beginning equal to a romantic reading of the destructive nature of war: a tabula rasa. They both stared into their desires, she colonizing her dream man, he, his dream woman. In time, it was as an armed struggle necessary for independence.

IV

> . . . the national liberation of a people is the regaining of the historical personality of that people, its return to history through the destruction of the imperialist domination to which it was subjected. —Amílcar Cabral, *The Weapon of Theory* Havana, 1966, Tricontinental

4.1 In 1942, Bienvenido Senior volunteered for the First All-Filipino Infantry Regiment, shipped off from Salinas, California, back to defend his homeland, but although through the act of war he returned an American citizen, he never spoke of the battles, the memory of dragging his dying brother, slimy with his blood, through mud and swamp, the horror of returning to the decimation of his family village, the pain of having to return to tell his mother the awful truth of her dead son and their lost people. He could not understand why he had survived, and he lived the guilt of that realization every day of his life. His was the lost history of seven thousand men, many engaged in espionage to infiltrate local villages, the covert and treacherous activities of spies, secret stories of stealth to create the conditions for victory.

4.2 The mask of race often hides the true hero, thus obliterating his participation in any history.

V

> Before it can adopt a positive voice, freedom requires an effort at dis-alienation. At the beginning of his life a man is always clotted, he is drowned in contingency. The tragedy of the man is that he was once a child.
>
> —Frantz Fanon, *Black Skin, White Masks*

5.1 Ben Junior entered college only to change his major along with his future plans every semester. In the next four years he would not accumulate sufficient credits in any area of study to justify under any bureaucratic or scholastic regimen the honor of a graduation ticket. And it was not as if he were a bourgeois son with certain prospects of employment; he had always had to work to support himself. He was in fact a true lover of learning, a bookworm, even a kind of young pedant, who roamed the library reading everything parallel to and intersecting with his studies. His absorption of any subject was a joy to his teachers, but there was no one area of inquiry that kept his attention. He was a migrant scholar moving from job to job, harvesting this, fishing that, gambling his future. No one in his family had ever gone to college.

5.2 His friends, and Karl Kang (who became his mentor) in particular, found this flitting from subject to subject a kind of innocent cavorting of a prodigious mind, recognized the playfulness of creative genius. Could his scholastic irresponsibility be channeled for a greater purpose?

5.3 Kang realized over time that no sort of professionalization could corral Ben's talents, and moaned to him: *You'd make a lousy lawyer. You can't just turn around midway and send the ball to the opponent's goal. You've got to use that kind of strategizing for your own team.*

5.4 To which Ben replied: *My team was losing anyway. My team is always losing.*

5.5 *That's the point. Your team is the underdog.*

5.6 It was also true that Kang would make a lousy lawyer.

VI

> "You think, therefore you are a thinker. You are one-who-thinks, white-creature-in-pith-helmet-in-African-jungle-who-thinks and, finally, white-man-who-has-problems-believing-in-his-own-existence." (mythical brother innocent to Descartes)
>
> —Wole Soyinka, *Myth, Literature, and the African World*

6.1 Karl Kang was hard at work on his political thesis regarding black nationalism when Delia came away from her spiritual meditations, pushed his papers away, and grabbed his crotch. This they knew was the best part of being married, this synthesis of their contradictions, his shimmying buttocks, her ample breasts, his strong arms and nimble hands, her wide lips. *Race is a category,* he whispered to her as he dug himself into the black soil of her rising rhythms. *Return to nothingness,* she rasped, rubbing his penis into a frenzy, clawing his hairless back, biting Buddha's nipples, drawing blood.

6.2 After, he spoke carelessly to her in Korean, and she answered unknowingly in Creole.

6.3 It may not be possible to cure the crazy ethnic, neither with the medicine of politics nor the medicine of culture.

VII

> At Bandung, to the astonishment and embarrassment of leftists all over the world, one of the two fundamental principles of the conference was religion.
>
> —Albert Memmi, *The Colonizer and the Colonized*

7.1 When the epiphany came as it tends to near the end of one's life, Bienvenido Senior saw his dead mother in a wreath of light at the foot of his bed and, fearing for his life, followed her out of his house in Daly City, along the silent avenues, and into a grocery market, losing her somewhere among the fruits and vegetables. Standing there barefoot and stupidly in his pajamas at three in the morning, he wept into the broccoli and the cantaloupe, the memory of her toil spreading like those fields in a tarmac of blinding light.

7.2 Ben had begun bringing his mother's meals to his father, trying to arrive before his father could hit the evening bottle, and holding forth with a planned question. But the next night, his father said: *I saw your grandmother last night. You don't have to worry about me. I know what I have to do now.*

7.3 Bienvenido Senior went to church, made his confession, tossed his whiskey habit, and organized a plan to build a new church in his old village.

7.4 Years later, Ben Junior would travel to the Philippines to visit his father, buried next to the church he had struggled to build with his bare hands during those years of martial law. Ben lit a candle in the church and sat to contemplate the rebellious zeal of their separate passions.

VIII

> I was made, by the law, a criminal, not because of what I had done, but because of what I stood for, because of what I thought, because of my conscience. Can it be any wonder to anybody that such conditions make a man an outlaw of society?
>
> —Nelson Mandela, Pretoria Court, November 1962

8.1 Ben San Pablo, Jr., saw his father off at the airport. He asked his mother, who waved at his side: *Why don't you go with him?* She shook her head. *He must go by himself.* She squeezed Ben's hand. *You'll understand one day,* she said, *when you, too, are free.*

8.2 The next day, Ben took speed, read *Das Kapital* cover to cover, and joined the Brigada Venceremos.

6: A Romance for Humanity

I

> I am First Lady by accident. I was not elected by the people, but here I am. —Imelda Marcos

1.1 So it was that as Ferdinand Marcos dipped his pen into the blood of his people, a revolutionary marriage was consummated.

1.2 The Occidentals say that all tragedy ends in death, all comedy in marriage, but what of a divine comedy, a marriage that anticipates its death, a romantic journey into purgatory, Dante pursuing his Beatrice, Orpheus his Eurydice? And what if the beautiful muse is Revolution herself?

> WHEREAS, on the basis of carefully evaluated and verified information, it is definitely established that lawless elements . . . are actually staging, undertaking and waging an armed insurrection and rebellion against the Government of the Republic of the Philippines . . .

II

> I'm like Robin Hood. I rob the rich to make these projects come alive . . . not really rob. It's done with a smile.
> —Imelda Marcos

2.1 It is said that Marcos signed his proclamation on September seventeenth, dated it the twenty-first, and announced it on the twenty-third. The dictator enacting evil vainly looks for the auspicious will of the stars.

2.2 Coincidentally, Ben and Olivia announced their marriage on the seventeenth, formalized it at city hall on the twenty-first, and celebrated the wedding on the twenty-third.

2.3 The twenty-first was a Thursday.

> WHEREAS, these lawless elements . . . have committed and still are committing, acts of violence, depredations, sabotage and injuries against our duly constituted authorities, against the members of our law enforcement agencies, and worst of all, against the peaceful members of our society . . .

III

> It's the rich you can terrorize. The poor have nothing to lose.
>
> —Imelda Marcos

3.1 The wedding invitations went out over the phone tree and as flyers posted all over Manilatown and Chinatown. The flyers' graphics matched the murals over the I-Hotel, strong-fisted people proclaiming a wedding of the people.

> WHEREAS, in the fanatical pursuit of their conspiracy and widespread acts of violence, depredations, sabotage and injuries against our people . . . these lawless elements have in fact organized, established and are now maintaining a Central Committee . . .

IV

> People say Mrs. Marcos is a great dreamer. Oh, yes, I dream not only at night when there is the moon and the stars, but I dream more so during the daytime without the moon and the stars. But I don't just dream. I do it. I'm an activist.
>
> —Imelda Marcos

4.1 The old lounge of the I-Hotel had to be scrubbed down, polished, and spiffed up for the occasion. Flowers and ribbons were laced about the room. Tables were spread with long cloths borrowed from a Chinese restaurant. Someone commandeered a red carpet and rolled it from the lounge to the front entryway. Tenants and activists scrambled to dress up the old hotel and finally themselves for the big day.

4.2 All day and night the smell of baking and roasting and stir-frying wafted through the hallways from every kitchen.

4.3 The old hotel, almost condemned, puffed itself up like a decrepit old Cinderella transformed by a dream.

> WHEREAS, in order to carry out . . . their premeditated plan to stage, undertake and wage a full scale armed insurrection and rebellion in this country, these lawless elements have organized, established and are now maintaining a well trained, well armed and highly indoctrinated and greatly expanded insurrectionary force, popularly known as the "New People's Army" . . .

V

> It is terribly important to do certain things, such as wear over-embroidered dresses. After all, the mass follows class. Class never follows mass. —Imelda Marcos

5.1 Olivia wore a red silk Mao jacket and matching pants, her hair braided with flowers down her back.

5.2 Ben wore a white embroidered barong and his best shoes.

> WHEREAS, these lawless elements, their cadres, fellow-travelers, friends, sympathizers and supporters have for many years up to the present time been mounting sustained, massive and destructive propaganda assaults . . . have so eroded and weakened the will of our people to sustain and defend our government and our democratic way of life . . .

VI

> Sometimes you have smart relatives who can make it. My dear, there are always people who are just a little faster, more brilliant, and more aggressive.
>
> —Imelda Marcos

6.1 Ben's stepbrother by his father's first marriage and Macario Amado were his best men.

6.2 Olivia's younger sister plus her seven revolutionary sisters were her best ladies.

> WHEREAS, these lawless elements having taken up arms against our duly constituted government . . . to the great detriment, suffering, injury and prejudice of our people and the nation and to generate a deep psychological fear and panic among our people . . .

VII

> I am my little people's star and slave. When I go out into the barrios, I get dressed because I know my little people want to see a star. Other presidents' wives have gone to the barrios wearing house dresses and slippers. That's not what people want to see. People want someone they can love, someone to set an example. —Imelda Marcos

7.1 The wedding march, a scratchy recording of the full orchestral version of the Chinese opera *Internationale,* blasted triumphantly from loudspeakers.

> WHEREAS, the Supreme Court . . . has found that in truth and in fact there exists an actual insurrection and rebellion in the country by a sizeable group of men who have publicly risen in arms to overthrow the government . . .

VIII

> I understand my people better than anyone. I study them all the time and even conduct experiments.
> —Imelda Marcos

8.1 Karl Kang wore a suit and red tie for the occasion and presided over the ceremony. It was thus that he admitted that he was the son of a Baptist preacher and had actually memorized the wedding vows as a child. But in deference to the revolution, he spoke thus, albeit the words of a prophet:

8.2 *Your friend is your needs answered. She is your field, which you sow with love and reap with thanksgiving. And she is your board and your fireside. For you come to her with your hunger, and you seek her for peace.*

8.3 *When your friend speaks his mind you fear not the "nay" in your own mind, nor do you withhold the "aye." And when he is silent your heart ceases not to listen to his heart; for without words, in friendship, all thoughts, all desires, all expectations are born and shared, with joy that is unclaimed.*

8.4 *When you part from your friend, you grieve not; for that which you love most in her may be clearer in her absence, as the mountain to the climber is clearer from the plain.*

8.5 *And let there be no purpose in friendship save the deepening of the spirit. For love that seeks aught but the disclosure of its own mystery is not love but a net cast forth; and only the unprofitable is caught.*

8.6 *And let your best be for your friend. If he must know the ebb of your tide, let him know its flood also. For what is your friend that you should seek him with hours to kill? Seek him always with hours to live. For it is his to fill your need, but not your emptiness.*

8.7 *And in the sweetness of friendship let there be laughter, and sharing of pleasures. For in the dew of little things the heart finds its morning and is refreshed.*

> WHEREAS, these lawless elements have to a considerable extent succeeded in impeding our duly constituted authorities from performing their functions and discharging their duties and responsibilities in accordance with our laws and our Constitution to the great damage, prejudice and detriment of the people and the nation . . .

IX

> The Philippines is in a strategic position. It is both East and West, right and left, rich and poor. We are neither here nor there.
>
> —Imelda Marcos

9.1 Olivia said:

I do not offer the old smooth prizes,
but offer rough new prizes.
These are the days that must happen to us.
We shall not heap up what is called riches;
we shall scatter with lavish hand all that we earn or achieve.
However sweet the laid-up stores,
however convenient the dwellings,
we shall not remain there.
However sheltered the port,
and however calm the waters,
we shall not anchor there.
However welcome the hospitality that welcomes us,
we are permitted to receive it but a little while.
Afoot and lighthearted, take to the open road,
healthy, free, the world before us,
the long brown path before us,
leading wherever we choose.
Comrade, I give you my hand!
I give you my love, more precious than money.
I give you myself before preaching or law.
Will you give me yourself?
Will you come travel with me?
Shall we stick by each other as long as we live?

> WHEREAS, it is evident that there is throughout the land a state of anarchy and lawlessness, chaos and disorder, turmoil and destruction of a magnitude equivalent to an actual war between the forces of our duly constituted government and the New People's Army . . . whose political, social, economic

and moral precepts are based on the Marxist-Leninist-Maoist teachings and beliefs . . .

X

The Philippines is where Asia wears a smile. Beautiful products can only be made by happy people.

—Imelda Marcos

10.1 Ben said:

If I speak of hunger,
is that not a love poem?

If I speak of shelter
is that not a love poem?

If I speak of the labor of my parents
and your parents
and their people before them,
is that not a love poem?

If I speak of enslavement
of genocide
of blood spilled
on the road to freedom,
is that not a love poem?

If I speak of your fearless voice
and the talent of your hands never at rest,
is that not a love poem?

May I be forever fed and sheltered
in the freedom of your labor
and the song of your voice.

WHEREAS, the Supreme Court in its said decision concluded that the unlawful activities of the aforesaid lawless elements actually pose a clear, present and grave danger to public safety and the security of the nation . . .

XI

And my scientists tell me that these forces are so powerful that we can use them to protect you, our American friends, against Soviet missiles. —Imelda Marcos

11.1 Jack, Aiko, and Stony sang a revolutionary wedding song especially composed to honor the nuptials.

11.2 Refrain:
Warrior woman and warrior man
Battle axe and silver sword in hand
Side-by-side you race into the fray
In righteous revolution, proclaim a new day.

WHEREAS, in the unwavering prosecution of their revolutionary war against the Filipino people and their duly constituted government, the aforesaid lawless elements have . . . succeeded in bringing and introducing into the country . . . a substantial quantity of war material . . . and other combat paraphernalia . . .

XII

Why should people be afraid that we use a few small pellets of uranium at the nuclear power plant in Bataan? Don't they know that we're surrounded by uranium? We have the world's fourth largest deposits of uranium. Yes, we're all radioactive—must be the reason why we have so many faith healers!
—Imelda Marcos

12.1 Karl Kang asked the people—that is to say, everyone in attendance—to repeat after him:

12.2 *By the power invested in the people, we pronounce you, Bienvenido San Pablo and Olivia Wang, partners in life. All power to the people!*

WHEREAS, in the execution of their overall revolutionary plan, the aforesaid lawless elements have prepared and released to their various field commanders and Party workers a document captioned "REGIONAL PROGRAM OF ACTION 1972" . . .

XIII

Bakit mayroong mga Pilipino na naninira kay Presidente at kay First Lady? Hindi ba nila alam na kami ang Tatay at Nanay ng Bayang Pilipino? Kung kamote ang Tatay at kung kamote ang Nanay, kamote ang Pilipino! Ang kamote ay hindi nag-aanak ng kamatis.

—Imelda Marcos

13.1 Upon pronouncement of the good news, Tino's barbershop quartet of guitars and ukuleles, plus a drum set, broke into a stepped-up Filipino rendition of the wedding recessional.

WHEREAS, in line with their "REGIONAL PROGRAM OF ACTION 1972," the aforesaid lawless elements have of late been conducting intensified acts of violence and terrorisms . . .

XIV

My economic theory is that money was made round to go round. Money was made to encircle man so that he would blossom with many flowers. The whole trouble is, the center is money. All the heads of people thinking about money. All the hands of people reaching out for money. All their poor little bodies working for money. They are running in all directions for money. —Imelda Marcos

14.1 Ben and Olivia stood to greet their well-wishers in the traditional receiving line.

14.2 A man unknown to Ben came forward with congratulations, and Ben queried: *Are you a friend of Olivia's, or perhaps a friend of one of the manongs?*

14.3 The man replied honestly: *Hey man, I heard there was food, so I came on in.*

WHEREAS, in line with the same "REGIONAL PROGRAM OF ACTION 1972," the aforesaid lawless elements have also fielded in the Greater Manila area several of their "Sparrow Units" or "Simbad Units" to undertake liquidation missions against ranking government officials, military personnel and prominent citizens . . .

XV

I always go with the flow. That is why I don't tire easily. Have you noticed how when you're traveling from the West to the Philippines, you don't get tired, but when you travel from here to the West, you're exhausted? This is because in one instance you're going with the current of the Gulf Stream; in the other instance, you're going against it.

—Imelda Marcos

15.1 As if by some miracle, the tables were suddenly filled with every kind of food imaginable: luscious roast duck, plump tofu with cashews, garlicky pancit and adobo, steamed rock cod in ginger and scallions, crab in black beans, stir-fried vegetables of every sort, an entire roast pig that the manongs had managed to bury in a pit in the alleyway, and mounds and mounds of steamed rice.

15.2 The old men of the I-Hotel were an assortment of cooks and short-order chefs from Chinatown restaurants and the galleys of the merchant marine.

15.3 Do not be fooled by the poor old man who hides a cleaver in his sleeve.

WHEREAS, in addition to the above-described social disorder, there is also the equally serious disorder in Mindanao and Sulu . . .

XVI

I get my fingers in all our pies. Before you know it, your little fingers including all your toes are in all the pies.
Imelda Marcos

16.1 Macario stood before enormous sugar-egg-and-flour twin peaks, a baking feat orchestrated by himself with the help of several tenants to create what Macario called Mao's mountains: Taihang and Wangwu. The frosting on the twin cakes was a celebratory red and gold, while the inside was rich, dark chocolate. Macario explained Mao's story of the foolish old man who wished to remove the mountains obstructing the view before his house by digging the soil away, that the foolish old man explained to the wise old man that eventually the mountains would be dug away, if not by himself, then by his sons and their sons and their sons' sons. Thus, Mao explained the foolish work of a billion Chinese people intent on removing the twin mountains of feudalism and imperialism.

16.2 The guests eagerly carved away at the chocolate mountains, although many interpreted the twin mountains to represent the wedding couple: Olivia in red and Ben in gold.

16.3 Mountain fables may move from mountain to mountain.

> WHEREAS, the Mindanao Independence Movement with the active material and financial assistance of foreign political and economic interests, is engaged in an open and unconcealed attempt to establish by violence and force a separate and independent political state . . .

XVII

If Imelda can make it, everybody else can make it.
—Imelda Marcos

17.1 Macario proposed a toast and recited thus:
May the road rise to meet you.
May the wind be always at your back.
May the sun shine warm upon your face,
The rains fall soft upon your fields.
And until we meet again,
May the people hold you in the palms of our hands.

May the people be with you and bless you.
May you see your children's children.
May you be poor in misfortune
Rich in blessings.
May you know nothing but happiness
From this day forward.
May the road rise to meet you.
May the wind be always at your back.
May the warm rays of sun fall upon your home,
And may the hand of a friend always be near.
May green be the grass you walk on.
May blue be the skies above you.
May pure be the joys that surround you.
May true be the hearts that love you.

> WHEREAS, because of the aforesaid disorder resulting from armed clashes, killings, massacres, arsons, rapes, pillages, destruction of whole villages and towns and the inevitable cessation of agricultural and industrial operations . . . a great many parts of the islands of Mindanao and Sulu are virtually now in a state of actual war . . .

XVIII

To know Asia is to feel Asia. Asia must be felt with the heart in order to be understood.

—Imelda Marcos

18.1 Ben serenaded Olivia with Beatles songs on the piano, surprising everyone with popular tunes like "Yesterday" and "When I'm Sixty-four."

> WHEREAS, the violent disorder in Mindanao and Sulu has to date resulted in the killing of over 1,000 civilians and about 2,000 armed Muslims and Christians . . .

XIX

Every Christmas, I ask myself what else I may give the young, and my answer always comes down to love and more love.
—Imelda Marcos

19.1 Olivia pushed Ben to one side of the piano bench and played several stanzas from a Chopin mazurka, her fingers flashing across the keys.

19.2 *Show-off,* he snarled, pushing her away to play "You've Got a Friend," cackling at her horrified reaction.

WHEREAS, because of the foregoing acts of armed insurrection . . . and because of the spreading lawlessness and anarchy throughout the land . . . and finally because public order and safety and the security of this nation demand that immediate, swift, decisive and effective action be taken . . .

XX

People say I'm extravagant because I want to be surrounded by beauty. But tell me, who wants to be surrounded by garbage? Beauty is love made real and the spirit of love is God. Only a crazy man wants to be surrounded by garbage, and I'm not crazy just yet. —Imelda Marcos

20.1 Tino's band joined in, then changed the tune to dance music, at which point all the guests crowded onto the floor.

WHEREAS, in cases of invasion, insurrection or rebellion or imminent danger thereof, I, as President of the Philippines, have, under the Constitution, three courses of action open to me, namely: (a) call out the armed forces to suppress the present lawless violence; (b) suspend the privilege of the writ of habeas corpus to make the arrest and apprehension of these lawless elements easier and more effective; or (c) place the Philippines or any part thereof under martial law . . .

XXI

> I have only ever dreamt of a small house with a picket fence by the sea. But how can I stop what I am doing? It becomes a romance not only to a president and a husband but a romance of principles and commitment. A romance for humanity. This is perhaps what makes me so controversial. I am beyond logic and rationality.
>
> —Imelda Marcos

21.1 At some appropriate moment, the band serenaded the wedding couple, following them out the entrance of the I-Hotel in a spray of rice and a flurry of rose petals.

> WHEREAS, I have already utilized the first two courses of action . . . but in spite of all that, both courses of action were found inadequate and ineffective to contain, much less solve, the present rebellion and lawlessness in the country . . .

XXII

> I have a different way of thinking. I think synergistically. I'm not linear in thinking. I'm not very logical.
>
> —Imelda Marcos

22.1 On Kearny, the gold Mercedes Benz awaited them, decked out like a float with flowers, balloons, crepe paper, and revolutionary slogans. *Venceremos! All power to the people! Unity through Struggle! Makibaka! Long Live the Revolution! Viva la huelga! Si se puede! Save the I-Hotel!*

> WHEREAS, the rebellion and armed action undertaken by these lawless elements of the communist and other armed aggrupations . . . have assumed the magnitude of an actual state of war against our people and the Republic of the Philippines . . .

XXIII

> The only gold my husband has is in his heart.
>
> —Imelda Marcos

23.1 They drove to the Golden Gate and watched the sun set over the bay.

> NOW, THEREFORE, I, FERDINAND E. MARCOS, President of the Philippines, by virtue of the powers vested upon me . . . do hereby place the entire Philippines . . . under martial law and, in my capacity as their commander-in-chief, do hereby command the armed forces of the Philippines, to maintain law and order throughout the Philippines, prevent or suppress all forms of lawless violence as well as any act of insurrection or rebellion and to enforce obedience to all the laws and decrees, orders and regulations promulgated by me personally or upon my direction.

XXIV

Win or lose, we go shopping after the election.

—Imelda Marcos

24.1 Olie said: *I married you for my green card, you know.*

24.2 Benny said: *I married you for the Benz.*

> In addition, I do hereby order that all persons presently detained, as well as all others who may hereafter be similarly detained for the crimes of insurrection or rebellion . . . for crimes against national security . . . and for such other crimes as will be enumerated in Orders that I shall subsequently promulgate . . . shall be kept under detention until otherwise ordered released by me or by my duly designated representative.

XXV

Daig ko pa si Cinderella.

—Imelda Marcos

25.1 Sneaking back to Kearny Street, Ben swept Olivia up and carried her ceremoniously across the threshold of the I-Hotel. He smiled when she did not protest.

25.2 Tucked into their single room, Olivia handed Ben a gift, a wrapped shoebox. *I've been saving this for you.* She smiled. *Guess what it is.*

25.3 *Too light for a gun,* he quipped.

25.4 Ripping it open, he pulled from the tissue paper the right side of a worn shoe, its rubber sole, red canvas, and laces caked in the white paint of the I-Hotel.

> IN WITNESS WHEREOF I have hereunto set my hand and caused the seal of the Republic of the Philippines to be affixed. Done in the City of Manila, this 21st day of September, in the year of Our Lord, nineteen hundred and seventy two.
>
> FERDINAND E. MARCOS
> President
> Republic of the Philippines

7: National Liberation

I

. . . the concept of competition belongs to a world of hunger, because competition belongs to an underdeveloped world, because competition belongs to a world where hunger and poverty have become institutions . . . you have been forging your own revolutionary consciousness . . . you have been helping to create the material base that along with education and consciousness will allow us to live according to truly communist norms, that is, according to truly fraternal norms, truly human norms, in which each man and woman will see others as his brothers and sisters . . . we have seen what can be done through human collectivity; we have seen what you have been able to accomplish in three months, a small army of young people working here enthusiastically, because you did not see work as a punishment, but rather as an ennobling activity, one that inspires man, that can fill him with happiness. That is work when it is not slave work; that is work when man is not exploited. . . . The plants that you have sown here will remain on the earth; your example will remain with our youth; and the heartening response of the new revolutionary generation will remain with our revolution.

—Fidel Castro, April 29, 1967

1.1 Let us speak of the sugar cane itself, rising in great clustering mastheads from the rich red earth, jointed like bamboo, stalks progressing from murky reds and purplish yellows to the green-grass spray at their waving peaks.

1.2 And to the people who cut the cane, who walked into its green moisture at dawn to level the fields with their swiping machetes, the instructions were simple:

1.3 Approach the cane with a firm grasp on your machete and swipe the stalk at its base, severing the cane at the ground. Hack the cane in half. Cut away the leafy top. Do not stand so as to cut your own leg. Achieve a technique so that your body creates a rhythm, so that your body becomes as a machine.

1.4 Forget that your hands and wrists will swell and blister; that you will soon be covered in tiny cuts from your own machete and from the cane's sharp leaves; that your skin will redden, then turn to deep brown from the intense sun; that sweat will pour from your body and reside in soiled puddles in your dusty clothing. Forget the one million arroba mark promised to the revolution. Forget that you will cut cane next to the most worthy of your comrades, the Brigada Boliviano, the Brigada Vietnamita, next to men who fought with Fidel, or even next to Fidel himself.

1.5 However, it was not the strenuous insistence of backbreaking and tedious labor alongside his comrades Cubanos that impressed Ben San Pablo; it was instead their deep love for Cuba. There was no way to get around it. He did not love the place of his birth, and every one of his companions Americanos also only expressed hatred for their imperialist homeland. And among themselves, the hostilities between the Third and the white worlds were hidden from their Cuban hosts. How then would they ever return to wage a revolution?

1.6 He tried to explain his concern to Olivia. *It's like Che said: the true revolutionary is guided by strong feelings of love.*

1.7 *Oh Benny, get over it.*

II

> What a luminous, near future would be visible to us if two, three or many Vietnams appeared throughout the world with their share of death and immense tragedies, their everyday heroism and repeated blows against imperialism, obliging it to disperse its forces under the attack and increasing hatred of all the peoples of the earth! . . . If we, those of us who on a

> small point of the world map, fulfill our duty and place at the disposal of this struggle whatever little we are able to give—our lives, our sacrifice—must someday breathe our last breath in any land not our own yet already ours, sprinkled with our blood, let it be known that we have measured the scope of our actions and that we consider ourselves no more than elements in the great army of the proletariat . . .
>
> —Ernesto Che Guevara, *Message to the Tricontinental,* April 1967

2.1 What is the duty of the revolutionary if not to make the revolution? Should the revolutionary hunker down on constant watch, the posted guard ever ready with the appropriate armory and flags and drums for the eventuality of the uprising spurred by the grand announcement of imperial death? Or should the revolutionary, like his counterpart mole in the Federal Bureau of Investigations, study the evidence with meticulous insistence, drafting and redrafting the intricate puzzles of conspiracies, creating counter-conspiracies and confusion to anticipate the moment of revolution? Or should the revolutionary, knowing the inevitability of the demise of his enemy, percolate ideas into the populace until such a time when such brewed ideas will caffeinate the minds of all? Men of action with their short lives, typically from ages seventeen to twenty-seven, have no such luxury. Yet some push on doggedly until the age of thirty-nine.

2.2 What is the revolutionary if not the revolution itself, the insurrectionary focus, the revolutionary condition, the incendiary spark? History has shown that on an island, it may be only six men; in a small country, a force of one hundred; in a country of eight hundred million, eight thousand will do.

2.3 *We may have to plan,* said Ben, *for the possibility of an insurrection in which we hold out in the I-Hotel.*

2.4 *You know we have our stash hidden,* suggested a member. *We could easily funnel it into the hotel, arm the place to the teeth. Once under attack, we could draw all of Chinatown in, set up multiple operational bases.*

2.5 Olivia appeared in the doorway in the full bloom of her pregnant self, tapping her living belly as she spoke. *What kind of bullshit are you talking? Have you asked the tenants? These guys'll kick you out on your revolutionary asses. Have you even asked Chinatown? Ask me. I work in Chinatown.*

2.6 The continued belief in the heroic individual who can change the course of history is a contradictory although romantic message to the collective cause. How many Ches will it take? Is the revolutionary dead? Who then will come forward in our time of great need?

2.7 Function may make the functionary, but only the historic individual may make history.

III

> It is absolutely essential that the oppressed participate in the revolutionary process with an increasingly critical awareness of their role as Subjects of the transformation . . . if they come to power still embodying that ambiguity imposed on them by the situation of oppression—it is my contention that they will merely imagine they have reached power. Their existential duality may even facilitate the rise of a sectarian climate leading to the installation of bureaucracies which undermine the revolution. . . . They may aspire to revolution as a means of domination, rather than as a road to liberation.
>
> —Paulo Freire, *Pedagogy of the Oppressed*

3.1 Karl Kang had argued: *This is not Cuba. The material conditions are not ripe in the U.S. You are working against a majority that represents a basically provincial American state of monolingual people. Even if you mobilize the working class, they don't give a damn about the Third World or blacks, much less Asians. It may take many years, most likely not in our lifetimes.*

3.2 Olivia argued: *Through our mass work, we can speed things up, but we need direction.*

3.3 Ben argued: *Others are organizing as we speak. If we don't delineate a clear line, we'll lose our voice.*

3.4 *Whatever line you take,* said Kang, *your success will pivot around the categories of race.*

3.5 Macario Amado stood at the bottom steps in front of the J-Town Collective on Sutter. It was his turn to do security. Down the street, Angela Davis sat in a car with three bodyguards, waiting. Suddenly two women erupted from the building, arguing.

3.6 Olivia said, *This may be a joint meeting, but we didn't agree to bring Angela.*

3.7 The other woman said, *This was an opportunity that came up.*

3.8 *You know we're aligned with Mao, and she's* CP *with the Soviets.*

3.9 *That's not why she's been invited. She's not coming to discuss our lines.*

3.10 *Well, she should, because I just read your position paper, and theoretically, it's pretty weak. With a position like that, you're bound to lose cadre.*

3.11 *Listen, this is not a closed meeting over lines. It's a mass meeting, so bringing Angela is part of educating the masses. We've got a packed room up there, waiting to meet her.*

3.12 *This is what you call mass work? Aiko, everyone knows that you're not doing mass work. You're just trying to get your crim degree.*

3.13 Two of Angela's guards emerged from the car and approached Macario. *Ah, say man, we can't have Angela waiting in the car like this. You have to let us know what's going down.*

3.14 By this time the argument between the two women was "fucking bitch" this and that, so Angela's guards said to Macario, *Later, man.*

Later, agreed Macario, watching the car speed away with the signature shadow of Angela's perfect natural.

3.15 The purest definition of the vanguard is as a fighting unit in armed struggle without which no vanguard may become a vanguard, in which case the struggle over its political life and organization may become an end in itself. High revolutionary fervor may be inversely proportional to a situation that is not in fact revolutionary.

IV

> . . . Chile now faces the need to initiate new methods of constructing a socialist society. Our revolutionary method, the pluralist method, was anticipated by the classic Marxist theorists but never before put into practice. . . . Today Chile is the first nation on earth to put into practice the second model of transition to a socialist society. . . . The skeptics and the prophets of doom will say that it is not possible. They will say that a parliament that has served the ruling classes so well cannot be transformed into the Parliament of the Chilean People. Further, they have emphatically stated that the Armed Forces and Corps of Carabineros, who have up to the present supported the institutional order that we wish to overcome, would not consent to guarantee the will of the people if these should decide on the establishment of socialism in our country. They forget the patriotic conscience of the Armed Forces and the Carabineros, their tradition of professionalism and their obedience to civil authority.
>
> —Salvador Allende, *First Message to Congress,* May 21, 1971

4.1 Olivia's words came between breaths. *I hate to admit this, Benny, but if Allende couldn't do it, how can it be done?*

4.2 *We've got to learn from this. Failure can be a springboard.*

4.3 *Oh, oh, oh, bullshit.* She was breathing hard.

4.4 Ben peered with the midwife between Olivia's thighs. *Are you concentrating?* he admonished Olivia.

4.5 *Can't you tell? This is how I'm concentrating,* she groaned. *But while we're learning, the enemy is also learning. Ohhhhh, Benny, we're not naming this baby Salvador.*

4.6 *Olie, it's got a shitload of hair! It's time to push!*

4.7 *I'm tired, Benny. I don't know if I can do this anymore.*

4.8 *Olie, this is no time to give up. Push!*

4.9 *What's that smell from the kitchen?* Olivia grimaced.

4.10 *It's the manong. He's frying chicken.*

4.11 *It's making me sick.*

4.12 *You're going to be really hungry after this. Come on, Olie, push!*

4.13 The manong came across the hall with two long bamboo chopsticks, parting the small crowd waiting patiently at the door, and stuck his head in. *How's it going?* he queried.

4.14 *Push!* shouted Ben.

4.15 *Push!* shouted the manong. *Push!* joined in the enthusiastic crowd in the hallway.

4.16 *Olie, it's a boy!*

4.17 *It's a boy!* repeated everyone in the hallway. And this was repeated to everyone in the stairwell and passed out a window to everyone in the street. Below their window, a band started up a raucous serenade.

4.18 *Olie, it's not over yet, you gotta push out the placenta.*

4.19 The manong clacked his chopsticks. *No problem. You pass that placenta to me. I tell you, the oil's perfect!*

8: Death of a Revolutionary

I

> ... The Great Society is not a safe harbor, a resting place, a final objective, a finished work. It is a challenge constantly renewed, beckoning us toward a destiny where the meaning of our lives matches the marvelous products of our labor.
>
> —Lyndon Baines Johnson

1.1 Ben looked over from his typewriter at Olivia in bed, who was listening absently to Malcolm, now a three-year-old, yelling and running up and down the corridor outside with a playmate. He saw the pain beneath her forced serenity and thought to distract her. *Why am I writing this?* He threw his arms up in frustration.

1.2 *Because it's what you're good at: figuring out what the others are thinking and interpreting what we're thinking and eventually creating the right thinking so we can merge into one new party. It's like drawing up a constitution.*

1.3 *You sound so sure. All anybody does is argue back, criticize every fucking comma. Where's the merging?*

1.4 *On paper, no one's a match for you. Admit it: you love kicking ass.*

1.5 *Strategy before tactics is not kicking ass.*

1.6 *If you don't think, we can't organize. You leave the tactics to me.*

1.7 He looked at her—her diminishing figure, the dark hollows of her high cheeks, then looked away.

1.8 *Hey,* she jabbed at him, *it's a good thing for you I saw that aurora borealis. Without me, you'd be nothing.*

1.9 *Bitch.*

1.10 *If you can't tough this out, you know where you can go.*

1.11 *Not much time left to change the world.*

1.12 *You have a deadline. Get back to work.*

II

Justice is incidental to law and order.

—J. Edgar Hoover

2.1 *How did we ever get to be leaders of anything? We never went to war or killed anybody. Never kidnapped anyone to save anyone.*

2.2 *Some guerilla force we've been, hiding out in the I-Hotel.*

2.3 *We stopped being clandestine long ago, but we're still illusive.*

2.4 *Think we've been infiltrated?*

2.5 *Why not?*

2.6 *I thought Y was a spy. I got her purged.*

2.7 *She was struggled out.*

2.8 *She was screwed up. She was sleeping around with all the men. After we purged her, she overdosed. Someone said she didn't have any family but us.*

2.9 *It's not your fault. There were bigger issues.*

2.10 *Maybe we could have handled it differently. Did you sleep with her?*

2.11 *She was a liability.*

2.12 *She broke the rules, but she wasn't the only one. Only she got purged. Was that fair?*

2.13 *Look who's talking about fair? At the time, you'd have said it was just.*

2.14 *We were right at the time.*

2.15 *Judgments can't be made in the absence of history or culture. That's about as just or as unjust as it gets.*

2.16 *We made our judgment out of fear. I don't have that kind of fear anymore.*

2.17 *Be honest. You've never known fear. You're the commandante.*

2.18 *Fuck off.*

2.19 *Olie, you're so full of shit.*

2.20 *I've been thinking, and it's not that I'm not going to be here to see it. I wouldn't tell anybody but you, but I don't think we're ever going to win this thing. It's all about the struggle. But we can never win.*

III

A man is not finished when he is defeated. He is finished when he quits. —Richard M. Nixon

3.1 *I really believed that we could change things, that if you thought it, I could make it happen. I believed in your mind. I was the van. You the guard. Was I wrong?*

3.2 *What if the shape of my mind took extreme turns, would you have followed anyway?*

3.3 *I'm not stupid.*

3.4 *That's what they all say. Besides, it isn't* my *thinking.*

3.5 *That's what they all say.*

3.6 *Change will happen because its possibilities are embedded in history.*

3.7 *Do you still believe history is inevitable? Why am I dying? Because cancer was embedded in my body?*

3.8 *I don't know.*

3.9 *They'll change everything, you know. When it's all said and done, they can change the history. We'll be like the Gang of Four. They'll only remember that we purged people, that Y died, that I was a fucking bitch.*

3.10 *Worried about your legacy, aye Olie?*

3.11 *Fuck yes. You'd better make me a martyr.*

3.12 *I've already written your eulogy.*

3.13 *Benny, did I just imagine all this?*

3.14 He lifted her emaciated body from the bed and carried her over to see Malcolm, sleeping in a puddle of toys and blankets. *No,* he said.

3.15 *He has your eyes, Benny. That's why I married you, for those eyes.*

3.16 He brought her back to the bed.

3.17 *That stuff you use. I know all about it. For Malcolm, you've got to stop. I'm going to help you stop.* And she directed him as if she knew all about it, which perhaps she did, directing the needle, then holding the syringe's plunger with her free hand.

3.18 *This better work. No, look this way. I want to see your eyes one last time.* She whispered so that he only thought he heard: *Great resolution and irony.*

3.19 He wrapped his face in the great cascades of her hair and wept.

1973: Int'l Hotel

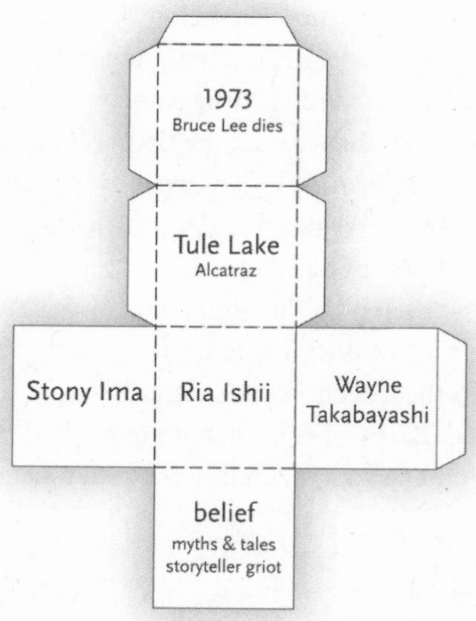

1: Turtle Island

It's not easy to get into a boat with three people you don't know and go rowing off toward your destiny. If someone said, "Hey, get into this boat; it's going to change your life," would you do it? That's the trickery of being young. You figure, what the hell. I've never done this before. You've got time. Youth's supposed to have adventures. Even when there're folks who come rowing back from that trip and tell you what could happen or even warn you to turn around, you think you'll make your own mistakes but not those. But they never tell you everything. The past is always saved in someone's ego, so the really complicated and difficult things can only be known by living them out yourself. When it's all said and done, you too will save the hardest stuff inside your knowing ego. And you won't do it out of meanness, or duplicity, or vanity, but maybe because you just forget and get tired, because you've got to be an elder with a certain distance that they call wisdom, or because they never ask you anyway.

A group self-identified by their Asian features gathered at Pier Thirty-nine under a full November moon, dancing through the usual lace of San Francisco Bay fog. Of course, depending, they could have been mistaken for Indian. It wouldn't be the first time someone recognized the features that claim the same genes that crossed the Bering Strait or canoed across the Pacific. Different tribes is all. The giveaway was probably the hundred-pound sack of Calrose rice. Wayne Takabayashi, a kid, probably high school, in skinny jeans and a pair of black canvas low-tops, was sitting on the sack when Stony Ima sauntered up, lugging a box on his shoulder. "Hey," said Stony to Wayne, "you waiting for the, uh, operation to the island?" He pointed his nose in the direction of Alcatraz. At that hour, it had the surreptitious feel of a dark spy operation, but no one had the code words.

Wayne looked up at a long-haired dude with a headband. "Yeah, who sent you?"

"Olivia. You?"

"Who's Olivia?"

"Does it matter?"

"Guess not. You know JB?"

"Yeah, everyone knows JB. So where is he?"

"Don't know. Where's the boat? Supposed to be transport, you know."

"How long you been here?"

"Half an hour at least. Shit."

"Hey," Stony pointed to an Asian woman walking toward them. "That's not Olivia. Know her?"

Wayne shook his head, waiting for her face to be revealed in the dark. "I don't know. She looks familiar." She had that long, straight hair parted in the middle that tumbled over a navy blue peacoat, but they all pretty much looked like that.

Ria Ishii walked purposefully, her hand gripping the handle of a large canister. Wayne noticed it was a gallon can of Kikkoman shoyu. She put it down next to his sack of rice and said, "So, this must be the place."

Stony shook his head. "Can't be too sure." He pointed at Wayne. "He's been waiting a half hour already and no boat."

"Well," said Ria. "Maybe we're not late."

"That's one way to see it," nodded Stony. "Shit, it's midnight."

Wayne pulled on his beanie and tugged his jacket tighter. The neons from the wharf reflected off the black waters, obscured intermittently by low clouds of fog hunkering over the surface. The wind blew cold against the ocean spray misting his face.

Stony, who had worked up a walking sweat with his load, was wiping the steam off his spectacles. "Good idea, the rice," he approved.

"Yeah, what'd you bring?" asked Wayne, nodding at Stony's box.

"Case of Spam." He smiled. "I figure they're camped out there. This is camping food, right?"

"I guess so." Wayne shrugged. Then he noticed that he and Stony were both staring at the gallon can of soy sauce. They were momentarily mesmerized by the light that bounced off the slapping waves and glinted over the can's gold and red-orange carapace.

"Salt substitute," Ria defended.

No one said anything. They all looked out across the bay at the island, the dark concrete fortress perched on its rocky base, the lighthouse beam sweeping in a constant pulse. Maybe they imagined it, but they thought they could see tiny bonfires and smoke trailing darkly across night skies in the cold wind. When the last prisoner departed from the old penitentiary, he left the island to a single caretaker and his dog. After six years, Alcatraz was again occupied. Now the Rock was Indian land.

Ria broke in, "I met an Indian out there on the street who just pulled in from Oklahoma. He's got a boat hitched to his station wagon."

"No shit. The message is traveling," nodded Stony.

"He needs help with the boat. I told him I'd send him some help. But maybe he could be our way over."

Wayne pointed. "They've got the Coast Guard patrolling. See that boat over there with the lights?"

"That must be why we're stuck here. Something fouled up."

"How about it?" Ria pursued her idea. "One of you stay here to watch our stuff?"

"I'll do it," said Stony. He pointed at Wayne. "You could probably use the exercise."

Wayne was jumping around a bit to warm up. "Yeah," he agreed and accompanied Ria, following a small crowd of late-night revelers emerging from a wharf bar.

"I'm Ria," said Ria.

"Wayne," said Wayne.

"I know I've seen you around somewhere."

"Yeah," said Wayne. "Me too."

They found the Indian dozing at the wheel in his station wagon. The back was packed to the gills with stuff. They knocked on his window.

"Hey." He recognized Ria. "I thought I'd catch some snooze. I been driving for almost three days straight, and anyway, I can't leave the boat. Too risky."

They helped him unhitch the boat, pulled away the protective tarp to reveal a wooden flat-bottomed boat painted a deep green. Wayne scrutinized the boat's name, painted in golden letters. In the dark it took awhile, but he finally read: *The Turtle.*

"I'm Jack. Jack Denny. Some call me Turtle, too," said Jack, shaking hands all around.

They filled the boat with paddles, a small outboard motor, fishing gear, a sleeping roll, and a duffel of clothing. Jack shouldered the front, with Ria and Wayne coming up on either side. They marched down the old pier to the end, Jack's boots making rhythmic footfalls, dancing to avoid puddles of fish blood and the drenched scatter of paper trash and beer bottles. The stink of fish and crab wafted about. At that hour, it was just them and the barking sea lions.

Stony was sitting on the rice and blowing plaintive sounds through a narrow bamboo flute. "Night guard came round," he announced and tucked the flute into an inside pocket in his jacket. "Asked me, was I one of those Indians, and did I know it was illegal to go over there."

"What'd you say?"

"Said I was Japanese, just night fishing like usual. Then for some reason, he started talking about raw fish. Said he knew all about it. Lived in Okinawa. Used the dipping sauce, too."

They all stared at the gallon canister of soy sauce again, and Ria smiled. "Hey," she said, introducing the boat's owner, "this is Jack."

They took the boat down a ramp to a docking slip and gently set *The Turtle* into the ocean. It bobbed there in the dark water, and they could see it would soon become like a piece of straw in the big bay. Even so, Jack looked out and said confidently, "Pretty calm out there."

"Yeah, well, good luck," said Ria.

"So we brought these provisions, see." Stony came forward with his case of Spam. Then everything got arranged in the boat—Jack's stuff, plus the rice and shoyu.

Stony looked up. "Oh man, here comes the guard," he rasped.

"How are you folks tonight?" said the guard.

Stony said, "These are my Japanese friends I was telling you about."

"Fishing crew, eh? Where you heading?"

Stony said, "Oh, Marin side maybe, do some rock fishing."

Wayne picked up one of Jack's rods and handed it to Ria, who examined it like she knew what she was doing. She stepped out in front of the guard to obscure Jack and made casting motions. Under the watch of the guard, one by one they all climbed into the boat. Stony retrieved the rope, and Jack took the paddle and pushed off the dock. Wayne got the other paddle and tried to match Jack's movements. Ria waved good-bye to the guard, who called out, "Bring me back some sa-shimi!" After a short distance, they could hear his mutter travel along the waves: "Crazy Japanese."

"Thanks for covering for me," said Jack, a red man but yellow enough.

"So, now what?" Ria asked.

"So, now we go claim the Rock," said Jack.

"Oh shit," said Stony, looking back at the dock that was receding into the dark distance. "Why not?"

"O.K.," agreed Wayne.

"Just so everyone knows," said Ria, "I've never been in a boat. I'm from the South side of Chicago."

"Aren't there lakes there?" asked Stony.

"Lake Michigan, but I never sailed it. How about you?"

Stony said, "Just some fishing with my dad in L.A. off Pedro."

"O.K., that's something," said Jack. "How about you?" he asked Wayne.

Wayne shook his head.

"The *Turtle* here," announced Jack, "is making her maiden voyage in the Pacific Ocean. First time she's touched salt water."

"Congratulations," praised Stony.

"And not to make you nervous or anything, but I can't swim either," said Ria.

Jack glanced forward to Ria in the bow. "The *Turtle*'s never let me down, but if there're any other last confessions, we'll hear them now."

Stony said, "Ria, you wanna go back?"

"No, no." Ria practically stood up in the boat, waved, and pointed. "Let's go take that Rock."

"O.K."

Wayne asked, "If we pretend to be fishing, will they leave us alone?" In the distance, they could see what looked like a patrol boat cruising by the east end of Alcatraz.

"Maybe." Ria stuck a rod out and pushed a bit of line into the water, watching its skimming trail follow behind.

Jack and Wayne traded paddling from one side to the other, keeping a distant beeline for the dark Rock. Jack suggested, "Sink the paddle in like this and push back."

Wayne copied Jack's motions and probably thought about the last time he did this, on a canoe ride at Disneyland, but this was hardly the time to admit it.

"Why," Ria asked Jack, "did you decide to come? Oklahoma to Alcatraz is a long way."

"It's time."

"You do Nam?" Stony asked, noticing the medals pinned to Jack's denim jacket.

"That too." Jack paused. "You know the story of the Modoc and Captain Jack?"

Jack jerked the cord back a bunch of times until the motor coughed into life. They all settled into the *Turtle* and stared hard at the destined Rock. The story bloomed around them in a translucent fog.

Who knows—if that night guard hadn't come around to talk about raw fish and make sure they paddled out to fish it, whether three Japanese Americans would have gotten on a little green boat with a Modoc Indian. And it was the damnedest thing how you could be Indian or Japanese but be just plain invisible. Now, some might say that making it through the Coast Guard blockade that night was a condition of this invisibility, but others will tell you that storytelling in itself is powerful magic, can get you from point A to point B, and you don't know how it happened.

Captain Jack, the man Jack "Turtle" Denny was named after, was the chief of the Modocs when they lived on the lava beds around Lost River and Tule Lake along the far northern border of California with Oregon.

That was around 1870, a hundred years ago.

"You know how the U.S. Army can have all the manpower, the guns, the copters, the bombs, and napalm and still be losing the war?"

"Yeah, man."

"So it was the same with Captain Jack and the Modoc braves. It was the costliest battle of the time. Government sent in everything and still they couldn't dislodge the Modoc people from lavaland. Hell, they couldn't even see the Modoc warriors who just disappeared into the landscape, merged into the black rocks and sage."

Outboard motor puttputted its concerted rhythm, and the battle rose from the inky ocean in great detail: bloody guts of the killed and wounded, a frayed army of white soldiers shredded by their own crazed departure through jagged rock. And only a single Indian—his head blown up by his own curiosity—fallen. But like every Indian victory, it's still just a story. If the Modoc could hold the inhospitable lava beds, what pride should remove their claim? The same would be true of the Rock, unsuitable for any occupation other than a penitentiary or an Indian reservation—no transportation, no running water, no sanitation facilities, no oil or mineral rights, no industry, no health care, no agriculture or game, no education. It could be rock, could be lava beds. Story's the same.

Winning a battle could get you a peace treaty, but not necessarily the one you want and not necessarily the one they'll keep. The price of peace, if it has one, is never cheap. "So," said Jack, "when the negotiations went sour, the Modoc council voted to kill the white general." Now, the operative word here is *voted,* not *kill;* people forget that war is a collective action. The story is that Captain Jack voted to negotiate the peace but was in the minority. And then he was called a "fish-hearted woman" for voting that way. Well, he went back into that peace-tent meeting with five other Modoc representatives and asked to get the Modoc lands back—those same lava beds and the Lost River, and once again, General Canby said no.

"At that moment," continued Jack, "Captain Jack took out the revolver hidden near his so-called fish-heart and shot the general in the face. You could say the general lost face, but not Captain Jack."

Ria interrupted. "I swear it's not the story, but I'm going to be sick."

Jack said, "You'll feel better if you just concentrate on looking out into the distance at the island." But when they all looked, they were staring the Rock in the face, its cliffs rising in gigantic shelves above an impudent turtle.

"What do you think?" asked Stony. "Go that way?" He pointed east.

"Got to be a landing somewhere."

Wayne lifted his right foot from the bottom of the boat and shook out his low-top. "You generally get this much water in the boat?"

Everyone looked down and saw the water seeping through. Stony saw Jack's dismayed expression and jumped down and started scooping the water out with his hands.

Wayne pointed with an oar. "Over there. We can make it."

As the boat approached a rocky outcrop, Ria tossed Jack's duffel, and then his sleeping bag. Jack jumped out and yelled for the rope. "O.K.," he yelled, pulling the tether and directing their escape. "Let's go. Grab his hand!"

When they were all safe on the rocks, Jack looked out at the *Turtle*, slowly filling with water but considerably more buoyant without its passengers. "Maybe we can tie the rope somewhere," Stony suggested, searching around.

"Nope." Jack shook his head. "*Turtle*'s gotta go. Had enough, I guess." He let the rope slip away, and they watched the boat bob around with the provisions—Calrose, Spam, and Kikkoman, the fishing equipment, and the paddles, flung like helpless arms.

"Hey!" a yell came from above.

The four looked up, wet to their waists and almost too frozen to move. A light passed over, blinding them, and then someone said, "Welcome to Indian land."

Someone else added, "Land of the free. Home of the brave."

The fifth day of the takeover would be dawning in a few hours. The feeling of excitement and purpose was palpable everywhere. How many times in your life do you feel that kind of power, the sort that unifies a people in collective pride and knowing? This time, you and your people get to choose. It's not an idle feeling, but one that you pursue in various forms, like singing the same song or cheering the same team or praying to the same spirit. A connective wave carries you to the same infinite space, and you feel more alive than you have ever felt.

Looking up from the bonfire, Ria saw the smoke meet the full moon. Two more astronauts had walked there only days ago, but no one seemed to remember. It was just another Apollo, another moonwalk. On Earth, Indians walked on Alcatraz. "One step for man, one giant leap for mankind."

Around the fire and after a change of clothing, the storytelling continued. The Indians of All Tribes had a comparative story going about Turtle Island. It seems like several tribes have a variation of this creation story, how the Earth was born from a tiny plug of soil on the back of a turtle. There are usually three animals who go in search of land. Some say the questing animals were an eagle, a loon, and a muskrat. Others interchange beaver and otter. Others put in for the toad. But there's pretty much some agreement that it was a turtle's back and always some minor amphibious animal who came back to the surface of the water with a precious plug of earth. Maybe it's a creation story, but maybe it's also a story about sacrifice and quest.

The morning rose over the island, and they had not slept. They walked to the eastern edge of the Rock and looked out toward the wakening city. Stony drew the flute from inside his jacket. Jack eyed it and asked, "What kind of flute is that?"

"Japanese call it a yokobue." Stony set the thing to his lips and pierced the morning with its birdsong. He blew a high-pitched wild yodel that converged with the barking sea lions, the low horns of passing ferries, and the clang of scattered buoys. Then Stony coaxed Jack: "You never finished your story about Captain Jack."

"Oh, yeah."

Don't think that if you kill a general, the U.S. Army will let you go. History tells us that the white man's pride is located in his laws, such that he will justify his pride and his greed, his great paternity and his superiority, with the great writ of his laws. Everything must follow accordingly. The white man will only give up or lose something if forced to do so by his own laws; in this way, he cannot lose face and continues secure in his pride that his law must be just. And so Captain Jack and four of his fellow Modoc warriors were tried and hung. Two braves, however, escaped the gallows and were imprisoned in Alcatraz. The Modoc brave Barncho died here, but Slolux lived to follow his people to Oklahoma. "Slolux," said Jack, "was my great-grandfather."

A great sunrise blushed behind the hills and towering buildings of the city's peninsula. Wayne pointed to a green speck rowing away from the Rock. Ria scrutinized the floating vessel. Stony said, *"The Turtle?"* then asked for confirmation, "There are two guys rowing, right?"

"Who are they?" asked Ria. "Hey! Come back!" she yelled into the bay uselessly. "That's Jack's *Turtle!*"

But when Stony blew his flute in melodic tribute, they seemed to look back in the direction of its cry.

Jack waved and said, "It's O.K. They're Indians."

"How do you know? From the island?"

"Yeah," he nodded. "Finally, they got away."

"Huh?"

"Shit," said Stony. "What are they going to do with your shoyu?"

2: Crane

For some people, this life begins with an interest in philosophy. Never mind that they don't know exactly what philosophy is; they just think it's something that can be figured out in the mind, like a twirling star that's an idea that blossoms into a grand explosion. Depending, that explosion might be a revelation or a revolution. Something inside the mind tells you that your thinking can be powerful. But then, the thinking has got to be put into practice, and how many middle-class activists checked into factories to find out what it's like to work? Even though this may have been a rite of passage, the truth is, really not many. How many graduate students of philosophy and political economics? Maybe there were others, but one was Ria Ishii.

A few days after arriving, the Indians would celebrate their first Thanksgiving on Alcatraz. By then the Coast Guard had abandoned their blockade, and the three Japanese Americans caught a ride back to the mainland. Jack stood by on the dock and gave the key to his station wagon to Stony with some instructions about the carburetor and said, "Catch you later, man." Stony drove everyone home to the beginnings of their separate destinies. Or, you could say their separate quests but same promises. A quest is at first just a question, something like: *what is my purpose in life?* Then the quest is to go out and find the answer, that plug of earth that can grow into a continent.

Sometimes, though, what you've got in the way of useful skills is the ability to sew, which you learned in junior high school when you started with the gym bag project and ended with the sequined gown with matching boa that you designed for the school musical production of *Guys and Dolls.* Well, Ria had those skills in her fingers, but up her sleeves she also had the skills of a young organizer who had fought to mobilize a boycott to redistrict Chicago's South Side wards to integrate schools, and who later organized tenants to bring down slumlords. Hard to imagine someone so young entering this arena in junior high school, but it's true that by the time she arrived at UC Berkeley, Ria was what you call a seasoned activist. So yes, technically, Ria could sew; socially, she could organize; and theoretically, Ria could think political economics: Marx and C. L. R. James, to be specific; she did her MA thesis on the Haitian revolution.

Of course, this information was scratched from her resume, and the manager, who couldn't tell the difference between a Japanese and a Chinese, gave her the job because he thought if she could speak English, she could be an interpreter. What did he know? His factory had forty seamstresses, three cutters, and three packers, all Chinese. By the time he figured out that Ria couldn't speak Chinese, she had convinced two other college students to join up who could speak Chinese, and they were agitating for a higher pay scale and better benefits. Once, they got almost all forty seamstresses to go to a union meeting of the International Ladies' Garment Workers' Union. But that was once. The Chinese ladies humored the students and went back to work.

Mrs. Lee explained things to Ria. "Union or no union, it's all the same. You got to get paid by the piece. Sew faster. Make more money."

The students reconnoitered and went out to do their homework like they were taught to do. It was true. Some Chinatown contractors made the seamstresses sign fake time cards to show that they were meeting the $1.65 per hour minimum. Union dues might get health benefits, but not much more. In Chinatown, you could at least leave your sewing machine to pick up from school and feed your children or check in on your sick auntie. Your boss was a paternal or a maternal figure who gave favors, made concessions, and took care of everyone. No one wanted to buck the system because no one wanted to lose her job. If you didn't speak English, what were your choices?

The statistics were bleak. Average pay for a six-day week was less than $2,900 annually. That might be a $1 an hour. No overtime. No vacation. No sick leave. Probably no health benefits. Limited English and no prospects for other work. All the women worked to supplement the family income, most of them married to service workers and many married to old retired men.

Mrs. Lee explained again to Ria. "When I come here, my husband's already sixty-five, but he got the money to bring me over and make himself some kids. But what does he know about nice clothing and a refrigerator? How long he's been a bachelor?"

One day Sandy Hu, who was a poet, dancer, singer, and performer, came by to ask Ria for a favor. "Ria, do you think, in between your organizing and all, that you could stitch me a Mao jacket?"

She sat down next to Ria's machine and sketched out her idea. "It can't be just any utilitarian jacket though. We're not going plebian here." She looked at Ria significantly. "I know you don't approve."

Ria sucked her breath in.

"Listen, don't get huffy, because I saw those polyester dresses you were piecing together for the JCPenney clientele, and that's not going to make no revolution in no part of the world." Sandy pulled out a roll of chartreuse silk.

Ria said, "We'll need to stiffen up the collar area to make it stand up."

And that's how it started. The sewing ladies back at the factory studied a picture of Mao and copied the style, measured Sandy, and cut the patterns out of Chinese newspapers. When the silk chartreuse Mao jacket was done, everyone else wanted one too.

It's funny how these things happen, how suddenly one collar leads to the sleeves and to the pockets, a range of sizes—small, medium, large, and extra-large, plus fabric choices and slight stylistic changes. The Sandy Hu design was sold and commissioned everywhere. With this initial capital, Ria, the students, and Mrs. Lee bought seven Singer sewing machines at an auction of some failing shop and rented out basement space in the I-Hotel.

As it turned out, the basement was the site of an old sweatshop. The cutting tables were still there, the industrial lamps, the dust of thread and discarded fabric, spindles and bobbins, ghosts of old sewing ladies. One of the students remembered his mother used to sew there. Ria wandered around the windowless basement and thought she could hear that former generation of sewing machines clacking away in the past. In the meantime, she found a cache of old unused hotel blankets and sent it over to the Indians on Alcatraz. It took weeks to clear out accumulated junk and months to kill the rat infestation. Ria called her ex-boyfriend, Mo Akagi, who accommodated her request for an evening rat patrol, bringing in his cohort with pellet guns to take out rats the size of cats.

Then one day, they became the I-Hotel Cooperative Garment Factory. Pretty soon the sewing ladies were going to and fro, and the machines were whirring with industry and purpose.

There's something about the thrill of a new business venture that makes you understand the draw of capitalism. You put the money in the bank and keep your accounting sheet, and you watch the numbers go up and down—you wonder about that surge you get when you move from red to black, from negative to positive, from three digits to four and then to five. But in this case, the thrill was collective; for the first time sewing ladies who had nothing had something: ownership and responsibility. Of course, at first, only Ria and the students felt that way, and in some respects, because they were proving what the books said about cooperative efforts. Their charge was to make the sewing ladies believe in the same thrill. In the beginning, the sewing ladies waited around for the students to decide and run things, perhaps skeptical but withholding judgment. The students went to school; they spoke good English. Let's see what happens. But as events developed, the sewing ladies had to realize the inexperience of youth.

Everyone hovered over the budget and tried to figure out where the numbers should go and why. What were their priorities? If they spent money here, what should be sacrificed or withheld where? It didn't take much time or coaxing to figure out that the sewing ladies were way ahead of the students in the way of financial savvy.

"No! We don't need that. What we need that for?"

"That vendor ask too much. We get better price!"

"You go back and argue for lower. Go back!"

"We not making enough money. We got to do piecework to make extra money."

"You go get contract for us."

"Get contract for pants. We do pants fast."

Ria and the students were sent scurrying. Everything went into high gear. Everyday they were out there knocking on doors for work. They found out what it really meant to be a Chinatown garment contractor, the middleman who had to negotiate terms with the manufacturers. In the end, there would be little profit margin for the contractor, who beat a path between the sweatshops and all the seamstresses sitting in their tiny one-room apartments trying to put extra pennies on the table. They got the sewing ladies to come along to meet the manufacturers, and they took field trips to the department stores to compare prices.

"This dress we make for $2! Look, selling for $30!"

They figured out that the manufacturer bought it from them for $2, sold it to the retailer for $10 who in turn marked it up another 200% and sold it back to them for $30.

"First, we get rid of contractor. Next we get rid of manufacturer."

Ria smiled. But could they make 100,000 dresses for national distribution? One dress at a time.

The women wandered through women's apparel, fingering the details on the blouses, pushing successive sizes of every imaginable style of jacket, dress, pants, and skirt along the racks. Mrs. Lee said, "In America, you have everything you want even if you don't want it. Biggest problem for America is what to choose."

Ria thought about Mrs. Lee's observation. "What do you mean, biggest problem?"

"Choose is easy," said Mrs. Lee, yanking at a sweater sleeve. "But really choose?" she asked. "No one in all world knows how. You come to America, everybody gets more confused. You have everything!" She gestured around at everything. "You," she stopped and looked at Ria significantly, even accusingly, "even have choosing foods for only cats!"

At night, Ria petted the factory cat, adopted to keep the rat population in check, and who came to sleep in her lap while she sewed. Lately Ria was there nightly, sewing piecework to make up for their deficit. Mo came around, sometimes as late as midnight, to find her sewing under a single lamp in the back.

"What are you doing here at this hour?" she asked.

"Rat patrol." Mo fingered the trigger on his pellet gun. "Thought I could do spot checks from time to time."

"Thanks," she said. "Just don't kill our cat." She went back to her sewing.

"Ria." Mo set the gun down and straddled a chair in front of her machine. "I'm worried about you."

She looked blurry-eyed at him over the spindle of thread and blinked.

"I know you're here every night. You're killing yourself."

"JB and I broke up."

"No shit."

"Is that why you're here?"

"No, really, I didn't know." He stared at his boots for a moment and tugged at his leather gloves. "Is that why you're here?"

"No. See that pile?" She pointed at a stack of denim fabric pieces. "If I can finish that tonight, we'll be o.k. for another week." She lifted the pressure foot and fed another piece into the machine, joining the seams, mechanically guiding the evolving puzzle into a wearable garment.

"The ladies do eight hours, Ria. You're doing something like sixteen."

"No, they probably do another eight at home."

"Yeah, but they get paid."

"I get paid too. It's just different."

Mo watched her fingers flip and turn, pause and push, backtrack and cut, the artistry of the craft spinning up the same article again and again and again. "You're killing yourself, Ria," he said again.

"Look, how cute." She held up a pair of baby overalls. "Mo, listen, I love this work. I love what we're doing. You should see the women when they come in in the morning. They're beautiful. It's so different from when we began. I'm living for that. I can't let it fail."

Ria's already red eyes welled tired with tears, but Mo's responses were as automatic as her sewing. He reached for his gun. *Spsst. Spsst.* The pellets flew out in quick succession. The cat leaped from Ria's lap and pounced on the dying rat.

Olivia Wang marched downstairs from her offices in the I-Hotel and got in Ria's face, as she was often known to do. "So you're organizing a cooperative, but you need to make sure you aren't replicating capitalist models."

Ria argued back, "Of course we're replicating capitalist models. How are we supposed to pay ourselves? Do you have a better plan?"

"I saw that Mao jacket you designed. You're creating bourgeois fashion."

"Yeah, and we're turning Maoism into an exotic commodity."

"That's right. And that's because you have no clear line."

"Show me a clear line, and I'll show you the tension on a zigzag."

"Don't get smart with me."

"Olie, don't bring your cadre in here and confuse the issues. Believe me, I struggle with this every day, but it's not like textbook Lenin."

"You have a responsibility to these women, and you're playing with cooperativism."

"No, Olie, the women have a responsibility to themselves. And yes, we're playing with cooperativism. You know a better way to figure things out?"

Olivia was quiet, but only for the moment. She and Ria always had a respectful hostility going. Their own histories connected back when they worked for SNCC. Being two of the few Asian women in an organization working for black civil rights, some thought they were interchangeable, or even the same woman. Interchangeability bonds you in humbling and exasperating ways, but the assumption of sameness may be grounds for a fight and certainly for competition. Olivia faced Ria off with militancy. Ria faced Olivia off with experience.

Similarly, everyone in the various organizations went tooth and nail at each other. Sometimes physical fights broke out. But what was at stake? The ultimate stakes for revolutionary change were high indeed, but the forks in the road were often so minor that only the most sophisticated thinkers understood the nuances. Ria and Olivia might argue that their decisions were based on the resolution of theoretical struggle, but how many others came to conclusions based on friendship, loyalty, and feeling? Ria and Olivia could jab at each other and come away whole, but how many would be casualties in these fights, where they had joined a group and therefore a struggle to match their passions with their beliefs like first love? To be scorned or threatened or put on trial by those you love for something you believe so passionately is a long hurt and a quiet dying.

Ria and Olivia were immune to these feelings as long as they could be in control, but control was something Ria was learning she needed to lose. The sewing ladies had begun to teach her something valuable about losing control and about dealing with change. After all, the sewing ladies had experienced big changes, lost their language and their homes to a new home. Whatever was useful to know in Hong Kong was not similarly useful in Chinatown. Mrs. Lee said, "Our factory is new idea. We get free to think new." She shook her finger with a warning: "Don't get stuck again."

The sewing ladies called a meeting, and by then Ria and the students were doing the listening. Mrs. Lee said, "We think new."

"We got to get child care."

"We make child care. Right here."

The students looked at each other. They were just trying to get the hang of running a sewing factory. "Are you sure?"

"Yes."

"Also, we want American lessons."

"American lessons?"

"Yes, good English and thirteen colonies."

"You know, thirteen colonies, Declaration of Independence, and fifty stars to pass citizenship."

Meanwhile, two male students were in the back of shop trying to kill two rats caught in a garbage can. They were beating on the rats with a broom and making a commotion, yelling at the rats who wouldn't die by the broom. "Goddamn fucking rats."

The sewing ladies looked up from their meeting, and Mrs. Lee shook her head at the disturbance. She took something out of her purse and handed it to another sewing lady. Ria saw it was one of those Chinese New Year firecrackers. The sewing lady walked over to the students and cursed one of them. "Stupid Steve," she yelled, lit the cracker, and tossed it in the can. KABOOM!

When Olivia said, "You're supposed to be creating a viable model," Ria replied, "You have no idea." Ria stood up and went to a chalkboard on the side wall. She wrote: *referendum, recall, initiative, civil rights.* In a second column she wrote: *market, price, renegotiate, percentage, cheap, stingy.*

"What's that?"

"English lesson for today. Got to know the definitions and spelling. First column is for American history. Second is for garment business."

The next day, one of the manufacturers came in with work to drop off. Mrs. Lee whispered to another sewing lady, "He's the one that's cheap."

That sewing lady stopped her machine and turned around to the next sewing lady and passed on the word. *"Cheap."*

"Cheap."

"Cheap." Pretty soon all the ladies had stopped their machines. They stood up and approached the young man, who was telling one of the students his time requirements, when he'd be back to pick up the work.

Mrs. Lee started in. "We need to talk."

"Yes, we study market. This next batch, we renegotiate price."

"Your price too cheap."

"You got too high percentage. How we going to eat? Put food on the table?"

"You are stingy!"

"You give us higher price."

The women surrounded the man. He looked out, trying to get help from the student negotiator. Ria sat in the back at the last sewing machine and held her breath to keep from laughing.

One day Mrs. Lee said to Ria, "What your ma say about your work?"

"Oh, I don't know."

"I know you can sew, but this factory can't last."

Ria tried to protest.

"No, don't try to fool me. I know. Everybody knows." Mrs. Lee tapped Ria on the knee. "Some are saying you are killing yourself so we have to kill ourself too. This is beginning of the bad end."

Ria's face fell.

"But," Mrs. Lee smiled encouragingly, "I think different. You are too smart to be here. We don't need more dresses. We need more brains." She pointed to Ria's head. "Go back to school. Better to finish."

"I am finished."

"No, you are not finished."

"I'm not?"

"I'm finished. Next week I get U.S. citizenship. Thanks to you."

"That's wonderful."

"Look." Mrs. Lee pointed to a *Vogue* magazine photo of a thin blonde model wearing a silk chartreuse Mao jacket. "See?" she pointed.

"Hey!"

"You can't win," said Mrs. Lee.

"No?"

"Somebody steal your idea. Steal your culture. Every time." She paused and laughed, "O.K., Mao's not my culture, but I am Chinese."

Ria shook her head.

"But don't worry. More ideas where that came from." Mrs. Lee nudged her. "Listen, I tell you something. American Revolution is happening two hundred years ago. What's two hundred years?" Mrs. Lee spit air into the air. "But," she gestured, "first time is the last time. Can't make same revolution twice. Look at me." Mrs. Lee looked into Ria's eyes. "I know what you think, but I am not the revolution."

Ria laughed. "Yes, you are."

Mrs. Lee shook her head. "I know students think East is Red, but this is not the East. So you better go. Go figure out a new way."

"New way?"

"Yes. We say the sun rises in the East, but now we live in the West. Now I am American. I'm not leaving. You go make a sun rise in the West."

Ria looked confused.

"O.K., manner of speaking." Mrs. Lee waved her hand. "You study, you find out."

"If I go, then what?"

"We got a plan. We're going into child care service. Chinatown Child Care." Mrs. Lee made like it was a banner across the I-Hotel. "Quit sewing. I never liked it anyway."

A while later, Sandy Hu sauntered in with the same *Vogue* magazine and threw her copy on Ria's table. "Did you see this?"

"Yeah."

"We should sue! I had the idea first."

"Sandy, it is Mao's jacket."

"O.K., but don't just sit there. Start sewing! How many have you even sold?"

"One hundred? Two hundred? I thought we saturated the market."

"Are you kidding? Selling at the Nihonmachi fair?"

But by the time everyone wanted a stylish Mao jacket, the I-Hotel Cooperative Garment Factory was another ghostly memory of whirring machines.

3: Cormorant

Every once in a while, someone disappears. In the meantime, the world turns in strange serendipity, and destiny, if there is such a thing at all, is not a simple destination, a straight predictable line to some inevitable end. Maybe you do get to turn, turn again, and turn back, dance a two-step, waltz in three-four, or chant a wakening that opens up a space of possibility, the great yawning mouth of your future. And maybe when you get there, it's not the future at all but the constantly evolving present.

Sometime after the first Thanksgiving, the band Creedence Clearwater Revival bought a boat for the Alcatraz Indians, and the trek across the bay from the island could get you a hot bath and some occupation R&R at Warren's Bar in the Mission. This was news to Stony Ima when he accidentally found Jack "Turtle" Denny coiled up in a fetal position with his head bleeding onto the sidewalk. He rushed Jack over to the hospital and hung around intensive care for three days until Jack was finally somewhat lucid.

"Hey man," Jack looked at Stony with one eye. "You saved my life."

"You're supposed to be occupying an island."

"Right. Supposed to die defending Alcatraz."

"What the hell happened?"

"Can't remember. Guy came at me with a pool cue. Next thing I know, I'm here."

"Shit, you lose your memory?"

"I remember you."

"Remember this?" Stony held up a key.

"Where is it?"

"Parked at my mom's place in the Sunset."

"I was going to look you up."

"Mom's telling me to sell the heap," Stony teased, "Complaining it's rusting up her driveway."

"Maybe she's right. Time to sell it."

"What's it worth? Nothing. Blue book'll give you a flat zero. At least it can take you back to Oklahoma."

"Got a pen?" Jack painstakingly carved some name and numbers onto a piece of paper. "This guy'll give you a good price. Tell him it's from Jack Turtle."

Stony took the information.

"Take the money. Are you listening? Half is yours." Jack closed his one eye.

"Jack, let's talk about this later."

He shook his head. "Other half, put away somewhere for me. One of those double-digit interest accounts that I can't get my hands on for another year." He smiled. "By then, who knows?"

"Are you kidding?"

But Jack had drifted off to a morphine sleep.

When Jack's contact handed Stony the large envelope of cash, he thought the guy must run a penny-ante operation, paid him a hundred with one-dollar bills or something. He wandered into a bank with the envelope, thinking about what he would do with fifty dollars, and if putting fifty for Jack in a double-digit account was even worth the time. But the bills turned out to be hundreds, and Stony watched in stupid disbelief as the clerk counted out a pile of crisp Benjamin Franklins.

When he ran over to the VA hospital where Jack had been removed to, there was what seemed to him to be an Indian powwow going on in the hospital room. Someone handed him a drum, and he beat his way through the chanting and bobbing bodies to make sure that Jack was alive. He handed Jack his Bank of America account book, which looked like a small passport, but there was too much commotion and too many Indians to talk freely. Jack smiled and nodded. "I had a dream."

"Oh yeah?"

"You get your carapace"—he pointed at his skull—"busted like me, dream's gotta mean something."

Stony nodded.

"I dreamed you went to Japan."

Stony pulled out his handy bamboo flute and took his place in the ceremony around Jack's bed. And just like that, Jack's dream unfolded.

JB had told Stony to get in touch with Kaz Ono when he arrived in

Tokyo. Kaz would get him over to Sanrizuka to meet the students and the farmers holding out against the takeover of their land for a new Tokyo airport. He got passed over to a Zengakuren student named Atari, who spent a long evening and several beers bemoaning what he saw as the dissolution of their movement. At some point, Atari looked at Stony as if it finally dawned on him and asked, "Where did you learn to speak Japanese?"

"My mom's a Japanese schoolteacher, a kibei. You know, born in America, raised in Japan. My dad was issei. He died a while back."

"Maybe that explains it. Your Japanese is all mixed up. Old. New. And dialects from all over Japan. Where were your parents from?"

"Let's see. Mom's Hiroshima but educated in Tokyo. Dad was from some place called Amami."

"Really?" Atari's eyes opened like he was seeing Stony for the first time. He pointed at his own nose. "I am from Amami!" He drew a map for Stony. "This is Amami-Oshima," he pointed.

"Hey, it's not even in Japan."

Atari nodded. "Closer to Okinawa." He leaned over and spoke almost confidentially. "I'm finally leaving Tokyo, going home. After that Red Army battle in Karuizawa last year, I can't be a part of this anymore. If you come, I will be there."

"I promised JB to check out Sanrizuka."

Atari agreed about first things first. He wrote detailed instructions about how to get to Amami and passed Stony along to some filmmakers who were trekking back and forth with documentary material on the farmers' holdout. They took him over to what was becoming the Tokyo-Narita International Airport. They pointed to immense swatches of farmland being turned into long landing tarmacs, previously the site of prolonged battles between protestors and police. It was pretty much over, they admitted. Their films could not stop the destruction of these farming villages. They would be moving on to another project up north in the mountains of Yamagata-ken. Did he want to come along?

"Sure," agreed Stony. "Why not?" He followed the filmmakers to Magino-mura, wandered around in the rice paddies with his flute, slept with all the women, and watched them watch the rice grow. The camera captured everything in speeded-up real time. After a season of police skirmishes, guard towers, gasoline moats, sticks, and helmets near Tokyo, the filmmakers were now talking about a season of film that might take a thousand years. He could dig it, but he was on Turtle's budget; he followed the rice through one cycle, cut and harvested, and when the snow began to fall, something told him it was time to move on.

He pulled out a picture he had been saving. He had torn it from a magazine. It was a photograph of a wooden statue of a Buddhist figure sitting with one leg crossed over the other thigh and the right elbow leaning lightly onto the knee, fingers curved against the cheek in a contemplative gesture as if pointing to the serene features of its sleeping head. "Miroku bosatsu." Someone recognized the famous bodhisattva. "You have to go to Kyoto to the Koryu-ji to see it. But why this bosatsu?"

"I don't know," replied Stony. "Just got this feeling." He felt for the flute in the inside pocket of his jacket, shifted the backpack over his shoulder, and trudged out onto the frozen road dusted with snowflakes. He discovered that all roads in Japan eventually lead to train tracks, and those tracks lead to a station. In a sweet moment, a train schedule could whisk him from a platform and make him disappear.

But in the next moment, he found himself at the Koryu temple facing the Miroku bosatsu. If the filmmakers in Magino were going for a thousand, here were thirteen hundred years burnished into sculpted wood in shades of deep purple and red. Thirteen hundred years in that tilted position of infinite meditation until one day the future Buddha may awake to offer compassion to a wounded world. No doubt about it: Stony asked Miroku for a sign, for some kind of message for the future, and then he left to cross all of Kyoto's historic streets, up and down, back and forth, until his movements became the woven fabric of the ancient city itself. If Stony was searching for Miroku's sign, nothing seemed to pop up, at least not immediately.

Meanwhile, he followed the sound of a shakuhachi to a shop in some part of the city he could never find again. The sage in the shop peered through the drooping folds of his ancient eyes and handed Stony the shakuhachi. "Do you play?" he asked. "If you play this one, you will not be able to stop." He chuckled his warning.

Stony drew the bamboo pipe to his lips, and the air from his lungs poured into the instrument like sweet liquor resonating back through his fingers, into his body, until empty space surrounded him in clear totality. When he could finally pull the shakuhachi from his lips, many hours had passed, perhaps many days. He did not know. His stomach rumbled with hunger; his lips were raw and parched. The old man was no longer there, but a young girl sat in his place. She said, "Grandpa said to give you a good deal since," she paused, "he felt perhaps he tricked you."

"No, he didn't," answered Stony when he could finally speak. "This is the real thing." He dug into his pack for the Turtle bills and walked away with the shakuhachi.

Now, perhaps it was finally time to follow Atari's instructions to Amami. Stony found them as specific as his map of the Japan islands and their distance from the Ryukyu archipelago. A small ship left from Kagoshima, and he trundled on with the other passengers, heavily laden with bundles and supplies. He sat with them on tatami mats in the large open innards of the ship. During the twelve-hour trip, they shared food and tea, played cards, gambled, and slept. As the morning rose over the ocean, Stony could feel the air change, felt the damp warm wind fondling his neck and finally billowing through his shirt. Looking with others over the deck, the water spread turquoise toward beaches littered with pink and white coral, and thick walls of deep foliage rose in dense green mountains, clouds slipping by in soft smiles. If it hadn't been for the shakuhachi secured to his belongings, he might have jumped into the ocean and swam to shore.

Stony found Atari out in the shallow surf with a net, scooping out schools of shiny fish. "Well, you finally came. I've been doing some research in anticipation."

"Oh?"

"Yes. I think I've found your father's family here in Amami. Maybe it's a coincidence, but it's just a walk up this beach."

"My dad never said anything about Japan. I mean, he died before we could talk about it. Died young of a heart attack while diving for abalone."

"He was a diver? That makes sense." They both looked out over the coral reefs and watched a large tortoise emerge from a bubbling swirl and pull its heavy body to land. Broken coral and shells, ground over millennia into pebbled, gross, and powdered sand, peppered its underbelly, and the foamy surf rushed from behind to erase the jagged trail.

"Yeah." Stony remembered his dad. "Died in the Pacific ocean."

"Come on," nudged Atari. "I'll take you to his old house." They trudged through the crunch of sand, picking up and discarding shells. Stony felt the pelting sand tossed up at the back of his calves and rubbed away the sandy prickle like black and white and toasted brown sesame seeds. Atari pointed. "That house over there."

Stony nodded and followed his own shadow toward a simple structure, its wood turned gray from the sea-salt wind, but when he looked over his shoulder to make some remark, strangely, Atari had disappeared.

At his calling, he could hear the answer of a woman inside. "Hai!" she called out and slid open the door. She appeared with an old wooden pestle for grinding sesame seeds, but suddenly dropped it in shock. It clattered to the floor and rolled over the threshold. Stony saw in a moment her entire life pass before him in a flash of great beauty, the same burnished age of the Miroku flying through serene and wrinkled time to terrible grief. She crumpled in the doorway, throwing her frail body at his feet and wept and wept.

Later he would understand. A woman came to the door and apologized. "She thinks you are my father, her husband returned after so many years." She showed Stony the photograph of her father, his father, once a young man. "The resemblance is remarkable," she agreed. "He left before the war never to return. We never heard from him again." Her voice trailed off.

That night he dreamed a dream. He saw himself staring at himself in a mirror in a future time, an older man much like his father as an older man, or was it his father? But it was his own voice, his breath pushed through his lips that formed the question in the mirror: *Is that all there is?*

That morning, he walked to the beach and stood barefoot in the clear shallow waters, feeling the waves surround and leave his feet. Stubbornly he thought he would stand his ground in the wet sand until the balls of his feet stood on sand posts, toes gripping and heels sinking, two long striations cut out across the sand chasing each receding wave. Looking down the long beach, he saw the patterns of other sinking pieces of debris: seashells, coral, broken glass and pottery shards, discarded bottles and buoys, driftwood, miles of trash circling a jagged coastline around the island, and sinking. For one long moment, or maybe forever, he felt himself pressed between the praying palms of two supporting hands—one palm, the breathing surf before him, and the other, the roar of cicada at his back.

O.K., so someone there could say that Stony took two tabs and slipped Jack one, but that in itself would not account for everything.

Like they say, every once in a while, someone disappears.

By the time Stony Ima resurfaced, Alcatraz was lost to the white man again and Congress had designated it a national park.

4: Muskrat

The story begins with a stick of straw that, tied to the body of a horsefly, becomes a toy that pleases a little child, in exchange for three oranges that quench the thirst of an old woman, in exchange for a roll of silk again exchanged for an ailing horse that, given water, recovers to be exchanged for a weedy plot of earth that, cultivated, yields rice and recognition and, best of all, the love of a woman. This is how a poor man is rewarded by the gods for belief and compassion—belief in the value of a stick of straw and the compassion to relinquish its value without question. Some journeys begin with a stick of straw.

Wayne Takabayashi climbed four flights of stairs and walked down a dark corridor toward a distant rectangle of light thrown across the floor by a single lighted office. He stepped toward the pecking on a typewriter and the intermittent zip-clunk of the carriage return. When he got to the door, he stood in the rectangle of light and observed his father bent over a manual typewriter set on a desk among piles of papers, paper cartons of food, and coffee cups. Stacks of books and notebooks and boxes were all around the office in walled piles. A narrow path led to Professor Tom Takabayashi's chair. He looked away from his work, probably not because he felt his son's presence but because looking away into the dark hallway was a way of pursuing his thoughts. "Oh." He recognized his son. "What are you doing here?"

"Yeah, well, what are you doing here? Kinda late, don't you think?"

"Trying to get this article done for the journal."

"Why don't you move down to the first floor? The elevators don't work."

The professor shrugged. "They made them inoperative a week ago, but this is the only floor with electricity."

"Can they do that?"

"Hmph." He shoved aside the stupid question. "No heat though." He was wearing his heavy jacket.

"Roughing it, aren't you?"

"I've been thinking I could burn these books and get a nice fire going."

Wayne held up a red thermos. "Maybe this'll warm you up."

The professor recognized the family thermos that his wife, Jean, always filled with coffee, tea, or hot chocolate and sent along to every event: late-night meeting, football game, campout, rally, march, sit-in. Maybe he remembered the last time he'd seen it. Jean had sent it with him to, if necessary, bail out Wayne. She had filled it with soup, figuring that her son hadn't eaten. Wayne had passed the thermos, with sandwiches, around to the others of the Haviland Twenty who had taken over the Crim School for an overnight protest of its forced closure. Now the School of Criminology was just the ex-associate dean—one Professor Takabayashi, exiled to one cold office in an empty campus building slated for demolition.

"Here." The professor gestured. "Pull up a box." He shifted several stacks of books on the floor to form a makeshift table and set a mug and a tin of cookies on top.

Wayne poured his father a cup of coffee and set the thermos down. He looked over the books on the top of the stacks, among them his father's edited journal, *Crime and Social Justice.* It already had the round stain of a coffee mug imprinted into its cover. On top of another stack: *"Walden,"* he read, "and *Civil Disobedience."*

The professor smiled, took a sip of coffee, and closed his eyes. "Guess I've been exiled to my Walden."

"Not much nature here." Wayne watched the steam from the coffee swirl into the cold air.

"Forced self-reflection. Could be a pond, a jail, or a cold empty building. I wrote about it in this issue." He pointed to the journal. "Penitence, the eye of God, the Panopticon, and state centralization of incarceration." He leaned over the stacks of books as if they were a campfire. You could even say his face glowed. Wayne's father used to be a dean, with an entire office of assistants and secretaries and graduate researchers. He probably had never even made his own coffee. Now, when he signed off on the last lingering thesis or dissertation, what would be in store for Wayne's father?

The professor watched his son munching dejectedly on a sugar cookie. "I know what you're thinking, but this is not the first time I've been through this. Law is capricious. Like he said"—he pointed to Thoreau—"law never made anyone free. Men make the law free. So citizenship didn't keep me out of camp, and tenure didn't guarantee my job."

"Yeah, but why did you have to be the test case?"

The professor stared into his coffee and chuckled. Maybe he saw the face of his older brother John float to the surface. He remembered John's face outside the kitchen window of that place they lived in in Idaho, digging up potatoes during the war. "You know the story about your uncle John?"

"Which story?"

"During the war. When he was studying up in Seattle, and the war broke out."

"Yeah, he went to jail."

"There was an eight p.m. curfew for Japanese. He decided to contest it. Walked around all night thinking he'd get arrested, but nobody bothered him. So finally he went into a police station and told them they had to arrest him. By the time his trial came along, the rest of us were in camp at Tule Lake."

Wayne nodded. He probably knew the story, but he wanted to hear it again. That's the way it is with some stories. You have to hear them again and again. They've got to get embedded in your psyche so you carry them as part of your life. So Wayne urged his father on into the late night. "So then what?"

"So your grandparents had to be escorted out of Tule Lake and up to Seattle to testify for John, but when they got there, authorities didn't know where to put them up. Technically, they were prisoners, so they were put in prison. My pop to the men's side, Mama to the women's."

"I remember. She got thrown in with the prostitutes. She was scared, so she played 'Beautiful Dreamer' on the piano for them. They loved her."

"When John saw our mother get up to testify for him, he didn't recognize her. The women had done up her hair, and she was wearing a load of makeup."

"Did that help Uncle John's case?"

"She was supposed to testify that he was brought up simply as a Christian Quaker." He passed Wayne the tin of cookies, and they both laughed.

Wayne poured himself some coffee too. Both son and father sat staring into their muddy cups. You might say they were looking for the bottom of Walden Pond. The bottom would be thick with its mossy silt, but you could imagine a depth that is infinite, and it was that imagination, one of hope and moral truth, that they both reached for.

The professor continued, "John asked to do his jail time in Arizona, but they had no way to get him there from Seattle, so he volunteered to get there on his own."

"Coulda disappeared."

His father nodded. His brother's features rose again in his coffee. By the time John was hitching rides to a federal prison outside of Tucson to join pacifists, Hopi Indians, and other Japanese American war resisters, his family had gotten permission to relocate out of Tule Lake to an Idaho farm. For one last time, in Idaho, John came through the door with his duffel and sat down for grace and dinner, and for one last time, they were a family again. The next day, the future professor drove his brother out to the highway and left him there with his thumb hanging out.

Wayne fingered the last issue of the *Crime and Social Justice* journal. All the other contributors must have been Marxists, but this never bothered his father. A few years ago, Wayne had been busy reading Marx and Lenin, attending study groups, and trying to put out an underground newspaper for one of the political collectives. He flipped through the contents and recognized the author of one of the articles. "What ever happened to Aiko Masaoka?"

"Distinguished graduate."

"She wasn't there with us for the Haviland takeover."

"Heard she went to North Vietnam with some delegation."

This time, neither had to remind the other of the story they both knew. Of course, like every story, you could hold details on your end of it that only get revealed in the exchanging. So this must have been the time to get both sides.

"How long's it been?" the professor asked.

"Four years, maybe."

"Already? You were still in high school." The professor remembered that Wayne had interrupted his lecture.

"Dad," Wayne had said in a quiet panic, "I've got to talk to you. I'm in some trouble." The professor turned the class over to a TA and walked out with his son, walked over to a café on Telegraph, sat across from his son, just like this night, gripping a coffee mug, and braced himself for the worst. He'd been so involved in problems at school, his son's adolescence seemed the least of his worries. Maybe this would be payback time. But sometimes the worst is really a crisis of conscience.

The political collective had advanced from Marx to Lenin to Mao to Che to armed revolution. Or at least that was the theorizing. If Wayne went to the meeting that evening as he was expected to, he would have to struggle with the others about this question, about their decision to arm themselves. He was expected to spend weekends practice shooting and training in weapons and explosives. "They're," his voice had trembled, "taking it to another level."

"Another level!" the professor's voice exploded. "Sons of bitches!"

"I don't think I can do it. You, Uncle John. If the draft were still on, I'm thinking I'd be c.o., too. How am I going to struggle with them?" The professor must have remembered the trauma in his son's voice.

"They've got you, haven't they? Got you scared."

"No, no," Wayne denied, then admitted, "yes."

"It's all right." He tapped his son on the shoulder. "Listen." He got up. "You're not going to struggle with anyone. You don't have to go back."

There are moments when your father makes a decision for you that you could not yourself have made, and you remember that decision for the rest of your life. Wayne had not understood until that moment that he did not have to go back. He pulled his sleeves in front of his eyes, wiped away the welling tears in relief, and walked out and home after his father.

Weeks later, Aiko Masaoka and others had asked the professor about Wayne, that they hadn't seen him in J-Town again. Was he ill?

"You sons of bitches, fooling with young minds." The professor pointed a father's wrath. "If I catch you doing the same thing here in this school, there'll be hell to pay."

"I didn't know you told them that," Wayne marveled.

"Hmph." His father put down his empty coffee mug and remembered his deadline. "Have you seen your mother?" he asked.

"Yeah."

"Good."

"How's school?"

"I think I'm going to do geography."

"Makes sense. Land and people." The professor picked something off his desk and handed it to his son. "How do you like that?"

Wayne took the pen. It had a fancy casing, blue with gold trim and a gold point.

"Grad student gave it to me as a gift. Signed his thesis with it. You take it. I'll just lose it in this mess."

"Thanks." Wayne looked like he wanted to say something more, but his father had returned to his typewriter, his head nodding in assent and his right hand waving him on.

The next day, Wayne ran into a petite Indian woman in a pink sari. Actually, he didn't just run into her, he fell on top of her as he ran to catch the Telegraph bus and lost his footing on the oily pavement. Disentangling himself from pink cotton, he tried awkwardly to help her small body up from the ground, grabbing her in all the wrong places. "I'm so sorry. I'm sorry. I'm sorry," he babbled endlessly.

But she was laughing, in fact laughing hysterically, as if it were the funniest thing. She sat on the pavement and wiped away the tears of her pain that turned into laughter. Suddenly a wind whipped through, blowing at a clipboard she had been carrying and scattering its sheath of papers across Sproul Plaza. "Oh!" she exclaimed and jumped up, running after the flying papers. Wayne ran around too, stomping and grabbing and collecting. The damn things swirled around everywhere, slapped against trees and bushes and passing students. As he retrieved the papers, he caught sight of the pink sari fluttering across the plaza and among the crowds in a widening circle.

When Wayne re-encountered the Indian woman in the middle of Sproul again, she was breathless, her hair blown about and sticking up in places. He looked at the messy handful of papers and realized they were signed petitions. The top petition clearly had the wavy imprint of his old low-top across the face of it.

"Thank you. Thank you! I'm so grateful. If it weren't for you—" She pressed the papers to herself.

"What do you mean? It's all my fault."

"Oh," she seemed to remember. "That's right." Then she began laughing again.

"Let's go sit somewhere and rearrange those," he suggested.

“O.K.” She pointed toward the student union. “Less wind in there.”

They sat down and spread the papers across a table, trying to arrange them by page number. “We seem to be missing a page.”

The woman’s face fell, and Wayne got up. “Let me go look for it.” She followed him out, and both went searching about against the buildings, in the bushes and gutters. Wayne collected trash as he went and finally rummaged through the trash cans before he discarded everything.

“It’s no use. The wind had some need of it perhaps.” She gestured to the air and turned toward the student union again. “Let’s go back and have something to drink. By the way, my name is Roshni.”

Back at the table, Wayne looked over the petitions. “Twenty-five signatures on a page,” he moaned. “That’s a lot.”

“Well, we’ll just start another page.” She pushed a blank petition his way and searched around for a pen. “I seem to have lost my pen as well.”

Wayne pulled out the pen his father had given him. “What am I signing?”

“You are signing for an end to nuclear armaments.”

“Good idea.”

“Listen. This is serious. You have to mean it.”

“O.K. I mean it.”

She pulled the paper away from under his pen. “No, no. Maybe we’d better have a good discussion so you will really be sure.”

“Is this going to take a long time?”

“Do you want to sign with an informed opinion?”

Wayne sighed, “Oh, all right.”

“So this year, my country, well, one of my countries, India, set off an underground nuclear bomb at Pokhran in Rajasthan. Can you imagine? Such a place so rich in history, architecture, clothing. Now, I have no proof of this, but I believe that the Rajasthan desert is the very birthplace of the Gypsies.” Roshni wandered into history, then back to her present concern. “They are calling this bomb a P-N-E.” She pronounced each syllable clearly.

“What’s that?”

“A Peaceful Nuclear Explosion.”

“No such thing.”

“Exactly.” Roshni slapped her hand on the table.

At that moment, someone came by and interrupted their conversation. "Are you Roshni?"

"Yes."

"Someone said to look for you, that I should sign your petition."

"Yes, yes, of course. Please sign here." She took Wayne's pen and offered it to the young man.

He quickly signed where Wayne had started to sign. "Thanks," he said and left.

"Wait a minute." Wayne put up his hand. "Did he mean it?"

"I certainly hope so."

"I'm confused."

"Yes, I know. So let me explain."

Many hours later, Wayne was still confused, but without stirring, he had traveled through time and around the world. The last time he had experienced this sensation of complete transportation was on a leaky boat to Alcatraz. That time the storyteller was a Modoc Indian; this time she was, well, what was she? Indian?

"Well, technically, yes," she said. "I was born in Mumbai—what you call Bombay—raised in Karachi, educated in Beirut." She paused. "Do you know your geography?"

He named the nations: "India, Pakistan, Lebanon."

"Oh, very good. Most Americans are confined to this big island and don't know where anything is in the world." Then she continued. "Then I was posteducated in Durham, North Carolina, and adopted by a family in Oaxaca. Now I'm here. Now that is where my body has been, but" —she gestured with small tilts of her head—"my ancestors were from Persia and China, and my mother was born in Japan."

"So your mother's Japanese?"

"You know, it's not always where you were born that makes you something." Roshni pulled out a folded piece of paper from a small satchel. "Look at this. You will be interested in this, I'm sure." She unfolded the paper and spread it flat for Wayne to see.

Wayne recognized the flyer announcing a meeting of the AAPA. "Asian American Political Alliance?"

"Yes." She nodded.

"And?"

"I went to this meeting. I thought, finally, I have found my people."

"Asian American?"

"Yes, wouldn't you agree?"

Wayne scratched his head. By this time in the storytelling, he had experienced the partition of India, the civil war in Lebanon, and a civil rights sit-in in the American South. In North Carolina, she was considered to be a Negro and instructed to sit at the back of the bus. He had followed Roshni's defiant body, whether by chance or purpose, into the streets of Karachi, where thousands of fleeing refugees filled the streets, stood on Beirut's riviera watching American Marines slug across the pristine beaches with machine guns, and secured in her arms a Negro grandmother who swooned at the sight of her grandson thwacked across his head by a policeman's baton.

"They were very polite, of course, but also very firm," she continued.

"Who?"

"This AAPA." She pointed at the flyer. "They took one look." Roshni paused as if asking Wayne to look at her. "And they said no, you must be mistaken. So I had to leave."

Wayne tried to remember if he had been at that meeting.

"I had so much to talk about, especially this campaign against nuclear weapons. We Asian Americans must be against this destruction. I'll never forget my mother's face when she heard about the atomic bomb dropped on Nagasaki. I told you she was born there. Well, I was too little to know about the bomb, but I knew my mother's face. I'll never forget it because the next time I saw that look on her face was when she died."

Wayne picked up a stack of blank petitions. "Let me help you. I'll try to get these signed. To make it up to you."

"You will? But you don't have to make anything up to me. That's not a reason to help."

"All right," he said with some exasperation. "I'll do it to prove to you that I mean it."

Many weeks later, Wayne searched for the pink sari, some sign of Roshni in the plaza. He found her at a card table draped with a poster of a large peace sign. He handed her a thick stack of signed petitions. She looked carefully through the signatures and smiled happily. "But"—she frowned—"Did you sign? You had better sign too."

"Are you sure?"

"Yes, yes," she laughed. "I'm sure."

Wayne signed and then he handed the pen to Roshni. "Here," he said. "I want you to have this. My dad gave me this pen, and every signature here was signed by the same pen."

"Thank you," she murmured. "It's beautiful." Then, without hesitation, she untied a woven bracelet from her wrist. It had a pattern of beadwork delicately woven in colored yarn. "This was made by Indians in Oaxaca," she said, tying it to Wayne's wrist. "We call it a rahki, and giving it means that you become my brother."

And once again, Roshni transported Wayne into the past to 1905, when the poet Tagore urged Muslims and Hindu to exchange rahki bracelets to prevent rising hostilities created by the English when they ordered the partition of Bengal. "We say," she said, "that the most important relationship is that of the brother to his sister, and the sister to her brother."

They were silent for a long time in the noisy hubbub of the plaza. You figure the defiance of peace was right there in that center where a pebble or maybe a muskrat dove into Walden Pond, and the duplicating waves resonated across the living surface with the extending mystery of a mandala.

After a time, Wayne asked, "Why did you laugh so hard when I fell on you that time when we met? You must have been hurt."

"Oh yes, I got a big purple bruise. You don't want to know where," she laughed. "It's disappearing gradually. But you know, you tickled me, so I forgot about it."

Wayne looked at her and turned a bit red.

"Oh," she shrugged. "You're my brother now, so we can talk about such things."

Perhaps it was a few days later on a Sunday when Wayne walked out of his house to find a gray-haired woman applying a car jack to the front right frame of her car. She was cranking the thing up like she was the Triple-A come to the rescue, except that she was rather dressed up, wearing a skirt and stockings and with her hair done up nicely in a French roll. He might have walked on, but her blue Chevy was parked in front of his house, and she wasn't what you would call a spring chicken.

"Uh, need some help?"

"Oh my, yes." She looked up. "If you could crank this up, I'll go get the spare in the back trunk."

"Wait, I can get the spare."

"Well then." She passed him the keys to the trunk and continued cranking.

By the time he got the spare out and was rolling it over the sidewalk to the front of the car, the woman had her foot to the wrench and was unscrewing the lugs.

"Hey, let me do that." He ran over and applied pressure and managed to unscrew the first lug. Then he started in on the second.

She corrected him: "Wrong direction."

"Oh, O.K." Wayne had never actually changed a tire before, but under her directions, the entire procedure went quite smoothly.

By the time he was lifting the flat tire into the trunk, the woman pointed to his front porch and asked, "Do you mind if I sit for awhile?"

"No, of course not."

"I guess I don't have the strength I used to."

"I never changed a tire before," Wayne admitted.

"Oh, well, it's not rocket science." She stared at him a moment and asked, "Are you one of those young people who want to change the world?"

Wayne stuttered, "Well, maybe." He sat down next to her.

"I knew an old lady way back when who was a suffragette. And she told me that she was sure that all wars would end when women could vote because women were the only ones who would vote war out of existence." She paused and shook her head. "Didn't happen that way, but that's O.K. dear." She patted Wayne's knee. "You keep on trying."

They both stared out to the street at the car with the spare tire.

"Well, I guess I'm late now," she sighed.

"Where were you going?"

"My meeting. Quaker meeting."

"My grandparents were Quakers."

"Mine were Mennonite," she said, "but I've been going to the Friends since before the war. One day I went up those creaking steps and over that creaking old floor and sat down. At first no one talked, and then the talking began, and I just listened, but I thought, oh yes, I have found my people."

Wayne went inside and returned with two glasses of water. "Oh, thank you." She continued, "So I started to go regularly to meetings, but then I wondered about all their talking. They could talk for hours. Talk and talk, and I thought, well, nothing will come of this. It's just talking, but when all the talking was finished, everything happened very quickly. I learned a lot from this. That was how I went to Tule Lake to teach."

"The internment camp?"

"Yes, you know, where the Japanese were sent during the war."

"My father and his parents were sent there."

"Oh yes? A terrible injustice," she said angrily and looked down the street. "Have you lived here a long time?"

"I'm just renting a room for now."

"I have old friends who live a few blocks from here. They are nisei. You are a sansei, are you not?"

Wayne nodded.

"The Utsumis. Do you know them?"

Wayne shook his head.

"Would you like to meet them?" Before he could protest, she handed him the keys and said, "You drive. Here. Let's go. Oh, I'm forgetting my manners. I'm Alma, and I'm so pleased to meet you."

As she had said, he drove a mere three blocks to a house similar to the one where he lived. "A long time ago," Alma remembered, "I came to this house every Sunday. That was just after the war."

Wayne followed her up the path to the door. "This house belonged to the Utsumi family before the war, so after the war, they came to reclaim it, but the people in this neighborhood were very hostile to the returning Japanese." She turned to look at Wayne significantly, and although he didn't respond, she emphasized, "Oh yes, that was how it was in those days."

They stood on the porch and Alma continued. "So my friend Laura Kennedy and I would come every Sunday when the neighbors would be home, and we would come to this door, and Marianne and Bill would come out with us, and the four of us would walk to the neighborhood church and sit together in the front pew." As Marianne herself opened her door, Alma exclaimed with delight, "We integrated that church!"

Wayne shifted awkwardly as Alma and Marianne hugged and he got introduced to a nisei woman who could have been his aunt.

"Oh, you're just in time," Marianne led them into the kitchen. "Bill is flipping pancakes."

So that was how after a while, Wayne found himself occasionally at a Quaker meeting, or at Sunday brunch with the Utsumis, or under the hood of one of Alma's several vehicles that were always in various stages of disrepair. Bill said, "Alma is a natural mechanic. If you want to know what's wrong with your car, let her drive it around the block."

One day Alma showed Wayne a photograph. "I've been trying to clean up my house, and look what I found."

Wayne stared at an old black-and-white photo of a group of around a dozen people gathered somewhere, perhaps in a garden or at the front of a house. He pointed: "Is this you?"

"Yes, and this is Marianne, and this is Bill."

"And the others?"

She named the others one by one, a mixed group of African Americans, Japanese Americans, Caucasian Americans. "This is our group!" she said with an exclamation.

"What year is this?"

"Well, after the war—1947 maybe."

"What did your group do?"

"Direct action!" Alma practically yelled. "After the war, there was so much prejudice and hatred of the Japanese, so we would choose places to go, like restaurants, and we would all go in and sit down together to be served. Oh yes!"

"Like a sit-in?"

"Oh yes."

Wayne smiled broadly and repeated, "Oh yes!"

"I also found this," she said. "It's yours."

"What is it?"

"Pink slip to that old Ford pickup back there. Now that you've got it running, it ought to be yours. I certainly don't need it."

"I don't know, Alma."

"Oh, take it," she said. "You're going to need it to do that geography of yours."

Wayne tugged with his teeth and untied the woven bracelet he had never removed since Roshni had tied it to his wrist. "It's time to pass this on."

Sometime in the summer after graduation, Wayne drove by Alma's place with the truck with camper shell on top, packed with all his equipment and supplies. "Hey, Alma, I'm headed south to Mexico. What do you think?"

"I think you should go. Just come back once before I die."

"Alma, you're going to live to be a hundred."

"I guess you're right, because I intend to see the millennium." Alma had her hair done up in a bun on the top of her head, something like a topknot. Roshni's woven rahki was carefully tied around her silvering knot of hair. .

Wayne gave Alma a big kiss on the cheek.

Well, you try to imagine the near future and what might be exchanged for an old Ford pickup.

5: Tule Lake

When it's all said and done, you might have a compilation of events, and you might have a story with meaning. Someone says, don't worry about the details, just get the stories. Someone else says, get the details and the hard facts, and then you can build a case for a story. Someone says a good story helps you to remember, but someone else says that everyone remembers differently. Everyone's got a version of the same story, or maybe there's no such thing as the same story; it's a different story every time.

But those're just stories that may or may not be important in themselves. What about the stories that are visions of the world, visions of reality that hold people inside, inside the reality of the world, inside their minds that see that world, and in society among each other? What about those stories that tell you how to live and how to stay alive and how to die? Which are the stories you take inside your mind to live by and to create a world, to teach your children, to wake to in the morning, to face each day? Some say those aren't just stories; others say that's all they are, just stories, and that's plenty enough.

In the Japanese American version of the Turtle Island story, you got a crane and loon and muskrat that go searching for a plug of earth in a lake that turns out to be a dried-up, desiccated lake called Tule Lake. You didn't imagine that enemy non-aliens, or for that matter anyone native to that land, would be exiled to any real lake, not Walden Pond, not an orchard of apples, not a jewel in the desert, not a mountain with a heart. Still, you know that it is the people who occupy the space, whether a reservation or a concentration camp, who draw the water, plant the apples, build from the raw jewel, cause the heart to beat.

Now, if after a hiatus of seven years you can bring the same three strangers back into the same boat, I'd say that's synchronicity. Of course, you'll say that's just some storytelling, some O. Henry kind of surprise ending, some paradox or irony or koan to contemplate long after the story's told. But how many times do you wander into the stories that turn out to be your own life, and someone says, *I know that story; it turns out like this.* And you say, *No it doesn't; my life is different; it's got its own consequences, its own endings.* Don't be so sure.

There's not much at Tule Lake that anyone can see, just open, endless, dusty acres of land with sage and broken junk, some of it piled into hills, most scattered across the terrain. In one direction, you see what the Japanese called Abalone Mountain. In the other, Castle Rock. If you make it out to one far end, you might be able to see the snow on Mount Shasta, but the vision of snow will make your throat parch under that harsh sun, with not a tree or cool spot in sight. If you scratch your boot toe in the dry earth, you might scrape up these tiny pink seashells from another time. No matter, the revelation of a scorched earth transformed from a wet one won't make you swallow anything but your own dry spit.

They were calling themselves pilgrims.

Ria turned to Wayne and said, "I know you from somewhere."

Wayne nodded, then both of them said simultaneously: "Alcatraz."

In an impromptu stage area, a guy with a headband in a happi coat was playing a flute. He dedicated his flute song to the memory of a sansei named Sen Hama, who died several years ago in a motorcycle accident up there on Castle Rock. He had been one of the first pilgrims to Tule Lake. Ria and Wayne remembered a piercing birdsong wailing across the San Francisco Bay.

Stony approached his old boat companions, an arsenal of bamboo flutes in a large brocade pouch behind his shoulder like an archer's sling. "Hey," he said, "you're not going to believe this but"—he pointed with his flute somewhere out there between Abalone and Castle Rock—"Jack Denny's living on a ranch right over there."

Wayne still had Alma's old pickup; it had survived crossing the Mexican border and back. Now the old *Turtle* contingent piled in and took off in the direction of Stony's pointing flute. Jack met them like it was just four stories ago. He said, "Welcome to Modoc Country."

They answered, "Land of the free. Home of the brave."

Jack announced, "We got a sweat going here. How about it?"

This time maybe they thought they knew and trusted each other, even though it had been seven different years of separate experiences. Their lives had walked in parallel lines until they bent in ways that led them to cross at this particular moment in time. Maybe over the years, they had passed each other without knowing it, met folks who knew them by degrees. Maybe it was the meaning of Tule Lake, and that alone was enough. They all passed through that smoky fog of sweet sage and crawled into the coal black heat of Jack's sweat lodge.

Jack pitched in the red hot rocks with a big fork, and the open flap went down. Now, you've got to sit in the pitch-black sauna of the Earth's womb for four seasons. Each time the flap opens, more red hot rocks are added, some sage and some cedar, and a splash of river water. Incense rises, and the steam spits. And the heat envelopes you until you bleed your dirty waters, grab the earth, and sink your cheeks into its cool dark soil. The hot darkness squeezes you like a wet sponge, and your waters get replaced for visions.

In the first vision, Jack recognized a man who is his uncle in his younger days. Uncle Albert is tracking something that looks like giant footprints across the desert. Al used to tell stories of meeting up with the Sasquatch itself, but he could never completely prove what he had seen. He could only draw you pictures of this big hairy beast that rose taller than a grizzly on two big feet.

But one day, he tracks it to a barbed-wire fence, and when he looks up, there is a tower rising into the sky with a soldier posted up on its lookout, pointing a gun in his direction. "Hey, get away from that fence," the soldier warns.

He backs away. "What's this place?"

"U.S. Government property."

Uncle Al takes a better look at the property and sees people, in fact an entire tribe of them—men, women, and children—coming and going from tarpaper barracks. Later, he would climb up to Castle Rock and get a bird's-eye view of the whole situation.

"What reservation is this?" he asks.

"Hey," the soldier barks. "You aren't a Jap are you?"

The flap came up, and the light filtered in with a dusty breath and another set of burning rocks. The flap went down again with the promise of another vision.

This time, Wayne recognized his grandmother, although long dead before his birth. Maybe he knew her from old photographs. She sits at a piano playing the Stephen Foster tunes that his father had said she knew.

Behind her on benches are children trying to sing along. *I dream of Jeannie with the light brown hair.*

A white woman moves into view and sits at the piano next to Wayne's grandmother. Scrutinizing her features, Wayne saw that it was Alma, with brown hair but still done up in that French roll of hers. The two women nod at each other in agreement and together play the Shaker tune "Simple Gifts."

When the song ends, the children come forward with a small box, a gift for Alma. It is a necklace crafted from the pink and white seashells sifted from the earth around the barracks. "Alma," they say. "We picked these shells all by ourselves!"

"I picked this biggest one."

"But we didn't go near the fence. No, we didn't."

Wayne's grandmother places the gift around Alma's neck, and they all accompany her as far as the gate, waving to her beyond the stationed soldier, watching the barbed-wire cut across her diminishing figure.

The flap came up a third time with the same ceremonies, and the third vision commenced.

Ria saw a nisei couple with a baby standing at a dock before the ramp of a large cruise ship. The workers scurrying around and the passengers climbing the ramp are all Japanese.

When the man speaks, Ria recognized the voice of her father. He is handing her mother a thick envelope. "This is the repatriation paperwork sent by Mr. Wayne Collins," he says. "Don't lose it."

"What about yours?"

"I have mine. And Ria is fine." He puts his finger in the tiny hand of the baby girl. "She's an American." Then he takes her in his arms and bounces her a bit.

"We were always American," Ria's mother speaks firmly. "I will write to you when we arrive in Chicago."

"It'll be just another year in Tokyo or maybe here in Yokohama, and I'll be there," he promises. "I just hope there'll be work for me."

"We can't work for the occupation forever. One day the Americans will have to leave Japan."

The ship's horn blasts, and they look up in resignation. Ria's father passes Ria into her mother's arms. Ria saw over her mother's shoulder her father's waving hand, waving and waving and waving.

And so the flap flew up the fourth time, and Stony anticipated the last vision. He saw a Japanese man knock on the door of a camp barrack. A young woman with a small child, a toddler girl of about two or three years, appears at the door, and he removes his hat and bows. He steps into a bare room where the woman offers him a seat on a crate next to a simple wooden table. She sets a kettle on the potbellied stove, then comes to sit at the table. "Ima-san," she says in Japanese. "I'm sorry it's such a sad place to receive you."

"That's not true." He shakes his head. He watches the little girl dance around the room. "See, Yasuko-chan makes this a happy house."

Now Stony understood they were his mother and his older sister Yasuko. His mother was already a widow when she arrived in camp. She says, "You know Seiji died just as she was born. She never knew her father. Now we've come alone to this camp. But"—she gets up to pour hot water for tea—"I thought you must have taken the last boat back to Japan. You did not have to come here."

He shifts on the crate uncomfortably, then says, "I was so wrapped up in my studies." He places a book on the table. It is a worn copy with the thin leather cover rubbed to lighter shades of brown along the spine and corners. "I want you to have this. It's one of the only books I brought with me to camp."

She picks up the book and marvels. "Tanka poetry," she smiles with some embarrassment.

He tugs a small piece of newspaper clipping exposed in the pages of the book. It is the notice of the honor of the woman's Imperial award for her tanka and the poem itself.

"You kept this?"

He nods.

"Ah, well," she sighs. "And now we are at war." She pushes the book back to him across the table. "I cannot accept such a precious gift."

He stops the returning movement of the book. "To be honest," he says, "I could not get on that boat. I could not return. Even now I don't know if such a thing is possible."

She looks at him with some confusion.

And he begins, "Seiji was my good friend, so." He stops, his words stuck. He rises from the table and reaches for his hat.

She steps forward with the book of poetry in both hands. "Ima-san," she says quietly. "I am very honored by your gift."

The flap to Jack's sweat lodge opened for the ending ceremony, by which time they emerged to dusk, the last glimmer of purple and red vanishing with the setting sun.

"Funny," Ria said. "I knew I was born in Japan, but I never knew why."

"Same here," said Stony. "I knew I was born in camp, but I never knew why."

The next day, they all climbed into the cabin and the bed of Wayne's pickup and took the roads into the lava beds, and Jack pointed out all the significant sites of the Modoc War: Captain Jack's stronghold, lava tubes, petroglyphs. But the Modoc War was just one rebellion. Like the story goes, you can win a rebellion but not for long. And then there was the Vietnam War. Jack said, "I'll tell you a secret, why the war had to end."

"Antiwar protest?"

"Yeah, that, but really it was because we"—he pointed to himself, a vet—"we refused to fight. Got sick of the killing and just stopped, you know?"

Funny how a group can be bound by refusal and resistance. Maybe something does get passed along. Could be ghost stories, something in the deep places of your psyche that's always hungry, hungry for intangible things that get defined later. You might go on a quest to find the answers, but sometimes those ghosts are right there next to you, following you around, holed up inside your being. Then one day, it all gets sweated out.

Jack pointed to a stretch of marshland. "Stop over there." They all climbed out of the truck and trudged behind. Jack dug his hands into the mud and water and pulled up a tall clump of the grass. He walked back to the truck and retrieved an empty coffee cup, stuffed the slimy soil and grass into the cup, and handed it to Wayne. "This is tule. Indians use this to make baskets, hats, canoes."

"Cool, I'll take it." Wayne took the cup of tule and handed Jack the keys to the truck. "Can you use a truck?" he asked.

"You're kidding, man." Jack put his hands up.

"No, I'm not. It was given to me to give away."

"Only if I can paint it green," said Jack.

They piled into the back of the newly dubbed *Turtle* with Jack in the driver's seat. He pumped the engine into a slow roar and tried the horn. Everything worked. Wayne pulled his cap over his head and secured the tule, and Ria passed around the water and a bag of chips. *The Turtle* revved into reverse and forward, Stony seated on the tail and blowing a high wail through his yokobue, and the marshland refuge came alive in answer, a thick, winged, and screeching chaos of thousands of ducks and swans and geese.

Indians will tell you that, yeah, there are prophecies and they do come to pass, but they'll also tell you that prophecies are like any other story—they can be changed.

1974: I-Migrant Hotel

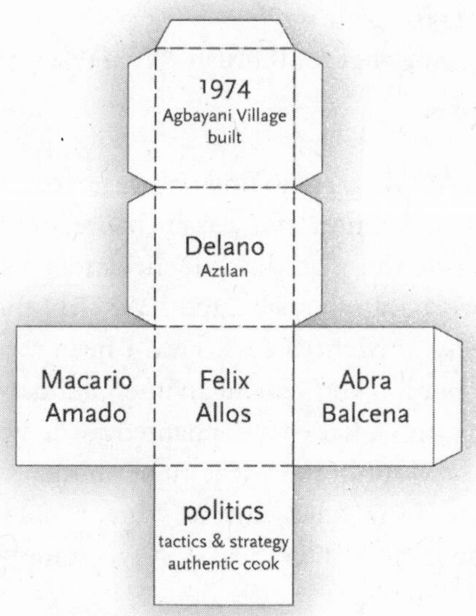

1: Grass Roots

It's morning, and I'm knocking on Macario's door. Who's Macario? Just a kid, but a smart kid come a long way, and I'm not talking just over the bridge from Berkeley, so we elect him vice president. Vice President of the International Hotel Tenants Association. O.K., I set him up for this, but I still got to pay my respects. There he is standing in the door with his toothbrush. "Felix," he says.

"Mr. Vice President," I say.

"Felix, cut the bullshit," he laughs, but he sees my suitcase and asks, "Where you going?"

"It's time," I say.

"Time?"

"Yeah, I got to go back to my grass roots."

"Luzon? Ilocos?" he asks.

"What the fuck I go back there for?"

"You Visayan?"

"Now you trying to insult me?"

"Felix." He's waving that toothbrush. "Where are you going?

"Delano."

"Oh."

"I been thinking. Now come to find out we got this new landlord. This Enchanted Seas Corporation. If it was enchanted sea*sons*, maybe I could deal with that, season this place into an enchanted restaurant. But who's got a business incorporating enchanted seas?" My thumb points to me, the boss. "I been to enchanted seas. Hey, I been to *dis*enchanted seas. What does a corporation know about an international hotel like this one? They could turn it into a five-star enchanted castle with a sea moat, and where we gonna be? Out in the street on our butts."

"Felix, like you're always telling me, we've got to study the situation. We just found out about Enchanted Seas. Give us some time."

"Do you read Herb Caen?"

"In the *Chronicle*? Yeah?"

"Herb says it's a Hong Kong investment company. How come Herb knows, and we don't know nothing shit?"

"Because." Macario drops the toothbrush to his side. He shrugs. "We don't know nothing shit." He looks dejected.

Now I feel bad. I don't want to be so hard on him. It's not his fault. I equivocate. "Maybe that's the writing on the wall," I say. "At least the last owner was a Democrat. You can always find the Democrats, in the capitol buildings, cutting ribbons, kissing babies. But this multinational corporation. What you gonna do? Catch a plane, go picket Hong Kong?"

"It's not going to be easy."

I shake my head. "So." I pick up my suitcase. "I go to Delano, help my union brothers build a retirement place. Who didn't pick grapes? Pay union dues? You did your time, you get a place to live. That's how it should be."

Macario agrees. "That's how it should be."

I point down the hall to the kitchen. "Back of the shelf, got a bottle of bagoong. I make it myself. That's for you. But don't lose the cover." I wave the air like there's a fart. "And the wok, you keep it."

"You coming back, right?"

I thump Macario's chest. "You save the hotel, maybe so."

"We can't do it without you, Felix."

"I taught you everything I know." I pause for a moment. "Well, not everything."

We laugh.

I pat him on the shoulder. "Now you got to—" I wave him away, because who wants to make a scene?

He finishes my sentence. "—study the situation."

I can feel his eyes following me down the long hall. I turn the corner and slip an envelope under Abra's door. She's out already, taking her kids to school.

Outside, the air comes brisk down Kearny, but the sun is out. I cross the street to get a final look at the I-Hotel, my home off and on for maybe fifty years. I see Frankie step into Tino's and pull off his hat, in for an early-morning shave and trim. After Tino's, he'll hang out at the Lucky M and shoot a round with maybe Benny or Noy Noy. For lunch, you can find him at the Silver Wing, then a stroll down to Portsmouth, like he owns the street. Maybe he does. For Frankie, it's still the 1930s. Pinoy about town in his pinstripe double-breasted McIntosh every day. He's gonna die in that suit.

Me, I zipper up the old jacket and pull down my cap with the huelga boycott button. I got a Greyhound to catch. Delano's south, over there down the I-5 headed Bakersfield way.

Come to find a couple months later, who shows up in Delano, making the turn at the old gas station and headed down the dirt road to Forty Acres? It's Macario in a Chevy station wagon followed by a caravan of maybe five more cars. Bunch of kids fall out of those vehicles with their sleeping bags and hammers. "Hey, Felix." Macario waves. "Put us to work."

"Welcome to Agbayani Village," I say to Macario and the kids. O.K., not kids. I should say *students,* from the university. Maybe they get extra credits for making the trip, so I know I got to give them their extra credits. "Let me tell you about Paolo Agbayani."

I tell them Paolo Agbayani was my union brother. We join AWOC in the same year and stand together in the picket line. What's AWOC? Practically all-Pinoy union: Agricultural Workers Organizing Committee, affiliated with the AFL-CIO. We start the Great Delano Grape Strike of 1965. Then the boycott. When's the last time you eat a grape?

No one can remember.

"Right," I tell them. "Don't forget it. We Pinoys in Delano started the whole goddamn thing."

Paolo Agbayani's like me. Working all his life, and finally got nobody but himself. So we got each other. We're on picket duty over at Perelli-Minetti ranch when Paolo keels over. He's leaning into his picket sign when I catch him falling, grabbing his heart. "Whatsa matter, Paolo? Get help! Get him some water! Maybe it's heatstroke. Paolo!"

"Viva la huelga."

"Paolo!"

"Mabuhay."

We say of the brothers like Paolo that he was a soldier of the soil. This soil here is where he fought his battles and finally died. So what we are building here is Paolo Agbayani's final resting place, the home where he should have lived. That's how we put everyone to work, digging foundations, laying bricks and tile, sawing roofing beams, setting pipes for plumbing and electricity.

I say to Macario, "You sleep over at Filipino Hall, but come over to Schenley camp, and I make you a good meal. By now you miss my cooking?"

"Shit, how'd you know? I gotta come three hundred miles to get a meal."

"What? You don't come to build my retirement house? I kick you out."

"Ah man, Felix, how long we gonna hold out? I'm losing weight."

"What are you doing here anyway? We finally evicted?"

"Not yet."

"What about Abra? How's Abra?"

"She's holding the fort while I'm here. She'll be here in a few days. Got to wait until her kids get summer vacation. Then I gotta go back."

"She driving herself?"

"Bringing the old yellow Bug."

"It could fall apart any minute."

"You know she fixes it herself."

I think about Abra running the I-Hotel, telling the old guys where to take their business. "Abra's tough."

"Tougher than me."
"That's for sure."
"We've been studying the situation, you know."
"That so?"
"Yeah, Enchanted Seas is a mafia godfather out of Thailand. Samut Songkhram."
"Samut what?"
"Songkhram. He's got a monopoly in Thailand on the sale of whiskey. All the Siamese police and generals are in his pay."
"That's Thailand. What's it got to do with us?"
"He's been buying up all the hotels around the I-Hotel."
"You ever eat Thai food?"
"No."
"They got this lemongrass coconut stew with chili. You just slip the white fish in there real gently. Serve it in a hot pot cooking on your table."
"Shit. You'd get evicted for some Thai food?"
"Think about it. Levi-Klein, Simon Solomon, the old owners. Latkes and matzo ball soup. How can you compare?"
Macario throws his hands up. "I thought you gonna help me."
"How many times I got to tell you: the way to a man's heart."
"I'm going to send you in to poison this Songkhram bastard."
"Now you talking."

End of a working day, I'm dishing up the food.
"What's this?"
"This my creation. Call it 'roots on a bed of rice.'"
"But what's this?" The brother is pointing at a large round root on his plate.
"Rutabaga," I say. "How about a beet? This one's daikon. Maybe you like gobo or yam?"
He's fishing around. "I'll take the carrots. What else you got?"
"Fifteen kinds of root vegetables. Try turnip. Try parsnip. Try onion. Everything that grows under the earth."
"You add some worms?"
"For protein. What you expect?"
"Shit, Felix. This stuff is too healthy."
"You gotta watch your cholesterol, Freddy. I'm just looking after you."

Macario says, "It's pretty subtle. Did you want me to bring that bottle of bagoong?"

"Hell no. These guys on a no-salt diet. Just following doctor's orders. Sometimes you got to force the palette by tasting the thing itself. You concentrate on that rutabaga; you can taste the true soil of Delano."

"That's deep, Felix." Macario forks his roots.

"Deep is Sixto's garden. Go check it out. Everything below the ground. Nothing topside. Go figure. Sixto must like to dig."

Lenny says, "You don't know? Fermin's chickens got into Sixto's garden. Ate everything topside."

Sixto yells from somewhere, "Next time I kill your goddamn chickens!"

"My chickens kill you first!"

Then Candido says, "How come you don't cut these up?" He's looking at his roots on his bed of rice. "Looks like dicks and balls."

Everybody's laughing. As a matter of fact.

I say, "Tell me the truth." I get my knife ready. "You want them cut up?"

"Hey," Pete remembers. "I seen this somewhere on television. No lie. Fertility soup."

"It's an island recipe," I nod. "Gonna enhance your chances."

Guffaws go all around.

"Bullshit."

"Could use some hot sauce."

Instead of saying grace, everybody's dancing.

You be surprised how roots fill you up. It doesn't take much. By the end of the meal, everyone burping and sitting satisfied. That's when our brother Philip Vera Cruz gets up and starts to put it all into what he calls the context of the larger struggle. He gets up and starts talking like he's talking to the three, four guys at his end of the table, but everybody gets quiet so they can hear, because they know Philip's our leader, our vice president next to Cesar Chavez.

These days, who doesn't know Cesar Chavez? But who knows about my union brothers Philip Vera Cruz and Larry Itliong? Who knows the context of the larger struggle that goes back seventy-five years to the Philippine-American War of 1899? Phil's gonna tell you, like he always does. Why guys like me are here, what we did, and why. How come we got to toil in the soil for fifty years to make some growers fat and wealthy? Help them take their agribusiness into every fertile valley in the state, from San Joaquin to the Imperial, and we retire to nothing? When the legs won't stoop no more, put our old feet on the road and say, *Walk*. If you lucky, they give you a shovel and say, *Go dig your grave.* Phil's gonna make you hear with new ears. First you strain to hear him, but then very gradually he's a quiet storm booming through your own chest.

But what Philip says I get to later.

A couple of days pass, and Abra and her two little ones arrive. Happen to be twins, boy-girl pair. I got names for them: Andie and Emil. I don't see them for a while, so I see them bigger, coming up to Abra's elbow and maybe passing soon.

I'm using up the sugar ration making sugar cookies. I'm teaching them to dig up Sixto's garden. "Dig here. You gonna find golden treasure."

Abra comes in with her sweaty brow. Hair all pushed inside her hat. Cheeks and arms peppered with sawdust. Skin glowing underneath. I think, how much more beautiful they get? "I could use a drink, Felix."

"From the tap O.K.?"

"That'll do." She turns the glass and takes it down in one swallow. What am I, a bartender? Then she fiddles around in her jeans pocket. "I just remembered. I forgot this." She hands me a folded envelope.

I shake my head. "I give it to you."

"No, you take it back. I can't accept it."

"O.K., it's not for you. For them." I nod at her twins. They got the little yellow potatoes all lined up like a line of train cars.

"Uncle, look how many."

She pushes the envelope back. "We already had this discussion. You know the rules. Don't try to get any ideas."

"I don't got no ideas. Just what I can see."

"Hmph." She eats my sugar cookie.

"You working for this collective. I don't say nothing to no one about this. It's like me. I'm a union man. But they not paying, so how about they help take care of the kids? Every night you making meetings. What happens to them?" I look at Abra's twins. Now they got the radishes lined up too.

"I'm the only one with kids. And they do help when they can."

"I could help."

"We decided we couldn't cross that line, remember?"

"You decided. Not me."

"O.K., I decided."

"Maybe it's not too late."

"It's not about being late. You know that already."

I shake my head.

"O.K." She waves the envelope. "I'll give this money to the collective."

"What?" I say. "They take it and send it to the Commies in the Philippines to fight martial law." I snatch back the envelope. "O.K. O.K. I'm against martial law, but what about the larger context of my struggle?"

But I forget to tell you what Philip Vera Cruz says. It's this kind of speech about our history. Make it real to you, we got to put our real lives inside real history. I tell you my version right here:

Back in 1920, I'm in Oahu with Pablo Manlapit. How many thousands of us Pinoys and Japanese strike against the plantations? Pau hana. We close them down until they spread their lies. Lies about Manlapit. Lies about how we Orientals look alike but we never get along. Separate the Pinoys from the Japanese. Use the Koreans against the Japanese to break the strike. It's a lesson you learn. I tell Macario and Abra. This is how you could fail in the end.

But that's not all.

In Hawaii, I get to be persona non grata, so I come to California to see what trouble I can make here. By then, Pinoys about the only folks not being excluded. Then, in 1934, I'm in Salinas with Rufo Canete, and maybe three thousand of us strike the lettuce fields. They deputize a white army, burn down our camp, and drive us out of town. You think they don't pay someone to come to bust your head open for a lousy extra thirty cents? Pay an army before they pay you. That's the next lesson.

Then the next year, they tell me my country's going to be free and independent. Guaranteed—just wait another ten years. But meantime, I change from being a ward of the American government to an alien ineligible for citizenship. I say, what's the difference? Except now they want me to go back to where I came from. What do they know about where I came from? They never know except I'm a brown brother. That's the next lesson.

We put the labor of canning and picking together because that's how we work. Move up the coast from the Imperial Valley on the Mexico border to the Wenatchee next to Canada, harvesting every fruit and vegetable along the way. You see us coming. A big army of hands moving north. From there, we ship out of Seattle to harvest the sea. Before I ship out in 1936, I'm in a Chinatown restaurant when I see Placido Patron take out his pistol and shoot Virgil Duyungan and Aurelio Simon. Placido's an Alaskero contractor, and he don't believe there's enough work to go around if Virgil continues to do our union work. You always got your own people to take out a gun for money. That's another lesson.

Five years later, in 1939, back in Stockton, we take on asparagus, celery, brussels sprouts, and garlic, and we win something. Then in 1948, we go for asparagus again.

And then in 1965, we take on grapes. First we win in Coachella. Then we go to Delano. This time in Delano, we gonna get a real union contract. We don't call our union Filipino, but that's what we are. So our union rep, Larry Itliong, talks to the Mexicans and asks, what gives? Dolores Huerta says yes, we strike. Helen Chavez says yes, we strike. All the women strike. What makes men men are women. Finally, Cesar Chavez comes to Filipino Hall, and the rest is history. Maybe that's the last lesson. You could be starting something someone else has to finish. And maybe it is never finished. And maybe down the road they forget everything. Who started it? Why did it start in the first place?

Later, our union leader, Philip Vera Cruz, comes into the kitchen. I make him his coffee like he likes it, very black. Then he spoons in the sugar and stirs. We sit outside staring into Sixto's garden and talk.

I say, "Now that Larry left, it's not the same."

"Yeah. Maybe we argued, but I miss him."

"Those were the days I'm doing scout work. We get the numbers on the train cars going north, then Fred and I take his beat-up Rambler and chase them up the 1-5. Meet them at the pass going slow and take turns with a shotgun, shooting out the generator lines." I cock my imaginary rifle. *"Blam! Blam!"*

Phil shakes his head. "Grapes went over the high Sierras and arrived stone frozen."

"And how about Rudy doing all kind of undercover work. Never got caught except over there at Terra Bella."

"Never got caught that time either." We both laugh, remembering.

I'm in the car telling Fred to slow down and pick up Rudy. Rudy's standing barefoot in the same booth where he phones us his SOS. See, he's lost his shoes to hide his tracks. But Fred sees the cops on the other side. "The union can't be involved," he says, so he's got to drive through. When we make the U-turn back, the cops have Rudy, so we leave. Later we find out, Rudy gets away. What's Rudy's story? He's hitching a ride and gets picked up and propositioned by one fag, so he gets in a fight. His shoes? Well, the guy takes his shoes so Rudy can't chase him down. Cops believe Rudy's story and give him his ride home to Bakersfield. Can you believe it? Next day, Terra Bella vines wilting in the sun. All the water lines to the pumps destroyed by acid. Goddamn coincidence.

I say to Phil, "Those days are over. After Larry, you the last one to fight. Keep the old spirit."

"Larry made a big sacrifice. He had his reasons for leaving."

"But look what happened. You win Delano but lose Salinas."

"Who's the real loser? UFW? Teamsters? No." Phil shakes his head. "It's the workers." He looks tired.

"And Cesar. He went away too."

"Took the headquarters to La Paz."

I nod. "Boondocks. In the Philippines, guerillas go into the mountains, but this one's some mountain retreat. If I were a saint, I go up there, too."

"No, Felix." We look at Sixto's garden and the dead terrain of Forty Acres. Must be ninety-five degrees in the shade. "We are not saints." Phil and I laugh.

I say, "How come you still here?"

"Someone had to stay. Build this Agbayani."

"One day the job is finished."

"One day."

The next day, Macario pulls up with his station wagon. Taking his volunteers back up the I-5 to San Francisco. I look in, and there's a space for me. "Maybe I better go with you," I say.

Macario says, "Maybe."

"Go back to my roots."

"Thought you said your roots are here in Delano."

"This my grass roots. I-Hotel my brick roots."

"O.K., Felix, hop in."

Abra comes out with my old suitcase. "You forget this?"

Macario looks at Abra and shakes his head.

Kids think they know something. They don't know nothing. If I leave it to them, my brick roots come down one by one. I get in the car and say, "Maybe I got this recipe."

Macario asks, "Can it kill you?"

"If you greedy, eventually."

"That's the one we want."

2: Halo-Halo

"Manong." The kid jumps out. "Take my seat in front." He holds the door open for me. When I get treated like this? I got to take advantage. Macario turns to me from his driver's seat. "Gonna ride shotgun?"

"Why not? I'm the only one can shoot a gun."

"Don't be so sure."

I look at Macario, but don't say nothing. Kids think they preparing for the revolution. O.K., prepare, but I been here before. In fact, in this Chevy wagon chasing the heat up I-5. History is repeating itself. But this is a different Macario.

"What's it been?" I ask. "Maybe I know you now five years?"

"Remember? I came down to Delano in a caravan with Pete Velasco. We brought a load of provisions for the strike."

"Ha! Velasco's Fiasco." I laugh. "How many times that truck broke down?"

"Met you at Filipino Hall. You were in the kitchen."

"Adding water to the soup. How long I'm waiting for provisions? Depend on you guys, we gonna starve."

"You always had food from that beautiful garden."

"I'm talking rice. Meat."

"Pete managed to keep some big fish on ice."

"How much ice left? Nothing but water when you arrive. Ha! I remember now. You struggling in with the cooler full of water." I demonstrate him stumbling in. "I open the cooler up and pull the fish out. Leave you there with a hundred pounds of sloshing water." I slap my knees. "Ha ha!"

"Shit, I got all wet."

"Stinking fish water."

"But that fish you made was good."

"Bulonglong style. I got the recipe from Johnny Bulonglong himself. You too young to remember. Used to be Ilocano owned the Golden Gate, across from the hotel."

"Felix, I got a favor to ask."

"What's that?"

"Don't talk about food yet. We just got in the car."

"Don't worry. I fill this car up with the aroma of food. You don't need to stop to eat never."

Everyone's groaning in the backseat.

"O.K. O.K." I'm quiet for a long time. But what we gonna talk about? I think about Macario, just a curious college kid come to check us out. That was back in 1968. That year we getting national attention for the grape boycott. Then Cesar stops eating. He's going to fast like Mahatma K. Gandhi. Suddenly Delano looks like India. Farmworkers like Indian people under the imperial thumb of the Great Encyclopedia Britannica. That's the stuff. The media eats it up.

"Did you come to Delano before or after RFK?" I ask.

"After. He was already dead. Assassinated in L.A."

"Robert and Ethel try my soup. Thin soup with handmade bread. That's how Cesar breaks his fast."

"Felix."

"Thin vegetable soup. Cesar is vegetarian."

"I don't believe it."

"What? I no lie. Strict vegetarian. No dairy even. Guy like that."

"How come we talking food again?"

"What's the problem? You not vegetarian."

Grumbling.

I change the subject. After all, I'm a peaceful guy. Just like Cesar. "That's not the first time you come to Delano. Hey," I remember, "next year you come with Ben San Pablo."

"Ben came with me to get Cesar's endorsement for the strike at Berkeley."

"Oh yeah, you students striking too. What was that about?"

"To get a Third World college."

"You get your college?"

"No. That's when I quit to work in the community."

I nod. I meet them all. Macario, Ben, Abra, Olivia, Ria. Kids are looking for something they can't find. Hotel's a magnet for them. Like Sixto's garden. Digging and sweating. I say, "That time in Delano you work in the Pink House and stay at Philip Vera Cruz's place in Richgrove."

"Phil talks with Ben and me all night, every night."

"I know the talk," I say. "Phil can get into it. Smart kids like you and Ben."

"Some nights I think you were there, too?" He's asking.

"What time I got for philosophy? You forget I'm the cook. Got to get up around three a.m. Fix grub by four a.m. for the first contingent of pickets. Besides, Phil got that goddamn dog Aguinaldo, never stops barking. All night. Barking. Barking. Who can get any sleep?" I slap Macario's knee. "That's why you have to talk all night."

"Ben and Phil did all the talking. Mostly I listened."

I think, that's Macario. Always listening. That's his talent.

"Those were the nights."

Maybe Ben's the brainy one. Thinks and writes what he thinks. Phil's like that too. But me, I got to cook. Otherwise I can't think. Maybe Macario's got to cook too. Could be. I say, "Now you and Ben got to practice what you talk. Like I say, 'proof of the pudding.'"

Macario remembers, "Then we got a call. Had to rush back to the hotel because of the fire."

"That's right. I knew Pio Rosete, one of the guys who died in the fire. What you think? To this day, I know it was arson."

"Too much of a coincidence. Fire's the night before Solomon's supposed to sign a new lease agreement. Next day, he won't sign."

Yeah, I make a quick decision and take the ride back with the kids. Phil comes too, but he's already promised. He's going to teach a class at Berkeley. Make some speeches for the UFW. I'm just thinking it's time to see my old home before it burns down completely. I go to San Francisco, check into the I-Hotel just like old times, and for a while, I never leave. I get a room on the second floor. Not the burnt end. On that side, it's all charred black. Whole place smells like smoke. Somebody thinks they saw Pio's ghost. Maybe it's just soot rising. Solomon says the place is a firetrap. Gives us three months to vacate.

About a month later, it's April 18 at 5:12 in the foggy morning, middle of Union Square. What are we doing at this goddamn hour? Mayor Alioto is about to start his Earthquake Party, sixty-three years after the great 1906 San Francisco earthquake. How many thousand San Franciscans there to feel the kick-off? This is one crazy city.

But suddenly, there's Macario and how many others rushing the podium. They pull out their banners: *Save the I-Hotel! Fight the Eviction of Elderly Tenants! Shame on you, Simon Solomon!*

At precisely 5:12 a.m. Macario speaks: *Mayor Alioto and the people of San Francisco. The Great Earthquake destroyed our city. It destroyed all of Chinatown, but we Asian Americans labored to rebuild this great city. Now another kind of earthquake seeks again to destroy our communities and to replace our homes and neighborhoods with financial buildings and parking lots for the rich . . .*

That's the mayor's Earthquake Party.

I admit. I'm surprised. Life takes that kind of turn. A clumsy kid who just listens suddenly gets some guts. Spits out the cork in his throat. Maybe Phil's thunder in his chest makes its way out.

"Tell me the truth." I say to Macario. "What you come to Delano for? Searching for something?"

"What do you mean?"

"First time, didn't you have a girlfriend? What happened?"

"Didn't work out."

"She was a nice girl. Smart, too."

"Hmm."

"What was her name? I forget her name."

"So did I."

"You forget her name? I never forget my girlfriend's name."

"O.K., Felix. You can talk about food again."

"Food and women. It's all the same thing."

Back in the day, I know Lucy. Of course, Lucy is not the only one. I know Nancy, Mabel, Dorothy, Betty, Doris, Lilly, Marilyn, Greta. I got them waiting in every town up and down the Pacific coast. You ask anybody who knows. Anywhere there's dancing, I got my special partner waiting. I buy up all her tickets for the evening, and we make the floor our floor and the night our night.

Old Frankie and I, we reminisce about the old days. I say, "You remember Lucy?"

"Oh yeah," he smiles big.

"She was my girl."

"Nah, Felix, I got to be honest with you after all these years. She was my girl."

"Frankie, I'm talking about Lucy Lightning over at Danceland. I could drive in from Delano or maybe Coachella on the weekend, and she would be waiting. Every other fellow had to fall away."

"That's Lucy. You come in on Saturdays as usual."

"As usual."

"So you warm her up. I come in on Sundays."

"Listen. After we finish on Saturdays, she got to get new shoes. She got to observe Sunday as a day of rest."

"I tell you, Felix. You just make the floor smooth for me."

"When I arrive, the crowd on that dance floor parts for me, and Lucy is right there walking to me with her open arms."

"On Sunday, I meet Lucy at Pershing Square, and we stroll around. I buy her ice cream at the soda fountain, then we make our entrance at Danceland."

Now I know Frankie's lying. Mostly because he's still alive and he's still wearing the same suit without evidence of ever being roughed up, or better yet, shot. How many fights I get in to keep company with Lucy? Those days, a Pinoy walk down the street with a white woman has to be ready with some bravado. Maybe Frankie had himself a pistol. Oh yeah. I can believe it. But the ice cream soda fountain thing, no way. I romanced my Lucy with halo-halo.

I take my time with Frankie. Explain about the halo-halo. Give him the benefit of the doubt. After all, Frankie's been around the block more than once. Course these days, all we doing is circling it. He's got his stories. I got mine.

O.K., most tropical fruits not available at the time. But I don't go with no can of fruit cocktail. Substitute succulent peaches for mangoes. Peeled grapes for macapuna. I make the sweet beans and corn myself. Maybe banana. A dollop of tapioca. Squares of lime Jell-O. Shaved ice. Make it rich with thick sweet cream. Top it off with a maraschino cherry. You make it to the bottom of the parfait glass, could be a surprise of rum or brandy.

Frankie says, "Felix, we talking women or food? Lucy or halo-halo?"

"All the same thing. When I think about those dancing days, I think halo-halo."

Frankie shakes his head. "You come up to my room. I show you something."

I follow Frankie upstairs. His room's same like mine, just down the hall. Narrow two-by-four gets you room for a single bed, chest of drawers, standing closet, little sink. You get your window overlooking Jackson or Kearny or maybe the alley on the backside. We paying fifty dollars a month. What you expect?

Frankie takes off his jacket and adjusts it on a hanger behind his door. Then he sets his hat on a hook up on the wall. He rolls up his sleeves and pulls out a small suitcase from under the bed. I sit in the chair. Frankie sits on the bed. Suitcase is filled with envelopes and postcards with foreign stamps.

"Love letters?" I ask.

"Look how many," he says. "I got another suitcase filled."

He fingers through the old papers, some of them going yellow. Pretty soon I see what he's looking for, but his eyes are bad. He misses it and gets down to pull up the second suitcase. While he's busy going through that one, I pick up some postcards and read them. "Francisco," I read. "Since when you called Francisco?"

He takes a close look. "See, this one signed *Maria Carmen.*" He points to the picture on the other side. "Rio de Janeiro. Sugar Loaf."

"What's this say?" I ask.

"She writes to me in Portuguese. 'Beijos,'" he reads. "Means, you know." He smiles and puckers up. He closes his eyes like he's remembering. But then he says, "But that's not the one." He throws the card back into the pile and continues to rifle through another stack.

When he's not looking, I tug out the envelope that has the return address on Temple Street in Los Angeles. You can't mistake the letters, L. L., in curlicues. I slip the envelope into my jacket.

I pick up another postcard. "You go to Macao? I was there too." I pick through the stacks. There're cards and envelopes from every port city in the world. Nagasaki. Hong Kong. Singapore. Madras. Karachi. Cape Town. Lisbon. New York. Montevideo. Lima. Honolulu. Brisbane. To name a few. Talk about circumnavigation.

I stick around a bit more while Frankie gets lost in his love letters. Spread out all over his bed. Pretty soon I think he forgets why he invited me up. He's reading them one by one like it was yesterday. I make my quiet exit with Lucy Lightning. I don't know why I take Frankie's letter.

Can't be much to it. Lucy don't have much education. Poor Okie girl rides in on a jalopy out of the Dust Bowl. Guys like Frankie spend their days washing dishes and busing tables on the ocean, got a girl in every port and nothing left but two suitcases of correspondence to prove it. I don't know why.

Macario nudges me. I'm back in the car. "You asleep?"

"No."

"What you thinking about?"

"Halo-halo."

"Figures."

"Halo-halo is like a performance. Like theater. Everything goes in stages with lots of color: red, green, orange, white, purple. Then texture: smooth, crunchy, slippery. Then character: sweet, sour, nutty, cold. You think: funny, romantic, nostalgic. When it's over, you bite your frozen tongue. Draw blood. Tragic."

"Goddamn, Felix. Where we gonna get halo-halo on the I-5?"

I tap my head. "Only in your mind."

"Man, you drive me nuts."

"You know, I think Cesar's right. If you gonna ask the whole world to quit grapes, you can go the whole way and eat nothing."

"Was that the point?"

"Back in the sixties, guys like you starving to be too skinny for the draft. Then others eating, eating, to be too fat. Some guys guzzle one quart of soy sauce to get high blood pressure. Eating, not eating, you put your life on the line. That's the recipe for revolution."

Macario lights up. "Maybe that's what we'll propose. Someone go on a hunger strike for the I-Hotel." He's nodding like it's his idea. "You volunteering?"

"No way!"

Someone in the back wakes up. "Shit. Didn't you say Cesar's vegetarian? Easy for him to cut out one more food group."

"O.K., we start slowly. One food group at a time."

Now the argument starts.

"This is when my cultural nationalism kicks in. Comes to food, I am Pilipino."

I'm staring out the Chevy surrounded by agribusiness on either side of the I-5. Maybe it looks like desert and sage, but they own it. They just need some water.

You think about it. Food is the basis for everything. Without food, it's all over. Kaput. They don't lie when they say you are what you eat. If you can't get nothing to eat, you are nothing. Nothing. They also don't lie when they say you eat to live. And you live to eat. What's someone's culture but the way he eats? Everybody living from meal to meal, even if it takes somebody three days to get to the next one. Call that the culture of poverty. Maybe you a nomad or you tied to the land. It's how you get your food. It's how you organize to get your food. Keep your food. Keep your food for yourself. Who grows it? Cultivates it? Sells it? Cooks it? Who gets fed and does not get fed? Who throws it away? Who eats the leftovers?

What's the story of the world? How come Magellan comes to bother folks like us in faraway islands? It's to make their food taste better. Once you taste a secret, you go running after your tongue. It can't be helped. Once you know this principle of the world, then everything becomes clear. You take Marx. You take Freud. You take Einstein. You take Suzuki. The politics of food. The sex of food. The relativity of food. The Zen of food.

I tell these radical kids, eventually all the answers can be found in food. Are they listening? Follow the food, I say. You born in the city. You forget your connection to the earth. And I don't mean just Watsonville or Delano. That's what guys like me have, the knowledge. We never stop. Everywhere we go, we touch the food right at the source. We digging the earth, sowing the seed. We pulling the weeds. Then cutting cane or slicing pineapple. Shucking lettuce or cutting asparagus. Dirt under the nails, under the blisters, in the grooves of our hands. It never washes out.

Then harvesting grapes. When grapes are ready, there's nothing more beautiful and luxurious. I don't say this like I'm the grower. I say this because who cannot appreciate the miracle of planted food comes back every year with your encouragement? These grapes are my grapes, my children. The small, sour, purple ones crushed for Gallo wine. Large, green, seedless Thompson for Dole fruit cocktail. The reds for Sun-Maid raisins. But that's just the earth.

What about the sea? Pulling in the live salmon. You see the great silver bodies kick out from the surf like wild mustang. We slit the soft bellies and pull out the eggs. Red orange, slimy grape clusters shudder in your hands. You holding salmon caviar in one hand and the caviar that makes the wine in the other. Holding it tender like babies because this stuff will travel to the man's table. Who's gonna put it there? I'm gonna put it there. Set the caviar on thin crackers with lime zest. Pour a chilled bottle of sparkling wine. Make him look gracious in a room full of beautiful women, tinkling glasses, fluttering candles, and chandeliers. I'm holding my hands out with the open palms of sea and land caviar. Holding them out like offering. Then take it away. Close the fists and squeeze. Squeeze hard.

3: Pig Roast

One day Macario comes by my room. He's holding a small cardboard box. He says, "Look what I found back of the closet in Joe's office."

I scrutinize the label on the box. "Crematorium," I make out. Then "Pio Rosete."

Macario pulls open the cover. Inside, there's a plastic sack of gray ashes.

"It's Pio," I say. "What's he doing here?"

"Maybe nobody claimed him. No next of kin."

"How long it's been since the fire?"

"A while."

I scratch my head. "That's what the guys say."

"What?"

"Pio's ghost coming around bothering them. Sometimes he's got his banjo. Other times, maybe you playing rummy, and you lose your card. You find it somewhere else you never expect."

"Guys are cheating."

"That's what they're saying. Pio was a good cheater."

"You believe it?"

"If you get him on your side, maybe you could win."

Macario chuckles, but then he looks at the box and gets serious again. "So now what?"

"Maybe he knows who set the fire. We never think to ask him."

"Look," Macario says. "You figure this out. You knew him." He hands me the box and walks away.

I put Pio down in the chair and sit in my room. Now I get these ashes for a roommate. "Pio," I say. "You remember that song? How does it go?" I hum a few verses. Pretty soon I remember the whole song and sing everything. I think, did he get burned up with his banjo? Probably. Nothing left of his old room. I think, that's Pio all right. How else could I remember the whole song?

Over time we get a committee going to figure out something for Pio. Put his spirit to rest once and forever. Also we gonna honor the other guys who died: Salermo and Knauff. We do a thing on March 16, anniversary of the fire. Everybody agrees. Too late for a funeral. Who's gonna mourn? We got our own troubles. There's gotta be food and music. Somebody says lechon baboy. Gotta be authentic pig roast over coals. I say, "What the heck you talking? We gonna burn the I-Hotel down this time for good."

Alfred suggests, "How about doing it Hawaii style, in the pit? That way there's no open fire."

"In the imu?" I say.

"Watchu call it?"

"Imu. Pit. Same thing. Before you bury the pig, you gotta burn wood and rocks for maybe four to five hours."

"Felix, you don't worry about the logistics. You the cook. You just tell us what to do. We do it."

Bunch of guys sign up for the food committee. Other bunch for the music. What can I say? It's a democracy.

But then someone says, "You want my humble opinion, Pinoy pig better than Hawaii pig."

I smack the side of my head because I know what's coming.

Someone else has to say, "Humble opinion? What's a humble opinion?"

"Lechon baboy got that crispy skin."

"You don't know what you talking. Kalua pig comes out so tender melts in your mouth. And the flavor." He smacks his lips.

"Think about it. You turning that baby on the bamboo pole, take turns for how many hours? Take it easy. Drink beer. Gets to be that deep red color. You get the reward: the crispy skin."

"Skin? What about the rest of the pork? Wrap it up in banana leaves and slow cook. O.K., you work to dig the pit, heat the rocks, bury it good. But after that, you go play, afternoon surfing, forget about it. Come back, you got yourself one luau."

"Yeah, you do that. You try surf in the fucking freezing bay."

Now we got an argument. Everybody on the food committee taking sides. They split down the middle. I throw my hands up. Revolution, O.K., but what cook believes in democracy?

Macario asks, "What's the matter? How about Pio's celebration?"

We go down back of the hotel—basement used to be a diner joint in the old days. Got the old counter and the six original stools, stove, fridge, everything. I clean it up and every now and then cook up a storm. Macario takes a stool, and I get a pot of rice going. Anyway, rice is basic. Then open up one of those square cans of Spam. Cut it up. Then green onions. Chop that up. Fry up the Spam with the onions. Meanwhile, open a can of chili beans. Could be turkey or beef. Could be Stagg. Heat up the chili.

"What're you making?"

"Hiro's dish."

"Oh no. Not that."

"Why not? I tell you this is the most original stinky thing you gonna eat. Beats anything Pinoy."

By now he knows this might be the only thing can cheer me up. "That bad, huh?"

"Maybe we go back to the first idea."

"What's that?"

"We do a funeral."

I prep the last ingredient: natto. Stinky, brown, snotty, fermented beans. Macario says smells like concentrated dirty socks. I tell him Hiro should know. Japanese invented this. Who'da thought? Same ones invented Zen. Whip the natto up with soy sauce and mustard. Crack in one raw egg. Whip it up some more. Touch of cayenne. Macario closes his eyes. I got to smile. I feel better already. I get the bowls ready. Pile up the rice, the chili, the fried Spam, the natto. Sprinkle more chopped scallions on top for garnish. For Macario, minus the natto.

Now we hunker down. Eat first. Think later.

Macario says, "I thought the guys decided."

"What they gonna decide? Pit or spit?"

"I know how you feel. I got the same problems."

"What's that?"

"CPA. ACC."

Now I got to laugh. You hang out across the street from the hotel, you can see the dynamics clear as day. Picture this: middle door is the International Hotel entrance. Got the original square pillars and the old buttresses. These days painted nice. Door to the left is the Chinese Progressive Association.

Door to the right is the Asian Community Center. O.K., depending on your point of view. You coming out the hotel entrance, door to the left is ACC, and door to the right is CPA. Both of them trying like crazy to be on the left. What's the difference? Same difference. Some days maybe they got the same program. Showing the same goddamn Chinese movie. *East is Red.* You get confused. Go down one side. Go down the other. Same long-haired kids. Same posters of Mao. Same PRC flags. Through the looking glass.

I look around. "Which side we on now?" I ask.

"ACC," Macario answers.

"Are they pit or spit?"

"Shit."

"You know, before we got the three-year lease, didn't have this kind of problem."

"Everyone was too busy working on the hotel."

"I think I'm missing the noise. Pounding, sawing, scraping, sanding, screwing-screwing, banging-banging-banging." I get excited. "Heh heh!"

Macario shakes his head. "Dirty old man."

"Even missing the smell. Ammonia and fresh paint. Insecticide and rat poison."

"That's a lie. You hated the smell."

"O.K." I gesture with my chopsticks. "I'm lying."

Macario is watching the sticky brown spiderweb grab the Spam and chili in my bowl. I slurp it up. The web sticks to my lips.

I say, "Saving the building is not the same thing as saving the hotel. Maybe anyone can save the building. Harder to save the hotel."

"O.K.," he agrees.

"That's why"—I got to stop to wipe my mouth—"the guys got to argue pit or spit. Same arguments everywhere. No matter what, we got a three-year lease, time to take care of ghosts and shit like that. Maybe we succeed, but no matter what, three years is"—I kiss the air—"poof."

Macario sighs. He doesn't know. He's too young. Three years is still a big percentage of his life. "So," he asks, "pit or spit?"

I slap the table. "We gonna do both. Two pigs. Same size. Same weight. Two roasts. We get a panel of impartial judges. Maybe blindfold them. But you got to do it from live pig to roast pig. May the best pig win."

I'm already cleaning up. Wiping down the counter.

"Felix." Macario hands me his empty bowl. "Did you just decide this now?"

"Hiro's dish. It works every time."

"What about my problem?"

"Sorry. You got to find your own dish."

Macario's waiting in front on Kearny with the Chevy. Another pickup behind him, and Alfred's driving that one. Butcher's crew, about half dozen guys piling in. Alfred's got two double-size Samoans in the truck. They're so big, he's driving squeezed outside the window even. Pretending to drive with one arm over the top of the wheel.

I look in the truck. "Cozy, eh."

Everybody looks at me and smiles. All they can do to turn their heads, but Alfred says, "O.K." He's always enthusiastic. "Where're we going?"

"You don't know?" I ask.

"Hey," he says, "lucky we got the truck."

Macario comes over. Consults with Alfred. "Claudio says he knows. Some place in Salinas."

"I'm following you, man."

As usual, I sit shotgun with Macario. He's looking at a paper bag with something in it on my lap. "What's that?"

"Pio."

"We're not leaving him out there, are we?"

"What? Pio's party right here in San Francisco. He's just going for the ride."

"Choose the pigs?"

"You never know."

"Right."

So we driving with the butcher's crew and Pio south to Salinas. Macario looks back in his rearview mirror and says, "What about the Samoans?"

"Alfred's buddies. He says they got the knowledge."

"What do you figure? Truck cabin must be holding seven hundred pounds."

The guys are looking back at the truck. "And that's not including Alfred."

"Don't go too fast. Truck has to brake, it's going to flip over us."

"That's why we got to get those pigs. For counterweight."

In Salinas, locate the Hamilton Farm. Family operation. Everybody gets out to negotiate. Hamilton says, "I'm not in the pig business."

"What about those pigs over there?"

"What about them?"

"Look like pigs."

"They're not pigs. Boars. Wild boars. Goddamn animals come down and tear up my crops. I shot the mother, then found this litter. Thought I'd raise them for meat."

"O.K., that's the kind we want."

Butcher's crew flanked by the Samoans all nod, then confer. "Too small. Even if we take all seven, can only feed seven."

Macario looks on. "They're not that small."

"Come back in a couple months," says Hamilton.

"How big was the mother?"

"Big. Hundred fifty pounds. Got her butchered into hams."

"That's it."

"We get big daddy."

"You want to hunt them out, be my guest. Goddamn infestation." Hamilton points. "Follow their trails into those hills over there. Plenty out there, if you can catch them."

Macario looks at me. "Hunt?" He addresses the butcher's crew. Tattered bunch of old Chinese and Filipino guys got their knives in the back of the car. Sharp and ready to go. They standing there puffed up with their arms crossed over their chests.

"We came here to get pig. We get pig."

"Save the fifty bucks. Get free ones in the wild."

"Maybe we need some preparation. When's the last time you hunt?"

The Samoans put in. "Don't worry. We gonna take care of business."

"That's right. We take care of business."

One of the old guys, Lee, says, "My cousin lives in downtown Salinas, old Chinatown. We get some lunch and get ready."

"Got to hunt around sundown. That's when the pigs come out."

Macario asks, "How long is this going to take?"

"Depends."

"Don't worry." The Samoans slap Macario on the back and hug Alfred. "We gonna take care of business."

"Right. Whatchu worry? We not born yesterday."

"Hunting is an old habit."

"You gonna see the real stuff."

Everyone is getting excited.

It's taking three days. Daytime, guys cutting bamboo and making long spears. Digging holes and making traps. Making maps and telling stories. The one that got away. How many get away? Sleeping late, eating at Lee's, drinking beers.

During the day, I say to Macario, "I take you on a tour of Salinas. I used to live here, cooked in that big house on the corner."

"That one?"

"Yeah, you know John Steinbeck?"

"*Grapes of Wrath*?"

"Yeah, that's his old house."

"Are you kidding?"

"John likes my tarts. I know he comes down to the kitchen at night. Steals the tarts. Strawberry tarts. Boysenberry. Rhubarb. One night I catch him, so I make a pot of coffee, and we get to talking. Some time I tell you about it."

We stand on the corner. House needs some painting. Garden's a mess. I shake my head. "Used to be beautiful. Wonder who owns it now? Nobody remembers."

"Rich growers in Salinas must hate Steinbeck."

"Those days, who knows he was gonna write? Who's side he's on? Just a kid like you. Going to Stanford sometimes."

"Felix, how old were you?"

"Oh, about the same as John. I was going to Berkeley, but I had to quit."

"Felix, you never told me that."

"You didn't know I was a fountain-pen boy?"

Macario's impressed.

"You know John died couple years back, 1968. You think that's ironic?

We start the grape strike, and he dies. All the time, Pinoys, Mexicans, we were there too. We were there first, before the Okies and the Arkies. Segregated camps, but still there. Nothing changes for us."

By the third day, Lee's cousin is getting anxious. Even though I'm helping him, Samoans eating multiply two times three. And then we all chowing down too, after chasing wild boar. And nothing to show for. Chasing is an exaggeration. How fast can these guys run? Samoans run in slow motion with thunder feet. Old guys not far behind. Bunch of retired savages. I quit after the first night on the grounds I'm the cook. But then, I got to hear the stories.

"Felix, you missing everything."

"So Claudio, he's got the idea we climb into the trees, and sure enough, we can hear them grunting around, and got an entire herd of them, right there under him."

"So I come around other side, getting ready. How close am I? Really close. But then, what the fuck! Claudio comes crashing down."

"Lucky for him the branch is slow falling. Otherwise he got one broken head."

"But goddamn! Those piggies scatter, bunch of squealing rats."

Alfred says, "And I see these manongs with handmade spears going in every which direction. Incredible scene, man."

"Shiiit," Claudio shakes his head guiltily. "We lost our chance."

"What about the traps?"

"They must be working."

"What you catch?"

"Raccoon."

Finally, the game is up. Fish and Game comes around. "You guys have a hunting license?" he asks.

"See this tattoo?" one of the Samoans asks. "This is my hunting license."

"That's a nice tattoo," Fish and Game says.

Next day, Macario and Alfred do some research. Drive up to a meat processing plant just outside Salinas proper. Make the guys choose the pigs. Haggle over the weight. Pinch the price. Pigs are clean, pink. No hair. No blood. Blue FDA stamp of approval. Tuck them in ice back of the truck and use them for counterweight. Throw in one of those decorative California banana trees never seen a banana. Throw in the bamboo spears that can double as spits. Stop for rocks. I pat Pio on the top of his box. Back of the Chevy, the butcher's crew's got their heads tossed in crooked directions. Everybody snoring.

Back at the I-Hotel, roasting crews are getting anxious. "Shit. We think you never coming back. Run off with fifty bucks and get drunk."

"We did that too."

"Hey, man," Alfred says. "We went hunting."

Crew examines the pigs. "Hunting for a butcher shop?"

"It's a long story."

Roasting crews haul off their respective pigs to separate kitchens. Something going on about the basting sauces. It's all top secret.

I can't be involved. I carry Pio upstairs and put him on my chair. I can't remember when I fall into my bed.

It doesn't matter because it seems like it's five minutes, and someone pounding on my door. "Felix! Wake up!" It's Alfred. "Guys said I got to bring you over to the site. You got to supervise, you know, the imu."

"What time is it?"

"Three a.m."

"Go away."

"Pit's dug. I got a shitload of wood back of the truck."

I remember Pio on the chair. "Goddamn," I say. "Who's idea was this?" I never take off my clothes anyway. Roll off the bed. "Come on," I say to Pio. "Let's go."

Outside, it's night. Street's dead. Usual Barbary Coast neons. In the truck, I ask Alfred, "Where's the pit?"

"We found the perfect location."

"Golden Gate Park?" I speculate.

"Couldn't get a permit for a fire there." Alfred shakes his head. "First, we thought about an open lot in the Western Addition, but it's not clandestine enough." He pulls the truck up under the hacked-off end of the Embarcadero Freeway. "This," he points into the dark freeway underbelly, "is public no-man's land. Hoboville. Skidrow guys always warming up around cans of burning material. Who's gonna notice one more fire?"

Out of the dark, the imu roasting crew emerges and runs off with all the wood on the truck. They got the rocks in the pit and the wood stacked up like a Boy Scout teepee. Pour a gallon of lighter fluid all over everything. "Watch out! Stand back!" Match gets tossed in and *whooomp!* That's no hobo fire. Smoke is curling around the concrete ceiling, mixing in with the fog. Except for the smell, could be fog. Joining the cat feet.

Everybody standing around that pit with their eyes on fire.

How many hours later, you got perfect oven conditions? Someone takes a machete to the banana tree. Lines the pit. Sets the hot rocks inside the pig carcass.

"Wait," I say. I run to the truck and open up Pio's box. Dip my hand into his ashes and grab a handful. Run back.

"What's that?"

"Special pepper and herb seasoning," I say. "Trust me." I sprinkle it into the carcass with the rocks.

"Is this cheating?" Someone asks.

"No way," I say. "I do the same for the spitters."

Wrap up the pig in leaves and wire and set it into the imu. Bury everything. By then, the sun's up, but crew's buried too, inside their sleeping bags around the imu. Ready to catch some zs.

But that's when the spit crew arrives.

"Hey, where you figure they buried their pig?"

"Can't you tell? Over there." Points to the sleeping bags. "They circling it like covered wagons."

They kick the guys in the sleeping bags and open their beers. "Hey," they yell. "Surf's up!"

Some in the bags roll over, but others get up and like to punch the daylights out for some nightlight.

"O.K. O.K. Calm down. Go back to bed."

Spit operation is simple. Pretty much cement blocks and two empty quart-sized cans. Dent the cans to make two rests for the bamboo spit. Pull the spit through the pig. Get your coals white hot. Prop the spit up on the cans on the blocks and turn. Keep turning and turning.

For my part, spit pig gets the same pepper and herb treatment. I slap my hands together, and Pio flies around the pig like pixie dust.

Macario arrives around ten a.m. He smells the air and says, "I've seen it on the way. The Tenderloin is emptying out, and every hobo is walking in this direction."

Band arrives. Guitars, ukuleles, banjos, violins, flutes, accordions, and drums. Once they get going, they never stop for nothing. One guy can leave to eat, but someone always replaces him. And Frankie's already managed to find a girl to dance with.

The ACC is busy pulling a banner over the side of the freeway. Says: *Celebrate the Rise of the I-Hotel!*

"Where's it rising?" I ask.

"Don't you get it? Like a phoenix from the ashes."

Not to be outdone, the CPA pulls another banner over the other side of the freeway. *Liberate the Holiday Inn for Low-Income Housing! Long Live the I-Hotel!*

I see Abra. She makes these blue ribbon pins for the three impartial judges and pins the damn badges on them like this is going to be their finest moment. It says: *Save the I-Hotel Roast Pig Judge.* Got to be some kind of joke. She winks at me.

Meanwhile, Julio comes by with a wad of cash and a notebook. "Pit or spit?" he offers. "You might as well put in the pool like everyone else."

"What are the odds?"

"No odds. How we gonna know a thing like that? Split up the winnings with the winners." He nudges me. "Come on Felix, your opinion counts. If someone knows it, it might help one side of the pot. Your opinion might be the odds."

"Are you kidding?" I wave him away. "What I got to do with that kind of trouble?"

Now that they got the badges of courage, I can see the judges are in trouble. Everybody going up to them and toasting them like the grooms in some wedding. "Hey, Jack," someone says. "Here's to pit cooking!"

"Jack," someone else says, "You drink to pit, you got to drink to spit."

"Fair is fair." Another toast.

"Hey, Ken! Looks like you need a drink, warm up those taste buds."

By the time Ken is looking very happy, Julio even tries to get him to join the pool.

"Julio," I say. "Ken's a judge. He can't be in the pool. It's a conflict of interest."

"What's the conflict? Either he wins or loses, depending."

"That's right," Ken agrees. "Depending."

I shake my head. Ken is a student at Boalt Hall, knows how to argue all the sides. So I can already tell he's never gonna be a real judge. Real judge's got to go with blind truth, not various possible truths. "Hey," I pull Ken over, "you wanna hear some stories about this guy?" I point to Julio. "How many years he makes it as a bookie?"

"I always come through for you, Felix." Julio gives me his smile.

"I met you first time over at La Plantera," I say.

"Oh yeah. Benny was the bartender. Kept that bar polished like he owned it."

"He did."

"Downstairs was where the action was. Gambling twenty-four hours."

"Max Duling was always there. Remember?"

"Card hustler," I explain to Ken.

Julio expands. Points to his eyes. "Max Duling was cross-eyed. You looking at his eyes, you don't know where he's looking, but his hands were moving fast."

"You remember the red light?"

"Upstairs, Benny had a button on the bar. If the cops come, he pushes it. Downstairs we quick put away our money and the cards. When the cops come down, all they find is a bunch of men watching boxing movies on an old projector."

"That's how come I met you."

"That's right. I took your bet on the Bolo Puncher that very night. The movie convinced you. You see?" He nods to Ken. "I make him a killing."

I say to Ken as I point to Julio laughing, "Don't trust him."

Suddenly, there's a commotion. Looks like the bamboo spit is on fire. Guys running around frantically trying to save the pig. Running with the spit and the two-hundred-pound pig this way and that. Red cinders flying everywhere. I see it before it happens. Cinders rain on the sleeping bags, and a couple catch fire. So now we got a pig and two sleeping bags on fire. We pull the kids out of the bags. Everybody's yelling.

"Water. Where's the water?"

"How come we got a fire going and no water?"

"Try beer!"

"Try your fucking pee!"

Someone thinks they can take another sleeping bag and snuff out the pig fire, but now it's on fire too. Fire's flying up.

The phoenix from the ashes banner catches fire and flies off into the street. I see the kids running around the street stomping out the new pieces of fire.

Now you can hear the sirens coming our way. When the fire truck gets here, the fire fighters run out. They're all decked out in their heaviest uniforms, ready for a conflagration. A tribute to Coit Tower. They laugh, but the spit crew is yelling. "Save our pig! Save our pig!" So they hose it down.

I go over to examine the pig. Steam is coming up all around. You would think it would be soggy, but actually the steam helps.

The spit crew is hovering over their pig, holding their hearts like they the fathers at the end of a long, tough labor. Claudio hands me a knife, and I make a critical incision. I announce like the doctor on the scene, "Skin is still crispy. Maybe this is an improvement. You got the effect of the imu without the imu."

"It's done!" someone yells.

"We did it!" The spit crew is dancing around like the fire was their idea.

Somebody in the back says, "I think Felix is saying it's edible."

Meanwhile Team Pit is unearthing their baby. They pull back the banana leaves, and already I know. The bones have collapsed inside the meat. It's that tender. Hard to say it has the look of a pig. Even the head has disintegrated. As a chef, I'd say poor presentation, but what the heck. "Very tender," I say.

I get up, and everyone is dancing around me. The firefighters are eating. The Samoans are eating. The judges are too drunk to eat. For some reason the band never stops playing. Like it's the *Titanic*. The musicians just back away from the fire and keep playing. Play through the whole goddamn fiasco. Jubilant fiasco. I see Frankie over there dancing with Abra. Abra's twins dancing too. Alfred dancing with Macario.

I watch the pork roast slip into hungry mouths. See the happy crunch of the burnt skin and the flaked feathers of meat slip away. Shiny grease coating every lip. Pio's magic making them remember. Remember every goddamn song they ever heard or sang in their lives. And they will sing and sing and sing until the night falls and the fog creeps back under the Embarcadero.

4: Empty Soup

This particular year Abra's twins are maybe five years old. After you get to be my age, you start counting again. My case, it's Abra's twins keeping count. Year number five and we still sitting tight in the I-Hotel. Boy is Emilio. Girl is Andrea. For Abra, it's all about history: Emilio Aguinaldo and Andres Bonifacio. I call them Emil and Andie. It's a twin life. Those two are never apart. Stuck together like some kind of glue. Got to do everything together. Get everything equal. Wake, eat, play, sleep together. Sometimes they're hugging. Sometimes they're fighting. You see them rolling around in the corridor like cat and dog. I yell, "Andie! Emil! I got something for you."

And just like the revolutionary generals they are, they get up to attention and run down to me. By now, they know I got some treat for them. This is proof that the cook is the most powerful personage in the nation.

Abra says, "You've got to stop it, Felix. They think they can get rewarded for fighting."

"After five years of life, they pretty damn smart. Who gets reward for being good?"

"Seriously, Felix."

"Look," I say. "They fight because they're hungry. Maybe starving. Get it? Remember what Imelda said. 'Let them eat cake.'"

"Felix, I don't think it was her who said it."

"Trust me. I'm there when she says it."

"Serving her cake in the Malacañang I suppose."

"Chocolate cheesecake. My recipe, but now the infamous Imelda cake."

"That's not your recipe. That's my mom's."

"But where did your mom get it?"

"*Ladies' Home Journal,* I bet."

"That's right! How long your mother reads the *Journal*?"

"How should I know? She was a Filipino war bride."

"I been reading it since Jane Addams was a columnist."

"You are so full of shit."

"If I could vote at the time, I vote for women to vote." I pause and look Abra in the eyes. "Abra, I got to ask you a personal question."

"What's that?"

"Are you a feminist?"

"Is this a trick question?"

"All questions can trick you."

"What do you mean by *feminist*?"

"That's what I want to know."

"Can we talk about this another time?"

"My days are numbered."

"How many days you got?"

"Oh, I don't know." I sigh.

She smiles. It's a beautiful smile. How can you resist?

"I got a plan," I tell her.

"What's that?"

"I take out a million-dollar life insurance plan, and we run away and get married. We have the best honeymoon. I make you the Imelda cake and anything else you love to eat. Then, I die happy. Leave you and the twins with all the money."

"Felix, you're gonna live forever."

"Don't forget I make you this once-in-a-lifetime offer."

"Crazy manong."

"You hear from your mother? Where is she?"

"In Cebu."

"What does she say?"

"I can't talk to her anymore. Remember?"

Now I remember. Abra's father dies last year. Abra goes with her mother and her little brother back to Cebu. Takes the father's ashes. What happens? Martial Law. Tanks coming down the streets. Mother and brother stay in Cebu, but Abra has to come home to her kids.

"They almost got you in Manila. You got lucky. They take you, and I never see you again." Fifteen soldiers with machine guns surround my beautiful Abra, escort her off the plane.

"I'm an American citizen," she says. "I demand my right to counsel with the American Consulate."

"Why did they pick you?" I wag my finger at her. "You looking suspicious?"

"I don't know. I thought there must be spies. Suspected I had those papers in my bag."

I shake my head. She's got newspaper clippings from before censorship and a summary from the CP. Shit like that. Lucky for her it's in an envelope marked in big letters, INSURANCE.

"What's this?" Soldier's interrogation demands.

Abra's got balls. "Can't you read?"

Maybe he can't. Any case, some papers with numbers on top, so he says, satisfied he can read, "Oh, yeah." Fifteen machine guns hustle Abra back onto the plane. Mother's in the crowd watching, but she can't know. Can't wave. Can't even look. Can't say good-bye. Can't write or telephone. How long it's gonna be? That's last year. Why does Abra remember fifteen machine guns? Not three. Not seven. Memory's like a dream. I don't tell her, but I have a suspicion—could be fifteen years.

"I know your father." Sam Balcena was a fountain-pen boy like me. Came to study about the same time at Berkeley, then dropped out in twenty-nine with the Depression. Ran around with the great author Carlos Bulosan, both card-carrying Communists. Sam's writing for the *New Tide* in those days. Friends with union guys like Chris Mensalvas. Maybe that's why Abra's got the bug.

"What if they arrest you that day at the Manila airport?" I ask. "Who is going to take care of the twins? Do you think about that?"

"Yeah." She looks guilty.

"Abra," I say, "You don't have to worry. I'm an expert on twins."

"What?"

"I raise twin boys from the day they are born. Feeding, shitting, burping, bathing. I know all about it."

"You never said you had sons."

"Not my sons. I just raise them. You know what they say? Chief cook and bottle washer. That's me."

"When was this?"

"Oh, back in the day. I been meaning to give you this." I hand her a book. One of those thick pocket editions of classics. "My story. It's all in here." I tap the worn cover.

"*East of Eden*?"

"Wouldn't you know? John writes my story, and it's a best seller."

Couple of days later, Abra comes by the kitchen. "What are you cooking up?" she asks.

"Take a look." I got a giant pot on the stove filled with water.

She looks inside. "You boiling water?"

"Not just any water." I get the long ladle and stir it around. I got a small bowl to the side. Carefully ladle a couple of tablespoons into the bowl and hand it to Abra. "Try this."

"Hot water, Felix."

"You're not concentrating. Close your eyes."

She takes another sip. "Maybe lead from the pipes," she says. "It's gonna kill us eventually."

I shake my head.

"Hey," she says. "I started reading the Steinbeck. That's not you in the book. It's a Chinaman named Lee."

"What does anyone know about the difference between Chinamen and Pinoys?"

"Felix, this Lee character has a queue. And he talks chinky. It's disgusting."

"How far you read?"

"Maybe a couple hundred pages. Took that long just to get to his part. I'm not reading this racist shit about a stereotype."

"Keep reading. John's long-winded."

"Seven hundred pages, Felix."

"Klinker's on page seven hundred."

"I'm giving you your book back."

"Look." I'm stirring my pot. "You take a rest from *Das Kapital.*"

She gives me her look.

"Oh, you think I was born yesterday? Katipunan ng mga Demokratikong Pilipino. You go to some mountain retreat, come back with the revolution." I wave my hands. "That's good. I support it. One hundred percent."

"You do?"

"Of course. Why else you come to this roach-infested hotel? You trying to save me, no?"

She shakes her head. "I don't know why."

"Listen, this *East of Eden* is maybe same stuff but easier. What they say? 'All books lead to Rome.' Way of saying, same place. In this case, California. John and I, we figured it all out. Trust me."

Just then, Emil and Andie run in. "Uncle Felix, what are you making?"

"Making soup. Wanna try?" I ladle out the hot water into two bowls. They scramble to sit at the end table next to the window. I hand them two spoons. "Wait. Hot. You got to blow first."

I see Abra watching the twins. Steam from the bowls, swirling around their dark little heads, silhouettes in our dusty window. Outside, city street noise like the soft crash of distant metal. Watching them blow.

Maybe it's a couple of weeks. Abra's got a job with Mrs. D., waking up at four a.m., leaving at five, starting work at six, making it over to the Mission, some sweatshop with all Filipino ladies making jewelry stands out of felt and Styrofoam. Making dollar and fifty an hour. Probably talking unionizing in between. Comes home by three p.m. smelling like glue, just in time to pick up the twins at school and start organizing to save the I-Hotel. Organizing every day until midnight. Sleep four hours, then start again. Something's got to give.

I see Abra. I ask, "When's it happening? "

"What?"

"The revolution."

She's gotta show optimism, so she says, "Soon, Felix. Soon."

"How long I gotta wait?"

Then one day she says, "Felix, you didn't tell me there's a character named Abra in that book."

"Abra, you a slow reader, but I give you a break."

"Read it on the bus yesterday."

"What you think?"

"I thought I was named after the province of Abra, where my dad's from."

"Funny. I thought you got to be Abra Cadabra."

"I heard that joke before, Felix. All through school." She's growling like some animal. "Be careful."

"No sense of humor."

"See this?" She pulls out a knife from her jeans pocket.

"Fucking switchblade. Are you crazy?"

"Carry it with me all the time, ever since junior high. You know the name of this knife?"

We both say it same time: "Abracadabra."

"Pretty tricky," I say. "You want to see knives? I got knives, too."

She's packing up the blade. "That's why I didn't finish high school. Got kicked out for 'possession of a deadly weapon.'"

"I thought you're pregnant with the twins."

"That too." She adds, "I guess I'm not nice like the Abra in the book."

"Oh, maybe not so different," I say.

Another day she says, "Felix, I finished the book. I have a question."

"What's that?"

"Who is Lee, really?"

"Lee is me."

"No, be honest. Think about it. In the story, there is Cain and Abel. Cain kills Abel, right? Every character is either Cain or Abel. Killer type or killed type. Except"—she points at me—"for Lee."

"It's a Western concept. Good, evil, sin. What you expect? Chinaman's outside of it."

"Hmmm," she grunts.

I go back and read the book again. She's right. I suggest to her, "If Lee is me, Felix Allos, then I tell you what. I'm leaning toward Cain. I got the killer in me."

"Felix," she says. "Let's get this straight. Lee in the book is fiction."

"Change the name to protect my true identity."

"I'm not convinced."

"O.K. John takes some liberties."

"Is that so?"

"One day I tell the real story. It's even better."

"That's a start." Abra's serious. "This is what I want to know. What is Lee's story? Does he even get a story? What is it?"

I go to the kitchen and boil up my big pot of water again. Lately I'm just boiling water. I look inside the pot and think about the Chinaman Lee in the book. What does he do in this situation? He goes to Chinatown and consults with the tong elders. Did I forget? You're goddamn right, that's what I do. I talk to the manong elders. I talk to Wahat and Virgilio, most learned manongs in the I-Hotel. Why not?

I say to them, "Stop writing poetry and playing pool. This is an emergency."

Pretty soon we got a group together. Alfred, George, Devin join up too. Got everybody reading John Steinbeck.

Abra asks, "Where have you been?"

"Abra," I say. "You got your study group. I got mine."

Study group argues about everything.

"First of all, what about this title? How come *East of Eden*? Why not *West of Eden*? We're not West?"

"Hey, you ever see an apple tree in Salinas? Nothing but lettuce for miles and miles."

"I know this very woman Katie in Salinas. She was some kind of whore. Ouwhee!"

"I heard she had Siamese twins. Are you sure about this?"

"How does a white woman have Siamese twins? Ha ha ha!"

"Maybe it's your kids. You Siamese by way of being Pinoy."

"It's possible. Felix is Chinese by way of being Pinoy."

"This never happened. Miss Katie was a great lady."

"My question is this: You got your Adam and your Eve in Paradise, right? So they having great sex all the time, right? Rolling around in Paradise. What happened?"

"Something about the apple of knowledge."

"This is the key. If you have knowledge of sin, it's sin. If not, not."

"Innocence is bliss. That was the Philippines before the Spanish."

"Fucking Spaniards. How come we got to go believe in their knowledge hook, line, and sinker?"

"Did you forget? They got the cannons. Bigger balls."

"Hey, you wanna see bigger cannons?"

"California is like the Philippines. Another kind of paradise."

"You know every town I go to, up and down California, it's always like this: Chinatown next door to whoretown. You got your bars, your gambling, your dancing, your prostitution. All same street. One happy family. How about that?"

"Maybe Eve's serpent's a Chinese dragon. It's making perfect sense."

"That's it! There's your answer. In the book, Lee's the serpent. Wise guy brings knowledge to the white people."

"Maybe so."

"Chinese dragon raises the twins. Maybe they learn the secret handshake."

"You thinking sex is sin, but you got to get to the bottom of this story. The sin we're talking here is murder."

"Worst kind. One brother kills the other brother."

"Why is Cain killing?"

"He's not listening to the Chinaman."

"Because he wants his father's love."

"No. It's because of the land. He wants the land."

"He's already got land."

"Wants more land. Greedy capitalist."

"You know what the real story is, right? There's always a woman involved. I saw it happen myself. You remember the Samson brothers? Johnny Junior shot his brother Babe. There was this girl. Anyway, she ran off with another guy. What was her name?"

"Maybe there's something to this. My brother, he stays back in Binolonan, works for my father, raises a family there. Me, I come here and send every penny back to my father. Keep the family going. Never make anything for myself. Can't go back. Am I jealous? Sure, I'm jealous. I would kill to take my brother's place."

Study group discussions go like this. I'm thinking there's never gonna be an answer for Abra.

One day, Virgilio comes in serious with a piece of butcher paper. Spreads it out on the table and says, "We gonna figure this out today, but we got to write it down."

Everybody's staring at the butcher paper with nothing on it. Looks like my pot of boiling water. "Virgilio, you the poet. You write something."

"Poetry," Virgilio says, "can be like a list."

Alfred says, "That's deep, man."

"Now I'm thinking like this. Top of the list, on one side you got Cain. On the other, Abel." At the top of the paper on the left, Virgilio writes *Cain* and then *Abel* on the right. "So now you got to figure, Cain is the farmer and Abel is the shepherd." Under the Cain side, he writes *farmer* and under the Abel side, *shepherd.* "You following my drift?"

"How about gatherer, hunter."

"Settler, nomad."

I say, "Vegetables, meat."

Guys roll their eyes. "Only thing he thinks about is food."

"O.K., try flora, fauna."

Virgilio says, "This is the obvious. Try to think harder."

"Domestic, wild."

"House, hotel."

"Earth, stars."

"Land, sea."

Someone says, "Inventor, explorer."

"Politician, soldier."

"Slave, conqueror."

"Citizen, alien."

"Outcast, wanderer."

"I don't get it. No difference."

"Think about it. You get kicked out your country. You an outcast. What you call it?"

"Exile."

"Right. That's Cain. He gets kicked out, but Abel, that's his life, following the herd. You could be wandering around like an ordinary hobo, no reason at all."

After that, it opens up.

"Immigrant, migrant."

"Sailor, pirate."

"Indian, cowboy."

"Peace, war."

"You can put in ideas?"

"Why not?"

"Knowledge, sin."
"Justice, liberty."
"Science, religion."
"History, prophecy."
"Physics, math."
"Comedy, tragedy."
"Novel, poem."
"Life, death."
"Hell, heaven."
"Man, God."
"That's it. Every time Abel dies, he turns into God. What a concept."

To make a long list short, it goes on forever. We got to tack it up to the wall and leave it there to cogitate. You come into the room every few days, got more stuff on the list. You see guys next to the list arguing the fine points.

"How come we got peace on this side? It's Cain who killed Abel."

"It's like this. Cain side is the idea about peace. Once you kill, you gotta make rules about not killing. Peace comes after war."

"That's the tricky thing. You can switch it, and nobody knows the difference."

One day I see: pragmatists, idealists.
Next day, it's: democracy, autocracy.
Then: nationalist, internationalist.
Then: Capitalism, Socialism.
Then: bourgeoisie, proletariat.
Then: Socialism, Communism.
Then: Russia, China.
Then: China, Russia.
Then: Mao, Marx.
Then: CPA, ACC.
Then: Aguinaldo, Bonifacio.
Then: IHTA, KDP.
"What's KDP?"

"Short for Katipunan ng mga Demokratikong Pilipino. Pinoy student Commie radicals.

"What's it mean?"

"Means we kill them."

Now we got one war on our hands.

I say to Abra, "We got infiltration in our study group."

Abra says, "Felix, you don't have a study group." She points at our wall. "You got a list."

"It's a poem. Says it all."

"Who wrote in the stuff at the bottom?"

"What does it matter? Matters only if they got the sides right. Like you said: killer type, killed type." Emil and Andie run by. "Both side twins. Come from the same womb. No escaping."

"You wrote that in, didn't you?" Abra looks accusing.

"Me? How do I know these things?" I shake my head. I'm walking away.

"Felix, what about the Chinaman Lee who raises the twins? Did you figure it out?" She's got her hands on her hips.

"Working on it. By and by."

"You know what I think?"

"What?"

"Steinbeck was a fucking chauvinist pig. All the women in the book are stereotypes. Sexy and evil. Or sexless and pure." Abra's getting excited. "The only good woman in the book is Lee."

"He's not a woman."

"Isn't he?" By now she's yelling. "Can you believe that? He never gets married. He never has sex. He just reads and cooks and takes care of the house and raises the children. I don't believe it!"

I get quiet a long time, thinking.

Abra walks over to me. "I'm sorry."

"No, you got it right." I nod my head. "Book is like this hotel. Bunch of men raising another bunch of men."

Abra touches my arm. Then she hugs me. I feel her warm body next to me, my arms around her back, her breasts pressing next to my chest. I pull her into me. How long it's been. Everything fitting into the perfect spaces. My muscles fill out. My lip touches her ear. My hands get electric.

"Felix." She's pushing away. "No!"

Next thing I see her running away. I look down at my stupid penis. How did it get so big?

After a while, I knock on Abra's door.

"Go away."

"Abracadabra."

That's the open sesame. Next thing, she's there in the door with the switchblade. "Felix, remember you asked me that personal question a while back?"

"What's that?"

"About being a feminist."

"Stupid question."

"I'm a feminist."

"Don't worry. Like being a vegetarian or a Communist. It could pass."

"I'm telling you this because I think you're my friend and like my father. Are you going to listen?"

"O.K."

"I'm a lesbian."

"I know."

"You know?"

"I'm not born yesterday."

We laugh.

I think Abra cries, so I say, "Now that's settled, can I hug you?"

"No!"

It takes a few weeks, but finally I knock on Abra's door again. "Abracadabra."

Door's open and behind Abra, I see the twins sitting on the floor coloring.

"I'm boiling water," I say.

"How long is this going to go on?" she asks. "You know what the twins say?"

Emil says, "Uncle Felix is fixing empty soup."

Andie says, "You got to use your imagination."

Emil says, "We gonna starve."

"I finally got the recipe," I say.

Alfred and Devin are coming by with the butcher paper with the poem. They tack it up in the kitchen. I'm cutting up vegetables. I got a pork knuckle thick with cartilage. I got one fat fish head. I got beans. I got more bones. I got oxtail. I got chicken feet. I got the fish sauce and the bagoong. I got limes. I got seaweed. I got coconut milk. I got peanuts. Alfred throws in a carrot and the fish head. He says, "Land. Sea."

Devin checks the poem and tosses in a potato and some beans. "History. Prophecy."

It goes on like that. Like chanting, we throw in everything: farmer, nomad, comedy, tragedy, life, death, proletariat, Capitalist, Communist, Socialist, man, God, evil, good, Mao, Marx, science, religion, peace, war, young, old, women, men, son, father, daughter, mother, brother, brother, sister, sister.

5: Rations

About this time, Joe and I take Macario downstairs to the Paddy Wagon. Paddy Wagon's a strip joint with a bar and a couple of pool tables. Every night Joe's there, so to talk to Joe, you gotta spend some time in the Wagon. "Come on," I say to Macario. "You got something against naked ladies?" But it's not about the strippers, because you got to be blind and drunk to appreciate these old-timers. This one is looking fat, but you got to give it to her. She can move. Everything on her jitters. We sit at the bar and buy a round of beers.

I say to Macario, "Joe and I go back, back to Bataan."

Macario's impressed.

"But," says Joe, "I knew you before the war. Remember, I trained you."

"He's lying," I say. "I teach him all his moves."

"Moves?" asks Macario. He's watching the fat woman sway her hips.

"Boxing," says Joe and points at me. "He was a lightweight."

"Don't believe him," I tell Macario. "See his nose?" I point to Joe's crooked nose. "Who's fault is that?"

Joe laughs. "One day, it's pointing left. Another, pointing right."

I say, "But I give you this. I got Joe to thank for getting me work on the docks." That's back in the day with Harry Bridges and the Longshoremen.

"Those days, boxing comes in handy."

I nod. How many times we got to stand our ground, get some promises, and make all the sides keep them? "Joe, we get our noses busted in the day."

"But not without busting some ourselves. Now you hanging out with the Mexican Gandhi. Got no satisfaction." He punches the air.

"New tactics for new times."

"You never gonna see me turn the other cheek."

I guess not. Joe's living his life on the front lines. I-Hotel's gonna be his last battle. I look up and see the stripper's got one breast exposed, hanging sideways.

Joe growls at Macario, then laughs. "Felix and I," he says, "we seen some battles."

"Sign up for the war same day."

"U.S. Army Forces in the Far East. But we got split up. Felix, I never knew what happened to you. Then come back to find out you survived the war."

Macario asks Joe, "You walked Bataan too?"

"No way," he spits. "Nobody gonna tell me to surrender. I'm not in my own country? I head for the mountains, join the guerrillas. Fight with Juan Pajota."

"Who?" asks Macario.

"Pajota. Captain of the Philippine Guerrillas. If you're on the right side"—Joe looks at Macario significantly—"guerrilla's not a dirty word." Joe orders more beers. "Did you see that movie? The one with John Wayne?"

Macario thinks about it.

"O.K., so you see Anthony Quinn. That's Pajota. True story."

"Who's John Wayne?"

"Hell if I know. He's John Wayne. What's a war movie without him?"

"They make another movie. Same title. *Bataan.* This time with Robert Taylor."

"Oh yeah, I remember, and that Cuban guy married to I Love Lucy."

"Desi Arnez? He plays a Pilipino?"

"No, this time they got real Pinoys."

"Maybe you know the guy? Alex Havier?"

"He plays Pajota?"

"No. He strips down to his Moro origins, puts on war paint, and runs through enemy territory to find MacArthur."

"Does he find MacArthur?"

"Are you kidding? By that time, the General has left." Joe looks at Macario. "Didn't they teach you that shit in school?" Joe stands up to attention and raises his glass. "The General's parting words to the Pilipinos."

I motion to Macario, and we all stand and toast in unison. "I SHALL RETURN!"

The stripper looks our way, tosses Macario her g-string.

Joe continues, "Did they teach you how we lost Bataan?"

Macario shakes his head.

"There was no food. No new rations. American forces are sick and starving while the Japs take Corrigedor and the General runs. And this guy"—Joe points to me—"he's got to march to his death."

"Macario," I say, "it's like this. You marching four guys in a row for four days. One of the four days, one guy in your row, he's not gonna make it."

"Worse," says Joe. "If it's Pinoys, three guys don't make it." He points at me. "Felix's the only one. Other than the shit in his pants and the worms up his ass, he don't get a bullet in his ear, a bayonet to his chest, or his head chopped off. Don't drop dead from malaria or beriberi or dysentery or dehydration. Don't get executed on the spot."

Macario stares into his glass like blood is collecting there.

"So, tell him what happened," Joe nudges me. "So he don't think you're just lucky."

"I'm just lucky," I say.

We order more beers. Another stripper appears.

"Tell him," Joe says again.

"I roll over into a ditch."

"Heat exhaustion."

"They don't see me."

"Otherwise, he was killed dead."

"Left for dead, anyway. Next to other stinking bodies. Nighttime, I crawl away."

"He gets rescued by a beautiful Pinay."

Macario raises his eyebrows.

I say, "It's true."

"Then what?"

"I get rescued. Then I put on my Pinoy disguise."

"You join the guerrillas too?"

"No, I go to Manila and work as a cook."

"Hey," Joe says, "you never told me this. First time I'm hearing it."

"Joe," I say, "you remember Fely? She's a dancer. My beautiful Pinay. Runs Club Tsubaki in Manila with Clara Fuentes." I look around at the Wagon. Beats this joint by twenty times.

"I just heard about her. Why would I go there? Place was crawling with Japs. Whole officer club of them."

"I'm working for Tsubaki in those days, replicating the taste of Nippon."

"Fucking traitor."

"You don't know. Fely and Clare, doing Mata Hari's work."

"Spies?"

I nod, watch some sailor pushing a bill into the stripper's cleavage. "Making pillow talk with the Japanese clientele."

Macario looks skeptical. "Meanwhile, you're slicing sashimi and frying tempura?"

"How did you know? Keeping the sake warm." We all toast again before I continue my story. "Message comes through the kitchen. We're cooking our network from there. How else you think Pajota gets the word? We know who's coming through, when they ship out, where they go."

Joe is nodding. "Now I remember. Madam Tsubaki, aka Clare, got caught smuggling goods into Cabanatuan."

"What's that?" Macario wants to know.

"POW camp," says Joe. "I helped to liberate their American asses. End of the war, maybe only five hundred of them left alive. We put their emaciated bodies on carabao carts."

"Joe's a hero," I say.

"I'm no hero. Threw a couple of grenades. Stopped some Japs in their tanks before they stopped me. Stupid bastards."

By now we're all pretty drunk. I get up and hand a dollar to the next stripper.

Joe says, "Pajota, now he was a hero. Held the bridge and killed everything in sight." He nods sadly. "Heard he died a few weeks ago. Died trying to get his citizenship."

"You fight for America. You get to be American. That's your ticket. You get on the citizen ship."

"Every race got to sacrifice some folks to get on the ship."

"Toss them overboard."

"Let them rot in the hold."

"Got to be one thousand of us to one of them."

"With odds like that, how can you lose?"

"You know in the movie what Pajota says?"

"It's not really Pajota."

"What difference does it make?"

"What's he say?"

"He says, 'It don't matter where a guy dies, as long as he dies for freedom.'"

"You believe that?"

"Of course I believe that." Joe looks hurt. "What else is there to believe?"

Macario and I get up to leave, and Joe waves us on.

Macario says, "Ben says Joe's a liability."

"What do you say?"

"I don't know."

"You know that's Joe's girl."

Macario looks confused.

"You don't see any strippers tonight?"

He shakes his head. All he sees is Bataan, dying POWs, war, blood in his cloudy cup.

"Her." I gesture back at the Paddy Wagon. "The last one." I swivel my hips to remind him. "Yeah, he takes care of her. Has a room on the first floor. How old is she? Fifty? Sixty? Maybe oldest stripper on the block. She has been, but he has been, too."

"Has been where?"

I pull Macario over. He's stumbling up the stairs. "Has been. Over there. You don't know? I got to explain?"

How many years Joe's running the I-Hotel? Maybe not forever, and nobody knows how he starts. Gets the manager's room with his private bath and all the keys, decides if there's room for you at the inn, collects your money. For some, there's always a room. For others, don't bother. For Joe, it's about loyalty and protection. You in his brotherhood, you stay there. Sometimes I think, who else could do this job but Joe? Think about the tramps and lowlifes coming through. Pimps and hustlers. Addicts and ex-cons. Joe might give you a slim chance, but he wants it respectable and quiet. He's keeping the rooms for his brothers. Nobody breaks Joe's rules.

How many times I see Joe arriving at somebody's door with his baseball bat. Guy might be naked. He's got to run out the hotel or take his medicine. How many rules Joe's got to break to keep this kind of peace?

Over the years, Joe's rubbing shoulders with the guys who rise to the top. In case you forget, city's a port. Tough guys rise from the dock to do the work of the people. Longshoremen with connections up and down the coast, up to organizing us Alaskeros. An injury to one is an injury to all. And just in case, he coaches boxing to every new generation. So when the I-Hotel gets threatened, he gets the ear of the mayor himself, old family friend. Probably taught this kid his jabs and hooks. Don't let the mayor forget where he comes from.

"O.K.," I tell Macario, "Joe's got his abilities."

I remind Abra. "Joe stands up for you. Gathers the men and tells them how to treat you young women. Noli me tangere."

"Right," says Abra. "He was standing there with his baseball bat and yelling."

"He says to us, what if these young ladies are your daughters? How do you feel?"

"He said, if he found out that anybody touched us, he was going to bash his head in."

"Manner of speaking."

"He hates the students."

"He lets them rent their storefronts."

"That's not his decision anymore. The hotel is run by the tenants. You're an association. He's not the boss."

"Who's gonna tell him?"

One day, Abra tells him. She's the treasurer, doing the books. She says to Joe, "You can't take money out of this fund without consulting with the tenants. It's their money. They made the decision to put it aside. Don't you remember? It's in the minutes."

"Minutes? What I got to run a hotel on minutes? I got hours and days and weeks. Every day we get closer to getting evicted."

"What did you do with this money?"

"Repairs. Broken window. Rat control. Don't you know?"

"Where are the receipts?"

"Are you telling me how to run my hotel?"

"It's not your hotel, Joe. You get a salary, and that's it. You can't mix up the money."

"What do you mean, it's not my hotel?"

"O.K., it's yours, but the money's separate."

"Who are you to say?

"I'm the treasurer."

"Oh yeah?" He grabs the books from Abra and rips them up. "Get out of my office." By now Joe's reaching for his baseball bat.

By the time I get there, Joe's got his batter's stance.

Abra stands him off. "Joe, you come and get me. Come and get me."

I see Abra's hand ready to pull abracadabra.

"Hit me, Joe," she snarls. "I'm gonna put you through that wall."

Shit, I think, *it could happen.* "Joe!" I yell from behind him and grab his neck, pull him back.

He struggles forward, but I yank to choke him good. By now, I got some assistance. How many old guys piling on Joe to hold him down? If you multiply our years, it takes maybe four hundred years of us to contain the bastard, save Abra, our damsel in distress. Decrepit bunch of old fogeys piled up like cannon fodder. What's more humiliating?

"Get the fuck off me!" Joe's yelling.

Now we're on top and down—who can move?

"Wait, I'm stuck."

Moaning and groaning. Huffing and puffing. How much exertion can an old heart take?

Abra's standing there, looking disgusted. I'm underneath, my ear pressed to the linoleum. I can hear her stomp away.

After that, I know Joe has got to go. We let Joe slip out to run some errand, then same old crew lines up at the door, waiting.

"It's like this," I say to Macario. "When you have the experience of starving, really starving, your gut knotted into a hard fist, you feed yourself first. If you got it, you hide your food. You steal from anyone who has it. Guy dies, you strip him clean. You eat anything that moves. Grubs, bugs, lizards, rats. Guys like me and Joe, survive the thirties, then Bataan, how you gonna trust us?"

"That's not an excuse for Joe stealing the hotel money."

"Macario, how much we need to buy back the hotel? One million? How we gonna save that much? What did Joe steal? It's peanuts."

"That was your money, too."

"You ever eat rat?"

"We catch a lot of them in this hotel."

"So maybe you did."

"Felix." Macario's looking worried.

"I got this recipe from a cook at Cabanatuan."

"Hey." Pete runs in from the street. "Joe's on his way back."

Joe steps up and gets his surprise. Same old fogeys—O.K.: *retired warriors*. Two rows of us standing there at the door, looking like we mean business. Someone's got Joe's baseball bat. Another's got his suitcase ready. Hands it to Joe. "Sorry, Joe, we can't let you back in. You got to go."

"Joe, you come in, you got to deal with me."

"Joe, I bust your face."

"Joe, time's up."

He points his crooked nose in my direction. "Fucking traitors."

I watch Joe walk away with his suitcase, head down Kearny, pass the Paddy Wagon, and cross Jackson. I know what's in the suitcase besides some clothing: boxing gloves, boxing medals, WWII bronze star, old photograph of young, buff, boxing Joe, another of his infantry, copy of the Rescission Act of 1946, pinup of Miss July 1952, bottle of Johnny Walker Red, canned corned beef, can of Spam, can of beans, can of tuna, can of sardines, can opener.

6: Ng Ka Py

I am reading the book *America Is in the Heart,* by Carlos Bulosan. My friend Wen gives it to me to read. "You haven't read this book?" He can't believe it. If anybody knows books, gotta be Wen. Li Po–poet type teaching at SF State. Says Bulosan double features with *Grapes of Wrath.* For triple feature, try *Native Son.* Well, I say, Carlos is my friend, but maybe you never get around to reading your friend's book. What are friends for? Give you the digested version to make life easy. But you read Carlos's life, and you think: your life is bad? Comes nothing close. Every page, Carlos is suffering; starving; broken by work; beat up; pounded; stabbed; near dying, escaping; getting TB; cheated; losing his country, his friends, his family, his innocence; nearly naked; losing his dream. O.K., nothing we Pinoys don't know, but maybe our hell all rolled into one heart.

Wen asks, "So what do you think?" Maybe you remember, Wen collaborates with me on a cookbook. Everything authentic. His poems and brushwork illustrations. My recipes.

"It's an inspiration," I say. "Now, we gonna call our book: *America Is in the Stomach.*"

Jack's my official ghostwriter. He says, "Like hell we are."

"Try this," I say. "Ng ka py. Recommended for poets. Helps you write." It's a black liquor I got corked in an old Manischewitz bottle. I pour him a shot. "Also medicinal."

"Shiiiiiiiit!" Jack coughs. "What's that?"

"My own recipe. Twenty secret herbs."

"Mostly absinthe," says Wen.

"Fuck. Is that legal?" asks Jack.

I say, "When I'm working in Salinas, I'm making it for John Steinbeck all the time."

"More bullshit. I don't believe it."

"Look how much John writes. And figure how many centuries of Chinese poetry." I pour some for Wen.

"That's right," says Wen, lifting his cup. "Yuan Hung-tao is said to have drunk this with some local fish, writing thereafter a poem about it."

"How about it?" I ask. "I'm divulging the twenty secret herbs, plus the local fish."

Macario drives over the Golden Gate to Wen's big house on the Marin side to pick me up. "O.K. Felix, ready to head back to our side of the world?"

I take one look at Macario's car and say, "Hey where'd you get this limousine?"

"What are you talking about?"

"This car. You pick it up special to make an impression for me?"

"You don't recognize my car?"

I'm looking closer. "No shit!" It's the same Chevy wagon, newly painted black, all the dings and dents pushed out and sanded over, no more rust spots. The whole thing is all buffed up and polished. I walk around to get the big picture. Busted headlights all replaced. New side mirrors. Cracked windshield replaced. Broken passenger-side handle fixed. Bumpers seem new too. Nice chrome finish. And matching hubcaps. Heck, new set of tires. I whistle. "What's happening here?" I puzzle. "You been dipping into the hotel treasury too?"

Macario opens the door and says, "Just get in, Felix."

Inside, how can you not notice? Upholstery all renovated. Front seats are black leather. Backseat's not leather and a different color, red, but near new too. Plus fancy red steering wheel, new rearview mirror, new carpets, new radio system. "You been busy," I say.

"Don't go spreading rumors," says Macario. "In fact, don't say anything at all. Not a word, you understand?"

I keep looking around me. "Hey, look at this. Even got new ashtrays." Funny, nothing inside is matching exactly. "How come they each a different color?"

Macario is looking out his new mirrors, trying to catch the ramps to the Golden Gate. "Felix, promise you'll keep quiet?"

"Depends."

"Baby Wah Ching," he says.

"I notice. Lately they're hanging around. You got your personal baby bodyguards. Now you're big time."

Macario groans. "I just did them some favors."

"I remember. You go down to juvie and get a couple of them out."

"Should have left them."

"So now they repay you the favor."

"I never asked them for anything in return." Macario's fuming. "Now, look at my car."

I look over, and he could maybe cry. Now it explains everything. One day you wake up and every car down Kearny bashed in. Parts probably missing here and there. What about the guy who steps out, sees his car sitting on axles? All four tires, gone. I nod, "Looks like a gangster car. What they call him? Bugs Malone."

"He never had a Chevy station wagon."

"Probably shiny black undertaker job. Whatchu you call it?" I'm thinking. "Dead Giveaway."

"Yeah, well, shoot me now, Felix."

I think maybe he's right. Macario's wagon's got about a hundred new pieces liberated from the system. Baby Wah Ching don't have an idea about brand names. I say, "I don't know much about automobiles, but can you put Ford parts into Chevys? Goes to show, you can weld anything to anything."

"Goddamn. I've got to get rid of this thing now."

"Maybe we park it here on the Golden Gate and walk away."

"They'll be looking over the bridge for the suicide."

"You kidding? I said walk away."

Macario looks at me, and I slap my knees and just about die laughing.

"Shut up, Felix. Look who's following us."

I shoot a look into one of the mirrors. Now I see one side is square style; other side is round. This is some kind of Chinatown art project. I see the cops framed in the square mirror. "We just look normal."

"Like hell we do."

Cop car speeds around us, and Macario relaxes. After that, we drive around streets I never seen, then park the car. "Where are we?" I ask.

"Daly City."

"Now what?"

"We take a bus to the hotel."

"This is farther than Marin."

Macario and I take public transportation back to the hotel. I think out loud to Macario. "Bus is like the hotel. For the people."

Macario nods. "Sorry about the car, Felix."

I shrug. "Forget it." I continue my thinking. "You know this eminent domain? Got sides to it."

"Yeah," Macario agrees.

"City can use the power to take away anything for the public good, but who can say what is the public good? More like political good."

"Public good in our case would be to house the poor and elderly after working all their lives."

"Makes sense to me."

"The city has to be made responsible for public housing." Macario's pounding on his knee, practicing his speech. "They can use eminent domain to obtain our property, but they've got to use it for low-cost housing for the people. That's what we're trying to argue."

"That Songkhram character's never gonna sell," I say. "His Chinatown lawyers acting like they know what's best for the public good of Chinatown. Maybe he's turning Kearny Street into a tourist attraction." I shake my head.

Maybe we shoulda seen it coming. The rich got a problem, they can always sell it to another rich guy who needs that problem to solve another problem. Years down the line, you gonna look at the hindsight and think yeah, now you see the whole picture. But the whole picture is always there. Somebody shoulda seen it when Simon Solomon dumped the I-Hotel on Songkhram. I send Macario out to study the situation. He comes back and says, "Student protest in Bangkok. Staged a revolution. Something like two hundred thousand came out. Military killed and wounded hundreds of them. So now Songkhram is looking to escape. Save his ass by sinking his assets here." What else did he buy besides San Francisco real estate? He buys a winery in Napa County. Whiskey magnet, my ass.

I uncork my ng ka py right there in the bus and offer Macario a taste.

"Not that stuff." Macario waves it away.

"My own brew," I say. "Medicinal tea."

He smells the bottle and shakes his head. "Is this the stuff you're thinking could poison Songkhram?"

"Why not?" I turn the bottle and just moisten my lips. "But we don't know who he is. How come you don't challenge him to a fight? Come out in the open and fight man to man. You send the message." I push Macario with my bottle. "Felix Allos versus Samut Songkhram in the ring for ten rounds. I beat his ass."

I know Macario goes to hide his stolen-parts car in Daly City. Must be some kind of a joke. Respectable Pinoys all living in Daly City these days. Manilatown's thing of the past. Nothing but old codgers like me living off social security. What do Daly City Pinoys care about us? They're like the baby Wah Ching, just arrived from the old country and thinking their rules apply. Baby Wah Ching working for the old tongs; Daly City Pinoys taking sides with the dictator Marcos.

This time, Macario and Abra in the kitchen. Got the pot of rice steaming on low. Then chopping the onions, peeling the garlic, measuring the soy sauce and the vinegar, dumping in the chicken parts. Final touches, bay leaf and paprika. I sniff the air above the pot and nod. "O.K."

"I found my dish," Macario says.

Maybe Macario's looking worried, but Abra's just looking hungry. "He said you said this works every time."

"Could be." I point to my head and nod, then ask, "Whatchu working out?"

"Politics."

"Nothing new."

By now, Macario's dishing out the rice. "Support groups're accusing us of being sellouts."

I'm imbibing the sweet aroma of rice, but I say, "What support group?" I think must be three hundred support groups out there. Friends of the I-Hotel. Workers Committee to Support the I-Hotel. Committee to Struggle with the I-Hotel. I-Hotel Ping Yuen Tenants Committee. Chinese Affirmative Action I-Hotel Committee. U.S. Postal Workers I-Hotel Support Committee. People's Church I-Hotel Support Committee. Low-cost Housing Tenants Association. I-Hotel Business Tenants Support Committee. Garment Workers I-Hotel Support Committee. Poets for the I-Hotel.

"You know which ones," says Abra. "The Maoist ones."

"You aren't Maoist?"

"Yeah, well."

I ask, "How come sellouts?"

Abra takes my plate and gives me a good ladle of adobo. "For working with the system and trying to get the city to use eminent domain to buy us out."

"Who else got the money?"

"They come to meetings and say that we got to liberate the hotel from the system."

"Easy to say." I shrug and dig in.

"What's screwing us up is this buy-back plan."

"We can never buy back the hotel from the city after it takes it away from Enchanted Seas. Not even for half of what they pay them off. It's never going to be realistic."

"Whose idea this buy-back?"

"Maybe Joe's. His private deal with the mayor."

"Joe's not here anymore."

I close my eyes, savor the flavors. "I think Joe had an idea. He knows there's no money, but there's money somewhere. Somewhere, there's always money. That's what he's thinking. Hey," I say, "this not bad."

"Thanks, Felix."

Everybody gets quiet eating. Nothing but the sound of eating. Forks pushing around the food, rearranging the chicken and sauce on the rice, scooping it up into satisfied mouths.

Finally I say, "Joe might be thinking like this. Eminent domain, buy-back, realistically, it can never happen. Something gets proposed, goes to court, court agrees, knocks it down, you get an appeal, goes back to the city, win, lose, buying time—not buy back, just buying time."

"You mean, we're just using stalling tactics."

"You never know. We could win."

"What kind of line is stalling tactics?"

"Line?"

"It's like this, Felix, a line is . . ." Macario is looking for words.

I cut in, "You think I don't know what you're doing? I don't know what your line is? How's your party line gonna help me? You get a party, but what do I get?"

Abra and Macario poking around the bones on their plates.

"Felix is right," Abra says. "Every group is using the hotel to test their line."

I know the problem. How many old tenants we got left? Used to be fifty. Now, maybe thirty. Every support group attached to one or two tenants, hauling him around from rally to rally like the real thing. I don't say nothing because what's an old guy got besides this kind of family, this kind of attention? What does he know about party lines? But he is not stupid. Didn't survive all these years without learning something.

"Besides," Macario says, "what about our own party? Abra, it's just you and me at the hotel. Central committee has pretty much said, 'You're on your own.'"

Abra mutters, "Abandoned."

Kids look tired. When do they sleep? Every day running around trying to hold off the eviction. Meetings every night. Strategy sessions. Going to court. Protesting every place. City Hall. Redevelopment. KMT headquarters. Harassing Songkhram's lawyers. Signing petitions. Posting flyers. Making speeches. Speech at Glide Memorial. Speech at college rally. Speech at garment workers' union. Meeting with supervisors. Meeting with the mayor. Meeting with Human Rights. Meeting with HUD. Arguing with every support group. Setting up the phone tree. Sending spies out to keep tabs on the police. Doing surveillance, make sure no one tries to burn down the building again. Then, maybe taking Frankie to emergency; got an asthma attack. Getting Wahat some heart medicine. Getting Benny his social security papers. Going over to the police station to pick up Lee, who gets drunk and sleeps in the street again.

I think I know the situation. "In the context of the larger struggle," they call it. Bigger battles to fight. Save those nurses from jail. Address the oppression of the Pilipino professional class. Oppose the Marcos dictatorship. Rally the exiled for democracy. What's the I-Hotel? Just thirty old men.

Abra looks at my empty plate. "Want seconds?"

I hand her my plate. "This reminds me of adobo I eat in the war."

"Is that good or bad?"

"The best. My beautiful Pinay saves my life with this same adobo. Just the sauce and a little rice." I demonstrate. "Spoon at a time."

"Did you tell Abra that story?" asks Macario. "About how you survived Bataan?"

"I escape to the mountains, join Luis Taruc and the Hukbalahap."

Macario looks confused. "That's not the story you told Joe and me. What happened to Fely, the Mata Hari dancer?"

Abra looks shocked. "You fought with Taruc and the Huks?"

"What's so surprising?"

"You never told me you fought with the Communists. What've you been hiding from me?"

"Guerrilla force just like Mao fighting the Japanese." I shrug at Abra and Macario. "That's the lesson."

"What?"

"United front. Philippine Scouts, Philippine Guerrillas, Huks, Chinese, Americans, USAFFE. Could be Nationalists. Could be Socialists. Could be Communists. Could be Imperialists. We drive out the Fascists together."

Macario's looking like the adobo's doing the trick. He's clearing the table, washing the dishes. Later, I'm hearing him at a meeting. He's calling for a united front. The support groups ratify a united front agreement. *Agreed: I-Hotel struggle represents the needs of a working-class minority over private property. Agreed: Public officials must be held liable for human needs over capitalist needs. Agreed: Actions against eviction must be nonviolent to protect elderly tenants.*

Abra's splitting a bottle of beer with me. "Why didn't you tell me you fought with the Huks?"

"Not much to tell. I get rescued by them. Run away into the mountains. Hey." I look at Abra. "You got me to remember guerrero woman just like you.

"Did Joe know about this?" asks Macario.

"Why does he need to know? By the end of the war, Huks and Philippine Guerrillas fighting each other. Maybe if I don't leave, I kill Joe. Win the war. Lose the country."

"What about the beautiful Pinay?"

"I'm too late." That's all I can say. What is there to say? I'm holding her in my arms. Her blood doesn't stop. Her heart stops.

It's a Wednesday night. August 3, 1977. Abra and I are looking out my window. "How many down there you figure?"

"Back in January for that protest, the newspapers said five thousand."

"Looks like the same." Every second I see more people coming to the street, both sides. "Who's not down there?" I say. "Even gay rights. You bringing gay rights?"

"Actually," says Abra, "that was Wahat. He went to the Exotic Erotic Ball in his Igorot loincloth."

"I guess he makes a big impression."

"He also brought in the Indians."

"Looks like the whole city coming to save the hotel."

"I hope so."

The chanting never stops. It's coming out of loudspeakers everywhere. The whole place is wired for sound.

THE PEOPLE UNITED CAN NEVER BE DEFEATED.
THE PEOPLE UNITED CAN NEVER BE DEFEATED.
STOP THE EVICTION! WE WON'T MOVE!
STOP THE EVICTION! WE WON'T MOVE!
WE WON'T MOVE!
WE WON'T MOVE!
WE WON'T MOVE!

I'm feeling the excitement. They're telephoning and radioing the whole city. People pouring in to Manilatown. Put their bodies up against the I-Hotel.

Still, we got to anticipate the whole night and maybe how many days? I get prepared with supplies for three days. It's August, so I got a deal in Chinatown: boxes of summer cantaloupe shipped out of the Imperial Valley. Abra and me sitting in my room, slicing the melon with the sweet orange meat.

"You sure they're coming?"

"We got word they're organizing their posse. Riot gear and billy club units. Calvary too."

"Coming with horses?"

"Yeah."

Finally, we hear the sirens. Sirens coming from every side of the city, getting louder every minute. The fire is going to be here.

On the street, thirteen rows of human bodies linked around the hotel.

WE WON'T MOVE!
WE WON'T MOVE!
WE WON'T MOVE!
WE WON'T MO
WE WON'T
WE WO
WE
W

From above, we can see police on horseback swinging clubs like machetes. Dark horse bodies press into the people. Press and lunge. We hear the crowd groan and resist. Every cry travels up to us. Abra shuts her eyes.

KEEP CALM!
KEEP CALM!

Then screaming. Yelling.

What are you doing? We're not armed!
Help this woman! Help her up!
Stay calm!
Don't resist the police. We are nonviolent. Remember, we are nonviolent!
Hold your places!
Stand firm!
We need a doctor here! Get this person some help! He's bleeding!

Outside my door, I know the corridor is filled with the second contingent. Wet towel's tucked under the door to stop the teargas. My mattress is outside, blocking the landing. Folks packed in like sitting sardines, arms locked and waiting. Police's got to drag them out one by one. Then finally, there's us. The last thirty tenants, each one sitting in our rooms, waiting. That's the plan.

What am I thinking? That they never get this far. That this time, like the other times, they give up and go away. Drive their cars with lights and guns and clubs away. Trot their horses back to Golden Gate Park. Go home to their families and children. Go home to TV and dinner. Let me stay here and live the few more years I got to live.

How can so many people fail?

Now I hear how the sirens have stopped right in front of the I-Hotel. Right in front of my room. It's the same fire truck saved our pig under the Embarcadero. It's the same goddamn firemen ate that same pig. I think, no fire here today.

I say to Abra, "They gonna shoot us with water."

Next moment, we see the fire ladder extend, lands at the second floor corridor window. That's their plan. Toughest guys, Samoans included, resisting at the front door look up. They're bypassed by a ladder. Firemen and police scale it like it's a siege. Coming up to our floor in heavy boots, protective gear, goggles, with clubs and axes. Looking like monsters.

We hear the commotion outside. Smashing glass, hatchets going through doors, breaking locks.

All right. Everyone out! Get up, get going! Time's up.

Bodies dragged away, bounced downstairs.

Abra's sitting on my bed, and for first time I see her crying.

"I'm sorry, Felix. I failed you."

"Whatchu talking?" I touch her hands folded tight in her lap. "You cannot fail. You can only live your life. You gonna see when you're my age."

They're at my door. Knocking even.

I take a last swig of ng ka py, wipe my mouth, and say like I'm stupid, "Who is it?"

"Sheriff's department. It's time to leave."

"Leave?"

"Yes, that's right. Open up right now."

Abra wipes her eyes and pulls open the door. Her body is back to being fierce. Abracadabra in her back pocket. She says, "You keep your hands off this gentleman. We will leave quietly. But keep your hands off." She pulls me up from the bed, holds on to my arm. We walk out together.

I don't tell Abra the rest about not failing. It's gonna be about remembering. I remember my union brothers. Same year, Larry Itliong dies, and Philip Vera Cruz—he quits the United Farm Workers. I figure it out later when I see a picture of Cesar Chavez, honored guest of the Philippine nation, on an elephant with Marcos. We get betrayed by saints and gods. Before that, maybe I could return to Agbayani. Now, I cannot.

We walk slowly down the old corridor. Mattresses and waste and broken pieces of the hotel everywhere. We go by Frankie's room, and I stop to look in. I see Frankie's two suitcases torn open, the letters and postcards thrown up and scattered everywhere, love letters flying out the broken window.

I'm getting confused. Something inside my gut is grabbing me. I hold on to Abra now. I think I see Pio's ghost back in the hotel again. He's walking out slowly right there in front of me. Maybe he's got his banjo. I think we send Pio away for good, but now I see even ghosts getting evicted.

By the time we leave the hotel, maybe it's dawn. Foggy light competing with the neon. My gut is killing me. Abra whispers, "Felix, Felix."

I bend over at the gutter, and everything inside me pours out. I cannot stop it. I heave and weep. I know everything is leaving my body: noodles in gelatin broth, Dongpo pork for Wen, lemongrass coconut stew with chili, Sixto's fertility roots, Phil's sweet black coffee, Johnny Bulonglong's fried fish in soup, Cesar's thin vegetable broth with handmade bread, Delano grapes, Alaskan salmon and salmon caviar, halo-halo for Lucy, Hiro's natto chili Spam on rice, lechon baboy and kalua poaa for Pio, Imelda's chocolate cheesecake for Abra and the twins, Joe's cans of Spam and corned beef, Macario's chicken adobo, ng ka py and twenty herbs, local fish, and empty, empty soup. Abra hangs on to me like she's holding on to a waterfall. Pretty soon I'm only spitting blood and tears. Abra's holding on to this empty sack. Keeps whispering, "Felix, Felix." My guts running in a river down Kearny to Jackson.

I don't tell Abra that maybe in the end, you can't remember nothing, and nobody else remembers nothing. But goddamn, we never give up. All we ever do is survive. I see through my bloody snot the last of my brothers walking away down dirty streets, trash spinning with love letters, looking up at the old hotel and looking away for the last time, Frankie still in his pinstriped McIntosh, walking away with Pio, maybe hang out over at Portsmouth, then moving on, circumnavigating. And that's the end. Like Pio's ashes. Ghosts. Only I never think it can hurt like this.

1975: Internationale Hotel

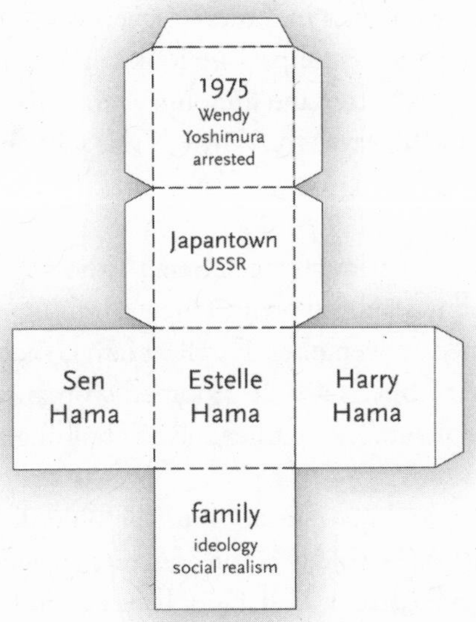

1: Arthur Hama—Liberty

This year, 1974, November marks an historic summit in Vladivostok. Students of the Cold War will recognize that it is only two years since the signing of the Anti-Ballistic Missile Treaty in Moscow, and that negotiations for the SALT II or Strategic Arms Limitation Talks also continue. Two leaders of the great superpowers, the general secretary of the Union of Soviet Socialist Republics, Leonid Brezhnev, and the American president of the United States, Gerald Ford, meet to agree to limit the nuclear arsenals of their respective countries. It is agreed that each side will have no more than 2,400 strategic launchers and strategic bombers, and that only 1,320 of these may have multiple warheads. They also reach an accord to prohibit any underground testing of nuclear weapons exceeding 150 kilotons and to share data from any future testing. These agreements are in the continuing international spirit of détente and the efforts to dismantle the nuclear arsenals that support what would be the ultimate catastrophe of Mutually Assured Destruction.

Far from Vladivostok, in what could be a sister city, San Francisco, a daughter of Russian émigrés in America peels open a tissue-thin envelope pasted with Japanese stamps. She looks up from the precise handwriting in the enclosed letter and announces to her son, "Art is dead."

"Yeah, God, but art? Never thought I'd hear you say that."

"No, I mean your father, Arthur. He's died."

Sen Hama carries the heavy wheelchair to the top of the stairs. His brother, Harry, follows behind on crutches, climbing each step with jutting but determined movements. Estelle Hama, their mother, waits at the top of the stairs. She is a well-groomed woman whose stark white hair radiates in a halo around her head. She's holding a small bouquet of homegrown roses.

Reaching behind and majestically into the blue sky and this extraordinarily clear San Francisco day is the concrete structure of Coit Tower, rising 210 feet over Telegraph Hill. Coit Tower is built to honor the firemen who saved the City of San Francisco from the fires after the Great Earthquake of 1906. Designed in 1933 in the style of art deco, the Works Project Administration invites twenty-six artists to paint the interior frescoes. Defaced and defamed in the 1950s, the tower is closed to the public for seventeen years. A caretaker opens the tower to the Hama family for a private viewing.

Estelle watches her sons struggle with their separate burdens, but she does not move to help. Her eyes are rendered with a glow of pride and resolve. Sen arrives at the top and waits with the wheelchair at his mother's side. When Harry finally huffs awkwardly to the top, Sen taunts his brother with a grin, "I beat you again."

Harry replies, handing his brother the crutches, "You had a head start." He turns his spindly legs and plops into the leather sling of the wheelchair. "One of these days, they'll put a ramp up, and I'll get a motorized chair, and then I'll beat your ass." He twists a glance back at Sen.

Sen cuffs him lightly over the ear and pushes the chair forward. "Harry, you're so full of shit."

Estelle walks resolutely ahead, followed by her sons, Sen pushing Harry in his wheelchair. They turn into the circular confines of the tower's first floor, their eyes adjusting to the somber light, slowly following the industry of the American people of San Francisco, California. The morning light, cast in filtered angles through narrow, recessed windows, illuminates frescoed images of powerful working people. The people working in factories, on farmlands, on railroads, and in shipyards. Hardworking people building America. Their strong muscular bodies and their faces, every one set with grim determination, pose for eternity in vivid earth colors across the curving corridor.

Estelle pauses before a library scene, ascending tiers of men reading the current headlines of artistic disputes and domestic turmoil. A man in the foreground reaches for a copy of Karl Marx's *Das Kapital.* "Bernard Zakheim," Estelle announces the name of the artist.

"Must have gotten in trouble for that." Harry points at Marx from his chair.

"Well, at least they didn't paint over it," says Sen.

Estelle remembers, "Someone painted a hammer and sickle. Maybe on one of the beams." She looks up. "I think they had to remove that, unless you spot it somewhere. Oh," she remembers, "someone wrote, *Workers of the World Unite.* Now that was definitely expunged."

Estelle moves across the corridor to the murals on the opposite wall. "I assisted on this mural here. Punched and set up the tracing. Prepped the paint. Kept the sponges wet, the brushes ready. Another guy prepped all the plaster. It had to be done in swatches. Like this area. See the gun? The holdup? The artist has to work fast on fresh plaster, and you can't make any mistakes. He's got to finish an area by the end of the day. That's why it's called *fresco,* for *fresh.* I was a student of Victor Arnautoff, who painted this city scene. This is Arnautoff himself here." She points to the artist's self-portrait next to the newspaper stand with the *Daily Worker.*

Sen pulls Harry in his chair back to get the big picture, then wheels him forward to see the details.

Estelle continues, "This is the street scene outside the Monkey Building where Art and I lived. All the artists lived there. Diego Rivera lived there while he painted the art school mural and the Stock Exchange. Your father and most of these other artists here all worked with Diego. Some even went down to Mexico. That's how they got their commissions in this tower."

"Monkey Building?" Harry laughs.

Estelle's memory wanders back. "Art shared a studio there with a Chinese painter. I forget his name. I think it was Lin. Lin had just come back from Paris, definitely a fellow traveler, someone who knew people like Chou En-lai."

"What year is this?" asks Sen.

"The Depression—1933?" she asks herself, then asserts, "1934."

The young men nod, but they have no real idea about this time period before they were born and when Arthur Hama worked as a painter and a political organizer for the Communist Party and later as a longshoreman.

Estelle reaches back. "I met Art in New York at the John Reed Club. They had just formed. He was a protégé of the artist Kuniyoshi. I knew Kuniyoshi. Well, everyone knew Yasuo in those days. They were friends: Isamu Noguchi, Hideo Noda, and Eitaro Ishigaki. When Art left for San Francisco, I followed him, but I didn't want him to think I was following him. My excuse was I was studying with Arnautoff. But when he turned up in jail on a vag charge, I was there with the bail money."

"*Vag*?" asks Harry.

"Vagrancy. In those days, they used it as an excuse to arrest protestors."

"Guess nothing's changed."

Estelle continues, "When Art wasn't painting, he was working for a Japanese newspaper, the *Rodo Shimbun.*"

"Communist?"

"Yes, of course. The paper supported the longshoremen and the strike. Look over here." Estelle searches around for another corner, then points to a wall of stalwartly defiant marching men. "There it is, the 1934 General Strike. By July, all the unions up and down the coast joined the longshoremen. Everything closed down. It was going on right as these murals were being painted. Just as we were finishing, everything heated up. I was running between the ILD offices and the Hall of Justice with copies of the Bill of Rights and, imagine this," she pauses in her own amazement, "thousands of dollars of bail money in my purse."

"ILD?"

"Labor Defense. We collected funds, posted bail, went to court, defended prisoners. In those days, every day I pulled folks out of jail. They'll always try to demoralize a movement by framing and arresting people. So you've got to create a positive defense to keep up the momentum."

Estelle steps into the past and grabs Arthur Hama by the arm to keep him from falling. Blood encrusts his head, his left eye is swelled shut, and a purple bruise runs across the left side of his face. He turns a twisted look at Estelle and says, "So, it is you."

"Come on. We've got to get you to a doctor."

Arthur limps forward. "I still got one eye, and they didn't break my fingers."

She pulls her fingers through his. "Still got paint all over them."

"It's not blood?"

"What's the difference?"

Estelle continues to tell Arthur's story to her sons. "We called it Bloody Thursday. The ship owners hired scabs, and the police deputized vigilantes. They beat up and arrested everyone. Threw gas bombs and fired live ammunition. Someone dubbed the city 'San Fascisto.' Two workers were killed." Estelle is quiet for a moment, remembering one of the men killed, a fellow Communist whose body she is asked to identify. She continues, "The Red Squad targeted Art because the day before he'd cut down a cop twice his size to save a comrade, and got away."

"Jujitsu," smiles Harry, slashing the air with karate chops from his chair.

"But this time, they really beat him up. He was a bloody mess."

"How many guys you save with bail money?" Sen queries his mother.

"Oh, there were lots."

Estelle hears Arthur's parched voice again. "You know what the jailer said when he let me out?" He looks woozy, as if he will pass out.

"Hang on," she says. "I'm calling a taxi."

He grips her arm for a moment and manages to say, "Jailer said, 'Your Red Angel's come for you.' That you?"

Estelle stares hard into the mural, at the only black man represented in these frescos, standing solidly with fellow workers.

Sen nudges Estelle. "But out of all of these guys you bailed out, you married the Japanese guy?"

"We couldn't get married, you know that."

"Our father was a Japanese Bolshevik troublemaker consorting with a white woman."

Estelle smiles. "That's right. I'm a hakujin."

"A Communist with loose morals."

"My morals were never loose."

Harry sighs, and Sen rolls his eyes, but they follow her obediently from mural to mural. Estelle disappears outside momentarily with a glass cup procured from her purse. Sen watches her from the entrance pumping water from the brass fountain into the cup. She returns with the cup, moving through the anteroom before the elevator. Here she points out the map and the birds. "Otis Oldfield," she identifies the artist. "Both Art and Lin studied with him."

She heads through a door and up a stairwell. Sen parks Harry in the wheelchair before the stairs and follows her up. He turns back to Harry, asking, "You coming?"

Harry shrugs, grips the handles on the chair, then the wall and doorway and banister, and makes his slow, tortured way up the stairs. He follows the San Franciscans of the 1930s who are painted into the walls who also climb the stairwell with the cable cars.

Estelle pauses at the curved top of the stairs and points to a figure with black hair. "That's Art," she says. Then she turns and points to a figure of a woman with a golf club in the mural across. "And that's me."

"Mom's just like you, Harry," jokes Sen. "Full of stories."

Harry struggles to get within viewing range. He scrutinizes the faces. "Could be Mom before her hair turned white."

Estelle places the glass of water at the corner base of one mural and arranges her small bouquet of roses. It's a flurry of yellow, orange, and red flowers to match the earth tones of the mural above. "This is it."

Sen and Harry see the mural for the first time. "How come you never showed us this before?"

"The tower was closed so long, and . . ." Estelle is silent. She remembers that she writes to Arthur in Japan, asking if he didn't want to see his sons again. He writes back a short but very vague excuse: he's traveling. In anger, she tells everyone that Arthur has died, and by the time she tells her sons, almost as if in passing, she too believes the lie.

The family trio steps back, scanning the accomplishment of the mostly unknown artist who worked in the collectivity of this project. Only they know that the artist is a father and a husband. Their eyes move intently with the figures of the painting—golfing, hurdling, on horseback chasing a polo ball. At the ceiling, a large sun casts brilliance over the burnished red tint, zigzagging with the prance of horses, across the flesh of athletes, and drawn finally to the red skirt of the female golfer.

Sen thinks aloud, "Seems like the Communists are all downstairs."

"The theme up here was sports and family life," defends Estelle. "We don't just work, you know."

"Really?"

"How old was he when he painted this?"

"Maybe Harry's age. Twenty-five. I was only twenty."

They are quiet in concentration for a long time. They scan the figures and the brushstrokes for memory and for knowledge. They try to recapture the moment of the painter painting. He is a young, aspiring, and Estelle reminds them, starving Japanese artist in America, painting a scene for public works.

Arthur Hama looks over his shoulder from his scaffold and notices a young and very pretty Estelle watching him. She says, "You're missing jujitsu there."

"This is an American scene."

"You're American."

"Born here, bred there."

"How about it? Take me to the study group tonight? I need to brush up on my dialectical materialism."

"Can't. I got another meeting."

"What's that?"

"Japanese Workers' Association."

"How about tomorrow night?"

"Tomorrow's the Nisei Democratic Artists and Writers League."

"Are you playing hard to get?"

He turns back to his painting but changes the subject. "You're Russian, aren't you?"

"My parents were from Vladivostok."

"Do they know you're hanging out with an Oriental?"

"Hey, I could be part Chinese or something, coming from Vladivostok and all."

Art looks over at Estelle, pretends to size her up, but says, "My favorite writers are all Russian."

"Well, that's a start."

"Pushkin, Bakunin, Tolstoy, Dostoevsky, Kropotkin, Eroshenko."

"Eroshenko?"

"Never heard of Eroshenko? He was from Vladivostok, I'm sure."

Harry interrupts Estelle's memory. "What about the judo? Was he a blackbelt?" Harry's twisted elbow jerks with excitement.

Sen quips, "Harry, with your genes, maybe you'll be our next Bruce Lee."

Harry's fist jabs Sen in the stomach.

"Ouch."

"It's all about upper body strength," Harry insists.

"You fight like an insect," Sen complains. "I should know."

"Preying mantis-style," nods Harry.

Estelle ignores the banter and answers, "Art hung out with the Okinawans who were Communists and blackbelts. They taught him their moves. Oh, he could hold his own. He became a longshoreman, you know. Before the war, he was the only Japanese longshoreman around here. The Monday after Pearl Harbor, the FBI came and pulled him right off the docks."

"You bail him out again?"

"They had to let him go. He came out fuming. You think your brother Harry has a temper."

Sen shoots a look at Harry. Harry only looks innocuous and vulnerable.

Estelle continues, "Here, Art was a citizen, a Communist, antifascist, anti-imperialist Japan, but thrown in with the Japanese nationalists suspected of espionage. The day they released him, even before we got home, he made us stop to send a wire to Roosevelt to offer his services to destroy the Japanese imperialists."

"Didn't do much good."

"No. We got on those trains like everyone else."

"You didn't have to go."

Estelle doesn't reply, but Harry answers for her. "Mom didn't think twice about it."

Sen smiles. "Harry, you're such a romantic." He looks pointedly at his mother, but he doesn't have to remind her. While Arthur is in jail, the California Communist Party secretary calls a meeting of the Bay Area nisei CP members at the Hama household. It's announced that, in the interest of unity in the fight against imperialism, all members of Japanese ancestry and their non-Japanese spouses, meaning Estelle, are suspended from membership for the duration of the war.

Estelle looks absently through the mural as if seeing another panorama. "As soon as we got to camp, Art was trying to enlist, trying to rally the antifascists. He joined Military Intelligence and was shipped off to Camp Savage in Minnesota. Several months later, you were born." She squeezes Sen's shoulder. "For the next years until they dropped the bomb, Art was fighting in Burma."

"What did you do?"

"I stayed behind in camp, raised Sen, taught grammar school, and painted. That's when I went to pencil and watercolors, partly because it was cheaper and more accessible. But I found my true medium. Art, of course, stopped painting entirely, but I never painted so much as during those days."

Estelle steps forward and crouches to rearrange the roses one last time. The thorns hook against the leaves and shake several orange and yellow petals to the floor.

"What year did he leave?"

"Nineteen fifty-one."

"It's been twenty-three years. A long time."

"How old would he be?"

"Sixty-six."

"In 1949, we had a plan to go to Paris to continue painting. But Harry was just born, and we had no money, so we thought Art would go alone. But he thought he'd better see his mother first, so he returned to Hiroshima instead. She was alive then, but he must have seen what happened after the bomb."

Arthur Hama returns from Hiroshima with a film of the devastation, taken by a Japanese filmmaker. He is advised that it is illegal to show this footage, but he finds his purpose is to defiantly show it everywhere. His audiences watch in silent horror as the film pans the ravaged expanse of his old home city. Now Hiroshima is a teetering net of crumpled steel structures, ghostly shadows of human beings vaporized in an instant. Deformed, crippled, and burned bodies, their wandering forms pass naked against an endless and desolate canvas. He becomes obsessed with a mission to reveal the truth about the atomic bomb.

"Estelle," Arthur holds his head in his hands. "I fought the entire war to defeat Japanese fascism, but I can't justify the way we ended the war."

"And now Russia has the bomb too."

"It's a disaster."

"You can feel the hate rising all around us."

Arthur begins to travel for the World Peace Council. One day, he leaves America and keeps going.

"Well," says Estelle, "shall we go to the top now?"

The elevator rises two hundred feet to the top of Coit Tower, but there is a final flight of stairs to climb. Estelle walks up ahead, but Sen parks the wheelchair and scoops up his brother in his strong arms. "Come on Harry," he sighs. "This time, I'm not waiting for you. Let's go."

As they ascend the stairs, Harry asks, "Our dad left for Japan in fifty-one because of McCarthy and red-baiting, right?"

"That's what they say, deported under the McCarran Act. Look it up."

"I will. That's why Mom worked so hard to repeal it, right?"

"Yeah, but he was a U.S. citizen. My guess is that they could only threaten him with deportation. Think about it. He had medals from his service in the war."

"So why'd he leave?"

"He was on a mission."

"Yeah."

"Then he met a woman, Harry. She's the one who wrote Mom from Japan."

"Bastard."

"Guess that's why we never heard from him again."

"And all this time, I thought he was dead. Did he keep painting?"

"I don't know. Shit, Harry, you're heavy." Sen carries Harry to a window outlook and leans him against the stucco.

Estelle is already looking out. She points toward the cityscape and the white pyramid jutting into the skyline. "See the Transamerica over there? That's where the Monkey Building used to be." They walk the circle of the tower, peering across the city at each point: the Bay Bridge extending from the Ferry Building over Treasure Island to the East Bay, Alcatraz at the center beyond the docks, the Golden Gate with its red suspensions flowing over toward the Marin Headlands. It's a living mural of the city on the clearest, bluest day of that crisp November.

On the day Arthur Hama dies, May 18, 1974, India conducts its first nuclear underground explosion at Pokhran in Rajasthan. It is a device of about fifteen kilotons detonated at a depth of 107 meters, producing a crater reportedly having a radius of sixty meters and a depth of ten meters. India confidently describes it as a Peaceful Nuclear Explosive, or PNE. It is more commonly reported as the Smiling Buddha.

"Here's an odd story about Art," Estelle says. "He could speak Esperanto."

"What?"

"No really. He ran away from home at age fifteen to follow Vasily Eroshenko to Peking. Eroshenko was a writer, an anarchist, and proponent of Esperanto. He was also blind. Art studied with him, and Eroshenko gave him money to return home."

When they come full circle around the tower's lookout, Sen scoops up Harry once again and follows his mother down the narrow and curving staircase. From his perch in Sen's arms, Harry looks back one more time in the direction of the Transamerica. He sees that his mother must have saved one last flower. The red rose is perched against the window at a crooked angle.

2: Estelle Hama—Equality

In this historic year of 1975, thirty-seven years after its inception as the Dies Committee, later known as the House Un-American Activities Committee and later as the Internal Security Committee, the American Congress votes to abolish this once very powerful committee. Significantly, it is remembered that in the years following World War II, HUAC concentrates its efforts to investigate Communist and left-wing organizations. The most famous of these investigations are that of Alger Hiss, accused of being a spy, and that of the Hollywood Ten, writers and directors accused of Communist affiliations.

Furthermore, in 1950, HUAC sponsors the McCarran Internal Security Act. This act, also known as the Subversive Activities Control Act, is enacted in response to hearings by Senator Joseph P. McCarthy's Senate Permanent Subcommittee on Investigations, charged with uncovering evidence of Communist conspiracy and infiltration. The McCarran Act requires U.S. Communists to register as foreign agents, denies them passports, and excludes them from defense-industry employment.

Attached to the McCarran Act is Title II, authorizing the president of the United States, in the case of a national emergency, to apprehend and detain any person suspected as a threat to internal security. The precedent for Title II is the 1942 Executive Order 9066 signed by President Franklin D. Roosevelt to authorize wartime internment, in particular of American citizens of Japanese descent.

Estelle Hama stands before a framed copy of the 1942 poster that announces evacuation orders: *Instructions to All Persons of Japanese Ancestry.* It is the entry to the first art exhibition of her wartime work, all the collected drawings and watercolors of her years in a Japanese American concentration camp. The exhibit is sponsored by Japantown Art and Media or JAM.

Harry wheels up to Estelle and gestures to the work lining the walls and partitions. "I knew it was big, but I really didn't know. All these years you just had them in stacks around the house."

“They look so different framed.” Estelle bites her lip.

“Sen did all the framing. I was up there at JAM helping him. I typed the titles. You know me. Search and peck.” He smiles at his mother, gesturing with his fingers.

“I didn’t give them all titles.” Estelle looks confused.

“I know. I did.”

“I’m not sure I approve of your taking such liberties.” Estelle gives him her look, and Harry rolls away sheepishly, waving to a group of guests arriving for the show’s opening.

Sen hangs the paintings tightly, mere inches between each, to maximize the small area of the room. All the work is at Estelle’s eye level, and she moves slowly from drawing to drawing, painting to painting, memory to memory. The story of her days in camp unfolds as if it was yesterday. The harsh charcoal renderings seem the most real to her. She is surprised to see that a few of the sketches are actually letters, messages she sent on thin tissue paper to Arthur. Severe creases cut across the paper like memory, surviving Sen’s efforts to press them under glass.

Sen appears at her side.

“Where did you find these?” she points at the letters.

“They were between everything else.”

“I should have paid more attention.”

“Harry rolled everything out of the house on his lap. Turned out to be a gold mine.”

“What didn’t you put up?” Estelle looks around the room, flustered.

“Oh, the repeats.” Sen laughs.

“This is not an exhibition,” she complains.

“No, it’s a story finally revealed.”

“I was obsessed,” she almost whispers. “Who was going to know what happened to us? No one was coming to bail us out.”

Sen puts his arm around his mother’s shoulders. They stare into a portrait of themselves. Estelle is cradling her newborn at her breast. She’s sitting on a wooden crate next to a potbelly stove in a mostly empty barrack, except for a line of diapers drying above. Their figures are contained in heavy charcoal shadows.

“I was never so lonely in all my life.”

Estelle and Sen turn to the recognizable squeak of Harry’s wheels, but his voice precedes him. They can hear his animated conversation approaching with a small contingent of well-wishers.

"Have you noticed?" asks Estelle. "Harry's becoming such a politician."

Sen groans. "Lucky he's confined to that chair."

"Can you imagine?" smiles Estelle, quickly wiping her eyes.

"Insufferable."

The group comes forward.

"Estelle!"

"It's, what can I say, very moving."

"Congratulations. Sen, you did a great job here."

"Yes, I don't think Estelle would have done this on her own."

"And mind you, Estelle can do just about anything on her own."

"It's a beautiful tribute to your mother."

"Estelle, aren't you proud?"

"This brings back such difficult memories. You capture so much here."

"We're very grateful to you."

"Everyone must see this."

"I remember this one," someone points to a watercolor. "You gave it to us for our Title II poster."

"When was that? Nineteen sixty-seven?"

"That's about when we started. It took four years, but we got Title II repealed in seventy-one."

"You know, Estelle said it then, but I didn't believe her."

"What's that?"

"Estelle, you said we ought to go for reparations. But now I'm coming around. I think that's our next battle."

Harry says, "Mom's a visionary."

Sen says, "It never ends."

Estelle says, "No, it never ends. By the way," she adds, "did you notice that Alger Hiss was reinstated into the Massachusetts bar? Twenty-five years later, the tables finally turn on Richard Nixon."

"Sometimes it takes twenty-five years."

Harry gestures around at Estelle's paintings. "Sometimes it takes thirty."

Estelle looks on at her two sons. They form a tableau against a backdrop of events they cannot know but must learn to remember. Sen stands cross-armed with a strong stance, nodding at the comments of a visitor. Harry glad-hands folks and rolls forward to give them the tour. There's a woman standing to one side. Estelle thinks she might be Sen's new girlfriend, but as the evening grows, it seems more likely that she's interested in Harry.

Estelle's eye follows the succession of drawings to a particular scene in the makeshift camp hospital: she and another woman are lying on cots; both women contemplate their pregnant mounds, rising beneath the sheets. Estelle stares into the memory hidden in the drawing.

The woman turns to her and asks, "Your first?"

"Yes."

"This is my fourth."

"I could use your advice."

"Concentrate on your breathing. It will get you through the pain. It will come in waves. You have to ride it through."

"I see."

"What are you hoping for? Boy or girl?"

"I'm not particular."

"Names?"

"If it's a girl, Karla. If it's a boy, Sen."

"Sen?"

"My husband's choice. After Sen Katayama."

"I see." The woman becomes quiet and closes her eyes. She does not talk to Estelle again. Perhaps she has heard of Katayama, who is the founder of the Communist movement in Japan and buried in the Kremlin after an illustrious career in the Communist International.

Estelle smiles to herself. At least Arthur didn't insist on some Russian name like Vasily.

Someone is tapping Estelle's shoulder. "Hey, Estelle. I'm glad you finally agreed to this showing. It's been a long time coming."

"Oh, Tom, thanks for coming."

"Actually, I've got a favor to ask of you."

"O.K."

"There's a young sansei woman who's been in the news, arrested with Patty Hearst just a few days ago. Have you heard?"

"You know, I think I recognize her. She was my student when I taught those art classes at CCAC. I didn't last long, though. She, however, was very talented."

"Well, that's interesting. You know, she was born in camp."

"About Sen's age."

"Right. Estelle—" Tom pauses.

"She's going to need help."

"I thought you'd understand."

"Maybe we can solicit for bail money tonight."

"Thanks Estelle, you're amazing."

"Come here." She takes Tom's arm and draws him to a watercolor scene of toddlers playing in the sand. "That's Sen. These are his playmates. All born in a concentration camp."

"Estelle, she's in deep trouble. Maybe ballistics, kidnapping, and a murder hold-up."

"It doesn't matter. She deserves a fair trial."

Estelle backtracks several drawings and finds the darkest one in her memory. It's the night of the camp riot.

In Estelle's collection, Sen finds sketches of this painting and the painting itself recreated over and over again. He places all of them in a line across the floor and asks her to choose the one that most represents the event. She chooses not a pristine watercolor rendition but a dark angry charcoal. Days later, Sen finds himself in the library wanting to compare this drawing with something he has already seen. He finds a similar expression in a famous painting by Francisco Goya entitled *The Third of May.* In Goya's painting, a peasant among others, their bodies in bloody pools at his feet, raises his arms in a wide v just before his execution.

In Estelle's drawing, she faces a soldier pointing his bayoneted rifle and ready to shoot. She clutches a baby in one arm, and raises the other arm in protest. Like Goya's peasant, the child is swathed in light. And while her own face is darkly shadowed, Estelle's hair is starkly white in the same light that bathes the child.

"Halt! Who goes there?"

Estelle's heart grabs tightly at the sight of the soldier and his rifle. The stark searchlights blind her. She's nearly run into his bayonet. The baby must sense her fear, must hear her heart thundering at her breast. She can feel the child recoil and shudder, but he doesn't cry.

The soldier doesn't shoot. She thinks, *He doesn't shoot.* She's frozen in the dark night. The MP lowers his rifle. His young, white features relax to see another white person, a white woman. If she had not been white, what would he have done? He doesn't know that she no longer sees herself in him.

"We're on their death list," she sputters. "I tried to barricade the door. My neighbor's been killed in the confusion. Please protect my baby. Please."

"This is the night," Estelle explains to Sen, "my hair turned completely white."

"The night you turned hakujin."

"They called me keto baba. Maybe it was symbolic."

"What do you mean?"

"Well, like becoming a witch. Persecution goes back to the Inquisition."

Sen chuckles. "Why didn't my hair go white too?"

"I was never so scared."

"A tough lady like you?" Sen wonders about the woman who dodges bullets and tear gas to deliver men and women from jail.

"Maybe that's how tough people are tough," she speculates. "You lose what you don't need."

They stare across the room at Harry. He senses their attention and wheels around and waves. "Yeah," Sen nods.

The young woman who shows interest in Harry wheels him over. Harry introduces her. She wants to interview Estelle. They talk. Harry and Sen look on. At some point she asks Estelle, "How do you compare your experiences with, say, Dachau or Stalin's Gulag?"

Harry and Sen brace themselves for an onslaught, but Estelle replies calmly. "Well, I'm alive, aren't I?" She smiles and walks away to greet another friend.

Harry whispers up to Sen, "Is Mom still a Stalinist?"

"What do you think?"

As the guests trickle away, Sen stands alone in the gallery with Estelle.

"Where's Harry?"

"That reporter. They went off somewhere for drinks. Said he's going to educate her."

"That was a stupid question." Estelle smiles wryly. "When are you going to get a girlfriend?"

"I *had* one. It was her birthday night before last."

"I see."

"I was over framing at JAM, and—"

"You forgot."

"When I looked, it was three a.m."

Estelle shakes her head.

Sen looks around. "Well, do you forgive me?"

"For losing your girlfriend?"

"No, for the way I put up the show."

"Diego Rivera said that the role of art is propaganda. Art is a revolutionary weapon."

"I turned your work into a weapon."

Estelle laughs. It's a big laugh. Then she says, "I forgot why I drew and painted in those years."

"You were a witness."

"Maybe that, but really, to survive."

"Now I know where your hair color went."

"Oh?"

Estelle swings slowly around the room. The dark charcoal and pencil lines and the rich earth watercolors call from the walls to her white halo.

Sen turns out the light.

3: Sen Hama—Fraternity

Nineteen seventy-six marks the Bicentennial of the great American Revolution that begins with the signing of the Declaration of Independence in Philadelphia by the Continental Congress. In the seven years following this declaration, the American colonies fight for their liberation from the British imperial monarchy, finally defeating King George III, Great Britain, and its allies. In this same bicentennial year, Jimmy Carter is elected president of the United States, and Alexander Solzhenitsyn, the Nobel Prize writer and author of *The Gulag Archipelago,* recently exiled from the Union of Soviet Socialist Republics, comes to live in Cavandish, Vermont.

"What would you know about Stalin?" Estelle fumes.

"It's what we don't know that worries me," argues Harry. "Why would Solzhenitsyn lie about this?"

"Solzhenitsyn writes fiction."

Sen is up in the loft of the Kearny Street Workshop gallery that was once the famous nightclub the Hungry i. On the Jackson Street side of the I-Hotel's brick structure, Sen has contributed to an expansive mural dedicated to the hotel tenants—now retired elderly Filipino and Chinese migrant workers. JAM and Kearny Street are preparing for a joint exhibition of photography and silkscreens. Sen prepares the colors for his silkscreen. He wants a gradated effect using a split-font technique. He can hear the argument downstairs. He remembers when Joseph Stalin dies, Estelle cries. He cries too, but Harry is a baby then. He looks over the side of the loft and sees Harry wheeling around with a paint roller on the end of a long pole and emphasizing his words in large swipes. His mother paints at an easel. "Hey, Harry," Sen interrupts, "when are you going to be done? We need that wall finished by tonight."

"Fiction?" Harry pushes the pole in emphasis.

Sen groans. He knows what's coming.

It's been a while, but he remembers the last night the "reporter girl" comes to dinner. He's forgotten her name now, but that's what they all call her, even Harry. By this dinner, she and Harry date regularly. She's always at the house. Sen can't remember why he's at that dinner too, but he is. He remembers that Harry is waving some typewritten papers around. Harry says, "Listen, you've got to read this. It's great stuff."

The reporter girl looks embarrassed and says, "Harry—"

"Really," he insists, "I think you should get it published."

Estelle takes the papers from Harry's excited hand. "Harry, you're going to get ice cream all over it." She looks at the title page with interest and sits back in her chair to read. Pretty soon she's immersed in her reading, chuckling and smiling. When she's finished, she looks up and says, "It's really a wonderful story about you and your uncle. Is he still alive?"

Harry's girlfriend smiles. "Actually, he's not my uncle. And that's not me but my friend who told me the story."

"But you write *I.*"

"Yes, because it seems more natural, and I also had an uncle who was like that, but of course that didn't happen to my uncle. Well, it's a bit embellished."

Estelle pushes the story across the table and says tepidly, "I see." She stands and begins to clear the table.

"So," says Harry, "what do you think? Best American Short Stories, right?"

"I wouldn't know." Estelle moves away with a pile of dishes. "You know I don't read fiction."

Sen, Harry, and the reporter girl all watch Estelle walk away coolly into the kitchen. Sen looks at the reporter girl, who sits moving her ice cream around her dish in disappointment and confusion. Meanwhile, Harry rolls after his mother. Their muffled voices can be heard from the kitchen. Suddenly, the reporter girl jumps up and runs out of the house. Sen picks up the story from the table and starts to chase after her. He stops midway, shrugs, and returns to finish his ice cream.

Sen calls down from the loft to Estelle, hoping to divert the storm. "Maybe you could come up here and check the colors for me?" he asks his mother.

But Harry is relentless. "What's wrong with fiction?" He's already heard the answer how many times, but asks as if it's a new argument.

"Fiction twists the truth. It's all lies. It's because of fiction we get in trouble. It's because of fiction that we get put in jail, get persecuted, framed, lied to by politicians."

"Right, that's how Solzhenitsyn got into the Gulag."

"You haven't thought about how he got into the U.S. His sort of anti-socialism is very convenient propaganda."

At that moment, someone appears through the gallery doors with a large box. "Hey, Sen, you here?"

"Yeah!" Sen yells from above.

"I brought my stuff." Leland Wong is one of the exhibiting artists. He sees Estelle at her easel and says politely, "Hi, Mrs. Hama. Hey, Harry."

She waves at him with her brush.

Sen points, "How about you use that far wall over there? Harry's still painting that side."

"Hey," Leland says, "I got some spots we can use for lighting. What do you think?"

Sen comes down to look at the spotlights. "Hey, where'd you get these?"

"Let's just say we borrowed them on a long-term basis."

"Long as they don't come get 'em this weekend."

Harry says, "Hey, Leland, you read Solzhenitsyn?"

"What?"

"Tell my mom. *The Gulag* is nonfiction. It's based on real-life testimonies and Solzhenitsyn's life in the camps."

"I don't know, Harry."

"Way she talks, you'd think fiction was fascism."

Leland looks at Sen, who shakes his head. "Harry, leave Leland out of this." He looks at Estelle, who's ignoring them. "You want to cross swords with the Stalinist, be my guest."

Harry swings his painting pole around like it's a lance. "Sir Estelle, I've thrown down my gauntlet. What say thee?"

Estelle parries her brush back at Harry. "Watch it. You're spattering."

Sen looks at Leland. "Don't mind them. This is a regular thing." He looks out the door. "Hey, where's your work?"

"Out in the truck. Give me a hand."

They go back and forth, bringing in framed silkscreens and photography.

"Line it up over here so we can take a look," says Sen.

They stand back from the wall and pause to look, but Leland says, "I gotta go pick up Nancy's stuff, then Rich's. I'll be back." He runs out.

Estelle walks over to take a closer look. She pauses in front of each piece. "I like the photography," she says. "Why is he doing this comic book stuff?"

"I like it," says Sen.

"I like it too," says Harry. "I like the colors."

Both Sen and Estelle stare at Harry, whose face is sprayed with tiny dots of white paint. He rolls back to his wall painting.

Estelle gestures. "It's farcical. Too commercial."

"You haven't seen underground comics," says Sen. "It's not what you think."

"Farcical. Fictional." Harry slaps paint into the wall and mutters out loud.

Sen says, "Social real for you is like the party line."

Estelle counters, "I don't tell people what to paint."

"This is not art for art's sake. It's got a message, if you want message."

"Silkscreens have a history," Estelle informs. "They go back to the WPA and before that to the Bolsheviks, when those artists wanted to develop a cheap and accessible way to create posters, but they did it with a certain aesthetic in mind."

"Right, and it's art made accessible to the people. What could be more accessible than comics?" Sen argues.

"It's not serious."

"This is not serious?" Sen stands in front of a piece with a large mushroom cloud. Bursting forth and resting in its pillow is a chubby, Buddha-like baby.

"It deflates a tragic image to the level of the comic book superhero."

Harry rolls back into the conversation. "This one here is my favorite." He points. "Godzilla." In this scene, Godzilla roars with a fiery tongue, a giant lizard looming over the remains of the Hiroshima dome. In one pincer hand he grips Nixon, who is hugging a red, white, and blue missile. In the other hand Godzilla grips Brezhnev, who is hugging a red missile marked with the hammer and sickle.

They stare at the cartoon images of the great leaders, one of them now defunct.

Sen asks, "Do you buy this idea about the bomb?"

Harry asks, "What's that?"

"That Truman dropped the bomb to scare the Soviets and to keep Stalin from entering into surrender negotiations with Japan."

Estelle nods. "I think that's true. Japan had already lost the war."

"That's why two hundred thousand people died?" Harry flails around. "How can you continue to support these alignments? It's not about people. It's just about ideology."

"You don't understand. It *is* about people. It's not about individual choice. Once a position is discussed and a decision made, the unity of the Party and the united action of all the people are its strength."

"But what about the Hiroshima people?" Harry wails.

"We're not talking about them. The decision to bomb was not Stalin's. It was Truman's. It was an American decision based on racism, anticommunism, and American imperialism."

"Ism, ism, ism," Harry gestures erratically.

"Oh, you're impossible." Estelle throws up her hands.

Sen remembers his project up in the loft and runs upstairs. He applies paint and squeegees it across the silk, lifts the frame, examines the print, then removes and places it on the drying rack. He places another sheet of paper, carefully matching the masking tape markings on the table. He thinks back.

His roommate JB smokes as usual. They both nurse their beers, but Sen doesn't smoke.

JB says, "The work you did for the poster presentation was really great."

"Thanks," says Sen. "Glad to help."

"Have you thought about joining?" He means joining the J-Town Collective.

"Yeah, but I don't need to join to help out."

"You've got a point."

"Listen, I got this name Sen, after the founder of Japanese Communism." Sen takes a long draft from his mug. "You know what I'm saying?"

"Yeah, man. I can relate." JB lights up another cigarette.

Sen coughs. "Growing up, I had to go to mass meetings. I was ostracized in school because my mom was an open Communist. Kids ran around yelling, 'Kill the Commies!'"

Sen remembers being nine years old and complaining to his mother about not having any friends. Estelle is on the phone strategizing for the next meeting. She puts the phone down momentarily and speaks to her son optimistically. It's like a continuation of her phone call. "It's easy, Sen. Just say hello to someone new every day, and pretty soon, you'll have new friends."

This works for Harry but not Sen. Sen is unbearably shy.

Sen and JB order another round of beers. "Ever hear of the W. E. B. DuBois Club?"

JB shakes his head.

"Yeah, well, I was in that for a while, until Czechoslovakia."

Estelle warns, "Don't get recruited into one of those ultra-leftist Maoist groups. Lenin warns about ultra-left sectarianism that destroys unity."

"But," Sen protests, "I'm not even in the CP. What does it matter?"

"I'm just warning you," Estelle says. "All these groups springing up have nationalist tendencies."

"But you live in Japantown. You turned Japanese ages ago."

"Look what happened to the SDS," Estelle continues. "Splintered into factions."

"I organized antiwar demos with them," says Sen. "I never joined."

"I know. New Left," Estelle sighs. "Infantile leftism."

"What do you mean? You supported it."

"Until they became a liability. A distraction, really."

"Why do you stay? The Party's over. Harry's right. You can't possibly support the Soviet Union anymore."

"Change doesn't come overnight. You don't know the struggles we've been through and what we've achieved. If you look back, you can see a history of failures that are really steps to revolution. You can't abandon the Party just because times are difficult."

"They abandoned you."

"That's been rectified, and I struggled for that change."

Sen continues to slather each paper with a streak of color and to lay the copies in the drying trays. He remembers an ex-girlfriend.

They drive south out of the city. He's leaving her off at Stanford, where she goes to school. He remembers the moment when he knows their relationship ends. He drives through an area of rolling hills and pasture.

She says, "Look at this beautiful land. It's so gorgeous."

He smiles to agree. It's a beautiful sunny day.

"Just think of it," she says enthusiastically. "One of these days, this will all belong to the people."

Harry's voice intrudes. Sen thinks his mother and brother can only go at each other for so long. It's always the same. Soon Harry will blow up.

Sen starts the process for the next color. The scene is from a photograph. A young sansei, Goro Tanaka, carries an elderly issei man down the steps from the senior center. Sen captures the image while he works at the center. Over time, Sen becomes the driver who takes the elderly to their doctors' appointments. He also carts around meals to old folks who are homebound and unable to cook for themselves. Some days he digs up the soil in the community garden to help the old men plant tomatoes. He moves between community work and his paid job at the People's Warehouse. All of his silkscreens are idyllic scenes from community life. He realizes that his work creates an opposition to his mother's dark representations of imprisonment.

Harry's voice rises to the loft. For some reason, they are back to talking about fiction and, now, the reporter girl. "Who's to say that her story is not art?" Harry says.

"It might be," Estelle concedes.

"It's the art of storytelling."

Estelle nods and continues to paint.

"Storytelling was no reason to run her out of the house."

"I didn't run her out of the house," Estelle protests. "If she wanted, she'd be back. Don't use me as an excuse."

"Excuse?" Harry continues, "What about your storytelling? How come you told Sen and me that our dad was dead?"

"But he was dead. Dead to us as a family. He made choices, Harry. You were only three when he left. Sen was eight. He kept asking when Art would return. I couldn't bear it any longer."

"You lied to us! That's fiction!" Harry throws down his paint roller. Sen comes down the stairs. He watches Harry roll angrily out the gallery door.

He looks at his mother, who tries to concentrate on her painting. "You knew that was coming," he says to her. "It's not about Arthur," he assures her, because she looks hurt.

"I know," she replies. "He's still mad about losing his girlfriend."

"It is your fault, you know."

"My fault?" Estelle looks up indignantly. "If she liked Harry that much, she'd still be around."

"No, I mean, it's your fault that Harry can't see that. He thinks he's like everyone else. Plus he thinks he's invincible. He's got no idea of his limitations. You did that."

"I treated you the same as Harry."

"I know." Sen nods. "What happened?"

"You liked to read. Harry never seemed to have time. You're more introspective. You still like to think more than to act."

"I'm theory. Harry's practice."

"Worked out fine." Estelle gestures. "No one is going to hand Harry anything. I knew that the day he was born with the cord around his neck."

Sen remembers Harry as a kid on an office chair with wheels, whirling around until he's dizzy. Harry wants speed. Sen thinks he wants speed too, but he knows his own limitations. Sen remembers being nineteen and taking his first motorcycle out to the Arroyo Seco speedway. He wants to be a race car driver. There's an opportunity to test a new Ford GTO. It can go 200 miles an hour. The trainer says, "Don't go faster than 150. You got that?" But Sen doesn't watch his speed, and it is exhilarating. When he looks, he's going 170. He can hear the trainer at his side yelling furiously at him through his helmet. When he stops the car, he's still yelling. "I told you! Not over 150! You wanna race, first thing you gotta learn is to follow instructions. You're not racing material. Get out of here!"

"But—" protests Sen.

"Get out!"

Sen leaves angrily and takes his motorcycle to Salinas. He parks next to an old saloon and goes in. Inside, his eyes adjust to the dark, and he finds himself among a group of Mexican workers. Beer and tequila make the rounds, and Sen forgets he's not racing material and takes off again on his bike. Somewhere down the road, a cop stops him. "Just a routine check," the cop says. "Let's see the registration on that thing. We got a lookout for stolen bikes."

"The bike's mine," Sen says.

"You'll need to prove it."

"Fuck you."

"That's not the right attitude, son." The cop grabs Sen, pulls him forward, and drives his knee into his stomach.

Sen falls into the dirt. His stomach clenches and releases in waves from the punch of the cop's knee but also from the beer and tequila. He heaves a fistful of vomit onto the cop's dusty black boots.

"Oh, shit." The cop looks down at his boots. "Now you really made a mistake there," he grumbles. He shakes off the vomit and walks to his car.

Sen can see him strutting back with his stick. When the cop gets close, Sen balls up his fist and punches hard into his crotch. As the man staggers and falls back, Sen jumps back onto his bike and races away. He returns to the bar and the Mexicans who are still trading tequila shots. "Don't worry," they say. They all go next door into a shack. They drag his motorcycle into the shack. "No problem, see?" they say.

But Sen can hear the cop asking outside, "You see a chink kid come 'round here on a bike?"

"Hey, I got a plan," whispers one man. "I take my bike and go that way. Make a diversion. You get ready and go that way. Ready?"

"You sure?"

"Yeah, we fuck the fucking gringo," he sneers.

Sen gets ready.

"Buena suerte," says the man and takes a last shot of tequila. Sen can hear him charge out of the backside of the shack and circle around and away. Soon he hears the commotion and rev of the police car behind. Someone even yells, "There he goes!"

When the sound of the car is in the far distance, the rest of the men yell, "Go!" and Sen goes. From country roads, he slips into the traffic of Highway 101 but keeps to the speed limit.

Sen returns to his silkscreen. He wonders why he likes this work. Maybe it's the intricate and precise mechanics—tracing the exacto knife in fine lines on stencil, peeling up the film, filling negative space with positive color. He thinks the silkscreen process creates limitations, planned layers and discrete spaces, boundaries where color can and cannot go. He scrutinizes his picture of a young man carrying an old man down stairs. He realizes it could be himself, carrying Harry.

Estelle comes up to look at his work. She says, "I'm not sure about the colors."

"What do you mean?"

"Maybe a little more strength in this area," she says.

"I like it subdued."

"Hmmm," says Estelle. "Just a bit more muscle."

He adds the color that Estelle suggests. They compare the results. "I still like it subdued," he says. "It feels more real to me. Just the way it is, like everyday life."

Estelle ponders the difference. "This one is more . . . " she searches for the word.

"Heroic," answers Sen.

"Yes." Estelle nods and returns to her painting.

Sen follows her downstairs. He looks over Estelle's painting. It's Harry in his wheelchair charging with the long pole. Ludicrously, the paint roller hangs at the end. Facing Harry's pole is Godzilla holding a large pinwheel.

"See," says Estelle. "I can do comics, too."

"Harry imagines that he walks like everyone else."

"But he does, doesn't he?" Estelle continues with a rush of strokes against her easel.

"Now, Mrs. Hama, you've got to admit that that's fiction. It's like, what do you call it, the 'dream work of revolutionary ideas.'"

"I didn't think of that."

"You've battered him about so much, you've transformed his consciousness."

"Not bad." Estelle smiles. "That's why Harry doesn't have to do art."

Sen laughs. "Harry is a work of art."

4: Harry Hama—Humanity

On April 4, 1977, President Fidel Castro of the Republic of Cuba arrives at Vnukovo Airport in Moscow and is hugged planeside by Soviet President Nikolai Podgorny, General Secretary of the Communist Party Leonid Brezhnev, Premier Alexei Kosygin, and Foreign Minister Andrei Gromyko. Presidents Podgorny and Castro repeat their call for an end to apartheid governments in Rhodesia and South Africa and their pledge to support anti-imperialist forces and armed struggle on the African continent. During President Castro's visit to Moscow, Secretary Leonid Brezhnev confirms the failure of the American Secretary of State Cyrus R. Vance's mission to negotiate constructive limitations of strategic nuclear weapons. This is a grave setback for the American President Jimmy Carter, who pledges in his election campaign for the elimination of all nuclear weapons on earth. While the American government presses for diplomatic resolutions over armed revolution in Third World conflicts, and for the USSR to conform to human rights agreements under the 1975 Helsinki Accords, President Carter now favors the development of the neutron bomb, also called an enhanced radiation warhead, a small thermonuclear weapon that theoretically produces minimal blast and heat but releases a large amount of lethal radiation, destroying life but leaving buildings intact.

The day after the Cuban president's historic visit to Moscow, sixty handicapped persons take over the fourth floor of the San Francisco regional offices of the United States Department of Health, Education, and Welfare. The Federal Building itself is an old construction built in the 1930s under the Works Projects Administration of President Franklin Delano Roosevelt's New Deal. As Harry Hama and others on wheelchairs take their strategic positions within the building, they pay homage to FDR, a closet cripple. Similar nationwide protests are staged in Washington, D.C.; Los Angeles; Chicago; and New York. Only the San Francisco contingent remains camped out in their HEW offices for the next twenty-eight days.

Harry Hama's appointment is with the HEW regional director, Joe Maldonado. He wheels in with three others, also in wheelchairs.

"Mr. Maldonado," Harry addresses the director, "The Rehabilitation Act was passed by Congress in 1973 over President Nixon's veto, but it was never implemented. The disabled community supported the election of Jimmy Carter with the understanding that he would instruct the new HEW secretary, your boss, Joseph Califano, to implement those regulations to enforce our civil rights. We are especially concerned with Section 504 of the act, which prohibits discrimination of any qualified individual by reason of his or her disability from programs or employment supported by federal funding."

"Mr. Hama," the director interrupts. "I am aware of the provisions of the act."

"Mr. Maldonado," Harry returns, "then you are also aware that President Carter was inaugurated in January, and it is now April, and we in the disabled community are tired of waiting. It has already been four years since the act itself was passed."

"Harry." The director put his hand up.

"Joe?" Harry answers.

"What are you guys trying to pull? I've had one meeting after the next with your people all afternoon. Don't you already know that I'm on your side?"

Harry pulls up his arm and glances at his watch. He waves a paper in front of the director. "Can I read you the provisions in Section 504?"

"You can read the whole act. My hands are tied until it's signed and the funding is released."

Jim in the wheelchair next to Harry offers, "Let me read it."

The director sighs as Jim reads in a steady monotone. Harry nods to an attendant behind him and excuses himself. In the hallway outside the office, he sees other disabled protestors and says, "O.K., pass the word. We're going to stay here tonight. We're going to stay as long as it takes." He watches two deaf people sign to each other, and a blind person down the hall taps away in excitement. Three people on crutches with large backpacks wave and follow Harry back toward the director's office. One of them says to Harry, "There're maybe three hundred of us out on the street by now!"

"How many inside?"

"Fifty?"

"That'll do for starters. You got fifty sleeping bags?"

"We got six here, two apiece. Got to smuggle in more."

"Do what you can. I got mine." Harry is sitting on his bag, which is folded under him like a cushion. "What about the walkie-talkies?"

One of the men on crutches shifts the pack behind him and gestures. "Right here. We got at least two sets. One set for inside. And one split to the outside."

Harry checks his watch and smiles. "Half hour to closing."

The counselor at City College smiles. He's a handsome black man with a large Afro. He says, "Harry, do you attend a church?"

"Why?"

"Well, you could talk to the pastor. My pastor, for example, would be very understanding."

"About what?"

"It's possible he could offer you some jobs around the church."

"That's your advice?"

"On the practical side of things—"

"I came in here to arrange my classes, and this is the sort of counseling I get? I need an action plan for the next two years to transfer to State, and I could use a scholarship, and you want to talk about church? Who do you think I am?"

"I didn't mean—"

"That's all you have to offer? You call yourself a counselor?" Harry bangs his fist on the man's desk. He swings his chair around and storms out the door. "Get me another counselor!"

Harry rolls his chair in reverse and feels the slight tilt of the chair to one side, accompanied by a yell. "Ow! Ouch! Ouch! Ouch!"

He quickly maneuvers the chair forward again and circles around to see a young woman hopping on one foot around her cane. "Oh, that hurts. That hurts," she whimpers.

"I'm really sorry," Harry apologizes. It's the second day of the HEW sit-in.

"You should be looking where you're going," she admonishes.

"You should be looking where you're going."

"What did you say?" she asks.

"Are you deaf?" he taunts.

"Are you blind?"

"No, you're blind."

"How do you know I'm blind?"

"Because you have a white-tipped cane, and you're wearing dark glasses."

"Goddamn cripple."

"How's your foot. Are you crippled now, too?"

"Maybe you broke my toe."

"Let me see your toe."

"Are you a doctor?"

"I'm considering it."

She removes her shoe and sock and sticks her foot up. Harry reaches for the bare foot and examines the toes. "You're lucky I'm not fat and not in one of those electric chairs. Those weigh a ton. You know, like a steamroller. Then these puppies would be smashed." He presses each toe, and she winces.

"I don't want to be a cripple."

"Better than being blind."

"How do you know?"

"Because I'm a cripple. Crippled's the best disability, I'd say."

"Oh, you're crazy!" She taps around with her cane and then gets down on the floor searching for her shoe, but Harry reaches over and takes it. "O.K.," she says, "where is it? Give me my shoe."

Harry wheels away and says, "I think we should get that foot of yours on ice."

"Where are you going?" She hobbles behind with one bare foot sticking and peeling off the marble floor after him. "Come back!"

Harry can hear himself among the ten CANE protestors locked inside the director's office of the Western Addition Redevelopment Administration. "THE PEOPLE UNITED WILL NEVER BE DEFEATED!" The director sits at his desk with his hands clasped, staring into space over the heads of the protestors chained to each other and sitting on the floor. Only Harry in his wheelchair can see the director's bored, simply waiting for the police outside to bust open the door. The police break in, and there is a flurry of commotion as they cut through the chains and drag out each protestor. Harry watches the eighth protestor pulled away and waits patiently for his turn, but no police come back to take him out. Harry yells out the door from the office, "The people united will never be defeated," but the sounds of protest and struggle fade down the hallway. "Hey!" he yells. "Hey!" No one returns to make his arrest.

The fifth day of the sit-in is a Saturday, and the federal building is empty except for the disabled protestors occupying the fourth floor with the guards. Around noon, they are all eating pizza and by late afternoon, a card game is going on, and there are wheelchair races down the wide corridors. Harry is around the corner from the commotion. He can hear the cheers go up and then from behind him, "Don't back up. I'm right here."

He turns his head and sees the blind girl. "How's your foot?" he asks.

"The swelling's gone down," she answers, then asks, "Why aren't you racing with the others?"

"You wanna borrow my chair?"

"Oh, you've got a radio?" She hears the channels changing.

"Yeah, I was hoping to hear the game."

"Game?"

"Baseball. Dodgers are playing the Giants this weekend at Chavez Ravine."

"So you're a Giants fan."

"No, I'm not. Do I look like a Giants fan?"

"How should I know what you look like?"

He scoffs, "I bet you do know. How did you know I wasn't racing?"

"I didn't hear your voice, and besides, the right wheel of your chair squeaks."

"Damn," he says. "Batteries must be going."

"So you aren't from San Francisco?"

"I am. But the Dodgers are my team." He turns up the volume on the portable radio, but the sound only grows dimmer. "Damn."

"Oh, that's too bad," she commiserates.

"I missed the game on Thursday."

"Oh yes," she needles him. "What with this sit-in going on and all."

He ignores her. "Don Sutton pitched, beat San Francisco five to one." He pries open the radio and dumps the dead batteries out in disgust.

Her hands reach forward, touching the radio, then snatching away one of the fallen batteries. "I'm hungry," she says. "Aren't you? There's still some pizza left, I bet." She walks away.

Sometime later, she stops him in the corridor. "Oh, there you are. Where are you going?"

"I was thinking I'd grease this wheel so that I become invisible to the blind."

She's hugging her sleeping bag and says, "Hey, I've got something for you." She whispers, "Is he around?"

"Who?"

"The guard."

"No."

She pulls out a long flashlight hidden inside her bag. "I borrowed this from him."

"Come on," he says, escorting her around the corridor to a quiet spot.

They trade out the batteries and tune in the radio.

"It's the fourth inning," he says. "Two zip. Dodgers winning."

Harry joins the busload of folks heading up to Tule Lake to visit the old site of the segregation center used to incarcerate Japanese Americans during World War II. They pitch tents and set up camp. The next morning, Harry can hear the gunning of a motorcycle outside his tent. He hears the motor go silent and the voice of his brother, Sen: "Hey Harry, get up. I could use some grub."

Harry peeks out of his pup tent with a sleepy eye. "How did you know I was here?"

Sen crouches down and looks at Harry with some amusement. "Well, you got your car parked out here like a beacon." He points to Harry's chair outside the tent.

Harry pulls himself outside and props himself up. He yells out, "Hey, anyone for breakfast?"

Someone stirs in another tent. "Shit, Harry, go back to sleep. It's only five a.m."

Harry looks at Sen and shrugs.

Sen smiles. "Wanna take a ride?" He points to a mountain outcrop that juts out of the landscape. "Let's see how close we can get to that."

"Castle Rock." Harry nods.

Sen gestures with his head to the back of his Kawasaki 500, and Harry struggles to swing his limp legs over the back saddle. "Hang on," says Sen. He guns the motor, and the two putter away over the sand and gravel of the dry lake bed.

Sen and Harry circle, looking for trails that the bike can climb. They zigzag around in the cool morning air. The July sunlight breaks over the skies with the promise of temperatures up to ninety degrees by the afternoon. "Hell of a place to be imprisoned," remarks Sen.

"Nothing left. No barbed wire. No guard towers. Not even the foundations of the barracks," notes Harry.

"I'm starved," says Sen. "I've been on the road since midnight."

"Let's head back," agrees Harry.

They head down a slight incline for several hundred yards when a rattlesnake slithers across the road. Sen swerves to avoid it, then corrects his direction, but it's too late. The bike slides off into a gully, then skids into a fast downhill. Harry slips from the back of the saddle and sees the shiny body of the Kawasaki skid, hit some rocky impediment, and flip in a large wheelie. When Harry comes to, he's staring at a small pile of tiny white seashells. In the distance down the rocky slope he can see the white motorbike on its side. "Sen?" he calls. He can't move one of his legs at all, but he pulls up on his elbows and presses the hard dusty surface with this forearms and hands. He can see Sen's figure sprawled near a bowl of sagebrush. It takes all his effort to drag his body in that direction, crawling like a slow lizard. "Sen," he calls. Sweat and blood obscure his vision. To crawl those few yards to reach his brother takes a lifetime. When he reaches Sen perhaps thirty minutes later, he knows the twisted position of Sen's neck is not natural.

Around the tenth day of the sit-in, the disabled protestors gather for a meeting. Someone says, "We need to keep up our spirits and our momentum."

Another says, "I could sure use a bath."

"I might have to leave to see my doctor."

"Seeing your doctor is a valid excuse, but not a bath."

"If he wants a bath, let him leave."

"But don't bother to come back."

Harry breaks in, "Congressman Burton was here, and he got us a telephone line out to get medical supplies and food. He also says he's going to conduct hearings right here."

"That will be good press coverage."

"So we've got a congressman involved, how about the mayor? The governor?"

"Harry, you know the mayor."

"I know him from before, when he was supervisor. He helped us fight for access at SF State."

"I suggest we send Harry out to talk to these guys. Send Harry to Sacramento. Get some promises and support."

"I could use some help," says Harry. "Maybe an assistant."

"I volunteer."

Harry looks to see who's volunteering; it's the blind girl.

"By the way," she says, "my name is Clara. I'm with the Center for Independent Living in Berkeley."

When they return from Sacramento with a declaration signed by Governor Brown, Clara asks Harry, "How are we going to get back into the federal building?"

"Let's go to city hall."

At city hall, the receptionist says, "Hey Harry, haven't seen you in a while." She winks. "You know, we're all for you."

"Thank you. So, is he in?"

"Have you got an appointment?

Harry smiles.

"I'll see what I can do."

In the next hour, Clara and Harry are in an entourage following Mayor Moscone down the walkway from city hall to the federal building across the street. The disabled protestors lining the front of the building cheer and part the way.

The mayor looks into the cameras and says, "We have 120 demonstrators here who are being denied medical and hygienic assistance, and this in the building that professes to support the health, education, and welfare of the people. I'm personally sending in showers, towels, and soap, and I want them installed."

A reporter approaches the mayor and asks, "Sir, what do you say to the commissioner who said yesterday that he's not running a hotel here?"

"These demonstrators are not going to leave. Four are on a hunger strike. We're putting their lives at risk."

Estelle is seated at his bedside. Harry opens his eyes then shuts them again tightly, pretending to sleep.

"Harry," Estelle says with exasperation. "Open your eyes."

Harry opens one eye and looks sheepishly at his mother.

"If you're going to try to kill yourself, make a better effort next time," she says.

"Sorry," he says.

"I didn't mean that," she apologizes.

"I know," he says. "But I deserve it."

"That's right," she replies.

"I had a vision," he says.

"Oh?"

"I saw Sen."

"We're Communists. We don't see dead people."

"I know." Harry chuckles drowsily. "I always knew I wasn't really a Communist."

Estelle smiles.

"He told me I wasn't going to join him in heaven. I was going to hell."

"Heaven? Hell? Miserable defectors," Estelle sniffs.

"That's when I threw up."

"They still had to pump your stomach."

"If we don't believe in heaven or hell, what do we believe in?"

"What a foolish question. We believe in history and," Estelle thinks for a moment, "and in names."

"Names?"

"Harry Bridges. You were named for Bridges, and until last night you were as tough and stubborn as Harry Bridges."

Harry pushes himself to sit up. "I guess I miss Sen."

"I miss him too." Estelle takes Harry's hand in hers. "But"—she squeezes him hard—"you've got your own promises to keep."

Back in the federal building, it's the end of another day of sit-in and protest. Harry says, "For a blind girl, you weren't such a bad assistant at all."

"I'm a qualified individual. I just need access to my job." Clara follows Harry down the corridor, then a turn and a turn again. The conversations, singing, and card games echo away and become distant. She unzips and zips together their two sleeping bags. Then she helps Harry from his chair. "Here," she says. She unties his shoes and places them to one side. She unbuttons his shirt and pulls it gently away. She unzips his pants and pulls them away as well. She folds everything neatly in a pile, then tucks Harry between the soft folds of the bags, plumping up the down for a makeshift pillow.

"You know when I fell in love with you," he says. "It was really only a few days ago."

"Oh? When you found out my family used to live in Chavez Ravine?"

"Well, that, but it was when I saw your face all wet with beer."

It's a secret, but in between negotiations and meetings, Harry and Clara sneak into Candlestick Park. He even brings his mitt to catch foul balls. Willie McCovey hits a foul, and Harry puts up his mitt in anticipation. Amazingly, the ball falls straight into the cup of beer held between his legs.

Clara's fingers run across his face, around his ears, and through his hair. "Don't make those funny faces," she complains. She mimics him gritting his teeth and sticking out his tongue.

He smiles. "Just testing."

Her hands spread across his chest. "I know massage, you know."

"Yeah," he says.

She crawls under the bag, and he can hear her muffled voice. "I can see in the dark, you know."

"Yeah," he says, "yeah."

Several years later, Harry and five other disabled people in wheelchairs chain themselves to the front gate of the San Diego bus transit yard, demanding that the system adapt all buses with wheelchair lifts. The buses and their drivers are stuck in the yard for hours until the police come and disengage the protesters from the tangle of heavy chains and wheelchairs and the chain-link gate. They are all booked and fingerprinted and released. The next day, Harry and others return and chain themselves to the actual bus bumpers.

When Estelle comes to bail Harry out of jail that day, she says, "Harry, have they ever put a person in a wheelchair in jail?"

"Come to think of it, no. I'm the first."

"Finally." Her smile is large. "They wised up."

1976: Ai Hotel

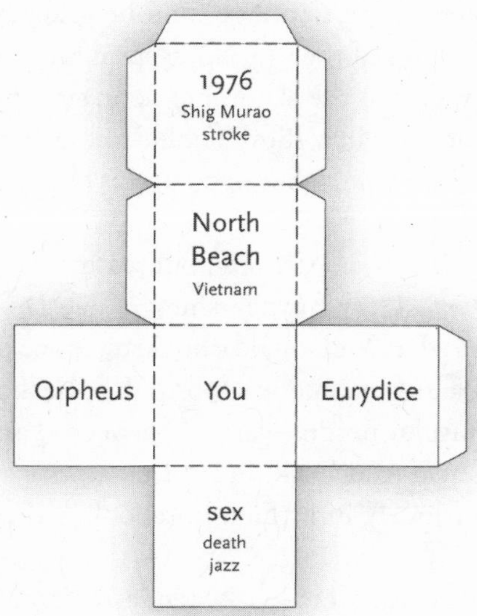

1: Devin & Yuri

Observe how Master Konnyaku, a scrunched and mottled clump of brown and gray fur, licks one of his remaining three paws, rubs its wetness across an empty socket. The fish head's now a neat pile of small bones and translucent scales. A long night of rain breaks, and the wet world framed by your teahouse door drips and breathes with quiet clarity. Sit here on the ledge with your bare toes swinging across the wet tips of grass and weeds, and watch the world wake—drunken snails and worms snatched by morning birds. Light flickers from a dream. Now pick the moonflowers creeping up the trellis, and scribble a poem on a J-Town fan, offered to lovers parted by death.

Devin climbs the ladder to his loft. He's built this structure to gain some space in this tiny room in the I-Hotel. Below, he's got a desk and shelves. Above, his mattress and eight-track cassette system, a necessary wall of music to keep his world insular. In this year, it might be a *Witch's Brew.* But still the human sounds are invasive. Joe's housing a dingbat prostitute next door to keep the men occupied. The insipid trill of her throat and the heavy groaning saturate the porous walls. Sometimes the eight-track speakers are not enough, and he grabs his hard penis and pumps it to the rhythms of the squeaking springs and the pounding bed, passes out. Then wakes to the slamming door, sits up high in his loft to greet his flaccid member in a slimy pool, demoralized again. A copy of Kant's *Critique of Pure Reason* lies open on his chest.

In your teahouse hideout, no *Critique,* but scattered collectibles perhaps. *Junky, Dharma Bums,* Gary Snyder, shunga, *The Divine Comedy.* Then two books discovered at McDonald's bookstore, one by Dick Nagai, the other, Imo Yashima. Asian American porn. Who'da thought. Settle naked side by side. Konnyaku nestles warmly between. Pass a sweet pungent joint. For a laugh, you read Dick; I read Imo.

Devin writes furiously in a thick notebook, writes to Yuri, the girl across the hall.

Yuri, his poems whisper anxiously, tenderly, caressing her name, her shy smile.

Yuri appears, often with an apprehensive look. Hi, she says to Devin as he arrives with the key to his room.

Hi.

Well, she says, see you later.

He watches her leave. He watches her arrive, sometimes with a guy. Always a different guy. A buff movement type who wears his jacket and boots casually like his cool masculinity. Sometimes the guy is there for many days, smell of pot and cigarettes seeping from under the door. Then one day he's gone, and Devin's poetry follows Yuri stumbling from her room, making a weaving path to the corridor bathroom, pours through the shower water, suds and bathes her body, follows every drop of water passing against her gentle curves and crevices and slick black hair.

He appears at his door as she returns, her hair turbaned in a towel. Hi. She looks embarrassed, then annoyed. Her eyes are red from crying, and she turns away. He can hear her sobbing behind the closed door.

Yuri? He knocks.

Go away.

Are you all right?

I'm fine. Go away.

He returns to his loft, settles into *A Love Supreme*, and writes again to Yuri, always and only to Yuri, his endless and intense feelings penned into page after page. Yuri, he moans, and somehow she appears there sitting in the loft, where they discuss in the minutest detail *Love's Body*. Freedom is poetry, he tells her. And she replies, Freedom is fire. Yes, yes, he writes it all, their conversation speaking urgently, a battling dialogue pressing extraordinary tension, rising with increasing excitability, breathlessly pressing the pen into and across the skin of her pages.

Konnyaku twirls around in his stuttered three-step and accommodates himself on your bare stomach. Quote passages from *Nephew of Nippon*, volume I. The protagonist is Dick Katai. Follow him around like a modern-day Genji in prewar L.A., dragging his great katana of a penis from Little Tokyo to Boyle Heights. Meanwhile, I hang out with Imo in the Central Valley, a farm girl siren who entices every migrant worker who ever picked a tomato.

The days grow into weeks into months into a year or two at least. Maybe Yuri has visited with Devin, listened to Miles on his eight-track, shared a couple of chashu bao. She looks at his shelves of books. Did you read all this? Herbert Marcuse. I think I had to read him for a class. I never finished it. I wish I were brainy like you.

Devin feels confused. But, he says. You are really smart. I know you are.

Oh Devin, you're sweet. She smiles wistfully. I've got to go. Study group, she sighs. I never know what they're talking about. Everyone knows I'm stupid. Maybe you can help me one of these days? She fumbles around in her purse, pops something between her teeth, gulps, and licks her lips.

Yeah, sure.

She doesn't invite him to come along, but he wouldn't go anyway. Doesn't he know more than they do? What is he afraid of? The FBI at his door, threatening to take his parents away. Are you or have you ever been a member of the Communist Party?

He watches the door close behind her, but thinks, hasn't he had several conversations with Yuri about advanced industrial societies and technology? He wants to find the entry in his notebook. When she leaves, he frantically searches through notebook after notebook for the exact passages. All night his mind flips through his past writings, switching about in philosophical eight-tracks. Sleepless.

Sleepless nights follow sleepless nights. Until one dawn, he steps into the corridor and sees Yuri's door left slightly ajar. The door, he senses, is open for a reason, left open for him. Yes, of course. She's been calling him. Yuri? he answers. A lava lamp is the only light, billowing globules rising in changing colors, casting shadows over scattered clothing, dirty dishes, cartons of leftover takeout, empty bottles of beer and cheap wine. The stink of sweat and beer and garlic and sex throbs there. Something grabs his tongue and attacks the nipples on his chest. Yuri? Her sheeted figure appears as a sarcophagus across the bed, her arms folded across her breasts, neatly tucked in. And yet her head hangs twisted to one side, pillowed by a book.

She is his muse, but her lips are cold and her body is hard and her mind is frozen.

Dick and Imo are fast reads. Chase the rising tension to the inevitable climax, swapping the balderdash of hard and wet, large and throbbing. Dick performs between lawnmowers and over raw sushi bars. Imo behind tractors and in hot tubs of steaming water. Rub the rural into the urban. Twist Dick into Imo and Imo into Dick. Make the books collide, nisei to nisei, every forbidden act strangled into quietness.

Who wrote this shit?

Bona fide nisei, wouldn't you say?

How do you know?

Turn the page.

Executive Order 9066. Dick and Imo go to camp.

Devin pulls the pillow book from under Yuri's head. She has pasted a cover of soft pink fabric and cushioned her book with felt padding. Within the pages, he reads a compendium of lists. List of friends. List of family. Significant dates. List of addresses where I have lived. List of foods I have eaten. Places visited. Movies. Songs. Bands. Concerts. Colors. Clothing. Books I have read. Books I want to read. Books I should read. Likes. Favorite things. Dislikes. Facial types. Body types. Animals. Dreams. Books. Boyfriends. Boyfriends I have slept with. Names I'd rather have. Stupid things I did. Movie stars I love. Things I should like but don't. List of resolutions. List of broken resolutions. Things I hate about myself. More things I hate about myself.

Devin cannot find himself under any list, negative, positive, lukewarm, or nondescript. He replaces the book beneath her head.

Dawning light searches through the blinds for dusty life, smacks his face wet with tears. He grabs her body in his arms, runs from the room, up and down the corridors. Yuri! Yuri! Yuri! Screaming until every door is open and every room is filled with the long wail of his shuddering and horrific grief.

2: Virgilio & Momo

Set your tape recorder on the table with bananas and fish. Press PLAY/REC. Rolling.

Manong, you got a story to tell?

I got plenty. Whatchu wanna know?

Any story you got to tell. We gonna record you for posterity.

Ha! You sitting on your posterity!

Laugh while manong reaches for the fish and slowly picks it clean from the bone. He nods and eats. Pulls apart more fish, working meticulously, tail to head, leaving the best for last, licking his fingers, licking his lips. Not bad. You cook this yourself? If Master Konnyaku could speak, this is what he might say.

Thus move from manong to manong with tape recorder, bananas, and fish, recording posterity captured in the dark filaments of spinning ribbon. Collect the audio cassettes in piles and stacks, hour by hour into hundreds of hours, a rising clutter displacing the graceful serenity of the tokonoma, Konnyaku's clumsy stalking toppling everything, golden locks of precious ribbon caught in his stubborn claws. Arrive to find him tangled in tape spaghetti, charging around with no escape, one hysterical one-eyed cat, looking like the wedding car, flying nuptials, trailing streamers and empty cans. Chase him in circles and into the garden. Konnyaku! Konnyaku! Until finally the stuff is extricated, tossed into the irises.

Sit quietly with Konnyaku, smoothing back his patchy fur, calming his racing heart. Contemplate voices lost to posterity, the eternal presence of the past captured in a wadded brain of plastic tape.

Manong Virgilio steps out into the corridor and catches Devin, holding Devin holding Yuri, holding both into silence, speaking incantations in Tagalog mixed with dialect as if Devin must naturally comprehend. Virgilio speaks quietly, continually, loosening Yuri from Devin's crazed grip and heaving sadness, extracting her body, a naked doll from a child's arms, carries her away.

Take heart that despite Konnyaku's taped turmoil, hundreds of manong hours still remain. Press PLAY and settle back to listen.

What's that?

Turn up the volume.

Hear that? Manong's eating. Chewing, chewing.

Now what?

So, manong, when did you come to America?

Long time ago. Chewing, chewing.

When was that?

Back then. Chewing, chewing.

Hmmm.

Dessert time. Peeling the banana.

Listen to long hours of chewing, chewing, clinking dishes, smacking lips, gulping beer, burping, burping, grunting. Fall asleep, then awake again to the same. Chewing, grunting, smacking, burping. Not bad. You cook this yourself?

You think it's got to come naturally, but only eating comes naturally. Talking manongs may not be your project. Pass this on to another poet.

Devin knocks at Virgilio's door.

Virgilio, you there?

Yeah.

You got time for an interview? Devin holds the tape recorder up for Virgilio to see. It's your turn. Are you ready to talk?

Oh, Devin, you back? Where you been?

Langley, you know. I went crazy there for a while.

I know. Happens to the best of us. You come back O.K.

Yeah.

You can still hear those voices?

No.

Voices are not so bad. Keep you company. But, one time I'm hearing her voice. But she's not there. Not anywhere. Can't be, but it's her voice. So I follow it.

Whose voice?

Momo. My beautiful peach girl. A long time ago I know her. I'm working for her father out there Central Valley way. It's a good job. He's got peaches, apricots. Other vegetables too. I'm doing all the work. But how can you only work and not see Momo? I'm seeing Momo, and my heart is melting. How can a heart love so much? I never felt this way before. And Momo is seeing me, and you think it can't happen, this love at first sight. For Momo and me, this is how it happens, and I never know so much happiness and so much loving. Once you feel this, you get the feeling of sadness because how can you keep the happiness? So we go crazy for each other and think maybe we will run away. But what kind of job I got, going from place to place, picking fruit? And her folks got plans for her, sending her to Japan to get an education and a Japanese husband. It's all planned out. But we are making love all the time, every opportunity. We cannot stop. Every secret place. Back of a truck. In the ditch. Up in the trees. Between the crates. Under the house. Sometimes morning. Sometimes middle of the day. Every night. How can we stop? Like two magnets. My mind doesn't work. Only my body, like I can't breathe, my heart busting out of my pants. And that's the way it is every day for days and days, like a marathon we never stop, and maybe I should know she's pregnant, got the rise in her belly, but I'm loving her even more, even when we know what we got is impossible, the more impossible, the more we need what we can't have, the more we got to make this loving, crying together, crying so much we mixing salty with sweet with bitter, like trying to scratch a way inside to some place where we stay together forever. You gonna run your machine or what?

Oh. This is your story?

Coming up best part. So one day I'm coming to meet her in a hideaway spot in the garage, and I don't know why I never think this has to end even though she's crying all the time and I'm licking away her tears and telling her we gonna escape and go away and never stop this loving. And so—

Virgilio?

Been a while, but the pain is the same.

Get your junior poets going off in every direction with separate tape recorders doing what the professors call an oral history project, collecting manong voices, history from the people who lived it. The audiocassette pile grows even larger, but Konnyaku avoids it now. Listen to all these new tapes. No more chewing-chewing, but new developments. Manongs talking pidgin. Manongs talking dialect. Seven hundred islands of seven hundred dialects, mixing it all up, speaking in authentic manong voices. What are they saying?

How the hell we know?

We lost control of the project.

They been taking the tape recorder and passing it around. Say we mess them up with too many questions.

They say, we can do it ourselves. When they remember, they say, just press PLAY/REC. Easy.

Devin waits. Virgilio's breath stutters up, holding tightly to the old pain. They stare a long time at the double twirling wheels in the plastic window of the tape recorder, concentrating on the recording machine, waiting.

Virgilio breathes in deep. So then I think Momo's joking with me. How's her feet dangling there? I got to climb up and cut the rope. I got to get her down. I got to get her neck straight. I got to make her speak to me. I got to hold her in my arms. I got to make her breathe. I got to feel her breathing on my neck. Got to taste her lips. Touch her breast. Touch all her spots. Touch where she's got the baby. No. No. No. How could she do this? How? How could she leave me behind like this? You know?

Bring the professors to the teahouse for tea. Stir it up and make them comfortable on cushions and at peace with nature, then press PLAY and make them listen to hours and hours of manong voices, seven hundred dialects from seven hundred islands. Who's going to transcribe all this? Who knows what they are saying? How is this different from chewing-chewing?

Invaluable documentation.

You got the right idea because these guys are dropping dead every day. Time's a factor here.

I think I know a guy in linguistics connected to Pacific Island studies.

Maybe there is someone at Manila University.

We need to get a grant. This will take time and money.

I'm on sabbatical this year. I can't take this on for another two years.

This is seminal work.

Seminal.

Devin and Virgilio cry. Sob into the microphone.

Maybe we should stop.

No. I got to tell you this. I got to take you back there. So like I started to tell you, I'm hearing her voice. I can't stop hearing her voice. So I follow her voice, and maybe I'm following her voice for many days, I don't know how long, going this way and that, never stopping, and her voice takes me there.

Where?

To where she is. Who knows, but I go there, maybe to hell, to the dead world, and then I see my Momo there like a dream, her beautiful face, her young body, everything glowing, I see her. I swear to you, I see her. And don't you know, I do everything just the way they tell you you gotta do it. You got to walk away and never look back, so that's the way she follows you out of the dead world, back to the living world, but Devin, this is what you need to know, what I didn't know when my Momo called to me: the dead cannot come back. They stay dead forever, and that's the truth, so even though she's calling to you and you follow her voice to the dead world, you got to look back and see the truth. Light a fire, and look back. You got that choice.

But what did you do?

I never look back.

But—

Can't you see? Behind me? Momo's always there following me, following me until this day, following me, now this old man, forever. She's always there, but never here. That's how I lose my life to her.

How many tape recorders can you find? Start with ten, then get ten more. Mr. Chang's got a whole collection. Drive all over the city, across the bay, radio station's giving them away, haul them all back to Bush Street. Spend a fortune in D batteries and fill the teahouse with portable tape recorders, wall to wall. Insert the manong voices into every tape recorder, and press PLAY. PLAY. PLAY. PLAY. PLAY. PLAY. PLAY . . . Konnyaku steps delicately across the player floor, one eye circling circling, pressing his crooked hip into the warm motors, paw snatching at the turning tapes.

Slowly, manong voices grow tape recorder by tape recorder, first chewing together, then burping, lulling quiescence, lips working the oil of fish and spit, then singing, joking, moving in crazy half beats, sad and melodic, talk talk talk, babeling posterity, singing, speaking simultaneously, unison of jabber jabber jabber, multiplying stories in multiplying dialects, multiplying memories, multiplying songs and jokes and lies, then running wild, staccato, pontificating, stylistic thrills and swoops, strutting and shining, exaggerated pose and cackle, then rising conflicts, battling voices, ha!

Back out and fall into the irises, shoved out by the multiplying sounds, Konnyaku cowering, burrowing his head into your crotch. How many manongs packed into one teahouse? seven hundred? ten thousand? Even with the volume low, their resounding convention rumbles, ten thousand muttering, chewing voices collecting in a crescendo, a crazy rising din, muscular waves of thudding sound pressing at fragile walls of borrowed wood, blowing out the speakers, paper screens ripping in sudden poofs, busting out in frightening wails, screaming herds collecting momentum, exploding ten to the ten times scratching tearing ripping breaking bruising cracking kicking swearing stomping punching twisting growling punching pounding beating pounding fucking fucking fucking fucking. Pick up Konnyaku with every remaining patch of hair porcupined into the air and run away, out the garden, through the gate, down the steps, down Bush Street, run like a fool, run like a fool.

When the police arrive, the landlord's fingering the stem of a crystal spout of Drambuie, catching the last recorded groans and stuttered jabber jabber crying sobbing groaning, dying, whimper wheezing choking sweet sweet single blue banjo twang and ache, spent, moseying away. Anyway, how the hell long can a ninety-minute tape last? *Click click snap pop blam zfwit zpit fooo . . .*

3: Sophie & Egan

Descend into the bowels of Arthur Ma's basement, six light bulbs hanging in an abandoned fortune cookie factory. Arthur uses the old vats to mix paints and wash brushes, and uses the heating grills like palettes. Every inch of wall space covered with his oil canvases, monstrous figures splattered aggressively in distorted robust strokes of dirty color, a relentless series birthing one cruel vision after another. Arthur sits disheveled, eyes bloodshot, under one of the light bulbs at an easel sketching all his monsters, tossing the writhing demons into piles spread over the floor. Let the eyes adjust to Arthur's dim underworld, and follow George through the labyrinth of paper, canvas, paint, booze, drugs, and related paraphernalia to the center.

Hey, Arthur.

Arthur growls.

What happened to the nudes?

Models cost money. Taps his head. Free.

Free's a concept.

Sophie?

Gone away to Tokyo.

But stop. Remember the first day you met Sophie. George Baso pops his head into the teahouse and says, Let's go hang out in Arthur Ma's Chinatown basement and write poetry.

Pick up some manju and black coffee at Benkyodo, trot out of J-Town, and head over to Chinatown.

How come the basement? What if I'm writing about nature?

All the more reason. When did you last study what's underground?

Descend into the same bowels of Arthur's basement, same six light bulbs hanging in an abandoned fortune cookie factory, but in those days illuminating a world of nudes, sketches, and oil canvases of every color and kind of woman in every lascivious, languid, odalisque, or standing position, squatting, bending, turning, same robust strokes of thick intensity birthing one feminine vision after another. Arthur stands in the basement center at his easel pressing his brush in quick gestures, glancing back and forth at a seated model, her bare breasts and head turned to catch a swatch of light passing through the barred window at street level. Though in the basement with six low-watt bulbs, everything seems bathed in light.

Hey Arthur.

Hey.

Stand with George respectfully, looking indirectly at the naked woman, wondering where to look. Look at Arthur's painting.

Arthur waves his brush and says, That's Sophie.

Hi.

We're here to write poetry.

You've come to the right place. Sophie is poetry. Then he gets up, walks over to an old cabinet, and pulls out a dusty bag. Been saving this for you.

Look in the bag and pull out tiny strips of paper. *You have a secret admirer. Love asks no questions. A rainbow requires rain. Love like wildflowers is found in wild places.*

Grab a seat and write.

Sophie and Egan meet on Telegraph at Moe's reaching for the same used book: *The Tao of Love at the Spring Palace.* His smile is eloquent. Her body flushes.

I think I might have been here first, he taunts.

Recuperating quickly, she retorts, This may be the only copy. I've already checked at Bancroft.

Studying?

Art.

Of course.

What do you mean by that?

Well, maybe you'd consider sharing.

What? She grabs the book from the shelf. It's large and square and heavy.

He also claims it with a firm grip on the other corner.

She tugs it away. He tugs back. Back and forth, until she tugs as forcefully as possible, the volume slipping from his hands and she falling in a backward thrust, tumbling against the shelf. He rushes forward, creating an umbrella with his arms and shoulders as the entirety of the great arts of China, every porcelain vase and inked landscape in book form, topple around her.

Are you all right? I'm really sorry.

She scrambles around, picking up the fallen books, too embarrassed to speak.

No, he says. Please just sit for a moment. This is all my fault. He picks up and rearranges the books. He smiles sheepishly. Saved you from the Great Wall.

The last book is the book in question, *The Tao of Love,* tossed open to a random page, a Ming print of a Chinese couple seated, with their genitals tenderly pressed together, in a pavilion surrounded by water lilies, a weeping willow falling gently over its roof.

On the way to the I-Hotel, check out Arthur's studio from time to time. Pose naked for Arthur because it seems natural in the presence of so much nakedness. Must be like being in a nudist colony, you say to Arthur. Sophie's usually there in a hippy smock sketching complicated figures, but always working on the same large abstract oil painting, a radiating presence of heat and color, the only art that's not human and naked in the basement. Learn that Sophie was one of Arthur's students from when he was at the Institute. Still working on that same painting, he gestures at her continuing work. Masterpiece. I can't work so slow, he shakes his head. I get bored.

So what about all these nudes?

I tell you a story. My father was a Confucian scholar right here in Chinatown. Everything was by the Confucian book, but he had all these daughters, seven beautiful daughters and then me, his only son. If he had lived, he'd still be having daughters. I was the wild card, the mistake, but Chinese don't think that way. So I was really spoiled. You can imagine. But you think about the pressure of being the only male heir to a Confucian scholar. Maybe you can play the patriarch, but the truth is my mother and my seven sisters ran the show. My father and I were just hanging around like a couple of jewels in the crown. So every opportunity I snuck away, crossed Broadway, did acid, found enlightenment, became a Taoist.

Think about your teahouse and Zen. Taoism's a further complication. Scratch your head.

If George is there, he gets agitated and paces around. Typical. You ask about nudes, you get Confucianism.

O.K. O.K., Arthur says and thinks. Confucianism serves the patriarchy. It's a complicated set of laws to preserve a bureaucracy with the patriarch at the top. But Taoism serves the matriarchy. The Confucian patriarch generates kids to build his kingdom. The Taoist matriarch generates energy to prolong life.

Probably all bullshit, George snickers.

Take a look at this. Arthur hands George a book.

I can't read Chinese.

Handbook of the Plain Maiden Su-nu. It's in all there. Arthur taps the cover. The spirit of the valley never dies. She is the mysterious gate. The great secret of the Tao is the key to longevity.

Egan turns, wraps his limbs around Sophie, who turns again and wraps herself around him, bodies slipping over and around, under and down.

Roll your body over in an arch like this.

Grab my thighs. Tighter.

Pull down on my hips.

Your hair's tickling my butt.

Hang on.

What is this?

Can't you tell? Yin and yang.

Who's Yin?

Beats me.

Are you the white tiger or am I?

I'm the white tiger. You're the green dragon.

Are you sure? Let me see that book.

No, don't move. We've created a sculpture.

Like contortionists in a circus.

I need to move. I think I might fart.

Farts are yang.

Take several trips into Arthur's basement before finally figuring out his arcane connections from Taoism to nude portraiture. It's all explained in the Chinese writing, the lessons of Su-nu, who instructs the Yellow Emperor on the art of the bedchamber. Arouse the woman, taking her with increasing pleasure through the ten movements, observing the exercises of pleasure and health but keeping one's vital energies. Practice this art, and live to 150. Elixir of life. The Yellow Emperor became immortal, ascending to heaven after intercourse with twelve hundred women. Some accounts figure thirty-six hundred. Arthur figures a thousand nudes will take him to a hundred. He's not greedy.

Sophie asks, What about women?

Women don't have to worry. You're the source.

I guess so.

Everyone looks at Sophie's protruding belly bumping into the basement clutter of Arthur's documenting canvases, her mountain rising month by month.

Later George says, Arthur's been hiding Sophie until the baby comes. She's got a room back of the basement. Her folks have a flower business in Alameda. They think she's in L.A.

Who's the father?

That's the thing. It's Egan.

Egan?

Arthur's son. You didn't know? Arthur had a son. Fell in love with a beautiful black woman a while back. One day Egan showed up.

Where is he now?

Vietnam.

Egan, Sophie whispers and rolls away with the book. Five signs. Five desires. Ten movements. Nine positions. Thirty methods. Have you been doing your homework?

Let's start with the five signs. First your vital energies rise, and you blush. He laughs. You never stopped blushing since the bookstore. You are just one long blush.

You rat. O.K., what next?

Let me see that book.

No fair cheating.

One should kiss lightly.

The nipples become hard, and you sweat around your nose.

Softly embrace.

Tongue becomes thick and moist, and you swallow.
I get really wet.
Then I should caress you softly.
My throat is dry, and I swallow constantly.
Now rock lightly back and forth.
Rock me, yes.
I'm rocking you, baby.
Reversed Dragon, she rasps.
Eight times shallow. Two times deeply.
All your ailments will vanish.

Push aside the sliding door to find George pacing in the garden. Come on, he says. Sophie's baby's due.

Stare through the big window at a dozen tiny swaddled newborns in a dozen crib trays on rollers. Scrunchy heads with sleeping eyes, dozing, little mouths yawning, wailing, groping, opening and closing around imaginary nipples. Tiny hands folded inside oversized sleeves.

Which one is it?

Maybe that one. Looks like a dark version of Arthur.

They all look the same.

It doesn't matter. We won't see it again.

Why?

Sophie's giving it up for adoption. Arthur got the word about Egan. KIA.

4: Stony & Aiko

Before there was ever a teahouse, there was Daruma living in the pantry. Walk in one day to grab a can of tomato soup, and he's sitting there on the floor, sitting cross-legged in monk's robes, large round bald head, messy beard around his chin, and two bushy white rabbit-tail brows patched above each eye. One eye opens like a searchlight and looks around.

Stumble away in shock and drop the can on your own foot. Ow! Goddamn fuck!

Now both eyes open, and his whole body shakes with laughter.

Who are you? Who let you in? What are you doing here?

He stops laughing and seems to think about this, then grunts and breathes deeply, returns to a stoned pose.

Back away to think about this situation, closing the pantry door momentarily and reopening it to check, just to check. Open the can of soup, add water, and heat to a simmer. Check the pantry again. Divide the soup into two bowls, and put one bowl with a spoon inside the pantry door. Leave the house and walk around J-Town for a couple of hours trying to sort things out. Go into all the temples, and ask if they're not missing a certain monk with bushy eyebrows. Return to find the empty bowl with the soupspoon placed outside the pantry door. Worry about this situation for about a week, then give up.

Couple weeks later, George comes around with a friend. This is Sesshu, he introduces him. He's an artist from Japan. He needs a place to stay so I said he could stay with you.

No way. I already got a monk in my pantry. See?

George and Sesshu look inside the pantry. No shit.

Sesshu says, Shit.

Monk says, Shit.

Sesshu sits down in the pantry with the monk and nods. It's very good.

George, no way he's going to stay.

It's very good.

George shrugs. Sit at the kitchen table and pull at your hair, pull your glasses off and rub your eyes, slap your face and pull at your cheeks, replace your glasses and refocus. George is still there. He's at the pantry door listening to Sesshu and the monk, whose conversation sounds like grunts and jabs, low staccato and hissing, then haah haah haah haaaaaahhh. He looks over and says, They're talking some heavy shit, heavy, heavy shit.

In a prison cell in Soledad, California, Stony composes a letter to Aiko.

> *Dear Aiko, angel of my recovery,*
>
> *I received your last letter dated January 8 and have read it again and again, every chance I get. That's true about all your letters, and I have my favorite letters already. I've even memorized parts of them and carry your words in my mind constantly. Especially your descriptions of traveling in North Vietnam and meeting those righteous people fighting for their liberation.*
>
> *I have drawn a small calendar, and I am crossing out every day until my parole. I promise you that first thing, I'm headed out to L.A. to see you. I admit I'm a little nervous about meeting you in person for the first time, but maybe it had to be this way, having this time in the joint to reflect and the sweet miracle of knowing you through your letters. I am reading and studying up, doing my push-ups daily, preparing to be there, fighting at your side.*
>
> *Your yellow brother in revolution,*
> *Stony*

Now there are two Japanese living in the pantry. Wonder how many Japanese can fit in one pantry. It's like this, says George, Japan's an island with no more space. Comparatively, your pantry's a mansion.

It can't be the poorly stocked pantry unless the bare shelves inspire hunger, but Sesshu emerges cooking Japanese cuisine—udon in clear fish stock, mushroom buttons and dried minnows in miso, raw tuna dipped in wasabi and shoyu, salted napa and daikon, blocks of tofu spattered with grated ginger, giants bowls of hot steamed rice. Wash everything down with green tea.

Now, Sesshu announces, we go out.

Now? It's past midnight.

In Japan, it's tomorrow.

Head out to Post Street escorted by two Japanese, a young skinny artist-type with a stringy goatee squeaking forward in slip-on Keds and an old monk in dark robes, the clatter of his geta on cold cement bouncing back and forth across the dark empty streets lined with sooty Victorians. Slip into a bar, but the bartender's already announcing last call. What'll it be?

Sesshu says, Jack Daniels.

Monk adds, Rocks.

Notice your friend Kats nursing a final scotch, and introduce Sesshu and Daruma to a J-Town local. Kats's family owns the fish store over there on Post.

Fish? Sesshu lights up. I need fish. My art, he points to his nose, fish.

How about it, Kats? This place is closing up. Let's take them over to see your fish.

Heard Miles Davis is in town.

Most likely end up at Jimbo's after hours.

Most likely.

Kats opens up the dark store, shows Sesshu the fridge with the giant fish, then opens up the back storage, and if the sound of a horn was distant at first, now Bop City's wailing through the back wall. Kats pulls away some boxes smelling of dried bonita and toasted rice, reveals a loose board, pulls that away, crouches low, and sneaks through. Follow him in to where he's got some crates snug in the cold packed earth, covered tubs of curing pickles, ikura, and kasu, and take a seat for the jazz concert of your life, not first-row seats but under the stage itself. Sense the weight of the man above, his feet keeping rhythms in the creak of the old wood punching down onto your head, the energy of blowing reaching down into the ground rising between your feet, through your crotch, and rushing between your eyes and out your brain like a blowhole into his blowhole. It's too much for a man to take. Trade seats with Daruma, and watch his eyes pop and his eyebrows catch fire. Far fucking out.

Settle into the sweet stink of jazz and seaweed and fish, and pass around a bottle of sake for the next couple of hours until Kats says, Time to get outta here before they bring in the morning produce.

Follow Kats out through the narrow aisles stacked with sembei, nori, and canned takenoko, and once outside, nod to scattered couples leaving Jimbo's next door. Hey, where's Daruma? The monk's been left behind. Think momentarily he'll be happier in the fish market, but Sesshu returns to fetch his roommate, running back into the dark store then back again to report. Sesshu's eyes are wide with glee. He says, Come look! We find great treasure!

Return to the back of the store to find Daruma pulling books out of the trash and stashing copies in his robes. Kats looks at the heap. The titles are all in Japanese. My sister's doing spring cleaning. Must be tossing this stuff. Used to be my dad's, but nobody's reading it now.

So, says Sesshu excitedly, we can take! He looks around. There are more in boxes stacked everywhere. Must rescue books, Sesshu announces with determination. He picks up a box and shoves it into your empty arms. Follow your crew huffing under heavy boxes filled with kanji, pantry reading material you guess, turning up Buchanan in single file. Turn back to catch a glimpse of Miles and his entourage, swinging their horn cases, moving slowly away down Post.

One day, Stony walks out the gate at Soledad, heads away from his past: slicked-back hair and toe-pointed shoes, running the J-Flats with the Baby Black Juans, dropping acid weekly and smoking pot daily. Time to leave all that behind, clean up his act, join forces with the people. Time to find his revolutionary woman. Time to meet Aiko.

Sesshu and Daruma are busy turning the pantry into a library, substituting the Campbell's soup system for some kind of Japanese Dewey decimal. Sesshu's pointing and Daruma intones like it's a sumo match: Hokusai. Utamaro. Eisen. Kuniyoshi. Kunisada. Shuncho. Hiroshige.

You got richest collection in all of Japantown. Maybe don't have this even in Japan. Stolen by American missionaries. Bombs away. Can you believe it? Sesshu grabs you like you need to be woken up. Greatest art of the Edo! Floating world, but, he spits out his skinny chest to emphasize, better yet, shunga!

Shunga?

He snatches a volume from the shelf, stab-bound at one end by thread. This, he says, enpon. He searches for an appropriate translation. Ancient

Japanese-style *Playboy*. Here, he opens to a page, spreads smooth the colorful block print on yellowing rice paper, ornate Japanese couple in swooping hair with dazzling combs, flowing layers of silken robes in patterned details, falling away to indiscreetly reveal the conjoining of the largest genitalia you have ever seen.

Holy shit! Cockeyed thoughts rattle your brain.

Sesshu asks, How do you think?

Big. You gesture for comedy.

You don't believe?

Daruma steps forward, parts his robes, and reveals his tremendous equipment.

Nod with honored appreciation.

Daruma points to another page and mutters something to Sesshu.

He says, this position extremely difficult.

Turn your head to ascertain how the bodies could twist around each other, the legs bent in opposite directions, but the penis making its appropriate entry.

Don't try this unless you are expert.

Daruma grunts seriously, points to his nose, and grins.

Now, Sesshu pronounces, I find my inspiration. You?

I find I'm horny.

Horny?

You know.

That's why you gonna write poetry. I do art. Women come very curious about poetry. Curious about art. Poetry, art, eventually, shunga.

What kind of art do you do?

Abangyarudo.

Go with Sesshu to Kats's fish market and get the fish for Sesshu's abangyarudo art. Sesshu turns the house into a workshop, slicing fish, slapping and gluing it with leaves and dead branches from the backyard onto canvases, and painting it all over with thick wild swatches of color, shellacking everything into shiny, hard, three-dimensional surfaces. Voila!

Beautiful, you say, looking at fish preserved in variously rotting stages.

No ugly. Ugly. That's beautiful.

When he's got about twenty abangyarudos, he says, Now we go to Venice, open exhibition, sell everything. You got a car? I show you the way.

Venice?

He gets a map of California out and points to Los Angeles.

Fill up Macario's old station wagon with twenty abangyarudos with two crazy-assed Japanese, Daruma chanting scriptures, seventy miles per hour all the way down 101. Then, somewhere near Soledad, pick up an Asian cat with a paper bag of his belongings, on the highway, thumb pointing south.

Stony, where you headed?

L.A.

Mind if we take a slight detour?

Sequoias, says Sesshu, pointing to the map. Turn left.

Stony joins Daruma in the backseat, surprises the monk with his fine Japanese. Hey, Daruma says in Japanese. Why does he make sense?

He's speaking Japanese, says Sesshu.

Ah!

Pretty soon Stony and Daruma must be talking heavy shit. Talk enlightenment through Fresno and on east into the Sierras, right up to the redwood groves covered in a thick blanket of snow. Suddenly jump out of the car and chase now three crazy-assed yelping Japanese into the snow. Rub crotches against the giant sequoias for energy and longevity. Spin snowballs to hit the upper branches of one sequoia, dislodging a snow pack over Daruma peeing freely into the crisp air. Pass around the shochu, and pack snow into dharma statues. Find an empty cabin and sit around the potbelly stove, drinking tea and shochu, eating Sesshu's riceballs and pickles, talking more enlightenment.

Sesshu says to you, Read a poem.

Wait, says Daruma, and pulls out a piece of bamboo from the folds of his robes. Yokobue, he says and hands it to Stony. Play.

Stony looks at the bamboo flute, confused.

First time easy, Daruma says. Play yokobue with poem, he commands.

You read. Stony blows.

Heavy shit, nods Sesshu.

Heavy, says Stony.

Shit, says Daruma.

Sesshu says, Stony, you Asian American yakuza, that's right.

Everyone agrees, and Daruma produces another bottle of shochu.

Sesshu continues, Stony, we got a job for you. You gonna kill dharma bums, Ginsberg first, then Snyder. Then, Sesshu points at you, he's gonna be number one Asian American poet.

Daruma grunts agreement.

Stony says, Nah, I'm on parole.

Oh, too bad. Sesshu pauses. Just you remember. His voice slurs and rolls around the cabin, kisses the belly of the fire.

What?

I forget.

Stony knocks on Aiko's door.

She's wearing a Mao jacket and cap and holding a shotgun extended across the back of her neck. Behind her the speaker system swells with orchestral strings, traditional zithers, triumphant horns, rolling cymbals, and the marching drums of the *Red Detachment of Women.* Stony could swear the whole room is glowing and pulsing red, that the entire cherubic yellow nation is welcoming him home. His chest pounds with the pride of eight hundred million people.

You're late, she says.

Never too late for the revolution.

She smiles and turns. Of course she's barefoot, and he follows her jaunty step, watches her pull the shotgun to her shoulder, focus on an unseen target, practice her stance. She cocks the twelve-gauge, *click clack,* and gently pushes it under the bed.

She tugs at his jacket, packed with her letters stuffed into every pocket, the most precious held next to his heart. She pulls them out and reads one or two, hands grazing his pounding chest, glancing at his lips that read back the parts he's memorized. His eyes fill with tears and longing.

Once a revolutionary, his lips form the words.

Her fingers find his lips, circle and touch his teeth, Now a comrade. She pushes her hands into the warmth of his jacket, padded thickly with all its paper, stamps, penned confessions. Everything has been said.

He pulls away her cap, her lustrous hair falling, pops open one by one the frog ties of her Mao jacket. Beneath, he's surprised to discover she's clothed in a second layer, a thin silk red pajama. Her revolutionary cast of accompanying dancers fly by with red ribbons, and she smiles. This begins in stages, touching through the scarlet layers, reaching within, feeling, exchanging soft, then wetter, kisses. Chu chu. Pa pa. Uun uun.

Time to put the shunga and its big promises on the bed. Twelve pages of twelve months turning fragrant pine over pristine snow to fluttering, fading cherry blossoms to erect murasaki irises to plump yellow chrysanthemums and crimson maples. Detachment's red thunder fills the room in powerful splendor, a symphony in four movements. Bodies roll and twist and turn, impossible contortions, grow dizzy with the visions of postered faces plastered to every wall: Mao to Marx to Ho to Lumumba to Lenin to Fidel to Malcolm to Che, zapping around and around, all the revolutionary men hard with anticipation.

Ha ha, fu fu, breathless
Little revolutionary sister
Movement man
Nicha wet and nicha sticky
Gusu wet and gusu rubbing
Slow nururi wet and slipping
Ha ha, uun uun uun
Zuppo sucking
Splashy piccha
Your love waters
Uh, uh, ah ah, uh uh
Ahh ahh
Aahh
Sloshing zupo zupo sloshing
Slippery nuru nuru slippery
Stand tokki tokki erect
Go deeply
Dig me there
Bicha bicha wet and bicha bicha slapping
Faster faster
Deeper deeper
Twitching biko biko muscles
Uun uun, ahh ahh ahh
Byokku byokku
Byokku byokku

Drive up to the Venice art gallery and unload all of Sesshu's abangyarudo, no doubt rotting and degrading under shellac. *Ephemeral* is what the gallery copy notes. Sesshu emerges with a wad of cash and hands you half.

What's this for?

For your teahouse.

What teahouse?

Maybe, he shrugs. You never know.

One day, Sesshu sends a postcard from Paris, and about the time Daruma floats away from the pantry, the three-legged, one-eyed Master Konnyaku stumbles in, his big balls dragging around under a crooked tail.

5: Clio & Abra

Hanging out with the poetry boys—Jack Sung, George Baso, Paul Lin, to name a few—on the roof of the I-Hotel, pass around the Christian Brothers and shout obscenities at the moon, you bunch of howling gangster coyotes dropping your pants to moon the moon, rising to exchange the sun's dying horizon. That's when the women catch you with your pants down, and you got to zipper/button up and return to being cool. Record the historic moment up on the roof of the I-Hotel when Jack, George, Paul, and you step forward to meet Sandy Hu, her Lady Murasaki, Clio, and me. Gust of wind flying through our hair, whipping up flared pants over worn boots, zipping around tank tops, rhinestones, and lavender leather. Sun down, moon rising. Make no mistake about it.

Abra's late but makes the second set, waves from the back of the bar, trying to catch Clio's eye. Even if Clio's seen Abra through the stage lights, she's ignoring her, trying to forget her earlier disappointment, working at the intricacies of the strings buzzing beneath her fingers, forcing her instrument to moan and wail. The rasping charge from the guitar reaches to the back of that dark underworld, and Abra feels it stab her in the gut, taunting and cruel.

At the table, Abra swivels the ice in her Coke, watches Clio take her time before taking a seat. Abra leans over for a kiss, but Clio pulls away, orders something hard on the rocks.

Abra's contrite. Meeting went longer. Then I had to mimeo flyers, distribute them. We've got a court date coming up, then a rally. Sorry. Who were you talking to?

New drummer. Vicki's replacement.

Oh? Where were you last night?

Practice.

I waited.

I thought you had a meeting.

I went over to your place. You weren't there either.

Band had to discuss things. Looks like we have a gig in L.A.

Why does the drummer keep looking this way?

How are the kids?

Sleeping.

Who's watching?

They shouldn't wake up.

Shit can happen. You'd better go.

I will. Just give me some time.

Look, Abra, it's not working out.

You promised. We promised. We can't let things get between us.

Things? You mean kids? You mean meetings? You mean politics? Does your collective approve of me? Do they even know about me?

I haven't asked you to join.

This L.A. thing is important to me. We might a get a record deal out of it.

They're just using you.

Who?

Those white girls. You're the only one with real talent.

Maybe I'm using them.

Didn't you tell the drummer about me?

What's there to tell?

Up on the roof, share the Christian Brothers with the poetry sisters, who oblige you with a small sample of their work. Listen to Clio's lyrics for a song about a hound-dog daddy who abuses and rapes her, about that daddy getting what's coming to him. If Clio could hook up her guitar and a mic, she'd blast the message into every tong association in Chinatown, every strip bar in the North Beach, every men's room in every office building in the financial district. Huddle under that rising moon, quiet and contemplative after Clio's emotional rendition, but the poetry brothers are already pretty drunk, and therefore giddy, stupid, and insensitive.

Well, I'd say as a rock song, it works for shock value, but I don't do rock. I'm more a jazz man myself.

It's not really a poem. It's a song.

Now let's be honest. Do all women have this imagination of their fathers doing it to them? What do you call it? Electra complex?

That Freudian shit is for white people.

Shit, what's this saying about Asian men? That's what I wanna know.

Why you wanna make us out to be assholes? When're you gonna give us a break?

When we write poetry, we write about how we love you.

Finally we stand up to the white man, and you blame us for your bound feet.

You fucking pigs! Clio yells and runs from the rooftop, poetry sisters all close behind.

Where're they going?

Just having a constructive conversation.

Thought she wanted my opinion.

Actually, I liked it.

Abra cradles Clio's lovely head.

Before I leave, Clio says, one more time.

Wild girl, grab me till I'm sore.

One more time, cherry bomb.

Bodies soft and smooth, but every movement hides a muscular and brutal edge, a slow tearing away, kneading out every hurt and unkindness, accusing hands grabbing and scraping, greedy to feel the ending, the long relentless twang holding out for as long as possible. Never stop. Make this feeling eternal. Make my hurt in hurt complete.

And yes, the flowing landscape of breast and hip matches buttocks and nape. And yes, the tongue burns with the salty slime of lemon peel, acidic and bitter. And yes, wet centers meet, aching and tender, dark iris to dark iris. And yes, fingers and palms play the body, one string, one nervous lip, one tense nipple at a time, then two, then multiple lips and nipples, fluttering, keying the melody and the deep bass all at once. Ordinary hands seen in the light of day, working hands—writing, typing, cooking, gesturing hands—now darkly languid yet urgent, pressing, slipping, spreading and knuckled, a secret talent, a secret eros. Praying, preying hands, lifting belly in a bittersweet sea.

Lean over the edge of the roof of the I-Hotel and see the dark figures of the poetry sisters charging down Kearny, a twinkle of poetry dust sparkling in their wake. Shout drunkenly, Asian sisters! Come back! We love you! Your idiotic cries roll off into the warmest night of that San Francisco summer.

And rising above the sweet lapping of the bay, you think the moon is a moon, but it is not. It's a blushing jellyfish alive in a cobalt sea, a belly-fish lifting, a great pulsing womb sucking, it's tentacles following, burning the hand that enters, entangling about the fingers, drawing them upward, plunging, tactile sensations traveling, the knowing shudder of the inner heart, the jelly's cruel, spasmed grip, sputter of white ink.

6: Bard & Huo Lian

Imagine the commotion on Columbus under the awning at City Lights, excited public primping for an imagined paparazzi, poet literati emerging from the netherworld of our pacific Barbary, scratching forty-eight-hour beards, replacing lipstick gloss, pupils punched from black confetti. The night is yours, name aglow in City Lights, published book of collected poems displayed prominently in the window, and, appearing tonight, reading and book signing by you, the author.

Where the fuck is he?

Paul, the editor, is pacing around nervously, wondering if someone's finally killed you off for your innocence. Arthur is the paparazzi, moving through the crowd and flashing photos of your historic moment. Hiro is uncorking, pouring, and drinking the wine, and about an hour into the scheduled event, George raises his glass, proposes a toast, and proceeds to read all your poems, starting on page one.

Make love, not war. What does this really mean?

It happens during rehearsal, Huo Lian playing the Japanese prostitute who's fallen in love with the young clerk, played by Bard. They've modernized the old eighteenth-century Chikamatsu play originally written for Bunraku puppet theatre, kept the Japanese costuming and the powdered faces but with a tattered, Brechtian edge. Separated by greed and the social desires of others, the star-crossed lovers find no recourse except the promise of life together in death. It begins in the scene where Bard is hidden under Huo Lian's robes, touching her feet tucked beneath her buttocks, and travels to the last scenes of michiyuki when their bodies gasp together in the final throes of passion.

I flubbed the last lines, Bard apologizes.

We just need more time, Huo Lian answers.

Maybe if I come over to your place.

Yes, you'd better. Only a few days to opening.

I have a confession to make. I flubbed my lines because—

I know. Maybe we can use it to our advantage.
I didn't understand the play until that moment.
I still don't understand the play. I don't understand my feelings.
What are you feeling?
Possessed. I feel taken over by ghosts.
Are you afraid?
Are you?

Someone says, Stop George before he reads the whole book.

Paul gets up and talks about how you and he went through piles of your papers and finally culled them down to this.

Hiro gets up and talks about how he first met you, how he walked into this storefront on Post Street just before they tore the street down and found you trying to run a used bookstore in a condemned building. Nothing in there but Japanese porn, but the real stuff. Seriously, the woodcut originals. Hiro toasts his glass like he should know, then points to your photo on the book cover and says, This guy could sell one volume of porn and live on that money for how many months? That's what he did. Sold one lousy book, then turned the CLOSED sign in the window and disappeared. Who knows where the hell he goes?

The night goes on like that with stories about how folks met you, what you did together, what people remember, jokes and lies and folklore, filling up the time, roasting your present spirit though absent body.

Bard says, The next time I'm under your robes, I'm going to touch you here.

And I thought you had a foot fetish.

I'm Korean. We don't have foot fetishes.

I never dated a Korean.

You told me you never dated an Asian.

Dated. Just no boyfriends.

And?

I can't stop staring at you. Matching noses. Matching foreheads. Matching lips.

Matching bodies.

All day long I speak my lines to your lines. We who love each other are cursed alike. May we be reborn in the same lotus.

We hurry toward our end, hoping our two souls will find the same dwelling. Do not mistake the way, do not lose me.

Are you making love to Ohatsu or to me?

Who are you?

I don't know.

I think I'm afraid of Huo Lian. Maybe Ohatsu is easier. Maybe Ohatsu is more forgiving.

Ohatsu wants to die with you.

And Huo Lian?

Huo Lian is complicated.

Why is that?

I've lost all my boyfriends, you know. They think I'm like Ohatsu, but I'm not. Sometimes you get between someone's idea of beauty, and you feel so ugly.

Well, that's what you get for going with white guys.

Admit you don't want white girls too. Your body shames you. Your mind screws you.

And us?

It's different. You know that. This, she grabs him, belongs to me.

I guess you got me.

No, we have to share.

Tokubei's given it up to you.

And Bard?

Bard is complicated.

Huo Lian nods in disgust, Bard already has a fiancée. She fingers the ring on his hand, then pounds him on his chest.

We're just rehearsing, remember?

Feel this. Are we rehearsing?

We're rehearsing.

Keep rehearsing.

Don't stop.

The storytelling peters out, and the bottles turned on end dribble out their last liquid hyperboles.

George says, Hey Paul, you want me to sign his books? I can forge his signature. Hey, lemme sign that book for you. Least I can do for our friends.

Let's go get some grub.

I could use another drink.

Wonder what happened to him? Maybe he just forgot. Got the dates wrong.

Did you check the teahouse? He's probably in there screwing.

Don't worry. He'll turn up. He always turns up.

Maybe he's writing another book.

Bard says, since doing this play, I got an idea for another play based on a famous protest poem using Korean pansori singing.

No one is doing anything Korean. You should work on it.

It's an allegory called *Ballad of Five Bandits,* about corrupt officials who represent actual politicians in the current South Korean government. It could be dangerous to do it.

All the better.

The poet who wrote it, Chiha Kim, is a political prisoner in Seoul now on death row. I have this idea that he plays the drum side of the song from prison.

Huo Lian says, O.K., that's your project. Here's mine. I'm working on a film using cuts from Hollywood films that stereotype Orientals with that yellow peril shit. I did this edit on Super 8. She sets up the projector. Check out Fu Manchu and Anna Mae Wong.

Film's silent. Let me play some pansori for you. It's similar to the chanter in bunraku, except the singer's accompanied by a drummer.

Black flickers over white, black Betty Boop lips and black fu manchu caught in slanted poses beneath dark inscrutability, hatch a plan, a poisoned death, the throaty vibrato of the pansori driven by yelps, sighs, and the deep slap of the drum, satiric tragicomedy condemns the poet but sings forever over his execution. Enclosed by sound and image in a dark room, tense and frantic sensations grip inky erogenous zones, and play and memory return to desire.

I can't be in the dark with you.

It's rehearsal time again.

The hungry group leaves City Lights and treks toward Chinatown for cheap chop suey and lots of it, probably descends into Woey Loy Goey's greasy basement.

So, George says, Ginsberg claims a poetic connection to Walt Whitman through, you know, sex. So Ginsberg fucked this poet who fucked this poet who fucked this poet who fucked Whitman.

Who are you fucking these days? It could be important. Any poets?

I'm celibate, man.

I wanna poetic connection back to Lady Murasaki. Think you can arrange that?

How about Basho?

Li Po?

O.K., Li Po.

Shit, what's Whitman? One hundred years? Li Po's gotta be over a thousand. That's a lotta fucking-fucking.

You ordering or what?

Barbequed pork egg foo young.

Steamed pork hash with salted duck egg.

Almond duck.

Seaweed soup.

Black bean sauce with beef tripe.

Braised catfish Cantonese style

Steamed squab with sausage and black mushroom.

Beef chow fun.

Cashew nut chicken.

Is that going to be enough?

We're going to eat ourselves to death.

You forget the steamed rice?

Wontons to start.

Get ready to die.

It's the night of the understudies. Bard and Huo Lian make their excuses. Anyway the show is ending in a few nights, and they should give others a chance at the lead roles. No one knows that they sneak back into the theatre and hide in the wings behind the curtains, folded together with the stilted language forming with precision on their lips, the staged movements passing through their heaving bodies, relentless desire, moans ground into skin, stifled gasps timed to theatric gasps, the final journey into the dark forest, their lovers' anguish lamenting the play's inevitable dissolution. The clatter of wooden clappers and the frenzied stammer of the shamisen announce their descent into hell. Tokubei binds Ohatsu to the emblematic pine and palm growing from a single trunk and strikes his knife, recklessly hysterical, slices at her tender throat and then his own, and in the dark wings, Bard and Huo Lian die their ecstatic slaying again and again. You are mine alone, forever, and it will never be like this again.

Return late from the Delta to the I-Hotel with two tired old manongs and forty-six inches and twenty pounds of prehistoric sturgeon caught with ghost shrimp on a two-inch hook off a rental boat near the Dump Gate across from Vieira's Resort.

Shit, you say as you push back the door of the teahouse and Konnyaku jumps at your fishy body. You knew there was something else you were supposed to be doing tonight.

7: Renee & Ken

Hiro's horn-rimmed glasses, framed by a scraggy bush of graying hair and stringy beard, appear in the door of your bookstore. Hey, he says. You back?

Oh, yeah.

Where you been?

Kyushu.

How about the Philippines? You go there?

No.

Why not?

I go there, they'll say I'm not from there. I don't have to go where I'm from but never been, right?

And they say I don't make sense. Hiro flips through your sparse merchandise on makeshift shelves. What were you thinking when you opened this place?

At the time, seemed like a good idea.

Shoulda got yourself arrested like me for selling indecency. What is this place but a funky Edo porn shop?

Oh no, these are all ancient instructional manuals.

Hiro chuckles, You came home in time. They're gonna ram their balls through that wall any day now. I was thinking I was going to have to break in to save your shunga and shit all by myself.

One more time, you and Hiro haul the shunga out of your defunct bookstore back to the floating pantry. Take the sign down that says USED RARE OUT-OF-PRINT BOOKS and turn the CLOSED sign around in the window forever.

Take a pot of rice, bottle of Coke, couple raw eggs, and a bowl of this slimy stuff Hiro calls natto down to the teahouse. You stick to rice and tea, but Hiro whips up the raw eggs and natto with shoyu in his bowl of rice and digs in, swapping the rice goop with swigs of Coke. You didn't eat this in Kyushu? he asks. He puts a glob of it in Konnyaku's bowl. See, he likes it.

He's Japanese.

Maybe you're Japanese too.

Coming back next time as a cat.

You believe in reincarnation?

Who knows?

Maybe death is easier if you get to come back.

I thought the thing is you got to find a way not to come back. Get to nirvana and leave the earth behind.

Yeah, but maybe you got some unfinished business.

Konnyaku's got some unfinished business. Look at what's left of the ugly cat—half a tail, one eye, three legs, patches of hair here and there.

I think his business is finished. Hiro pours your tea into what's left of the brown egg slime at the bottom of his bowl and chugs it down. I been reading this *Tale of Kieu,* call it the epic poem of the Vietnamese nation. Read the national tale and know why they could fight the Chinese, the French, the Japanese, and the Americans for two thousand years and finally win.

Reincarnation?

Unfinished business.

Ken walks out of Boalt Hall in a paisley shirt, khakis, gold suede shoes, and with a law degree to boot, then passes the California bar and founds the Asian Law Caucus. Up to and in between, there's showing up at the first class, then pot, acid, mescaline, and hanging out at the beach making blue, green, and purple sand candles, paying for the biker upstairs to bike to L.A. to buy a brick, divvying up the brick into baggies and lids and sending the whole mess back to a contact at the UCLA library for general sales to support life back in Berkeley and pay for law school, and showing up at the last class and acing all the exams. And wedged in between all that, there's draft counseling in J-Town and Chinatown and the I-Hotel, strategizing evasive tactics to avoid the draft, getting the paperwork lost in the draft boards, analyzing the lottery numbers, 1 to 146 most likely to go, writing testimonies toward the sanctity of life, putting blood in a stool test to get signed off for colitis, guzzling a quart of soy sauce to push up the blood pressure, pink panties to get fag status, peanut butter up the ass for the anal exam so when the doctor inspects and says, What's this? you scrape it off your crack, lick it from your fingers, and say,

Shit? And beyond that, there's pro-bono work on behalf of every radical left formation liberating material from the dirty capitalists, advocating for their right to chain themselves to public property.

Then, one day, Ken meets Renee.

He says, You know, you really look familiar, like a girl I once knew.

Oh?

Yeah, her name was Yuri.

You goddamn fucker, you! Renee flings herself forward, punching his face and grabbing his necktie to choke him.

What the fuck! He grabs her hands and pushes her backward, but her feet come forward kicking. He's got to grab all her parts and twist her arms back, and she's still struggling. Are you crazy?

You're the one! You killed my sister! Drugged her up and left her to die!

What are you talking about?

How many of you are there? You fuckers!

Calm down. Calm down. You got the wrong person.

Do you know old she was? Not even twenty. How could you? How could you?

Listen to me! It wasn't me. It wasn't me.

Renee's body sinks into sobs.

I'm sorry. I'm sorry.

Hand Hiro another Coke and settle in to listen to his rendition of the *Tale of Kieu.* Kieu, who is beautiful and talented, falls in love with Kim, promising to marry him, but to save her family from slavery, sells herself to another man who sells her into prostitution, leading to servitude, slavery, other marriages, the nunnery, and finally back to Kim. Up to and in between, her sister Van marries Kim in her place, and Kieu, now a prostitute and later a slave and concubine, attempts suicide and fails, marries again but as the second wife becomes a slave to the first, then marries a general but accidentally betrays him, causing him to be defeated in battle, is ordered to marry again, attempts suicide and fails again, finally escapes into a life of religious meditation, however finally marrying her first love, Kim, becoming his second but platonic wife. Wedged in between all that, Kieu discovers that, though a vision of human perfection, she's the incarnation of a previous existence of passion and loss, and the more she fights her karma, the greater and more bitter her failure. Beyond that, she's a woman in a man's world, but with four marriages, first- and second-wife status, rape, prostitution, and a stint of concubineship, the good news is no kids. That's the long and the short of it, says Hiro.

National epic, you nod. I don't get it.

I think it's like this. You keep coming back to fight, fight cruelty and injustice, and maybe you never win, and if you get lucky, you figure it all out before you die and before they put you in a rest home.

When you're just a kid like Kieu with your whole life ahead of you, how you supposed to know?

It's the shit they never tell you.

Renee emerges an average student from a low-end but middle-class family background in a suburban San José neighborhood in the postwar fifties, gradually gets drawn into civil rights and radical left politics, becomes an active Asian American movement radical, joining a new left communist group from which she is eventually purged, then marries a movement attorney. Up to and in between, she has a long-term relationship with a fellow traveler, associates with radical Third World feminism, marries the fellow traveler to solidify their political comradeship as directed by party leaders, but agrees not to have children, is followed into political activities by her sister Yuri who, unable to overcome severe depression and personal insecurities, becomes lost to drug addiction and casual sex, dying in an overdose; meanwhile, Renee looks to support from the party only to be purged for her suspicion that some of the members have slept with her sister, divorces her cadre husband, enters a long period of psychological therapy and bitter soul searching. Beyond that, she earns a masters in sociology at San José State while working a full-time job with the county.

Ken draws Renee closer.

I don't know if I can, she says.

It's been a month. Come on.

Two miscarriages. That's all I can think about.

Stop thinking so much.

Like I'm setting us up for failure.

Maybe we've got to stop trying so hard. If it happens, it happens.

Do you think?

What?

I'm too old.

Don't say that.

I lost my chance. I wanted this so much, just to make this life happen inside me, and now I can't. It's too late.

Come on.

I can't feel anything. I just can't.

Go to the hospital to see Hiro lying there in ICU with tubes up his nose, serum dripping into his veins. Stand next to Ken and Renee who take turns sleeping in the room all night, looking haggard, red eyes, unshaven.

Uncle Hiro had a stroke, says Ken.

Happened in the basement at City Lights, says Renee.

Sometimes he seems to wake up, but I don't know if he can hear.

I brought him this bottle of Coke, you say.

Thanks.

Return to the teahouse, and sit in the dark with Master Konnyaku, watching the fog hunt through the grass and tall weeds, creep silently under the house. Think about Hiro and a conversation about Thich Quang Duc, the sixty-seven-year-old monk who, in 1963 on a busy Saigon intersection, sat in the lotus position, smothered in gasoline, and lit himself afire. Hiro hands you a book; he's always handing you some book. *Vietnam: Lotus in a Sea of Fire.* As Americans, maybe we can never understand this, he says. Full engagement with life. An act of sacrifice to open the heart to love.

1977: I-Hotel

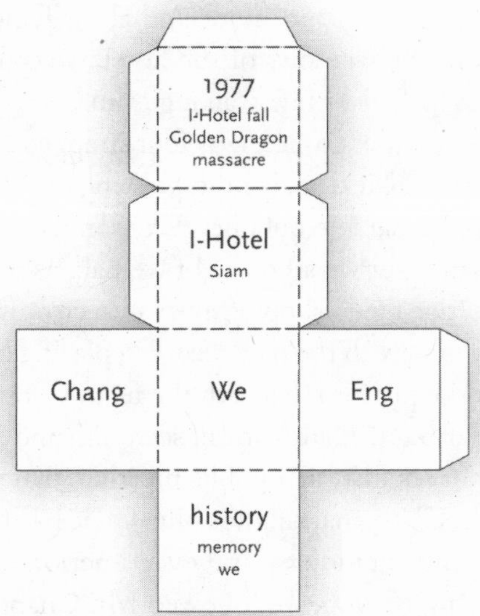

1: And this will conclude our transmission from the International Hotel

By the time we attached our destinies to the I-Hotel, it was an International Hotel in its third incarnation, the first hotel built before the Civil War in 1854, the second built after in 1873, and our building, rebuilt after the great earthquake in 1906. Our I-Hotel was as old as, although in some cases younger than, its tenants, and though we had repainted, re-plastered, and remortared all or significant sections of our aging home, we knew from crawling into all its secret places, the fragile locations of its deteriorating infrastructure, the rusting plumbing, bursting with sewage and flooding our basements, the need for vigilant inspections of electrical wiring and gas piping. We patched. We repaired. We renewed and celebrated. We pumped the old place with new blood and spirit, and the stubborn structure took its vitamins, wore our new cloak of banners and fiercely colored murals, brandished a renewed position of power, became a fortress and a beacon.

Who's to say why walking into an old forgotten building could have the strange effect of swallowing our minds and electrifying talents we never knew we had? From the windows of the hotel, we could see Mr. Chang arriving from across the bay by bus, walking from Chinatown with an array of portable cassette recorders, as many as four strapped across his shoulders and chest like an armed Mexican bandit, pressing the recorders' keyboards and speaking into external microphones. We wondered where we had met or known Mr. Chang, but we all thought we had, as if in déjà vu we recognized his diminutive figure slipping away into crowds. Wasn't he always there, the Chinese man with the tape recorder, placing his equipment near the pedestal or on the platform beneath the feet of Mario Savio or Bobby Seale or Warren Furutani? Hadn't we all seen him and forgotten his presence at that rally, that march, that public meeting, that protest?

Now we saw Mr. Chang parking his blue Civic hatchback loaded with cabling and recording equipment, and over a period of two years before that fated day in August 1977, we followed Mr. Chang into the hotel as he orchestrated our many hands into skillful technicians, wiring every inch of the International Hotel, passing our cables down and around its dark corridors, between walls and floors, in and out of rooms, from the basement to the roof. We mapped that brick structure with a complex nervous system of cabling that led to amplifiers, loudspeakers, IFB connectors, multiple microphones, recorders, transmitters, and a master control in a hidden broom closet on the last floor. And this system responded to our reporting voices, communicating our information to every location inside and outside, our message sent through hotel and street corridors, transmitted from our roof in pirated waves and retransmitted from a 304-foot tower overlooking the hills of Oakland. If our intention had been to blow up the building, we might have caused it to implode and fall in on itself, sucked into its eventual hole. Instead, our wiring caused a great explosion of live sound, our voices and our protest resonating and rippling in waves into the far reaches of the City, across the Bay and through its fingered peninsulas. And the center of our great uproar was a gigantic organic voice box of our own making; it was our I-Hotel.

Mr. Chang loved all the possibilities of recording live sound, the miracle of embedding events into the rolling filaments of plastic tape, but his preference was for the cheaper simplicity of sound. Others of us became attached to the way the same plastic tape could embed images, learned the workings of F-stops on thirty-five-millimeter cameras or the stops on new-fangled video port-a-pack cameras, the strong shoulder and steady arm required to pan an event, the necessary zoom to catch intimate human details, the agility of the chase, the danger of shooting and being in the line of shooting. We may have noticed a young woman, deftly moving in time to the crowds, as if her body was always riding the crest of a wave and her eye constantly seeing the world through its recording lens. And similarly, we thought we recognized Judy Eng's figure as if by déjà vu. Hadn't she always been at every significant press conference and event concerning the I-Hotel? Even though we might not have recognized her face hidden behind a camera, wasn't her body always in the middle of every eventual fracas, documenting the truth? Even as our eyes followed with significant attention the manong's story or the politician's lie against the backdrop of our beloved hotel, had we not pulled back to see the larger picture itself, of those of us who recorded the recording?

If we, the audiophiles and filmophiles seeking to be powerful through every new innovation in our adopted fields, had wired the I-Hotel to hear and see, how then would it speak? But of course we knew our voices, like our eyes and ears, to be many and multiple at any one time, but on the night of August 3, 1977, and into the following morning, our voices sounded as one voice, and the I-Hotel spoke, and, although for the last time, spoke loudly.

Arthur Ma arrived in a fishing vest stuffed with extra microphones, additional battery packs, and electronic paraphernalia, and so the evening began, Arthur and his Third World Newsroom crew, attached to Mr. Chang's intricate sound system, recording and transmitting every moment from every location inside and outside, over and underneath the I-Hotel. Though we immediately recognized the cadenced voice of Arthur Ma, most of us did not know his face or physical person. Arthur Ma was a familiar and unmistakable radio voice, but tonight, he would be our voice. And from ten p.m., when the red alert was sounded, calling the people to save the I-Hotel, Arthur Ma, followed recklessly everywhere by Judy Eng and perhaps a half-dozen other cameras, described every event that we could possibly see or feel for the next ten hours.

"We have received calls to the hotel warning us that police are gathering in large numbers at the Civic Center."

"We just got word that the Bay Bridge has been closed to traffic to prevent East Bay folks from crossing to bring us assistance."

"It's now eleven p.m. and folks are beginning to pour into Kearny Street."

"We've learned that the police assault was scheduled for twelve thirty a.m., but it's now one in the morning, and we estimate about two thousand supporters are outside on the street."

"Medical personnel who should be inside the hotel assisting tenants, please proceed to your stations. We will be initiating a lockdown of the hotel in the next five minutes."

"The police are arriving!"

"Legal support teams and floor and hall monitors, please take your positions."

"Members of the press who will be covering events inside the building, this is your last call."

"They're coming! They're coming!"

"Protest leaders, please take your positions. Everyone, hold tight."

STOP THE EVICTION! WE WON'T MOVE!

STOP THE EVICTION! WE WON'T MOVE!

"It looks like there are about 250 police in riot gear. They've got several paddy wagons at the rear of their contingent as well as ambulances."

"They've blocked off Kearny Street on both ends. Access to Kearny has been completely closed."

JUST LIKE A TREE STANDING BY THE WATER, WE SHALL NOT BE MOVED. WE SHALL NOT BE MOVED.

"Two buses have just arrived, filled with the sheriff's deputies."

"Our human barricade is at least twelve rows deep. Our arms are linked, and we are standing ready."

THE PEOPLE UNITED WILL NEVER BE DEFEATED!

THE PEOPLE UNITED WILL NEVER BE DEFEATED!

"The assault by the police has begun. Police are forming themselves into a wedge and trying to shove their way to the entrance. Our human barricade is holding strong."

"The police are returning in a second wedge. They are attacking our people with their clubs! Trying to rip us away, prodding and punching us with their sticks!"

"Despite their sticks, our people are holding tight."

"The foot police are backing off. But now about a dozen police on horseback are moving forward. They're pressing their horses into our people, swinging their clubs and hitting folks!"

"We just saw a woman take her bare fist and punch a horse in the nose!"

"From their positions on horseback, the police don't seem to have much leverage with their clubs."

"But the horses are frightening. Their bodies are huge, and the police are forcing the animals into our human barricade. Their large hooves are falling into our people! We can see their panic and horror, grimacing pain."

HANG IN THERE! HOLD STRONG! WE'RE BEHIND YOU!

"The police seem to be retreating momentarily. Despite everything, the human barricade is relinking arm in arm and remains firm. We are set in our determination to stop this eviction."

STOP THE EVICTION! WE WON'T MOVE!

STOP THE EVICTION! WE WON'T MOVE!

"Here they come again! This time they are really beating folks on the head and in the stomach!"

"People are getting hurt! A woman has fallen to the ground! A man's face is covered in blood! More bloodied faces! This is turning ugly! We need medical support!"

"Members of our defense leadership request that demonstrators disperse."

EVERYONE PLEASE DISPERSE! PLEASE TAKE YOUR POSITIONS ON THE OPPOSITE SIDE OF THE STREET!

"We've agreed on nonviolent resistance. Our leadership insists that we've got to draw the line between defending the building and allowing the tenants to be hurt."

"If the police resort to tear gas to disperse the protestors, that could be deadly to the elderly tenants inside the hotel."

"There will be no bloodbath!"

DEMONSTRATORS ARE ASKED TO MOVE AWAY FROM THE HOTEL ENTRANCE.

WE WON'T MOVE!

WE WON'T MOVE!

"As we can hear, there's stubborn resistance to the order to move. Many believe we can hold out until sunrise when the rest of the city wakes up. They're hanging tight."

"They're telling us to move, but there's no place to move to. We're completely trapped. Police are on every side!"

"It's 3:15 a.m., and the fire department has arrived with fire trucks."

"Police are climbing the truck ladder to the roof of the hotel. Protestors on the roof are trying to throw off the ladder from the roof!"

"Now they've got a truck with a telescoping light. The entire street and hotel are lit up like daylight. The light is blinding!"

"We can see clearly that there are about twenty tenants and supporters on the roof blocking the stairwell down into the hotel. Police are attacking and handcuffing each protestor."

"We have word that the police have sealed off the back of the hotel with three foot patrols."

"Now police are scaling the ladder to a third-floor window. They're breaking the glass and entering a room! We're told it's tenant Joe Bungayan's room. The glass to his room is shattering!"

"It's four thirty a.m., and the police have breached our human barricade. They are battering down the front entrance, pulling apart the plywood and two-by-fours used to secure the doors. Everything is splintering! They're destroying the doors!"

"Inside we've prepared another barricade using mattresses and tables. This should slow their progress into the hotel. We estimate another hundred protesters inside the hotel sitting in the corridors, blocking the way to tenants' rooms."

"The police are also taking sledgehammers to the storefronts. They're banging on the doors of the Kearny Street Workshop and the Chinese Progressive Association."

"We just got word that the police crashed through an adjacent hotel wall and are dragging out members of the CPA through the rubble."

"The last storefront, the Asian Community Center, seems to be impenetrable. The police keep at the door with their axes and sledgehammers, but it won't give! They must have put up a steel wall!"

"We're radioing in to the ACC telling them to open the door. We've learned that the doors are supported by sixteen-foot two-by-fours wedged from the doors to the opposite wall. We're requesting that ACC members give themselves up. We don't want to give the police any more excuses to use violence."

"The Sheriff's deputies have been called to enter the hotel and evict the residents. The police are standing on guard in the front."

"Two busloads of deputies, about sixty men in riot gear, are positioning themselves in front of the hotel."

WHERE WILL YOU LIVE WHEN YOU GET OLD?

WHERE WILL YOU LIVE WHEN YOU GET OLD?

"We've got at least fifty supporters sitting on the landing blocking the second floor to the tenants' rooms."

WE WON'T MOVE! WE WON'T MOVE!

"The deputies have spotted the president of our hotel tenants' association, and they're trying to pull him out of the crowd. They've got him in a chokehold. Our people around him are trying to hold him down. The deputies are pulling at him. They're hurting him. They're choking him. He's fighting back, holding on. They're twisting his legs. They've got him! Three deputies are dragging him away."

"There's stubborn resistance here. It's taking at least two or three deputies to pull each protestor out. One by one they're removing us from the hotel."

"Protestors are being removed from the hotel and dumped on the street on the other side of the police barricades."

"The Sheriff himself is now entering the hotel. He's got a sledgehammer, and he's bashing one of the tenant's doors. It's splintering under the force of his battering ram. Someone is crying inside. Other deputies are proceeding to other rooms and following his example."

"It's six a.m., and the first tenant is leaving his room, accompanied by his medical team."

"He's a long-time tenant of the hotel. He's in a state of shock. He's being guided out the hotel entrance. He's raising his arm to shield his eyes from the blinding spotlights. Folks are applauding and cheering him."

LONG LIVE! LONG LIVE!

"Another elderly tenant is leaving the hotel. He's glaring defiantly at the police. He's yelling something at them. He's cussing them out!"

"The tenants are now being escorted out. One by one they are being forced to leave their home. Some of these tenants have lived here for over fifty years."

LONG LIVE! LONG LIVE!

"Our people outside are cheering, but the tenants are in a state of shock."

"This tenant's face is awash with tears. This is a heartbreaking scene."

"The tenants are leaving with nothing. No baggage. No belongings except what's on their bodies. They haven't been given any time to collect their things. Not even a blanket."

"One old tenant is collapsing. He's collapsing! We need medical assistance for this man. This is urgent! The strain of the eviction has been too much."

"We're laying him down on the sidewalk on top of an old banner. We've ripped down a second banner to serve as a blanket. The banner says in Chinese characters, *Liberate the I-Hotel!*"

"The last tenant is being escorted from the hotel. He wants to make a statement."

I am crippled, and I am deaf, and I am very old. I am alone here, and they put me in the street. I want freedom, the principle of American democracy in the richest country in the world. Do you think our mayor has a place for me? No. No. Because I was happy here.

"Although the mayor promised to provide housing for the tenants after their eviction, there is no one here offering housing to anyone. There are no promised buses or housing assistance."

"A contingent of tenants can be seen walking away down Kearny. They have no place to go. Where will these suddenly homeless people go?"

"It is eight a.m., and the Sheriff has handed over the I-Hotel to the Enchanted Seas Investment Corporation."

SHAME! SHAME! SHAME!

"Nine hardhats from the Giant Debris Box and Wrecking Company have arrived with a truck of plywood. They are beginning to board up the hotel storefronts along Kearny Street.

"It's eight thirty a.m., and Pacific Gas & Electric has arrived to shut down electrical power and gas mains."

"The hotel has gone completely dark."

"And this will conclude our transmission from the International Hotel."

We saw the morning rise over our I-Hotel in a sea of rubbish: broken glass, splintered wood, horse shit, lost pieces of clothing and shoes, abandoned scarves, face masks and helmets, torn posters, paper flyers and shredded banners, blood and vomit. It's not known, but the very last person to emerge from our hotel was Mr. Chang. Hidden in our master control in the broom closet on the last floor, he continued to transmit our final sounds, the last weeping gurgles, and the long sigh of our dying hotel. Shut away in a dark closet for ten hours, Mr. Chang had seen and heard everything, and he had made it possible for us to also hear and see everything. When the single light bulb in his closet went dark, he pulled away the two-by-four that we'd fashioned across his closet door and unlatched the bolted lock. He packed up the equipment in two large suitcases and moved slowly through the debris of our hotel. Similarly, Judy Eng secured her lens cap and packed away her camera, and Arthur Ma wrapped his microphone in a soft piece of cloth and stuffed it into the deeper recesses of his fisherman's vest. We had seen and heard and experienced everything as it happened, believing that we were framing a vision of real events in real time, hearing and watching history happen, holding our machines up to the event with our hearts pounding in our fingers. And we all walked out and away, invisibly, firmly gripping our recording machines with their live, insinuating, and damning evidence, every moment engraved into plastic film.

And that was when the life of the I-Hotel was finally snuffed out—our hearing gone deaf, our seeing windows blinded, our fierce voice silenced.

2: Where will you live when you get old?

A little after ten at night on a Wednesday in August, the third day of that summer month in 1977, we got the call, the red alert. Maybe we had our suspicions or had been warned, had seen the extra commotion of riot cops training on nearby Folsom and Nineteenth, heard the rumor of reserved parking for police cars in all the downtown garages, had the inconvenience of getting rerouted because of closed freeway ramps, saw the mounted police grooming their stallions over on Market. Their mobilization was gaining momentum, but we too began to activate our own preparations, phoned the next ten people on our list who would phone the next ten and the next ten, spreading the alert over hundreds of telephone lines across the city and the bay. One by one we emerged from our slumbers, exchanged our pajamas for heavy padded coats and work jeans and helmets, put down our evening beers, shut down a summer rerun of *Baretta* (French connection detective and his pet cockatoo), abandoned our books, our pool cues, our rum and Cokes, our horny lovers, rushed away to bang on the doors of our neighbors, gathered our walkie-talkies, filled our pants pockets with coins for the phone booth and bus fare, our jacket pockets with face masks, Hershey bars, corn nuts, and beef jerky, attached our armbands with safety pins, and marched to cars and buses and bicycles and motorcycles, revving up all our motors and churning our wheels and our feet, heading out into the late evening streets, walking our bodies and our collective determination toward a single three-story brick building on the corner of Jackson and Kearny. We would save the International Hotel.

Thus we emerged from every living crevice in our hilly city, every tenement, blighted Victorian, public housing project, cheap hotel, single or collective rental, many of us the forgotten and abandoned people whose voices were muffled in the underbelly of working poverty, stuffed into the various ethnic ghettos, we the immigrants from the Old and New Worlds, from the black and white South and tribal America, we the dockworkers of the long shore, we the disabled and disavowed vets, we the gay and leathered, we the garment workers, restaurant workers, postal and clerical workers, we who praised the Lord in his house at Glide and his People's Temple, we of the unions, tired and poor, we the people.

But why save an old hotel?

Because if we remembered the history of our city, we would remember how frontier towns began: with a trading post and a saloon with a second floor of lodging rooms. In time, we saw erected a jail with our troublemakers, a courthouse with our records, and a bank with our money. The trading post became a dry goods store, and the saloon a restaurant and hotel. That was our basic town. After that, we'd add a church and a school, and possibly some local professionals—a doctor and a lawyer. But when we took everything away and thought only about the second floor of lodging rooms, we remembered that people have always come from distances and had to be accommodated, given shelter and a bed, and what we used to call board. And it wasn't as if you could get this board for nothing; you had to pay or have something to exchange. That exchange was its own respectability, a kind of citizenship.

This basic town got complicated and multiplied into a thing we call a city, with every kind of reinvented trading post and saloon and lodging that over time we could imagine. And we supposed that the history of any city could be told through the comings and goings of any trading post or saloon, but thinking as we do, as people coming to the city to find work to pay for shelter and board, whether just for ourselves or for our families accompanying or left behind, it was the lodging that most concerned us. And we could see how city life and hotel life were inextricably connected, that what the city had to offer had a home in the hotel. Over time, we'd forgotten that hotels in our city have long served as temporary but also permanent homes, that living in hotels had been a normal consequence of living in our city. From the inception of our city, our city life could perhaps be translated as hotel life, the way that we as young, single, and independent people could arrive to find work in the industry of the city, find the small cafés and bars, theaters and social clubs, laundries, shops, and bookstores, all within walking distance or perhaps a cable stop away. Even if we did not actually live in hotels, we may have participated in, if not considered, the simple luxuries of hotel life: the bustling social life of our streets, the hotels' communal restaurants and social galas, the convenience of maid service and bedsheets changed, the possibility of being completely freed from any housework, the possible leisure to think or to create, and finally the anonymity and privacy of a room of our own. Hotel life defined the freedom of the city, but such freedom has been for some reason suspect, and there are always those who want to police freedom.

Finally, like the society that evolved in our city, there have been, of course, hotels for those with money and hotels for those of us with not so much money. And even though the city required our labor and allowed us housing in cheap hotels, in time we came to know that laboring people are necessary but considered transitory. Eventually, it was thought, we'd just go away or become invisible. So even if hotels depended on our constant occupancy, we were not considered permanent or stable members of society. We did not own our homes. We may have had families, but hotels were suspect places to raise children, and so we were suspect families. Our communal lives in hotels with shared bathrooms and shared dining, shared genders, shared ethnicities, and heaven forbid, shared thinking that might lead to shared politics, were also suspect. Hotel life might even be subversive. A famous scholar who studied our hotel life warned us that when there are no homes, there will be no nation. But what did he mean by *home?* And, for that matter, what did he mean by *nation?*

By the time we got the red alert to place our bodies in a human barricade around an old hotel that held seventy years of our city's hotel history, we were already the displaced people in the city's plan to impose a particular meaning of *home* and a particular meaning of *nation*. Since our hotel life was considered suspect morally and socially, our hotels should naturally be replaced by proper single-family houses built in locations distant from the city, and our hotels and all our businesses that serviced us should be replaced with what the city was properly useful for: trading posts, jails, courthouses, and saloons. And no one should be allowed to live over a saloon unless he was just passing through. A commercial room was simply not a dwelling. These edicts were substantiated by zoning and blight laws allowing the city to use eminent domain to liberate our homes for the public good, even if the public good meant giving up our property for the wealthy few. Almost as quickly as an earthquake, our neighborhoods located in the Fillmore and South of Market were already razed and being replaced by forty-eight-story multinational corporate trading posts. Even if we were expected to build, maintain, clean, and service these posts, we weren't expected to live anywhere nearby. Be at work promptly at eight a.m., but please, please disappear by five p.m. But this was an impossible request because we could not leave, and we had nowhere to go. So that night in August, far past our five p.m. curfew and into the next morning, we gathered around the I-Hotel to face four hundred officers of the police, sheriff's, and fire departments all dressed up in riot gear, to demonstrate that we had not disappeared and that we were finally fed up. What was the total cost to us as taxpayers, not just in overtime and equipment, but everything—everything it took over how many months in anticipation to deploy the full force of the city's and county's final retribution? No doubt more than a million dollars, the insipid worth of the structure we defended.

Had we not ourselves elected these men of good intentions: the mayor who ran out of promises, the judge who ruled for eviction despite a hung jury, and the sheriff who carried out a law he thought to be unjust? Did these elected officials also think that our city was only useful for trading posts, a courthouse, and a jail?

Armed with only our bodies, we faced our officers of the law—heavily protected by face helmets, gloves, sticks, given height by their tall animals, speed by their motorcycles, reach by their aerial ladders, and ultimately power by their deadly weapons. We saw the barricades part for the Sheriff himself, driving up to the I-Hotel. He emerged from his vehicle as if it were his powerful steed and stood in the blinding spotlights of that evening, young and handsome, dressed informally in a gold turtleneck sweater and casual jacket, bidding his dinner partner a sweet goodnight. Perhaps it was a brash double-oh-seven gesture lost to our angry chanting. We knew he had been convicted for contempt of court, spending five days in his own jail for refusing in January to carry out the court order of eviction of the tenants of the I-Hotel. Was he not one of our own people, our own gallant knight, and would he not once again take a stand in our favor? Had he not himself complained that the laws of our society were written to protect those with property and money? Would he later justify his part in the eviction based on having, as an officer of the law, to carry out the law, just or unjust as it may be?

As two thousand of us were eventually bullied away from the hotel entrance, we saw our sheriff enter at the head of his deputies, leading them into the hotel and the final phase of the eviction, breaking into the doors of each of the hotel tenants and ordering them to leave their homes. And yes, we knew that each room was a tiny home, a place of final refuge for a lifetime of work, and that the room, though housed in a hotel, was still a home.

So when we saw our sheriff place his sledgehammer to the first door, banging and splintering the old dark wood into jagged pieces, we were ourselves diminished by every stroke of his hammer. We heard the wretched sobbing cry of horror, an anguished plea but also a warning, *No! Don't do it! Don't do it!* But our sheriff had made his decision, perhaps, he justified, to take responsibility by being an actor in this painful event, to mitigate what he imagined could have been a more violent end. But we would never forget his violent presence on that night and the sad betrayal of his actions.

Shame! Shame! Shame! we cried.

Where will you live when you get old?

Where will we live when we get old?

3: We won't move

We grew up here, and we lived here: in Chinatown under colorful pagoda roofs and serenaded by flower drum songs down Grant Avenue; in Filipinotown in heroic Bataan bars and courted with sampaguita flowers along Kearny Street; in Japantown between jazz spots and cherry blossom festivals around Post and Buchanan. We lived in the centers of our city's Oriental tourist attractions, our li'l towns described as "exotic Kodak moments" in *Sunset* and other travel magazines. We were always smiling for our customers, saying that if they visited our towns, it would be the next best thing to traveling to the real countries, even if some of us had never even been there. We supposed that joining our city's tourist industry was part of our contribution, a survival feature that came out of the consequences of how we got here, but that's a long story. And once we got here, well, that's another.

Maybe we all look alike, and maybe the laws lump us all together so we got to stick together, even though we're really different and can't understand each other and our folks back in the old countries hated each other's guts. A good war will always get people to line up on one side or the other of the enemy lines, but those lines don't last forever, especially if you can't tell who is who without their uniforms. And when we all got stripped down to our bare bodies, it turned out we could be black, brown, red, white, or yellow. Now if we were going to have to work with the rules of a color wheel, well then maybe we should get to define what our color is. But creating that definition turned out to be a complicated and impossible task no matter how we circled around it or tried to confine it, and we argued long and hard about this until perhaps we've never really resolved it. Maybe there's no resolution; the problem of the color wheel in America has a long and deep history, and just as we pass on our physical attributes to every new generation, we also pass on that long legacy of hatred and assumptions.

But as we started to say, we lived here, many of us born and raised. While our towns' borders were porous for outsiders, we ourselves were confined within—for example, a Chinatown bounded by California, Kearny, Broadway, and Powell. We didn't cross those streets alone unless we wanted to get beat up. But then again, everything we thought we needed was contained within our towns—our foodstuffs and medications, our banking, our old country associations, our schools, our churches, our newspapers and means of communication, our extended families. Although outsiders may have thought we operated large secret societies within our towns, there were very few secrets that everyone among us didn't already know—our real and paper names, our real and assumed social positions, our political affiliations, our mistresses, our favorite and illegitimate children, our failed business negotiations, our good and bad habits. We were an open book written in a hundred dialects.

By the time the city came to tear down, rearrange, encroach upon, or, as they liked to say, "redevelop" our towns, it's not as if we didn't know it was happening. After all, we were the first merchants, the town patriarchs, the educated sons and daughters, the rising professionals, the veterans of war, whose hard work and sacrifice proved that, given opportunities, we could be worthy citizens. We were notified, and we made our moves to protect our gains and mitigate our loses. We may have been called upon to negotiate these changes, and we did so as honorably as we knew how. But even though we returned to worship, enroll our kids in language school, buy our food, get our haircuts, and, on occasion, gamble in our towns, perhaps we'd moved out to neighborhoods with nicer houses or better schools. And yet, we still returned to gather our kids into drum and bugle corps, drill teams, and scouting clubs, teach the folk dances and martial arts, and sponsor our yearly festivals. We knew where we came from and the value of knowing that, but the war had taught us that nothing stays the same forever, that the world outside, though hostile, was possible, and the safe haven of our li'l towns might not contain everything we wanted in our lives. And anyway we weren't going back to where other folks thought we came from.

But our kids thought we'd betrayed them, and they couldn't appreciate our hopes for their future. Pushy goddamn kids got turned on to the radical politics of the times, protesting everything in sight, giving up the opportunities of college educations to go back to the towns we had worked so hard to get them out of. What's a movement? We argued with them and said, *It's getting from one place to the next*, and how long have we been doing that? But did they listen? If in the early days we supported saving the International Hotel and the lives of the old men who lived there, we became uncertain of our support by the end. It had gone on too long with too much bad publicity for our communities, as if we couldn't control our radical kids who were just looking for a cause and strutting Communism. We weren't against taking care of our own; after all that's the way we were raised, to respect our elders and to take responsibility for our families. So when the I-Hotel came to its end, most of us watched from afar, saw the commotion on the evening news or in the morning newspapers, hoped our kids weren't hurt or jailed, shook our heads at an ending we might have predicted. But when we saw the elderly tenants thrown out on the streets, maybe we saw ourselves, our own stories of struggle and sacrifice connected to their stories, and we knew that whatever our kids had been trying to do, we could agree on this one thing—the honor due to those who've gone before.

So maybe while our kids had come home to sleep off the long working hours of their protesting days and nights, we went out to inspect the very last building that remained of what used to be Filipinotown, the absolute end of our old hometown. We walked down Kearny and remembered when one side of that street was Ilocano and the other side was Visayan; how on this street corner, we used to sell the *News* for three cents or the *Call* for five cents a copy, or how we used to hustle shoeshines on Sundays. We remembered how we could run into a union foreman who would promise us two seasons of work canning in Alaska, and how we could make about five hundred bucks for four-and-a-half months of work. Or maybe we'd get ten bucks to spar at a boxing gym and got to know the local featherweight champs. We remembered how the old-timers at Julian's taught us to play pool and palalasi, and how we learned to pay our respects by pouring a round of whiskey in small paper cups at the end of a good game. We remembered where we used to eat—at the Sampaguita, the LVM owned by Nina, the Bataan Café owned by Ramy, the Mandalay Club owned by Ness, the PI Clipper before it became the Silver Wing owned by Mimi and Jimmy, and the Bayong Sikat Café. And we remember how we learned to cook fish from Johnny Bulonglong at the Golden Gate. Then there were the bars, Blanco's, La Plantera, and Mr. Bing's owned by the Tolentinos. We used to get our haircuts at Noy Noy's, do our dry cleaning at Lapu Lapu, get our suits tailored by Babe Samson, and our cigarettes at the Mango Smoke Shop. We knew which establishments were Tagalog, which Ilocano or Visayan, and depending, we stuck with our kabayans.

We stood in front of the old door that had been Julian's and thereafter the Lucky M Pool Hall and Mike's Barbershop, and finally we remembered how the old-timers always dressed up. They could be cooks or busboys, but they came into the pool halls in their dapper McIntoshes and platform shoes. They hung their coats on hangers, never loosening their ties but throwing them carefully over their shoulders, removing their fancy cufflinks and rolling up their long silk sleeves. Then they washed their hands and chalked up their cues. We could hear again the knock and clack of wood on wood and the clatter of tumbling balls into the corner pockets, the accompanying guttural chuckles of satisfaction.

But then our memories were suddenly distracted. Devin wasn't an old-timer, certainly not one of our old manongs, but he was still a tenant evicted from the I-Hotel. Maybe he was the youngest tenant and continued to hang around Kearny, having lost his home and thinking he should still be doing surveillance, just in case. Devin was accompanied by Eddie Yu, the last and only old tenant of the Victory Hotel. The Victory Hotel was in fact right next door to the I-Hotel and also owned by Enchanted Seas Investments, but no one paid much attention to the Victory. No one thought to barricade it with their bodies since Enchanted Seas had long accomplished its eviction except for one last Chinese holdout, Eddie, who still lived there without lights, heat, or even water.

We followed Devin and Eddie, shouting excitedly and running down an alley to one side of the I-Hotel. We saw these puny men, one young and one old, pick up two long two-by-fours, holding their wooden weapons before them like great lances and running to attack a slowly approaching bulldozer, its gigantic wheels churning, exhaust spouting up its pipes, steel blade heading to wreck the back wall of the I-Hotel. And ridiculously, we stood with them and challenged the great machine as it plunged forward, shoving bricks and mortar and steel rods into a gaping wound, but it was too late.

4: The people united will never be defeated

These were the years when we were young and foolish, our bodies lithe, our minds awake, and our smiles innocent, and the International Hotel was a great brick building with four possible entryways. We picked a door, possibly any door, a conscious decision or an intuition, and upon entering, we found ourselves captured within a place we recognized as home, not the home we'd left, but the very home we hoped to find. Or perhaps it was a home with what we might call potential, so that we knew we could give up our energies to making it what we imagined it should be. For some of us, it was family and purpose, for some a realization of our talents, and for others, it was an idea, and not just any idea.

We could argue that there were never only four doors, that there were plenty more, that there were doors within doors, and probably a few back doors and escape passages. And over time, the doors may have also changed, but by the end of our great struggle to save our International Hotel, we could speak of four radical youth groups who had weathered the long haul and had given our youth to these days.

Traveling north on Kearny from Washington toward the lucky numbers 848, we may have been enticed to enter Everybody's Bookstore, displaying its radical collection of books inside the Asian Community Center, ACC for short. We may have lingered among the many volumes and pamphlets by and about Marx, Lenin, Engels, Stalin, and Mao, amazed to see such an open array of Communist literature. Perhaps we recognized a bold display, or perhaps we were merely curious about what we understood to be a forbidden literature we had never read. We browsed through the volumes wondering what would happen if we read them, what could be so dangerous about the words held within. We might have picked up a copy of a newspaper, *Wei Min Bao,* and realized that these were also the offices of the Wei Min She, the Organization of the People, its slogan *Serve the People.* Maybe we stuck around and eventually returned to buy and read books, to join study groups, to work on the research for a book about Chinese workers in America and in the process worked on a campaign to mobilize support for striking Chinatown workers in a small electronics sweatshop called Lee Mah.

But perhaps we headed for the center door with numbers 848, the entrance to the International Hotel itself, stairs leading to the second-floor offices of the International Hotel Tenants Association or IHTA. And although the offices of the Union of Democratic Filipinos or the Katipunan ng mga Demokratikong Pilipino, KDP for short, were not located here, their associated members were here busy at work. We may have come to support the opposition to the Marcos regime and martial law in the Philippines, or perhaps we became involved in the campaign for justice for two Filipina nurses accused of murder at a VA hospital in Michigan. More likely we were here at the I-Hotel to support the elderly hotel tenants, the manongs, in their struggle against eviction.

Or perhaps we approached 848 Kearny traveling from the south from Jackson, in which case we might have entered another door, that of the Kearny Street Workshop or KSW. Perhaps we found ourselves in the workshop's dark room developing black-and-white photos of scenes around Chinatown or portraits of the elderly hotel tenants, or maybe we became involved in the process of making silkscreen posters protesting the war or producing revolutionary T-shirts. During the day, we might have climbed the scaffolds on the Jackson side of the I-Hotel, filled in the colors of that great mural with its giant portraits of fierce manongs. And during the evenings, we returned to pass around a bottle of wine and read our poetry, to work on the publication of a feminist anthology.

But we may have also bypassed the KSW and slipped instead into the door of the Chinese Progressive Association or CPA, attracted to the large posters of Mao Tse-tung, the beautiful landscapes of China, the display of Chinese pamphlets and literature, and the schedule of sponsored events. And within that center, we would find the offices of the IWK or I Wor Kuen, meaning Righteous Harmonious Fist, so named after the Boxer Rebellion. Perhaps we stayed to report and write for the IWK newspaper, *Getting Together*, or maybe we went into Chinatown to canvass for tuberculosis health reporting. We may have been involved in draft counseling and organized protests against the Vietnam War, or we helped to start food programs for the Chinatown elderly and advocacy for social services and naturalization papers. We worked on cultural programs and

Chinese film nights. We may have helped to organize the tenants at Ping Yuen public housing and to create tenant support groups from other hotels to rally around the I-Hotel.

By now we understood the joke about the Red Block on Kearny and swimming around in radical alphabet soup—KDP, IWK, WMS, KSW, IHTA, CPA, CCA, EBS. On the face of it, we were all radical activist revolutionaries, and we were all united to defeat a capitalist-imperialist system of greed. We threw ourselves into the concerted work of myriad social and political projects, and we worked our butts off. Our commitment and our passion were irreproachable. We were in these years full-time revolutionaries, and we only thought about the revolution we were building, the fierce resistance to a system that served the few and propertied and wealthy, a social system that had failed our immigrant parents and grandparents, had denied their human rights because of their class and color. We learned to educate ourselves in a literature and culture of resistance, and finding ourselves gathered together at the very center of our Asian communities, we also began to educate ourselves in the practice of that resistance. And that practice gave us experience and power. We were young and powerful, and we were the future.

Well, that was the face of it, because over time, despite our agreed ideals, we came to hate each other. For some strange reason, once we entered one of those four inviting radical doors of the I-Hotel and gave our lives to any one of the projects within, our lives were transformed. Our transformation from individuals into collectives was precisely the thing that gave us power, but power has many sides to it, especially the power of a group. Feeling power, wielding power, demonstrating power. A group could act as a single fist or as an open handshake. Well, handshakes were not the tenor of our times. Perhaps it could be said that four mighty fists emerged from four doors to confront a common enemy, to fight in concert the foes of the I-Hotel, but we admit that very often the left fists did not follow the right fists, the punches did not follow the hooks and jabs; we could not agree on our tactics and strategies, and outside of the safety of our doors, we avoided or passed each other in hostility, rushing off to our separate tactics and strategies.

We could blame this all on Lenin and Mao, the two leaders whose theory and practice had led to real revolutions, to the overturning of old social structures, and we were avid readers and interpreters of their theories and practices. They were our heroes. We thought they had realized our dreams. Thus we may have followed their principles of democratic-centralism, meaning in theory that we should all participate in our arguments but finally follow in the fierce unity of our majority decision. And we also believed that our arguments were necessary to our collective struggle, that each group was pursuing a line of thinking that would eventually be proven or disproven in practice, that at the end of our struggle, we would finally unite in common unity. Our struggles would make us stronger, more powerful. But we were young and inexperienced, and our fighting was very real, our ideas held just under the tender surface of our new skin and flared in our nostrils. We wanted to be right. We wanted to win.

After we had worked together for our beliefs in twenty-four-hour days without rest, bonded ourselves to each other through the inner struggles of self-criticism within our groups, confessed our social sins to our brother- and sisterhoods and lost our individual selves to our collective purpose, we finally could only be with each other. And we found ourselves fighting about if we should collude with the so-called system and its elected liberal officials, if our struggle should be defined as working with the working class or our oppressed Asian communities, if this or that hotel tenant was an advanced worker, if gay lib protestors were bourgeois degenerates, if our loyalties were with the PRC or the USSR, if any of us were reformists, revisionists, or sellouts, if our art and writing must always have political purpose, and we were very sure that depending on our correct analysis of these definitions, we could then make decisions to act that would be ultimately unbeatable. But however we may have accounted for our thinking and our actions in these years, this was how we fought and spent our youth.

On the weekend after the fall of the I-Hotel, after we had all spent that long night into the morning hours locked in combat against the police, we regrouped before the hotel that had been our home, the center of our radical movement. Though physically exhausted and spent emotionally, we returned dutifully to our posts, returned to pick up the pieces and to continue the fight. We would not give up.

One of our groups had rented a truck with loudspeakers and parked it across the street from the boarded-up hotel, now surrounded by a small contingent of police guarding its entrance. A member of the WMS stood before the microphone and began to speak, but a member from the IWK suddenly jumped on the truck and grabbed the microphone away, at which members of the WMS defended the possession of the microphone. And that was the beginning of our melee, every group jumping onto the truck to fight the others. An alphabet soup of punching youth, kicking and pushing, beating out the long years, months, and days of our frustrations, strangling the deep disappointment of our failure, finally spilling the blood we could not in nonviolent civil disobedience. The police across the street who now guarded our four doors pointed at our stupid battle and laughed. But we continued to fight, our humiliation pounding away, erasing our young years, our awakening minds, our innocent smiles.

4: Do you speak English?

We have always arrived, they say, in waves, waves of yellow people splashed against American shores. A very few of us can say that we made the trip out of curiosity, but everyone else must probably admit that we've been forced across the Pacific, caught in the shifting consequences of war. That war might be violently active or violently passive, hot or cold, political or economic, but nevertheless, war. They've called us sojourners, immigrants, FOBS, refugees, exiles, even the brain drain, but we are all the ordinary or extraordinary veterans of cycle upon cycle of global conflict. In 1965, after the passage of new laws by the American Congress abolishing immigration quotas based on race and exempting family reunification from any quotas, word spread quickly. How many of us attached ourselves to our families and new possibilities, avenues of escape and prosperity in another world? Thus we surged forth, in a post-1965 wave multiplying our numbers tenfold from 20,000 to 264,000 every year. We were Chinese from Taiwan, Hong Kong, Singapore, Malaysia. We were Filipinos, Koreans, Thai, and Japanese. In another decade, our wave crested again higher, as we Vietnamese, Laotians, Cambodians, Hmong, Nepalese, Burmese, Indonesian also joined our distraught destinies to life across the Pacific. And in this same time period, the contours of Asia officially pushed southward so that we of the Indian peninsula, we Indian, Pakistani, Bangladeshi, also entered as *Asian* Americans.

Our waves landed us in scattered locations across the American nation where we recreated our memories of home in old and new ghettoed communities. How many thousands of us landed right here in the great City of San Francisco, merging our new lives with old lives, our new wave splashing against the last wave, encountering the familiar along with the odd stink of the anachronistic and yet the bravura of tired experience and sacrifice? Even though our families here made it possible for us to join them, their old wave did not really want the trouble of our new wave, did not want our neediness, our foreign dialects, our true stories. They did not want our troubled nightmares, the brutality of our memories holding a serpentine grip around our daily actions, the cynicism and dishonesty of our survival strategies, or the fervor of our grasping capitalism. But neither we, nor they, could know this before we arrived, and here we were anyway.

Maybe we emerged late from our jobs that Wednesday night in August, making our way along Kearny or Jackson, and noticed the growing commotion on the streets. We had seen the signs in Chinese, read the headlines in the local papers, heard the strident voices speaking in Chinese from a loudspeaker on a moving truck calling us to protest injustice. We weren't strangers to protests and certainly not to injustice, but the problems of those old men in that old hotel seemed distant from our problems. Maybe we even knew this Samut Songkhram who, though Thai, was Chinese after all, heard stories about his powerful godfather's reach. Where we came from, it was not wise to fight such men. Maybe we felt a sincere connection to their plight but feared involvement, or maybe we shunned their politics. We may have hung around long enough to witness the American police plunging their horses into the people, whipping their sticks against so many soft faces, or even to see the final hours when the folks inside the hotel were carried out and thrown into the street one by one, but most likely we hurried away, fearing any chance of arrest or assault. We had come too far and sacrificed too much to risk such involvement.

However, exactly one month later, we found ourselves hanging out for a late-night snack only four blocks away from the International Hotel at the Golden Dragon on Washington. We were among the late-night customers, looking for a hot bowl of pork won ton or maybe a good seafood juk. We had worked the last shift, closing our own places, busing the last tables, or maybe we had seen the last showing of a Chinese opera, or lost a day's wages in a foolish gamble, and didn't feel like returning to a crowded room with snoring men or interrupting a quick tryst. Or maybe we were not drunk enough to sleep and still needed a beer and something to fill our bellies. The Golden Dragon was dependably open, even at two a.m. We could spot it by the lanterns, but the green and yellow dragon tile we could only imagine in the dark. Golden dragons wound around the columns and reflected from the mirrors behind which we sat inconspicuously, in corner booths in the loft above or on the ground floor.

We were among the seventy-five or so patrons out and about in Chinatown on that Labor Day weekend. Of celebrating labor days, we knew very little. For us, it was just another laboring weekend.

We could not see but only imagine the two double-parked Plymouths, engines purring quietly outside on Washington, expectant, and the four young men, not even twenty years of age, who jumped from these cars hidden behind ski masks, one with a .45 semiautomatic, a second with a short barrel 12-gauge pump action shotgun, a third with a long barrel 12-gauge pump action shotgun, and a fourth with a silver-plated .38 revolver. It's said that the Joe Boys had come to settle tong business. Our old world had followed us into a new world, and yet we were saved because we understood the excited command in Cantonese: MAN WITH A GUN! And we dove instinctively beneath our tables. The deadly ammunition sprayed the innards of our Golden Dragon, leaving a fetter of broken glass, splintered dragon plaster, and torn human tissue, sputtering blood.

We ran down the back stairs, through the confusion of the greasy kitchen, and away through back alleys. We ran and ran. By the time we could hear the sirens of police cars, we were approaching our temporary beds. We would never be questioned, our presence on that morning never known. Invisible, we would slip into the clammy reek of our tiny rooms, rouse our counterparts from their sleep on our communal beds, push them off dutifully to their morning jobs, and fall into restless slumber in the rising heat pressed without intermission into damp mattresses.

6: August 3, 1977

In the final hours, we join this great gathering of human bodies, our bulwark of flesh surrounding an old brick hotel—materially worthless, symbolically invaluable, yet tonight still the Movement, fortified by passion and stubborn hope. See us collide and congregate, rally our puny human forces for the greater good. We've given our lives to this old place, but tonight we know our imminent failure, know that we may fall beneath its crumbling structure and with it, its crumbling memory. Public memory inscribed and archived as dates and naming. Secret memory withheld forever or revealed coyly, indiscreetly. Gossip. But as we tumble into the gravesite left by its demolition, perhaps our memory may flutter skyward, the City exploding and swirling away from our center—Manilatown, Chinatown, Japantown—spinning away with phallic impressions of Pyramid and Coit, spanning bridges of Wharf, Bay, and Golden Gate, dotted islands of Alcatraz and Angel, Victorians in soft undulating pastels, the rich green of Park and the endless blue of Bay, away and away and away. America. America.

And in time we may remember, collecting every little memory, all the bits and pieces, into a larger memory, rebuilding a great layered and labyrinthine, now imagined, international hotel of many rooms, the urban experiment of a homeless community built to house the needs of temporary lives. And for what? To resist death and dementia. To haunt a disappearing landscape. To forever embed this geography with our visions and voices. To kiss the past and you good-bye, leaving the indelible spit of our DNA on still moist lips. Sweet. Sour. Salty. Bitter.

I HOTEL

Afterword

In the 1990s, Amy Ling, then professor of English and Asian American literature at the University of Wisconsin-Madison, sent me a questionnaire she hoped would turn into an essay that would be part of a collection of essays by Asian American writers. The answers I returned disappointed Amy—she sent me a more full-bodied response written by another author. Comparing my work to the other author's, it seemed to me that we both had answered everything with the same ideas, except my answers were in shorthand. I decided to answer Amy with something she really didn't want at all, something she could reject outright. So I wrote an article about a book I'd never written. That led to thinking about that unwritten work. It was about the Asian American movement, mostly as I knew it in Los Angeles. But by 1997, I had come to live in Santa Cruz, and I thought I should explore the San Francisco/East Bay area where my parents grew up and where I was born. I shifted to a new center for this now real project: the International Hotel in San Francisco Manilatown/Chinatown, the site of political activism and community service for almost a decade until 1977, when residents of the hotel were forcibly evicted.

The I-Hotel, as it was known to its residents and the greater city, housed mostly elderly Filipino and Chinese immigrant bachelors, men who had come to work and make their fortunes prior to World War II and who, because of antimiscegenation laws, exclusion acts prohibiting Asian immigration, and a life of constantly mobile migrant labor, were unable to find spouses, have children, and to settle in the United States. In the 1960s and 1970s, the I-Hotel was sold to force the eviction of the residents and to redevelop the site as the extension of a West Coast Wall Street. In an effort to save the hotel and the surrounding Chinatown and Filipino communities, Asian American activists staged dramatic protests with thousands of participants and made the hotel a center for political activities and community service. The I-Hotel became a magnet for a multitude of political action groups in the San Francisco Bay Area, a center and symbol for the Asian American movement.

Against the backdrop of the Vietnam War and the political and social changes of this period, Asian American students and community activists, influenced by the civil rights movement, the Black Panthers, and international revolutionary movements, gathered to create what became the Asian American, or Yellow Power movement. From this came Asian American studies, with departments in colleges and universities across the country, communes and cooperatives, drug rehabilitation programs, bookstores, newspapers and journals, theaters, filmmakers, cultural centers, artists, musicians, politicians, law cooperatives, educators, historians, underground Marxist-Leninist-Maoist collectives, and literary and political movements. For the Asian American community, this was a flourishing time of new creative energy and political empowerment.

Since beginning this project, I have spent countless hours in Asian American archives, wandered around the old brick-and-mortar sites, read books, viewed films, listened to music, speeches, and rallies, and had both long and short conversations with over 150 individuals from that time. Researching a period in this way is passionately involving, so much so that you begin to live it and to forget why you began the project in the first place. At some point, I realized that I was supposed to be writing a novel, and the research had to stop.

I began to create a structure for the project. I found my research was scattered, scattered across political affinities, ethnicities, artistic pursuits—difficult to coalesce into any one storyline or historic chronology. The people I spoke with had definitely been in the movement, but often times had no idea what others had been doing. Their ideas and lives often intersected, but their ideologies were cast in diverse directions. Their choices took different trajectories, but everyone was there, really *there*. Thus the structure I chose for the book is based on such multiple perspectives, divided into ten novellas or ten "hotels." Multiple novellas allowed me to tell parallel stories, to experiment with various resonant narrative voices, and to honor the complex architecture of a time, a movement, a hotel, and its people. While the book has become inevitably big, it yet seems to me to be a small offering, a rendering to be continued and completed by others.

Author's Acknowledgments

In the way of institutional support to accomplish research for this project, I would like to acknowledge: faculty research grants awarded by the Committee on Research and the Institute for Humanities Research at UC Santa Cruz; *Amerasia Journal* at UCLA and Russell Leong and Mary Kao; Asian American Studies Collection at UC Irvine and Dan Tsang; Asian American Studies Collection at UC Santa Barbara and Gary Colmenar; Asian American Studies Department at San Francisco State University and Malcolm Collier and Marlon Hom; Asian American Studies Library at UCLA and Marjorie Lee; *The Car Show,* KFPK Pacifica Radio, and John Retsek; Chonk Moonhunter Productions and Curtis Choy; City Lights Books and Paul Yamazaki; Eastwind Bookstore and Harvey Dong; Ethnic Studies Library at UC Berkeley and Wei Chi Poon; Filipino American National Historical Society and Fred and Dorothy Cordova; Fine Arts Gallery at San Francisco State University and Mark Johnson; Freedom Archives and Claude Marks; *Hokubai Mainichi* Archives and J.K. Yamamoto; Hon-Kun Yuen Archives and Eddie Yuen; Japanese American National Library and Karl Matsushita; Kearny Street Workshop and Nancy Hom; Manilatown Heritage Foundation and Emil de Guzman; McHenry Library at UC Santa Cruz and Frank Gravier, Martha Ramirez, and Beth Remak-Honnef; National Japanese American Historical Society and Francis Wong and Peter Yamamoto; Philip Vera Cruz Audio Archive and Sid Valledor; San Francisco State University Special Collections and Helene Whitson; Steve Louie Archives and Steve Louie; Urban Voice and Boku Kodama; Yuri Kochiyama Archives and Yuri Kochiyama. Also, I'd like to recognize the work of Sudarat Musikawong, who worked for the project as a research assistant through UCSC, creating a database and copying many hours of audiotapes from the H. K. Yuen audio archives. Also, a special nod and thanks to Warren Furutani and Jessica Hagedorn for shared material, to Sina Grace and Leland Wong for their graphic renderings, to Linda Koutsky for art design, to Anitra Budd, Allan Kornblum, and Kristin Thiel for editing, and to Claire Light, Molly Mikolowski, and Patricia Wakida for grant and publicity consulting support. Many thanks to the remarkable staff at Coffee House Press and the staff in Literature and Humanities at UC Santa Cruz for their careful and meticulous work, to Lourdes Echazabel-Martinez and Ronaldo Lopes de Oliveira for translations, to Jane Tomi Boltz and Fred Courtright for their legal expertise, to Craig Gilmore and the Facebook Fan Club for making me feel famous, and to Micah Perks for being my colleague in the crime of fiction. For Richard Sakai, there are no words to express my humble heart. And finally, a wave to Amy Ling, in the heavens, whose prodding gave rise to an article about an unwritten book; now that book is written.

Along the way, generous readers have agreed to read and comment on early drafts of some or all "hotels": George Abe, Shoshana Arai, Anjali Arondekar, Chris Connery, Eddie Fung, Emil de Guzman, Estella Habal, Alex Hing, Ted Hopes, Makoto Horiuchi, Ruth Hsu, Betty Kano, John and Mary Kao, Allan Kornblum, Lelia Krache, Russell Leong, Jinqi Ling, Zack Linmark, Steve Louie, Roshni Rustomji-Kerns, Stephen Sohn, Andy Chih-ming Wang, Rob Wilson, Paul Yamazaki, Judy Yung. I mention their names to thank them for their critical contributions, care, and time. Many more people have joined this journey, but I have decided not to name names. I have been humbled by so many stories, some revealed with bravura, others insinuated obliquely, but much also silenced from pain, fear, or loss. If this fictional representation seems larger than life, perhaps it is because the work and lives of these activists have been largely invisible. In part, I came to know a kind of collective invisibility of folks in the movement who, in this labor for social-political change and revolution, gave up their youth, personal aspirations, and predictable family and social lives. My thanks and gratitude for the stories recuperated from this great labor cannot be conveyed except through this fiction, but it's still entirely my fault.

—Karen Tei Yamashita

KAREN TEI YAMASHITA, the author of four previous books and an American Book Award and Janet Heidinger Kafka Award recipient, has been heralded as a "big talent" by the *Los Angeles Times,* extolled by the *New York Times* for her "mordant wit," and praised by *Newsday* for "wrestl[ing] with profound philosophical and social issues" while delivering an "immensely entertaining story." A California native who has also lived in Brazil and Japan, she is Professor of Literature and Creative Writing at the University of California-Santa Cruz, where she received the Chancellor's Award for Diversity in 2009.

Also available by Karen Tei Yamashita

The Illustrators

LELAND WONG'S prints and photography have been widely published and exhibited both nationally and in the California region. During the 1970s he became involved with the Kearny Street Workshop and remains active in San Francisco's Asian American community as an artist, screen printer, and photographer.

Illustrations for all chapter frontispieces and karate poses (pages 267, 270, 273, and 276).

SINA GRACE is the author of *Cedric Hollows in Dial M for Magic*, and the comic book series *Books with Pictures*. He also provided illustrations for Amber Benson's *Among the Ghosts*, a children's book for Simon and Schuster. He lives in Los Angeles.

Illustrations for "Chiquita Banana" (pages 262–264) and "War & Peace" (pages 244–250).

Permissions Acknowledgments

Anonymous: [#35 "Leaving behind my writing brush and removing my sword, / I came to America"] and ["Ox"] from *Island: Poetry and History of Chinese Immigrants of Angel Island, 1910–1940,* translated by Him Mark Lai, Genny Lim, and Judy Yung. Copyright © 1980 by the History of Chinese Detained on Island Project. Reprinted with the permission of the University of Washington Press.

Frank Chin, excerpts from Act I from "Chickencoop Chinaman" from *Chickencoop Chinaman & The Year of the Dragon.* Copyright © 1973, 1974 by Frank Chin. Reprinted with the permission of the University of Washington Press.

Kahlil Gibran, "On Friendship" from *The Prophet.* Copyright 1923 by Kahlil Gibran, renewed 1951 by Administrators C. T. A. of Kahlil Gibran Estate and Mary G. Gibran. Used by permission of Alfred A. Knopf, a division of Random House, Inc.

V.I. Lenin, excerpts from *What Is to Be Done?* Reprinted with the permission of Foreign Languages Press.

"Si hablo del hambre . . ." ("If I speak of hunger . . ."), translated by Lourdes Echazabel-Martinez. Reprinted by permission of the translator.

Mao Tse-tung, excerpt from "Changsha," translated by Willis Barnstone, from *The Poems of Mao Tse-tung* (New York: Harper & Row, 1972). Translation copyright © 1972 by Willis Barnstone. Reprinted with the permission of the translator.

Paul Valéry, excerpt from "The Graveyard by the Seal," translated by C. Day Lewis, from *Selected Writings of Paul Valéry.* Copyright 1950 by New Directions Publishing Corp. Reprinted by permission of New Directions Publishing Corp.

Funder Acknowledgments

Publication of this book has been made possible in part by a major donation from Richard and Amber Sakai. Support for this title was also received from the National Endowment for the Arts, a federal agency. Coffee House Press receives major general operating support from the Bush Foundation, from Target, the McKnight Foundation, and from the Minnesota State Arts Board, through an appropriation by the Minnesota State Legislature and from the National Endowment for the Arts. We have received project support from the National Endowment for the Arts, a federal agency. Coffee House also receives support from: three anonymous donors; Abraham Associates; Around Town Literary Media Guides; Bill Berkson; the James L. and Nancy J. Bildner Foundation; E. Thomas Binger and Rebecca Rand Fund; the Patrick and Aimee Butler Family Foundation; the Buuck Family Foundation; Dorsey & Whitney, LLP; Fredrikson & Byron, P.A.; Jennifer Haugh; Anselm Hollo and Jane Dalrymple-Hollo; Jeffrey Hom; Stephen and Isabel Keating; Robert and Margaret Kinney; the Kenneth Koch Literary Estate; Allan & Cinda Kornblum; the Lenfestey Family Foundation; Ethan J. Litman; Mary McDermid; Sjur Midness and Briar Andresen; Schwegman, Lundberg, Woessner, P.A.; John Sjoberg; Mary Strand and Thomas Fraser; Jeffrey Sugerman; Stu Wilson and Mel Barker; the Archie D. & Bertha H. Walker Foundation; the Woessner Freeman Family Foundation in memory of David Hilton; and many other generous individual donors.

This activity is made possible in part by a grant from the Minnesota State Arts Board, through an appropriation by the Minnesota State Legislature and a grant from the National Endowment for the Arts.

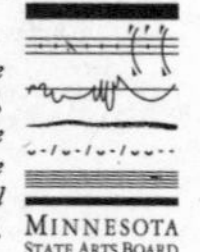

To you and our many readers across the country, we send our thanks for your continuing support.

Good books are brewing at www.coffeehousepress.org

Coffee House Press

THE COFFEE HOUSES of seventeenth-century England were places of fellowship where ideas could be freely exchanged. In the cafés of Paris in the early years of the twentieth century, the surrealist, cubist, and dada art movements began. The coffee houses of 1950s America provided refuge and tremendous literary energy. Today, coffee house culture abounds at corner shops and online.

Coffee House Press continues these rich traditions. We envision all our authors and all our readers—be they in their living room chairs, at the beach, or in their beds—joining us around an ever-expandable table, drinking coffee and telling tales. And in the process of this exchange of stories by writers who speak from many communities and cultures, the American mosaic becomes reinvented, and reinvigorated.

We invite you to join us in our effort to welcome new readers to our table, and to the tales told in the pages of Coffee House Press books.

Please visit www.coffeehousepress.org for more information.

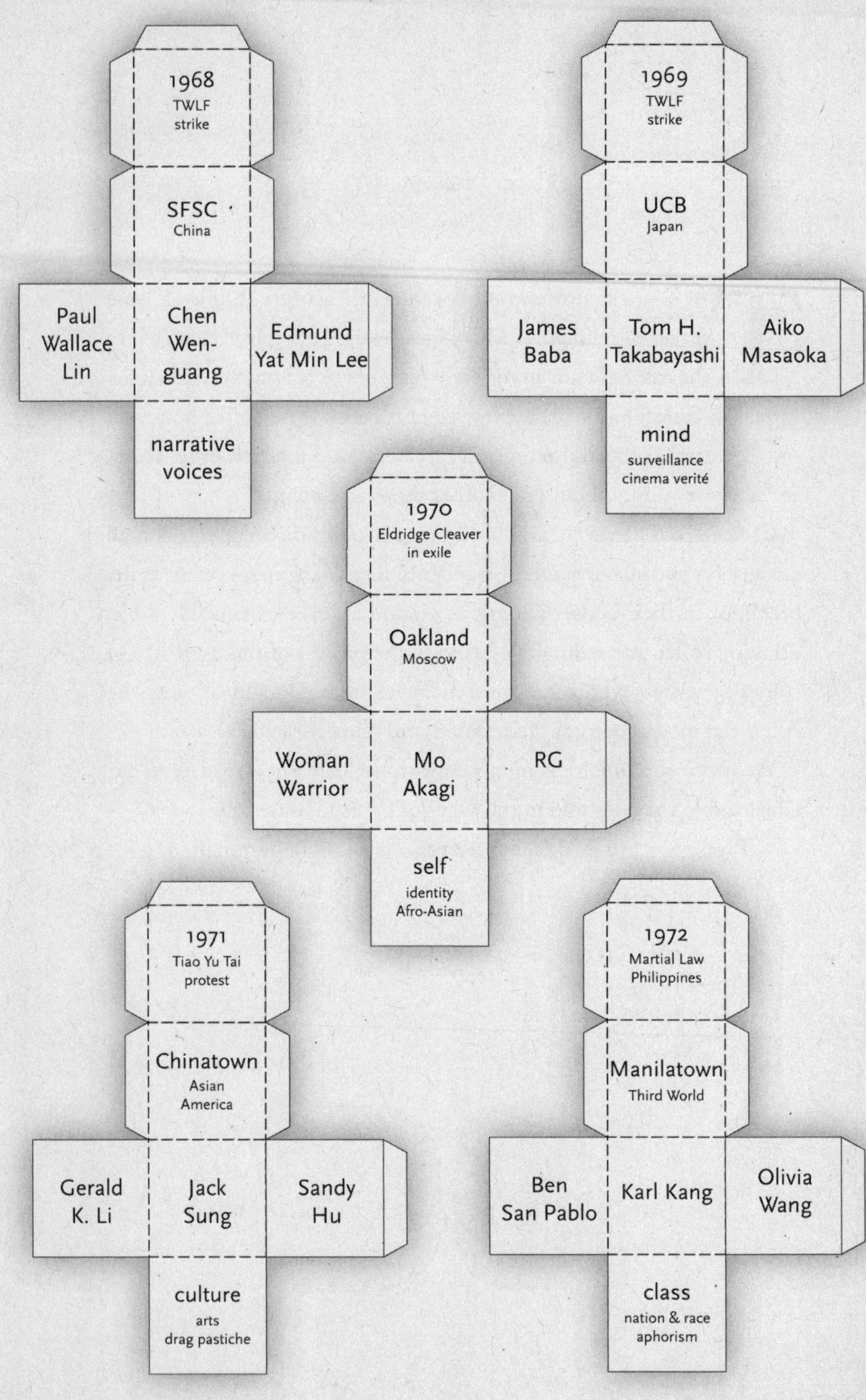
1968
TWLF
strike
SFSC
China
Paul Wallace Lin
Chen Wen-guang
Edmund Yat Min Lee
narrative voices
1969
TWLF
strike
UCB
Japan
James Baba
Tom H. Takabayashi
Aiko Masaoka
mind
surveillance
cinema verité
1970
Eldridge Cleaver in exile
Oakland
Moscow
Woman Warrior
Mo Akagi
RG
self
identity
Afro-Asian
1971
Tiao Yu Tai
protest
Chinatown
Asian America
Gerald K. Li
Jack Sung
Sandy Hu
culture
arts
drag pastiche
1972
Martial Law
Philippines
Manilatown
Third World
Ben San Pablo
Karl Kang
Olivia Wang
class
nation & race
aphorism